THE ENGLISH TEMPLAR

THE ENGLISH TEMPLAR

A NOVEL

Helena P. Schrader

Authors Choice Press
New York Lincoln Shanghai

The English Templar

Authors Choice Press
an imprint of iUniverse, Inc.

iUniverse books may be ordered through booksellers or by contacting:

iUniverse
2021 Pine Lake Road, Suite 100
Lincoln, NE 68512
www.iuniverse.com
1-800-Authors (1-800-288-4677)

Originally published by Minerva Press

First Published 1999

ISBN-13: 978-0-595-43271-4
ISBN-10: 0-595-43271-9

Printed in the United States of America

Prologue

Najac, France, March 1302

How long could it take an old woman to die? Marie sat before the fire, her embroidery frame in front of her, and stitched with the rigorous efficiency unique to her.

The light was fading already, and she sighed to think that another day had gone by with so little accomplished. The entire household was lamed by the impending death of her mother-in-law. Eleanor de Najac, the sole survivor of her once rich and respected family, had been failing for almost a year, but the deterioration in her health since Christmas had been dramatic. She had taken to her bed on Epiphany and not left her chamber since. By mid-February she had been unable to keep down solid food. But she would not die. Marie jabbed the needle into her frame and pulled the yarn through the canvas with short, sharp flicks of her wrist.

She was flanked by her two daughters, Natalie, who had turned fifteen on Christmas day, and ten year old Félice. Natalie was conventionally pretty for a maid her age, with fair hair, a small, upturned nose, round cheeks and pouting lips. With a sideways glance, Marie noted with disapproval that Natalie had put on some sort of paste to cover the pimples along her hairline.

'If you don't let your blemishes breathe they will fester and leave scars,' she told her daughter sharply. 'Go and wash that paste off at once!'

'But, Mama, my Montfranc cousins—'

'No "buts"! I told you to remove that paste and I expect to be obeyed instantly.'

With an almost sarcastic curtsey to her mother, Natalie departed through the tall, peaked doorway giving access to the great hall. She resented her mother deeply, but she knew better than to defy her.

Marie now spared a glance at her younger daughter. Félice had a mop of undisciplined, red curls that never seemed to be tamed, no matter how tightly they were braided. She had a heart-shaped face with a widow's peak cleaving her high brow, but to her mother's displeasure her nose had already taken on sharper contours than her elder sister's and her eyes were a light golden brown. In short, Félice was not destined to fit the fashion in looks, and she was certainly not gifted with the needle. Even now she made faces while she worked and squirmed ceaselessly in her chair.

'If you don't learn to sit still, Félice-Marie, I will tie your ankles and knees to the legs of the chair until you do learn.'

Félice went rigid.

Satisfied, Marie turned back to her own work. Her thoughts returned to her dying mother-in-law. Eleanor's husband, Geoffrey de Preuthune, hardly left her side, which at least kept him from being underfoot, but Marie resented the fact that her own husband, Louis, also kept close so that he could attend upon his mother at short notice. Louis had even refused to go out hunting with his firstborn and heir, Petitlouis, though the weather was splendid and they could use the meat. Marie was still weary of Lenten fare, though Easter had been celebrated in a subdued atmosphere last week. Maybe Petitlouis would be lucky, she tried to cheer herself.

Tucking her needle into the canvas and deftly rolling the yarn together, Marie stood and shook out her skirts.

Striding to the window niche she pressed herself to the window to try and peer through the thick panes of glass to the outer ward below. The sun had sunk below the hills to the west and the entire ward lay in shadow. As was normal this time of year, the temperature had also dropped abruptly, and she could feel the damp chill rising from the river bed on the valley floor. The steep bank down to the Alzou was wooded and the snows of February still lingered deep and dirty.

'May I go and check in on Grandmama?' Félice enquired hopefully.

'Your grandmother is surrounded with people looking after her. The last thing she needs is the likes of you disturbing her peace,' Marie retorted sharply. What did the girl possibly think she could do? It was bad enough that Louis thought he had to check on his mother every two or three hours.

Marie's mouth tightened and the lines at the corners became more pronounced than ever. She had never understood why Eleanor enjoyed such popularity with her family. She had been an indulgent and lax mistress (which accounted for the fact that everyone, from the kitchen boys to her fat, worthless waiting woman, fawned upon her) but Marie could not, for the life of her, see why her husband should be so devoted to his mother.

Not that an eldest son shouldn't revere his mother, but Eleanor de Najac had slighted her eldest son, failing to show him the respect he deserved as her heir. Instead, she had blatantly favoured his younger brother. Even now, while Louis waited on her hand and foot, day in and day out, she asked incessantly after Jean. It had gone so far that even Marie was beginning to wish Jean would finally come – if only to put an end to her mother-in-law's nagging. And then maybe she would be willing to stop clinging to a life that was useless to her and an increasing burden to everyone else.

Her thoughts were interrupted by a loud sniff and she noted that Félice was sitting with her head hung between her hunched shoulders, apparently crying.

'Stop that snivelling or I'll give you something to cry about!' Marie warned. 'Put your needlework away and fetch me all the herbs I need for a good hot hippocras. Your brother Petitlouis will be cold and thirsty when he gets in from hunting.'

Félice was too relieved to be released from the needlework and her mother's presence to protest. Her mother, of course, was testing to see if she knew which herbs were required for hippocras – which she didn't – but Félice was confident that the gardener or the almoner would tell her if she asked. She dipped her mother a hasty curtsey and scampered from the room, her tears for her grandmother apparently forgotten.

Rid of her younger daughter, Marie could at last sink into the large, armchair before the banked fire, lay her head back and close her eyes for a few moments of complete rest. It was so exhausting trying to run this household with all the servants utterly spoiled by the years under Eleanor's lenient hand. Marie was an energetic person by nature, but the need to constantly set a good example – even for Louis and her children – was wearing her out. And it wasn't as if anyone were ever grateful to her for all she did. Oh, no, they all complained either openly or secretly – even Louis criticised her in his weak, whining manner, 'suggesting' that 'maybe' she should not be 'quite so harsh' in this or that. Louis had cut a pretty figure in his armour when he was young, she reflected, but he hadn't worn it for years and his girth now was too great for the slender hauberk of his youth. Denis de Ladurie had been even more dashing.

The banging of the door brought Marie to her feet, flushing with a guilty conscience. She was relieved to find it was only her eldest son. He had burst into the room through the east door which led directly to the wall walk. He smelt of fresh air, horse and leather, and his raw-leather jerkin was stained and hardened with blood.

'Damned, clumsy horse! I swear I could see that gully coming and I was concentrating on the stag. You've got to let me buy a new stallion, Mama! Thunder stumbles too damn often. What if it had been a tournament?' It was a rhetorical question and he knew better than to press the subject of a new stallion too hard. His mother had started to scowl so he rapidly changed topics, still breathless and exhilarated from the chase. 'We nearly had him! My quarrel must have grazed him, but he didn't even falter!' His admiration for the great stag and disappointment at not having made the kill were equally poignant.

'Take off your muddy boots, Petitlouis! This is the solar not the scullery.' Although she would have denied it furiously, the voice Marie used was not so sharp as that which she had used with her daughters. She was proud of this seventeen year old, her first-born, who would certainly be knighted this year or next. He had the beginnings of a beard, which he diligently encouraged, and if he were not as tall and muscular as she would have liked, he was nevertheless athletic and virile. She had heard rumours that one of the girls in the village was carrying a child she claimed was his.

'Go and change into clean clothes. I won't have you coming to dinner in that old jerkin. You should also look in on your grandmother.'

Whereas Marie saw no point in Félice hanging about her grandmother's deathbed, she thought Petitlouis should do his duty since he would be the ultimate heir of Eleanor's entire estate. It was only right that he show his respect and maybe Eleanor would make some provision for him to assume one of her estates early. Then he could buy his own stallions, Marie reasoned. She was certain that Petitlouis had no real sense of how expensive his demands for stallions, armour and Spanish saddles were. It would do him good to live on a fixed income.

'Is Grandmother still hanging on?' Petitlouis asked with the callousness of youth. 'You don't suppose she's waiting to be hereticated, do you?' Petitlouis had meant it as a joke but, as with the jokes of many teenagers, it went frightfully awry.

Petitlouis knew that his great-grandmother had been burned at the stake as a Cathar heretic. His grandmother had been held and interrogated by the Inquisition for two years, but released since she was innocent of heresy. She had, to Petitlouis' knowledge, always behaved like a devout Catholic which was why he thought he was joking. Marie, however, had long harboured suspicions about the depth of her mother-in-law's piety. In the last years she had not heard mass more than twice a week at the most. Worst of all, there had been that old hag in the village who had sent for Eleanor when she herself wanted to be hereticated. The fear that there was truth in her son's words made Marie overreact.

'I'll make you wash your mouth out with soap for that!' she shouted shrilly. 'How dare you imply such nonsense!' She lashed out with her hand as well as her tongue, striking an astonished Petitlouis on the face with a slap that left the flat of her hand stinging and a red mark on his white jaw. Then she stormed out of the solar by the connecting door to the hall.

The wooden clogs which she wore over her soft leather shoes during the working day clunked angrily upon the wood of the dais and echoed in the rafters overhead. In the lower hall, the grooms of the chamber were starting to set up the trestle-tables for the evening meal, and they glanced up in astonishment at the sudden appearance of Madame. The look on her face boded ill, however, and at once they made a show of working more vigorously. Marie took a deep breath, squared her round shoulders and started down the length of the hall.

What on earth made Louis say such stupid things? she wondered, eyeing the men setting up the tables, looking for something to criticise. He was indeed a handsome youth, but sometimes she wondered if he was missing something between the ears! To even imply that his grandmother was a heretic could cause new rumours to spread about the family, and it was Louis and Petitlouis who would suffer the most from such innuendo. What if the Inquisition came back to Najac?

She had reached the end of the hall and to her right the door led along the north wing to the chapel and, beyond, to the chambers of the household. To her left was the doorway into the north-west tower where the children had their chambers and ahead was the steep, straight stairway leading down to the ground floor.

The braying of horns from the main gate distracted her. She remembered Natalie's remark about her Montfranc cousins and scowled. Louis's sister Alice had married a certain Antoine de Montfranc. They were a Norman family which had supported Simon de Montfort in his crusade against the Albigensians and been rewarded with substantial properties in the Languedoc. As an Albret, Marie looked down on such families, but at least the Montfrancs weren't parvenus like her father-in-law.

Geoffrey de Preuthune's father had been one of the Lionheart's knights, who had somehow been stranded on Cyprus and Geoffrey owed his own knighthood to Saint Louis' generosity during the Seventh Crusade. God knew, it must have been the saint's illness at the time that had induced him to raise the son of an English adventurer and a Cypriot peasant woman to the French nobility! But that was another topic; the arrival of the Montfranc brood was the issue at hand.

Louis' sister Alice had died in childbirth three years ago, but Louis had courteously sent word of their grandmother's impending death to her children. If they arrived *en masse* (for Alice had been a prolific breeder and fully nine of her children had survived infancy), Marie would have her hands full.

She rapidly descended the stairs and stepped out on to the landing leading down into the inner ward. She instantly regretted it. A stiff, cold breeze was blowing and tore at her gown, surcoat and veils, driving icy fingers up her sleeves and down her neck like a lewd, devil's hands, grasping for her private parts. Marie had no eyes for the last rays of light which gilded the scattered clouds to the west and painted their bellies blood-red in an otherwise sapphire sky or the evening star rising in the east. From out of the inner gate a party of horsemen was just emerging from the shadows. The castle dogs had come to life and were collecting in the ward with frenzied barking. Grooms were running to take the horses and men-at-arms were clattering down from the guardroom with lighted torches.

There were six riders, all well swaddled in heavy, hooded cloaks that seemed black in the dim light, except for the lead rider, whose cloak was a dirty white. He had flung the hood back on to his shoulders and the chain-mail coif encasing his throat and head glistened in the torchlight. His face was turned away from Marie and she could see the lacings of the leather band that held his coif in place, an old-fashioned style she had not seen for years. Then, glancing around the ward, the lead rider turned towards her and Marie found herself gazing at a handsome, middle-aged man with a full beard. It was not anyone she knew, certainly not one of her husband's Montfranc relatives, and that caused her to scowl. The last thing they needed was strangers in the house! Why hadn't these men been stopped at the outer gate and politely turned away? She had given orders to that effect weeks ago.

Whoever he was, she would explain to him that her dearest mother-in-law was on her deathbed and they could not entertain guests. She started down the stairs into the ward as the rider leaned over his pommel and swung himself stiffly from his horse. In that instant, his back was turned to her and she could see the great splayed cross of the Knights Templar clearly blazoned upon the back of his cloak. With a gasp, Marie halted on the steps. It was almost twenty years since she had last seen her brother-in-law, Jean, but it still startled her that she had not recognised him.

She took a deep breath. He was one guest they could not turn away, and she resumed her descent at a rapid pace to dispel the chill. The men of her brother-in-law's escort were also dismounting, and the grooms were starting to loosen girths as Marie came up.

'Jean!' Marie called sharply to be heard above the clatter of hooves, the barking of dogs and the jabber of men.

Jean turned at the sound of his name. He was chilled through and bone-weary. He could hardly stand on feet that had turned to blocks of ice and legs that had not unbent from the saddle for almost ten hours straight. The woman approaching him across the ward was short, buxom and broad of hip. Her small nose was lost in her fleshy face and her lips were hardly visible above her double chin, but the lines that ran from her nose to her mouth stamped her face with a look of perpetual dissatisfaction. From the quality of her silk veils and the mink trim on the sleeves and neckline of her surcoat, Jean surmised that she must be his sister-in-law, but she bore not the faintest resemblance to the pretty girl his brother had proudly brought home decades ago. 'Madame.' He answered her greeting.

'Welcome to Najac.' Marie offered him her cold cheek, and Jean dutifully touched cheek to cheek.

'Is my mother still alive?' He could contain himself no longer. He had not ridden from Strathclyde to the Languedoc in three weeks to exchange pleasantries with his sister-in-law.

'Yes, your mother is alive – but very feeble. You have made it just in time. I did not know when to expect you,' Marie was explaining. 'Your chamber is not made up, but I will send someone at once. Do you wish to warm and refresh yourself in the hall until all is ready?'

'No, I'd like to go up to my mother.'

Jean glanced over his shoulder to the tallest and largest corner tower, at the junction of the south and east wings. All his life, his parents had shared the chamber on the first floor and the faint warm light that spilled from the narrow window of the stairwell reassured him. 'But my brothers need hot wine and a good meal,' Jean added turning back to Marie.

'As you please,' Marie replied sourly, for some unknown reason resenting his insistence on seeing his mother at once. 'Your men can go on into the hall.'

Marie was now shivering with cold, so she hastened towards the tower which housed her in-laws, leaving Jean to follow as best he could on his frozen feet. Marie took a torch from the wall bracket at the base of the stairs and held it in one hand and her skirts in the other as they wound their way up the tight spiral stair.

Marie knocked at the door of her in-law's bedroom but did not await an answer before sweeping into the room. This chamber soared two storeys to a central keystone carved with roses. The corbels supporting the ribbed arches were delicately carved and two large double-light windows, flanked by deep window seats, opened the room to light and long views. It being a winter night, however, the room was lit only by a fire, which caused a thousand shadows to dance and leap in every corner of the hexagonal room.

The room was much more richly furnished than Jean remembered it. In his youth, his parents had lived frugally. Now oriental carpets with their deep colours covered the floor, including the steps up to the window seats. The plastered and painted walls were hung at this time of year with tapestries that held back the chill. Saracen cushions softened the stone benches in the windows and obscured the seats of the wooden chairs by the fire. The chest at the foot of the bed was massive oak and exquisitely carved with a hunting scene. The bedside table was laden with goblets, pitchers, bowls and plates. The drapes of the great bed were of amber velvet, stitched with black Catherine wheels, the device of the de Preuthune heraldic arms.

At first glance Jean could not even find his mother. She was lost behind the half-drawn curtains in the goosedown pillows of her bed. He saw instead his mother's old maid, Eleni, bending over the fire to test the temperature of something she was boiling over it, and he saw his father with a book in his hands sitting beside the bed.

Geoffrey de Preuthune was seventy-one years old. His hair and beard were completely white and his face was eroded with time, like his Cypriot homeland, into a landscape with deep gullies and prominent peaks. His eyes were sunken under brows that seemed to jut out more decisively than ever in his youth. His nose was a ridge dividing his face in two and his cheeks were cut with crevices, but his lips were firm.

Geoffrey looked up from the book which he had been reading aloud to Eleanor, expecting his eldest son Louis. Though his hearing showed the first signs of weakening, his eyes were still sharp and they glittered intelligently under the white brows. Jean clearly saw the light in them leap with elation, and in the next instant Geoffrey was thrusting the book aside and pushing himself up from his chair. 'God be thanked! Jean!'

To Marie's indignation, Jean pushed past her and fell into his father's arms. Geoffrey gripped his son with an intensity that brought tears to the younger man's eyes. From the day he had learned his mother was dying, his principal concern had been his father. They would not have sent for him if there had been any chance of his mother recovering. There was nothing he could do for her. But how was his father going to survive without her?

Geoffrey and Eleanor had been married fifty years. Of course, many couples lived in open indifference or even hostility decade after decade. Many noblemen took mistresses. Many noblewomen retired to convents. Many couples lived apart. It wasn't being married for fifty years which mattered, but being in love all that time. Jean knew of no other couple who had so consistently and unerringly remained devoted to one another. His parents were indivisible – and now they were about to be brutally divided. Jean feared that his father would not survive the amputation of his heart.

Geoffrey had never doubted that Jean would come if he could, and in his heart he had been certain that Jean would come. But Geoffrey's common sense had reminded him that there could be no guarantee the friar entrusted with the message for Jean had ever reached the western coast of Scotland, where Jean was stationed. And the former Templar novice knew all too acutely that a Knight Templar would have to gain the express permission of his superior to leave his commandery and travel home for a visit. Furthermore, a family crisis was no legitimate reason to give a Templar leave. A Templar left his family behind when he joined the Order and his only family ties were, theoretically, to his brother Templars. Since Jean was commander at Mingary, he needed the permission of the preceptor of England (who was also responsible for Scotland and Ireland) to come to Najac. Geoffrey had reminded himself that there could be any number of reasons why William de la More would not feel he could afford to be without a commander in western Scotland for months on end.

Holding the strong, hardened body of his son in his arms, Geoffrey was filled with gratitude that he had been granted this rare pleasure of seeing him again – possibly for the last time. He had loved all his sons when they were young, but as they grew into adults he had become closest to Jean, even though Jean was always farthest away. It was not just that Jean had joined the Temple, in which he himself had served for years as a novice, or the fact that Jean had lived in the Holy Land and Cyprus. It was simply that Louis spent all his life looking over his shoulder to see what other people were thinking of him. Everything he did, he did to please someone else: his mother, his wife, his neighbours, his king. Jean did what he thought was right regardless of what people thought of him.

With a last, grateful hug, Geoffrey drew back and turned towards the bed. 'Eleanor, Jean's made it.'

The voice that answered was weak and cracked: it was the voice of an old woman and that shocked Jean, who had last seen his mother riding astride a prancing mare as she waved goodbye from the quay at Aigues-Mortes ten years earlier. 'I heard,' the voice said.

Jean pressed forwards to the bed and leaned over the shrivelled figure sunk among the pillows. His mother's hair was grey, her skin flecked with age marks, her lips bloodless and her eyes underlined with smears of blue like bruises. She was too weak to even try and sit up. 'So they let you come,' she whispered with a faint lifting of her lips as her eyes devoured his beloved face.

'I didn't ask,' Jean told her, aware that his correct father stiffened slightly at his insubordination. 'I sent word to de la More of where he could find me.'

Jean took her hand in his and bent to kiss her on the lips. It was more than filial affection: the Rule forbade a Templar from kissing even his mother on her lips and his mother knew it.

She squeezed his hand. 'You're ice cold and look like you've hardly slept in weeks. You must be hungry. Look and see...' She turned her head towards the sideboard to see if there were any remnants of food remaining which she and Geoffrey had not already consumed.

'I ran into Niki in the ward. He is fetching me something,' Jean reassured her.

'Then sit and tell me about Scotland. Does it ever stop raining there?'

Jean looked over his shoulder and his father indicated his own chair. Geoffrey was content to take a back seat, to let Eleanor and Jean have as much time together as possible. He would have time for Jean after... afterwards. He went to stand beside the faithful Eleni, whose greetings to Jean had been no less joyful, though lost to the principals in their preoccupation with themselves. Also unnoticed, Marie had withdrawn, leaving her in-laws alone together.

Jean unbound the band holding his coif and shoved the chain-mail off his head to reveal an ill-shaved tonsure. Then he sat holding his mother's hand and chattered. Eleni fed Eleanor her evening porridge and Niki brought Jean mulled wine, bread and paté, which he prepared diligently for the one-armed knight before silently and unobtrusively kneeling to unbuckle his spurs.

*

19

As the evening passed, Jean became aware that spasms of pain racked Eleanor's body with increasing frequency. Each time it hurt him, and more than once he glanced towards his father, wondering how he had watched Eleanor suffering for month after month. He felt guilty to think that she had held out so long partly out of hope of seeing him. He wished that she had not drawn out her own suffering for his sake. He wished she would stop fighting death.

Eleanor tried to listen to Jean but she could not concentrate. The pain was worse than ever now and she felt a chasm starting to open under her. Finally she interrupted her son. 'Jean?'

'Mama?'

'Is your father there?'

'Yes, of course.' Jean was already preparing to surrender his place to his father.

Eleanor held him back. 'Ask him to go for Louis and the children.'

Jean's heart stopped briefly. She was surrendering, and, even if he had wished this only minutes before, it was terrifying to face it. He turned to speak, but Geoffrey had already heard and understood. Tears were running down his face but he nodded and left the chamber. He had hoped and prayed for an end long before Jean had even known that his mother was dying.

No sooner was the door closed behind him than Eleanor grasped Jean's hand with the strength of desperation. 'Jean, you must help him. Stay for more than the funeral. Stay…'

She wanted him to stay for ever, but whenever she had asked Jean to sacrifice his Order for her sake he had denied her. She could not make the same mistake again. She must be content with what he could give. It was good that he was here. She did not want Geoffrey to be alone the night after she died. But what about the weeks and months and years to come? Damn him! The old corroding bitterness she had always felt against the Templars rose like acrid bile in her throat.

Louis crashed into the room, breathless from running up the stairs, and flung himself on his knees beside his mother's bed. Jean was mildly shocked by his brother's appearance. He wore expensive velvet robes and a beaver-trimmed surcoat with an embroidered border, but for all that he looked like a provincial merchant – flabby of face and belly. He had soft, pasty skin which suffered from too little exposure to the elements and an over-long fringe of hair around a receding hairline.

'Mother! Mother!' he cried melodramatically – or was he really desperate for her attention?

'It's all right, Louis,' Eleanor rasped from her bed, her hand seeking his hand.

He grasped her hand and covered it with kisses and tears. 'Mother, what are we to do without you?'

'I've lingered long enough,' Eleanor insisted, and Jean resented his brother's lack of consideration. Couldn't he see how much she suffered? Didn't he grasp that Eleanor needed to let go? Their job was to make it easier for her, not more difficult.

'Louis,' Eleanor addressed her sobbing son, 'please remember that the people of Najac were always loyal to me and my family even when we were in disgrace. We owe them a debt.'

Louis was nodding and assuring her that he would always remember without even understanding what she meant. Eleanor sighed. It was too late to explain it all. She had made many mistakes in her life... She pulled herself together.

Marie had now entered with her surviving children: Petitlouis, Natalie, Norbert and little Félice. Eleanor called Norbert over, asked the frightened twelve year old to give her a kiss and then told Eleni to take him out. She had never been able to establish a bond with him and he was clearly discomforted. When he was gone, she turned again to her first-born.

'Louis, you are to provide for Eleni for the rest of her life. Full livery and maintenance. Don't forget – she left her family and her homeland for my sake. She is to be given more than a beggar's portion. Is that clear?'

Louis nodded, and Eleanor continued, 'You inherit on your father's death.' She said this more for Marie than Louis, but she felt Louis stiffen at the reminder and she could feel Marie's resentment chilling the air from where she stood. 'If and when he decides that the burden of my full estate is too much for him, he will retire to Chanac.'

She paused to let this sink in. Chanac was at the northern edge of the Cévennes and it had once been designated her dower portion in the days when she had had brothers and no one thought she would inherit the entire Najac estate. She and Geoffrey had often retreated there when they wanted time for themselves, away from the pressures of the world and their family.

She continued, 'Your father has been generous enough to agree that Petitlouis can assume control of our manor at Pompignan at once – but then he has no rights to other support. You understand?'

Louis was nodding vigorously, and Marie was notably mollified.

Pompignan was one of the more prosperous manors and it was near Toulouse, an ideal location for Petitlouis to establish himself.

'Do you understand, Petitlouis?' Eleanor demanded, trying to raise her voice, though she succeeded only in rasping more harshly.

Marie gave her elder son a shove and he stumbled forwards to kneel beside his father and stutter out his thanks.

Eleanor had to be satisfied. She did not believe that Petitlouis would live within his means nor that his parents would make him learn to. They had always spoilt him and they would continue to do so: no one's dying words would change a relationship of seventeen years.

So she continued. 'I have settled one hundred louis tournais on each of the girls, Marie. They are to be used towards the dowry regardless of what else Geoffrey or you decide to give them. But there is one stipulation: your daughters must consent to the marriages you choose for them. Saint Louis himself promised me that he would not force me to marry against my will. If a king can show so much respect for the wishes of an unknown ward, then I expect you to show your own daughters equivalent respect.'

It was a long speech and the antagonism that prompted it rendered Eleanor all the more exhausted when she finished. She had seen all too clearly that Marie treated her daughters without compassion or sympathy and it angered her. She did not understand how a mother could be so preoccupied with her sons. Her own mother had been her best friend and she had tried to be a friend to her own daughters and granddaughters.

Natalie and Félice listened to their grandmother with bated breath. Both knew that with Eleanor's demise they were losing their most compassionate champion, but, while Natalie thought she would soon have the comfort of a husband, Félice knew that she was about to be left alone and friendless. She sneaked a glance at her mother to see what effect this impassioned speech had made and a chill went through her. Her mother's eyes had narrowed and her lips were clamped together, causing little sacks of skin to stick out more prominently on each side of her chin. Félice tried to swallow the sob that welled up in her chest but her gasp cut through the room like a cry.

Marie at once spun on her and hissed for her to get hold of herself or leave the room, but Eleanor wasn't dead yet.

'Marie! Follow your own advice! Come to me, Félice!' Eleanor removed her hand from Louis', to his distress, and held it out to Félice.

Félice ran to her grandmother, conscious that her mother would make her pay for this but it didn't matter. She jostled her father aside, indifferent to his feelings.

'Ah, Félice.' Eleanor smiled faintly, grasping the little girl's hand. Why did she feel better just at the girl's touch? Clinging to Félice, she let her eyes scan the others again: weak, shallow Louis, who let himself be governed by the sour-faced, self-centred Marie; spoilt Petitlouis, who now shuffled from one foot to the other, anxious to escape a scene that was boring and vaguely discomforting; poor wishy-washy Natalie, whose dreams never went further than a dashing, handsome lover in shining armour. Eleanor felt the pains clutch and gnaw at her innards again and with revulsion she smelt her own sweat. She could not bear to have them around her any longer.

'Leave me,' she murmured. 'Louis, Marie, Petitlouis and Natalie.'

The latter two were evidently relieved, but Marie was offended and Louis hurt to the quick.

Eleanor saw the pain and then the resentment in Louis' eyes as he looked up at her and then cast a look of seething jealousy at his younger brother. She was sorry for him, but she had no strength to take his feelings into account. 'Please, Louis – you have your Marie. Jean and Geoffrey have only me.'

Louis swallowed this explanation superficially but Eleanor knew that the resentment would fester. What did it matter? Jean would be far away and there had never been any love lost between the brothers anyway.

Natalie and Petitlouis were already gone; Marie put her hand on her husband's shoulder and squeezed gently, signalling him to obey. As Louis rose and backed away, stifling his sobs, Marie snapped her fingers at Félice. 'You too, you stupid girl! Your grandmother wants to be alone with her Templars!'

'No!' Félice and Eleanor spoke simultaneously.

'Let Félice stay with me,' Eleanor reinforced, afraid she had not been heard.

Marie cast her daughter a look fit to kill but made no remark, concentrating instead on supporting her wounded and insulted husband through the door. This was a night she would not forget – especially the fact that Eleanor had not once called for the priest. She crossed herself hastily, convinced now that Eleanor was indeed a heretic.

Eleanor breathed out when they were gone and the pain that had knotted and twisted her stomach seemed to ease into a dull, tolerable ache.

'Come, lie beside me here, child.' Eleanor patted the bed on her far side. She wanted to make room for Geoffrey and Jean on the other side. Félice ran around to the far side of the bed and climbed up with alacrity. It was odd, Eleanor noted, that the girl felt no shyness at the approach of death. Norbert's – even Petitlouis' and Natalie's – discomfort in the death chamber had been far more natural. But Félice now snuggled beside her and very gently laid her arm across Eleanor's chest.

'Thank you, Grandmama,' she whispered, apparently not in the least offended by the body odour which Eleanor herself found so offensive.

She turned to the two men and saw that tears were streaming down Geoffrey's face again, glistening in his beard. Jean was not crying. She remembered him telling her that he had not been able to cry for Master de Beaujeu either as the Templar Master lay dying of his wounds at

Acre. Poor Jean. He had seen too many friends die, but he was strong. With her free hand, she reached out to her husband.

'It's all right, Eleanor,' he told her in his strained voice. 'You don't have to suffer any longer. Let go.' He bit back a sob. He meant what he said, but he couldn't help crying for himself.

'Jean, take your father upstairs.'

'No!' Geoffrey tried to protest, to cling to her.

Jean slipped his arm around his father's waist. 'Mama is right. There is nothing more you can do or say. Come.'

He had left Beaujeu's chamber before the moment of death and he was grateful for it. He had seen other men die and he knew that he could not bear to see the life depart a beloved face. He could not bear to let his father watch his mother die. Geoffrey could not fight them both. He was far too weak.

His knees gave way and Jean had to half-carry, half-drag him to the door. Fortunately, Geoffrey's powerful Cypriot squire, Niki, was lurking there and in a quick, easy motion he swept the old man into his arms and carried him to the chamber above.

Left behind in the death room were only Eleanor and Félice.

'Aren't you afraid, child?' Eleanor asked after a few moments with a guilty conscience.

'Why should I be afraid, Grandmama? You won't hurt me, not even after you are dead.' Félice reflected for a moment. 'But you won't feel the pain any more, will you?'

'Not the physical pain,' Eleanor admitted. 'But what about the pain of parting? It's not only those who are left behind who are separated from their loved ones. What am I going to do without Geoffrey? And Jean? And all of you?' The questions were rhetorical.

Félice seemed to take her time reflecting upon the question and then she answered in a clear, strangely mature voice, 'I think the dead must experience time differently. It won't seem that long before Geoffrey can join you. And you will find it is not so hard because even if he can't see you, you can be with him.'

'But what good is that if I can't talk to him? Comfort him? Laugh with him?' Eleanor protested, suddenly fighting against the smothering force she thought she had been prepared to accept.

'You can talk to him and comfort him,' Félice insisted in her strangely confident, mature voice. The voice reminded Eleanor of someone else. 'He won't hear the words, perhaps, or he may think he's dreaming but you will find the means to comfort him. He will sense your love, your presence.'

'Oh, Félice, will you look after him for me?' Eleanor cried out to the little girl who seemed so much older than herself. 'Jean won't stay for long and then Geoffrey will be so lonely. I know young girls would rather be with young men, but will you remember your grandfather now and again? Ask him to teach you Greek. It would please and distract him.'

'Of course. But you mustn't worry, Eleanor.' Félice's voice seemed so much older and yet it was the same and so wonderfully familiar. 'Geoffrey has something he has to do, something important for his soul. You wouldn't want to deny it to him.'

Eleanor recognised the voice. It was her mother's voice. She tried to open her eyes but the weight of her eyelids was too great. There was a great weight dragging down her entire body. She struggled against it in sudden panic and broke free so abruptly that she sat bolt upright. After so many days of laying on her back, the act of sitting up made her dizzy. She looked back over her shoulder to her granddaughter.

Félice lay with her arms around her grandmother. Eleanor saw her own tired, bloodless face lying on the pillow surrounded by unkempt strands of grey hair, and shuddered in revulsion. She reached out to the little girl and called to her. 'Félice.'

Félice nodded, but pressed her eyes closed. Tears were glistening on her eyelashes. 'Goodbye, Grandmama,' she murmured, and kissed the leathery, splotched face on the pillow.

Part One

Chapter One

Poitiers, August 1307

Notre-Dame-la-Grande was filled to overflowing. Not only was the nave packed but the two narrow side aisles were equally crowded and some of the more nimble students had managed to climb on each other's shoulders to reach the window sills, where they perched precariously.

Félice had detached herself from the twittering cluster of nuns and fellow boarders from the convent of Saint Radegonde and wormed her way forwards to a place between two of the brightly painted columns opposite the pulpit. She was grateful that the abbess had agreed to let them come to the service, but she had no desire to stay with the others. Most of them came only for the sake of getting out of the convent and had no interest in the actual attraction: a sermon by Father Elion.

Father Elion's reputation for inspiring rhetoric had preceded him to this university town housing the pope, but so far Clement V had not appeared. Almost no one else of consequence in Poitiers, however, was missing. Félice noted that the entire faculty of the university had come *en masse* and secured the best places directly under the pulpit. The bishop was in his seat in the choir and his staff of priests, deacons and monks clustered around him in the ambulatory, spilling into the side chapels. Although the pope was absent, the red of a half-dozen cardinals stood out dramatically among the throng of black, brown and white habits. Almost equally outstanding amidst the sea of habits was the cluster of Templars, in their austere but striking armour.

The Templars were standing in the alcove immediately to Félice's right, and she was distracted by them at first. She knew that the Grand Master had arrived in France from Cyprus at the pope's command and was here in Poitiers to consult with him about a new crusade, but she had not seen him until today. Knowing that the Grand Master was responsible for her Uncle Jean's banishment to the wilds of Scotland, she was particularly curious about him.

Master de Molay was easily recognisable among the half-dozen knights because he was the only Templar not in armour, wearing instead the white Templar habit trimmed in red. His once brown hair was now grey and so thin that he had no need of a razor to maintain his tonsure. His beard fell in an ever thinner strand to a point just above the red cord at his waist. His expression was stern, a frown carved permanently upon his features by the lines of his face. He had pale eyes and an over-sharp nose. None of that surprised Félice, who had been raised to dislike the man, but she was astonished that he looked so nervous.

Then Félice remembered the rumours which had circulated at the university: that the pope had summoned not only de Molay to Poitiers but also the Grand Master of the Hospitallers. According to the rumours, the pope was interested in seeing the two military orders merged into one. Maybe that was de Molay's problem: he was afraid that he would be replaced as the head of the united Order by the more dynamic and charismatic Hospitaller Master, Fulkes de Villaret. De Villaret had not answered the pope's summons because he was too busy conquering the island of Rhodes, wresting its control from a notorious pirate captain.

The Templars were in the midst of a discussion while they awaited the start of the service, and as they made no attempt to keep their voices down, Félice made no attempt not to listen.

'Of course, it's astonishing that a man who was thought dead or, at best, a fugitive in Ireland has been able to defeat the English in a series of skirmishes, but a couple of mountain ambushes do not win a war!'

De Molay's tone was irritated and almost petulant, Félice thought. She wondered which of the knights had provoked this response and, scanning their faces, drew back in initial shock as she was confronted by a man with a hideous scar running diagonally across his face, dislodging his nose.

This knight responded to the Grand Master in heavily accented French and a voice that was far too loud for the environment. 'Robert the Bruce is no' winning a war – he's winning a kingdom! He's demonstrated tha' we can tweak the leopard's tail – and get away wi' it!'

'There's no need to shout, Sir Duncan,' The Grand Master rebuked in a schoolmaster tone. 'And no good tweaking a leopard's tail either. Sooner or later the English king will be provoked into a serious response and that will end as all the other campaigns have – in the humiliation and despoliation of Scotland.'

'Can ye be so sure, my lord? Edward I is dead, an' his son is made of a different cloth.' There was something in the way he said this that made Félice sense an implication to his words which she did not grasp.

The Templars exchanged looks and shifted somewhat uneasily.

The Scottish knight continued, 'You could be betting on the wrong horse, backing Edward II against Robert the Bruce.'

This seemed to make the Grand Master pause. He passed his hand over his mouth and smoothed down his beard in short, nervous pats. Then he shook his head. 'I must consult Master de la More. He will know the new English king. I will send for him at once.'

'I could go, my lord.'

The eagerness in the offer was impossible to overhear, and Félice leaned forwards so she could see around the pillar to the speaker. It was an exceptionally tall, young knight with curly, light brown hair and a clear, well-structured if somewhat bony face.

The Grand Master seemed as astonished as Félice by the quick response of the young knight and turned around to look at him with an expression of vaguely reproving surprise. 'Sir Percy, your commandery is on Cyprus and it is there that you belong. I will be sending you back with dispatches some time in the next four to six weeks.'

'I could be to London and back by then, my lord,' the knight persisted stubbornly and, so Félice thought, foolishly. He must have noted that his superior did not approve of his desire to travel to England and would have been better advised to let the issue drop.

'No!' de Molay, as Félice had expected, was sharper now and scowling. 'You will do as you are told.'

The knight pressed his lips together, inclined his head and took a step back.

De Molay, mollified by the show of obedience, turned to one of the other knights near him and remarked,

'I think it would be wise to send—'

Félice did not hear the rest because at that moment Father Elion made his entry and a ripple of excitement seized the entire great church. Félice lost all interest in the banal conversation of the Templars and strained to get a glimpse of the famous Dominican.

Standing on tiptoe and shifting first left and then right as the crowd in front of her also shifted excitedly, she managed for an instant to get a clear view of the Dominican friar. By chance, the priest had turned to look in her direction and she saw him full in the face. He had a distinctive face – gaunt and hawk-like. He too was tall, taller even than the young Templar, but, unlike the Templar, who stood straight and relaxed, the Franciscan hunched his shoulders like a vulture.

She forced herself to suppress her instant dislike as foolish and focus her intellect upon the man's words as he began his sermon. He was indeed a gifted speaker. He spoke with genuine intensity and he used his voice adeptly, varying tone, pitch and volume. But his themes were hardly original. He railed against wealth, reminding his audience that Christ had been born in a manger of humble parents and had abjured all wealth. Only those ready to cast off their worldly possessions and renounce their inheritance were privileged to follow Christ.

At the end of the sermon, Félice felt a vague sense of disappointment and uneasiness. She was glad when the service was over and the great throng started to shuffle their way towards the portal. Around her, the students, monks and secular clerics were animatedly discussing the sermon. Virtually no one seemed to share her disappointment. Quite the contrary: from the enthusiasm of the reception, one might have thought he had presented a brilliant new thesis. Had she just been too stupid to hear it? Félice tried to listen more intently to the students disputing behind her. They were repeating Father Elion's phraseology, flattering by imitation, but she could still detect nothing particularly original in the words they praised so highly.

The crowd clogged the door and the impatient tried to elbow and shove their way forwards. Félice hated crowds and drew back somewhat, letting the others go before her.

It made no difference to her that the abbess and the other girls had passed out of the portal well ahead of her. It was midday and she was not afraid to walk the streets of Poitiers from Notre-Dame-la-Grande to the convent of Saint Radegonde alone. On the contrary, she was glad to be on her own and not have to listen to the giggling gossip of the other girls and the nuns.

Outside the church it was a bright sunny summer's day with flying clouds. The market around the church was alive with vendors, citizens and dogs who seemed astonished by the sudden swarm of clerics pouring out of the old church. Félice turned her face up to the sun, soaking in the warmth and letting the breeze lift her short veils from her shoulders. She wore her hair bound in white ribbons which criss-crossed down her thick rope of frizzy auburn hair to the waist and a short, white veil, held fast with a simple circlet of silver on her forehead. Like all the girls boarding at the convent, she wore a pale blue linen gown with tight sleeves and no collar or trim and a white smock which was loose, sleeveless and ended at the knee. This too was devoid of any embroidery or adornment and thus the object of much scorn among most of the girls. Félice did not share their dislike for her school uniform. She knew that it marked her as a maiden attending the convent school and that it thus gave her a degree of protection in the streets of Poitiers. Not even the boldest apprentices or the most shameless drunks were wont to harass nuns and the girls in the care of the nuns were almost equally immune – unless their own behaviour invited other advances.

Félice turned and started for the head of the Rue du Marché. She was startled to hear someone calling her.

'Mademoiselle de Preuthune! Mademoiselle de Preuthune!'

She stopped and looked about somewhat disturbed, and then saw, on the other side of the crowd still streaming out of Notre Dame, a student waving at her. It was Umberto di Sante. Félice flushed brightly and the pounding of her heart was insistent, no matter how much her mind ordered her body to remain calm.

Umberto was seventeen with a clear, regular face so well proportioned that it was almost angelic. He had dark brown hair, silky and straight rather than the rats' nest of frizzy curls that was her despair. The son of a prominent and wealthy Sicilian family, he had a gallant manner and a natural charm that dazzled the fifteen year old Félice despite herself.

Now he fought his way through the crowd and breathlessly reached her side. 'Did you hear the sermon? Wasn't it splendid?'

'It was very well delivered but the content was rather banal.'

'Banal? You can't be serious! In *that* crowd – the Bishop practically crippled from the weight of the jewels on his cope – to preach against wealth! And then did you see the way he kept looking at the Templars? He was criticising not only individuals who hoard their wealth but institutions as well – like the Templars and the Benedictines!'

'It may have been courageous but the message was hardly original,' Félice insisted. She had never learned to agree with someone just because he was male. Her education had been almost entirely in her grandfather's hands until her mother had sent her up to Poitiers the previous year. Her grandfather had encouraged her to tell him what she thought and why. She always had to tell him *why* she thought what she did.

'It wasn't supposed to be original,' Umberto pointed out enthusiastically. It was the fact that Félice did not agree with him which made her so fascinating. Umberto had never known a woman of any age or status who did not assure him that he was certainly right since he was ever so much cleverer than she. 'It was supposed to be a reminder of what Christ taught us thirteen hundred years ago! Come, I'll walk you back to the convent,' Umberto suggested, directing their steps away from the crowded square towards the Rue du Marché.

Félice fell in beside him gladly. She could think of nothing more pleasurable than discussing anything with this young man and enjoying the summer's day in his company. By mutual accord, they kept their pace slow, as if too absorbed in their discussion to move forwards.

'But there is absolutely no certainty that Christ ever *did* say it was easier for a *camel* to pass through the eye of a needle. My grandfather says that it is probably a mistranslation or false transcription from the original Greek and that Christ probably said "rope" not "camel".'

They turned into the Rue de la Cathédrale.

'Rope or camel, neither can pass through the eye of a needle and so the lesson remains the same,' Umberto retorted quickly.

'A rope is made up of single threads and each of them can pass through the eye of a needle individually,' Félice pointed out. 'But something else bothers me far more.'

'And that is?' Umberto paused to look her straight in the face. He too was flushed from the pleasure of her presence. He found her curly hair, touched with sinful red, exciting. Her wide-set golden eyes were warm enough to melt his heart. With some internal discomfort, his eyes waited anxiously for every breath of wind that pressed her smock to her chest and enabled him to make out the small but pronounced curves of her breasts.

'That material wealth is of this world. That means that at death and at the moment of resurrection we are *all* beggars possessing nothing but our naked bodies and our souls.'

Umberto fell in beside her again and focused his eyes upon the cobbles of the street. He dared not be distracted by her sexuality at the moment for he could not readily find a retort to her argument.

'Certainly, we are all equal after death but it is the deeds we have committed in life which determine the judgement meted out. So too it is the wealth we possess in life which will be considered and not the poverty induced by death itself. Only that poverty which we *voluntarily* assume will count in our favour on the Day of Judgement.' He now looked up and smiled a little triumphantly, pleased that he had, after all, so rapidly found a refutation of her objection.

'But if rich people give up their wealth for the sake of entering heaven, then surely it is a selfish act and not one really deserving reward?' Félice persisted. 'I don't consider it particularly virtuous for rich people to give up their wealth merely for the sake of getting into heaven. Surely you know the story about the woman at Masyaf who carried coals in one hand and water in the other to extinguish the fires of hell with the one and destroy heaven with the other.'

'What?' Umberto was laughing at the absurdity of her speech and the charm of her flushed cheeks. He often felt like laughing when Félice was excited by an idea, because then her cheeks grew redder and she wet her lower lip with her tongue, making it shine brighter, and sometimes, when she was very excited, her chest heaved and he could see her breasts rising and falling.

Fortunately, Félice had no idea that Umberto was sneaking glances at her chest. She was uncomfortable with sexuality in any form and wanted Umberto to like her for herself – for her mind and her soul, not her body. She excitedly continued with her story, anxious to impress Umberto. She knew that he liked radical ideas. 'The woman said she wanted to destroy heaven and hell so that people would do good and avoid evil not for reward or fear of punishment but for their own sake. Surely that is what Christ wanted?'

'Who was this woman?' Umberto enquired with a look of scepticism.

'Some woman in Masyaf.' Félice dismissed the woman irritably. She wasn't interested in the woman: she wanted Umberto to discuss the *idea*.

'A Mohammedan!' Umberto exclaimed reproachfully. 'Who told you such a silly story?'

'It's not silly. My grandfather, who was knighted by Saint Louis,' she reminded him proudly, 'told me the story.'

Umberto knew better than to criticise Félice's grandfather. So he chose instead to change the subject. 'Look, His Holiness is at the baptistery!' They had reached the end of the street. Ahead of them loomed the cathedral but to their right, across the cathedral square, was the Baptistery of Saint Jean, built in the fourth century when the city was still Roman. 'What do you suppose he is doing there?' Umberto asked with genuine curiosity.

Félice felt considerably less interest in Clement V than Umberto did. Since she had come to Poitiers, she had seen the pontiff on various occasions and received his blessings twice. He was a thin man who seemed to suffer from a perpetual head cold and was always coughing or wiping his pointed nose. She did not like him – which was, her mother would have said, proof of her heretical blood. But she could see that she would never get Umberto to return to the content of their discussion. Umberto was attracted to clerical power like a magnet and had only come to study at Poitiers – a relatively obscure university – in order to be near the pope. So she pretended an interest in the pope, and together they strolled towards the baptistery.

'Mademoiselle de Preuthune!' For a second time, a voice called out to her.

This time, vaguely conscious that she should have headed directly for the convent rather than letting Umberto drag her along in his wake, she started guiltily and turned about. Coming across the cathedral square, his cassock fluttering about him as he strode towards her, was the dean of the cathedral himself.

The dean, Monseigneur Michel de Saint Laurent Sérvre, was a man in his early forties. He was a vigorous man, built more like a smith or a longshoreman than a priest. He had broad shoulders, thick, muscular arms and a stride that shook the earth. He trod as if an elephant were abroad. More important, though not a man of noble birth, he was a relation on his mother's side of the king's most influential minister, Keeper of the Privy Seal, Guillaume de Nogaret. It was no secret that he was designated for the bishopric of Albi as soon as the present incumbent finally succumbed to the sickness that had incapacitated him for months.

Félice dipped her knee and bowed her head demurely to the powerful priest.

'The Reverend Mother is looking all over for you, mademoiselle!' the dean told her sternly. 'She was about to send out search parties. Report to her at once, and for your sake let us pray the Virgin inspires her with mercy.' He dismissed her with a quick flick of his hand.

Félice dropped another curtsey and with a hasty, almost inaudible 'Adieu' to Umberto, she collected her skirts and ran across the cathedral court, heading for the Convent of Saint Radegonde beyond.

Umberto, embarrassed to be discovered by such a prominent churchman in a potentially compromising situation, also bowed and started to take his leave, but the Monseigneur had him firmly by the elbow and started to lead him forcefully towards the cathedral.

'Not so fast, young man. I intend to take a stroll in the cloisters and you will accompany me.'

Umberto could hardly say no, and a part of him was even excited. It was not every student who took an afternoon stroll with the Dean of Poitiers Cathedral. His colleagues never need learn the reason or the content of the discussion. He fell in beside the dean and paced himself to match the stride of the senior cleric.

'I've been watching you for some time, di Sante,' the dean commenced before they had reached the cathedral. 'You're an ambitious young man.'

Umberto was flattered – and impressed that the dean had been able to detect this, given how little contact they had had with one another.

The dean shoved open the door of the cathedral. It banged it loudly; the echo vibrated in the soaring arches overhead, but the dean was not in the least distracted. He marched across the nave with only the barest hint of a genuflection towards the altar, heading to the door leading out into the cloisters at the base of the transept opposite. The fact that mass was being read in the choir disturbed him not in the least. They entered the tranquillity of the cloisters where the pure romanesque arcade framed the bubbling fountain in the centre of the garth with its clipped grass.

The dean had no particular affinity for beauty and he started pounding his way over the graves of deceased priests as if he were intent upon wearing away even the simple crosses with the Christian names and dates.

'You selected the books for copying not merely on the basis of the condition of the pages but on the basis of *content*.' The dean willingly revealed one of the reasons he was impressed by Umberto.

Umberto noted this with satisfaction, remembering that he had explained before he was asked the reason why he recommended the copying of various volumes. At the time, he had thought the dean uninterested and even irritated;

now he was gratified to learn that his effort to attract attention had been more successful than he had dared hope.

'You have a good head on your shoulders,' the dean continued in a matter-of-fact tone. 'Your professors assure me of that.' He glanced at the young man next to him and his eyes narrowed a bit.

The boy had a face too pretty by far. Monseigneur Michel was not himself a good-looking man: his face was too round, his lips too thick and his nose too stubby for that. But then everyone had their faults, Monseigneur reminded himself, and he continued, 'It seems to me that you have a great number of options open to you.'

Umberto's blood quickened in his veins. Never in his wildest dreams had he thought he might obtain patronage and opportunity so early. He had only been at the university for three years. Many youths studied for ten without attracting particular favour. And, while his family was rich enough to secure him a church benefice or a position in a monastery in Sicily, Umberto couldn't bear the thought of ending there, so far from the seat of power.

'You will have given thought to your own future,' the dean continued. 'What is it you actually want out of life?'

Umberto was embarrassed to admit the dreams that filled him. He could hardly tell a man who had not yet gained the bishop's staff that he aspired so high. He reduced his sights accordingly: 'A university chair—'

'I thought you had more sense than that! Do you want to spend the rest of your life arguing about how many angels can stand on a pinhead?' The disapproval was patent.

'Well, no, I just—'

'Let's not play stupid games with one another. You're too good for that. You known damn well that power lies not in the universities, much less the parishes. There are only two real routes to power – the papal court or the crown. You can serve the pope or the king of France – and to be honest that is one and the same thing at the moment since the king controls the pope. To serve the king is the more direct means of gaining reward.'

Even Umberto was taken aback by the directness of this speech. To be sure, all the students talked among themselves about Clement's utter subservience to Philip IV, but they always kept their voices down and looked over their shoulders when they spoke.

'The king has urgent need of intelligent clerics who are willing to follow his lead without any mealy-mouthed prevarication. He's going to have special need of them in the near future. Did you like the sermon by Father Elion, by the way?' The dean stopped abruptly and asked the question out of the blue.

'Yes. Very much. The man has brilliant rhetoric and real courage. The Bishop did not look pleased,' Umberto added with a touch of a smile.

The dean laughed heartily. 'No, the bishop was not unduly pleased, but that hardly matters. The king is impressed by Father Elion. He is a man who has a nose for the seat of evil and the fanaticism to root it out.'

Umberto wondered how the dean knew this, but already the dean was continuing.

'The king is a very devout man, you know. He cannot abide heresy.'

This was hardly a secret. Philip IV had not hesitated to accuse pope Boniface VIII of heresy. The king had then proceeded to have the pope arrested – by troops under the command of de Nogaret. Pope Boniface had died not very long afterwards – whether of poison, fear or merely despair was a matter of much lively speculation among the students.

'Now,' the dean continued purposefully, 'for a young man eager to rise rapidly in the Church, there are a number of options. The most obvious course – and therefore the one most unimaginative youths pursue – is to become attached to the papal court.'

Umberto was anxious to show that he was not so 'unimaginative' and now spoke up. 'My family supported Charles of Anjou. I intended—'

'Anjou may be the king's brother, but make no mistake about his influence. The king wants his brother to become Holy Roman Emperor in order to increase his own power. Charles de Valois is a cultivated, intelligent man but he has none of his elder brother's ruthlessness.'

Umberto had not noted that Anjou conducted the campaign in Sicily with particular mildness, but he knew better than to contradict.

'What you need to do, di Sante, is to join the Dominicans. That is the order most favoured by the king and all his confessors have been and will be Dominicans.'

The idea of being the confessor of a king had never crossed Umberto's mind but he liked the image instantly.

'There is a problem.' The dean stopped abruptly and turned to confront Umberto so directly that the young man took a step back in shock. 'You must enter holy orders – you must become a priest – and you cannot have any female casting a shadow over your career.'

Umberto blushed against his will. 'You misunderstood. I saw Mademoiselle de Preuthune alone before Notre Dame and I merely offered to escort her back to the convent. We have—'

'I am Mademoiselle de Preuthune's confessor, di Sante. You don't need to tell me that she is not only still a virgin but a sincerely modest maiden. But listen carefully: there is no woman in Poitiers who is more dangerous for you than the Preuthune maid.'

'Monseigneur! I don't understand. Of all the maidens now at the convent, she is the most genuinely interested in learning—'

'The girl is much too intelligent for her own good! She has a better mind than nine-tenths of the students at the university! You don't have to tell me that. And she reads Greek – which I dare say is more than you can do. But that is *exactly* why she is dangerous. She's not a girl you can use and discard. Her father is a respectable nobleman, her brother is on his way to becoming one of the leading tournament champions of France, and, to top it off, her grandfather was knighted by Saint Louis himself. I happen to know her grandfather, di Sante; he may be over seventy but he is fearless. If you dishonour the girl, you can be sure that he will not hesitate to go to the king himself. Do you want to end like Abelard?'

Umberto blushed and unconsciously slipped his right hand protectively over his genitals.

'No. You don't. Look, if I know anything about Sicily, you ploughed more than one furrow before you left home. No one says you have to stop. There are more girls than you can count who would pay a pretty penny to take you to their beds. You have the kind of face girls like.'

Umberto swallowed awkwardly, unsure if he were expected to admit that he regularly took advantage of this fact.

'I see you haven't been fasting.' The dean read his expression correctly. 'No one is going to blame you for that. Not even after you take higher orders. You don't think the whores of Poitiers live on secular customers alone, do you? But in the name of God, keep away from maids like the Preuthune. The most important rule is: never sleep with a woman who hasn't spread her legs for dozens of others. Whether she's whore or just a woman of low birth or morals, never, never give a woman the chance to claim convincingly that you are the father of her bastard.'

As abruptly as he had addressed Umberto, the dean seemed to tire of him. He stepped back. 'I hope you have fully understood me,' the dean remarked almost wearily, and then waved him away. He hardly looked at Umberto as the youth dipped his knee and backed away in a state of confusion.

Chapter Two

St Pierre du Temple, 12th October, 1307

As the sun turned coppery and sank behind the clouds on the horizon, Sir Percy de Lacy was grateful to find the turning towards Saint Pierre du Temple. There was a chill wind blowing off the Massif Central and the trees here were almost naked. The yellow and brown leaves collected deep in the ditches beside the road. They reminded him that it was late in the year to find a ship at Marseille bound for Cyprus.

For the hundredth time he shook his head mentally at the Grand Master's curious indecision. Three times in the last month, he had summoned Sir Percy and given him sealed dispatches for the seneschal of the Temple, only to change his mind the next day, take the dispatches back and order him to wait again. He could have been to England and back twice over while he waited!

Sir Percy had been born and raised on the marches of Wales, the fourth son of a cadet branch of the powerful de Lacy family. He had joined the Templars at seventeen and had been sent to the Holy Land two years later. It was now six years since he had been home. In that time his father had died and his eldest brother had assumed his inheritance and married. Percy would have liked to go home. Not to stay, but to visit, to meet his sister-in-law and nephew, to tell his brothers his adventures and hear all the news from family and friends. He would have liked to call in on his cousin, the Earl of Lincoln, and meet King Edward II so he could form his own judgement of the controversial prince. He resented having to cool his heels in Poitiers for over three months, and the thought that he might be too late for the voyage to Cyprus this year was particularly frustrating.

He tightened his calves upon the flanks of the greying stallion he had been issued at the last commandery and urged it to a trot. The big-boned warhorse pretended not to feel anything and Percy at once resorted to his spurs. He was used to better horseflesh and disliked having to push and drive this stallion forwards. Maybe they would have better horses at Saint Pierre, he comforted himself.

No sooner did the low walls of the Templar manor come into view in the last light of dusk than Percy knew he would be unlikely to find any decent horseflesh there. The 'commandery' distinguished itself from any rundown fortified manor or priory only by the banner flying from the gatehouse. The walls themselves were in disrepair, he noted professionally, and the smell of dung hung oppressively upon the air.

'What sort of a pigsty is this?' his squire enquired, screwing up his face.

The youth, Ramon, was not a Templar but a waged squire. The eagerness with which the young man had volunteered to accompany Percy to Cyprus led the knight to suspect that the young man was running away from something. He had not made any effort to discover Ramon's past, however, suspecting that he wouldn't like what he found. Besides, they would have ample time to get to know one another on the ship to Cyprus.

'Saint Pierre du Temple,' Percy answered, and drew up his stallion to pull the bell at the gate.

It seemed to take an inordinately long time before a peephole in the porter's lodge was shoved open and an cracked voice asked, 'Who goes?'

'Sir Percy de Lacy, Knight of the Commandery at Limassol, travelling with dispatches from the Grand Master. I need accommodation for the night.'

He had not finished all that before he could make out muffled voices, screeching and creaking and then the gate started to slowly swing open. Through the gate, he could see a boy darting across the courtyard, his brown, lay brother's habit held up so high that his bare calves and filthy bare feet were exposed. The old porter was bowing his bald head at Sir Percy, and welcoming him exuberantly.

'We had no reason to expect such an exalted guest, sir. We hardly see any guests at all. The last time a knight was here must have been back in... in... let me see.' He scratched his scabby head. 'In '06, at Michaelmas, on account of our rents. But then it was Sir Denys from Saint Gilles. He always came at Michaelmas and Easter until he got the gout. Since then the commander at Saint Gilles prefers Sergeant-Commander Brother Gautier to bring the rents over himself.' As if he had just noticed that he was talking too much, he added, 'Shall I take your horse, sir?'

Percy jumped down, glad to get out of the saddle even if this poor house was not likely to offer much luxury in the way of accommodation. 'Ramon will see to our horses.' He indicated his squire. 'If you will take me to your commander.'

'I sent Brother Gaston over to fetch him – there they are!' The porter pointed to a low, blunt-headed door with a weathered stone frame which gave access at ground level to the line of buildings along the west wall.

Percy scanned the little complex around him. The largest building was a towering tithe barn to which the deep ruts in the muddy courtyard led. He supposed that the bulk of this year's harvest was now stored there. A low, half-timbered stable cowered beside the tithe barn and an external well with watering trough was located between the stables and the kitchens. Adjacent to the kitchens but at a right angle were the living quarters of the little community: a two-storey construction of whitewashed field stone. A humble chapel crouched just inside the gatehouse.

The commander in the black habit of a sergeant, followed by the boy Percy had seen scampering across the courtyard, hobbled across the courtyard. His face was weathered, the fringe of his tonsure grey. 'Welcome to Saint Pierre, sir.' He bowed, and Percy, who towered a good eight inches over the sergeant, bent and gave him the kiss of peace on both cheeks.

'I hope we will be no inconvenience. I am on my way to Marseille.'

'It is our pleasure. You come from the Grand Master, Gaston tells me.' The sergeant indicated the boy, who stood beside him gazing up at the knight with awestruck eyes.

Gaston was twelve and he had never seen a Knight Templar before – not in real life. He had often imagined them in his daydreams: in spotlessly white mantles on great, fierce stallions, the Cross of God blazoned on their chests, their lances red with Saracen blood. Gaston had fought a thousand battles against the Turks and Egyptians. He had rescued endangered knights and earned his own spurs and helped free the captive cities of the Holy Land. Sir Percy did not disappoint him. For one thing, he was taller than any man Gaston – who had been born only sixteen miles away and never left the parish – had ever seen. For another, he wore steel knee guards, a bassinet with a gleaming crown and ominous chain mail neck guard. The two-handed longsword which hung from his heavy leather belt looked big enough to spit an ox.

'You will be tired and hungry,' Brother Gautier was insisting. 'Come into the refectory. We are in the midst of our evening meal.' Percy had not thought it was so late and looked, somewhat surprised, over his shoulder towards the western horizon.

'We eat at sundown,' the sergeant explained. 'To save on oil and candles. These have been hard years for us. The drought destroyed most of our crops and when the spring floods came more than half the livestock was swept away and drowned. They were too weak to swim and save themselves.' He shook his head. 'So many families were ruined and they all come here begging for alms. They never believe that we have nothing ourselves.'

Percy nodded gravely. He had been shocked by the poverty of France. It wasn't just the contrast with Cyprus. One couldn't compare France with the richest Mediterranean island. But Percy had been raised to think of France as infinitely richer than the rugged hills of the Welsh marches where he had been born. Yet he had never seen so many beggars in England or so much squalor. When he had remarked on this to fellow Templars they too had referred to the drought of the previous year and the ensuing famine. For all he knew, he reminded himself, Herefordshire was now populated with beggars too.

Percy left his helm, bassinet and shield on his saddle, giving instructions to Ramon to bed down in the loft of the stables after the meal. The squire made some remark under his breath, but led the horses away dutifully.

The refectory was a vaulted undercroft with very small, deep windows, which smelled heavily of smoke. By the light of a half-dozen torches and two candles on the high table, some two score brothers took their meal at trestle-tables. As far as Percy could see, the brothers were all serving brothers. There was neither another sergeant nor a priest among the brown-robed men with bare or sandalled feet who followed him with curious eyes and open mouths as he accompanied the commander to the high table.

'Have you no priest?' he asked in a low voice, somewhat concerned.

'Father Roger is in the reading pulpit.' The sergeant indicated the niche set some six feet above the floor, reached by a wooden stair. There stood a very young man in the robes of the priesthood, staring at Percy with no less wonder than the serving brothers.

At the head table, Sergeant Gautier turned to face the hall of astonished Templars and announced, 'This is Brother Percy. He is on his way to Marseille and will spend the night with us. Father Roger, if you would be so kind as to continue.'

With this he sat down and indicated the place next to him for Percy. A serving brother, reeking of sweat, grease and garlic, was already laying a place for Percy: a trencher composed of thick-sliced stale bread, a chipped pottery mug with what smelled like sour wine and a rusty-looking spoon and knife. As discreetly as possible, Percy untied his own eating utensils from their place on the right hip of his sword belt and speared a stiff-looking dried cod.

The droning of the priest now made conversation impossible and Percy registered that the Rule was apparently observed scrupulously in this backwater – even if the serving brothers shovelled the homely meal into their mouths without paying attention to the lesson being read. From the way they hunched over their trenchers and the eagerness with which they grabbed the food with their dirty hands, it was clear that they were the sons of serfs. Scanning their uniformly crude faces, low-set brows, wide, fleshy noses and big mouths, Percy suspected that half of them were related to each other and certainly they all came from the surrounding countryside. Percy suspected that even the priest, stumbling over his text and reading in a mumbling monotone, was a man of local and low birth. It was a sad commentary on the state of the once great order, he reflected, and a sharp contrast to the Holy Land, where serving brothers were often born freemen and were usually skilled craftsmen.

At the end of the meal, the brothers filed out of the refectory to the chapel, and the nervous young priest hastened down from the reading pulpit to conduct the service of vespers.

'We always read vespers and compline one after the other,' Sergeant Brother Gautier explained somewhat apologetically. 'Then we can retire for the night.'

Percy nodded. He already understood: they saved on firewood and wine by skipping the cosy interlude between vespers and compline in which the brothers normally sat together and chatted before the rule of silence came into effect for the night.

The chapel must have been nearly two hundred years old. It was squat and solid with only the narrowest of blunt-headed windows and naked of adornment. A testament to the austerity of the Order at its founding, it humbled Percy, who had grown more accustomed to the grandeur with which the Grand Master and the other officers surrounded themselves nowadays. The Temple in London where he had been received and undergone his novitiate was a city within a city and the Templar church, though humble compared with the abbeys and cathedrals of England, was still well lit by soaring triple windows along the nave and the clerestory windows in the circular choir.

Standing with Brother Gautier in the first pew, Percy could see that the priest looked hardly more than twenty and that his face was a welter of acne. He kept glancing nervously at Percy as he rattled through one service after the other as if he had learned them by rote. Once or twice he skipped over whole passages without apparently noticing.

After compline the rule of silence applied. Brother Gautier signalled for Percy to follow him and then led him up a flight of external stairs to the dormitory above the refectory. The long, raftered room was lit in the day by narrow windows set high in the walls but now they were shuttered against the chill of night. Two thick candles, one at each end of the hall, were lit by the first brother to enter the hall.

Percy was touched that, despite the financial distress of the little house, the rule about Templars sleeping with a burning candle was still observed. This paragraph of the Rule, like that requiring knights to sleep in shirt and drawers, had been intended to ensure that knights would be in a position to arm rapidly and without confusion if the alarm were sounded in the middle of the night. Designed for knights living on the outposts of Christendom, vowed to protect Christians from the incursions of a more numerous foe, it hardly had any relevance on this peaceful farm thousands of miles from the enemy and housing not a single fighting monk.

Brother Gautier led Percy to the upper end of the dormitory and took from an ageing cabinet a pallet and two blankets. These he carried to a spot somewhat separated from those of the serving brothers and directly beside that of the priest. Meanwhile, the serving brothers were emerging one after the other from the stair to the latrines on the floor below and starting to pull their habits off over their heads.

Brother Gautier started to unroll the pallet and prepare it for the knight, but, seeing that the sergeant was handicapped by his stiff leg, Percy took over from him and made up his own bed. He would have liked to ask the sergeant if his bad leg were the product of a wound he had received in the Holy Land, but the rule of silence prohibited him.

The bed made up, Sergeant Gautier kissed him on each cheek and made the sign of the cross before hobbling to the other side of the room and kneeling at the foot of his own pallet. Percy made his way first to the stinking latrine behind the kitchen and then past the two rows of serving brothers to his waiting pallet. The priest now knelt in his shirt at the end of his pallet, his scrawny, hairy legs sticking out on to the cold floor behind him. As Percy arrived, he made the sign of the cross and crawled in under his blankets.

Percy unbuckled his heavy sword belt and laid the great weapon beside his pallet. Then he went to remove his cloak. Suddenly, out of the darkness the figure of the boy, Gaston, emerged grinning. Apparently, he had been waiting for him. With eager if inept awe, Gaston began helping Percy remove his surcoat and hauberk. In his imagination, Gaston was now a squire rather than an illiterate serving brother.

Percy sat on his pallet and started to unfasten the buckles of his spurs. Gaston at once addressed himself to the foot nearer him, following Percy's example because he had never seen armour so close and did not know how it was all kept in place. He unfastened the garter holding up his chain mail legging and finally the points attaching the legging to the aketon. The leggings laid aside, Percy removed his aketon and with a nodded thanks signalled Gaston to return to his own pallet. Reluctantly, Gaston did as he was bid.

Percy wrapped himself, still in hose, braies and shirt, in the coarse blankets and shut his eyes. He drifted to sleep to the deep breathing and light whistling snores of the two score men in the great dormitory.

The shouting and clatter that woke him made him start up from his bed in confusion. For a moment he could not remember where he was and then as he recognised the long dormitory with the two rows of pallets lining the walls, he was even more confused. He could hear raw shouting and dull, ominous pounding. Around him several of the other monks were starting to stir. Someone cursed under his breath and another, elderly voice seemed to cry out in fear and then subdue itself.

The crash that came from the courtyard made Percy fling off his blankets and grab his aketon. Now he could hear more shouting, the imperative yelling of men giving orders, the thudding of numerous hooves on frozen ground, the pounding of boots on wooden stairs, the clunk of doors being flung open. He pulled the aketon over his head and tightened the laces at his throat.

Men were bursting into the dormitory. By the light of the two candles, Percy could see that they wore round 'kettle' helmets over mail-coifs and that they had naked swords in their hands.

Percy dragged his hauberk and surcoat together over his head even as the armed men were roughly kicking the serving brothers awake and herding the startled, bewildered men together.

Sergeant Gautier was on his feet and limping forwards in his underwear, calling out, 'What is this? Who are you? What do you want?'

'You are all arrested in the name of His Grace King Philip IV of France!'

While some of the serving brothers broke into a jumble of confused exclamations of disbelief, Brother Gautier protested in a raised, somewhat hysterical voice, 'Why? On what charge?'

The thought that these simple brothers could have done anything to offend the crown of France was so absurd that Percy instantly dismissed the claim as either a mistake or a ruse. Philip of France could hardly know that Saint Pierre du Temple existed. The Temple was, in any case, not subordinate to any king and owed Philip neither taxes nor obedience. Percy knew, however, that he no longer had time for his mail leggings and reached instead for his sword.

There came a shout, the sound of someone running and then he was tackled from behind and flung stomach first on to his pallet, pinned down by the weight of his assailant on his back. Even as he rammed his elbows backwards against his attacker, he saw a foot kick out and send the sword skittering across the flagstone floor out of reach. Another man had joined the first on his back, pressing his knee into Percy's spine. Another had hold of the back of his neck in a powerful, muscular grip and forced his face down into the blankets, nearly suffocating him. Someone was wrenching his arms behind his back and tying his wrists together. Percy knew when he was defeated since that too was something a good soldier learned to recognise and he stopped struggling instantly. The pressure on his spine and head eased at once. The men backed off him, pulling him to his feet.

He looked over his shoulder and saw that the men holding him were indeed wearing the livery of the king of France. It was ridiculous! What could they possibly hope to gain by a breach with the pope? Did Philip of France want to start a feud with Clement V to match the one he had had with Boniface VIII? Weak as Clement was said to be, even he would not tolerate such a flagrant affront to his authority.

The king's men were already herding the bewildered serving brothers and the priest down the stairs to the courtyard. One old man kept asking his brothers what was happening while Gaston kept looking anxiously over his shoulder to see what had happened to Percy. Serfs by birth, they had been born to docility and as monks they had vowed obedience. Such men, Percy told himself, could not be expected to distinguish between lawful and unlawful authority.

Brother Gautier alone was protesting to the captain in charge. He insisted that he and his brothers were innocent of all wrongdoing. Not one day in their lives had they ever been anything but loyal subjects of the king, he assured the king's representative in a shaky, strained voice. Terror was written on the aged sergeant's face and Percy felt sorry for him. Evidently, he was so frightened that he had forgotten that the Temple was subordinate to the pope alone.

'It's not for me to judge your guilt or innocence,' the royal officer told Brother Gautier matter-of-factly. 'I have my orders.'

'But who gave you the orders? What is the cause of all this? I don't understand,' Brother Gautier was wringing his hands.

'Take it up with the sheriff,' the man advised indifferently.

He was relieved that his mission had gone so well. The orders to attack a house of the Knights Templar and arrest all those within had made him break out in a cold sweat just six hours ago. He had been raised on the legends of Templars defending their castles against tens of thousands of Saracens, their small bands matching great armies, their rescue of King Louis II from destruction, their heroic defence of Acre. The captain knew that they were not allowed to withdraw unless the enemy had more than three-to-one superiority, and he could not know how many men they had in Saint Pierre – which was why he had mustered his entire company of nearly fifty men. In the event, it was almost ludicrous how easy it had been, he thought, shaking his head.

'You can be sure that we will take this up with the sheriff – and the pope! Someone – you, your sheriff or King Philip himself – has overstepped his authority.'

Percy's voice drew the captain's attention and he looked up, startled, at the man held by two of his subordinates. He took in the chain mail hauberk, the muscular shoulders and thighs and drew the correct conclusion. This man was a knight. 'Are you the commander, sir?'

'No, I am the commander. This is just a poor traveller. Here for a single night. Whatever crimes we have been unjustly accused of, they cannot apply to him.' Brother Gautier spoke before Percy could get a word out.

The captain looked from Brother Gautier to Percy, somewhat uncertainly. 'I am an Englishman, Sir Percy de Lacy of the commandery at Limassol on Cyprus, *en route* from Poitiers to Limassol,' Percy confirmed. 'And you have no business arresting *any* Templar since we are subordinate to no one but our own officers and the pope himself.'

The arrogance of Percy's tone angered the captain and he took refuge in the certainties of life: 'I have my orders and they were to arrest *everyone* inside this house. I don't give a damn if you are a bloody Englishman or the pope himself!'

And at this he turned his back on the two remaining Templars and clattered down the stairs into the ward, his men pushing Percy and Brother Gautier before them as they followed him outside.

The Templars stood huddled together near the shattered gate. The king's men had evidently forced an entry using battleaxes to hack out the lock and weaken the wooden panels before they smashed through them with a wagon. The serving brothers stood around docilely while the king's men tied their wrists together with a single, long rope. They were just about finished when the captain arrived.

He checked on the work and ordered Brother Gautier bound as well. Addressing his prisoner as the old sergeant stood with his wrists held out in front of him, he asked,

'You said you were the commander here. Where do you keep valuables?'

'In the treasury, of course,' Brother Gautier answered tightly, staring at his tied wrists in open disbelief.

'Where is that?'

'Why do you want to know?' Brother Gautier countered.

'Why do you think? My orders are not just to seize your lousy persons but your misgotten wealth as well!'

Brother Gautier's face went ashen. He was remembering the way the king had seized the wealth of the Jews just a year earlier. Philip's ruthlessness had impressed everyone – whether with inner glee or aversion.

Percy's reaction was to dismiss the possibility that these were the king's men at all. Common thieves, he thought, disguised as royal troops.

'Well, where is it? Is it in locked chests? Give me the keys!'

Brother Gautier clamped his mouth shut and lifted his chin. The captain reacted automatically, striking the old sergeant with an almost casual, backhanded cuff that smashed the monk's head to one side. But Brother Gautier let out not even a whimper. That angered the captain even more, and he delivered three more quick blows. Blood started to gush from the sergeant's nose but he held his tongue.

'Do you think I can't make you talk?' the captain shouted. He snapped up his knee and the sergeant crumpled on to the ground, moaning and writhing. The captain delivered one kick to his hip and another to the base of his spine.

The cry that the sergeant gave was like a howl, and Percy could stand it no longer. 'Brother! I am your witness! You cannot defend yourself! And nor can I,' he added sadly to himself.

The captain looked over, astonished. He had half-expected this young nobleman to protest at his actions. He had half-wanted him to protest because that would have given him an excuse to deal out similar treatment to the arrogant whelp. But if he were going to be so cooperative, the captain would have to reconsider. He looked back at the man at his feet.

'Did you hear what the knight said? Give me the keys.'

'They, they are... in the dormitory. In the cupboard.' Gautier spoke in gasps.

The captain sent one of his men back into the dormitory and ordered another to get the sergeant back on his feet. It seemed to take a long time, but eventually the man came back with a ring of keys. Satisfied, the captain left just a handful of men to watch the prisoners and set off with the others to open not just the treasury chests but the store-rooms, cupboards, and anything else that was deemed worthy of being locked.

The Templars watched in silence. What started as looting soon turned to vandalism as the royal soldiers, promised hoards of gold and caches of silver, found almost nothing of value. Even the church was not sacrosanct: the king's men ransacked it more thoroughly than any of the other buildings and, when the soldiers showed their meagre haul to the captain, he cursed violently and abusively with a scowl in the direction of the Templars.

Percy glanced at the priest and noted that the young man was trembling from head to foot and his lips were moving, apparently in prayer. He felt a profound contempt for this man who, as a priest, enjoyed the most exalted status of all the men at Saint Pierre. He should have been setting an example for the others. He should at least have made the effort to exude calm. Better still, he should have explained to his bewildered and frightened brothers that they could not be treated like this with impunity. He should have reminded them that they stood under papal protection. He should have at least tried to reduce the impact of this appalling assault on their dignity and livelihood by assuring them that they had powerful friends who would make sure that the damages were repaired and the losses made good.

Percy looked from the priest to the sergeant and he realised that they were both completely intimidated. Oh, Christ, he thought. Are these the mighty Templars who are supposed to be your fearless champions? But of course the image of the Templars was forged by knights not sergeants and priests – much less serving brothers. He looked around and saw that many of the brothers were cowering in instinctive terror and others were openly weeping. In none did he see a flicker of defiance or even outrage – except the boy. Gaston clenched his fists and his eyes met Percy's. 'They can't do this to us, can they, sir?'

'They don't have the right to do this, and I'm sure someone will pay a heavy price for such lawlessness!' Percy spoke not just for Gaston but to give the others courage as well.

'You mean they'll be made to give us back what they've taken?' one of the other serving brothers asked in a tone that was far from convinced.

'I should think more than that! They must pay for the damage that has been done!' Percy indicated the smashed gate and now the blankets, pallets and kitchen utensils which the outraged soldiery were dumping in the centre of the ward.

From the stables came the nickering of disturbed horses and then some shouts. With a tinge of guilt, Percy realised that he had forgotten Ramon. Apparently, the squire had slept through all that had happened up to now – or, having seen armed men, he had tried to hide himself. A few minutes later he was marched out of the stables, straw clinging to his hair and his clothes.

'What is this all about, sir?' Ramon demanded the minute he saw Percy.

Percy shrugged. 'You'll have to ask these men, who claim to be in the service of the king of France.'

'But the Temple isn't under royal jurisdiction!' the squire protested in a somewhat high-pitched tone.

Percy wondered if the youth was wanted by the crown and for that very reason had sought service with the Temple – preferably outside France. If so, he had just had some very bad luck.

'No, it isn't, but as you see they outnumber us and they are armed.'

Realising that Percy was bound and apparently resigned to his fate, Ramon made one last desperate effort to escape. He flung himself with all his strength to the left and wrenched free of the man on his right. But the surprise effect was brief. He was just a youth and the two guards were hardened veterans. The man he had evaded was ashamed to have been outmanoeuvred by a mere youth and, with a roar, leapt after him. The other man, who had never lost his hold, lashed out at the squire's knees with his foot. In an instant they had felled Ramon and, once they had pinned him to the ground, they thrashed him thoroughly. He howled and tried to protect his head with his arms.

'Does it take two grown men to subdue a boy?' Percy asked in raised voice.

The taunt worked. Instantly, they ceased beating the youth, and one of them bound his arms behind his back while the other came ominously towards Percy. Percy met the man's eye and braced himself for the blow. He expected it to come to his belly or groin after what he had seen in the last hour. But the authority of class still cast a protective shield around him. The soldier narrowed his eyes and ran his tongue over his crooked, discoloured teeth, but he did not yet risk laying hands on a nobleman without orders from his captain. He turned his back on Percy and stalked away.

Eventually even the captain had to admit that the run-down little manor had nothing more to offer. With an obscene curse and a kick to the pile of household goods collected in the centre of the ward, he gave the order to load the prisoners on to a wagon.

This startled Percy. He still could not bring himself to believe that these men were acting on higher authority, and he had expected to be locked into some cellar while the thieves took off with their disappointing plunder. If, however, the Templars were to be taken with the robber band, it suggested that the thieves wanted not only to get clean away but to eliminate all witnesses as well. For the first time that night, Percy felt fear in the pit of his stomach.

The Templars were roughly shoved towards the open wagon which the intruders had used to break through the gate. Two powerful draught horses were brought in from outside and hitched to the shafts while the Templars were ordered to climb into the wagon. While the serving brothers meekly scrambled aboard as best they could with their tied hands and long habits, Percy hung back. Now he searched feverishly for some means of escape.

Unfortunately, he was being observed. No sooner did his lingering become apparent than a man shoved him brutally forwards. They were all around him, clustered at the wagon, preparing to mount their own horses.

'Here!' the captain shouted and beckoned.

The man behind Percy steered him over to the captain. A horse was brought over and, for the second time that night, Percy submitted to the inevitable, lifting his left foot into the stirrup and allowing the man behind to shove him into the saddle. He was the only one they provided with a horse, he noted. One of the guards took up his reins and another man tied his legs together under the belly of the gelding.

Chapter Three

Friday, 13th October, 1307

It was starting to drizzle and the sky was lightening by the time the walls of Albi came into view. Percy recognised the city at once. He had passed through it only the day before and asked there for directions to the next Templar commandery. They had named three houses and he had aimed for Saint Pierre as the house closest to his goal of Marseille.

It had become increasingly clear during the long night ride that his captors were not robbers but royal soldiers after all, so Percy's fear receded as rapidly as it had risen. He had regained confidence that they were the victims of some mistake or some misguided tactic of the unscrupulous French king.

He did not underestimate King Philip's high-handedness. The French king had not hesitated to arrest a pope, and the more Percy thought about what had transpired, the more deeply he was convinced that Philip of France wanted to seize the Temple's reputed riches. Perhaps someone had told him that Saint Pierre du Temple was a depository for Templar treasures. Maybe he had hoped to seize such vast sums of money that he could pressure the pope into agreeing to taxation of Church lands. Taxation of the Church had been the cause of his conflict with Pope Boniface, after all. It was nothing but his insatiable greed which had prompted him to turn against the Jews the previous year, Percy reflected. The French king's treasury was empty and he seemed ever more desperate to find new sources of revenue.

Though the first farmers from the outlying countryside were still waiting for the gates to be opened at prime, the watch admitted the troop of royal soldiers and their prisoners without question – further evidence that their escort was known in Albi. Percy was grateful that the shops were still closed and the city only starting to stir. He was ashamed to be seen – even by strangers – riding with his hands tied behind his back and his feet bound as if he were a dangerous and contemptible criminal. The fact that he wore only his hose under his aketan made it all the worse.

The chambermaids emptying the chamber pots from the upper storeys of the houses, the apprentices and kitchen boys scampering along to the bakers, the beggars who had slept in the portals of the churches all looked in astonishment at the curious spectacle of a Knight Templar being led along like a murderer and a cartload full of Templar brothers being brought into town like livestock to the slaughter.

They turned into the narrow alley leading to the city jail. Percy felt a shock go through his body as he saw that two wagons similar to the one behind him already waited there. Had they made raids on more than one commandery? In a single night? Of course in the same night, he told himself, otherwise there would be no element of surprise. It was standard tactics, but the increased pounding of his heart could not be calmed.

They stopped and at once someone came and untied his feet. The pain in his ankles as he moved them again was not insignificant but he was too proud to let it show. He leaned forwards at once and vaulted to the ground. He had underestimated the impact of a night tied to the back of a horse. His feet were numb and he lost his footing at once. He staggered and, without his hands free to balance him, fell to the ground, to the general gratification and laughter of the guard. He flushed in embarrassment and anger, but also managed to get his knees under him and right himself. Meanwhile the other prisoners from Saint Pierre were being pushed off the back of the wagon and into the jail.

There seemed to be some discussion about where to take Percy and Ramon, but in the end they too were shoved after the others. As Percy was pushed past the porter of the jail, he turned and addressed the old man. 'I demand to see the sheriff and a representative of the Bishop of Albi,' Percy protested.

'Oh, you'll have ample opportunity to get to know the sheriff,' came the answer in a sneering voice. And then something particularly curious happened. The man called him, 'an ass-fucking heretic!' and spat after him.

Percy had not recovered from the shock of such an uncalled-for and perverse insult when he found himself at the entrance to the public jail. Before him, spread upon the stale straw, with chains around their feet or chained directly to mouldy walls were over one hundred Templars. It took his breath away. He shook his head to clear it and in that moment was roughly rammed through the door by the guard behind him. He tripped over the man at his feet and, seeing it was a priest, at once apologised. The priest looked up at him with wild, confused eyes. He was an old man with wisps of hair and an empty mouth.

Percy looked for a single prisoner who was not in the habit of the Templars – and he found none. Ramon, behind him, had apparently made the same discovery. Now he started to harangue their guards. 'There must be some mistake! I'm not a Templar! All the rest are Templars. If the king has decided to attack the Temple, it has nothing to do with me. I am only a hired squire. I have nothing to do with the Temple.'

'You were in a Templar commandery last night!' the guard answered.

'I just told you! I am a hired squire for that knight. He'll tell you. I never joined the Temple. Look at my clothes! Do they look like the habit of a Templar? This is a mistake.'

'Better check with the boss,' one of the guards muttered, but they put chains around Ramon's feet nevertheless.

Percy was led to the wall and his hands unbound so that they could be secured in iron cuffs attached to chains fixed to the wall. Iron shackles were then snapped around his ankles and a key turned in the lock. Percy just stared at his feet while the guards withdrew, squabbling irritably about who was going to report Ramon to their 'boss'.

*

It was a week before Percy was removed. By then he was wiser. Since the guards did not bother to separate the prisoners, they were able to exchange all they knew.

By the end of the first day there was no doubt that all had been arrested between midnight and dawn on the 13th, and there was good reason to believe that not just the commanderies in the vicinity of Albi had been affected. Since Ramon had been released and slunk out of the jail without a backwards look at Percy, there could be no doubt that King Philip had struck at the Knights Templar with his accustomed deliberation, efficiency and ruthlessness. Percy acknowledged to himself that he had underestimated the French king after all.

By the second day, it was clear what charges had been levelled against them. The Templars were accused of nothing less than abusing the sacraments, denying Christ, worshipping idols and engaging in institutionalised sodomy. They were accused of conducting initiation ceremonies which included forcing the initiate to deny

Christ three times and spit upon the cross. They were, furthermore, accused of having forced initiates to kiss the official in charge of their acceptance on the base of the spine, the navel and the lips. Sodomy was allegedly not only encouraged but routinely practised, even against the will of new brothers. And in place of worshipping Christ, they were supposed to worship some other 'idol' – although none of the arrested Templars could fully comprehend what this was supposed to be.

After four days it was apparent that the sheriff was following a very careful plan in his 'investigations'. While the few knights who had fallen into royal hands (most of the Knights Templar were either on Cyprus or in the provincial headquarters) were left chained to the walls, the eldest and the youngest serving brothers were interrogated first. Whilst the knights stood day and night, fed once a day on worm-eaten or mouldy bread and brackish water, forced to urinate and defecate upon themselves, the serving brothers, then the sergeants and finally the priests were taken away.

And when they came back they were often unconscious, usually carried by guards, and they whimpered and prayed through the hours that followed so that none could sleep. The prisoners were crowded too closely together not to be able to learn what had been done. Sometimes the victims themselves told of their agony. Sometimes the men around them inspected their wounds and reported to the others.

The two priests in their midst – the old man over whom Percy had stumbled as he entered the jail and the nervous priest of Saint Pierre, Father Roger – both had their fingernails torn off; it was assumed that priests could write and so were more sensitive in their hands than mere serving brothers. Percy could have laughed to think he had been contemptuous of Father Roger's fear on the night of their arrest. The acne-faced young priest had had a better appreciation of the situation than he himself.

The serving brothers were more likely to have the soles of their feet held to a brazier. On the second day after the arrests, they carried the first serving brother back into the jail whose bones were visible amidst the charred flesh. It was the bald Brother Thomas who had admitted Percy to Saint Pierre on that fateful Thursday night. If he survived, he would never walk again.

Other brothers had the bones of their feet crushed. The effect was the same, but apparently the torturers needed some kind of variety to keep themselves amused. Sergeant Brother Gautier was a particular delicacy. As he managed to tell Percy in the night after his interrogation, he had broken his hip and knee in a riding accident almost twenty years earlier while training for mounted combat. As a result, he had never been fit for service in the Holy Land and had spent his entire life on one manor or another, seeing that revenues were collected to support his luckier brothers. He had walked only with pain before, and now he would never walk again. They had taken his leg and twisted it until it not only came out of its socket but every bone snapped.

The faint hope that they would not dare treat knights and noblemen in the same manner as commoners was shattered on the afternoon of the 19th. That was the day they took the ageing Sir Etienne de Mendé to the torture chambers. They extracted his teeth one by one until he had confessed to everything they wanted to hear.

When the guards came and unlocked the chains at his feet, Percy felt such a terror of what was ahead of him that he could hardly control his bowels. Sweat glistened on his face. Someone murmured a blessing. Someone else said a prayer for him.

He could hardly walk. His muscles seemed to have frozen. He tripped over his own feet. He smelt his own stench and he was ashamed of himself. He was led along a dark, dank corridor, past a chamber full of torture instruments, and into a windowless room lit by a torch. Behind a plain wooden table sat the sheriff. At his right hand sat a monk in the habit of the Dominicans. The Inquisition.

To his surprise, a stool was waiting for him. At a gesture from the sheriff, Percy sank down on to it. The relief was less than he expected. His muscles were not used to sitting any more and the stool was low. His legs cramped at once and he had to clamp his teeth together to keep from crying out while he tried to shake the cramp from his legs.

During the entire procedure the sheriff and the Dominican stared at him like lizards – without the slightest flicker of emotion. The guards who stood inside the door made some crack to one another in a relaxed tone. Then it was over. He waited.

'Your name?' the sheriff asked.

Percy pulled himself together. He had had time enough to think about what he would say to this inevitable question. 'Sir Percival de Lacy, second cousin of the Earl of Lincoln, subject of His Grace King Edward II of England and Knight Templar of the commandery at Limassol, Cyprus. I hereby protest vehemently at my unlawful detention at the hands of a foreign monarch and demand immediate audience with a representative of the English Crown.' It sounded decisive and self-confident – if only his sweating, stinking body and shaking knees had not betrayed him.

Even so, there was evident surprise and consternation behind the table. The sheriff raised his eyebrows and turned to the Dominican. The Dominican leaned forwards and whispered loud enough for Percy to hear. King Philip had, of course, immediately informed his fellow monarchs of the outrageous crimes committed by the Templars and his own decision to put a end to the perversions which offended God. He had urged all his fellow monarchs to follow his example, arrest the Templars and investigate their crimes. As yet it was too soon to know the response of the English king, but he was due to marry King Philip's only daughter, Isabella, in just a few months. He was sure to follow the lead of his wise and devout father-in-law.

The sheriff looked more sceptical. He consulted the Dominican again after completely turning his back on Percy, and this time Percy could not catch any of what was said. Then they both nodded in apparent agreement and satisfaction.

The sheriff addressed him.

'Your request has been noted. I will pass it on to my superiors. For now, your cooperation in this grave matter is requested. I am certain that voluntary cooperation will be noted with favour by both your own king and mine. You are aware of the charges levelled against your Order?'

'I have heard what my brothers reported after their interrogations,' Percy answered cautiously.

'Do you agree that the denial of Christ is a vile and heinous crime?'

Percy crossed himself. 'With all my heart.'

'And the worship of some idol in place of our dear Saviour must offend every Christian.'

'It is repulsive!' Percy spoke with conviction.

'Yet both of these crimes have been confessed to by your brothers.' The sheriff leaned forwards over the table. 'How do you explain that?'

'A man will confess to anything to stop pain,' Percy retorted and at once wondered if he had blundered. Hadn't he just admitted that he too would admit to anything to stop pain? Wouldn't they at once recognise how weak he was? Wouldn't they exploit it?

'But a man who makes a false confession is condemned to the tortures of hell – and hell has no end. The tortures that we poor, imperfect instruments of His will can impose are finite. They can always end in death, and that is – for the truly innocent – a release into paradise. To confess to end earthly torture only to land in the perpetual and eternal torture of hell is the act of a madman.'

'Pain creates madmen,' Percy answered.

He had not prepared for these questions. He was not ready for an intellectual discussion about the nature of earthly and divine torture. He had no clue what he should say to defend himself. And so he said what he thought. Unbeknown to him, he was sitting straighter on his stool and he had lifted his head.

The Dominican felt a tremor of erotic desire go through him at the sight of the tall man with the symmetrical angular features and the thin, masculine lips. His tonsure was already covered with a fuzz of curly brown hair reminiscent of a man's pubic hair, the Dominican noted with a blush of desire.

The sheriff too saw through the soiled hose and filthy face to the harmony of the bone structure and the intelligence in the blue eyes. This was the first prisoner he could almost admire. He had felt pity for some of the older men because they were so helpless and frightened, but his predominant emotion had been disdain for the filthy, grovelling, cattle that had been led before him. They had been either too frightened to resist after they understood what was expected of them or too stubborn to confess except under extreme duress.

'You do not give credence to the confessions of your brothers?' the sheriff asked raising his eyebrows.

'How can I? I do not know what they confessed.'

'Ah.' The sheriff lifted the corner of his mouth. For some reason he was genuinely pleased to have a worthy opponent. 'Let me read them to you.'

He leaned back in his chair, beckoned to a clerk and gave him whispered instructions. The clerk nodded and hastened from the chamber.

At first they waited in silence, then the Dominican abruptly asked, 'Are you thirsty, sir? Should I have wine brought?'

Percy swallowed. If he drank wine now he would completely lose control of his tongue.

'No.'

He could not leave it at that. He was thirsty. Thirst too could drive a man to any extreme. He knew that from the desert.

'Water.'

The Dominican raised his eyebrows but a smile played on his lips too. He ordered the guard to fetch water.

'*Good* water!' he called after the man.

The water and then the documents arrived. Percy sipped the water. His hands shook as he raised the chipped pottery cup to his lips. He noted that his lips were chapped. He tasted blood as he drank but the water was good.

The sheriff read aloud. 'Your brother and *priest*, Father Roger of Saint Pierre du Temple confessed the following:

> When I took my vows before the chapter, I was led into a small room beside the chapter chamber. There I was told to remove my clothes. This I did without hesitation, thinking I would now receive the mantle of the Templars. But when I stood naked before the commander, he lifted his habit and ordered me to kiss his navel. I did so. He then turned his back on me and ordered me to kiss his ass. I did so. Then he gave me the kiss of peace.'

The sheriff set the parchment aside and looked expectantly at Percy.

Percy stared back and thought of Father Roger's hands. At the thought of someone tearing off even one of his fingernails, his muscles tensed. Seven of Father Roger's fingernails had been removed brutally. His hands were swollen like sausages and hot to touch. Blood and pus still oozed from them. And Father Roger was the son of serfs: the pride of his family, the one son who had been allowed to go to school and whose freedom had been bought by the Temple so he could enter the priesthood. Percy knew that now. Brother Gautier had told him about Father Roger after they brought the latter back from his interrogation.

'Well?' the sheriff prompted. 'What do you have to say to that?'

'That Father Roger is a poor, miserable man whom I pity with all my heart. May Christ have mercy upon him! He did not mean to lie but he was not strong enough to insist upon the truth.' Percy crossed himself. He did not think he was strong enough to withstand such torture either.

The sheriff shifted uncomfortably. That was too true. Then he suppressed his discomfort. Christ might be merciful; King Philip never. And it was to King Philip that he owed his position and his wealth.

'Brother Thomas, also of Saint Pierre, confessed to the following,' he persisted mercilessly. 'At my initiation I was forced to deny Christ three times—'

'As did Simon Peter on the day of the Crucifixion.' Percy interrupted without knowing what he did.

The stench of Brother Thomas's charred feet was in his nostrils. He felt nausea rising in his empty belly.

The sheriff looked at him with a mixture of anger and admiration. He was not used to prisoners interrupting him – unless it was with screams and pleas for mercy. But the remark was correct. And that gave him an exciting idea.

'You mean this was routine? Templars re-enact the denial of Christ which Saint Peter made on the day of His Crucifixion?'

'No!' Percy quickly saw the error he had made. 'I never denied Christ. I was never *asked* to deny Christ,' he replied firmly but the error had been made, the seed planted.

The sheriff and the Dominican consulted together in whispers and made copious notes. Percy sweated on the stool in front of them and his sweat chilled him. He noted that the room was cold for a man clad as lightly as he. The Dominican and the sheriff both wore fur-lined surcoats.

'Simon Peter never spat upon the Our Lord in His agony.' The Dominican entered the interrogation for the first time. He had a relatively high, frail voice.

'Not that I know of.' Percy retorted. 'I wasn't there.'

'You impudent bastard!' The Dominican sprang to his feet, furious. He thought Percy was mocking him.

The sheriff patted his arm and gestured for him to reseat himself.

'But your brother Thomas of Saint Pierre confessed to that,' the sheriff remarked calmly. 'After denying Christ three times, he was forced to spit upon the crucifix which was held out to him.'

'Read me his confession,' Percy demanded, trying to concentrate all his attention and intelligence on some way out of this spider's web of lies and torture.

'I was forced to deny Christ three times and then spit upon his image.'

Percy noted the difference between this confession and the last. The first confession had been wordy, as if Father Roger had spoken. This confession read like the indictment. They had not torn more than a yes or no answer from Brother Thomas. Or, rather, they had forced him to say yes after countless nos. Percy understood that but he knew he could not voice his thoughts. He took refuge in the familiar. He crossed himself. 'Christ have mercy. God have mercy. The Holy Spirit have mercy. My brother knew not what he did.'

The sheriff felt first a touch of satisfaction at Percy's calm but then reminded himself that he would sing a different tune if they were applying the glowing iron to his genitals. He shook his head slowly and leafed through the documents before him. 'I think you will agree, sir, that idol worship is not something that can be taken lightly, much less forgiven. Nor is it something an ordinary Christian could think up.'

'Not even the Muslims are idol-worshippers!' Percy retorted.

Of all the accusations against his Order this was surely the most ridiculous. Percy found it hard to even take it seriously. Sodomy was something which – at least according to rumour – did occasionally occur, even if it were not sanctioned, and it surely occurred no more frequently than in other religious orders. The denial of Christ during initiation might, in some provinces, really have been a part of initiation rites, Percy decided – as a test of the ability of new recruits to stand by their faith under pressure. But the thought that the Templars, who had spilled more blood in the defence of Christ's homeland than the rest of Christendom put together, might in secret worship an idol would have been hilarious if it were not so dangerous an accusation.

'Yet I have a sworn confession by a brother of yours who describes in detail how the chapter met at midnight, stripped off their habits and trampled on the cross. Then they crept naked, in single file, into a chamber opened by a secret key kept only by the commander. In the chamber the idol was kept and each brother bowed before the idol "like an Egyptian slave" I quote,' the sheriff stressed. '"Then after we had bowed three times, we kissed the feet of the idol." The idol, according to this report, was shaped like a big head with hands and feet but no body and with cat's ears.

After kissing the feet, each brother retreated backwards so the next brother could enter.'

Percy looked at the sheriff, the Dominican, and then he turned and looked at the guards on either side of the door. 'You can't seriously believe that?' Percy asked at last.

'Believe it? It is the testimony of a Templar – freely given I might add, without resort to torture.'

'You think that French noblemen, men who heard mass six times a day, men who fought in Christ's name, who when captured could gain life by denying Christ, but instead *died* by the hundred for Christ, secretly worshipped a head with cat's ears? Have you lost your senses?'

Percy felt that his protest was much too weak, but he could not find words for his sense of sheer disbelief. The notion of such infantile idolatry was not only too absurd, it was not worthy of the Inquisition or an officer of the crown.

'Let me repeat!' the sheriff said sharply to disguise his own growing embarrassment. 'This is a sworn confession – from Saint Pierre, I might add.'

'By whom, in God's name?'

'Brother Gaston.'

'Gaston?'

Percy could not place the name at first. Then it dawned on him. Gaston was the *boy*. The over-eager boy who had helped him out of his armour, the only one among the whole herd who had shown a spark of outrage and defiance. 'Gaston is a child!' he said out loud.

'He is twelve and so has reached the age of maturity,' the Dominican retorted with surprising intensity.

Percy was frowning. He did not remember seeing Gaston since the day after the arrest. Gaston had been removed for interrogation – but he had never returned. A shock went through him.

'Is Gaston dead? Did you torture him so long that he couldn't take it? Did you kill him?'

Percy, get hold of yourself, he warned himself. You are losing control. Calm down. Shut up. Get hold of yourself. He sat clutching the edge of his stool, shaking and sweating, waiting for a reaction.

'I told you the confession was not made under torture,' the sheriff replied calmly, his eyes narrower. 'What makes you think he might be dead?'

Calm! Calm! Percy warned himself. He took a breath, and swallowed. His throat was dry. He swallowed again. The Dominican did not offer him water now. The Dominican was staring at him with narrow, hostile, hate-filled eyes. 'Because he did not return. You took him to an interrogation and he has not returned since.'

'That is true. He was... cooperative. It was not... necessary' – the sheriff glanced at his colleague – 'to return him to the jail. You need not worry about Gaston.' A chill went down Percy's spine.

Why did he feel so certain that they had done something vile to Gaston? Surely he should hate the boy for making up such ridiculous stories about heads with cat's ears and feet! But he could not find hatred for the boy. He closed his eyes and pictured Gaston helping him remove his spurs – the last time he had worn spurs.

'Did you have illicit relations with Gaston?' The tight, jealous question came from the Dominican.

Percy opened his eyes and stared at the man. In that moment he knew this other monk had raped Gaston. Gaston had not been tortured into his confession. His limbs had been left whole. But he had been degraded and humiliated until there was nothing left of the idealistic youth, proud of his membership in a famous order. Percy did not answer. He stared at the Dominican until the other monk lowered his eyes.

The sheriff had been watching. He knew what his colleague had done. He had not witnessed it, of course, because he found it revolting, but he knew. And he knew that it brought excellent results like this lengthy and explicit confession. Furthermore, the boy could be produced as a witness. Cleaned up and properly worked over in advance, his testimony would melt the heart of the pope himself. Oh, Gaston was worth his weight in gold. Gaston was worth more than all the others put together – precisely because there wasn't a mark upon him. Gaston could never, never claim that he had been *forced* to confess. Gaston could *never* tell the circumstances of his confession – not without condemning himself to be hanged. That was the beauty of it. And still the sheriff found it distasteful.

He looked at Percy and he was sorry. He liked the young man. He had intelligence, dignity and humanity. It was a pity that he was on the wrong side. It would be a pity to break him, but, unless his king were prepared to defy his soon-to-be father-in-law and King Philip were prepared to indulge his future son-in-law – break him he must.

Chapter Four

Poitiers, February 1308

Sister Renée entered the convent warming rooms, where the boarders sat clustered together doing needlework while Sister Cécile read aloud from Saint Thomas Aquinas.

'There is a visitor for Mademoiselle de Preuthune.'

Félice sprang to her feet with undue alacrity, earning a scowl from Sister Renée, but she didn't care. She stuffed her needle into the canvas and took her mantle from a hook on the wall.

Outside the warming room, the convent was bitterly cold. It had been one of the coldest winters in living memory, and coming on the heels of the famine, had claimed the lives of thousands of poor across the country. Here at Saint Radegonde they were sheltered from the worst of the effects, but the old convent, built at a time when the nuns still kept a strict rule and for a climate that was predominantly mild, didn't have enough fireplaces to keep it warm.

The cross-vaulted dormitory in which the boarders slept was not even provided with a fireplace and as they passed through it they could see their breath. Beyond, they entered the infirmary cloister and here the wind added its teeth to the cold, howling around the pillars supporting the arches and filling their hoods with cold air that bit their ears. Frost glazed the brown grass of the garth and old snow gave the grotesque carvings of the capitals white mouths and eyes.

From the infirmary came the sound of coughing and sniffling. Dozens of sisters were down with colds and bronchitis.

Félice, however, had robust health and suffered more from chapped hands and dry patches on her face than from head or chest colds. Now she felt tentatively at her face, distressed that the red splotches were disfiguring her appearance because surely it was Umberto who had come to see her at last.

Umberto had joined the Dominicans just after Christmas. She had argued against it. The Dominicans were the Inquisition. They had burned her great-grandmother at the stake, held her grandmother for two years in demeaning conditions and now they were torturing the Templars. Those had been her arguments but there had been another factor which had made her heart protest against Umberto's decision. By taking vows as a novice he had moved a step closer towards irrevocable membership in the clergy and a step further from her. As a student in lesser orders, it would have cost Umberto nothing more than a small fee if he changed his mind and chose a life outside the Church. As a novice, the price of changing his mind was substantially higher. If he were to take final vows, the cost was virtually prohibitive. Only men with very powerful connections or purses could escape the clutches of a religious order of which they were full clerical members.

It was wrong, Félice supposed, to even desire a man destined for the Church but she loved Umberto and she was not ashamed of loving him. Wasn't her love for Umberto – for his learning, his mind, his wit and his humour – much more divine than her sister Natalie's love for one tournament hero after another? Natalie had fallen in and out of love a half-dozen times by the time she was sixteen. Félice loved only once: Umberto.

Félice crossed herself and whispered a short prayer that her sister had at last learned a different kind of love, for she had been married almost a year to a man of her mother's choosing. He had been neither a notably adept knight nor a good-looking man and Natalie had cried for a whole week before the wedding making a terrible scene. Her father had nearly given in to Natalie, but her mother had been iron-willed. Natalie had married Monsieur Engeurand de Marmande, potbelly or not, and she was due to have his child any day now.

No doubt Félice's mother was already looking for some man of equal 'virtue' for her. At sixteen she was patently marriageable and with her grandmother's one hundred louis she was even dowered. Félice harboured hopes, however, that this was too small a portion to make her marketable. If her mother could not find a suitable match with one hundred louis, it might be years before her father could afford to pay a dowry of his own because Petitlouis was constantly running up debts that Louis felt compelled to honour.

Petitlouis was one of a half-dozen bachelor knights in the Languedoc who was being lionised for his prowess on the tournament circuit. But though he routinely won substantial prizes – and the weapons and armour of his defeated opponents – he occasionally took expensive spills. He also felt compelled to have the flashiest armour, trappers and accoutrements generally, and believed that it was incumbent on his status as champion to lavish gifts on his friends, squires, grooms and even the water boys – not to mention the expensive gifts he gave the ladies he courted. The revenues of his manor met not half of his expenses so Louis dug deep into his pockets to pay the wages of Petitlouis' neglected seneschal and chaplains, for repairs to the roofs of his wind-damaged barns and so on *ad nauseam*. As long as that went on, Félice felt relatively safe.

And since Petitlouis showed no sign of wearying of this glamorous life, she assumed that she had at least three or four years before the issue of her wedding became acute.

In the interim, Félice believed that she and Umberto had a chance. She imagined Umberto finding a position with a great lord. The seneschal of a great estate received not only an annual salary but an apartment in his lord's castle, sometimes an entire manor of his own. A seneschal was expected to be married. Umberto's birth, education and charm entitled him to such a position, and every month Félice heard of enquiries made to the university by one lord or other asking after suitable candidates. The only question she had harboured had been how powerful and wealthy Umberto's lord might be.

But then Umberto had joined the Dominicans.

Umberto claimed to love her. He claimed that his decision was forced, upon him. He claimed that the pressure was too great for him to resist. And he claimed his decision was not irrevocable: 'Let me join them, let me learn all they can teach me, let me see *how* they work. I'm bored here. There is nothing more to learn – maybe in Paris or Salamanca, but not here at Poitiers. I've heard every lecture these stupid professors have ever made! I need to expand my experience. I can still refuse to take the final vows.' But since he had entered the Dominicans she had not heard from him.

Her footsteps quickened automatically as she approached the visitors' ante-room. Stepping down from the corridor, she saw the robes of a student and her heart started to take wing. He had already cast off the white of the Dominican novitiate! And then the student turned around and she saw her cousin, Hugh.

Hugh smiled at Félice, unaware of the disappointment his innocent presence caused. He was six months her senior and, because he had three elder brothers, his father had never taken much note of him. He had frequently spent summers with his grandparents, playing with Félice when they were younger, more brother than cousin.

As he had been born sickly and had three elder brothers, he had long been intended for the Church – in a causal way. And because his father really didn't give a damn what he did or what became of him, Hugh enjoyed a degree of freedom rare for a young man of his years. He had decided to come up to the university at Poitiers just to see what it was like. A genuine calling to the Church was the last thing he would have pretended, but he had to make a living somehow and he was certainly not suited to any profession requiring skill at arms. Hugh had never held a longsword in his hands and wouldn't have known how to string a crossbow if his life depended on it.

He had a pleasant round face with red lips and eyes almost lost in fleshy lids. He had the blond hair of the Montfrancs (their Viking blood, Eleanor had always claimed insultingly) and pale blue eyes that sparkled happily at Félice as he gave her a smacking kiss on both cheeks. 'You look like you're freezing to death, cuz! I'd better take you up to my garret. With the four of us, it's warm even in this weather.'

His father's indifference to him assured Hugh his freedom but unfortunately it was also responsible for the fact that he had practically no money. Modest as Félice's allowance was, there had been more than one occasion when she had been moved to 'lend' him a few sou. Sister Andrine, who was on chaperon duty in the visitors' anteroom, coughed reproachfully but she knew that Hugh was really harmless.

'Do you want some warm soup?' Félice thought to ask now. Hugh might joke about how cold she looked but his skin was still burning from the sting of the wind and his hands were stuffed into the opposite sleeves of his robes all the way to the upper arms so that he was clutching himself. 'We can go to the kitchen.'

'You mean warm soup exists somewhere in France?' Hugh asked wide-eyed.

Félice managed to smile. He did her good with his silly sense of humour but nothing could lift her heart, knowing that Umberto still had not come.

The alms kitchen was built next to the visitors anteroom and had a door opening directly on to the street so that beggars could be provided for without entering the convent. But Félice led Hugh into the corridor and then into the kitchen.

The kitchen was warm. Spikes skewered with pike were being turned over two great fires and a cauldron steaming over another fire gave off the aroma of leeks and carrots. Hugh grabbed his far from insignificant belly and moaned in delight.

The serving sisters glanced up from their work at the sight of Félice and Hugh, but it was not unusual for one of the boarders to bring a visitor to the kitchens and students were as common as flies. Sister Isabeau glanced up from her books with an irritable expression but when she recognised Hugh, she smiled. Hugh at once went over, bowed deeply over her hand and enquired after her health with every appearance of concern.

Soon Sister Isabeau had ordered one of the serving sisters to give Hugh a large bowl of stew and a thick slice of bread.

'And I've got some leftover raisin pies.'

Hugh clasped his hands as if in prayer and rolled his eyes towards heaven. 'Merciful Mother Mary, you have answered my prayers.'

Sister Isabeau cuffed him on the shoulder in rebuke whilst she laughed heartily. Félice sat down opposite him at the scraped and dented table, which still smelt of fish.

'I'm supposed to be bringing you greetings from your mother and father,' Hugh informed her between mouthfuls of stew.

'My parents? I didn't know you were in Najac.'

'I wasn't.' He took another mouthful. 'I was home to beg some money from Raimand.'

Raimand was the eldest of Hugh's brothers and the one with whom Hugh got along best. Because of the twelve year age difference Raimand viewed Hugh more as a cute mascot than a burden. 'Your parents were on their way to visit Natalie and just stopped over for a few days.'

'My parents are going to visit Natalie?' Félice could hardly picture it.

'It seems she's expecting shortly you know, and wanted her mother near her,' Hugh replied, tearing off a chunk of bread from the three-inch slice Sister Isabeau had put before him.

Félice looked sceptical and Hugh shrugged. 'That is what your father said.'

Félice could not imagine her sister asking for their mother, still less their mother being concerned about her daughter's whims. There had to be more to the story than this, but Hugh probably didn't know. Then another thought struck her.

'Was Grandpapa with them?'

'Good Lord, no! He remained at Najac. Your mother was fussing about how he would undoubtedly start interfering in the household again.'

'But if my parents were already on their way to Natalie just now—'

'The day before yesterday.'

'Then Grandpapa will be alone for his birthday.'

'In all likelihood, yes,' Hugh agreed.

'That's dreadful!' Félice declared. 'He turns seventy-eight in ten days' time. Who knows if he'll ever see seventy-nine.'

'To hear your mother talk, it is more likely he will live to be one hundred and nine.'

'That's only because she resents him!' Félice retorted unnecessarily.

Hugh was as aware as Félice herself that Marie suffered almost physically under the subordination to a man she considered far beneath her by birth.

'Hugh, let's surprise him! Let's go to Najac for his birthday! You know he'd love it – and it would do me so much good to get away from here.' Away from waiting for Umberto, away from the crushed hopes and frequent disappointments. Maybe she could sort things out at home. Maybe she could even talk to her grandfather about the affair.

'What?' Hugh asked. 'Just the two of us?'

'We can be there in a week and I know the abbeys where we can spend each night. You'll have a warm bed and a hot meal every night for the whole way!'

'And freeze my ass off on horseback ten hours a day!'

'Oh come on, Hugh! Think of all the things Grandpapa did for you when you were growing up!' Félice pleaded.

Hugh was not really as ill-disposed towards the idea as he sounded. He was not a notably good student and he had been depressed by having to return to his cold, smoky garret after being home for the week. The idea of Najac – without his Aunt Marie – was highly tempting. 'All right – if you can finance our dinners that is.'

'I thought you just saw Raimand,' Félice exclaimed with wide eyes and an angelic smile. Hugh looked so discomforted that she had to laugh. 'Of course I'll finance our dinners,' she assured him. 'And the tips for the stable boys.

Grandpapa will be so delighted to see us!' The thought really cheered her.

Hugh nodded and wiped the inside of his bowl with the last chunk of bread. Speaking with his mouth full, he added, 'Do you know some Dominican novice called Umberto something?'

Félice's heart stopped. She stared at her cousin.

'He wants you to go up to Notre-Dame-la-Grande just after nones. He will meet you there. You aren't going silly on me like Natalie, are you?' Hugh asked.

Félice flushed. 'What do you mean? Umberto di Sante is not some tournament dandy!' she said defensively.

'But he does have a pretty face,' Hugh pointed out.

'That's not why I love him!'

'But you *do* love him?'

'Is that a crime?' Félice demanded defensively.

'No,' Hugh admitted. 'But it generally doesn't do anybody any good. Actually, it just seems to make most people unhappy,' Hugh pointed out sensibly.

But Félice was not in the mood to be sensible. The fact that Umberto had sent for her was cause for unbounded joy and the unhappiness of the past weeks faded instantly into insignificance.

'Love didn't make our grandparents unhappy,' she pointed out.

'The exception proves the rule,' Hugh insisted lightly. He supposed there was no point trying to argue with a girl in love, but he personally thought it was all rather silly, this mooning about over someone who would never be important in one's life – whether it was a tournament champion or a Dominican monk.

*

Hugh escorted Félice up to Notre-Dame-la-Grande just in time to meet the scattered individuals who had attended mass at nones leaving the old church. Hugh had agreed to wait at a tavern across the square until Félice returned and then walk her home. Félice gave him change for his wine and then continued under the magnificent portal into the dim, incense-laden air of the church.

A lone acolyte was dousing the candles on the altar. Two old women still knelt in one of the back pews. They looked like peasants who had come in from the countryside and were probably seeking shelter from the wind as much as comfort for their souls. Then, halfway up the nave, Félice saw the white form of a novice at prayer.

She advanced steadily up the nave, her heart pounding and her brain turning over all the things she ought to say or not say. Part of her wanted to reproach him for not seeking her out sooner. Part of her wanted to thank him for sending for her at all.

She dropped her knee to the cold stone of the aisle and crossed herself. Instantly, the novice on her left took flight noisily. She glanced after him in alarm. Why send for her if he intended to flee? He worked his way out of the far side of the pew and fled into the confessional directly before him. Fortunately, Félice had been watching him in disbelief, his name on her lips. It did not escape her notice that he entered the priest's cubicle. She understood.

With a glance over her shoulder to see if anyone else had noticed the unauthorised flight of a Dominican novice behind the velvet curtain of the confessional, she moved much more slowly and deliberately to the other side of the confessional. The curtain was open and she pulled it closed behind her.

'Félice?' Umberto asked anxiously. 'Is it really you?'

'Yes, Umberto,' she answered simply, unaware of how low and melodic and calm her voice sounded as she fell on her knees. Her head was raised towards the wooden lattice-work that separated her from Umberto.

'Félice! Félice!' He sounded almost as if he were in pain. 'I had to speak to you again before I leave!'

'Leave? Where are you going?' Alarm was evident in her voice.

'Monseigneur Michel, the new Bishop of Albi, has asked me to accompany him. I couldn't say no. You must see that?'

Félice felt only numbness in that minute. Of course he couldn't say no. You didn't say no to bishops if you were a mere novice. And *certainly* not to Monseigneur Michel. But if he left Poitiers, if he had the patronage of a bishop, there was no hope for them. None at all.

'Félice. I love you! Oh, you can't know how much!'

Despite his admiration for Monseigneur Michel, Umberto was convinced that he had been wrong about one thing: the cheap women who satisfied his body could not replace this rose of virtue to whom he had given his heart. And how could the Monseigneur claim that a noblewoman was damaging to his career when all of Poitiers knew that the Countess of Périgord was Clement V's mistress? She had given birth to a son the previous year though she had not seen the count of Périgord in at least three years. Clement openly doted on the infant. Umberto was convinced that he need only climb high enough and have the right patronage and then there would be no problem about living with Félice.

'You must have faith in me, Félice. You must believe in me!'

'What good does that do me?' she asked him bluntly, near to tears.

'Félice!' He held his hand against the lattice-work and she responded instinctively, placing her palm against his. They could not really touch yet there was a warmth, a communication between their hands, their bodies. 'I swear to you, I will come back for you. We are destined for one another. I can sense that. Nothing and no one can separate us,' he told her passionately.

'No one but the Church,' Félice reminded him sadly.

'Oh no. It need not be so. Listen to me, Félice.'

He had bent his head against the lattice-work and was peering at her through one of the holes in the screen. Even in the darkness of the confessional, Félice could see the glinting of his brown eyes.

'No one – not your father, your mother or your confessor – can *force* you to marry. You must consent. If you withhold your consent no marriage is valid.'

'I was thinking of *your* vows.' Félice told him softly.

'Félice, trust me! We will be together again – for ever – as soon as I am... as soon as I have attained the security I need. It could take a couple of years, I know that, but we are both young.' He knew that he dare not tell her yet what he planned. She was still too modest and innocent. She might be offended at this point. But if she loved him... 'Félice, do you love me?' he asked in sudden alarm.

'You know I do.'

'Félice! Swear to me you will take no other! Swear you will love only me! Please, Félice! I can't bear to part from you without knowing you love me and will wait for me!'

What was a sixteen year old maiden supposed to do when confronted with such a request from the man she loved? Félice didn't think. She put her forehead to the lattice-work so she could feel Umberto's warmth through the wood and swore that she loved him, would always love him and no one else but him.

'You won't let your parents force you to marry someone else?' Umberto persisted.

His breath smelled of mint leaves and it caressed her lips through the lattice-work.

'I cannot stop them.'

'You can! The sacrament consists of obtaining consent from both parties. You know that! If you refuse, no marriage can be concluded.'

Félice remained sceptical. She knew how much pressure her mother could exert. Hadn't she been witness to Natalie's futile protests? But she promised that she would do her best.

'Félice!' he cried out one last agonised time and pressed his lips against the lattice-work.

Félice touched her lips to the opposite side of the wooden screen and they kissed for the first time – separated by the wooden fretwork of the confessional.

Chapter Five

Albi, March 1308

Edward II of England, along with the kings of Portugal, Castile and Aragon, expressed disbelief concerning the allegations Philip of France made against the Templars, so on 22nd November, 1307, Pope Clement V ordered a general arrest of the Templars on the grounds that the large number of confessions by French Templars made an investigation of the charges imperative. Edward II continued to protest and prevaricate, however, so it was January before the English king acted. By then, of course, the Templars in England had had enough warning for large numbers of them to 'disappear' – along with most of their valuables. Master de la More courageously remained in the London Temple with a few other brothers to defend the reputation of his Order against the accusations. Edward II, on the advice of his bishops, housed the arrested men in chambers suited to their rank and prohibited the use of torture.

Torture had no tradition in England, the English king blandly explained to the pope, and he had no one in his entire kingdom who was versed in the methods. Clement V immediately sent some of his best inquisitors and their skilled henchmen to make up this deplorable deficit in backward England. After four weeks of frustrated fuming at the king and virtually all the bishops of England, the inquisitors returned without having been given access to a single Templar.

It was at this critical juncture that the Bishop of Albi drew the pope's attention to the fact that he *had* an English Templar in his jail. Clement immediately sent Father Elion to Albi with instructions to secure the Englishman's confession to as many of the indictments as possible. He needed a confession by the Englishmen to at least two of the main counts, he stressed.

In the meantime, thirty-six Templars had died under torture. More than twice that number had died of the consequences, while others had managed to commit suicide one way or another. Philip IV sent furious orders to his sheriffs, ordering more care in the conduct of the interrogations. Dead Templars could not be put on trial, he angrily reminded his officers.

The sheriff at Albi shrugged with resignation. He knew his royal master. Philip was a man who could 'forget' from one hour to the next what his orders had been. In October he had wanted confessions regardless of the cost – and his tactic had worked. The confessions had swayed the pope and the kings of Sicily, Navarre, and the emperor of the Germans. But now that he had overcome their initial incredulity at the grotesque charges he had levelled against the Templars, he needed confessed heretics whom he could parade about publicly and put on trial. The first phase had been the breakthrough; now they were in the consolidation phase, which required different tactics. Father Elion was reputedly a master of the necessary tactics.

Father Elion studied the records of all the previous interrogations of Sir Percival de Lacy. After the first interrogation in October, de Lacy had not been brought before the Inquisition again until mid-December. At that time the papal bull ordering the arrest of Templars outside France had been issued, but Edward II had responded with protest rather than compliance. The sheriff had confined himself to suspending the Englishman by his hands, tied behind his back, and applying weights to his legs. De Lacy denied all allegations until he passed out after six hours of interrogation. Two days after Epiphany, they had extracted three of his teeth, but his responses became utterly incomprehensible and apparently delirious so they had been forced to discontinue the session. Thus, when Father Elion arrived in early February, the Englishman had not confessed to a single point of the indictment.

Father Elion knew that different men were sensitive to different kinds of pain so, for his first interrogation of de Lacy, he ordered the application of heat to the base of the Englishman's feet. They secured the prisoner to a table with leather braces across his chest, hips and knees. A thin sheet of steel was heated and, as the questioning intensified, was moved ever closer to the soles of the prisoner's naked feet.

Father Elion had been encouraged by the results. The English Templar's denials reached a pitch and volume that indicated he was near breaking point. But, unfortunately, the state of his feet was such that Father Elion was forced to break off the interrogation. Had he continued, the burns would have been incurable and the prisoner might have died; he certainly would not have walked again.

Not only had King Philip made it clear that he did not want dead Templars, but the other religious orders, including Father Elion's own superiors, were protesting with increasing vehemence about having to provide for worthless mouths. The other religious orders were required to take Templars into their own ranks after they had made their peace with the Church by confessing their heinous sins and receiving absolution. Brothers who could not walk were a burden which the other orders did not want to take on.

After de Lacy was sufficiently recovered from the ordeal involving his feet – he was allowed to lie, chained to a ring in the prison floor, rather than having to stand against the wall. Father Elion opted to apply heat again. For his second interrogation, he had the jailhouse smith forge a brand in the shape of the splayed Templar cross. He ordered the guards to bare Percy's chest and then had him strapped upon the table again. As they brought the brand nearer and nearer his heart, the Englishman screamed at them in sheer terror: 'No! Noo! Nooooo!'

His chest seemed to leap under the brand like a rabbit hit by a quarrel and then he went completely limp.

'You may have made a mistake,' the sheriff remarked to Father Elion calmly. 'It looks as if his heart has stopped.'

Father Elion leapt up and rushed to the prisoner. The stench of burnt flesh made him wrinkle his nose and hold his breath as he laid his head against Percy's ribcage. He heard nothing.

'Christ, no!' he demanded of the Merciful Saviour. 'How could He let this happen?'

Father Elion had never had a prisoner die while under interrogation. Both Pope Clement and King Philip would be furious. This one English Templar of all prisoners! Frantically he shook the corpse with the Templar cross burned into the left side of his chest. A gasp seemed to come from the lifeless lungs. He shook again, more violently.

Behind him the sheriff stood and opened the door to the chamber. He shouted down the long corridor outside, 'Fetch me the leech!'

But by the time the physician arrived he wasn't needed. The English Templar wasn't dead. They carried him back into the jail with his clothes.

Father Elion knew that he had had a close call and it made him both nervous and determined. He had been working on this case for almost a month and he had come out of two interrogations without a ghost of a confession. Though his methods continued to work flawlessly on other prisoners, he clearly had to do something different with the Englishman.

His sense of frustration was aggravated by the fact that he had promised Pope Clement that he would supply him with a batch of *presentable* witnesses against the Temple by Easter. He had selected seven men: a knight, two priests and four serving brothers, who made very credible witnesses – not senile old men or simpletons – and, furthermore, men who could, after rest and decent food, actually walk without assistance and stand more or less straight, and they were prepared to repeat their confessions without the instruments of torture being at hand. He was going to have to send the lot of them up to Poitiers within the next couple of days if they were to reach the pontiff by Easter. Because of the weather, the roads were nearly impassable at places. He had to allow at least two weeks for the transport of the prisoners to Poitiers.

Father Elion was determined to send the Englishmen to Poitiers at the same time – even if he had to be carried in a sack. There would be time enough for him to recover once he reached Poitiers. What was important now was that he confessed to at least two counts – without dying in the process.

Between his other duties, Father Elion went back through the notes of de Lacy's interrogations, looking for some weakness he could exploit. He wanted something he could use as the wedge with which to crack him open. After two days of searching, and when it was impossible to delay the transport of prisoners another day, he could not sleep after matins so he took out the notes of the interrogations yet again. Suddenly, it came to him with such clarity that it could only have been divine inspiration.

Father Elion flung himself on his knees, took his crucifix between his hands, kissed the figure of Christ and gave thanks feverishly. He had the key: Percival de Lacy said 'no' to everything they asked him. It was the only word he had ever uttered under torture.

★

When they came for him late the next day, Percy wanted to be sick. He turned over in the straw and retched but his stomach was empty.

One of his brothers laid a hand on his shoulder. 'God be with you, brother. He loves you all the more for – like Him – you are suffering for all of us.'

The guards had hold of his shoulders and were now dragging him up off the soiled straw. His brothers had dressed him, despite his protests, almost immediately after the branding. The rubbing of the cloth, weighed down with chain mail, had been unbearable at first, but they had insisted he would die in the unheated jail if he did not wear all he owned.

He still could not walk so the guards had to carry him between them. Percy closed his eyes and tried to collect his strength as they clumped down the corridor. But he didn't have any strength left to collect. Percy started shuddering violently as if he had a chill.

He could sense when they passed through the doorway to the torture chamber. The guards dumped him on the table. He opened his eyes and stared at the ceiling, just waiting. Would they remove his clothes again? They didn't. They started to buckle the leather braces over him. He screamed – one of the braces tore off half of the bloody scab which had formed over the brand as they went to tighten it.

'Move him up a bit,' the sheriff ordered simply and the guards took Percy under his arms, hauled him up the table a couple of inches and refastened the braces.

He could make out the voice of Father Elion talking in an officious but diligent undertone to someone. He could catch fragments of what was being said: '... an Englishman... important to prove it wasn't just the Templars in France who were... difficult because he is too weak to withstand...'

Percy twisted his lips in a sick smile. *That* was all too true. He was too weak, much too weak. Curiosity finally overcame him. He turned his head in the direction of Father Elion's voice.

The inquisitor was sitting where he always sat, next to the sheriff behind the table, and on his other side a young Dominican novice was nodding earnestly. The novice had lush, dark, wavy hair and a perfectly oval face with symmetrical features of astonishing beauty. He looked like Adonis must have looked, with unblemished skin and large dark eyes.

Father Elion felt Percy's gaze and glanced over at him. Their eyes met for a moment and Father Elion smiled at him. Percy felt a chill go through him and closed his eyes as he turned his head away. Now he just wished that they would get started. He couldn't bear not knowing what they would do to him.

The sheriff and Father Elion consulted and then Father Elion explained to the novice the device they would apply today. An iron stirrup was fitted around Percy's left foot, attached to an iron bar that could be twisted laterally. Since Percy's knees were made fast to the table, by rotating the bar one could slowly wrench the ankle around and eventually break the bones of the ankle, and even the fibula if enough pressure were applied. The beauty of it, according to Father Elion, was that no one had yet died of a broken leg.

The questioning started as it always did. Percy could not have told anyone why he didn't just confess. The Temple as he knew it – knights and destriers, fortresses and fighting ships, the sparkling white of Limassol against the turquoise of the Mediterranean or the mighty grey of the Temple of London – none of that existed any more. It was nearly five months since he had seen the light of day. He had not bathed or had a change of clothes in all that time. He had not tasted any kind of vegetable, fruit or meat – unless you counted the mould on his bread. He was not sure that he would ever be able to walk again – certainly not after they were finished with him today, he thought. He could not imagine that he would ever ride a stallion, hold a lance or a sword – be a knight again. The thought of ever facing someone he knew – his forceful and competent older brothers, his commander or brothers at Limassol, Master de la More in London or even the pope – was enough to make him writhe in an agony hardly less than the one produced with instruments of torture.

Percival de Lacy was dead. What was left was some creature not really human any more, who would never again be worth anything to anyone.

What did it matter if he joined the hundreds of others heaping abuse and insults upon an institution that had not been able to save him from this? An institution which could not possibly survive the systematic defamation of its goals and the extermination of its members? Why, in the name of a merciful God, couldn't he just confess?

But the nagging question, like all the questions they put to him, provoked a bitter, vehement protest which was so powerful that he *could* not confess. The allegations were lies! The confessions were lies! The Cathars had gone to the stake with raised heads because they believed in their heresies. They had confessed to *heresy* not to be reconciled with the Church but in order to escape a world they viewed as hell. How right they were! But he could not confess to worshipping an idol with cat's ears! It was an insult to his intelligence and his manhood. No, no, no!

The pressure on his left ankle had grown so overpowering that he could no longer flee into his thoughts.

'Did you deny Christ on your admittance to the Order?'

He clenched his fists and tried to brace himself against the pain in his leg. 'No!'

'Weren't you asked to deny Christ and spit upon the cross?'

He bit down on his lip and tasted the blood. 'No!' When was the damned ankle finally going to break?

'Did you worship an idol while you were in the Temple?'

He did not feel the tears that left marks on the filth of his face and glittered in the torchlight as they ran down his grimy unkempt beard. 'No!'

'Didn't your Templar brothers worship an idol?'

'Nooo!'

His fingernails were digging into the palms of his hands and drawing blood. He could hear his ankle bone creaking. Someone was retching and he could smell the stink of vomit.

'Do you believe in Our Lord Jesus Christ?'

Father Elion gave a nod to the guard as he asked the question and, instead of increasing the pressure gently, the powerful henchman jerked the bar over.

The sound of the fibula snapping was so loud that it echoed around the chamber. 'Nooooo!'

Father Elion smiled at the sheriff and looked with pity at Brother Umberto, who was trying to wipe the vomit from his lips on the cuff on his sleeve. The pretty youth was ashen and looked almost worse than the prisoner. Father

Elion reflected with a sense of superiority that Brother Umberto was too soft. He needed to harden up if he were to serve God.

Father Elion turned back to the prisoner. The English Templar was bathed in sweat that shimmered on the surfaces of his face and hands and gave a new overlay of stench to his body. He was whimpering now, rolling his head back and forth and whimpering, 'No, no, no!'

Father Elion stood and went around the table to stand beside the prisoner. He laid a hand on his shoulder. 'Well done, my son. Well done. You are at last on the path to salvation. *Deo Gratia*.'

Only then did Percy grasp what he had done. Even above the pain that devoured his leg, distressed his stomach and half-obliterated his mind, he became conscious of the fact that he had denied Christ. He started sobbing. Tears streamed down his contorted face, not tears of pain, for those oozed out of his eyes unconsciously – this flood was tears of humiliation and despair. He had just been outwitted, tricked into a confession against his will – something even worse than a confession to stop the torture. A confession to stop the pain of torture – at least for that instant – was intended.

'Now, now.' Father Elion patted the Englishman's bony shoulder as it shook under the sobs. Father Elion felt a wave of relief and satisfaction go through him. He was now confident that he had found the right method for breaking de Lacey. He had one confession already, and tomorrow or the next day, when he made up the report, he could decide exactly how to use this denial of Christ, but he needed a second confession. Clement had insisted that the Englishman confess to at least two counts. Or could he interpret that a denial of Christ was a confession to *both* having denied Christ at the time of his admittance to the Order *and* to worshipping an idol ever since? After all, he had not confessed to having denied Christ in the past; he had said he *did not now* believe in Christ. Ah, it was perfect!

But then Father Elion remembered something: the transport of prisoners for the pope had to leave first thing in the morning. Anxiously, he asked the time of his companions. The sheriff informed him that it was after midnight. He cursed abruptly. There was no time to lose. He had to write up the report so it was clear that the Englishman had confessed to two counts and then he had to read it back to him and get his signature affixed to it – all before dawn.

He turned on Umberto without the slightest indulgence now. 'You shame the habit you wear, Brother Umberto. Sit down and start taking notes. We have to get the report finished tonight.'

'Do you need me any more?' the sheriff asked, shoving his chair back and stretching his arms over his head as he yawned.

'No, not at the moment. Turn in, if you like. But you'll have to witness the confession and the prisoner's signature.'

The sheriff nodded. 'Send for me when you need me.'

'Shall we take the prisoner back to the jail, sir?' the senior guard asked the sheriff.

'No, leave him there. You can remove the braces if you like. He's not going anywhere.'

The sheriff started out of the chamber but stopped as he passed the guards with a backwards glance at the prisoner, who was still sobbing on the table. 'And bring him a blanket, clean water and a slice of good bread.'

The guards did as they were bidden and then sat down on the wooden benches by the door and tried to doze. It was strenuous work having to stand on your feet hour after hour applying just the right amount of pressure.

Father Elion started dictating to Umberto. He paced as he spoke and Percy could hear Umberto's pen scratching on the parchment. Father Elion was an eloquent preacher and he took pride in his style, but he was not a good extemporaneous speaker. He worked over his manuscripts carefully and memorised them. Now he had to keep correcting himself, improving upon what he had dictated. Umberto had to read out the text again and again and often he had to scratch out what had been written and start again. It took them nearly two hours to write a confession that satisfied Father Elion.

Umberto was by now feeling dreadfully tired and weak; after all, he had lost his dinner when he vomited and the stench of the prisoner and his own mess were making him nauseous. But Father Elion had no mercy. He knew that it was already between two and three o'clock. He ordered Umberto to make two clean copies of the confession.

'May I go up to the scriptorium to write, Father?'

'No! You'll sit right there and do as you are told.'

'I'm feeling ill, Father.'

'Guard, clean up this mess. Brother Umberto is as squeamish as a girl and can't bear the stink of his own vomit.'

The guard grunted. He thought such work beneath his dignity as a skilled torturer, but he knew better than to cross Father Elion when he was in such a mood. He went for a bucket of water.

Brother Umberto wrote up the confessions as carefully as he could but it took far longer than pleased Father Elion, who paced ever more furiously, ever faster. The guard cleaned up the vomit and sat down again. At last Umberto was finished. Father Elion checked it over, made one or two corrections in a clean, elegant script and then sent the guard to fetch the sheriff.

The sheriff came into the chamber with sleep still in his eyes, wearing a fur-lined robe over his nightshirt. 'It's five o'clock in the morning!' he grumbled. 'Couldn't this have waited?'

'No!' Father Elion insisted with fervour.

'Sir Percival! You need only sign the confession here and here and then you can look forward to a good hot meal and a warm bed.' After you reach Poitiers sometime in the next fortnight, he added mentally.

'No.' Percy's voice cracked as he answered and Father Elion thought he had misunderstood him.

He cocked his head. 'What did you say?'

'No!' Percy managed to say it more distinctly this time.

Father Elion stood speechless and the sheriff had to laugh. He had never seen the famed inquisitor look so flabbergasted. It was worth getting up before dawn just to see – and he felt a warmth for the damned Englishman rise up in him again.

Father Elion got hold of himself rapidly. Angrily, he signalled for the stirrup to be fastened to Percy's right leg. The sheriff sighed wearily and sat down behind the table, huddling into his nightrobe. It looked as if he were not going to get any more sleep this night after all.

Percy could hardly be surprised by Father Elion's reaction. He knew that his refusal to sign the 'confession' would not be meekly accepted. But he had never before had to withstand two torture sessions in such close succession. To be sure, lying chained to the damp, cold floor of the jail hardly counted as recovery, but the presence of his brothers had done more to restore him than he had realised before now. They always welcomed the men who returned from interrogation with words of comfort and encouragement. The men who had confessed were assured that no one blamed them, that it was only natural for a man to break under such pressure, that God knew what was in their hearts. And for the few Templars like Percy who had not confessed there had always been a reception of admiration and gratitude. The others seemed to believe that as long as some of their brothers held out against the torture, they would all be vindicated.

Percy missed the restorative balm of his brothers admiration and encouragement. His teeth chattered audibly now that the blanket had been removed, and he started trembling as they buckled the braces again. His stomach turned over. There was no one to say: 'Take courage, brother, our prayers are with you,' no one to strike up one of the Templar hymns which had given so many Templars in so many hopeless situations the courage to face the enemy.

In the dank chamber, putrefied by the stench emitted from his own body, Percy was utterly alone. To the men around him, he was not even worthy of hate. The guards regarded him as an object on which they honed their valuable skills. The novice viewed him with tangible revulsion, the sheriff with resentment for keeping him from his bed. Father Elion viewed him as a personal insult, an affront to the Church and God.

Father Elion was so angry at the English Templar's insolence that he allowed his personal feelings to guide what was usually a highly professional operation. He could not maintain his usually cool, neutral tone of voice but demanded in a burst of candid temper, 'Do you refuse to sign your confession?'

The guards took up the crowbar and wrenched it around sharply so that Percy screamed at the abrupt shock but could not answer the question.

'Do you refuse to sign your confession?' Father Elion demanded again.

The guards maintained the pressure, pushing against the resistance of Percy's bones, ligaments and tendons. The ligaments and tendons slowly started to stretch and tear.

'Yes!' Percy shouted at Father Elion.

Father Elion was mildly surprised to have wrenched a positive answer from him for the first time – and satisfied as well. Now he stepped closer to the Englishman and spoke directly into his ear. His voice was smooth and sounded almost solicitous. Percy could hear the smile on his lips. 'You realise that if you refuse to sign your confession you are, in effect, retracting it?'

'Yes,' Percy managed as the ligaments in his ankle were torn fibre by fibre from his bones.

'You confessed to heresy. If you refuse to sign your confession, you must be considered a relapsed heretic.'

Some part of Percy's brain registered that this was not true. He had never confessed to heresy. He had denied a belief in Christ but that was atheism not heresy yet he did not have the strength or breath for such a lengthy reply. He could only shake his head and protest, 'No!'

Father Elion ignored his response as if he had been silent. 'You know the fate of relapsed heretics? They have to be burned at the stake.'

Father Elion obviously relished informing Percy of this fact, but the pain which burned up Percy's right leg was so consuming that he had no room in his brain to contemplate an auto-da-fé. At that moment, he might even have welcomed the flames as an alternative to the wrenching of his bones. His body was loosening itself from the grips of his brain. Without even being aware of it, he was starting to sob and struggle against the braces that held him.

Father Elion had been in this situation scores of times before and at once his professionalism took over. With a mental self-reprimand for having allowed himself to get carried away by his emotions, he started to concentrate all his energy upon questioning the prisoner. He could sense that he was on the brink of victory.

'Do you want to be burned as a relapsed heretic?'

'No,' Percy gasped.

'Do you want to be reconciled with Holy Mother Church?'

Percy struggled against the pain, trying to retain his wits, but the question was beyond him. He couldn't decide if he should say 'yes' to show he was not hostile to the Church or 'no' to indicate that he did not need to be reconciled since he had never broken with the Church. But he *had* broken with the Church, he reminded himself – if only because he was tricked. He had denied Christ not more than a half-dozen hours ago. For that, even if it were only a mistake, he could ask to be reconciled. 'Yes,' he gasped.

Father Elion nodded now with increasing satisfaction and flexed his hands, which had cramped in the sheer intensity of his anticipation. He cast a glance back at the *Inquisitor's* table and saw that the sheriff was sitting up straighter and watching with open excitement. He too sensed that they were on the brink of success.

'Good,' Father Elion said aloud. 'Holy Mother Church loves you, my son. She is not vindictive. She will welcome you back into her arms if only you will tell the truth. Fight against the Devil, my son. Tell me the truth: did you deny Christ and spit upon the cross at your reception into the Order of the Poor Knights of the Temple of Solomon?'

Percy's head was rolling from side to side and his breathing came in gasps. The breath from his uncleaned, scurvied mouth made Father Elion take a step backwards to spare his nose. Umberto was gagging again.

Percy knew that he had denied Christ. It *was* the truth – even if the point in time was different from that in the question. And how could he do otherwise? he demanded of himself. How could there be a *merciful* Christ? A merciful Christ would not have allowed this to happen to his most devout servants! Percy felt a burst of fury so overwhelming that it almost blocked out the pain – or rather was one with it. He hated Christ. He denied Christ. He wanted to spit upon the Cross.

'Yes!'

Father Elion flashed a triumphant smile over his shoulder to the sheriff. The sheriff was on his feet and walking around the table. He wanted to be sure that he missed nothing now. He had to bow his head in respect to Father Elion for this session. This was a real confession.

'Well done,' Father Elion addressed the English Templar again.

Percy felt the isolation around him. He was aware that he had no one left in the world. He could never go back to his family in England after what he had become here, and now that he had turned against Christ he could not return to his brother Templars either. He no longer had a right to their respect and he could not accept their words of comfort because he had betrayed them.

'Just one last question,' Father Elion purred in the foul air of the torture chamber. 'And then – assuming you put your signature to the confession – you will be received back into the grace of the Church and provided with everything you need for the comfort and restoration of your body and your soul.'

He made it sound so inviting but Percy had no ears for his words: the pressure on his leg was still increasing, the fibula of his second leg nearing the breaking point.

'Did you and/or your brother Templars worship an idol?'

'Please,' Percy gasped. 'Please. Not my other leg.'

Startled to have him say anything other than yes or no, Father Elion at once signalled for the guards to ease up.

Percy let out a sigh of relief. His head and body went still and tears glistened on his cheeks. The sheriff felt a wrench of pity for the broken animal in front of him. He had once been such a proud and handsome young man.

'All you have to do is admit that you and your brother Templars worshipped an idol,' Father Elion told the human wreck on the table.

Percy shook his head and at once Father Elion made an imperative gesture. The guard sprang to obey, but, because he was not just increasing a pressure already applied, he made a slight miscalculation. The bone snapped with the same sharp crack as the first leg and Percy's howl rang through the room and careened off the walls with such penetration that Umberto blanched and broke out into a sweat.

Father Elion let out a stream of abusive curses at the guard. He hopped from one foot to the other, calling the man an idiot, a goat, a chunk of cattle meat, an ass. He had ruined everything! He deserved to have his blundering arm removed at the shoulder! He ought to spend the rest of his life hung upside down!

There was a knock on the door and the sheriff gratefully called, 'Come in!'

One of the Bishop of Albi's sergeants, his bassinet on his head and a cloak over his hauberk and brigandine, reported, 'We have the wagon you ordered waiting out front, my lord.'

The sheriff nodded and glanced at Father Elion. The inquisitor was still fuming, red in the face.

'Shall I see that the other prisoners you are sending to His Holiness are dispatched?'

'Yes!' Father Elion snapped. Then, remembering his manners, he added stiffly, 'Thank you.'

The sheriff followed the bishop's sergeant down the long corridor.

'Damn you all!' Father Elion shouted, kicking out at the guard who had made the fatal mistake of breaking Percy's second leg before he had confessed to idol worship. The guard jumped out of range just in time and Father Elion turned on Umberto instead.

'You baby! Have you wet yourself?' he demanded.

It was unfair. Umberto had not disgraced himself to that extent but he did feel ill. He couldn't bear to look at the prisoner. He looked instead at the table in front of him.

Father Elion's gaze fell upon the parchment spread out there and a shock went through him. He had become so carried away with his success in this last interrogation that he'd forgotten they had prepared an adequate confession on the basis of the previous one.

Ah, if only the bloody bastard would sign the confession they could send him up to Poitiers. Father Elion could then send a revised protocol in the next couple of days and replace some of the earlier pages. As long as the signature was on the last page, no one would know the difference. He grasped the writing board, and the last page of each copy. Dipping the pen in ink, he returned to stand beside the Englishman.

With his head, he signalled for one of the guards to unstrap the braces pinning the English Templar's arms to the table. While they released de Lacey's arms so he could write, Father Elion placed one hand on the Englishman's fevered forehead. 'Well done, my son.' He now gave the little speech he had given so many times in recent weeks. 'Now that you have confessed your sins, you can be assured of His forgiveness. You must, of course, do penance for such grievous errors, but Holy Mother Church is merciful.'

For the English Templar he added, 'I will send you to His Holiness the Pope. If you help the Holy Father investigate the crimes of your Order in England, I'm sure His Holiness himself will intervene on your behalf and see that your penance is milder than it would be otherwise. Now, sign here and here.'

Percy did not even protest.

Father Elion held the wooden board vertically on his belly and closed the fingers of the prisoner's right hand around the pen. Ink dripped down on to his fingers and, since he did not have the strength or will to lift his head and watch what he was doing, Percy scratched an awkward signature somewhat diagonally across the bottom of the page. He did it twice, as was demanded of him.

Father Elion smiled and patted him on the shoulder. 'Bless you, my son.'

Then he turned to the guards. 'Take him up and load him on the wagon with the other prisoners bound for Poitiers.'

While the guards dragged the English Templar off the table, the inquisitor had Brother Umberto witness the confession, then he folded it and set his seal upon it. He sent Umberto hurrying after the guards to give the protocol to the bishop's sergeant and, with a sigh of relief, headed for his own bed.

*

In the street before the jail, the open wagon bearing the prisoners for Poitiers blocked the road and the driver of a delivery wagon with firewood was cursing and demanding that the bishop's men make the way clear. The bishop's men returned the abuse and said they'd move when they were damned well ready, but they did, in fact, start to hurry.

It was a dull, overcast day with the smell of snow in the air and the escort were anxious to be on their way. The roads were icy, and if it started to snow they would be slowed down or even fail to make the first stage of their journey to Poitiers, Laguépie. They had little enough time if they were to be in Poitiers for Easter, and, with a glance at the sky, they locked the chains binding the prisoners' wrists to the side of the wagon one after another. The wagon had been specially fitted to carry the seven prisoners up to Poitiers: four men on one side and three on the other, all with their hands chained to the wagon and their feet chained together.

The first driver was already climbing up on to the box when the guards carrying the English Templar emerged from the jail house.

'This one too,' they told their colleagues.

'What? Our orders said seven!' the sergeant protested.

After the gloom and stench of the prison, Umberto stumbled on the steps leading down to the street but he held out the sealed document imperatively. 'This English knight just confessed during the night. It is very important he travels with the others. You must deliver this protocol to His Holiness.' In the fresh air and among these commoners, Umberto regained some of his dignity and enjoyed the importance of his mission.

The sergeant cursed and one of the men of the escort protested. 'There are no chains for an eighth man.'

'He's not going anywhere!' Umberto gestured contemptuously to the limp body the guards were dumping on the back of the wagon. 'Both his legs are broken.'

The sergeant looked over and confirmed this with a grunt and a shrug. 'All right.'

Percy had passed out at some point between the torture chamber and the exit from the jail house. The guards propped him up into a sitting position like the others, his back to the side of the wagon, and arranged his legs in front of him approximately as they should have lain had they been intact.

The guards jumped down, closed the back panel of the wagon and, with a wave, returned inside the jail house. The sergeant stuffed the parchment inside his brigandine and mounted his sturdy gelding. The other five men of the escort followed his example and they set off.

By mid-morning the first snow flurries started to swirl in the still air but they posed no threat to progress as the party had put the steep climb up from the river to the corniche behind them. They reached Cordes by mid-afternoon, where the escort stopped for a warm meal. When they emerged from the tavern, the snow had become noticeably thicker and wetter. The sergeant looked up at the sky with a sour expression and half-considered stopping here until the snowstorm was over. But the new bishop was not the kind of man who would go gently with someone he thought had neglected his duty. The sergeant pulled his bassinet back over his head and ordered a blanket spread out over the prisoners. They were supposed to be delivered alive, after all.

Within two hours he was starting to regret his decision, but to return to Cordes went against the grain. The snow was accumulating fast, sticking to the trees and collecting in the ruts of the already icy road. It was with considerable relief that they reached their destination, the Carthusian monastery at Laguépie. Here the entire wagon was driven into the tithe-barn and the horses unhitched. The prisoners were brought bread and fish soup. One at a time, they were unlocked and escorted to the latrines, then brought back to spend the night chained in the wagon. Percy was too much trouble to carry around so they left him where he lay. The others cursed him for fouling the straw in their wagon.

The next day their destination was Villefranche-de-Rouergue. It was a considerably shorter distance than they had managed the day before but the road was worse and fresh snow was bound to hamper progress. The sergeant ordered bags of sand put in the front of the wagon to give the horses and the wheels more traction. They set off after a breakfast of bread and cheese. The prisoners received only bread, but at least it was decent bread and freshly baked.

They made slow progress, winding up the long steep slope from Laguépie, and by noon it had started to snow again. The sergeant almost considered turning off their route to take refuge at Najac. But it meant a detour of roughly three miles and he decided against it. If they had to stop, then it would be on the route he resolved, so they continued. It was hardly surprising that just a couple of kilometres farther on, they came upon a wagon which had skidded off the road and was stuck in the ditch.

The accident had not happened very long before and when they came upon the victims, the owners were still stomping about in the snow, squawking and squabbling, as the Bishop of Albi's party approached. Seeing the helpless, mindless way the others seemed to be addressing the situation, the sergeant felt challenged to demonstrate his competence and resolution – an inclination reinforced by the fact that the victim turned out to be the widow of a wine merchant with a cargo of Bordeaux bound for Figeac. She was accompanied by her two daughters and a pack of incompetent servants. The widow's fur-lined cloak and the garnets in her ears informed the sergeant that the woman had money; she was not more than forty – a heavy but healthy woman with round, red cheeks and a merry look in her eye as she glanced up at him and exclaimed that surely he was her knight in shining armour come to rescue her from adversity.

The sergeant laughed and, leaning on his pommel, looked her in the eye. 'I'm no knight and you're no lady! But I'll be damned if I don't get you out of this mess.'

'You won't go unrewarded, my good man,' she assured him with a coquettish wink.

'You can be sure, mistress, I wouldn't lift a finger if I didn't think the rewards would be worth the troubles.'

The widow laughed happily and the sergeant swung down from his saddle with a shout to the escort.

In a very short time, he had things well in hand and ordered one of his men to get one of the bags of sand from the wagon and sprinkle it on the icy road to give the draught horses traction. The guard opened the back of the wagon, stepped over and between the legs of the prisoners to get to the sand bags and hefted one on to his back. A little more unsteadily, he retraced his steps over the legs of the prisoners, almost losing his balance once or twice, and jumped off the back of the wagon. He didn't have a hand free to reclose the back panel.

Percy stared at the snow on the road, which was abruptly beside him. Less than six inches separated him from the end of the wagon. If he managed to reach the edge, all he had to do was let go and he would fall three feet to the ground, on to the hardened, rutted snow covered by a layer of soft fresh snow. He had no illusions about the pain the fall would cause. His broken legs would be flung about like so many pieces of china in a skin sack. He supposed that he would scream and pass out and then the guards would come running back and find him, possibly mishandle him in their outrage. And then they would find a means of tying him to the wagon – maybe even subjecting his shattered legs to being bound together. He was better off staying where he was.

But the snow beckoned.

He lifted his eyes slowly from the road just behind the wagon to the road stretching back along the corniche to the south. Forest grew thickly on either side of the road. It was a mixed conifer and deciduous forest where the naked branches of the beeches rattled and scratched the snow on the pines and the oaks, still clad in their brown leaves, rustled in the light wind. The snowflakes swirled now faster and now slower, now thicker now thinner. Percy raised his face to the sky and the snow was like dirty ash falling through the white of the sky to melt upon his feverish face. He leaned his head against the back of the wagon and closed his eyes. He could hear the sergeant giving orders and then the crack of a whip and the grunts and groans of men trying to push the wagon out of the ditch.

'No! There's nothing doing. We'll have to unload,' the sergeant announced professionally.

That would take a long time – unloading, getting the wagon out of the ditch, reloading. Percy looked again to his right, at the clean white snow inviting him to abandon the wagon with the straw he himself had soiled and the stink of chained and broken men. It was particularly inviting to think of abandoning the men who hated him and themselves for what they had all done and become. He did not even know their names and they had not asked for his. They did not speak among themselves. They were alone with their individual guilt, self-loathing, despair and apathy.

Percy squirmed a couple inches nearer the edge. None of the others even took notice. Another couple of inches and he could feel the cold wind sweeping up from the road and chilling his entire right side. Another couple of inches and he started to hang off the edge. The cold grabbed at his lightly-clad buttocks.

He clung to the wagon, looking down at the drop to the ground. It would be worse than the moment when his bones broke. It would be like the branding – a searing overpowering pain. He would certainly lose consciousness. But if he could just keep his jaw together, if he could swallow the scream inside… He let go of the wagon.

He came to slowly. The pain in his legs was fierce, enough to wake him, but that was nothing new. Far more odd was the gradual awareness that he was still lying in the snow. He became aware of the snowflakes settling and melting on his face and the melted snow running down his cheeks to his ears. Then he became aware of the stillness. No one was around him shouting and cursing. He opened his eyes and saw only the snow sifting down out of the light grey sky in big, wet globs. He turned his head to the right and saw the road stretching between the forest as it had when he was in the wagon. Then he turned his head to the left. Over him loomed the wagon and between its wheels he could see the two draught horses and beyond that the snowy boots of men rolling great heavy barrels on to the road. The men were straining and now and then called out advice or curses at one another. Percy registered the voice of the sergeant giving irritated orders to someone. He closed his eyes and drew a deep breath.

After several minutes the cold of the snow started to pierce his consciousness from between his shoulder blades. He gathered his strength, clenched his jaw and concentrated on the pain this caused to distract himself from his legs. All his teeth were loose – which had been a blessing when they had extracted three of them to try and get him to confess – but now clamping them together caused his gums to ache almost unbearably and he tasted blood. With his tongue, he felt the gaps torn in the right upper side of his mouth and, while he explored the wound, he lifted himself on to his elbows and started to drag himself backwards towards the ditch.

His eyes could not focus but he didn't actually lose consciousness. Sweating and trembling Percy started to think that he couldn't take any more. Now he was torturing himself. No amount of begging and no magic words would release him from the pain. One arm at a time, inch by inch, he dragged himself on to his elbows, creeping towards the mercy of the snow-filled ditch.

His arms had once been powerful, capable of wielding a four foot long sword with precision or withstanding the impact of a lance smashing on to his shield with the full weight and momentum of a galloping horse behind it. Now they were hardly able to drag his own wasted body. Trembling from the exertion, he forced himself to continue, placing one elbow and then the other an inch or two nearer the ditch, pulling his worthless legs along behind his hips like dead game. Behind him, he could hear renewed shouting: 'Together! Push together!' The whip cracked and the horses snorted angrily. 'Again!' the sergeant ordered.

Percy reached the side of the road and started down into the ditch, into the deeper snow. He stuffed his head into the snow to cool it. Then he squirmed and slithered and, with a soundless, snowy thud, he was off the road and lying half-buried in snow in the ditch. The snow was falling more thickly than ever and the sun was sliding rapidly down the sky. The overcast heavens were turning greyer and greyer. He drew a deep breath. The snow had started to numb the pain in his limbs. He had lost all sense of feeling in his feet. He would – if he were lucky – be allowed to die here. If only it would snow a little harder so they could not follow his tracks from the wagon to the ditch.

The sound of cheering penetrated his dreamy state, and he registered that the guards had been successful in getting the other wagon out of the opposite ditch. He stiffened nervously. Now they would return to their own wagon and discover he was gone. He listened tensely.

'That was worth at least one cask of Bordeaux, my good man.'

Another cheer.

The sergeant apparently made some protest. Percy caught the words 'time' and 'snow', and opening his eyes, gazed up at almost black flakes against dark grey sky. It must be getting on towards four o'clock in the afternoon. But apparently the widow had a way with men like the sergeant, because, after she had spoken there was another cheer. Percy presumed more than heard that a cask was opened and jugs were filled and passed around. The jokes and laughter became ever more frequent.

The snow was so heavy now that Percy was almost covered already. From habit he said a prayer of thanks and relaxed. He would go unconfessed and unshriven to his death because the Templars had been denied priests since their arrest, but he was shocked to realise that he didn't even care. Just as long as they didn't find him and force him to go on living.

Chapter Six

Najac, March 1308

Hugh was getting increasingly nervous as the snow thickened and the light faded from the day. He would have preferred to have stopped at Villefranche-de-Rouergue. At Sanvensa he tried to urge Félice to request the hospitality of the village priest and continue the next day. Félice, however, could be incredibly stubborn. They were no more than seven miles from Najac at this point – at most an hour's ride – and she wanted to get home to her grandfather. They were already behind schedule and tomorrow was his birthday.

It was not that the roads themselves posed any serious problem for their horses, but after dark Hugh was sensibly afraid of robbers. The harsh winter had left so many peasants on the brink of starvation that crime was increasing by the day. The king's officers could not even start to counter it, no matter how many men they publicly hanged week after week. Hugh was all too conscious of the fact that Félice and he might consider themselves poor compared to their older siblings, but their well-fed horses arrayed in good tack and their fur-lined cloaks betrayed them as travellers of substance. There were probably hundreds of men living in this region who would kill them for their cloaks alone – as long as they thought they could get away with it.

And why shouldn't they get away with it? They were two lone travellers on an infrequently travelled road after dark on a night so snowy that even the tracks of their assailants would be obscured. Hugh had no illusions about his ability to protect either himself or Félice. The farther they rode and the darker it became the more frightened Hugh felt, and he cursed himself for not having insisted on following common sense.

They passed two wagons filled with jolly, inebriated travellers escorted by a half-dozen equally tipsy men-at-arms which were heading in the opposite direction and this reassured Hugh somewhat. Maybe any lurking cut-throats would have taken flight at the sight of the armed men. But shortly thereafter they were confronted by great splotches of red staining the snow and evidence of some mishap.

Hugh felt the hair stand up on the back of his head. 'Christ in Heaven! Someone was murdered right here! Look! You can see the blood and how they dragged him off the road! Jesus, the corpse is still there!'

Félice first felt the same terror Hugh did, but then she caught the scent of wine and decided that the red snow was coloured by spilt wine not blood. Following Hugh's outstretched finger, she expected to find something equally harmless: a piece of discarded tack or clothing, but she grabbed her pommel in terror when she realised that there was indeed a corpse beside the road.

Félice's mare shied to the left as she felt her rider's nervousness.

Hugh was looking frantically over his shoulders and then around at the forest, which loomed ominously in all directions. 'Oh, my God! Oh, my God! What if they're still here? Jesus, what are we going to do? Félice! What are you doing? Are you mad?'

Félice had jumped down from her mare and was approaching the corpse. She could not have said why but something about it wasn't right. Clutching her skirts in one hand and leading her reluctant mare in the other, she approached the body cautiously. And then with a shock she met its eyes and her heart stopped. The eyes had locked on hers and they looked through her to her very soul. She was more than naked. Her soul was on trial. The Day of Judgement would not be more merciless. The shock of that realisation took her breath away and blood flushed her face, but the fear was gone. Then Félice shook off her astonishment and rushed forwards, to fall on her knees beside the man.

Her eyes ran over the long, greasy hair and beard crawling with fleas, saw the cracked lips and the blood oozing from the corner of the mouth. The man's skin was so pale that it was almost translucent and grime outlined the thousands of lines carved into his face by pain. The eyes were sunk deep in their sockets. Félice registered the smears of dirt on the neck, the half-hardened, half-wet smear of blood on the left breast of what had once been a white surcoat. Though the red cross itself was all but obscured by filth, straw and dried vomit, Félice did not need to see it to know what she had in front of her. Her eye continued down the length of the body past the hose blackened with filth to the swollen, bruised and deformed limbs below the knee. She gasped and her stomach heaved as her nose registered the revolting mixture of sweat, urine, shit and rotting flesh that emanated from the Templar.

'Hugh!' she shouted over her shoulder, appalled that her cousin was still astride his horse and staring at her as if she had gone mad. 'Hurry! One of the blankets! No, bring me both the horse blankets and then ride for Najac.'

'Are you are crazy? You don't know who the man is! He might be an outlaw or—'

'Don't be stupid. He's a Templar and he's close to death. We have to get him to Najac!'

'A Templar! Jesus God! Have you lost your senses entirely? If we help him, we'll be arrested and excommunicated and probably hanged! Leave him alone! If he's close to death, then the best favour you can do him is let him die in peace!'

Hugh gingerly urged his horse close enough to be able to look down directly upon Félice and the man in the ditch. He now saw the broken legs.

'Ugh! He'll never walk again from the look of those legs, and we can't possibly move him without killing him. Leave him be!'

The eyes of the victim were fixed upon Hugh's face as he spoke and Félice was ashamed of what they must see, but Hugh avoided them. He kept his eyes averted, focused on the repulsive clothing and cast revolted but fascinated glances at the mangled legs.

Félice did not argue. She stood up abruptly and went to her mare. Hugh sighed with relief and turned his horse away from the embarrassing discovery on the side of the road. Then he realised that Félice was not mounting but dragging her saddlebag off her mare's crupper.

'Félice! What are you doing now?'

'I'd rather be excommunicated than damned!' she retorted as again she dropped down beside the Templar.

She detached the heavy, felt blanket covered with grey hairs and smelling pleasantly of horse to which the saddlebag itself was attached. She arranged this over Percy as gently as she could.

Hugh considered pointing out that she was talking utter nonsense: since an excommunicate could be neither shriven nor buried in consecrated ground, he was surely damned. But then Hugh decided that this was not the time or place for a discussion on theology. He decided on a more direct tactic. 'Félice! We could be attacked at any moment!

God knows what thieves and cut-throats lurk in the woods here.' Hugh looked around nervously again.

Félice had lost all fear for herself, distracted as she was by the Templar's more acute need. She was also aware that alone she could do almost nothing to help him. She raised her head and looked Hugh directly in the eye. 'This could be Uncle Jean or Commander Bourgneuf or any of the good men we have known over the years. I refuse to leave him here to die. If you won't help me, then I will have to get Niki or someone else to come back with me, but don't think Grandpapa will ever let you darken his doorway again if you refuse to help me now.'

'But what do you want of me?' Hugh whined hopelessly. 'I'm not strong enough to lift him on to a horse.'

'All you have to do is ride to Najac and get Niki. Tell him the situation. He'll know what to do.'

'All right. Let's both go.' Hugh was anxious to get away from this awkward situation. Maybe once they reached Najac, Félice would come to her senses or lose her courage or their grandfather would persuade her it was too dangerous. Or maybe the man would have the good grace to die before they could get back to him.

'No. I'll stay here until you or Niki or someone else comes back for us.' Félice could read Hugh's mind far too easily.

'Jesus God!' Hugh cursed. 'And what if some cut-throat comes and carries you off? You might be raped and murdered.'

'The longer you take getting help, the more likely that is. I hope you will hurry, Hugh.'

'You stupid girl! This is the last time I'm ever going to go anywhere with you!' Hugh told her furiously and dug his spurs into his startled gelding. Then he was pounding off down the road as if the devil were after him. He was afraid for himself and for Félice and also angry that he could not make her see sense and so was forced to do silly things like this!

Alone with the Templar, Félice was still not afraid. It was completely dark now but the snow fell soft and gentle, making the darkness cheerfully bright. It was not cold and there was no wind. Only Félice's hands were chilled and that made her realise that the Templar had neither head covering nor gloves – and no stockings or shoes.

She opened her saddlebag and started looking for something she could use to wrap his hands and feet. All she found was her flannel nightgown and, after a moment of hesitation, she took this out and then placed the saddlebag itself under his head as a pillow, to at least keep his head out of the snow. Then she tore her nightgown into four large pieces with the help of her knife. She could feel his eyes watching her every motion with calmness and understanding.

It was almost uncanny, she reflected, that he had not yet said a single word, yet she sensed that he was neither demented nor simple. She glanced over and met those eyes watching her, evaluating her, judging her.

She wondered who he was, where he had come from; was he sergeant or knight? The fact that he wore a chain mail hauberk suggested that he was neither serving brother nor priest but more she could not say. She could not even guess his age because the man's face was too marked with pain to be judged by normal standards. And how had he come to be here?

It was odd too, she reflected, as she lifted the horse blanket and reached for one of his hands, that he had not made any effort to ask for assistance. But he did not resist it either. He let her wrap first one hand and then the other in her rags. Then she swallowed her aversion and forced herself to fold back the blanket so that she could see his feet. Only now did she see the effects of the burning. She gasped and looked up at him in horror. She met his eyes but he said nothing. Had they torn out his tongue?

She leaned forwards and tried, very, very gently, to wrap his feet in her rags. It was his turn to draw in his breath sharply and his face contorted. She was hurting him and she couldn't bear it. She stopped guiltily and looked at him. He closed his eyes, surrendering to her care. After a moment's hesitation, Félice wound the flannel loosely around his feet and then lowered the blanket again.

After a while, she stood up and started pacing along the road to keep herself warm. She inspected the rapidly disappearing ruts of the wagon that had gone off the road and generally kept herself distracted until, feeling guilty, she returned to the Templar and, kneeling in the ditch, took his head on to her lap and spread her cloak over his upper body. They did not speak, but she felt him thank her with an attempted smile.

At last the sound of drumming hooves warned her that riders were approaching. She slipped out from under the Templar and went to stand in the middle of the road. She gazed to the south, from whence the riders were approaching. Either Niki was coming from Najac with help or she and the Templar were both about to be delivered into the hands of strangers who might do anything with them. *Now* Félice was afraid, but she did not regret what she had done.

A moment later she recognised the massive bay stallion that Niki rode and beside it her grandfather's ageing destrier. Her first thought was that Hugh had taken him as a fresh mount but then she saw Hugh lagging behind on a roan from the stables. At the same moment she registered that her grandfather himself was astride the old warhorse. She broke into a smile and started to run forwards. Maybe her mother wasn't just being cynical; maybe her grandfather really would live to be one hundred and nine! He certainly looked far from his deathbed as he drew up his stallion and swung down from the saddle. No, he did not spring down; he let his brittle bones down gently. And, yes, he was thin with hair as white as the snow that mingled in it, but he was not feeble as he advanced somewhat stiffly but determinedly towards Félice.

She flung her arms around him and leaned her head on his bony chest. 'Thank you for coming, Grandpapa.'

He squeezed her in reply; already, both of them were looking to the ditch.

Félice took his hand and led him forwards. The Templar's eyes were open again, glittering and penetrating. They met Geoffrey's eyes as they had met Félice's some two hours earlier, and Félice felt her grandfather start violently.

Just once before in his life had Geoffrey experienced a similar sensation. He had looked at his son Jean and seen his dead friend Raoul look back at him. That had been on the night Jean told him that he intended to join the Templars. The man who looked out of the ravaged face on the snow was a man whose life he had once saved. A man who had given his life for a lost crusade. A man who had then been as white and bearded as Geoffrey was now.

'Master de Sonnac!' Geoffrey exclaimed and went down on one knee as if in homage.

The Templar shook his head. 'My name is Percival de Lacy.'

Félice was relieved that he could speak.

Her grandfather nodded calmly. 'My grandson says both your legs are broken.'

'And his feet have been burned!' Félice burst out in indignation.

Geoffrey signalled for her to be still. 'May I see?'

Percy nodded, confused by the question when he was helpless to resist even if he had wanted to, but he trusted this man even more than the girl.

Geoffrey folded back the blanket and considered the legs clinically. He had seen countless battle wounds and more than one broken leg; it would have taken more than what he saw there to shock him. He glanced up at Niki and found that his Cypriot squire was already holding the splint and leather straps which had been made for his youngest son years ago. Niki squatted down beside Geoffrey and started preparing the splint.

'Monsieur!' Percy reached out and caught his arm. 'If you help me, you endanger not only yourself but your whole family.'

The sheriff had made sure all the Templars were read the royal writ which had placed them on the same level as outlaws and excommunicates. Any person who aided them was threatened with arrest.

In answer, Geoffrey put his hand to his sword hilt and drew out the great weapon far enough for Percy to see the hilt. It was a strange gesture and Percy could only gaze at the odd sword in puzzlement. The grip was composed of crystal encasing a finger bone as if it were a relic. Then Geoffrey dipped the sword and Percy saw that the pommel was white enamel with a splayed red cross set in it.

Percy frowned. Was the old man a Templar then? Perhaps one of the many noblemen who joined the Order for a fixed term of service before returning to their lands and families? He looked up at Geoffrey, questioningly.

Geoffrey smiled. 'My name is Geoffrey de Preuthune, Brother. And my oath was never to abandon a brother in danger or distress.'

Geoffrey turned to attend to Percy's legs, but Percy stopped him again, more desperately this time. 'Wait! You don't know what I've done.'

Geoffrey looked at him, waiting patiently.

Percy was sweating and his chest heaved in time to his short, shallow breathing. 'I denied Christ. I said I spat upon him. I... No, no, I didn't confess to idol worship. But I signed the confession. The inquisitor twisted what I had said but I signed it. I didn't even—'

Geoffrey didn't appear to be listening any more. He was examining the legs with his cool, wiry fingers and the expression of a physician. When Percy fell silent, he looked back.

'Do you want to know what I said to Master de Sonnac at Mansourah? I told him: "Christ died on a cross in Jerusalem but he was not the Son of God and not the Messiah."'

Hugh cried out in shock and half-expected lightning to strike at any second. Even the loyal Niki blanched and crossed himself. Only Félice was not shocked. She had never heard this but she knew that her grandfather had lost all his brothers at Mansourah and that he had had to kill his best friend to keep him from being further mutilated by the Muslims. She could more than understand that her grandfather might have been angry with God for the defeat the crusaders had suffered and for his personal losses. He had been only nineteen at the time.

Percy and Geoffrey stared at one another. Percy repeated the words in his head and wondered why he was not shocked. Was it that he had started to feel and think these thoughts himself as the weeks and months of his captivity slowly passed?

'I had not been tortured,' Geoffrey continued, reaching inside his suede leather brigandine studded with brass tacks and withdrawing a flask of wine. He slipped his left hand behind Percy's head and held the flask to his lips.

No wine had passed Percy's lips since the night of his arrest. The wine tasted strong and he coughed slightly. Geoffrey waited for the coughing to pass and then offered him the flask again.

'It will go to my head,' Percy whispered, feeling the effect even as he spoke.

'It is supposed to,' Geoffrey countered and pressed it to Percy's lips again.

Now Percy drank with a kind of dazed gratefulness. It seemed almost miraculous that someone could want to dull his pain rather than increase it.

When he had drained the flask, Geoffrey laid him back on his bed of snow and warned softly, 'Brace yourself, Brother. This will hurt more than the breaking did.' He took hold of two pieces of one leg and, with uncanny strength and skill in his skeletal hands, set the first of Percy's legs.

For the second leg they had to improvise a splint; by the time Niki lifted Percy out of the ditch and handed him up to a remounted Geoffrey, he had lost consciousness.

*

At Najac, Geoffrey had Percy housed in the chamber above his own and ordered Félice and Hugh to see to the horses, change their snow-soaked clothes and get something to eat. Meanwhile, between them, Niki, Eleni and Geoffrey undressed Percy, disposed of his clothes and then washed him, shaved off his beard and cut his hair.

When Geoffrey saw the wound left by the brand on Percy's chest, he lost his temper and cursed the king, the pope and God himself, but the outburst was short-lived. He regained his self-control and applied the same salve which his Templar brothers had used on his Greek fire wounds all those decades ago when he had been a novice/squire on crusade in Egypt.

It was not possible to apply the same salve to the soles of Percy's feet, however, because these – left untended in the unsanitary conditions of the jail for too long – had started to putrefy. Geoffrey had to slice open the festering boils and drain the pus and blood before he could wrap them in clean linen bandages.

Noting the foulness of Percy's breath, Geoffrey inspected his mouth and discovered not only the missing teeth but confirmed that he was suffering from the same disease that had killed thousands of crusaders in Egypt. He asked Eleni to go into the kitchen, sauté onions and mix them with yoghurt. She was then to press two lemons and bring the juice with the onions, yoghurt and fresh bread.

Félice knocked on the door but her grandfather sent her away. She was a maiden and Percy – no matter how much he had been mishandled, degraded and abused – was a young nobleman.

Only after he had seen Percy fed and laid to rest in the wide canopied bed, with Niki on a pallet on the floor beside him, did Geoffrey retire for the night.

Returning to his own chamber on the floor below, he undressed down to his drawers and shirt and, by the light of a single candle, he knelt beside his bed.

'Eleanor,' he addressed his dead wife, 'surely you would not have denied him shelter – even though he is a Templar.'

After a pause in which he listened to the silence, he was reassured. Eleanor had hated the Temple all her life but she had loved her Templars – himself and Jean. She would not have turned her back on the young man sleeping over his head.

'I have to do this,' he told her. 'Maybe it's the reason I haven't been able to die. I have to help him – and the others. You must see that.'

Then he bent his head, closed his eyes and said the Lord's Prayer before climbing into the lonely, cold bed to sleep alone.

*

Geoffrey's birthday dawned in glittering splendour. The snowstorm had swept on westwards and the sun rose upon a carpet of fresh, untouched snow almost twelve inches deeper than the morning before. The snow all but buried the cottages in the little bastide of Najac, and smoke slithered up out of the shapeless mounds of snow to leave grey smudges against the pastels of the morning sky. The dogs barked eagerly at the transformed world and even the villagers found delight in the winter splendour.

The villagers of Najac were all serfs of the lords of Najac and they had no need to fear the harshness of the weather. For almost one hundred years, in times of need the lords of Najac had provided for the villagers from the great cellars of the castle. This year too, as the villagers' own stores ran short and the first of their livestock died in the unusual cold, Geoffrey had ordered his daughter-in-law to distribute grain from their own storerooms. Marie had been furious but Louis had backed his father. His mother had reminded him of his duties to the villagers of Najac on her deathbed.

The children were the first to leave the stuffy, smoky warmth of their cottages and tumble out into the snow. They were soon dressed in snow from head to foot, and snowballs were hurled in furious battles that raged up and down the alleys to shrill cries of delight.

The clang of the basilica's bells brought some of the old people from their fires. The women draped scarves over their heads while the men put on their battered felt hats before they fought their way through the snow, up the path and past the castle to the church for mass.

By mid-morning the snowy main street of the village was already well-trodden and dirty from the villagers going about their business. Today was their feudal lord's birthday and there would be a meal for all the villagers in the great hall of the castle at noon, so they were anxious to get their chores finished early despite the weather. In the cottage near the eastern gate of the bastide, the laundress Raymonde was wringing out the laundry and hanging it out to dry on a line stretched from the corner of her cottage to the wall. Her hands were bright red and chapped, and her knuckles were already swelling with the arthritis that had plagued her mother and grandmother. The sudden arrival of armoured men cantering through the gate startled her, but only for an instant.

Registering their ecclesiastical livery, her lips turned down and she turned her back on them to continue hanging up the washing.

'You! Woman!' a loud, angry voice called out.

Raymonde calmly finished pinning a nightshirt to the line before turning around and facing the Bishop of Albi's sergeant.

'We're looking for an escaped Templar! He has two broken legs. He can't have gone far on his own. Someone must have helped him. Have you seen anything suspicious?'

Raymonde looked at the sergeant while she dried her hands on her worn apron. She had seen Sir Geoffrey ride out after dark and return with a heavy burden over his saddle. Sir Geoffrey had once been a Templar novice. Sir Geoffrey would undoubtedly help a brother Templar escape if he could. Raymonde nodded.

'What then, you stupid hag?' the sergeant prompted irritably. Ever since he had sobered up and realised that he was missing a prisoner, he had been in a frenzy. It wasn't just his job at stake – it was his very neck. He had to find that damned eighth Templar or God knew what the Bishop of Albi would do to him.

Raymonde lifted her hand and gestured vaguely. 'Just yesterday evening...' She started with the initial reticence of peasants in front of other classes.

'What?' the sergeant prompted impatiently.

'I had to go for more firewood, see?'

'No, I don't see,' he told her angrily. He couldn't stand the way these peasant women spoke in riddles.

'Then let me finish, young man!' Raymonde snapped indignantly.

'Christ give me patience!' He rolled his eyes.

'Late yesterday afternoon, as the snow came on thicker, I realised I needed to get more firewood in. You wouldn't have acted differently!' she scolded.

The sergeant rolled his eyes again and Raymonde continued with native stubbornness, 'I went out to collect firewood, see? We villagers were given the right to collect the wood by the Lady Eleanor's father in the year that King—'

'I believe you, I believe you!' The sergeant didn't give a damn if the old hag had been collecting wood legally or not. He had to find the missing Templar!

'Well, I went out not long before dusk, see, and I headed for the beech grove. You know, just before the turn-off for La Bruyère?' She gestured towards the south. She had seen both Félice and Hugh riding behind Sir Geoffrey and they, she reckoned, must have been coming from Poitiers, from the north.

'And?' the sergeant prompted.

'Well, I hadn't got very far – maybe a mile or a mile and a half – when I was overtaken on the road by five men – horsemen. They nearly ran me down!' Raymonde's tone was indignant. 'But when I wanted to protest about such unchristian behaviour, well, my good man – these were the kind of men you can't teach manners to.'

'Lords?'

'Good heavens! Whatever do you mean? These were the kind of men who would rather kill you than spit!'

'Mounted?' The sergeant sounded sceptical.

'Why not? There are always horses to be had for the right price.' She rubbed her thumb and forefinger together.

The sergeant had to concede that she was right.

'Go on!' he urged, although he was beginning to doubt if what she considered 'unusual' could have anything to do with the missing Templar.

'I almost turned back after that but I needed the firewood so I continued. Besides, following in their tracks made my going easier. That's why I know that the tracks abruptly turned off the road and headed into the woods.' She stopped as if this were tremendously significant.

The annoyed sergeant shrugged. 'And?' he prompted. 'What does that have to do with the escaped prisoner?'

'But the tracks lead towards the old quarry!' she exclaimed as if that explained everything. 'That's where outlaws often hole up for weeks on end. Haven't you heard?' she asked in disbelief. 'There are whole squadrons of Templars who never fell into the king's hands! God have mercy on us!' she crossed herself. 'And they roam the woods here about and in the Cévennes, of course, and by Clermont-Ferrand.' She gestured vaguely here and there. 'They must have seized this man you're talking about and spirited him away to the quarry!'

The sergeant felt a chill come over him and then a new pulse of hope. Almost against his will, he had to admit that she was making sense. Of course some of the Templars had escaped arrest. Everyone knew that. And if they had learned about the prisoner transport – and that wouldn't have been hard – they might well have decided to try to intercept it. Then during the incident with the wagon they could have struck. Christ's balls! The sergeant's head still ached from the wine he'd drunk and today the widow's charms seemed considerably less alluring than they had last night. But while they were all working to free the wagon it would certainly have been possible for these mysterious Templars to have swept down and freed the prisoner. It made sense. But why just the one? The others were chained, of course. Maybe they didn't have the tools to cut through the chains. Or maybe the escaped prisoner was particularly important. What the hell! He was lucky that they had only seized the one.

'Where is this quarry?' he demanded.

'Oh, it's easy to find.'

Raymonde led the little troop out of the gate and, standing there, gave such explicit directions that anyone would have got lost. The little troop swung their horses about and spurred through the snow without giving her a sou or a second glance.

Raymonde returned contentedly to her laundry. It was going to be a good day! There really were robber bands in these woods and they often used the old quarry for their camp. The Bishop of Albi's men would find evidence of fires beneath the snow and would follow the false trail for God knew how long! It was years since she had been so pleased with herself and a day's work.

It could only have been destiny that sent the Bishop of *Albi's* men here! Albi! Where they had tortured and burned so many of her ancestors! Albi, which had given her faith its name Albigensianism – and where that corrupt and foul body which called itself the Church of Rome had built a monument to its own oppression: a cathedral that looked more like a prison. Raymonde laughed. The Bishop of Albi's men would spend all day in the cold and the snow, chasing after a man who was warmly tucked away in good Sir Geoffrey's care at the castle. She glanced in the direction of Najac castle with satisfaction. That was a castle no half-dozen men of the Bishop of Albi could take! She laughed aloud in her delight. Let them search!

*

The Bishop of Albi paced back and forth across his study, his purple robes fluttering about him, the gold threads of the embroidery glittering in the candlelight. He was a formidable figure in full episcopal regalia, his mitre set firmly upon his head and his thick fingers laden with massive rings. But for all the jewels and silk, he still strode back and forth like an angry elephant, and the calloused guard feared the strength hidden beneath the clerical robes.

The bishop was red in the face and his eyes bulged slightly in his round, flat face. The guard had been sent back to report the loss of one prisoner to the bishop, while the sergeant proceeded with the rest of the detachment to Poitiers. They had lost a whole day looking for the missing prisoner and then decided they could not risk arriving late in Poitiers with the other seven.

The bishop had heard the man out with mounting fury and then demanded why in the name of God they had stopped to help the widow. 'You were already tasting the Bordeaux, weren't you?'

'No, Your Grace. We couldn't get past the other wagon, Your Grace.' The guard had been instructed to lie about this point and he had readily seen the sense of it. 'We had to stop and get it out of the way first.'

'And you couldn't leave one moron like yourself to watch the prisoners? How many men did it take to move one bloody wine wagon?'

The guard cleared his throat and flexed his hands nervously but he had no answer, and the bishop's look of contempt made him run his finger under his collar in embarrassment.

'Why wasn't the man chained?' the bishop bellowed next.

'We were instructed to bring a wagon for seven prisoners. There was no time to make chains for the eighth,' the guard responded defensively. 'I pointed out that there were not enough chains for the last prisoner, but Sir Novice' – he pointed to Umberto, who was standing as unobtrusively as possible to one side of the fireplace – 'said it didn't matter. He said the prisoner had two broken legs and wasn't going anywhere.'

The bishop spun about on Umberto. 'Is that true?'

Umberto swallowed his fear and lifted his head. His hood was flung back upon his shoulders and his head proudly emerged from the folds. His skin had a marble pallor and his eyes and cheeks were sunken and shaded grey.

'Yes, it is. Father Elion spent all night interrogating this English Templar and writing up the confession just so he could be transported. I assumed that your escort and the fact that the prisoner could not walk was sufficient guarantee he could not escape.'

'You are as innocent as a newborn lamb,' the bishop observed in a low, insulting voice that made Umberto flush.

He knew that he had been made to look the fool and now he feared for his career.

The bishop's gaze shifted from Umberto to Father Elion. The master interrogator looked extremely weary. His bony shoulders were hunched and his head hung low, the lines leading from the hawk-like nose to mouth standing out like gorges down the side of his face. His eyes were lost in the shadows of their sockets.

'The Englishman's confession is pivotal. He is the first and only English Templar to confess to denying Christ and to idol worship. I have his signed confession here.' Father

Elion drew one copy of the confession from his deep sleeves.

'A lot of good that does us now!' the bishop snapped back. 'Do you think the king gave such explicit orders about taking care not to kill the prisoners so we could let them slip through our fingers before they can be put on trial?'

'But he can't have got far. Not with two broken legs. Even if he was rescued by other Templars, they could not take him far in his condition,' Umberto protested. He had to do or say something to mitigate the impact of his error.

'No. Most likely the man never got farther than the woods at the side of the road. You—', the bishop spun on the guard, 'may choose to believe tall tales of phantom Templars still lurking in the woods, capable of miraculous deeds. The Templars I've seen couldn't save their own asses! It is by far more likely that the prisoner did no more than roll off the wagon and die in the snow!'

No one contradicted him. After a moment the bishop continued, 'As soon as the first thaw comes, you will search the woods on both sides of the road all the way from la Bruyère to Villefranche until you find the corpse. If you fail to find the corpse, then you will search every village and turn every farm and cottage upside down until you find the man. These villagers are all still heretics at heart. It would be like them to harbour a Templar precisely *because* they have heard that Templars have denied Christ. We may have to take hostages and publicly put them to the question. That, Brother Umberto, will be *your* responsibility!' The bishop pointed his stubby finger directly at Umberto, then stomped out of the room to say mass on this, the fifth Sunday of Lent.

★

For Percy, the first days after his rescue passed in a confused daze of pain and comfort. His legs, his teeth, the base of his feet, even his shoulders all screamed their agony the more distinctly that he was not half-drugged with despair. But Percy was also aware of being fed heavenly food – he had never known that Brussels sprouts, spinach and cabbage could taste so divine. He was aware with almost equal gratitude that someone provided a bedpan whenever he expressed the need. He sensed that his body was free of vermin and filth; and the smell of clean linen was almost as intoxicating as the wine they gave him. He was not so much aware of the bed as half-bewildered by the lack of hard, damp stone disturbing his sleep.

And then suddenly he woke up and the room around him was crystal clear. It seemed to be midday. Sun was streaming through one of the double windows, and a bird perched on the outside sill and pecked at the glass as if hoping to be let in. His eyes swept from the window to the splendid cross-vaulting of the chamber, supported by corbels carved with human faces. Then they came back to the somewhat faded cushions tossed carelessly upon the stone window seats, then to the dusty tapestries upon the wall and the threadbare rugs. Percy let his eyes sweep systematically around the room, registering the low fire with a steaming pot over it, the bedside table laden with remnants of a meal and then the fine silk curtains of his bed, brightly embroidered with silver towers and black ravens on pale blue. His bed was packed with soft wool blankets and at first he was startled by the great mounds that rose at the foot of the bed where his feet should have been. Lifting the covers, he discovered that a cage had been built over his legs to hold the weight of the blankets off his broken limbs. The legs themselves were properly set, he noted in wonder. He let the blankets down on to his bandaged chest. Everything suggested that he was in a substantial castle. Though the furnishings were somewhat old and worn, they nevertheless spoke of wealth.

The door latch clicked and the door creaked open. Percy looked over expectantly and smiled at the old man who entered. He knew that this was the man who had saved his life, set his legs and was responsible for the care he had received.

Geoffrey stopped short at the sight of the blue eyes looking at him. 'Brother! You look better today.'

'I am better. How long have I been here?'

'Three days.' Geoffrey told him, advancing to the bed and looking at his patient with satisfaction. He had never really feared for Percy's life, but the Templar had been feverish and it was good to see that the fever had broken.

'How can I ever thank you?'

'By surviving, by getting well, by taking up the fight against those that did this to you – to us: to the Temple.'

Percy didn't answer. Three days ago he had not wanted to survive. Now he was content to lie here in this cocoon of safety and goodwill, but if he got well he would have to leave. And where would he go? He could not face anyone who had known him before; and the Temple had been destroyed in any case. But if he could face getting well with uneasiness, he had absolutely no desire to go on fighting. He did not think there was any point in fighting. The men who had done this to him had not only the King of France but the Holy Church behind them. They would surely do it all again if he tried to defy them. Percy knew that he could not face the torture chamber again. He would rather kill himself.

Geoffrey sensed some of what was going on in his mind, and he laid his thin, wiry hand on Percy's. 'Don't worry about that now. You did not ask for my help so you owe me nothing. I helped you because I could not do otherwise. I vowed to help my brothers and I intend to do that as best I can. I regret only that I am so old and feeble. I'm hardly a figure to strike fear into the heart of the King or Nogaret, much less the Inquisition.' Geoffrey gave a self-mocking laugh, and Percy was ashamed.

'My lord, I think you would make the King and even the Pope burn with shame.'

'My name is Geoffrey. I should prefer you call me that.' The intensity of Percy's admiration embarrassed Geoffrey, and he drew up a wooden chair beside the bed and sat down, explaining chattily, 'This castle and lordship belonged to my wife. I am nothing but a landless Cypriot knight who had the undeserved good fortune to win the hand of my lady from Saint Louis, who was her guardian.'

'Cypriot?' Percy lifted his head slightly. 'I spent six years on Cyprus – at the commandery at Limassol.'

Geoffrey smiled. 'That is where I did my novitiate.'

'Then you are... were...' Percy tried to work it out. If he had been a novice then he was a Templar. But Templars could not marry.

'I refused to take my final vows,' Geoffrey explained. 'I was still a novice at Mansourah and was one of three Templars to survive. I carried Master de Sonnac out of the city unconscious across my saddle. When he offered to knight me and accept me into the Temple as a knight, I told him Christ was not divine.'

Now it was coming back to Percy. 'Christ died on a cross in Jerusalem, but he was never God's son...'

'That's right. The odd thing is that Master de Sonnac did not despair of me even then. He persuaded King Louis to knight me and gave me a letter that ordered any commander to admit me into the Temple – but made its use conditional on my understanding and accepting what had happened at Mansourah. Instead I met my future wife and gained the favour of the King and one thing led to another. I disappointed Master de Sonnac's hopes,' Geoffrey admitted. He could not regret what he had done; to regret was to deny Eleanor and she had every right to all he had given her and more. Yet now, sitting beside Percy and remembering Master de Sonnac, Geoffrey was sorry that he could not have done both: been Eleanor's husband and the Templar de Sonnac had wanted him to become.

'And do you understand what happened at Mansourah now?' Percy asked, fascinated.

'We should never have attacked Egypt. We should have confined ourselves to the *defence* of the Holy Land. By taking our crusade into lands that had never been Christ's, we had become the aggressor and so perverted our own mission of protection.'

Percy nodded, content with the answer.

'And what took you from Limassol to this barbarous country at such a fateful point in time, Brother?' Geoffrey asked, turning attention from himself to his guest.

'Please call me Percy. I was sent from Cyprus to the Grand Master with dispatches in midsummer and Master de Molay kept delaying my return so I could take the latest news back with me to the seneschal.'

'Jacques de Molay,' Geoffrey remarked vaguely, looking away. 'You know that he is said to have confessed to all the allegations of importance?'

Percy felt his stomach muscles tightening. The word 'confessed' triggered memories of his own confession and his body poured out ill-smelling sweat at the thought of the torture chamber. 'We were told as much,' Percy managed to answer stiffly.

Geoffrey touched his cool fingers to Percy's forehead and Percy relaxed. He did not continue the topic of de Molay. What was the point in telling Percy that de Molay had not been tortured? He had apparently confessed at the mere threat of torture or because he had been promised lenient treatment if he 'cooperated'. Geoffrey's view of de

Molay was warped by his son Jean's hatred of the man who had failed to support his predecessor Beaujeu when it was most important.

'But surely you weren't still with de Molay on the night of the arrests?' Geoffrey continued.

'No, I was making for Marseille with…' Percy was horrified to think that he had completely forgotten about the dispatches in his confusion and fear. 'Dispatches! They were inside my shirt,' he added somewhat lamely. He had never been searched and they must have been there for the whole period of his incarceration, but he could not remember anything about them.

'There were some remnants of documents in your shirt but they disintegrated at the touch,' Geoffrey told him. 'To the extent they were not soaked with blood, that is. I destroyed them.' Percy nodded and Geoffrey continued, 'So you were at some commandery in the Bishopric of Albi?'

'Yes. How did you know?' Percy had the feeling that his brain was no longer functioning properly. He couldn't follow Geoffrey's thoughts as easily as he should.

'Some of his men came looking for you.' Geoffrey tried to sound casual and relaxed but, pale as Percy was, he blanched and his hands cramped. For the first time since his rescue, Percy realised that he was still not safe. His host might be willing to risk his own freedom and life but he could not guarantee that they would not both be seized.

'We – or rather the good widow Raymonde Duval – sent them on a wild-goose chase and they have not been seen since.' Geoffrey tried to reassure him.

'They will be back,' Percy stated flatly. Of that he was as certain as death itself. 'They need me.'

'Why?'

'I am the only English Templar they have been able to "put to the question". I heard Father Elion explain that they needed my confession to prove it was not just the Templars of France who had fallen victim to heresy and perversion.'

'Ah, I thought I detected an English accent sometimes. And in your delirium Niki said that you sometimes spoke in a language he did not understand. My father was English. He went to the Holy Land with Richard the Lionheart and got stranded, so to speak, on Cyprus.'

Geoffrey studiously avoided the issue: that Percy was of particular importance to the Inquisition. He had not reckoned with that when he had brought him here. Not that he would have acted differently, but it did make his protection more difficult than Geoffrey had first presumed. He would have to consider whether it were safe to keep him here, so near the place they had found him.

'How did you come to be in the ditch?'

Percy explained.

Geoffrey was calculating. Percy's former captors had a rough idea where he had been 'lost' or they would not already have been in Najac. And if Raymonde had seen him ride through the village with a man in his arms, then half the village had seen him. He could hardly expect all the villagers to be equally loyal or equally impervious to offers of reward. He would have to think of a way to remove Percy to a location where the Bishop's henchmen would not be so likely to look for him.

But he hated to move him now, when he was still so weak. Besides the snow was yet deep and the cold bitter.

'How old are you, Percy?'

When they had first found him in the snow, Geoffrey had taken him for a man of at least forty. Now, shaven and rested, he looked much younger.

Percy had been reflecting on what would happen when they found him here. Now he took a deep breath and forced his thoughts away from the dungeon. He could not entirely escape it. It blotted out all of the rest of his life.

'I don't know.' he admitted after a moment in answer to Geoffrey's question.

Geoffrey started and looked at Percy with open alarm.

'I don't know today's date,' Percy pointed out.

'March 11th,' Geoffrey answered, relieved that his baffling reply had such a logical explanation.

'Then I am still twenty-five. I was born on the 18th March, the year of Our Lord 1282.'

'Then we will have a another birthday to celebrate soon,' Geoffrey remarked, thinking that at that age Percy's bones would heal faster. Already his gums had stopped bleeding and were becoming firmer.

There was a knock on the door and Geoffrey called, 'Come in'.

The girl who entered had masses of curly auburn hair confined only by a ribbon around the crown of her head. She had wide-set, golden eyes under clean, black brows, a long fine nose and well-shaped lips set in a heart-shaped face. She wore a gown of cream-coloured wool and over this a loose pleated burgundy surcoat that ended at her knee with a broad band of embroidery. She was not the kind of bright, shimmering beauty who took away one's breath, much less the kind of succulent, voluptuous female to inspire instant lust, but no normal young man could have failed to feel an instinctive attraction. The freshness of her skin and the litheness of her motions as she stepped lightly into the chamber reinforced those instincts.

Percy unconsciously tried to sit up and at the same time keep the blankets tucked protectively around a chest that had grown thin and frail from inadequate diet and lack of exercise. He surmised from her free hair and the quality of her gown that she was a daughter of the house.

She broke into a smile as their eyes met and Sir Geoffrey reported, 'The fever has broken. Sir Percy and I have been having a very pleasant conversation.'

Then he turned to Percy. 'You remember my granddaughter Félice.'

Percy froze. He started to remember. Before Sir Geoffrey had found him there had been someone else, a woman. Just after the prisoners' transport had continued without him, he had heard hooves. He had thought they had come back for him. Instead he found himself looking at a stranger: a woman. She had dismounted and covered him with a blanket. Then she had wrapped his hands and feet in rags. He stared at the enchantingly innocent maiden before him with open horror. He could remember the condition he had been in. As good as naked from the hips down and stinking with his own excrement. He turned his head away and closed his eyes in humiliation.

Hurt, Félice turned on her grandfather with a bewildered and outraged expression.

Geoffrey put his finger to her lips. 'Come, my dear. I've evidently talked too long and wearied our guest. His fever may have broken but he needs rest.'

Geoffrey pushed himself to his feet and, taking Félice by the elbow, led her back out of the room, closing the door behind them.

'Why does he scorn me?' Félice demanded in outrage.

'He is ashamed of what you saw, that is all. It is a good sign. It means he is recovering – not just his strength but his pride. That is something to be grateful for,' Geoffrey insisted, firmly escorting her down the spiral stairs.

'You mean he would rather I had not seen him at all? That I had ridden by?' Félice asked indignantly.

'No, he would rather that I had found him – or Niki or Hugh.'

'Hugh would have left him there!' she protested angrily.

'I know. But you must try to understand. At the time he only wanted to die. He didn't ask you to rescue him, did he?'

'No, but you can't mean we should have left him there to die! You—'

'Shhh!' He put his finger to her lips again, smiling at her burst of righteous temper. Of all his ten grandchildren, Félice was his favourite. She had her grandmother's intelligence and his own stubborn temper and sense of justice, but she could be as gentle as Jean and as merry as Will had been.

She stood before him frowning furiously and he wanted to laugh for joy.

'Félice, *Felicitas*! Do you know how much joy you have given an old man? I think that without you I would have become a senile old fool. You keep me young. And I need you for what lies ahead.'

Chapter Seven

Najac, March 1308

Marie could not comprehend what she had done to deserve the catastrophes which had overtaken her since the turn of the year. First, Natalie's husband had accused her of adultery with a knight of his household. Natalie hotly denied the charges – and then had proceeded to give birth to a baby with hair as black as coal when both she and her husband were fair. Marie and Louis had managed to convince the cuckolded husband that he should save the costs of buying an annulment and give Natalie a second chance. Fortunately, the child was a girl so he could hide her in a convent as soon as she was seven. If Natalie gave him no further cause for jealousy, things might yet work out and the scandal would blow over.

But this much scandal would make it harder to find a husband for Félice. Men always assumed that wantonness ran in a family. They would have to wait until things had died down a bit. Maybe they should send Félice to a convent? Ah, weren't there enough troubles without her senile father-in-law giving refuge to an outlaw?

Marie still could not fully grasp it. Every decent Christian was revolted and outraged by the revelations about what had gone on at the secret meetings of the Templars. She had always been suspicious of an Order that engaged in moneylending and other banking activities. And hadn't there been rumours at the time of the fall of Acre that the

Templars had negotiated secretly with the Saracens? And where had all their treasure disappeared to? It did not surprise her that the devout King Philip IV had discovered what abominable rites these over-secret, over-haughty knights practised. Every good Christian must rejoice that they were being brought to justice!

But no, her senile father-in-law had found one of the offensive heretics and given him refuge under her roof! By giving assistance to a heretic they were all tainted with heresy, and by defying the king they had placed themselves outside his grace. As the initial incredulity at so much stupidity wore off, Marie began to grasp how truly dangerous the situation was. This – more than a hundred Natalies – could completely destroy her sons.

Marie felt a chill crawl slowly up her back and she stiffened. She glanced first at her husband. Louis sat sunk in a chair with his shoulders hunched over his shapeless belly. He had puffy bags under his eyes and his jaw was slack. He was clearly in shock, not yet recovered from what Natalie had done to them and unable to grasp the magnitude of the disaster his father had precipitated.

She looked next at her eldest son. Petitlouis looked hardly less stunned than his father. His athlete's body did not sag and his massive shoulders were straight, but she could read the blank expression on his face. If Petitlouis could not solve something by challenging someone to joust with him, then he did not know what to do. Today Marie had no patience for him. Petitlouis would be no help at all in this delicate and dangerous situation.

So Marie turned her gaze to her second son. Norbert was approaching his eighteenth birthday. He had met her hopes of being taller than either his father or elder brother, and he had rugged good looks that – though less courtly – filled his mother with almost indecent pride. Norbert met her eyes now and she felt a surge of relief. Norbert understood that they were all at risk because of this madness of a senile old man. Marie did not bother considering her youngest child. Félice was only a girl.

'He has to go!' Marie told the others flatly.

'The Templar?' Louis asked, as if coming out of a daze.

'Of course the Templar!' Marie snapped back. 'We must go to the sheriff and report that your demented father mistook him for a beggar or I don't know what.'

Louis was staring at her in open horror. 'My father isn't demented – and no one will believe he is. We have to keep this quiet.'

'Quiet! The whole household knows – and probably every villager in Najac as well! It is a wonder it has not already been reported to the sheriff!'

'But it hasn't. There is no point making a fuss now. We must just send him away quietly.'

'I could take him on a wagon and dump him somewhere on the side of the road,' Petitlouis volunteered hopefully, his face lighting up in satisfaction at his own suggestion. 'In this cold he'll be dead in hours.'

Félice felt her stomach wrench and swallowed her revulsion. She had never been terribly fond of her brother Petitlouis but she had never hated him until this instant. Still, she forced herself to sit perfectly still and attract no attention.

Marie considered her eldest son with a touch of surprise. The suggestion was not bad.

'That won't wash us clean of guilt,' Norbert countered. Intensely jealous of his elder brother, he could not stand to see the look of respect in his mother's eyes. 'We need to take him to the sheriff ourselves.'

'How can we possibly do that without saying where we found him and that my father had taken him in?' Louis demanded of his younger son angrily. He much preferred

Petitlouis' suggestion. It avoided unpleasant contact with the royal authorities and left his father out of it.

Marie cast Norbert a look of thanks. He had given her a new thought and already she was regaining her courage.

'But everyone knows what your father did,' Marie told her husband in a soft, hissing voice. 'We can only dissociate ourselves from his action by showing we are prepared to sacrifice him.' If they played this correctly, she calculated, she would rid herself not only of the vile Templar but her father-in-law as well.

'What do you mean sacrifice him?' Louis demanded, rearing up in his seat. 'You can't mean you would tell the sheriff what he did?'

'And why not? Why shouldn't he pay for his actions?'

'He's an old man. He was himself once a Templar – and no doubt he thought of Jean. You can't expect him to believe these latest accusations.' Louis had trouble believing them himself, but since it was clear that the king was determined to crush the Knights Templar, he would not have lifted a finger to help one. His father was another matter.

'Your father can believe whatever he likes, but he has no right to endanger the rest of us by defying the king!' Marie told her husband with rising anger.

'He didn't understand what he was doing!' Louis insisted.

'Whether he understood what he was doing or not, he did it! And now, if he does not pay the price, you and your sons will!'

Marie could not understand why her husband failed to see the advantages of getting rid of his father. If his father were out of the way, he would come into his estate at last. Louis was fifty-two years old. Any normal man would have been chaffing to get hold of his inheritance.

'There must be some other way,' Louis insisted stubbornly. The thought of betraying his own father to the Inquisition was appalling. His mother had raised him to hate the Inquisition.

'Really? Pray tell me what it is.' Marie mocked.

'As Petitlouis says: we could dump the Templar somewhere on the side of the road far away from here. Or we could say my father mistook him for his own son, Jean...' Even to his own ears that sounded unconvincing.

'You haven't been listening! Everyone in Najac knows what your father did! No matter what we claim, we will be perceived as guilty unless we do something to demonstrate our exceptional loyalty to the Crown and the Church. Isn't it bad enough that your mother was accused of heresy? What do you think the Inquisition will think if you try to protect your father after what he's done? The Templars have been revealed as worse heretics than even the Cathars!' Marie could not have said where her rhetoric ended and where her genuine fears began. 'They have confessed to worshipping Satan in the shape of a cat! They denied the divinity of Christ! They spat upon the cross at their initiation and engaged in sodomy! Do you think the Inquisition will be lenient on the son of a Templar and a Cathar!'

Louis jumped to his feet, his fists balled. 'My mother was never a Cathar! She was cleared of all suspicion!'

'Did your mother even own a rosary? Did she attend mass regularly? Did she send for a priest when she was on her deathbed? No! She sent for your Templar brother! For all we know, he hereticated her before she died!' The suspicion had only just taken shape but it seemed brilliantly logical to Marie. Marie had no notion what beliefs the Cathars harboured. Maybe they too worshipped Satan in the form of a cat. Certainly, they were known to have engaged in every conceivable kind of unnatural sexual activity. It all made sense to her.

But his mother was sainted in Louis' eyes and, by attacking her, Marie had made a fateful mistake. 'How dare you even suggest such a thing!' he shouted at his wife. 'She was acquitted by the Inquisition! Saint Louis himself cherished my mother! My mother never, *never* entertained an impious thought!'

How little he knew her, Félice observed to herself as she watched her father rage. But at least he was prepared to defy his wife. Félice could tell that her mother recognised her mistake. Her face hardened and her lips were a bloodless line lost in sagging cheeks. Marie knew that it was pointless to argue with Louis about his mother so she hoped he would run out of things to say.

Louis did, but he was not prepared to reopen the discussion about betraying his father either.

'We will dump the Templar in a gully somewhere far from Najac.'

Félice was biting down so hard that her jaw hurt. Couldn't they hear themselves? Didn't they realise they were talking about murder? She saw again in her mind the eyes that pierced to her soul, and she was ashamed to think what they would have seen if Petitlouis, Norbert or – God forbid – her mother had been the soul they judged. Her father was continuing, 'No one is going to betray us now if they have not betrayed him already. And that is the end of it!'

He stamped out of the solar into the great hall followed by Petitlouis, who was pleased to have his suggestion accepted. He knew that if he waited around he would have to listen to his brother and mother tearing it apart.

As the tall oak door slammed behind them, Marie hissed, 'Idiot.' She was referring to herself for dragging

Eleanor into it. She might otherwise have managed to persuade Louis to betray his father, she supposed.

'There is no reason why we have to rely on them,' Norbert suggested softly.

'What do you mean?' Marie snapped her head around. Norbert was leaning against the wall with his long, booted legs crossed. He wore bright red hose, a blue tunic with hanging sleeves and a decorative hood that hung down his back but was never meant to be worn. His shirt was of canary-coloured silk, and one could almost have taken him for a dandy. But Norbert was more deadly than Petitlouis. Petitlouis always played by the rules. Norbert was gaining a tournament reputation of his own: he was a man other knights sought to avoid.

'We need only ride to the sheriff – or the Bishop of Albi – and report the situation. We can say Papa doesn't have the heart to report his own father but that we see it as our Christian duty. We can plead for mercy for Papa – and Grandpapa of course.' He shrugged to indicate that he didn't think it would do much good.

Marie felt a slight chill run over her. Norbert was prepared to sacrifice not just his grandfather but his father and elder brother as well. Of course. How else was he ever to inherit anything? His cold-bloodedness frightened – and excited – her. She had always felt a touch of disdain for Louis because he was so soft. In Norbert she saw the other side of strong men: they were ruthless. Norbert, she reflected, might even sacrifice her if he thought it would aid him in getting something he wanted. No, she corrected herself, he would never go that far. Norbert loved her.

'All right,' she agreed. 'Give me a last chance to convince your father to cooperate. If he does not see sense by tomorrow, we will go alone to Albi.'

A raised eyebrow suggested that Norbert thought she was wasting her time, but he let it rest. After all, he was asking his mother to betray her own husband and eldest son.

Marie stood and held her hands to her aching back. 'I must get some rest.'

Norbert nodded and then as an afterthought gallantly sprang to escort her up the steep wooden stairs leading from the solar to the chamber overhead. If he could work on her a little more, he might still talk her round, he reasoned.

Only when she heard the door of the chamber overhead close did Félice dare leave the window niche. She took the door in the east of the tower which gave direct access to the wall walk. She ignored the brisk wind that tugged furiously at her skirts and passed through the south tower with only a nod to the astonished watch, who had no time to get up from their game of dice before she had passed on. She had just entered the south-east tower when she ran into Niki on his way down the tower stairs. His arms were full of blankets and comforters.

'Niki? What are you doing?'

Niki looked back up the stairs and then back at Félice and replied illogically, 'Changing the bedcovers, mademoiselle.'

He pressed himself against the wall to let her pass. She entered her grandfather's chamber and found her grandmother's ancient and gouty maid on her hands and knees before her grandfather's chest.

'Eleni? What are you doing?'

'Nothing, child, nothing. Why aren't you in bed?'

Félice ignored her and started running up the spiral stairs. She burst in upon her grandfather without knocking.

Her grandfather was pulling a heavily quilted gambeson over Sir Percy's head while the Englishman sat in the middle of the room, his splinted legs stuck out in front of him. Geoffrey had wound heavy horse bandages around his legs and resplinted them. The Englishman wore a long woollen shirt and an even heavier tunic with elbow-length sleeves. A hooded camail with liripipe and dagged edges waited on the floor with a fur-lined cloak; all Niki's clothes from the look of them.

'Where are you going?' Félice demanded as Geoffrey and Percy looked over at her, the alarm in their eyes giving way to relief as they recognised her.

'To Chanac,' Geoffrey answered. It was the most obscure and impoverished of the Najac manors, located just north of the Gorges du Tarn. It had harsh winters and rainy summers and was cut off from the rest of the world much of the time. But the wild beauty of the countryside around it had always attracted Eleanor and Geoffrey and they had spent many happy seasons there together.

Félice considered this for a moment, remembered the look on her mother's and Norbert's faces and announced, 'That's not safe.'

'What do you mean?' Geoffrey asked with a frown.

Félice stepped nearer her grandfather. He straightened and met her eyes with a look of wariness that suggested he half-suspected what she was about to say. 'My parents just had a fight. Papa and Petitlouis were in favour of simply – forgive me, sir,' she addressed Percy who looked up at her from the floor with a flushed, drawn face and those penetrating eyes – 'leaving Sir Percy at the roadside to die. But my mother and Norbert insist on going directly to the Bishop of Albi and reporting what you have done. They say the whole village already knows and it won't do any good just to get rid of Sir Percy. They want to turn you over to the Inquisition.'

'The bitch!' Geoffrey spat out. 'The murdering, conniving bitch!'

Geoffrey had always known that Percy could stay only until his daughter-in-law returned. That was why he had been anxious for him to recover enough to be transported. He had anticipated Marie's demand for Percy's removal, and half-expected that she would have him removed by force – which was why Geoffrey was hastening to forestall her. He wanted to be gone by midnight. He also knew that his daughter-in-law resented and despised him. But he had not thought she would go so far as to report him to the Inquisition. But if she were prepared to go that far, his mind quickly proceeded, then Félice was right: Percy would not be safe at Chanac. That was the first place Marie would look for him – or send the Bishop's men to look for him. He nodded once and then redirected his attention to helping Percy into warm clothes.

Percy felt ill. He knew that he could not face the Inquisition again. He would kill himself first. He should kill himself at once, he realised, somewhat shocked that it had taken him so long to think of it. That was the only way to save Sir Geoffrey and the girl from arrest and possibly torture.

'I need a dagger,' he told Geoffrey softly.

Geoffrey went stock-still. 'What for?'

'Don't worry. I know how to use it.'

'To do what?' Geoffrey insisted sharply.

'To kill painlessly.'

'To commit suicide?' Geoffrey grasped Percy's bony shoulders in his long, skeletal hands and shook him with a force neither of them had expected. 'After all we've risked to keep you from dying, you would dare to throw your life away?'

Percy closed his eyes and didn't answer. They didn't know him and so could not possibly know whether he were worth saving. He wasn't even sure himself – rationally – that he was worth saving. There was an inborn instinct that clung to life, of course, but when he used his intelligence he saw only that he was a younger son, trained to arms and vowed to an institution which had been utterly annihilated. Never in his life had he done anything of sufficient value to warrant the sacrifice of others for his sake. He had not even, in the end, been strong enough to stop himself from adding his voice to the thousands who condemned the Order and thereby betrayed his brothers to further pain and endless humiliation. He had contributed to the ruin of the only thing that gave him status and purpose. Why should he go on living?

'Listen to me!' Geoffrey still grasped him in his claw-like hands, the knuckles white from the effort. 'I am an old man who has lived much too long already. On that point my daughter-in-law is quite correct. If I choose to die for your sake, that is my decision!'

Percy opened his eyes and looked straight at Geoffrey. 'And the Lady Félice?' he whispered.

Geoffrey looked over his shoulder at his granddaughter. At sixteen she still had soft, unfinished features and the half-mature body of a teenager but the look on her face was not adolescent, and it was Félice who answered for herself. 'I am neither a child nor a fool. I knew what I was doing when I sent for my grandfather. To have left you there would have been to deny Christ himself. If the Pope, the King and all the clergy of France are too blind to see that, then God have pity on their souls! I knew the risks.'

Percy shook his head. No one who had not faced the Inquisition could really imagine what it was like. But she had reminded him of something: it was as morally contemptible for them to deny him help as it was for him to expect it under the circumstances. Checkmate.

'Nor is the situation so hopeless,' Geoffrey stated. He had had a week to consider the alternatives. Chanac had been his first choice, but it was not the only possibility. On reflection, it had been a selfish decision, one which suited his own longing to retreat to the little fortified manor on the Lot. 'If Chanac is not safe, then... then I will have to take you...'

He glanced over his shoulder towards his granddaughter. It was better if she did not know where they went, then she would not need to lie. 'To somewhere safer still. Somewhere my daughter-in-law does not even know about.' He spoke as much to himself as to the others.

'Where has Niki got to?' Geoffrey asked generally.

'I'm coming with you,' Félice announced.

'Félice, please. We are in a hurry. Don't make things more difficult,' Geoffrey retorted with a touch of irritation.

'You'll be safer with me,' Félice told him, unintimidated. 'They won't expect a Templar to be in the company of a woman.'

'Félice, please,' Geoffrey came and stood directly before her. The stern, sad look on his face made Félice feel like a little girl again – as if she had disappointed him with some childish prank or lie.

'We are in a hurry – we *must* hurry. As you value Sir Percy's life, don't endanger it now with your wilfulness.'

Félice dropped her eyes and bit her tongue.

'If you want to help, go to the village and fetch Raymonde. I must talk to her.'

Félice nodded and turned away sharply so neither her grandfather nor Sir Percy could see her face. She left the chamber behind and descended the spiral stairs. At the foot of the stairs she stopped, tears running down her face. They refused to let her know where Percy would be. Her grandfather, despite everything, didn't trust her and that hurt her more than anything her mother had ever done or said to her.

*

It was a still, bitterly cold night with the stars stabbing the darkness between wisps of blowing cloud. The snow squeaked under her boots and was so dry that it hardly clung to her skirts or the hem of her cloak as she hurried along the street of Najac to the hovel near the gate which housed Raymonde. The air still smelt of smoke from the fires in the cottages but they were all dark and shuttered at this time of night. At the door to Raymonde's cottage, Félice hesitated for a moment. The door was old and sagged in its frame. She could hear the peasant woman's snoring through the cracks.

Taking a deep breath, Félice knocked. The snoring stopped and then resumed. She knocked louder. A startled snort came from inside. She knocked again, more insistently.

'Who's there?' Raymonde called in an evidently frightened voice.

'Félice de Preuthune. My grandfather sent me.'

She heard a bump and then the bolt on the door being shot back. Raymonde stood before her with her hair unbound and hanging in great, coarse strands of black and grey about her shoulders. She wore a flannel nightdress over which she had wrapped her blanket. Her feet were kept warm by old socks in desperate need of darning.

'My grandfather has asked me to fetch you.'

'Ah.' Raymonde nodded. 'Your parents returned this evening.'

'Yes.'

'And now that poor boy must be spirited away before the Inquisition can lay their bloodied claws upon him again.' She nodded. 'Let me dress.' She had already turned her back upon the young woman.

'Raymonde?' Félice held her cloak about her tightly, shivering in the draughty cottage, which stank of smoke and latrines. 'How did you know about... about the Templar?'

'I saw your grandfather bring him home. The whole village knows.'

'Why has no one reported him to the bishop?'

'Because it's none of our business what your grandfather decides to do,' Raymonde retorted irritably, then, relenting, she added, 'Besides he has been a good lord. You won't find anyone in Najac who wishes your grandfather ill. He loved your mother and did right by her.'

Raymonde was rolling another set of stockings over her feet without removing the socks she had on. 'And some of us would rather see the Bishop of Albi burn than give him the time of day!'

'But the bishop was only appointed at Christmas,' Félice pointed out, remembering her former confessor well. He was a practical man, more lenient than many priests she had known.

'This Bishop of Albi or any Bishop of Albi or *any* bishop deserves the flame! Have you ever seen a bishop do a Christian thing in his life? Bishops, dear child, are nothing but parasites. They live on the fears of the common man, sucking his last sou from him for the sake of mumbo-jumbo! Do I shock you?' She looked up from her feet and confronted Félice's frightened face, the eyes two dark pools of confusion in the night. 'Why do you think your grandfather has sent for me?'

'I don't know.'

'Because, my dear, I know other people who think as I do about the bishops, cardinals and popes – all those bloodsuckers! Preaching poverty and living in luxury! At least the nobility don't claim to be poor! And there are good lords, like your grandfather, but find me a good bishop! They don't exist! And as for the Inquisition...'

She stood and turned her back on Félice whilst she twisted her hair and swept it up on to her head before wrapping her wimple deftly. 'Did you know your grandmother's brother once killed an Inquisition judge?'

Félice tensed. She licked her lips and saw her breath clearly in the dark of the room. 'No.' Why wasn't she more shocked?

'That was a courageous act, fitting of your great-grandmother's son. But I am just an old woman and to help save anyone from their hands is a great privilege.' She took her cloak from a hook and started towards Félice. 'To save a Templar is a sacred duty.' She nodded.

'But didn't they take part in the crusade against the Albigensians?' Félice asked, confused.

'At the beginning, but only half-heartedly. And later they gave refuge to very many of our brothers, disguised them and even allowed them to live out their days under the protection of the Temple – though they did not join the Order or hear mass. Many Catholic knights who had sympathised with us and fought for us, like your great-uncles, were admitted into the Temple.'

Raymonde was ready and stood beside Félice.

'And there are others who think as you do?'

'All across the Languedoc, my dear child,' Raymonde said proudly. 'West of the Garonne and north of the Lot, there are only a very few – tradesmen mostly, who moved away. But between here and Chanac your grandfather will find many willing to help.'

'He can't go to Chanac,' Félice told her. 'It's the first place my mother will look.'

Raymonde frowned. 'That makes things more difficult,' she admitted, and then she opened the door and they stepped out of the dingy cottage into the clear, windy night. The moon had lifted above the ridge of hills to the east and the night seemed almost garishly bright.

'Where does your grandfather intend to go?'

'He hasn't told me,' Félice admitted in a voice which betrayed her hurt.

'Now, now. Don't take it like that. He only means to protect you.'

They started back along the slippery street towards the castle.

'I don't want to be protected!' Félice retorted. 'If only I had been born a boy!'

Raymonde smiled at her. 'Don't wish so wildly, child. A younger son is nothing to envy: no land, no home, no income but what he can earn at someone else's table. He must sell himself to the highest bidder – or grovel his way up the ladder of the Church.' She spat.

Félice had never looked at it that way before. 'But he does have the choice, doesn't he? He can *decide* to take service with one lord or another and decide whether he wants to sell his sword or his education.'

'The grass is always greener on the other side of the fence. God will have had his reasons for giving you the sex you have in this life. You must try to make the best of what you have if you want to escape to something better in the next life.'

'You mean in heaven.'

'No, I mean when you are born again on earth – unless, of course, like your great-grandmother, you can achieve the state of perfection before departing this life.'

Raymonde considered the maiden beside her with a cocked head. She could not picture such a blooming maiden in the role of a perfect, since that status was usually reserved for older, wiser women who had already seen the world and tasted sin and remorse in abundance.

'Listen to me, child. If God is so loving and almighty as your priests say, then how can there be famine? How can there be leprosy and why should innocent children die of colds and fevers? God is either not powerful enough to control the world He created or He is an evil, hateful monster! Look around you! Think of your poor prisoner, tortured to make him confess the lies the Church put into his mouth! How can a loving, almighty God let that happen?'

'But it is people who have done it to him. Evil people!' Like my own mother and brothers, Félice added mentally, thinking that Petitlouis wanted to dump Percy on the side of the road to die and that Norbert would hand him back to his torturers.

'Certainly, it was people who have done it to him. And the famine? The cold that takes the lives of the weakest? The diseases that reap good and bad with equal indifference?'

Raymonde stopped and turned on Félice angrily. 'Can't you see that nothing in this world fits the fairy tale those frocked liars tell you? Your grandmother was not so stupid!'

Félice did not answer at once. She glanced around at the starry night and village asleep in the snow as if expecting someone or something to emerge unexpectedly. But all was peaceful. She licked her lips and her breath billowed into the night. 'Do you mean there is no God at all? No loving God, that is?' It was a frightening thought that sent chills down her spine far more piercing than the chill of the night.

'Of course, there is a loving God but there is a hateful God as well. And this—' Raymonde gestured to the world stretching all around them under the cold and brittle heaven, 'is a battleground.' She let the words sink in before continuing, 'Each drought, each flood, each famine is a victory for the Evil One. And every good harvest, every blooming flower, every healthy child a victory for Him. Christ was his soldier – and they crucified him.'

'But His was the victory!' Félice protested with the fervour of youth. 'He gave us victory over death itself!'

'Did he? Then why does anyone cling to life? Shouldn't your priests and bishops be the first to rush to salvation by ending their lives here on earth?'

'No; only our lives on earth can determine if we are to be admitted into paradise or banished into hell. Earth is not a battlefield between good and evil except in our own hearts. If evil wins our hearts then our souls are lost for ever.'

'And if God is almighty, why does he ever let the Evil One win even a single heart?'

'Because God wants our love to be sincere – not the slavish love of creatures with no choice and no free will. If I cannot do otherwise than be good then being good is not an act of goodness but of compulsion.'

Raymonde had never disputed with anyone who could counter her arguments before and she gave Félice a sidelong glance that lay somewhere between suspicion and admiration. She would have to think about what Félice said when she had more time. Now, however, they had reached the outer gate of the castle.

In the inner ward Raymonde put a hand on Félice's shoulder. 'Go to bed, child. We can talk in the morning.'

*

Late on the afternoon of the first Sunday after Easter Geoffrey crossed the Gourdon by a wooden bridge below the village of Lys-Saint-Georges some eighty miles east of Poitiers. Just beyond the bridge, at the base of the steep bank leading up to the village and château, a little complex of buildings built of fieldstone with steep, moss-covered tile roofs came into view. The line of buildings running parallel to the road had roofs plunging almost to the ground so that not a single window gave passers-by a glimpse inside. Only a bell suspended in a stone frame above the peak of the roof indicated the presence of a chapel at the end of the building. A single blunt-headed window pierced the front of the chapel above a low, arched door.

The climate here in Poitou was milder and the snow not as deep as in Najac. On the road, traffic had worn and churned the snow until it was mixed with dirt, but the snow before the door to the chapel was undisturbed. If it hadn't been for the smoke rising in thick clouds from a squat, square chimney at the other end of the complex of buildings, one might have thought it deserted.

Geoffrey dismounted and stepped down from the road on to the snow before the door. He sank in up to his ankles as the brittle crust broke. He pulled a rope beside the door and heard the distant tinkling of a bell somewhere inside the complex.

The light was already fading, the clear sky turning pastel. The air was noticeably colder than it had been two hours earlier. From the church in the village, further up the hill, the bells started to ring for vespers.

The creaking of the door drew Geoffrey's attention back to the chapel and he turned around sharply to face a nun in the habit of the Augustinians. The face framed by the tight white wimple was perfectly oval and, despite the lines that marked it as no longer young, it was a well-made face. The expression was one of cautious welcome as the eyes widened and the face brightened.

'Sir Geoffrey!' The delight of recognition was followed almost instantly by alarm. 'Has something happened to Jean? He hasn't—'

'Not that I know of. To my knowledge, he is still in that part of Scotland held by Robert the Bruce – and, given the fact that king Robert is excommunicate, I expect the Pope has little influence over him. I have brought one of his brothers instead.'

Geoffrey turned and gestured towards the wagon which Niki was driving. 'An Englishman held five months by the Bishop of Albi. They broke both his legs, burnt the soles of his feet, branded his chest, extracted three teeth and kept him in a dungeon without light, heat, adequate food or hygiene.'

The nun crossed herself but almost before she had finished she was gesturing Geoffrey to take the wagon up to the turn-off that led to the hospital complex some two dozen yards ahead. While they manoeuvred the wagon down the drive, the nun returned through the interior of the hospital to unlock the iron gates across the entry to the courtyard. She closed and locked the gates behind them.

'Are you alone here, Sister Madeleine?' Geoffrey asked as she joined him again by the wagon.

The courtyard was deserted and he had not seen another living soul.

'No, of course not. There are now eleven patients and I have Jacques, who does most of the heavy work for me, and Thérèse, who helps where she can.'

She looked up at the wagon and her face lit up again. 'You must be Niki.'

'Yes, madame,' the squire agreed shyly.

Everyone recognised him because of the birthmarks marring his face but he remembered this nun as well. She had run a leper hospital near Paphos on his native Cyprus. She had been a beautiful nun then and Sir Jean had been in love with her and she with him – though of course it was a hopeless love.

Sir Geoffrey's eyes went to the wagon and then together he and Sister Madeleine went around the back and clambered up. From Limoges onward, they had not tried to hide Sir Percy but had bedded him amidst the other goods in the wagon. If asked, they told a plausible story about an accident for curious innkeepers and passers-by.

They had been on the road for almost two weeks and even healthy people were exhausted by travel under these conditions. Travel by wagon over rutted roads and cobbled streets rattled even intact bones and left most people feeling bruised by the end of a day, much less a fortnight. Despite the blankets and straw, lying all day exposed to the winter air meant that Percy's body was too preoccupied with fighting off the cold to heal rapidly.

Since these conditions were infinitely better than the dungeons of the Inquisition, Percy never said a word in complaint. Ironically, however, it was precisely because he was starting to recover that his discomfort was most acute. In Albi he had been unconscious or only semi-conscious much of the time. The pain had been so constant that it was like a drug which deadened his senses and awareness of what was happening between the climaxes of agony that were the interrogations. Now each jolt of the wagon sent stabs of pain through his shattered legs and ankles. He tasted the blood that occasionally drained from the wound in his mouth. His feet were swollen and his hands ached from cold. And his shoulders, wrenched when he had been hung by his wrists with his hands tied behind his back, felt the road through the wooden planking of the wagon. By the end of the day, they were so stiff that he could not move them without severe pain.

Percy waited stoically for Niki to lift him from the wagon for the night, and he was surprised to see a nun picking her way across the chests and crates to him.

'Welcome to Saint Lazarus du Lys-Saint-Georges.' Sister Madeleine welcomed Percy with a smile. 'You will be safe here until you are well.'

He started. Lazarus? Had they brought him to a leper hospital? Was that the price of evading the Inquisition? He raised himself up on his elbows, his shoulders screaming in protest which he ignored. 'Safe?'

Madeleine put her fingers to his chest and shook her head. 'You need not fear infection, sir. Look at me – and I have served the lepers for seventeen years. Nor have any of my servants ever become afflicted. In Paphos I had almost twenty lay sisters and brothers assisting me and not one of them ever became leprous.'

'Paphos?' he enquired. He had heard about the large leper colony near Paphos. 'You were at Paphos?' he asked.

'I established the hospital at Paphos, but I turned it over to the Order of Saint Lazarus the year after my father died. My brother asked me to come home and set up a hospital here. It was the right decision,' she answered the look of scepticism in his eyes.

The leper colony at Paphos had been given an entire manor, along with its income. Percy had ridden by once or twice and seen the fields of sugar cane and grain, the lemon and orange orchards, the olive groves and almond trees stretching in all directions. At Paphos the lepers had spun and woven their own cloth, produced their own farm and household implements at the colony's own cooperage, carpentry and smithy. They had even sold some of their produce in the markets of Paphos, Limassol and Nicosia. It was a palatial establishment compared to this.

'In Paphos everything was going well and Master de Villaret of the Order of Saint John guaranteed us the protection of and a stipend from the Hospital of Saint John. I had a very competent deputy in Sister Hillary, who took over when I left. Here in France it is much more difficult to provide the necessary diet and facilities – and my brother's purse is much smaller than the Master of the Hospital. But we have made a start and we progress. You will see, we follow very strict rules, all designed to prevent the spread of the disease from one limb to another or from one person to another. But I will have a pallet made up for you in my own cottage. Until you are strong, you need not even see my patients.'

Percy was utterly helpless and thus at the mercy of these people who had decided to help him – whatever their motives – but he found himself asking, 'Do you know the price of helping a Templar?'

The nun had started to collect her skirts so she could climb down from the wagon. 'Of course,' she told him, looking back over her shoulder. 'And the price of not helping,' she added with a smile.

Niki climbed over the front of the wagon, lifted Percy into his arms and followed Sister Madeleine along a path between the hospital refectory and the kitchen complex. They passed through a large, fenced-in herbal garden to a hedge and then through the hedge into the back garden of a thatched, half-timbered cottage nestling on the bank of the river.

The cottage was simple in the extreme, but it was clean, whitewashed and smelt of a mixture of pine smoke and herbs. The herbs were hanging in bunches from the rafters. The floor was not bare earth but was paved with rough-hewn boards covered with threadbare rugs. The windows were glazed – a luxury totally out of context. But the result was a cosy cottage which was not dingy.

'I am fond of luxury,' Sister Madeleine remarked, seeing Percy's astonished gaze wander around the room. 'And my brother is the lord of Lys-Saint-Georges. He has been generous.'

When a pallet had been made up in the main room, Percy was laid upon it. The wooden frame was placed over his legs and then blankets piled over him. The fire was blazing now, filling the room with dancing light and the crackle of twigs caught in the flames.

'I'll bring you dinner as soon as the patients have been fed,' Madeleine told Percy, and then turning to Geoffrey, she added, 'You, my lord, must go up to the Château and tell my brother that you have brought me a patient. Say it is your grandson and tell him it is not yet certain if he has leprosy. Many people come here thinking they suffer from leprosy when in fact it is something else entirely. They soon get well again on good food and regular cleaning. Then they leave. You need only tell my brother you have brought your grandson for observation and you will be made welcome. You can thereafter visit as often as you like but there will be no questions when the Templar is well again and your visits abruptly cease. You need only say that your grandson has been cured.'

'I don't know how I can thank you for this,' Geoffrey admitted.

He was acutely aware that Percy was in better hands here than if he had been taken to Chanac. At the lepers' hospital in Paphos Sister Madeleine had been assisted by a priest who had learned medicine in Alexandria during some thirty years of slavery following his capture in the Seventh Crusade. Madeleine had learned more from him about medicine than many practising physicians in France. Now that they were safely here, Geoffrey was almost grateful to his daughter-in-law for forcing him to make the longer, more dangerous but more rewarding journey to Lys-Saint-Georges. But though he had never doubted that Sister Madeleine would give Percy shelter, it did not mean that she deserved no thanks.

'It is I who thank you, Sir Geoffrey.'

'Whatever for?' He looked at her, baffled.

'This is the first time…' She hesitated and wondered if she dared count the two times she had given herself to Jean but then dismissed the thought. 'That I have been allowed to repay your son for buying me out of slavery.'

Chapter Eight

Poitiers, May 1308

It was mid-April before the thaw came, but then it came with a vengeance. The temperatures climbed to almost fifty degrees, seemingly overnight, and the snow melted so quickly that hissing and gurgling could be heard day and night. The melting snow and spring rains broke the banks of the rivers. Mills were damaged, fields flooded, livestock drowned. Fords and bridges were washed away, cutting off whole regions from the outside world.

When the floods receded and the entire countryside abruptly bloomed, Geoffrey rode to Poitiers and reported to his anxious granddaughter that all was well. At her pleading, he admitted to Félice the secret of Percy's location and assured her that he was making rapid progress under Sister Madeleine's skilled care. His burn wounds were no more than scars. He was exercising his shoulders and arms so that they no longer looked as fragile as an old man's. Geoffrey looked at his own frail shoulders wistfully as he spoke. And Percy could already manage a few steps on crutches. He would walk again, the question was with how much of a limp; and his ankles would always be weak, likely to break down again at any unusual pressure.

Then Geoffrey left for Paris where he intended to speak with various influential noblemen and churchmen with whom he was on good terms. He indicated he would check in on Sir Percy in another couple weeks or so. More he did not say.

Félice was left behind to watch the leaves unfold from their buds in the cloister garth and the willows along the Meuse turn green. She learned Latin, rhetoric and logic with the other girls, stitched endless altar cloths and copes and, when the weather permitted, walked to various shrines with the other girls and nuns.

On May Day, they all wove ribbons in their hair and donned their gayest gowns. They were not allowed out to bring in the May with the girls of the town but they joined in the dancing in the market square later. More than one of her fellow boarders came home with blushing cheeks and tales of stolen kisses from the gallants of their choice.

On the Feast of Saint Evodia the entire convent made the annual pilgrimage to the abbey of Fontgombault. No one could adequately explain why the nuns always travelled in a half-dozen open wagons like a cackling hoard of hens to Fontgombault on that particular feast day, but tradition is tradition. The event was more a picnic and outing than a religious event, and Félice loved the abbey at Fontgombault, with its alley of trees and the walled-in vineyards.

Yet the day left Félice feeling melancholy. She knew from a map that they had been more than halfway to Lys-Saint-Georges and her curiosity about the nun who had given Percy refuge quite obsessed her, but there had been no way she could separate herself from the others. By the time they returned to Poitiers, the wine which made the others giggle and titter had made her sleepy. She looked forward to her bed, but the porter stopped her and pulled her aside as they started for their dormitory.

'You have a visitor, Mademoiselle de Preuthune,' he whispered in her ear with a suspicious look towards the others to be sure no one stopped to hear what he had to say. 'He has been waiting for three hours already.' The tone was reproving, as if she were to blame. Félice was expecting her grandfather or possibly Hugh. The figure that rose out of the shadows as she entered was not, however, dressed in the shabby black robes of a student but rather the pristine white of a Dominican novice.

Her heart and steps stopped in the centre of the room. Umberto wore his cowl well forward, shadowing his face. She did not really see him until he stood directly before her and took her hands in his.

He looked dreadful. His eyes were sunken and deep, and dark streaks swept from the eyes into his haggard cheeks. His upper lip was dark with the beginnings of a beard and his throat and chin were shadowed with stubble. Worst of all, his eyes were bloodshot as she had never seen them.

'Umberto!' she cried out in alarm, and he dropped his head and started covering her hands with kisses.

'Félice, Félice! You are my only comfort, my only joy! So beautiful!' He lifted his head again and devoured her face with his eyes. She blushed in embarrassment, certain that her hair and veils were disordered and her gown far from fresh after the long outing. She had spilled wine on one sleeve and her surcoat had grass stains at the knees.

But Umberto had no eyes for such things. With a timid finger he reached out and, ever so gently, touched the curve of her cheek.

Félice felt the tip of his finger as if it burned. It burned down her cheek and settled on her chin. The heat of his finger set her blood on fire and the fire shot along her veins to her heart causing it to pump frantically. Her whole body was aflame, down to her last toe.

Umberto gazed at her in wonder. Was it possible that anything so perfect and so pure still existed in this world? Her skin was as flawless as the petals of a rose. Her cheeks flushed like the first hints of dawn upon a cloudless eastern sky. Her eyes were like drops of smoked honey. And her lips... were like the lips of Venus. He could not resist them. He bent and touched his lips to hers. No more than that. He did not press or force his tongue between her lips as the other girls had described their lovers doing. Yet it was enough. Félice was afraid that she would lose her balance, that her knees would give way under her. She did not know when she had stopped breathing but she was out of breath.

As he drew back, she felt his lips scratch hers. Startled, she put her fingers to them, astonished to find them chapped and split. Umberto's tongue darted out to wet them and they stung as they split wider. He tasted a trace of blood from a crevice.

'Oh, Umberto. You look so... so agonised!' Félice declared in concern and confusion.

It confused her that Sir Percy's eyes had been so much less tortured than Umberto's though his body bore the marks of merciless abuse. Umberto's eyes better fitted Sir Percy's body than his own inviolate one. Or had he been violated in a way she could not see?

'What is it?' she demanded urgently.

There was a bench against the wall and they sat down. Félice was conscious that Umberto pressed against her and clasped her hand with an intensity he had never shown before. She was aware of the excitement that the warmth of his body sent through her own, but she was determined to ignore such carnal responses. She sensed that for all Umberto's forwardness he was not here to seduce her. Umberto was clearly in pain and she wanted to ease it.

'Félice, I never knew...' He broke off.

He knew that he should not be confessing this, not to anyone. But he needed to talk, and to confess his feelings to any man would be a humiliation he could not dare. To confess to his confessor might cost him his future. Umberto was not so naive as to think that any priest employed by a bishop put the secrecy of the confessional above loyalty to his lord.

'The path I have chosen—'

'Have you chosen? Can't you still—?'

'No! No! I can't go back. Not now. Not any more. Félice, try to understand. We Dominicans have a sacred mission. It is a mission that... that demands incredible sacrifice. Not what you think! Not just obedience and poverty and chastity.' He dismissed these virtues with an irritable wave of his hand. 'It demands far, far more. For the sake of God we are forced to confront... to witness... to commit... How can I explain?' he cried out in agony.

He wanted to share everything with her, but he knew that she could not understand. He had to make her understand. He *needed* her to understand – and tell him that it was all right. If she, so pure and innocent as she was, would kiss him and soothe his raw nerves, then he knew he would have the strength to go on. And he had to go on. If he retreated now they would tear him apart like a pack of hounds that have run a fox to ground.

'Félice.' He turned towards her on the bench and clasped her hands between his. 'It is good that you do not know – cannot even dream of – the evils of which men are capable. The perversions, the depravity, the blasphemy to which some men sink...' He shook his head. He could not bring himself to tell her the truth.

I know more than you think, Félice reflected to herself. She knew now that men could tear out the healthy teeth of a prisoner and put burning iron to his flesh – to make him lie.

'There is heresy around us, Félice,' Umberto told her, diverting his own thoughts from the dangerous uncharted waters of doubt into the safe waters of righteousness. 'Far, far more than I even imagined. Who would have thought that the very Knights of Christ were themselves rotten with the vilest of all heresies?'

She started.

'I know, I know. You think of your uncle and your grandfather and you don't want to believe it is true. But… but I have been taught that you can trust nothing by its appearance. A man, a soul, can wear so many disguises. But to pierce through the layers of falsehood to the truth…' He had let go her hands and grasped his own head. 'Sometimes… I am not sure I have the strength!'

Félice waited but Umberto was staring into space, his eyes veiled, his tongue licking at his unhappy lips.

'The strength for what, Umberto?' she asked gently.

'For my profession. The bishop has entrusted me with so much responsibility already,' he told her and he did not bother to disguise his pride. 'I have been entrusted with a special investigation – entirely on my own. But… but it is very difficult.'

'If it were not difficult it would be no challenge and no achievement.' Félice was glad to be able to fall back upon a phrase they had often bandied about before.

Umberto's lips acknowledged her words with a smile and his eyes even lightened a little. She was helping him as he had known she would. He had been right to come to her – and there really was no need to lay his soul bare. It was good as it was. Encouraged, he pressed ahead. 'To date there have been thousands of confessions by French Templars, but not one Templar outside France has admitted to the vile practices we have uncovered. That is, one Englishman, a knight who fell into our hands by chance, did confess and we sent him to Poitiers just before Easter – so that the Pope could convince himself of the validity of the confession. But he escaped. Some say he was spirited away by Templars still at large and others that villagers – Cathar heretics – have given him shelter.'

Félice was afraid to breathe and afraid not to. Surely he would see how terrified she was.

'You have nothing to fear!' Umberto hastened to assure her, seeing that she looked as if she thought the monster could come and attack her in her bed. 'He had two broken legs and could do no one any harm – that is why he must have had assistance. Unless, of course, he died in the snow.'

If Félice had not known the story, she would have been thoroughly confused. In order not to give herself away, she insisted somewhat sharply, 'You aren't making any sense, Umberto. Try to tell me calmly, from start to finish, what has happened – and what this has to do with you.'

Umberto lifted her hands to his lips and kissed the palms hotly. 'You are right! You are always right. But why have I been frightening you with tales of free and escaped Templars? There can hardly be very many and we will track them down soon enough. You need not fear them. I promise you!'

He reached out and his fingers brushed a strand of her curly hair off her neck. He wanted to protect her from all harm and all evil. He wanted to keep her wrapped in a cocoon of security and luxury. No other man – not the brutal, bestial, disgusting creatures that called themselves men – should ever come near to her. Better she lived out her days in purity here than that she was exposed to the world beyond.

'I was entrusted with finding the Englishman or his body when the thaw came. But you know what the weather has been like. It was not until two weeks ago that I could even begin the search. And, you see, that makes it so difficult to find a corpse. It could have been washed away in the floods to God knows where! But if I do not find the corpse, then I must find the man. And to find the man I must question the villagers along the route where he disappeared.'

'Have you been questioning people in Najac?'

'Why Najac?' he asked, alarmed. 'That wasn't on the route.'

Félice felt her stomach turn over. She had given herself away after all. 'Because you said I had nothing to fear. I thought it was because you had already established no one knew anything there.'

It sounded ridiculous to her, but Umberto was too preoccupied with his own thoughts to be alert to disjointed logic. 'No, no. I've started farther south – near the old quarry where it is reported the Free Templars camped. But you see the peasants – they don't want to cooperate. They force us – truly force us – to apply harsher methods. And then it can happen… it sometimes happens that even under pressure they… they cannot tell us anything. A man who knows nothing cannot give information he does not have. But think how hard it is for me? How can I know who has information but is refusing to tell and who is truly innocent? So innocent people inevitably get hurt. Even women.' He added the last under his breath, the agonised screams of the woman still ringing in his ears.

Félice understood. He had tortured villagers – women – and she felt a revulsion that made her want to run away. But then she saw the beautiful young man she loved and she was filled with pity for him.

Umberto held his head between his fists, his elbows propped on his knees, and gazed at the tiles of the floor. They had hung her by her breasts and applied heat to her feet, but she had been innocent. He was sure of it. She had sworn to everything they asked, promised them everything, agreed to everything, but she had never in her life seen a man with two broken legs.

'Would it not be better to let this Templar go free than to harm innocent villagers?' Félice ventured cautiously.

'I can't do that!' Umberto protested, lifting his head sharply. 'Don't you understand? If I fail to find him, I am ruined! I will have failed the bishop and he is not a man who keeps unreliable men in his service!'

'But surely the bishop doesn't want you to hurt innocent people? They are his flock, after all. The bishop must be concerned about their welfare,' Félice argued hopefully.

'About the welfare of their *souls*!' Umberto told her impatiently. He was disappointed that she was so dull. 'He would rather expedite the souls of the devout to heaven than tolerate the heresy that still seethes latently among the common people of the Languedoc and thereby endangers their souls!'

'Kill them all – God will recognise his own.' Félice heard the words attributed to the papal legate at the sack of Béziers ring in her skull like the blow of a mace. It left her too dazed to answer and Umberto continued. 'You have no idea how many of the people we have questioned don't believe that the Host is the Body of our Lord! And then – quite apart from the English Templar – I must pursue the issue, arrest the offenders and see that they are properly tried by the Inquisition.'

As he explained self-righteously, Félice felt her stomach knotting up again.

'If I had known how pervasive this Cathar perversion was in your homeland, I would have feared for your soul long before now.' Umberto continued forcefully. 'It would be better if you did not risk going home. The very air is poisoned with demonic ideas! Promise me you will stay in Poitiers from now on!'

Umberto wanted her safe, far from all he had seen and done and associated with the Diocese of Albi.

'How can I promise that? I owe my parents obedience and must do as they please. Besides, I love Najac. It is home.'

'But for the sake of your soul, Félice—'

'Mademoiselle de Preuthune! What are you doing here? At this time of night? Brother Novice, you disgrace the habit you wear and your entire order!' It was the abbess herself who spoke.

Umberto might have bribed the porter but Félice's absence from the boarders' dormitory had been discovered and reported.

Both Félice and Umberto jumped to their feet, instinctively moving apart to make the circumstances less incriminating.

'Go to your chamber at once, mademoiselle! I will deal with you in the morning!' Félice dipped her knee and kissed the abbess's ring with a wave of gratefulness.

As she fled she heard the hissed reproaches and threats flung at Umberto and she prayed that they would be carried out. If his superiors punished him, he would not have to continue his search for Sir Percy or arrest villagers still clinging to Cathar beliefs. Maybe he would even be expelled from the Dominican Order…

*

The patients had been given their evening meal and the dressings had been changed. After the harsh winter and the spring floods, the weather had turned unseasonably warm so many of them still lingered in the courtyard, enjoying the breath of the cool evening breeze as they squatted on the steps of the refectory or helped feed and water the livestock.

Sister Madeleine wished them a good night and let herself through the gate to the herb garden. She paused to pull a handful of weeds and mentally noted that she must do a proper job of weeding on the morrow. Now she was weary and hungry.

Behind her cottage, she stopped at the well and drew a bucket of water. She pushed her sleeves up over her elbows and vigorously washed her hands, forearms and then, removing her veil and wimple, her face and neck as well. Refitting the veil, she went into her cottage, looking forward to supper.

Of late Percy had often set the table for them both. For over a week she had come home to find the bread sliced, cheese and cold meat arranged upon her pottery platters and wine already poured. But the table was naked.

'Percy?' she called.

There was no answer and as her eyes adjusted to the dark she realised the cottage was empty. She felt a short spasm of alarm and then dismissed it as ridiculous. Instead, she ducked out of the door leading to the river and let her eyes search the river bank. But in the gathering dusk and the shadows of the trees she did not see him. She stepped over the door frame and then gasped at the sight of a crutch lying across her path. It was as if someone had thrown it there. If they had found him and arrested him again they would surely throw the crutches away. She started running. The second crutch lay almost on the bank. She let out a little cry that turned into a short scream as the man suddenly loomed up from the river.

'I'm sorry.'

'Percy!'

He had apparently been sitting upon a large rock just a yard or so from the bank. He stood now with his feet in the fast, flowing icy water – without the support of either crutch. The shock turned to delight.

'Percy! You're walking!'

'If you can call it that. I'm not so sure.'

He sank back down on to his rock, and Madeleine could see that his face was tense and sweating. The trip to the rock had cost him strength and standing unaided still hurt intensely.

'But that's wonderful!' Madeleine bent and took the crutch into her hand as she advanced to stand directly opposite him on the bank. 'It's something to celebrate. I will open a bottle of Commandaria!'

Percy smiled without opening his mouth. He was ashamed of the gap left by the pulled teeth, and the effect was a smile which was a little crooked and as sad as it was happy. 'Thank you. I would like to sit here a while longer, if you don't mind.'

Sister Madeleine nodded and, leaving the crutch within easy reach of where he sat, she returned to the cottage. She cut bread and cheese and loaded these into a basket along with a bottle of the treasured Cypriot Commandaria wine and two pottery mugs. Then she returned to the river bank.

'May I join you?' she enquired.

Percy smiled again but looked around somewhat helplessly. There was not room for two on his rock.

'I'll sit here on the log.' Madeleine indicated a tree that had been uprooted and swept ashore during the flooding in April. She seated herself, removed her wooden clogs, her leather shoes and then, with her back to Percy, her stockings as well. Barefoot, she ventured into the stream. The hem of her habit at once soaked through and was swept away with the current so that she had to struggle against it to reach the rock. The shock of the cold water was invigorating and refreshing after her long day in the oppressive heat of the hospital. Madeleine laughed in delight at her own childish pleasure and then reached out her basket to Percy.

'You must be hungry. Take something.'

'Thank you.'

Percy helped himself to a slice of bread and some cheese before pouring Commandaria for himself. Madeleine then returned to the bank and sat herself upon the uprooted tree, wringing out her skirts contentedly. She no longer felt weary, and she looked forward to the picnic beside her.

Although Percy had always been sparing with words, she found his silence strangely ominous and she could not help asking, 'What are you thinking about out there?'

Percy started slightly. 'About a youth who let his brother drown.'

'What?'

'It was a spring like this. The thaw came unexpectedly and the rivers burst their banks. My brother Arthur and I went out for a ride. Arthur was a year older than I, but he was very sickly. From my earliest memories, I was always being scolded not to be so rough with Arthur. As I grew older, I was expected to look after him. I resented it greatly.

'My resentment was not made any less by the fact that Arthur was not particularly grateful for my help. He took it for granted. He knew that he had only to complain to our mother and I would be scolded or punished for any neglect or carelessness much less genuine roughness.

'Our elder brothers, Roger and Simon, were seven and eight years older than I. They were glamorous creatures, already knighted by the time I was ten, and taking part in the king's Scottish campaigns. I adored them both. I tried to imitate them in everything. They often went swimming at a stream some six miles from our castle, just above a little waterfall.

'That spring I had just turned thirteen. I decided to go swimming there, and Arthur insisted on coming with me. I was angry at him for tagging along. And alone, away from the watchful eye of my mother, I did not disguise my hostility.

'We tied our horses and undressed and plunged into the pool. Even I was totally surprised by the force of the current. I had misjudged the effect of the spring rains and there was a moment of panic when I was swept away towards the falls. I had to take vigorous strokes towards the bank, but then the danger was past and I found the wild tugging of the rushing water thrilling. But Arthur called out in alarm, of course, and I irritably told him to swim on.

'He protested that he couldn't. He started whining for help. He always whined for help. No matter what we did, he always ended up whining and saying he couldn't do this or that until I came and did it for him. I purposely turned my back on him. Suddenly his cries started to climb in pitch and took on a new quality. Too late I realised he was really in danger. I was frightened then and turning towards the cries I saw that he was clinging to a branch hanging over the river very close to the edge of the little falls. He had no foothold and was screaming inarticulately.

'I lunged back into the middle of the stream and tried to fight my way towards him, but the current swept me off my feet. I was shoved underwater by the current. Water filled my mouth and nose and ears. I felt as if I were being held down by the force of tons of water and at the same time I was being spun around. I crashed into rocks and logs and God knows what and then plunged over the falls. Somehow I surfaced behind the falls in the relative calm and managed to get to shore. I was bleeding from various cuts and abrasions and very shaken from my experience, but all I could think about was Arthur.

'By the time I got to a place from where I could see the branch he had been clinging to, he was gone. I started to call and search for him. I stumbled along down the side of the stream. I was much too upset to look properly, and even now I have no memories except of a confused crashing through the underbrush – naked, bleeding, soaked and shivering with cold. My teeth were chattering and my feet were torn to shreds by the time I found him. He was lying face down amidst various other flotsam against a low-hanging branch. I hauled him on shore but he was dead. I knew it, even if I refused to admit it at first.' The voice suddenly stopped.

Madeleine swallowed. She had not expected such an answer. The content unsettled her less than the narrative itself. Up to now Percy had not spoken of his family, his childhood or any aspect of his past. He was invariably polite. He never failed to thank her for even the smallest gesture, but he had never spoken about himself at all.

In the evenings they had spoken instead about her hospital and patients. Percy had asked about her family and, cautiously, about the Preuthunes as well. But she had always been the one to do the talking – often until she was embarrassed to have talked so much. She had herself been surprised by the flood of memories he unlocked with his quiet questions and apparent interest.

Not that he had ever pressed her or probed unkindly. He had even let her slide over the years of her slavery after the fall of Tripoli with a single sentence. Rather than asking about what had become of her with the voyeurism of most people who learned of her past, he had given her a piercing look of such profound compassion that it had brought tears to her eyes. She had jumped up and busied herself about the cottage until she was calm again, and he had changed the subject. For that she would always be grateful.

And now, abruptly, he had opened up his soul and told her something that belonged more to the secrecy of the confessional. What could she possibly say? Clearly, he did bear a portion of guilt for his brother's death. Clearly, he had been a mere boy and guilty of foolishness more than crime.

Percy was speaking again. 'My father didn't blame me for Arthur's death and even my brother Roger defended me, saying it could have happened to him no less than me. But my mother never forgave me.'

He paused again and then continued. 'Because his health was so delicate, Arthur had always been intended for the Church. After he was dead, my mother said it was my duty to atone for my sins by taking his place. She told me a lifetime of prayer would not wash away the sin of Cain, but I could at least try.'

'I hope your priest told her she had no right to insult Christ's mercy by measuring it against her own heartlessness!'

Percy smiled his crooked, closed smile and shook his head. Again there was a long pause in which Madeleine searched for some appropriate response and found none.

Percy continued, 'Monsieur de Preuthune and his son wanted to be Templars. For me the Temple was the lesser evil. My brother Roger suggested it to me and even managed to awake a certain enthusiasm. He told me how brilliantly they fought and how great King Edward's admiration for them was. Roger had a gift with words. He could make me see the walls of Jerusalem and the clouds of dust over the Horns of Hattin.'

Again he fell silent and Madeleine was left calculating that rather than betray an Order he had not particularly wanted to join, he had been tortured and humiliated for five months. He would bear the scars of what they'd done to him the rest of his life.

'Madame!'

The call through the woods made both Madeleine and Percy start. 'Madame!' It was the voice of Thérèse, a retarded woman who had been left at the door of the leper colony some four years earlier.

'Here, Thérèse!' Madeleine answered, taking her shoes and stockings in her hand and slipping her bare feet into her clogs.

'Madame, visitors!' Thérèse told her breathlessly as she crashed through the underbrush with the clumsiness unique to her.

'Very good, Thérèse,' Madeleine praised. 'How many?'

Thérèse looked blank and then she lifted her hands and with the left hand lifted three fingers of the right.

'Three,' Madeleine told her.

Thérèse smiled and nodded. 'Three,' she repeated, pleased with herself.

'Mounted or on foot?' Madeleine asked.

Thérèse looked blank.

'Horses?' Madeleine asked.

Therese nodded again.

'Stay here, sir.' Madeleine addressed Percy, and laying her arm around Thérèse's shoulder, she started back up to the cottage.

At the gate to the hospital, Madeleine found a maiden in a modest but quality gown and cloak, a serving woman and a groom. The maiden jumped down from her well-bred mare and handed the reins to the groom.

'Sister, I heard my grandfather, Geoffrey de Preuthune, has grown weaker. I came as quickly as I could. Can I see him now? Tonight?'

Madeleine glanced at the groom who glowered from his gelding, his weight resting on the high pommel of his saddle. Then at the ugly serving woman and then back to the maiden. Geoffrey had told her in glowing terms of his favourite granddaughter and how it had been she who had first found Percy on the road and insisted on helping him. This could only be she – with some word from Geoffrey she did not dare give in the presence of the others.

Madeleine answered cautiously, 'He is very ill, child.'

'Please!' Félice pleaded.

'All right, you may come in and wish him good night – but only through the grille. You must not touch him at this stage.'

Sister Madeleine backed up to open the gate wide enough only for one and Félice slipped through. To her relief, neither the groom nor the serving woman made any attempt to follow.

Madeleine told the servants to wait and then led Félice down the path to her cottage. She ushered Félice inside, closing and bolting the door behind her.

'Are you Félice de Preuthune?' she asked at once.

Félice nodded, relieved that the nun had been so quick to grasp both who she was and the need for caution.

Sister Madeleine's face lit up. 'What a pleasure to meet you at last! Your grandfather has told me so much about you! But you look exhausted.'

She noted now that Félice was dusty and sweaty. 'Sit down.' She gently pushed Félice on to the bench before the table. 'I'll fetch you a glass of water.'

Félice had never in her life been waited on by a superior and she at once jumped up, embarrassed. 'No, no, madame. I'm all right. I can—'

'Sit down.'

Madeleine pushed her back on to the bench more firmly this time. 'You've ridden far in this weather and I presume you had your reasons. No maiden would risk coming to a leper colony *without* good reason. Your servants – they are your mother's?' Madeleine asked on the threshold to the door.

'No, they are the abbess's,' Félice continued. 'I only obtained the abbess's permission to ride to Lys-Saint-Georges with the lie that my grandfather was on his deathbed. The abbess didn't believe me. She thought I wanted to meet some young man, which is why she sent her own as watchdogs.'

Madeleine nodded. She had lived long enough in convents to know how very difficult it was even for the boarders to get free.

'Wait just a moment. I'll fetch you that drink of spring water.' She was out of the door before Félice could stop her.

Left alone, Félice looked around the cottage, noting with surprise the little luxuries, from the carpets to the glazing. Félice was used to nuns and abbesses who lived in prosperous convents with stone walls, great kitchens, servants and silken habits. Her Aunt Eloise kept no fewer than two horses, three hounds and her own falcon, and retained a maid and a groom. It was not, therefore, the luxury *per se* that startled her but the mixture of altruism and self-indulgence. A woman who devoted herself to the care of lepers was in Félice's mind already half-sainted. And all the 'holy women' that Félice had ever heard about were obsessed with their charity to the point of denying themselves any creature comforts.

Sister Madeleine was not at all as she had imagined her to be. She had unconsciously expected a fanatical version of the abbess – someone so conscious of her own virtues that she was self-righteous and judgmental, admonishing others to follow in her footsteps or face damnation. She had half-expected Sister Madeleine to reproach her for leaving the convent and riding about the countryside. She had been a little afraid to confide her message to her for fear that she might side with the Dominicans against the Cathars. But now that she had met her, her fears dissolved.

Sister Madeleine was far too kindly and warm to tolerate any kind of cruelty – even against heretics. Félice decided intuitively that she would have taken Percy in even if he had not been brought here by her grandfather. She was not doing this as a favour to him, but because she couldn't bear to see people suffer.

Madeleine re-entered with a pottery cup of well water.

'So. This should make you feel better. I'm so glad you've come. I'm expecting your grandfather any day now—'

'You mean he isn't here?'

There was a crash behind them and they both spun around, frightened. The door to the river darkened and Percy ducked inside. Madeleine registered at once that he must have flung his crutches aside at the door. Her face clouded with concern. She could see that his jaw was clamped shut and his face gleamed with sweat.

But Félice's face lit up with delight. 'Sir Percy! You're walking!'

He could not get his teeth apart enough to reply. It took all his will power to take the next two steps and sink on to the bench inside the door. Even so the pain lingered and his chest heaved as he breathed again.

'Forgive me, my lady,' he managed at last. 'I wanted to—
'

Félice did not let him finish. She was too excited. 'But it's wonderful! I'm so glad. But, Sister, isn't my grandfather here?'

Percy closed his eyes and let his head sink back against the wall. Why had he thought she had come to see him? She had done her Christian duty, more than her Christian duty. What more did he expect?

'I'm sorry. We've been expecting him for over a week but he isn't here.'

'Oh, dear. What are we going to do?' Félice had been so certain she would find her grandfather here.

'What is it?'

'The Inquisition sent men to find Percy's body and when they didn't find it they started questioning the villagers along the route. They are using torture – and, of course, half the villagers still have Cathar leanings so they're being arrested for heresy. It won't be long before they start burning them again. We have to do something!'

Percy swallowed. He knew that he was supposed to stand up and say he would turn himself in. But if he did that they would want to know who had helped him. How long would it take before they tore the information out of him? And even if he took the names of his rescuers with him to the grave, would they be satisfied? Or would they continue their vengeful search for those who had defied them?

'Calm down,' Sister Madeleine urged, with a glance at Percy. She could read his thoughts on his face. 'We will have to give this careful thought. Your grandfather will know of something we can do. He... he anticipated this,' she admitted.

Félice was startled. 'But if he knew...'

'He didn't know. He simply said it would not surprise him if the Inquisition was vindictive enough to look for the corpse. He said he would have to produce one at the appropriate time. You mustn't worry.' She spoke to Félice, but her words were meant for Percy. 'So many died of famine this past spring – outlaws and journeymen and beggars.'

'Not with two broken legs and missing teeth,' Percy pointed out. He was trembling from the after effects of the exertion of walking unaided.

Madeleine looked over at him. 'What is the greater sin? To maim the body of a dead man or to mutilate the living?'

'The sin of maiming the dead is upon my head,' Percy pointed out tensely.

'And you would rather be clean of sin than save innocent villagers from the Inquisition?'

He lowered his eyes. 'No, of course not.'

Madeleine turned back to Félice and put her hands on her shoulders. 'Come, child. I'll escort you up to the château and see your watchdogs are out of the way before my brother can say anything that might give you away. Return to Poitiers tomorrow and don't worry. Everything will work out all right.'

Chapter Nine

Poitiers, June 1308

Geoffrey had dressed with great care for his audience with the Pope. Black suede boots set off the gold and diamonds of the spurs Saint Louis had buckled around his heels so long ago at Mansourah. They also hid his knobbly knees before turning back just above the knee to reveal a lining of light brown suede on to which black Catherine wheels had been sewn. He wore his best, long-sleeved hauberk which Niki had rolled in a barrel of sand for hours until the last fleck of rust was removed from each and every ring of chain mail. It was too large across the shoulders and chest these days, but it covered his thinning thighs. Over his hauberk he wore a marigold silk surcoat embroidered with black Catherine wheels, trimmed with black velvet at the armholes and hem. His broad sword belt glinted with thumbnail-sized topazes. His stallion wore not only a silk trapper in the gold and black of Preuthune, but the bejewelled Saracen saddle – still stained with blood – which Geoffrey had taken from the captured mare of an emir he had killed during the Seventh Crusade.

With resentment, Marie had to admit that he outshone the rest of them. Her husband had grown too fat to even fit into his armour these days, so he wore brightly patterned hose of different colours, a red silk shirt under a striped tunic and a surcoat with hanging sleeves and decorative cape and hood. True, she had selected the material and patterns herself, but today she noticed that so much silk of so many different colours only made Louis look ridiculous. And Petitlouis in his best tournament finery looked like the dandy he was beside his austere but martial grandfather. If only Norbert had been there – but Geoffrey had said the audience was no place for second sons. As if he weren't himself a younger son!

In the courtyard of the comital palace, the little party halted and dismounted. Papal grooms hastened to hold their horses, and a deacon bowed on the steps to the Lord of Najac and his heir, before indicating they should follow him.

They passed through the high, flamboyant portal into the cool interior of the palace. Geoffrey was relieved to escape the glare of the sun, which heated his chain mail until it burned to the touch, but he was distressed by the number of men in royal livery lounging near the entrance. The entire city of Poitiers was packed to overflowing with royal retainers, servants and hangers-on who had accompanied King Philip to Poitiers. The presence of so many royal archers and sergeants suggested that the king was in attendance upon the Pope at that very moment. Mentally, Geoffrey girded his sword tighter. He had not anticipated a confrontation with the king himself.

They were escorted down long corridors of glazed tiles. The wall hangings had been removed to reveal plaster walls vividly painted with lifelike scenes: a stag hunt, lords and ladies dancing a carol in a flowering garden, a tournament with ladies watching from a pavilion, the roof of which peaked on the hooks from which the tapestries hung in winter. There was even a scene depicting the capture of Jerusalem in the First Crusade and another of Richard the Lionheart fighting with Saladin. This, after all, had been Eleanor of Aquitaine's residence.

In a large ante-chamber lined with benches, the Preuthunes were asked to wait 'just a moment'. The room was crowded not only with courtiers in satin and cloth of gold, but clerks of every conceivable religious order – except the Templars, of course. The deacon ignored the great, double doors blocked by two pikemen in royal livery and disappeared through a door that led to a spiral staircase.

Sweeping the room with his eyes, Geoffrey recognised the marshal of the hospital, accompanied by several Knights of Saint John. The marshal was master of the 'Tongue of Auvergne' and the third most important officer of the order of Knights of Saint John of Jerusalem after the Grand Master and the Grand Commander.

In April and May Geoffrey had visited everyone with influence he knew – and he was not without good connections at court – but no one had been willing to oppose the king for the sake of the Templars. True, most of the peers of France acknowledged that the charges against the Templars were absurd, but now that Templar wealth had refilled the royal treasury, the pressure the king had otherwise exerted on their own purses had lessened. Individual noblemen were prepared to make individual pleas for their own sons, brothers and uncles – but not for the Order as a whole.

So Geoffrey had turned to the Hospitallers, hoping for support there. He had been informed by a polite but distinctly cool subordinate officer that they had asked for instructions from the Grand Master, but as yet had no reply. Of course not. No ships sailed for Cyprus or Rhodes in the winter months so word would not have reached Master de Villaret about the arrests of the Templars before the middle of April. It would be the end of June before the hospitallers in France could have instructions from de Villaret.

Fulkes de Villaret, who had been elected master of the Hospital on the death of his elder brother in 1305, was not only preoccupied with conquering the island of Rhodes but was even more ambitious than ever Jules had been. Jules de Villaret had also been an ambitious man – but one with a conscience. Geoffrey sometimes doubted the conscience of his brother and successor. It would not entirely surprise him if Fulkes de Villaret decided it was to the Hospital's benefit if the senior and more prestigious military Order were completely humiliated and degraded. Fulkes de Villaret might even speculate on being the heir and beneficiary – in manpower and property – of the complete destruction of the Knights Templar. Marshal de Ferrant, in contrast, had been at Acre. Geoffrey at once started towards Ferrant, signalling for Louis, Marie and Petitlouis to stay where they were.

'Brother André,' Geoffrey addressed the marshal of the hospital.

The senior hospitaller looked over somewhat surprised, not to say irritated, and clearly he could not place the white-haired knight in the severe surcoat.

'You don't remember me, Brother? Geoffrey de Preuthune, Lord of Najac.'

'My lord,' the Hospitaller said politely, evidently still unable to associate anything with the name.

'It is some years since we saw one another.' Geoffrey tried to make it easier for the marshal. 'On Cyprus.'

'Cyprus?' The Hospitaller seemed to become more interested. 'When exactly?'

'After the fall of Acre. You may remember my son better. Jean de Preuthune: he was one of Master de Beaujeu's companions and with him at his death.'

'Ah, of course. Jules de Villaret – may he rest in peace – was particularly friendly with him. What brings you to Poitiers, my lord?'

'I hope the same thing as you – the need to defend the Templars against this slander!'

Geoffrey did not need to hear the answer; the darted look from the marshal to one of his companions and the nervous way he licked his lips before answering said it all.

'We have no way of knowing what went on at Templar initiation ceremonies or chapter meetings. The confessions are quite overwhelming. I must say I am shocked. I never suspected such things—'

'No, not so long as Templars were spilling their blood so you could make it to the harbour and escape!' Geoffrey spat out.

He was so sick of the excuses, so sick of the way everyone hid behind allegations they knew in their hearts to be nothing more than the calculated concoctions of a greedy king. He hated them all. They had all allowed the Templars to die for the Holy Land in their stead but no one was prepared to lift a finger now.

'How dare you!' The Hospitaller marshal raised his voice and pulled himself to his full height. He was much taller than the slender old man. 'Repeat that slander again!' he ordered, making sure that around them courtiers and clerics looked over to see what was going on.

Geoffrey thought of Percy and knew that he could not afford to indulge his sense of indignation. 'Did I make a mistake?' he asked with a perplexed frown. 'I thought you were one of the Hospitallers who escaped Acre on the Master's galley?'

'I was carried aboard ship half-dead!' the Hospitaller told him loudly. 'Do you want to see my wounds?'

'Forgive me.' Geoffrey bowed his head.

Already the others were looking away again, uninterested. What did they care about the confused memory of an old man?

Geoffrey nodded adieu to the younger Hospitallers, who were gazing at him with various expressions ranging from amusement to disgust. With a last nod to the marshal, he murmured, 'And may *God* forgive you!'

He had almost returned to Louis when the double doors to the inner chamber banged open and the King of France strode out. As if a scythe had swept the room, the occupants dropped down on their knees before their sovereign. King Philip crossed the room without acknowledging the homage of his subjects; indeed, without so much as a twitch of his lips. His handsome, square face, framed by long blond hair, was as impassive as a tomb. He was trailed by a gaggle of nondescript men, among whom Geoffrey recognised the mastermind behind the king's secret police and terror apparatus: Nogaret. A man of low birth and plain looks, he was despised by the peers of France, hated by the Church and feared by the common people. The look on his face was mildly triumphant as he followed in the wake of his king, enjoying the homage intended for his master.

Almost immediately, a herald called for Sir Geoffrey de Preuthune, Lord of Najac, and Geoffrey advanced with Louis, Marie and Petitlouis through the double doors and into the great chamber. The Pope was seated upon his oversized throne, the white and gold silk canopy suspended some twenty feet over his head by golden poles.

The white and gold of his robes flowed abundantly over the arms of the chair and down the first step of the dais. He was flanked by no fewer than six cardinals in their hats. Various mitred bishops and abbots hung about on the fringes. Close behind the throne, a tall Dominican priest with a beak-like nose and hunched shoulders hovered like a vulture.

Even though Geoffrey knew the pomp and princely attendance had been staged for the king, he could not entirely escape the feeling of intimidation evoked by such a display of ecclesiastical authority. His heart was pounding in his thin chest, his pulse racing, and his face flushed. He knelt before the pontiff three times, despite the aching of his knees, before he reached the foot of the throne and knelt again to kiss the extended ring on a white-gloved hand. Then he stepped to one side to let Louis, Marie and Petitlouis repeat the act of homage.

'You requested an audience, monsieur,' Clement V opened in a schooled, nasal voice.

'I have come with my heir and my heir's heir to protest against the illegal, unjustified and merciless murder of three of my serfs!' Geoffrey answered in a voice that was much deeper and firmer than the collected clergy had expected from the somewhat fragile-looking nobleman with white eyebrows under a mane of white hair.

'The punishment of murderers is something for the civil authorities, monsieur. It has nothing to do with us.'

This was so obvious that the Pope was clearly somewhat uncomfortable having to state the obvious. Was the old man senile? Why hadn't his son and grandson prevented him from making a fool of himself?

'Not when the murderers wear the robes of priests!' Geoffrey answered grimly, and the Pope started visibly.

'That is a serious charge, my lord. An outrageous charge. Are you certain?'

'Your Holiness, I have more witnesses than could fill this audience chamber!'

Geoffrey gestured to the room around him and the cardinals and bishops started to whisper and murmur among themselves. Geoffrey was not certain but he thought he caught sight of the new Bishop of Albi among the agitated ecclesiastics.

'Have you taken these charges to the priest's superiors? To his bishop?'

'To my knowledge, Your Holiness, the Dominicans are directly subordinate to the papacy.'

'Dominicans!' the Pope exclaimed in apparent horror, and he turned to look at the vulture hovering by the back of his chair.

The tall, gaunt friar stepped forwards. 'Where, when and under what circumstances did these alleged murders take place?' It was the Dominican who put the questions for the Pope.

'In the village of La Fouillade, on the feast of Saint Petrus Kanisius, the shepherd Pierre was suspended with his hands tied behind his back and weights were tied to his genitals. His buttocks were burned to the bone with hot brands. He died the same day. In the village of La Bruyère on the Feast of Saint Florian, the widow Grazide Maulen was suspended by iron claws clamped on to her breasts above a coal brazier and questioned for three hours. She died the same night. On the—'

The Dominican interrupted him with a sharp gesture. 'My lord! Questioned for three hours? You are describing the justified application of intensified interrogation methods against individuals suspected of heresy! It is an affront to the Holy Church to suggest that the death of suspected heretics as a result of our fervent efforts to save their souls is akin to murder!'

The indignation in the Dominican's voice caused the very timbers of the chamber to vibrate.

'My serfs are dead, Dominican, and the *questioning* had nothing to do with suspected heresy! They were questioned concerning the whereabouts of a certain Knight Templar who escaped the hands of the Bishop of Albi shortly before Easter. What right does the Bishop of Albi have to question – much less torture and kill – my serfs merely because he failed to maintain sufficient guard of the Templars in his custody?'

Now there was a great stir among the churchmen and the Bishop of Albi thrust forwards angrily. 'The Templar was being transported to Poitiers – you will remember the incident, Your Holiness. The English knight. He could only have escaped with the help of others because he had two broken legs. It is not only my responsibility to find him but to punish those who, in defiance of Your Holiness, have given aid to these vile heretics. And furthermore, in the course of our investigations we have discovered—'

Geoffrey interrupted him sharply. If at all possible, the word 'Cathar' must not voiced. 'If you had reason to suspect that the Templar had been given refuge by my serfs, then you should have come to me! I am the lord of Najac and no one – not the Bishop of Albi nor the Inquisition – has the right to lay hands on my property!'

'Please, Papa,' Louis hushed, trying to calm Geoffrey as if he were a madman.

But the Pope agreed with the old nobleman. 'Yes, my son, you are quite right. I will have a word with the bishop – and of course you will be compensated for the losses incurred. But all talk of murder must cease. The Inquisition has a sacred mission. It cannot be held to account by secular authorities. Nor would it be appropriate to interfere. The English Templar is of particular importance to the entire investigation of the crimes committed by the Knights Templar. We require his testimony before a papal commission. It is your duty as a devout son of the Church to assist the Inquisition in every way possible.'

'Certainly. I will take them to the Templar.'

The exclamations that erupted now were anything but restrained.

The Bishop of Albi was practically jumping from one foot to the other as he demanded, 'Where? Where?'

Father Elion could not keep from rushing down the steps of the dais in relief. 'You've found him? You know where he is? *Deo Gracia! Deo Gracia!*'

Geoffrey let the tumult die down a bit before explaining calmly, 'I myself found him at the side of the road – in a bank of snow. I brought him home to my castle at Najac. He lingered almost a week, but I am no physician and by the time my daughter-in-law returned' – he indicated Marie with his hand – 'he was dead.'

'What?' the Bishop of Albi roared.

'No!' cried Father Elion in despair.

'Why didn't you report this to me at once?' the bishop demanded.

'The roads were impassable. I am an old man and my son and my mature grandchildren were all away. Should I have risked myself in a blizzard?' Geoffrey sounded indignant.

'But you could have sent word as soon as your son returned or the weather cleared!'

'I didn't see the point of telling you about a dead man,' Geoffrey told the bishop with a peeved expression and a shrug. 'How was I to know he was important?'

'But my men searched for him!'

'They talked to one of my laundresses, it seems, but they did not come to me so I did not learn of their interest until it was too late. I repeat, Your Holiness, it is an affront and a dangerous precedent if serfs are to be questioned without the knowledge of their lord!' He had pointedly turned away from the bishop to address Clement V.

'The Lord of Najac is quite right,' the pope insisted to the bishop. 'In future, you will consult the lords of any village before you interrogate the residents.' He made an effort to sound stern but no one in the room took the admonishment for more than the slap on the wrist it represented – least of all the Bishop of Albi, who only made an annoyed grimace and bowed his head to the pontiff in mock respect.

'Now, is that all, monsieur?' the pope enquired of Geoffrey.

'No.' Geoffrey surprised them all – not least Louis and Marie, who had been prepared for everything up to now.

'Your Holiness, I was myself a Templar novice when I went with Saint Louis on crusade. At Damietta I was wounded and at Mansourah I was knighted by Saint Louis himself.' He thrust his leg forwards and indicated the spurs with the *fleur-de-lis* of France. 'I did not join the Temple but I am convinced that the allegations against it are groundless. Even the English knight I found on the road repeated again and again – in his delirium – that he was innocent of these charges. He claimed to have confessed only because he could not bear the torture any longer. Surely the words of a dying man must be given credence, Your Holiness? What did the English Templar have to gain by lying in the last moments before he faced God? Only true repentance could save him at that moment and he died with the Lord's Prayer on his lips.'

The room was deathly still and Geoffrey could sense that he had managed to move most of the men around him.

'It is...' the pope started rather hesitantly, 'certainly possible that the Englishman was innocent. Possibly the poison of heresy, sodomy and corruption has not yet spread across the Channel or the Pyrenees. But am I to believe that all the hundreds of confessions – including that of the senior officers of the Temple – are lies?'

'I can remember the feel of Greek fire upon my skin, Your Holiness, and I know that I would have said anything to make the burning stop. *Anything*!' Geoffrey stressed.

He was staring straight at the pope: their eyes were fixed on one another and the rest of the room was forgotten.

'Leave us!' the pope ordered abruptly, sitting up and gesturing irritably to all the cardinals, bishops and abbots.

'Your Holiness—' Father Elion tried to intervene.

'*Especially* you, Father!' Clement hissed.

Geoffrey turned to Louis and gestured for him to withdraw as well. Muttering and whispering, they all withdrew through one of the various doors until the pope and Geoffrey were utterly alone. The pope then gestured for him to come closer.

Geoffrey mounted the first two steps of the papal throne and then waited. He was separated from the pope by no more than a yard. He could see that the pope wore white powder on his face and a touch of rouge. He smelled of sweet bath water. He remembered that this was a man who openly kept a mistress – a noblewoman thirty years younger than himself.

'Monsieur de Preuthune,' the pope opened slowly, 'you are a courageous man. You fought against the Saracen for your faith—'

'As did the Knights Templar for nearly two hundred years!'

Geoffrey's fervour, the unexpected hope that he might be able to influence the pope to intervene on behalf of his brothers made him forget himself.

The pope scowled and lifted his hand in startled reproach. He had not expected the same impudence from this nobleman he had had to suffer from the king and his ministers. Geoffrey bit his tongue.

'As we were saying, you fought against the Saracen for the sake of your faith, and we know that the Saracens outnumbered the army of Saint Louis many, many times.'

Geoffrey nodded, and the pope continued, 'But you do not seem to understand the nature of the enemy here.' He paused and looked sharply at Geoffrey.

'I was trained in the Temple, Your Holiness. We were trained never to retreat unless the enemy outnumbered us more than three to one. It was the Templars who were the vanguard of the Seventh Crusade. We attacked at Damietta, we attacked all along the advance – though King Louis had ordered restraint – and we attacked at Mansourah. Do you think I should fear now?'

'Yes,' came the blunt reply. 'We see you are a man of simple, straightforward faith. A man of the sword, you are not used to intrigue and the need for discretion. But you are a subject of the King of France and if you do not wish to die a criminal, then you would do well to forget your Templar past.' The pope leaned back in his throne and let this sink in.

Geoffrey could not tell if he were being warned or threatened.

The pope leaned forwards again and now he whispered. 'We too are the king's prisoner. The king would not hesitate to charge us with the same crimes he has levelled against the Templars or our predecessor, Pope Boniface VIII. We are powerless against him. Neither excommunication nor any other spiritual sanction impresses him. Do you think we haven't tried? Haven't you noticed how the city swarms with his soldiers?' he demanded.

Since the arrival of the king in Poitiers, Pope Clement lived in daily fear of kidnapping or outright murder. Hadn't Nogaret seized another pope by force and driven him to an early grave? Probably with poison.

Geoffrey saw the fear in the pope's eyes and the trembling of his thin hands. This self-indulgent, frightened old man was supposed to be Christ's vicar? Geoffrey's disbelief gave way to contempt. This old man cared only for his own survival – his survival, his comfort and the *trappings* of power. He was not even willing to fight for the substance of his authority. He was prepared to live a sham.

Ah, I should have known. Geoffrey cursed himself. A pope who keeps a mistress could have no interest in moral authority. He would be content so long as all his creature comforts were met and people *pretended* to respect him.

Geoffrey chose his words with deliberation and he spoke softly but distinctly, his eyes fixed on the watery, pale eyes of the pontiff. 'If you had not allowed the king to arrest all the Knights Templar in the kingdom, you could have called upon an army!'

The pope started. His pointed nose was running and a drop of water hung on the tip between the nostrils. 'What —'

'The Templars owed their allegiance to no king, only to you. You could have surrounded yourself with the best trained knights in Christendom – and then you could have challenged Philip – or any king – to any test of strength you liked. They would have died for you, Your Holiness, with the same élan and devotion with which they died for Jerusalem and Acre. You could have made kings dance to your tune or set them aside – instead of letting them treat you like a pawn.'

The pope had gone pale as he stared at Geoffrey. Hastily, he brushed the drop from his nose with the back of his gloved hand and looked away. He swallowed; Geoffrey could see the Adam's apple bobbing in his scrawny throat.

'With your permission,' Geoffrey said coldly and he backed off the dais.

'Wait!' the pope cried and Geoffrey waited, but it was too late. They both knew it was too late.

The pope swallowed and wiped again at his running nose. 'Go with God,' he muttered with a hasty hint of blessing, and Geoffrey made a suggestion of a bow before turning his back on the frightened man occupying the Shoes of the Fisherman and striding out of the audience chamber.

Chapter Ten

Poitiers, June 1308

In the forecourt of the palace the sun still blazed down hotly, evaporating the puddles left by rain the night before. With the departure of the king, many courtiers and guards had withdrawn but there was still the commotion of arriving petitioners and departing clerics. The Preuthunes had to wait for their horses.

Louis ventured to ask his father what had occurred during his private audience with the pope, but Geoffrey shrugged. 'Nothing particular.'

'Are you satisfied now?' Marie asked.

'Satisfied?' Geoffrey turned to his daughter-in-law. He had bought her cooperation by promising to retire to Chanac and transfer the rest of Louis' inheritance to him at once. The price was not too high for Percy's life, not considering the fact that Geoffrey had no desire to reside in any castle or manor where this viperous woman and her dangerous younger son might be. But he resented her greed nevertheless. 'How should I be satisfied knowing that henceforth my loyal servants and serfs will be subject to your rule? No, I am not satisfied, but I am old and tired. I have no choice.'

This speech made Louis visibly uncomfortable. 'As if we do not care for the welfare of our dependants! Didn't I feed all of Najac through the winter?'

Geoffrey felt the weight of his hauberk on his shoulders like a burden he could hardly bear. He felt the weight of his years. He had outlived his utility.

'You mean well, Louis, I know that,' he told his heir wearily. Louis might not be the son he had wished for himself but he was not the problem – Marie was.

Then, looking towards Petitlouis, he added, 'You would do yourself more honour to follow your father's example than to waste your income on such foppish finery.' It was a last, feeble blow, one that glanced off Petitlouis' conscience as easily as a blow of Geoffrey's sword would have glanced off the shield of the stocky tournament hero. Petitlouis did not even bother to answer except for a peeved sigh.

'We will go to see Félice now. Do you wish to join us?' Louis asked his father dutifully while the horses were brought up.

Geoffrey longed to see Félice. He would have gladly told *her* all that had happened this morning. But he could not speak freely in the presence of her parents so he shook his head. He would come back another day, another week.

'We can discuss Félice's dowry with the abbess,' Marie told her husband as she collected her reins.

Geoffrey lifted his head sharply. 'Has Félice decided to join the convent?'

'Félice will do as she's told!' Marie retorted sharply. Why did this interfering old man have to question everything she did for her children?

'I still control the dowry my wife left her!' Geoffrey responded sharply. 'And you will not see a sou of it unless Félice voluntarily chooses the veil!' Geoffrey could not bear the thought of Félice being forced to do anything against her will.

'Nobody is going to force Félice to do anything.' Louis tried to soothe his father. 'We've learned our lesson with Natalie—'

'Don't mention that whore's name!' Marie swung herself into the saddle.

'Madame! She is your own daughter!'

'I wish she weren't! Good day!' She brought her riding crop down on the flank of her mare and the startled horse sprang forwards, shoes sliding on the cobbles.

Louis was relieved that his wife was gone. He turned and embraced his father, feeling not a little guilty about the deal that had been struck. It was not honourable to turn out his father as they had done, but it was the price of peace with Marie and Norbert. 'You know you can always come to me if there is anything you need.' Louis told his father.

'Yes, I know, Louis.' Geoffrey left it at that. What was the point in adding that it would do no good to turn to Louis as long as Marie lived? They embraced again and then Louis and Petitlouis mounted and rode out.

The papal groom waited sullenly for Geoffrey to take his stallion at last. Wearily, Geoffrey collected his reins and pointed his boot into the stirrup. But the weight of his hauberk seemed to drag him down. The strength in his arms seemed to fail him. He could not haul himself into the saddle.

From behind, someone offered him assistance and a strong hand gave him a boost into the saddle. Red with embarrassment, Geoffrey turned to thank the man and found one of the younger Hospitallers standing by his stirrup.

'Are you alone, my lord?' The Hospitaller asked.

'Now, yes.'

'Are you staying in Poitiers?'

'No, I am bound for Châteauroux.'

'May I offer you the hospitality of my house? I am Henri de Corbière, commander of the Hospitaller Commandery at Saint Savin.'

Saint Savin was on the road to Lys-Saint-Georges and Geoffrey was so weary that he felt he could use the support of this vigorous, sympathetic man. But how could he stay with the Hospitallers after the way they had responded to his request for assistance today?

'It would be an honour, Monsieur de Preuthune.' Corbière urged.

Geoffrey didn't have the strength to resist. He capitulated. 'Thank you.'

*

The roads were crowded with tradesmen and farmers, and great puddles, though already drying on the fringes, still blocked much of the road, slowing progress. Geoffrey sank into his thoughts and let his companions lead the way. Wherever his hauberk was exposed to the sun, it grew so hot that it burned to the touch. Beneath the coat of mail, sweat soaked his shirt and gambeson, and the sun burned his face red. He was relieved when at last they turned off the road and passed under a gate with the eight-pointed cross of the Hospital.

They arrived as the bells were ringing vespers, and inside the complex they seemed instantly removed from the noisy, hectic world outside. They dismounted under a stand of ancient chestnut trees; a cool breeze rustled the broad leaves and gave Geoffrey the first hint of refreshment. Serving brothers in the black robes of the Hospital came silently to take their horses, while from the open doors of the chapel, the first strains of the plainsong could be heard.

'Shall I see you to your chamber, my lord, or will you join us for mass?' Corbière asked solicitously.

Geoffrey lifted his face to the breeze that was already drying the sweat on his face. 'I will join you,' he decided, but he let Corbière take his elbow and help him up the steps.

They entered the cool, dim interior, lit only from the clerestory and echoing with the chant of monks. Geoffrey sank down on to his knees just inside the door of the nave and Corbière, after a moment's indecision, left him there to take his place in the choir.

Geoffrey clasped his hands together and propped his forehand upon the entwined fingers. 'Christ,' he pleaded. 'Help me!'

He could feel the bitterness that had seized him after Mansourah bubbling up again. As if the bile from his stomach were poisoning his blood, he felt feverish with fury. It would not take much for him to shout again that Christ was not divine. Or worse.

In the past the enemy had been shrouded in the robes of Islam. It had been Muslim clerics who had ordered his father blinded. It had been the Muslim citizens of Mansourah who had mutilated his best friend. A Muslim army had massacred the wounded crusaders and killed every one of his Templar Brothers from Limassol. A Muslim arrow had pierced Master de Sonnac's eye and killed him. Muslim soldiers had brutally raped Sister Madeleine and sold her into slavery. Jean had lost his arm to Muslims who broke their word and molested the civilians who had taken refuge in the Temple at Acre. It was hard to understand how God could let the misguided followers of a false prophet defeat not only the invaders of Egypt but the defenders of His Holy Land.

But with time Geoffrey had come to terms with that. He had accepted that it had been presumptuous to expect God to compensate for their weakness of numbers. He had even come to recognise that Christ did not care more for Bethlehem or Jerusalem than any other city. What did He care for cities at all? His was the Kingdom of Heaven. He cared less for a thousand men who wore the cross on their shirt than for one who wore it in his heart.

But how could he let His own Church feast upon the blood and bodies of His loyal soldiers? How could He have chosen such a vicar? Could He want His Church represented by the cowardly and corrupt? Was it His will that His servants be hypocrites and sadists? There was more blood on the robes of His inquisitors than on the hands of all the murderers and heretics in Christendom.

Geoffrey started banging his forehead with his clasped fists. His faith was shifting under his feet. He was losing his grasp on it. He could feel himself sliding into the abyss. And Eleanor's cool voice was asking what he had expected. She had warned him that the Inquisition was as merciless and unchristian as the Turks. Why was he shaken to find that she was right? Why had his interview with the pope shattered his faith? What had he expected?

For all his years, Geoffrey admitted to himself, he was still the naïve, blue-eyed boy who believed God ought to be on the side of the righteous.

Once upon a time when he was a boy who witnessed the blinding of his father by Muslim 'justice'. He had thought that he could serve God and righteousness by taking the mantle of the Poor Knights of the Temple of Solomon and fighting to defend the pilgrims to the Holy Land. He had fought with conviction on the Seventh Crusade. And he had given his best-loved son to the cause he had abandoned for Eleanor's sake. Jean had been the better Templar. Jean had given his arm and denied himself the woman he loved. But how could either of them fight the Inquisition, the pope, the Church itself – in the name of Christ?

His brother-in-law had murdered an Inquisition judge.

'My lord?'

It was the voice of Corbière, and Geoffrey jumped as much from guilt as from surprise. Corbière helped him to his feet. His knees creaked and he was so stiff that he could walk only with an awkward, limping gait.

'I will send one of our serving brothers to massage your muscles, my lord. It will do you good. But first I think a little light refreshment is appropriate. Will you join me in my solar?'

'Thank you.'

Geoffrey let Corbière guide him, hardly taking note of the route they followed from the transept of the chapel up a tight spiral stair into a corridor connecting directly to the dormitory of the knights and then beyond that to the commander's quarters.

Geoffrey sank down into the cushioned chair indicated and drew a deep breath. The room smelled of dried lavender. The sun slanted through the double-light windows, casting a pattern of mellow light on the red-tiled floor. Corbière handed him a silver chalice already moist with perspiration from the chilled wine. Corbière seated himself in the chair opposite.

'I was in the ante-room while you had your audience with His Holiness.'

'Yes.' Geoffrey sipped the wine, at once on the alert.

'It was said by those who came out that you had given refuge to an escaped Templar.'

'Yes.'

'It was a courageous thing to do.'

Geoffrey shrugged.

'But everyone agreed that even you, my lord, would not have had the courage to admit it to His Holiness – in the presence of the Inquisition – if the Templar were not long since dead and buried.'

Geoffrey hid his face behind the chalice. That is what he wanted them all to think.

'But what,' Corbière continued, leaning closer to him and lowering his voice, 'if the Templar had still been alive and in your care? Would you not have chosen to condemn the Temple loudly as our marshal did?'

Geoffrey started so violently that he splashed wine on his face and had to wipe it hastily away with the hem of his surcoat, too embarrassed to look at Corbière. Then, after he had restored his dignity, he looked over and studied the Hospitaller, at his fine face and salt-and-pepper beard.

'All across France,' Corbière broke the silence but kept his voice low, 'Templars who had for one reason or another evaded the arrests of Friday the 13th, turned to their families or – if they had none – to their brothers in other Orders. Lay brothers and priests were given refuge by the Augustinians, Cistercians, Benedictines and Franciscans. But sergeants and knights turned naturally to the Hospital.'

Geoffrey felt the words warming and comforting him. 'Thank you for telling me this.'

'Perhaps we could publicly express scepticism about the charges against the Templars without endangering the individuals we have helped, but are we not vulnerable to similar charges for similar reasons? Are we perhaps already next on the list? The king must covet our lands no less than the Temple's. I suspect he only postponed an attack on us because he knows that we have indebted ourselves for the next thirty years to finance the operations against Rhodes. King Philip could indeed seize our properties – but they are devoid of cash and so heavily mortgaged that they would bring more harm than benefit to his treasury.'

This too made sense.

'You can accuse us of being timid,' Corbière admitted. 'But it is the opinion of my superiors that the existence of our Order is at stake and cannot be endangered by a defence of the Temple.'

'Surely that is the very reason you should protest! If the other Orders would stand together against the king...'

Geoffrey did not bother to finish. He knew that nothing could get the other religious orders to come to the Temple's defence. There was too much jealousy. The Temple had robbed them of too many fat bequests and wealthy recruits over the past two centuries. Oh God, how petty it all was.

'No one is prepared to risk the anger of the king for the sake of an Order that made many enemies with its privileges and its pride. For the Hospital, the decision has been made that, once Rhodes is secure, we will make haste to remove as many men and valuables from the king's grasp as possible, but we will not risk his wrath so long as we are vulnerable.'

Geoffrey nodded and set aside his chalice. Rationally, he could understand the decision the Hospitallers had made. He could not even pretend that the Templars would have behaved differently if the roles had been reversed, but he no longer had the stomach for the sweet wine. 'Forgive me. I am exhausted.'

Corbière at once got to his feet and helped Geoffrey stand. 'I will send a brother to attend you, my lord. Feel free to be my guest as long as you wish.' He rang a silver bell.

Geoffrey was led to a spacious and well-appointed guest chamber, evidently intended for high-ranking visitors. There were two double-light windows which cast golden light across the wooden floor. Wainscoting encased the walls to the base of the windows and the plaster above was decoratively painted with flowers and birds. Geoffrey went to each window and unlatched the small, iron-framed casement to let in fresh air from the garden below. Then he sank on to the window seat and gazed towards the setting sun, already orange and shapeless on the horizon behind a copse of trees.

A knock on the door brought him back from his directionless reverie. The middle-aged man who entered was dressed in the robes of a sergeant Hospitaller. He bowed to Geoffrey and offered his services. As he knelt to remove the knight's spurs, Geoffrey noted that he was missing three and a half fingers on his right hand. 'Were you in the Holy Land?' Geoffrey asked automatically.

'Yes, my lord, until the fall of Tripoli.'

With the stub of his forefinger and his thumb, the man deftly released the buckle of the spurs, but he hesitated a moment as he went to slip them from Geoffrey's heel, studying the diamonds set in the enamel *fleur-de-lis*. Geoffrey unbuckled his sword as the sergeant removed the second spur. He slipped the heavy sword belt off his hips with a sigh of relief, and it hung heavy in his hand as he held it out to the sergeant. But the sergeant recoiled at the sight of it and almost fell backwards off the steps of the window.

Their eyes met.

'Do you recognise it?' Geoffrey asked slowly. The man hardly looked old enough to have known de Sonnac.

'The... the... there was a legend that old Templars told...'

'Go on. And there is no need to fear it.' Geoffrey held it out insistently, his arm tired.

The sergeant timidly took the belt in his hands, careful to avoid touching the hilt, as if it were too sacred to touch. He stared at it.

'What legend?' Geoffrey pressed gently.

'There was a sword that held the finger bone of Saint John the Baptist in the hilt.'

'There is such a sword, yes.'

'It belonged to the Grand Master of the Knights Templar.'

'William de Sonnac, yes.'

'But when he died before Mansourah he was wearing a different sword. The sword with the Baptist's hand had... disappeared. Master de Beaujeu did not have it either. Some said that if he had had it, we would not have lost Acre...'

'The legend, as I heard it, said that no man could be *killed* so long as he held the Baptist's hand in his. The man who held that sword at Acre is still alive.'

'Are you...?'

'No. I was not at Acre. I was at Mansourah. Master de Sonnac buckled that sword around my hips personally – just days before his own death.'

'And were you...? Are you...?' The sergeant licked his lips, his eyes almost pleaded.

'I was a novice of the Temple; I did not take the final vows.'

'Do you believe these lies?' The sergeant's eyes flashed up angrily and his cheeks above his thick, curly beard reddened.

'How could I? My son was with Beaujeu. You wear false colours, don't you?'

The sergeant swallowed and then he bent and kissed the cross in the pommel of the sword. He lifted his eyes challengingly to the old man. Geoffrey drew himself to his feet and then embraced the sergeant. 'What is your name, brother?'

'Giles, my lord.'

'Corbière says you are not alone.'

'What do you mean? I am the only Templar here. All my brothers were taken! All of them! I saw seven of them taken in chains to the royal dungeon in Chauvigny. Knights who had spilled their blood for the Holy Land chained together like criminals!'

'But Corbière tells me that all across France there are others. I myself found a knight who escaped while being transported from Albi to Poitiers. He is… safe. Come, help me out of my armour. I feel it is nearly smothering me.'

'Forgive me!' The sergeant hastened to help Geoffrey out of his surcoat, hauberk and gambeson. He unbuckled his garters, removed his boots, unfastened and rolled down Geoffrey's hose, and folded back the covers of the canopied bed so Geoffrey could lie upon the clean, white sheets.

Geoffrey breathed more easily at last, the cool breeze evaporating the sweat of the day and almost chilling him. He bade the sergeant bring him wine and bread and then dozed off in the dusk until the sergeant returned.

Sitting up and covering his scrawny, knobbly legs with the sheets, Geoffrey took the silver tray of refreshments on his lap feeling much stronger already.

'Sit, Brother, and tell me about yourself.'

The sergeant did not hesitate. He sank on to the floor beside the bed and told Geoffrey the story of his life. His father had been a mason, his mother the miller's daughter. They had apprenticed him to an armourer who sold his merchandise to the Templars in Civray. He had fallen under the spell of the Temple and begged his master so long that he was released from his contract and allowed to join the Templars. He was trained as a sergeant and had been sent to Safid and then Tripoli. Wounded at Tripoli, he was aboard one of the last galleys to get out, and had been sent back to France to train recruits. That was how he had ended up back at Civray.

On 12th October he had gone with two lay brothers to buy remounts at the horse market held every fortnight at Chauvigny. He and his companions had been up early and gone to see the horses before they could be doctored. They saw the royal herald arrive with a decree to be posted and read aloud. They thought nothing of it, for they had no reason to expect an attack upon the Temple. But a Knight Hospitaller happened to be at the market looking over the horses and he read the decree. He read it, then came over and casually asked if they knew what was in it. They said no, so he informed them: the king accused the Temple of the most repulsive practices, including idol worship, blasphemy, heresy, sodomy – incredible crimes beyond imagining. The Templars were indignant. But no one could believe such slander! It was a disgrace! They would protest. The Hospitaller answered, 'You would be better advised to dispose of your habits and disappear.'

His two companions did not hesitate, but Brother Giles resisted the suggestion – until he saw the wagon filled with his superiors chained together in the straw. Then he was seized with panic – yes, he admitted it: he panicked. He tore off his surcoat and took refuge in the privy of the most disreputable tavern in Chauvigny. He hid there behind the bolted door, making gagging and retching noises whenever someone tried to get in. He hid there until dark and then slunk out of town just before curfew. He went first to Civray, but, finding royal troops guarding it, he went to the Hospitaller house at Le Réau. There he knew a sergeant who had been brought out on the same galley from Tripoli. The sergeant was afraid to inform his own superior, but sent Giles to Saint Savin. Corbière had explained the gravity of the situation and given him refuge. He later learned that not only were all his brothers arrested in Civray, but his two companions had also been discovered and turned over to the royal authorities.

'I am the only Templar from Civray not in their hands. And do you know what they do to them?'

'Yes,' Geoffrey answered simply.

'Once or twice the inquisitors have asked the Hospitallers to tend to my brothers after they were so mishandled they needed medical attention. Corbière let me go with the nursing brothers. My lord, I cannot tell you—'

Geoffrey leaned over the bed and grasped the sergeant by the shoulder. 'You don't have to.'

'But how can we sit here, knowing they are lying just fifteen miles away in abject misery – tortured, half-starved, denied the sacraments and even the confessional! Two of my brothers have died already – and they have been carted out like dead horses and dumped in a pit outside the city walls! No one gave them the last rites! No one read the requiem! And they lie in unconsecrated ground! I have begged Corbière to let me dig them up and give them a decent burial but he refuses. He says it is too risky.'

'He is right. It *is* too risky. If we are to do anything, then let it be for the living. God will not scorn the souls of men who served him. You know how many of our brothers suffered a similar fate when they died in Muslim hands.'

Brother Giles had forgotten that. He fell silent for a moment. Then he lifted his head again. 'But what can we do for the living?'

'I don't know yet, but if you have been in and out of the prison at Chauvigny, then you know where our brothers are and how well they are guarded.'

'The prison is impregnable,' Brother Giles groaned.

'To corruption?' Geoffrey asked with raised eyebrows.

Brother Giles looked up sharply. He had not thought of that, but then he shook his head. 'There are too many guards. It would cost a fortune.'

'Maybe but sometimes it takes only one corrupt man in the right place to make an impregnable fortress permeable. We do not need to storm it, after all, simply remove from it some relatively small, helpless, apparently lifeless but infinitely precious… things.'

Geoffrey felt life surging through his old veins. Perhaps he was not superfluous after all. Once he had wanted to be a Templar to defend helpless pilgrims on the way to the sites of Christ's Passion. Now he wanted to aid helpless

Templars trapped in the clutches of an unscrupulous Christian king. Could there be a better way for a man his age to die? What did he have to lose, in the name of God?

'Do you think there is a chance? Truly?' Brother Giles had risen on to his knees and was gazing at Geoffrey as if he were the Resurrection itself.

'I think it is worth thinking about. We must ask Corbière if he will allow you to accompany me. We will have to discuss our plans with Brother Percival and Sister Madeleine.'

*

Niki was fishing on the Gourdon and saw Geoffrey coming first. He called a greeting and then ran barefoot through the underbrush to tell Percy and Madeleine. Percy was behind the stables exercising with Niki's short sword and an improvised quintain from the back of a draught horse. At Niki's shouts, he hastily shoved the sword back into the scabbard and abandoned his clumsy games before anyone should see him at them.

'Sir Geoffrey is back!' Niki called breathlessly.

Percy leaned over the thick neck of the docile farm animal and swung his right leg over the rump to let himself down as gently as possible. For all his care, the jarring of his ankles and legs as he slipped the last metre to the ground sent stabbing pains up his shins and he caught his breath. Then, recovering, he led the gentle gelding back into the stables.

Madeleine came running from the dormitory, her white apron soiled with pus, blood and ointments. She stopped at the head of the steps, wiping her hands clean, her face turned anxiously to the gate. Niki was already shoving back the bolt and swinging open the gates. A moment later,

Geoffrey's stallion trotted contentedly into the courtyard, familiar with this barn and sniffing slightly.

Behind him on a bay gelding rode Brother Giles in plain civilian clothes.

Geoffrey jumped down and handed the reins of his stallion to Niki with a grin – and then a hug. Then he lifted his eyes and smiled at Percy, standing straight and unassisted just outside the barn.

'You are dead and buried, my boy, and the pope, the Bishop of Albi, and that damned Dominican, Father Elion, all accepted the fact as regrettable but hardly suspicious. They did not even ask to see the grave – much less dig up the corpse.'

Percy wanted to laugh but somehow he had forgotten how and managed only his crooked, tight smile. Then he started forwards and went to sink on his knees before Geoffrey in a gesture of gratitude that went beyond words.

Geoffrey caught him and embraced him instead. 'Come, let me introduce you to Brother Giles of the Commandery at Civray.'

The sergeant had been told about Percy and he dutifully bowed his head before the knight.

'And there are others – maybe there will even be more soon. Ah, children, there is so much to tell – so much to do!'

It was Madeleine who laughed. She had never seen the old man so pleased with himself.

They sat around her oak table late into the night, half-drunk on Commandaria, half on hope. They went through Madeleine's reserves of candles, discussing drugs that make men sleep and drugs that simulate death itself. They drew the dungeon of Chauvigny in the sand of the garden using pebbles for guards and they discussed every danger on the road from Chauvigny to Lys-Saint-Georges.

Niki nodded off to sleep some time after matins, and not long after that Brother Giles dropped his heavy head on his arms and started snoring. Madeleine blew out the last of her candles and started clearing the table. Percy disappeared out of the door to the river, and Geoffrey stretched and yawned contentedly. Then, pushing himself to his feet, he carried his pottery mug to the basin where Madeleine was collecting the dirty things.

'We can sleep in the loft, Sister. You should have more privacy here, not share this cottage with four rude men.'

'You are like a father to me, monsieur.' Madeleine answered, without looking at him, her tongue loosened from too much wine. 'And the others are my brothers because they are Jean's.'

Geoffrey sensed there was more to this remark than he wanted to know. He decided to ignore the undertone and glanced towards the door through which Percy had disappeared. He seemed to be taking a long time. He hoped that the younger man hadn't fallen. His legs must be more unsteady than theirs.

Geoffrey went to the door and discreetly looked out. He did not see Percy. He stepped out into the cool night. The heavens were studded with stars, the Milky Way a dirty smudge across it. He identified Orion and Cassiopeia and then brought his eyes back down, to see Percy standing on the bank of the river some ten yards away.

He made his way somewhat unsteadily down the worn path to the river.

'Are you all right?' he asked.

Percy looked over and gave Geoffrey his close-lipped smile.

Then he looked back towards the river. This whole night they had talked and planned and Percy did not know how much was wishful thinking and how much was meant in earnest. He knew that for his part he did not believe they could achieve anything. The odds were against them and he could not – not even under the influence of the Commandaria – believe that they would be successful in freeing a single one of the captive Templars. More likely they would themselves be captured or killed. Pray God it would be the latter!

But he knew too that he owed this old man his life. He was naked but for what this man had given him. He would do whatever Geoffrey wanted of him because he could not do otherwise. He owed him more than he could ever repay. Except by dying with him for the sake of his dream.

'I have no right to expect your assistance, sir.' Geoffrey remarked cautiously, sensing Percy's scepticism. 'Your duty is to return to Limassol and report to your commander.'

Noting that Percy jumped slightly, he added, 'King Henry of Cyprus dismissed the charges against the Order as absurd and categorically refused to order any arrests. You need not fear persecution there.'

Percy unconsciously shook his head. He had heard from Madeleine that his brothers on Cyprus were untouched by the events in France. But that was precisely the reason he could not bear the thought of returning. He could not face the pristine world of a Templar commandery where no one could imagine or understand what Philip of France had done. Percy pictured the regularised life with its strict rules, the monotony of training at arms punctuated by mass. He thought of the tedious chapter sessions in which infractions of the Rule were confessed and punished – crimes such as talking at meals or failing to properly tend one's stallion or coveting another man's newer equipment. How could he ever again take such 'crimes' seriously? Worse still, how could he take the nonsensical plans of recapturing the Holy Land seriously? Even before his arrest he had been conscious of how out of touch with reality his Order on Cyprus had become. His months in Poitiers had been enough to convince him that they were living in a dream world. He could not return there and pretend that they were still a powerful, rich Order destined to fulfil a sacred mission. He couldn't stand the lies any longer.

Geoffrey responded to the shake of Percy's head and the subsequent silence. 'I would understand if you prefer to return to your family in England. The English king is prepared to turn a blind eye to Templars still at large.'

But again Percy shook his head. He could go home even less than he could return to Cyprus. He could not face his family after what he had become. They were powerful border lords who had never seen the inside of a dungeon, much less felt the bite of shackles around their wrists and ankles. They would look at him askance and wonder if he hadn't really been guilty of some crime. They would be repelled by his scars.

'The decision must be yours,' Geoffrey said helplessly in the face of the enigmatic silence of the younger man.

There were moments, like this one, when Geoffrey felt no superiority of age. On the contrary, he became acutely aware that he had been carried away by his own enthusiasm and been babbling ideas like a green youth. He felt suddenly as if he were a boy awaiting the judgement of the older and wiser man. Geoffrey sighed, then looked sidelong at the gaunt man towering beside him.

Percy was dressed in some of Niki's cast off clothes. The wool was darned, stained and patched in places, and it stank of horse sweat from the afternoon's bareback exercises. Geoffrey had seen apprentices who looked less shabby but none who stood with shoulders so proudly squared. They were still thin, Geoffrey noted with a stab of pity, but they were starting to fill out again and if he got regular exercise with sword and lance...

Geoffrey drew a breath. 'Whatever you decide, you will be outfitted as befits your birth and rank with destrier and palfrey, arms and armour, decent tack, cloak and clothes.'

That would cost a small fortune – more than the annual income of a prosperous farmer or tradesman – and Percy opened his mouth to protest.

'I am not a pauper.' Geoffrey stopped him. 'Better you are well outfitted than my grandson should lavish yet more finery upon himself when I die.'

'And your granddaughter?'

The words came out without thought. Percy regretted them at once. He did not rightly know what he meant. Geoffrey need not buy destrier and armour for his granddaughter.

'Félice is at the mercy of my despicable daughter-in-law at present, and there is little I can do about it.'

Percy nodded, ashamed he had raised the subject. The girl was not his affair. 'I will help you, monsieur, in as much as I am able. But I beg you to understand, I will not let myself be taken again. I will kill myself first…' If I have the chance, he added mentally, his stomach turning over as he remembered the night of his capture.

'I will give you my sword,' Geoffrey answered, as if this would solve everything.

'You can't!' Percy spun back on him, split by guilt and shock. The sword a man received when knighted by a king was not a weapon one gave to virtual strangers. 'It was—'

'It is yours,' Geoffrey told him, and then he turned and retreated to the cottage.

Chapter Eleven

Lys-Saint-Georges, August 1308

Percy stopped briefly at Neuvy-Saint Sépulchre, but he left the Church abruptly at the arrival of the priest. He had not been to confession since his arrest and was uneasy in the presence of clerics. He felt guilty for not confessing but he knew that a confession of his sins would reveal his identity and might result in a new arrest. Furthermore, although he knew it was irrational to blame every man who had ever taken the cloth for the complicity of the Dominicans in his arrest and torture, somehow he did blame them. He blamed them for assenting and assisting in the destruction of another holy order out of greed and sloth and cowardice. But then what right did he have to expect courage of others?

He stepped out into the muted sun of a Poitevin August afternoon and breathed deeply of the clean air. The village was as good as deserted for it was harvest time. Every pair of hands, no matter how small or crippled with age, could be put to use. The wind brought the occasional shout or burst of laughter from the fields and the scent of hay.

Giles was standing with the horses, leaning against the stone trough and running his wet hands through his dusty hair. He straightened at the sight of Percy coming from the church but Percy smiled to indicate that he had no objections.

He took the reins of the light chestnut stallion Lord Geoffrey had given him, and at once the stallion started to back up and fidget. He was a high-strung, young horse, by no means suited to mounted combat, but he was one of the fleetest horses Percy had ever had the privilege to ride. That might yet prove to be a great asset to a man who had chosen a life of outlawry, Percy reflected, tightening the near rein so that the stallion turned tightly towards him and giving himself the necessary push to jump into the saddle. Such exertion still hurt, but only briefly.

Beside him, Giles had mounted. They turned into the road that led to Lys-Saint-Georges and picked up an easy trot. They rode past the teams of reapers stretched raggedly across the gentle hills, and Percy noted that the grain harvest looked plentiful.

Last year the harvest had been deplorable but at the time it had not interested him. His spirit had been on Cyprus and the harvest had only made him more impatient to be gone. The realisation that the season had turned had increased his annoyance at the Grand Master's evident indecision and vacillation. He had found it increasingly difficult to be respectful and obedient to a man of such obviously limited capabilities. Furthermore, he had been disgusted by the opulence and intrigues of the papal court and offended by the manner in which the Countess of Périgord had flaunted her relationship with the Holy Father. He had burned to be gone – almost as if he had sensed what would come in the autumn.

But, no, he had never dreamt what was coming, he corrected himself. He had hardly believed it even as he lived it. It had taken weeks before he admitted that it was not a mistake; months before he had given up hope of rescue. And when it came, he had almost ceased to want it, preferring the oblivion of death.

Percy thought back on that now with detachment. He did not deny his feelings but he was glad that he lived. He discovered intense delight in the way the light filtered through the trees on the side of the road. The motion of his stallion and the way the young horse tipped his head to one side or flicked his ears at unexpected sounds gave him pleasure. The scent of hay and the twittering of the birds – things he could not remember ever noticing before – filled him with contentment.

Before, he had often been impatient and dissatisfied, he decided critically. He had resented being the fourth son, resented his brother Arthur, resented that he had had to join the Church. He had spent too much time wishing he was someone or somewhere else. It seemed as though it was only this summer that he had learned to live and love each day, one day at a time, conscious as he had never been before that he might not see tomorrow.

Not that he did not look forward to tomorrow. That too was something he had learned this fateful summer. After his arrest, each morrow had been dreaded with an intensity which only those at the mercy of the Inquisition could imagine. Each day they did not come had been a blessing, but the fear that they might come tomorrow turned the future into a perpetual nightmare.

When he had been learning to walk again, each day had been a torment less defeating yet more exhausting than his imprisonment. In prison he had had no choice but to endure. At Lys-Saint-Georges he could have chosen to remain a sheltered, pampered invalid. But he had chosen to fight against his own indolence, had forced himself to rise above his own cowardice. He had often gone to bed almost sick from self-inflicted pain, dreading the morning.

Now, he told himself with a twisted smile, he was growing over-confident. At the end of June they had succeeded in extracting no less than seven Templars from the dungeon at Chauvigny by bribing one guard to 'poison' their water. When the prisoners had been discovered apparently dead in the morning, the provost feared some infectious disease. He had ordered the bodies removed in haste. Disguised as gravediggers, Geoffrey, Niki, Giles and Percy had removed the 'dead' Templars, dumped them on the back of a wagon and driven away. Two days later, Geoffrey had even had the impudence to return and demand their pay, claiming that they had buried all seven corpses beyond the city gates. In fact, all seven men were by then safe at the leper hospital of Lys-Saint-Georges, where Sister Madeleine nursed them back to health. Two of the serving brothers had chosen to stay and help Sister Madeleine; the remaining three serving brothers and two sergeants had gone to Chanac with Geoffrey.

Three weeks after their success at Chauvigny, Geoffrey had learned that two Templar knights were being held at Rodez – in the commandery itself, where the provost had confiscated the commander's quarters for his own use. Geoffrey was familiar with the commandery, having often stayed there as a guest while travelling, and he also knew the provost. The temptation had been too great.

Geoffrey and Percy had called on the provost and, while Geoffrey drank him under the table, Percy had – on a pretext – left the chamber and found his way to the prisoners, held in the Templars' own punishment cells under the chapel.

The two men were kept here in isolation, the provost had readily explained before he became incoherent with wine, because they had proved too effective in encouraging or inspiring their subordinates to resist the Inquisition. Since neither had broken under the torture of their bodies, they had been confined in absolute darkness and silence, abandoned to the torment of their own thoughts, doubts and desires. Percy found that the younger of the two men, hardly more than a youth really, seemed to have gone mad but the other provided lucid answers to his questions through the hole in the ceiling of the cell.

Since the Temple itself was locked and barred to the outside world and the prisoners chained to the wall, the provost felt there was no need to waste manpower on guarding the cells. The Inquisition had shown no interest in the prisoners for months in any case. Apparently, the recent protest by the pope against the jurisdiction of the Inquisition had made them back off.

The provost shrugged and shook his head, unable to understand why the pope should first allow the king to infringe upon his prerogatives by arresting all the members of a holy order and then allow the Inquisition to extract confessions that discredited the entire Church, only to change his mind almost a year later. It was all so inexplicable. Was one really to think that the Templars were heretics and sodomites?

Geoffrey shook his head and asked the provost what he planned to do under the circumstances. The provost shrugged. What could he do? The king had ordered their arrest so he held them – though it seemed a terrible waste. He fed them – through a chute in the ceiling – because you never knew when the Inquisition might demand to see them again – and it was better not to disappoint the Inquisition. Geoffrey had nodded sympathetically and said that the Inquisition was indeed unpredictable and at times irrational.

A week later, Geoffrey had come again, with an even better wine. He and the provost had talked about the 'good old days' when the women were willing and the wine more potent without making a man less so. They had reminisced about the provost's great success in bringing a particularly feared band of cut-throats to bay near Florac in the year of Our Lord 1276. That had been the peak of his career – the deed which had secured him his appointment as provost. No, he wasn't one of these worthless men nowadays who bought his post – even if, naturally, he had shown his gratitude to the king with a small donation towards the next crusade. Ah, Saint Louis had been a different sort of king!

Geoffrey had drunk to that, and Percy helped the unsteady man to the garderobe. Solicitously, the younger man had undone his belt so he could vomit more comfortably and then left him in privacy. Taking the keys from the belt and tucking them under his gambeson, Percy collected Niki and Giles, who were waiting like good servants in the kitchens. They opened the cells and removed the prisoners. Both prisoners were too weak to walk but the three rescuers managed to get them to the waiting litter, which Geoffrey had used, claiming to have haemorrhoids which made riding unpleasant. Percy had returned, replaced the keys in the provost's belt and sat down with Geoffrey before their host came back from the privy. To date, he had not even noticed that his prisoners were gone.

Yes, there was definitely a danger in becoming overconfident. Percy told himself sternly, though he could not wipe the smile off his face. Both knights, now safely at Chanac, were recovering well. Even the knight who had first appeared mad had rapidly recovered his senses after contact with understanding people – especially his companion had been restored.

This past week, Percy had gone to Poitiers. He was following a tip given them by a journeyman about a Templar priest allegedly held in the Carthusian priory at Availles just outside Poitiers. The tip had proved correct, if the circumstances remained obscure. Apparently, the Carthusian prior had a personal grudge against the Templar priest and had made an arrangement with the Dominicans which gave them access to the prisoner but left him in the custody of the prior – subject to the prior's own whims.

According to the garrulous gardener at the Carthusian priory, who had been happy to share Percy's flask of wine in the shade of the plane trees, the Templar priest was a devil worshipper. He was known to commune with the devil even now, despite the holy environment, and had even had sexual relations with the devil in the church – in the Templar church that is – before his arrest. The devil must have enjoyed it, the gardener told Percy with a breathy chuckle, because who else could have given the man the strength to withstand what the Inquisition had done to him? An intriguing question, Percy admitted.

Then, driven by a foolhardy urge to face his demons, Percy had ridden into Poitiers and attended a mass in the presence of His Holiness – and Father Elion. He had even gone so far as to put himself almost in the pontiff's path and had looked Father Elion in the eye. Both men had brushed past him as if he were a trivial annoyance, mistaking him for some awestruck provincial knight.

In retrospect, Percy assumed that the pope had not taken any note of him when he had been in Poitiers with Master de Molay last summer. And Father Elion – who had seen him for the first time after he had been in a dungeon for three months – evidently lacked the imagination to recognise him now that he was clean, shaven, and tanned. It helped, of course, that they thought he was dead. But if they did not recognise him, who would? The Sheriff of Albi very likely, but Percy was determined to avoid Albi for the rest of his life. And the Bishop of Albi might have given many of the orders that affected him, but he had never laid eyes on him. Percy felt invulnerable – though he knew that the feeling was dangerous.

They breasted the hill over the Gourdon and started down towards the river. Both horses sensed that they were nearing a welcoming barn and broke into a canter of their own accord. Percy had no objection to letting his stallion,

Renaissance, have his head for a moment, so he relaxed his hands slightly. Renaissance at once confidently picked up the pace. The hooves of the horses sounded loud and deep on the wooden planking of the bridge, Giles's gelding already lagging behind Renaissance. The clunking turned to chinking as their hooves left the bridge and started up the stone-strewn road past the leper hospital. Since he had recovered, Percy did not stay in the hospital itself but up at the château.

Almost too late, Percy saw the nun on the side of the road. She was wearing the pure white of the novitiate and had – in defiance of all rules and decorum – removed her veils. Her frizzy auburn hair fluttered unconstrained around the edges of her face and whole strands tried to lift themselves from the heavy weight of the curly masses hanging down to her waist to fly free in the wind. Percy drew up abruptly and Renaissance protested by rising up on his haunches and then lashing out with his hind feet.

Félice shrank in surprise and respect to one side, half stumbling into the ditch, which was deeper than she had expected. But the look she gave him was not reproving or angry as he deserved, only disbelievingly pleased.

Percy jumped down before Renaissance had come to a stop and the jarring of his legs almost took his breath away. He clamped his teeth hard, glad that the horse was between them, giving himself a moment to recover before they were face to face. And then the worst was past, and he ducked under the sweaty neck to approach her.

'Mademoiselle Felicitas, I did not expect to find you here.' Unconsciously, he used the name he associated with her rather than the one with which she had been christened.

Félice was clambering out of the ditch somewhat ungracefully, her veils in her left hand and her skirts in her right. 'Nor I you, monsieur.' Her eyes were taking in his silk surcoat of blue and purple over the gleam of quality chain mail. His blue suede boots fitted over his knee and his spurs were gold. She smiled up at him, for the first time in a position to register that he was exceptionally tall, still lean but not skeletal as once he had been. He had short hair – like a Templar – but he wore no tonsure and no beard. His broad brow, straight but insistent nose and high cheekbones dominated the structure of his face, but it was his blue eyes which attracted her fascination. My God, she thought gazing at him in wonder; how could anyone have tried to destroy this man?

Percy flushed under her scrutiny, unable to imagine what she saw. He evaded her eyes, ashamed as he remembered how she had first seen him. He wondered if that man – if you could call what he had then been human – would always lie between them. And then he looked at her sidelong, confirming what he did not want to believe – that she was indeed dressed in the habit of a Benedictine novice.

'Should I call you Sister, mademoiselle?'

'I don't know,' she answered with disarming candour. 'I can't seem to make up my mind. That's why I'm here. Oh, it's so wonderful to see you, monsieur! My grandfather said you were well, but... to see is different from hearing. Have you come to see Sister Madeleine? Will you be staying the night at the château?'

For all the poise and timeless grace she sometimes possessed, Félice was in fact only a girl of sixteen. Her words came out in a rush and her cheeks were flooded with the healthy rush of blood her heart sent pumping through her veins.

'Yes.'

Percy, dismissing the circumstances of their first meeting, responded to her innocence. He was fully a decade older and he had seen a good deal more of the world – even at her age. Flinging Renaissance's reins over his head to lead him more easily, he stepped off the side of the road and touched his fingertips to Félice's elbow. He indicated with a nod the drive leading to the leper house. Together, they walked to the back gate and let themselves in. Brother Giles followed, unquestioning.

They were greeted almost immediately by Brother Robert, who came hobbling out of the barn, pitchfork still in his hand, to greet Percy exuberantly. Félice was taken aback. No one had told her that the two new serving brothers at the leper hospital were former Templars, much less that they had been freed from the dungeon at Chauvigny by her grandfather and Percy. Now she was left to draw her own conclusions as first Brother Robert and then Brother Jacques, coming from the hospital with a bucket of slops, bent their knee to Percy and then bombarded him with questions about Sir Geoffrey and their brothers.

While Percy tried to still their thirst for news, not without a smiled apology to the waiting girl, a now alert Félice looked for the marks of torture on the servants' faces, hands and feet. Robert had deformed, toeless feet. Jacques, the younger of the two, did not seem crippled, but what Félice could not see was that he had lost his genitals after weights had been attached to them while he was held suspended by his arms behind his back – and that despite his having already confessed to most of the charges. Insatiable, the Inquisition had always wanted more 'evidence'.

When Jacques and Robert had exhausted their questions, Percy asked, 'Has either of you heard of a certain Father André de Messelière?'

The serving brothers looked at one another and then Jacques asked hesitantly, 'A Templar priest?'

'Yes.'

'There was a young man of that name who joined the Temple at Civray many years ago. But then he was sent to the university and I don't know what became of him.'

'You have no idea why the Prior of Availles might take an interest in him?'

'The Carthusians? They hated him because of a legal dispute over lands which both the lords of Messelière and the priory claimed. André de Messelière was an only son. When he joined the Templars, all his property, including the disputed lands, were added to the demesne of the Temple, of course. And the preceptor made sure that the claims of the Carthusians were rejected in the papal court. They never forgave him – or us – for that.'

Percy nodded sadly, a cynical twist to his lips. He had imagined much more sinister rivalries behind the vendetta against Father André. He should have remembered that greed for wealth was the most common reason for feuds.

But could the greed for land be so great that it would drive a man to revenge himself some thirty years later? His heart rebelled against the idea. Maybe the Carthusians thought King Philip would turn the land over to them if they showed particular zeal in persecuting a Templar. Or did they hope that they could drive the man to make confessions of copulation and cooperation with the devil? Such confessions would hurt the Temple even more than idolatry and sodomy. Philip might indeed reward the Carthusian prior for confessions of such a spectacular nature – assuming the Grand Inquisitor did not feel that his prerogatives had been infringed. Percy wanted to laugh in sheer despair over human nature.

'What is it, monsieur?' Brother Jacques enquired of him anxiously.

'Father André is being held at the Priory of Availles.'

At once Jacques crossed himself fervently. 'God have mercy on his soul! They are devils!'

Percy sighed. It was this willingness of simple people to assume that their enemies were in league with the devil which made it possible for them to believe the most ridiculous accusations against their fellow men. It was what had made it easy for Philip to blacken the name of the Templars and sow seeds of such overpowering mistrust that the common people were prepared to believe each new 'revelation' with greedy fascination. Perhaps, Percy speculated, it made their own sins seem more trivial if the Knights of Christ themselves could fall victim to the temptations of Satan?

'Can you get him out, monsieur?' The question came from Brother Robert.

Percy shot a look at Félice. She was listening with alert, concerned eyes. Percy knew that she had missed nothing of what had been said and from this one question she would piece together the rest. Her grandfather had not wanted her to know about their activities out of protectiveness, but Percy felt that to deny the truth would be an insult to her after all she had done. He turned back to Robert.

'I honestly don't know. I don't even know where to begin at the moment. If their own prior hates him and is so interested in him, than we cannot count on indifference or carelessness to loosen their defences. Greed was the cause of his special treatment, so perhaps we can use that in some way. But we hardly have the resources to tempt a Carthusian prior!'

He was thinking how cheaply they had bought off ill-paid guards and impoverished undertakers. A prior who lived like a lord would require sums of money he could not even start to contemplate. Worse still, Sir Geoffrey's resources were very nearly depleted after so many unusual expenses – not to mention outfitting Percy himself. And he had sorely overestimated the revenues of Chanac after the disastrous harvest of last year, the harsh winter and spring floods. Geoffrey was at the end of his means.

'Do you suppose the prior would take an interest in the hand of John the Baptist?' Percy asked. He meant it as a joke, but his delivery was so dry that the others missed the intended humour.

Félice caught her breath and her eyes went to his hip, only now registering that he wore her grandfather's great broadsword.

Robert scratched his head and screwed up his face, trying to gauge whether a Carthusian would place great value on such a sacred relic, but Giles nodded with thoughtful approval and Jacques enthusiastically embraced the idea. 'But of course he would! Think what a price Saint Joseph's tools brought when the abbot of Saint Sauveur sold them to raise money for a new roof in the summer of '04! If we had—'

Percy was trying to signal to him to cool his enthusiasm. He could hardly go to the prior at Availles and offer him a relic known to belong to the Templars without arousing suspicion and courting arrest. Nor did he have any intention of selling Sir Geoffrey's sacred sword for cash. Before he could explain, however, they were interrupted by the sharp, angry voice of Sister Madeleine.

'Brother Jacques! What's keeping you!'

Guiltily, Jacques ducked out of the conversation and started running back towards the hospital calling out, 'I'm coming, Sister!'

Madeleine stepped out the door, her face drenched in sweat and the front of her apron filthy. She caught sight of Percy and her face cleared slightly, but the frown remained and there was an irritated edge to her voice even as she greeted him. 'One of my patients is dying, monsieur,' she added with a reproachful look at Félice. 'I need Jacques' help. Would you be so kind as to see Mademoiselle de Preuthune up to the château where I sent her, and wait for me there?' Then she disappeared back through the low door of the rough hospital with a repentant Jacques at her heels.

Percy nodded to Robert and murmured that they would talk at a more convenient time, then he took a subdued Félice by the elbow and led her back to the road, while Giles brought the two horses behind them. Félice suddenly seemed to remember her veils and she hastily fitted them over her hair and tucked them primly around her neck so that not a strand of her auburn curls was visible. Percy noted his own disappointment with wariness.

'You see,' Félice confided, 'she sends me away when someone is dying. She doesn't think I can take it.' Her voice was tight with disappointment.

Percy looked more closely at her well-shaped face and saw the quiver of her nostrils and the working of her throat. She was fighting back tears.

'She underestimates you, mademoiselle,' Percy said comfortingly, remembering the fearlessness with which she had stayed with him on that snowy night despite the conditions and his repulsive state.

Félice did not meet his eyes but she shook her head vigorously. 'Not really. I… I can't bear to treat the lepers. I've tried, but when they are far gone… It's not even that I fear infection. Sister Madeleine has been treating lepers for many years and you can see how healthy she is. But… the sight of their corrupted limbs sickens me – physically sickens me. Sister Madeleine gets so angry with me because she says I upset the patients when I look away and make faces, much less when I gag and have to be sick.'

Percy could understand Sister Madeleine's point of view – but he had experienced much the same reaction at the sight of lepers as Félice and he had studiously avoided contact with the real patients during the entire time he had lived at the hospital.

'Sister Madeleine is an exceptional woman, mademoiselle,' Percy told her gently. 'You are, perhaps, expecting too much of yourself to measure yourself against her example.'

'But she had to learn some time, didn't she?' Félice lifted her face and looked at him challengingly. Her eyes were bright with both tears and defiance. 'She wasn't born with a gift of healing or even an interest in the sick. Her brother has told me stories about her girlhood. She was more spoilt and frivolous than I *ever* was!'

Percy would have laughed at the child who stamped her foot and shook her red hair if he could have done so without offending the woman who was trying so hard to be more charitable than he was himself.

'The girl who grew up here' – he nodded towards the little moated château with its twin, round towers guarding the narrow drawbridge – 'went through hell before she became the woman we know at the hospital.'

Félice dropped her eyelids over angry eyes and her cheeks flushed. She seemed to study the white skirts of her habit intently. After a moment she ventured, 'Has she ever talked to you about it?'

'Never and nor would I ever ask.' Percy's tone was both a warning and a rebuke.

'I didn't!' Félice defended herself hotly. She did not want him to think that she was so tactless. 'But surely that's not the only way one can learn real compassion?'

Percy stopped abruptly and studied the girl – woman – beside him. The habit of a novice shrouded her in false purity and made her seem trite. If he concentrated on her face, however, he was pleased to find that she did not have a soft, doll-like prettiness but an over-long nose and over-wide mouth that betrayed character – even whilst she chewed it with a line of teeth that were white but not all straight.

'Felicitas, you mustn't be so dogmatic.' He addressed her in a very low voice, hardly conscious that he had taken a great liberty of address, shifting to the familiar form and using a name he had coined for her. 'Compassion is not a quality you lack. But you must be yourself. Don't try to imitate someone else.'

Félice looked up at him, startled. Then, as if she had only just noted that Giles was waiting impatiently with two even more impatient horses, she briskly resumed the walk. She seemed to be thinking about what Percy had said, and he did not press her.

They crossed over the lowered drawbridge and Percy reported to the porter in the right-hand tower and requested the hospitality of the house. The lord of Lys-Saint-Georges knew him as Percival de Preuthune, Félice's brother, and thought it only courteous that he called in on Madeleine from time to time to thank her for the good care she had given him when he was suspected of having leprosy. Giles took the horses to the familiar barn, and Percy suggested to Félice that they take a stroll through the orchards behind the château. She readily agreed.

The orchard was composed of apple, pear and plum trees, all heavy with green fruit. They walked in silence at first.

Félice noted that Percy walked with an awkward gait: he hesitated for a fraction of a second between each step, as if bracing himself for the pain to come. The pain had long since ceased but it was the way he had learned to walk again and the gait remained as much a scar as the brand on his chest.

'Is it because of Sister Madeleine that you have entered the Benedictines?' Percy asked at last with a nod towards her habit.

'Yes and no. My mother finds it more convenient – and cheaper of course – to give me to a convent. I thought...' She hesitated to tell Percy about Umberto.

'What?'

'I find convent life tedious, but Sister Madeleine is an inspiring example. A life like hers does not seem so... senseless.'

'No. Definitely not senseless,' Percy agreed.

He admired Sister Madeleine. He was grateful to her. But he could not bear the thought of Félice taking the veil just to imitate her – or for any other reason.

As soon as he acknowledged this fact, he made himself examine the reason. What difference could it make to him if Félice were a nun or not? His own monastic vows made her unattainable – even if he had not been a penniless younger son with nothing to offer her. It was not out of desire for her that he wanted to keep her from the Church – much less the desire to see her become the property of another man.

He forced himself to consider this alternative. If she did not enter the Church, her parents would find a suitable husband for her. He pictured her as a young matron, a mother of red-haired children, hawking, hunting, running her estates. He found this picture far more acceptable.

'And would marriage be senseless?' he enquired gently.

'Marriage?' Félice seemed to jump at his words as if they frightened her. Was she still bound by her over-hasty promise to Umberto? Did she dare take another man without breaking that oath? And what were the consequences of a broken oath? Would God really wish her to be bound to a man who could torture innocent villagers to death? She wished that she could ask someone these questions, but she dared not tell anyone – least of all Percy and her grandfather. 'Marriage isn't senseless in itself, I suppose. But I am afraid—'

Percy did not understand. 'Your father would not marry you to someone unworthy or unkind.'

'But my mother would. And I probably would not even have a chance to get to know my husband first. I would not know if I liked him or not before it was too late.'

'It is wise not to expect too much,' Percy replied cautiously. 'But most husbands and wives learn affection for one another.'

Percy was reflecting on what he had seen in his own life. Love was neither a prerequisite nor a condition for marriage in his experience, but that did not mean the marriages were unsatisfactory to either partner.

'And you would have children,' he added.

'Do you know how many women die in childbirth?' Félice retorted with a sharp frightened edge to her voice.

She had been eight when her aunt Alice died giving birth to her fifteenth child – a daughter who died only weeks after her mother. Two years later, her mother's maid had died during the birth of her first child. The whole castle had heard her screams – getting first more shrill and terrified, and then more helpless and weak – for over two days. The maid had been sixteen and still bloated with her dead baby when they buried her. Both incidents had left their mark on Félice. She was terrified of pregnancy.

Percy sensed something of her terror and it disturbed him enough to make him stop and try to overcome his own resistance to her decision in favour of the convent. Out of the corner of his eye, he saw her white habit bend to collect a pear that had fallen early, and suddenly he smelt his own sweat and heard the sound of a novice vomiting. He stopped abruptly, dizzy.

'Is something wrong?' Félice asked, her eyes registering his pallor and then his heavy breathing.

Percy repressed his memories. This was irrational. The white of the Dominican novice who had taken the details of his confession and the white of this novice were unrelated.

If that were the source of his objection, then he must dismiss it out of hand.

'If you truly feel you have a calling to the Church...' He forced himself to admit that this was right.

'But I don't!' Félice admitted in despair, spinning around sharply, her veils billowing out from her face in the breeze. She looked up at him, her wide eyes framed by the white veils, pleading for understanding. 'I don't feel any kind of calling at all. I feel like a hypocrite in all this white!'

'Christ,' he whispered inaudibly and swallowed.

Now the sweat was clammy on his spine and under his arms. He looked away, across the fields beyond the orchard to a distant copse of trees. He struggled for several moments, aware that Félice was watching him as if she could already sense what he was going to say.

'Félice, please don't do it.' The words out, he turned back and looked her directly in the eye. He shook his head. 'Don't take vows you don't really mean – not to a Church that—'

'That can persecute and butcher her own servants,' Félice finished for him.

He closed his eyes, relieved that she had understood him, and they stood together in silence for a few moments.

Félice's problem was that, much as she understood Percy – or thought she did – she did not see how she could avoid entering the Church. Her mother seemed quite set on the idea after all the trouble she had had with Natalie; and then there was that vow to Umberto.

Félice glanced sidelong at Percy. 'I... I... am afraid I have to enter the Church whether I want to or not.' Her tone was sheepish. She was ashamed of her own cowardice and foolishness in the face of his impassioned plea not to prostitute herself to the institution that had tortured and humiliated him.

'Your grandfather would never let your parents force you against your will. You must know that. He told me that he controls your dowry – or at least a substantial part of it,' Percy pointed out.

'Yes, I know, but…' Félice still found it very difficult to talk about Umberto. Unconsciously, she was chewing on her lower lip and fidgeting with the twisted cord of her habit.

'What is it?' Percy encouraged gently. He could sense Félice's inner turmoil and couldn't bear not knowing what was tormenting her.

'Oh, I know it will sound so silly – so childish. It *was* childish but does that truly make it meaningless in God's eyes?'

Percy couldn't follow her thoughts, but her inner agitation distressed him. 'Félice, what is it? What are you afraid of?'

Félice knew that she could trust Percy's discretion. She knew he would never betray her and she was tired of carrying her secret around with her. She longed to share the burden with someone else, with someone as wise and experienced as Percy. He was a monk, after all. He must know a great deal about oaths. But, even so, she found that she could not meet his eyes when she spoke of Umberto. Umberto had joined the Dominicans and become one of the torturers!

'In Poitiers,' she started indirectly, 'when I was still a schoolgirl, we used to come into contact with the students at the university. There was a young Sicilian…'

Beside her, Percy had gone very still. It would have been wrong to say that he was stiff or tense yet he waited with so much attention that he could hardly have been breathing.

'It's not what you think!' Félice hastened to dispel the suspicions which she assumed he harboured. 'We were not lovers. Most of the time we only discussed philosophy and theology and logic. But... I was so young and so naïve. I *thought* I loved him. I thought it must be love because I was so excited to see him or be near him. You don't need to tell me how foolish that is.' She hastened to forestall his objections. 'I was just as silly as Natalie really. Falling for a pretty face and a glib tongue rather than a fine figure and a skilled lance.'

Percy found himself smiling faintly at her defensiveness. The very intensity of her shame was a token of youth – of emotions not yet tamed or tempered.

Félice did not notice because, now that she had started talking about it, she realised to her own dismay that she was indeed no better than her sister had been.

'And I was just as foolish as Natalie, thinking that one day I would marry my hero. He comes from a very good, noble family, after all, and he is clever and well mannered. I was sure he could be appointed steward of some great lord's estate – or treasurer or auditor or something similar. I built up a whole dream world!' she scoffed, angry at her own naivety.

'I dare say you are not the only maiden to do the same. I'm sure that my sisters fell in love and married a dozen men in their dreams before reality caught up with them.'

'But you see,' she spun round on Percy, desperate for understanding, 'I was too inexperienced not to be flattered when he vowed his love for me!'

'You need never be flattered by love, Felicitas. Flattery is only for those undeserving of the honour paid them.'

The answer caught her off guard and for a moment she lost the train of her thoughts, but her need to explain herself took precedence over the temptation to discuss this remark.

'He swore to love me for ever and begged me to promise never to marry anyone else.'

'And you did,' Percy supplied the ending. Félice was so very much a young, innocent maiden, both in her own words and in the manner of telling her story, that Percy could not be jealous.

'Yes. I did,' Félice admitted solemnly. 'I not only promised, I swore a sacred vow in a church,' Félice continued.

She clearly took this so seriously that Percy restrained his impulse to smile.

She looked up at Percy with wide, earnest eyes. 'But you see, *he* has taken holy orders. So we cannot marry. The only way I can keep my vow is by not marrying anyone at all – by taking holy vows as he did.'

'When was the last time you saw him?' Percy enquired, careful to sound as serious as Félice did.

'I saw him only last month, when he came to Poitiers in attendance on his bishop. He looked straight through me – not even acknowledging recognition much less a bond.'

The bitterness in her voice as she reported this suggested she was not as indifferent to this student as she had first made it sound. Percy registered this fact with unease which he quickly suppressed. Félice's affairs of the heart were not his concern.

Félice, however, was looking at Percy expectantly. 'It doesn't matter what *he* does, does it? My vow was made before God and I must honour it.'

Percy considered Félice at length. The sun had sunk below the horizon and the air had cooled a little. A light breeze stirred the leaves of the trees about them so that they whispered like a collection of gossips. Her wide, golden eyes were fixed on his face, prepared to accept his judgement of her actions without restriction.

Percy did not feel qualified to advise Félice on this issue. He was too confused about the status of his own vows which he observed as often in the breach as in the fulfilment. Still, he found it hard to compare the vows some selfish youth had imposed upon a trusting maiden with the vows he had made to the Church as a grown man. He drew a deep breath and gazed out towards the horizon, orange now with the sunset.

'Félice, I have no right to advise you. You made your vows before God and it is with Him that you must come to terms. But ask yourself this: does it make sense to take new vows which you know you don't mean in order to fulfil an older vow that has lost its meaning?'

Chapter Twelve

Najac, September 1308

Félice stood hesitantly in the portal of the church, letting her eyes adjust to the relative darkness after the sun outside. The wind that blew in behind her was laden with the heat of the long day and her body was damp with sweat under the white habit. Before her, the basilica waited, stagnant and stale, the stench of decay already starting to emanate from the body laid out before the altar.

Swallowing her revulsion, reminding herself of the lepers at Lys-Saint-Georges and how Sister Madeleine washed and dressed them for the grave herself, Félice forced herself to advance down the aisle towards the open coffin. At the head of the nave, she sank on to one knee, bowed her head and crossed herself fervently. She remained thus for some time, praying for more strength and composure, and then rose and advanced with stiff steps to the edge of the coffin. The stink was worse the closer one came, but she was pleasantly surprised to find that her brother's face was not notably corrupted. Petitlouis still looked like himself, although the lax muscles and waxy skin made him seem older than his twenty-three years.

He had been killed in a tournament accident. Flung from his horse in a joust. He had fallen awkwardly and broken his neck. He had been dead before his squire could reach him or his opponent dismount. The incident had caused a furore – happening as it did before so many noble spectators. The rest of the tournament had been cancelled by the sponsor, the Duke of Burgundy, and the pope had issued another condemnation of tournaments altogether, threatening participants with excommunication. Many maids and matrons had grieved openly for the fallen champion and the unfortunate Portuguese nobleman whose lance had lifted Petitlouis from the saddle had flung himself upon the corpse, weeping with remorse. But there was no question of foul play. It was simply one of the risks of the sport, an unfortunate accident.

Félice looked down at her overbearing, spoilt, spendthrift brother and tried to conjure up feelings of grief or even sadness. She knew that Petitlouis was not a particularly evil young man but she had always had a strained relationship with him. She had resented the fact that her parents had favoured him over all their other children and her brother had shamelessly exploited his position as first-born and best-loved to oppress his siblings. The memories of childhood tyranny and squabbles she could suppress as unworthy in the face of early death, but she could not forget the way he had casually suggested 'dumping' Percy on the side of the road to die. Admittedly, Norbert had been worse. He would have turned Percy over to the Inquisition but he was calculating and ambitious, Petitlouis simply callous in the extreme.

Félice could not help thinking that Najac was better off for never having to endure the lordship of her eldest brother. Petitlouis would have ruined his inheritance with his uncontrolled expenditure and his utter negligence of management. He would have bled his estates for his own sake without taking the slightest notice of from whence his income came or how it was earned. He would have been easy prey for every corrupt bailiff and steward because they could have enriched themselves at his expense without his even noticing. Instead, he would have tried to squeeze more from the serfs themselves.

Norbert was cold-blooded but self-interest would make him a better – if a harsher – lord. Félice sighed. She was grateful that her father was far from the grave. She would not have liked having her future determined by her mother and Norbert. They would not hesitate to sell her into slavery if the price were right. She shuddered in the oppressive heat and tried to concentrate again on Petitlouis.

Looking at his sagging face, she tried to understand why so many women had fallen for it. Petitlouis bragged of three bastard children – and he only counted those born to maidens he had deflowered because you couldn't be sure of the parentage of children born to married women. Two of the girls had subsequently been put away in convents – at the Preuthunes' expense. The latest of Petitlouis' conquests had arrived with her eleven month-old baby and insisted on attending the funeral. Marie had treated her less than courteously, calling her a slut and a whore and ordering her out of the castle. Louis had taken pity on her, however, and offered her shelter with Eleanor's old maid, Eleni. Félice resolved to seek her out when she had finished here.

And what more could she do here? Petitlouis had died quickly whilst engaged in the sport he loved best. He had had a short life but one in which he wanted for nothing. He had been rich, healthy, good-looking and loved – if not by his sisters, then by his parents and numerous women. Félice could not find any reason to be truly sad. To pretend would have been hypocrisy and before God there can be no pretence.

Dry-eyed, she crossed herself, and with a murmured, 'Au revoir!' to her brother, she withdrew.

Back outside the glum basilica, she took a deep breath of the clean air and felt much better. She let her gaze sweep across the panorama spread out before her as the slope fell steeply away from the basilica to the river. A summer haze clothed the hills beyond the river in indistinctness and made them seem more distant. She felt a melancholy that had nothing to do with Petitlouis' death. It was as if Najac itself had changed invisibly. She glanced up towards the castle behind its massive turreted walls. It should have made her feel safe and happy but without her grandfather, and with Norbert now assuming the role of heir, Najac had turned strangely hostile. The castle seemed not a place of refuge and comfort but of oppression and threat.

What nonsense, she rebuked herself, and, taking a fistful of habit in her hand, she started walking resolutely back up the slope towards the castle. Rather than returning to the inner castle, where her father mourned and her mother planned the future with Norbert, Félice directed her steps towards the garden.

She passed through the wooden door in the high south wall and was startled to find a fair-haired girl with a baby in her arms sitting on the bench just inside the door. The girl at once jumped up guiltily.

Félice, recovering from her surprise, remarked, 'You must be... Petitlouis'...' What word did one use in the circumstances?

'Yes, m'lady.' The girl dipped Félice a courtesy.

The girl did not look any older than Félice herself. She was short and plump of stature. She had red lips and blue eyes in a round face with a dimpled chin. Her hair was fair and her milk-heavy breasts seemed almost as though they would burst the seams of her made-over, worsted gown. She was pretty, to be sure, but she was also very common. Félice, against her will, understood her mother's dismissal of the girl. But she did not want to be like her mother.

'I am Félice, Petitlouis' sister,' she began. 'What's your name?'

'Simone, my lady.'

'And the baby?' Félice found it very difficult to make conversation but the baby seemed the most obvious topic.

'Louise, of course,' Simone said and smiled happily.

Félice smiled too and leaned over to look at the red bundle Simone held proudly in the crook of her arm. Félice did not know what to do with babies, however. They awoke no particular feelings in her, and this one, with its eyes screwed shut and its drooling mouth, seemed ugly.

Simone could not imagine a woman who did not adore babies and, in a simple-hearted bid to win Félice's sympathy, if not friendship, she shoved her precious bundle at Félice. 'You can hold her if you like.'

Félice could hardly refuse and suddenly she found herself holding an irritably frowning baby. She looked so nonplussed and awkward that Simone giggled. With the confident air of a wiser woman, the mistress set about telling the novice how to hold the baby, adding, 'Bounce her up and down on your arm a little. That will make her smile.'

Félice dutifully did as Simone bid, feeling even more ridiculous. She could sense that Simone felt superior to her despite her lower birth and morals, merely because she had known a man carnally and proved her fertility. Simone embodied the raw essence of woman, beside which the virgin nun seemed a pale and almost meaningless aberration. Félice felt naïve and indeed inferior. Never had she sensed the barrenness of religious life as acutely as now.

Beside her, Simone was chattering about Louise. 'At first I was afraid that Louis might be disappointed but he said that he already had two sons and a daughter suited him better. Besides, it would be hard to raise a son alone.'

'But what are you going to do?' Félice asked.

Simone shrugged. 'Oh, something will turn up.'

'Mademoiselle!'

Félice was rescued from her difficult conversation by a strange male voice and she looked over, somewhat unnerved not to have heard anyone approach. The man who bowed low before her was a stranger with dark brown hair receding from his high brow and a trimmed beard that gave his lean face pronounced elegance. He was wearing low, black, soft leather shoes, brilliant red silk stockings and a black tunic studded with pearls. The sleeves opened at the elbow and hung down, revealing a red shirt with pearl buttons from elbow to wrist. His belt was gold on black and, although he wore no sword, his dagger sat in a sheath of exquisite Toledo workmanship.

Behind her, Simone gasped and hissed in Félice's ear, 'That's the man who killed my Louis!' In the next instant, she seized Louise so roughly that the baby started to howl furiously.

The madonna-like image of an virgin holding a placid infant which had first presented itself to the stranger was shattered.

Simone fled the garden with her screaming child, leaving Félice to face the stranger alone.

Félice looked at the man in a new light, surprised to think that this slender and middle-aged man had defeated her athletic young brother. She did not feel any hostility towards him, however, and, embarrassed by Simone's behaviour, she hastened to apologise. 'Please forgive her, monsieur. She is a simple girl and she must have loved my brother very deeply.'

The man made a vague dismissive gesture with his hand and answered in heavily accented French, 'It is understandable, mademoiselle. As you say, she is young and without protection. The fate of a mistress can be hard indeed.' And with that Simone was forgotten as he continued, with open emotion and audible intensity, 'I am extremely grateful to your lady mother that she can bear the sight of me and allow me to show my respects to your gallant brother by attending the funeral. You are the Lady Felícia de Najac, are you not?'

Félice nodded.

The stranger continued, 'Let me introduce myself, I am Dom Pedro Alfonso Tellez de Meneses.' He bowed again. 'It is my fervent hope, mademoiselle, that you too can find it in your heart to forgive me.'

'I do not blame you for my brother's death, Dom Pedro,' Félice told him calmly. 'Jousting is a dangerous sport – which is why it appealed to my brother so much. I'm sure there is no way he would rather have died.'

'Ah, but to have to die at all, Mademoiselle Felícia! That is the tragedy! And so young! If there were anything I could do to bring your brother back to life, I would do it gladly – even if it cost me my own. I have vowed never to enter the lists again, never to put my hand to my weapons unless it is to fight the Saracen. Indeed, I have thought about joining the Templars...'

Félice started so violently that Dom Pedro hastened to assure her. 'The archbishops of Portugal have made a most thorough investigation of the Templars and found them unimpeachable! Not even a trace of corruption, mademoiselle, much less heresy! The charges raised against them, at least in Portugal, are utterly groundless. Utterly!'

'You need not defend the Templars to me, monsieur. My uncle is a Templar.'

Dom Pedro raised his eyebrows in surprise. 'I did not know. Your father never mentioned anything.'

'My father grieves for his first-born son, monsieur,' Félice reminded him. 'He has no room for other thoughts just now.'

'You are right, mademoiselle. An heir is a man's greatest treasure – and duty. I should have no scruples about joining the Templars were it not for the fact that I am without heirs. My wife was very ill for many years. She gave me only one daughter who died as an infant. It is my duty to produce a male heir before I enter a religious order.'

'Your wife has now recovered?' Félice asked politely.

Dom Pedro crossed himself. 'My lady wife died last winter. That is why I chose to come to France this spring. I hoped that a change of scene, new acquaintances and new experiences would distract me from my grief. I hoped to make a new start in life and look where I have ended! The blood of a gallant young man is on my hands! A noble family is plunged into grief!'

'You mustn't blame yourself, monsieur,' Félice insisted, feeling discomforted by the contrast between Dom Pedro's remorse and her own lack of mourning.

'You are an angel of mercy, mademoiselle!' Dom Pedro declared, suddenly seizing her hands and covering them with kisses.

When he then lifted his eyes, his head still bent over her hands, Félice felt a wave of uneasiness sweep over her. There was a passion in him which frightened her.

'You will forgive me, monsieur. I must attend upon my mother.'

Dom Pedro bowed lower and released her hand.

*

The day following the funeral, Félice's mother sent for her. Black suited Marie. It smoothed over the unsightly rolls of fat that had accumulated with time and the black barbette hid the sagging skin under her chin. She worked at her embroidery frame with unimpeded vigour and hardly looked up as Félice entered and curtsied to her dutifully.

'You sent for me, Mama?'

'Yes, where were you?'

'I went for a short ride,' Félice replied honestly.

'Hmm.' Her mother cast her a sidelong glance. 'Sit down. I need to talk to you.'

Félice did as she was told. Her mother continued to work, pulling her long thread through the canvas in short, staccato jerks. Félice waited.

Marie cast her another sidelong glance, a frown playing at her brows. 'That habit does not suit you. It makes you look insipid. I would never have sent you to school if I had thought it would turn you – of all people – into a pseudo-saint.'

'It was your wish that I enter the convent, Mama,' Félice retorted, finding it difficult not to let her anger show.

'My wish? Whatever gave you such a ridiculous idea! But I must say, riding about the countryside alone is hardly very saintly behaviour is it? Your habit is filthy with dust and horse sweat.'

Félice was fully aware that the habit she wore was now less than pristine white. She had worn it for days. She had planned to bathe and change before dinner. She did not bother to answer, knowing that her mother was not interested in her excuses. She never listened to her children and only sent for them when she had something to say.

Marie came to the point. 'You haven't taken final vows and that abbess of yours is a greedy old bitch! What she expects in dowry would please a count!'

'Are you speaking of any count in particular?' Félice asked without thinking.

'Don't be cheeky with me!' her mother rebuked her furiously.

She detested the way this daughter always came up with clever retorts. It had been a serious mistake to let her receive any education. First her grandfather had stuffed her head with Latin and Greek and now she had learned rhetoric and logic and God knew what else. She was completely taken with herself these days and thought she was cleverer than everyone.

'Dom Pedro has asked for your hand in marriage, and I dare say he is too good for you!'

Félice caught her breath and pictured Dom Pedro. She recalled the look he had given her as he kissed her hands and part of her was not surprised.

'He is Portuguese.'

'Yes, so what?'

So what indeed? Her mother didn't care if they ever saw each other again. A daughter married was a daughter off her hands. 'May I ask how old Dom Pedro is?'

'He is thirty-nine. A handsome, vigorous man, and I have never met a lord with better manners. He has substantial estates, as he explained to your father. I forget the details but there's a palace in some town and a castle. His estates produce olives, almonds, cork and, of course, wine. His expectations of a dowry are nil. He says that after robbing us of our heir, he could not dream of asking for a dowry. You can have no objections to such a match. Your father and I have already agreed.'

Félice smiled wryly. She had known what was coming as soon as the dowry was mentioned. Her mother could not resist selling her for nothing and keeping what should have been her dowry for herself and Norbert. But a dowerless bride could hardly expect much of a dower portion – estates settled on her alone. Without a dower portion, a bride had no financial security if her husband proved a spendthrift or drew the anger of his monarch. 'Has my father negotiated a dower portion?'

'What sort of question is that? You should be grateful that we have found such a pleasant, handsome, generous husband and not haggle like a Jewess! Your sister Natalie would have thanked me on her knees for such a husband

and all you can think about is gold and land! You are as mercenary as the pope!'

'That, madame, is blasphemy.' Félice pointed out.

Marie reached out and slapped Félice across the face. 'I will stand no more of your impudence! You are my daughter and you owe me not only obedience but respect as well!'

Félice's face went bright red with indignation, anger and hatred. The emotions blended together and made her blood churn, but she did not lose her temper. Her mother's power was finite. It ended the day she married.

Félice had taken Percy's plea to heart. She admitted in her heart that she could not honestly give herself to the Church and that her vow to Umberto could not justify a dishonest vow. She had vaguely dreaded a confrontation with her mother when she refused to take her vows and so she was in some respects relieved to be spared that fight.

She stared at her mother coldly, and Marie had the uncomfortable feeling that she had just made a mistake, though she could not see what it was.

'I owe you nothing, madame. But you need not worry. I do not object to the marriage you have arranged. When is it to be?'

'Michaelmas. Dom Pedro wishes to take you with him when he returns to his estates for the winter and he must cross the Pyrenees before the snows come.'

That was barely two weeks away.

Chapter Thirteen

Chanac, September 1308

Percy drew up and signalled for the others to cross the wooden bridge over the Lot before him. The days were noticeably shorter now. The sun was already behind the hills and there was a chill in the air to match the turning of the leaves. But he had no time for their beauty now. His eyes swept carefully and suspiciously across the countryside looking for any movement or trace of life.

There was not even a shepherd in sight, however, and it was a full week since they had shaken off their pursuers. A week in which Percy had zigzagged and backtracked, dividing his little troop of six into three and meeting up again at designated points, constantly watching for signs indicating that they were being shadowed or were under suspicion. He had done everything he could think of to ensure they were not followed, but he knew too that he was inexperienced in such manoeuvres and he did not feel entirely secure.

But both Brothers Giles and Charles were wounded and needed treatment and rest. Brothers Arnault and Guillaume were also at the end of their strength, both being elderly and still not fully recovered from the ordeal of their imprisonment and torture. Furthermore, Brother Guillaume's gelding was lame and getting lamer. Altogether, they were a sorry little troop.

Percy swung Renaissance around, turning his back on the main road, and trotted after the others, catching up with them on the far side of the Lot. He fell in beside Giles, whose face was grey and strained, the wound across his thigh was bleeding again.

Giles gave Percy a forced smile. 'I told you it would be all right.'

Percy nodded, adding, *'Non nobis...'*

And then he pressed ahead, to ride beside Brother Charles.

Charles was the younger of the two knights Geoffrey and Percy had rescued from Rodez. His arms had been repeatedly dislocated during torture, and this proved a weakness the moment he had to fight. In a clash with royal troops a fortnight ago, his right arm had been wrenched again from its socket and naturally he'd dropped his sword. Percy and Giles had barely managed to come to his assistance in time. They had been able to reset the arm later, but Charles rode hunched to the right.

Charles glanced over at Percy as he drew up beside him, and he scowled as he tried to sit more upright. 'I'm all right, monsieur.' At twenty, his pride was more hurt than his body. He felt as if he had failed to acquit himself and had not been able to take revenge upon his tormentors. This made him dissatisfied with himself and sullen towards the others. With an inward sigh, Percy left him in peace.

Bunched together, they started to ascend the steep, stony road leading up to the right. Behind the hill rising from the river, the road branched and in a cleft of the hill the village of Chanac snuggled. The grey stone cottages were swathed in a cloud of smoke emitted from the hearth fires stoked for the evening meal and hanging in the still air about the

---

[1] Templar motto: *Non nobis, Domine, non nobis, sed nomini, sed nomini tuo da glorium:* 'Not to us, God, but to you goes all the glory.'

cottages. The yapping of dogs greeted them as they clattered through the village towards the fortified manor that stood above the village, with a view back down to the Lot.

A square tower blocked the road beyond the houses but the iron-reinforced door opened with a protesting creak as they approached. The riders poured through the narrow gatehouse into the cramped ward of the manor and were greeted not just by the castle dogs but by every variety of servant coming from stables and kitchens and hall.

Someone was shouting, 'They've made it! They've made it!' The high-pitched voice of a boy was shouting, 'Hurrah!' Others called out, 'Welcome home!'

Percy saw Niki's hulking figure taking the stone steps up to the first-floor hall two at a time to call as he reached the door, 'Sir Percy's back!'

The returned Templars dismounted, helping hands readily crowding around to help Giles and Charles solicitously from their saddles.

Percy leaned forwards and swung his right leg over the croup to drop on to the ground. Now he let himself note how stiff and tired he was. He had not slept for more than a couple of hours at a stretch for over a fortnight and suddenly he felt as if he would fall asleep on his feet if he only closed his eyes. He caught at Renaissance's withers for support but the stallion took a step in the direction of the stables, dragging Percy with him.

Then a groom had hold of the reins. 'I'll take him, sir.'

Percy nodded and, with a pat of thanks to the loyal horse, turned away.

Sir Geoffrey had emerged from the door to the hall and was making his way down the steps with stiff-legged urgency. Percy went to meet him, and Geoffrey flung his arms around the younger man his eyes brimming with tears.

'Thank God! Thank God! I had all but given up hope. Never again, Percy! Not like that! It isn't worth it. We cannot risk what we have gained! What if you – or one of the others – had been killed or captured? What would have been the sense of it? I will not let you use force again, do you understand?' Like any worried father Geoffrey could not seem to decide whether he should scold, threaten or simply show his relief.

Geoffrey's concern and gladness at his return were like a salve for Percy's weariness, and he discovered he was not really exhausted after all. He held Geoffrey firmly in his arms, aware of the strength he still had in reserve, and contentedly smiled his tight-lipped smile. He could not remember his natural father ever showing so much affection for him. Then, as Geoffrey's tirade lost its strength, Percy drew back and asked earnestly, 'Is Father André safe?'

'How else do you think I knew you had clashed with royal troops? He's here and he's recovering. Sir Martin and Brothers Jacques and Marcel arrived here almost a week ago. They had expected you to be here before them, coming as they did by cart.'

'I did not want to risk bringing the bloodhounds with us. We've ridden to Bordeaux and back, and with luck they'll think we were English mercenaries paid by English Templars to get Father André out of France altogether.'

'That is not a bad idea. We will have to talk about it later. But I am quite serious about what I said: I will not let you use force again! From now on we use our wits not our arms to achieve our goals. We must exploit the weaknesses of others, their greed and their vanity.'

Percy sighed. 'We went through this before I set out. All our wit together was not sufficient to find a way of helping Father André except by breaking into the priory and taking him out at the point of a sword. And our resources hardly suffice to pay our expenses much less bribe anyone.'

'I've spent the last fortnight thinking of nothing else except how to solve that problem and now I think I know what we can do. But we can talk about that tomorrow, after you've had a good night's rest. For now, come and refresh yourself and then maybe you could go and see Father André. He has been nearly as concerned as I, asking after you every morning.'

'Brothers Giles and Charles need medical attention.'

'I'll see to it. Go on inside and get something to eat.'

With one last squeeze of Percy's arm, Geoffrey turned his attention to the others.

*

They had lodged Father André in a small room on the first floor of the keep. It was a square room with a low wooden ceiling and a relatively narrow fireplace but a double window facing the Lot. It was furnished with a curtained bed, an oak chest and a small writing table that crouched beneath the window.

Percy knocked and opened the door at a sound that might have been a welcome. He hesitated briefly in the doorway and then ducked into the room. He had removed his gauntlets and sword and now removed the leather-lined chain mail coif from his head. Still, the chain mail of his camail emerged from the neckline of his surcoat and the skirt of his hauberk was visible as his surcoat fluttered away from the central slit when he advanced into the room.

In the centre of the great bed, almost lost among the heavy embroidered curtains and velvet coverings, lay a white-haired, bloodless old man looking like a visage of death. His lashless eyelids flickered when he saw Percy and he followed him with glittering dark eyes. As Percy reached the side of the bed, he held out a deformed hand from which all the fingernails had been ripped away.

'My son.' The priest's voice was cracked and scratchy and he spattered saliva as he tried to form his words despite missing most of his teeth. Father André was forty-eight.

Percy dropped down on his knees in horrified respect and bent his head to kiss the twisted hand.

The priest reached out his other hand and rested it lightly on the back of Percy's head. 'You are Sir Percival de Lacy, are you not?'

Percy nodded.

'Then it is to you I owe my life and my freedom, Sir Geoffrey tells me.'

Percy refrained from nodding but his silence was acknowledgement enough.

'You have been denied confession for almost a year, Brother. Let me ease the burden of your soul.'

Percy had not expected that so he started slightly. Then hesitantly, almost timidly, he formed the familiar but long unspoken words in his mouth: 'Forgive me, Father, for I have sinned.'

The ritual proceeded fitfully. Percy confessed to making false confessions under torture; he confessed to wanting to die; he confessed to his anger towards God; he confessed to seeking death as he crawled into the snowy ditch the night of his escape. He confessed to all the violations of the Rule which had been occasioned by his arrest: the failure to hear mass regularly; the failure to observe silence after compline; the failure to give alms; a complete disregard for fast days – things he had continued to do even after he was freed. He confessed to lying, bribing and blackmail in his efforts to free the prisoners at Chauvigny and Rodez. But he did not confess to striking senseless two Carthusian brothers in order to gain access to the cell where Father André was confined or to killing three royal sergeants to enable Sir Martin to get Father André away later.

Father André was silent for a long time after Percy was finished. When he realised that Percy did not intend to say any more he asked sadly. 'Is that all, my son? Have you nothing else on your conscience?'

Father André himself had heard his jailers vehemently and hysterically promising damnation to anyone who defied them and he had seen through the bars of his prison window, a knight raise his sword. He had cried out in horror at the thought that the knight might kill a monk *for his sake*. But the sword had been inverted when it struck: the butt had crashed down on the skull of one man and then the next. It spoke of skill and strength that both monks were still breathing when he was carried out of his cell a few minutes later.

Three days later he had been witness again when royal troops overtook them on the road and surrounded them. Sir Percy and the other Templars had drawn their swords and fought a way clear for the cart. Then Sir Martin had lifted him out of the cart and carried him across his saddle while one of the serving brothers drove the cart in another direction. Behind him, the others were still fighting, keeping the royal soldiers from pursuit. He could not know how many died but he had seen blood on the swords of his protectors and heard screams that were already unearthly.

'My son, for all the sins you have confessed I can give you absolution, but for those sins you do not confess you can still be damned.' The voice, scratchy and broken as it was, was sad and the mangled hand gently caressed Percy's hair.

Percy drew himself up off his knees and stood towering over the priest. They gazed at one another without speaking.

Then Percy shrugged. 'Father, I cannot confess what I do not regret – much less repent.'

'My son, bring a stool and sit with me.' Father André gestured with his swollen and discoloured claw towards the stool before the writing desk.

Percy swallowed and then unwillingly took the stool and set it beside the bed. He sank down upon it and was now so low that he had to lift his head slightly to see the priest.

'Sir Geoffrey told me much about himself – and you. As much as he knows.'

Percy's lips twitched. Geoffrey knew only what he had become since his arrest. Only Sister Madeleine had learned fragments of his past.

'He told me the condition you were in when he found you.'

Percy did not answer. No thought was more humiliating than the memory of that night when the Lady Félice had found him half-naked and soiled with his own filth.

'You have yourself confessed the circumstances of your false denial of Christ and confirmation of the allegations against our beloved Order.'

Percy did not respond. What did Father André expect him to say?

'Brother, do you think I do not understand your plight?'

Percy looked down at his hands. They were untouched by torture. His fingernails were cut or bitten short but otherwise healthy and squarish on the tips of his long fingers. His palms were calloused from exercise with sword and lance. They were a knight's hands, not the mutilated hands of this priest.

'The torture, as we both know, was not at its worst when it was most intense. During the actual torture, I always felt His presence. Do you know how I withstood their questioning? I wish I could have told you the secret before you were forced to a confession you did not mean. I wish I could reveal the secret to all our brothers.' Father André's voice was almost elated. 'I blocked out even the questions. I never heard what they asked of me. And I answered with prayer. I said the Lord's Prayer aloud, or the Ave Maria, or the *Te Deum*.'

Percy tried to imagine this. He had not had the strength for so many words. He had never been capable of uttering more than 'yes' or 'no'; he did not remember pleading for his right leg.

'The worst torture', Father André was continuing, 'was between the interrogations. I was kept suspended in a tank of water for what must have been several days and then left in a cold cell, still soaked through with the cold water. That was how I lost my voice. Later, when I was feverish, they chained me to the outer wall of the bread oven. My back blistered from the heat and I was close to madness from thirst. I would have confessed to anything they asked me – but they were too stupid to put questions to me at that time. He was with me.' The priest crossed himself.

'And then…' The priest faltered, 'I only tell you this, Brother, because I hope you will understand. I was accused of having sexual relations with the devil.'

Percy nodded. The gardener had told him that.

'They heated a poker and they inserted it in my rectum.'

Percy put his hands over his ears and closed his eyes. 'And you wonder why I don't regret striking your jailers!'

The cry echoed around the room and died out. The fire crackled faintly as it sputtered, the room was growing chilly.

'My son, if I can forgive them, why can't you?'

Percy took his hands away from his ears and opened his eyes. He looked at the fragile priest lying in the great bed. 'Because', Percy told him slowly and deliberately, 'I do not pretend to be Christ. I do not forgive them. I do not even understand them. If I had known the whole of it, I might have killed them.'

'Please! Please! For your own sake fight such thoughts of vengeance and hatred! Did He not teach us to turn the other cheek? Did He not beg His Father to forgive them even as he hung nailed to the cross?' The priest's voice was impassioned, and then it changed. 'They left me hanging in my cell for days on end – suspended on a rope attached to the ceiling beam and holding my bound hands together over my head. And the whole time, I kept thinking how lucky I was not to be hanging by nails hammered into the palms of my hands! Nothing we suffered was comparable to His suffering.'

'Did the Romans put a hot poker up His ass?'

'Don't!'

'The Romans were heathens! The men who tortured us claim to be Christian!'

'My son, please! Forgive them! Repent of what you have done!' The mutilated hands reached out for his.

Percy could not resist them. He could not use his strength against this wrecked body with its mighty soul. He let Father André hold his powerful, calloused, bloodstained hands in his broken, fragile ones, but he could not share in Father André's grace. Percy was acutely aware that he had felt satisfaction during this last rescue – not merely because he had extracted Father André from the hands of his tormentors but because he had finally struck a blow against the enemy.

Slowly, sadly, Father André released the younger man's hands. He laid his head back upon the pillow and closed his eyes, exhausted. 'It's all right,' his ruined voice scratched out comfortingly. 'You can come to me whenever you're ready. You will forgive them with time and then you will feel remorse. You will come of your own free will and I will rejoice with you.'

For the priest's sake, Percy was almost moved to pretend a repentance he did not feel, but, even as he drew breath to speak, the words caught in his throat. He could no more pretend to regret inflicting injury on their persecutors than he could pretend that he had worshipped an idol with cat's ears. 'Forgive me, Father,' he murmured helplessly, dropping on his knee to kiss the priest's hand before withdrawing in hasty embarrassment.

*

Geoffrey went in search of Percy and found him scouring his own hauberk in a sunny nook of the ward. The young man sat facing the sun, his long booted legs bent to support the hauberk spread across his knees. He was using a wire brush to free hardened mud and rust flecks from the chain mail. Percy was hunched over his work and he did not hear Geoffrey crossing the ward in his soft leather shoes.

Geoffrey paused and watched his guest, noting the healthy tan on Percy's high brow and cheeks and the bleached brown of his wiry hair; but he was most impressed by the diligence with which Percy approached this menial task. Geoffrey could not imagine Petitlouis or Norbert tending to their own armour. Not even Jean would have assumed such a task as long as there were sergeants and lay brothers available.

Percy felt eyes upon him and looked over, somewhat startled. At the sight of Geoffrey, he set aside his work and stood up in respect. Geoffrey gestured for him to sit down and sank on to the crude bench beside him, sweeping the skirts of his long robes between his knees as he sat. He turned closed eyes towards the sun and breathed in the warmth of the autumn sun while Percy resumed cleaning his hauberk.

There would not be many more days like this, Geoffrey calculated. His thin blood felt the chill on the light breeze even through his loose, woollen sleeves. Already they had

had the first of the autumn rains and the mornings were moist and misty. Soon there would be frost. In another month the first snows would dust the peaks of the hills and then creep down the slopes to shroud the valleys. Geoffrey had never spent a winter at Chanac but he knew it would be harsh. That was one reason he was trying to gather as many stores as he could, buying up as much wine, sugar and dried fruits, salt and spices as he could afford. He sighed unconsciously.

'Is there any way I can help you, my lord?' Percy enquired, glancing sidelong at the white-haired man beside him.

Geoffrey's skin was flecked with age marks and it sagged around the creases of his face, but he still had his teeth and his hair was thick as a lion's mane. He looked far less fragile than Father André despite being thirty years older.

'We need to talk, that's all.' Geoffrey opened his eyes. 'The summer harvest is in – and we can be proud of it – but we must face the winter now.'

Percy's hand stopped its scrubbing and the *shish-chick* of the wire brush on chain mail was abruptly silenced. Geoffrey's words seemed to announce the return of Persephone to the underworld. The chill that went up his spine was the dank, stale coolness of the dungeon.

'Thousands of my brothers are still chained in the darkness and have never seen the summer.' Percy tried to keep the bitterness out of his voice. It was Geoffrey who had given him the summer and Geoffrey who had persuaded him to help the others.

Geoffrey sighed. 'I know.' Geoffrey looked at his gnarled hands, with the age splotches stretching over the bony knuckles. He hated being old. 'That is why we need to find some means of breaking into more dungeons – but not by force!' He was no less insistent than he had been the day before. 'We have to break them open with gold.'

'Gold which we do not have,' Percy reminded him with a touch of exasperation in his voice. He did not want to argue with Geoffrey. He respected him far too much for that but he was tired of this vicious circle. Geoffrey's resources were depleted. But they were six fighting men – if you counted Sir Charles. And that had proven enough this last time...

Percy resumed his scrubbing. His mind was far too good to let his heart deceive him for long. If he were honest with himself, he knew that they had been extremely lucky. Father André had been kept in a priory not a dungeon and his guards had been unarmed monks totally unprepared for an attack. The moment they had been confronted by royal troops, they had been very nearly overpowered. Four of the Templars were still suffering from the effects of their arrest and torture. Only Giles and himself had fought well – and now Giles was wounded. Oh, Christ, what good were six Templars against the might of the King of France? And their weapons, armour and horses all cost Geoffrey money. Percy's hand went still and he stared at the chain mail across his knees, wondering what was the point of fighting.

Geoffrey was watching him, enjoying the glint of sunlight on the mail where Percy had scrubbed it clean and the quiet competence of his hands as they worked. They were elegant, long-fingered hands, the hands of a nobleman or a scholar. But Father André had confided in Geoffrey what he had witnessed – the blows against two unarmed monks and the bloody clash with royal soldiers. Geoffrey's eyes shifted to the cuff of Percy's gambeson and saw the dark, hardened stains smearing the right sleeve.

Geoffrey did not share the priest's horror at what Percy had done, but nevertheless he was uneasy about the morality of shedding Christian blood. Nor was he comfortable with the thought of using the Baptist's hand to knock monks unconscious. He was also acutely aware that he was to blame for Percy having embarked upon this campaign to free captive Templars. He had to share the blood guilt, Geoffrey concluded. And no guilt would be greater than if the blood that stained the gambeson were Percy's own.

'Everything I have heard about the arrest of the Templars in England suggests that they were given ample warning and that the majority of the brothers – and their portable valuables – were brought into safe hiding in time.'

Percy nodded. He had no way of knowing if this were true or not, but he had heard the same rumours.

'Did you know Master de la More?'

'He officiated at my initiation,' Percy stated simply.

That surprised Geoffrey. Not every recruit was received into the Order by the provincial preceptor, but it made things easier. 'If you went to him now, do you think he would trust you?'

'I don't know. I was a youth, barely out of my novitiate when we parted. He will have no particular memory or opinion of me.'

Geoffrey considered this and then confided, 'He was with my son, Jean, at Acre and they were close. I think he would trust you for Jean's sake alone.'

'You want me to go to him?'

'Yes, to explain to him what we have done and what we would like to do and to ask him to put some of the Temple's money at our disposal so we can buy the freedom of other Templars.'

'De la More is in the Tower of London.'

'But he must have given orders for the removal of the valuables and he will know where they are deposited. Equally important, only he will be able to give you the necessary authorisation to collect money from those English Templars who evaded arrest and now guard the treasure.'

Percy considered this plan from all sides and agreed that they had little to lose and possibly much to gain. If he hurried, he could sail from Bordeaux or, if the weather turned bad, he could make for Calais and sail from there even in the dead of winter. At all events, he could be in London before Christmas. If William de la More was willing to help them, he could be back by February or March, possibly with the means to buy scores of Templars out of the clutches of the Inquisition – provided they survived a second winter in their dungeons. What was more, some of the English Templars still at large might be persuaded to join them. They would have arms and armour, even Templar horses, and maybe they would even know where stores of other arms and armour were which they could bring back to Chanac to refit the men they freed. The idea opened up a range of opportunities.

Percy nodded. 'Yes, of course. I will set out tomorrow for Bordeaux and try to take passage with one of the wine merchants.'

Geoffrey smiled but laid a hand on Percy's arm. 'Not quite so fast. There are two other favours I would like to ask of you.'

Percy waited expectantly, his hands still.

Geoffrey looked across the ward, to where two of his servants were chopping the great trunks felled in his forests into firewood logs. 'Once, over half a century ago, I was with Saint Louis on crusade,' Geoffrey started in a distant voice.

Percy had rarely heard Geoffrey reminisce. They had been too preoccupied with the present. He cocked his head slightly.

Geoffrey continued in the same distant voice, 'I wore the mantle of a Templar novice then. I was proud to be allowed to go on crusade, and dreamt of returning a Knight Templar. Instead, I denied the divinity of Christ to the master of the Temple and he – kindly but firmly – cast me out of the Order.'

Percy knew the story but this time he heard more than merely what had happened: he heard the pain and humiliation of the crusading youth echoing in the voice of the old man. Percy thought he could almost hear the pleading and avowals of remorse that youth had sobbed out in desperation. The images filled him with a melancholy sense of regret.

'Instead of being granted the mantle which signified for me all earthly virtue, I was sent back to Cyprus in what I considered to be disgrace – but it was a curious kind of disgrace. First, I was granted knighthood by Saint Louis; second, my orders to return spared me captivity and may well have saved my life, and – most curious of all – Master de Sonnac gave me a letter which he claimed would guarantee me readmission to the Temple.'

Percy found himself asking, 'Why didn't you make use of it?'

'Because Master de Sonnac made its use contingent upon understanding why the crusade had ended in ignominy. By the time I understood, I was married and lord of Najac. My ambitions had altered and I closed my ears to that part of my conscience which said I belonged to the Temple.'

'No man belongs to the Temple!' Percy countered with unexpected sharpness.

Geoffrey looked over at him, somewhat startled, but Percy would not meet his eyes. He lowered his lids and the shadows of his lashes cast dark circles under his eyes.

Geoffrey let it be, preferring instead to reach inside his own surcoat and remove a yellowed parchment with an unbroken seal. He handed it to Percy without comment.

Percy's eyes fell on the heavy red wax and recognised the seal of the master. He looked up sharply.

'Master de Sonnac said I could give it to any commander, and he would be required to admit me to the Temple – as a knight.'

Percy shook his head slightly. 'I'm not a commander.'

'But my son Jean is. I want you to take that to Jean at Mingary and ask him to authorise you to act as his proxy when you return.'

Percy was frowning slightly, making Geoffrey uncomfortable.

'Of course, if you do not want to make the long journey to Scotland, you could make the same request of Master de la More.'

Percy continued to stare at him for a long moment, and then he shook his head to free it of the bizarre images crowding the edge of his consciousness. In his imagination he could picture Geoffrey in the robes of the Grand Master. In his resentment at Jacques de Molay's indecisiveness, he could not help thinking that Geoffrey would have been the better master. Geoffrey, with his courage and his willingness to take risks, combined with his profound love of his dependants and brothers and his common sense, would not have failed them in this crisis. Geoffrey would never have confessed to the false allegations, not even under torture. More important, Geoffrey would have found a way to fight the Inquisition. As he was doing now.

'You do not think me worthy?' Geoffrey managed tightly, wetting his lips nervously.

'What? No, you misunderstand me.' Percy shoved his hauberk off his knees impatiently and faced Geoffrey directly. 'I was… thinking about something else entirely. You are more than worthy. You are worthy of much more.'

Geoffrey's face at once lit up. 'Then you will do it? You'll take the letter to Jean?'

'As soon as possible.'

'Ah, that was the other favour I wanted to ask you. My granddaughter is to marry at Michaelmas. She would like us to attend. Will you escort me – or would you rather avoid Najac?'

Percy felt the ground lurch slightly but then he got hold of himself quickly. 'No, I will take you there and continue on to Bordeaux. With luck I can be in London by Saint Nicholas.'

Chapter Fourteen

Najac, Michaelmas 1308

In two weeks there is no time to make new clothes, so Félice unpacked the gown her grandmother had worn at her wedding over half a century earlier. Taking the white silk in her hands, she imagined that she could smell the cyprus trees and hear the whisper of the palms. In the damp chill of Najac on a rainy autumn day, the silk seemed warm to touch, as if it still carried in its folds the warmth of the Mediterranean sun.

Eleni and her mother's maid helped her bathe, wash her hair and get dressed. Far from missing her mother's presence, she was relieved that Marie was preoccupied with the wedding feast and the few guests who had managed to arrive at such short notice. Marie would only have disturbed her. As it was, dressing in the tower room where her grandmother had died, Félice felt Eleanor's presence and it comforted her. Eleni reminded her as she drew the pink silk undergown over her head that Eleanor too had married at a court plunged in mourning.

With Petitlouis so fresh in the grave, it was inappropriate to make a great fuss, so very few people had been invited. But, of course, a daughter's wedding is a good opportunity to court the powerful so Louis had sent humble notices to the Counts of Foix and Armagnac and the Captal de Buch, confident that all would decline. And they had. The circle of guests was thus confined to the more humble, local gentry and the wealthy burghers of Cordes.

Félice did not mind the fact that the wedding would be small and humble. She had no particular desire to be the centre of contrived lewd attention for hours on end. Nor did she find any particular pleasure in stilted conversation with strangers. She regretted only that her grandfather had not appeared. She hoped that he would be pleased she was wearing Eleanor's gown.

They brushed out her hair and left it free in cascades of red-brown curls down her back. Then they fitted a delicate circlet of enamel leaves and roses on her brow and pinched her cheeks to make her flush. The bells were clanging out.

Louis, in severe mourning, wrapped one of his own cloaks with a deep hood over his daughter so she could make it through the rain without getting too wet. He escorted her from the castle to the basilica, where the family, guests and household waited in the chill of the cavernous church.

On account of the rain, Dom Pedro awaited Félice inside the basilica rather than on the porch. In front of the altar, they exchanged their vows and then immediately received communion and heard mass. Félice went through the ritual as if by rote, aware only that she felt no particular emotion and wondering if that were normal. After the priest had sprinkled them with holy water, Dom Pedro kissed her hand first on the back and then on the palm, and then they rose from the cushions before the altar to face the church.

The bells were pealing again. Félice advanced down the aisle towards the exit on Dom Pedro's arm. First her father and then Norbert leaned over to give her a kiss and their blessings. Norbert added something off-colour, which fortunately she did not quite catch. Marie looked smugly satisfied from where she sat. Raymonde was wiping her eyes on the corner of her dirty gown. The captain of the guard and the cook nodded to her encouragingly. Old Eleni was weeping and shaking her head, probably at the memory of Eleanor's wedding, Félice supposed.

And then her grandfather stepped into her path and flung his thin arms around her. 'Félice! My heart! My joy! May God grant you all the happiness of heaven.' His eyes were brimming with tears and he clung to her.

Félice felt Dom Pedro's scandalised stiffness, and she turned to him. 'This is my grandfather, Dom Pedro. He lives in retirement at Chanac.'

At once the Portuguese noblemen lost his stiffness and bowed low with a flourish, anxious to compensate for his earlier disapproval. How was he supposed to know that this plainly dressed old knight was the lord of the manor? 'My lord! I had no idea.'

Geoffrey looked at the Portuguese in his jewel-studded surcoat, the collar crusted with gold embroidery, and he tipped his head just slightly. 'I hope, sir, that you know how to value the treasure you have taken into custody today. Of all Najac has to offer, you have plucked the most precious.'

Félice blushed at such extravagant praise and raised her hand to gesture for her grandfather to be more moderate. Geoffrey ignored her embarrassment.

'You, who have known her so briefly, cannot begin to know what she is worth, but with time you will discover she is like a rose that opens up to greater beauty with each passing day and year. But unlike a rose, she will be as magnificent on the day of her death as she is now. I know. Her grandmother was a rose of the same variety.'

A smile played at his lips, and Félice decided that he had been speaking of Eleanor all along. If only she could have as good a marriage as her grandparents had had!

Geoffrey bent to kiss her again, once on each cheek and then on her forehead. His eyes held hers. 'Bless you, child.

Remember you are my greatest joy and no matter what it is – no matter how trivial it may seem to you or how shameful – you can always, *always* turn to me.'

Félice felt Dom Pedro stiffen at the affront.

'Monsieur, I assure you, your granddaughter will never have need to turn to anyone but myself!'

Geoffrey lifted his eyes and looked at his granddaughter's husband with sharp, hard eyes. 'Pray God that is so, sir!'

Then he stepped back out of their way, and Dom Pedro took her firmly by the elbow to escort her past this mettlesome old man.

For a split second, Félice's eyes met Percy's as he stood beside her grandfather. Félice stumbled and would have stopped if Dom Pedro had not firmly swept her forwards with him. Félice felt her husband's arm guiding and controlling her, but the pain which shot through her heart was so intense she believed it was physical.

My God, she cried out silently, my God! What have I done? What have You done to me? To us?

Chapter Fifteen

Bordeaux, November 1308

Bordeaux gave Percy a feeling of reassurance as they passed through the massive gates just before curfew. Behind them the garrison flung shut the tall wooden doors and rammed home the wooden beam. The flag that flew proudly – not to say defiantly – from the ramparts over the walls bore the Plantagenet leopards not the lilies of France.

Percy did not know Bordeaux well, but, following his sense of direction, he turned Renaissance in the direction of the port. Behind him a stolid pack horse and the fifteen year old Alfons followed docilely. Alfons was the son of the castellan at Chanac and he had been sent to serve Percy for the voyage to London, Mingary and back. At the time it had seemed a good choice since it gave the Templars more time to recover and assured that Geoffrey had a decent garrison if there were trouble. Alfons had been flattered at first, but his enthusiasm had rapidly waned as he learned how strenuous the duties of a squire actually were.

The houses started to crowd in upon them as they approached the port. The upper storeys hung over the street, blocking out the remnants of light, and refuse clogged the gutters. They had to ride in single file and Percy had the feeling that he ought to duck more than once to avoid a sagging dormer. Turning into a narrow alley which seemed to angle in the right direction, Percy noticed too late that women lounged in the doorways. He grimaced to himself and closed his calves around Renaissance's flanks so that the long-legged thoroughbred stretched his stride.

'What's the rush, monsieur?' a silky voice hissed at him.

'Afraid of showing us what you've got?' asked a ruder voice with a Norman accent.

'Give us the little boy at least, monsieur! He looks like he's got a lot to learn!'

Peals of laughter greeted this remark, and Percy realised that the whores had left their doorways and were sauntering towards Alfons, who sat with popping eyes and a gaping mouth upon his gelding, forgetting to urge it forwards.

'Alfons!' Percy called sharply.

The boy shut his mouth and kicked his mount forwards. The whores parted slightly but one caught at Alfons's leg as he rode past and expertly ran her hand up his thigh under his tunic. They all burst into new peals of laughter as he stiffened and reddened under her touch. Alfons kicked so hard now that the gelding trotted a few strides before catching up with Renaissance.

'He's not bad!' the woman called after them. 'But I bet you're better, monsieur! I'd do it for you for just fifty sou!'

Percy ignored her and turned his attention back to the end of the alley, which opened on to a square. A number of taverns spilled their light and the sound of male voices on the uneven cobbles. Percy drew up and looked about the square, somewhat disconcerted. Then he caught sight of the alley leading off the other side and rode towards this. Again the alley was narrow, but the only disturbance was the stench of piss and sour wine, and then they reached the quay.

More than two score ships were moored along the quay, their yards slanted at a sharp angle in order not to crash or entangle with their neighbours. From the canvas over the decks and the naked yardarms, Percy concluded that most were already laid up for the winter. But two of the outermost cogs were flying bunting and there were lights aboard.

Percy left Alfons with the horses and clambered over the planking stretched across the decks of the ships nearest the quay towards the outer ships. When he was within hailing distance of the watchmen, he announced that he was looking for passage to England. The watchman shrugged and sent him back to the *Neptune*. The captain always stayed there, the watchman explained, and he could ask him if he were willing to take passengers to England at this time of year.

They found the *Neptune* on the square with the other taverns, just as a gust of rain splattered down on them. Percy glanced up at the low cloud scudding overhead and on impulse decided there was no need to go in search of a hospice. Geoffrey had pawned Eleanor's jewels to finance their journey to England, and he had coin. The inn hardly looked as if it could cost them a fortune, and he needed to talk to the mariners anyway. So he sent Alfons into the mews to stable the horses and ducked through the doorframe.

He was greeted by the smell of fat, smoke and wine and the gruff laughter of men in their cups. He almost backed out again as his body reacted with alarm to the unfamiliar atmosphere. As a Templar he had been prohibited from entering such an establishment. Templars were required to seek refuge either in their own houses or with other religious orders. Geoffrey, like most noblemen, did the same, enjoying the luxurious guest houses and excellent cuisine of abbeys and priories when he was on the road. Percy had readily adopted this habit since his rescue until these past weeks, when he had preferred pitching his tent in forests or fields to frequenting places where large numbers of travellers gathered.

The narrow passage in which he stood, the beams low overhead and the plaster yellowed with age and smeared with smoke, filled him with revulsion. But, contemptuous of his own squeamishness, he advanced with long strides towards the doorway giving access to the public room.

As he ducked and stepped down into the room, a broad woman with massive arms glanced up from serving one of the tables. Rapidly and expertly appraising the quality of the chain mail encasing the stranger's throat and head and the finesse of the wool cloak, she at once nodded and smiled to him. 'Come in, milord! Come in!' She was anxious to overcome the hesitation she could read on his face.

The room was crowded and the air thick with smoke from the badly made fireplace. Percy glanced about sceptically for a vacant table but saw none. Any thought of leaving was foiled by the hostess bustling over and gesturing towards the end of a long table occupied by a gaggle of young clerics, three still in the white robes of the novitiate. Percy's stomach tightened.

'What will it be, milord? Our best Bordeaux? I swear you've never tasted better! And dinner? I have an excellent lamb pie, just the thing on a night like this.'

'I am looking for passage to England. I was told the captain of one of the cogs bound for London was here.' Percy was hoping that the cog was bound for anywhere else and that he could gracefully withdraw.

'Indeed, indeed! That'll be Captain Rowe! I knew you were an Englishman!' she added with a wink. 'Have a seat while I fetch your wine and dinner; I'll send Captain Rowe over. Are you alone, milord?'

'My boy's stabling the horses.'

'Then I'll have a glass of cheap stuff and the leftovers set out for him as well.' She gestured again towards the vacant end of the table with the clerics. Reluctantly Percy squeezed his way past other customers and between the tables and benches to the indicated place.

The table was sticky with spilled wine and gravy which had not been wiped away and the bench was wobbly on the uneven floor or uneven legs. Percy resolved to leave as soon as he had talked to Captain Rowe and he glanced around the room to see if he could identify the mariner. Unfortunately, all the guests, except the clerics at his table, looked like fishermen and sailors to his inexperienced eye. His attention was drawn back to the tonsured, inebriated youths at his own table.

He forced himself to look at each of the novices in turn. One had a horse face with prominent crooked teeth and a breathy laugh. Another had such horrible acne that his face was scarred and purple. The third was a strikingly handsome youth, and for a moment Percy thought it might be the novice who had been at his interrogation. But then he realised that these were all Franciscans and the novice at his interrogation had been Dominican.

Percy took a deep breath and was actually relieved when the wine jug was thumped down in front of him, along with a pewter mug. He was grateful for having something to do with his hands, and at once poured himself a tankard of ruby-red wine. He sniffed at it doubtfully, but it was not as bad as he had expected and he took a gulp. It tasted tangy but left a bitter aftertaste. He took another mouthful to obliterate the aftertaste.

From the far end of the table he heard a cheer, and he saw that three young sailors had joined the crowd of clerics. They appeared to be foreigners: two had the olive skin and the silky black hair Percy had often seen on Sicilians; the third had Moorish blood. A place was made for them next to the novices, and at once a clamour went up for more wine. Percy watched over the rim of his tankard, his stomach unsettled but his mind fascinated.

The sailors shed their short cloaks and revealed sleek bodies in tight-fitting hose, short, hip-length tunics and hoods with long, decorative liripipes. They even had outer sleeves slit open to the elbow to reveal inner sleeves like courtiers. On the finger of the Moor, a heavy gold ring glittered and a gold chain stood out sharply against the black of his throat.

Percy was distracted by the arrival of Alfons, who sullenly squeezed in beside him, complaining that the grooms in the tavern stables were lazy and stupid. He had had to do everything himself.

'That's what you are meant to do. I don't trust my horses to strangers,' Percy told him.

Alfons made a sour face and then sniffed around the room. 'Are we going to eat here? It stinks.'

'You don't have to,' Percy replied evenly. 'You're welcome to go without supper, if you prefer.'

Alfons gave him a look of sheer hatred and then busied himself with removing his own hood and cloak. The room was overheated with so many people.

The hostess arrived with two platters of food and set the better-looking plate before Percy. 'The boy's wine is coming,' she said without being asked.

Alfons had already fallen over his food as if he were starving. He hunched over his plate with his elbows on the table and used his unwashed fingers. Percy removed his knife and spoon from his belt and addressed his own meal. They had not eaten since morning.

As he ate, Percy occasionally lifted his glance towards the clerics sharing their table. He was fascinated by the self-assurance of the three sailors. They did not appear to be drunk, and, though one after another of the clerics staggered up and out of the door to relieve his bladder or stomach, the three sailors sipped their wine decorously, with extended baby fingers. Percy had seen such men on

Cyprus, but he had never seen them mingle so openly with the clergy. One of them had put his arm around the fairest of the novices. The novice seemed embarrassed by the gesture. First he fidgeted and then sat very still, flushed with more than wine. Percy drank slowly, staring at the youth until he glanced up nervously and met Percy's gaze. The blush turned his shaved head the colour of boiled lobster and he looked away sharply. He doesn't want this, Percy registered and shifted his gaze to the others.

The acne-faced novice was turned towards the Moor, who sat with his arms crossed, a haughty expression on his face. The novice's hands were under the table. The horse-faced novice was laughing ever more hysterically while the third sailor fondled him openly.

'Something stuck in your craw?' a deep voice growled at him.

Percy looked up at a big man with a mane of greying hair. He was red of face and shimmering with sweat. His tunic and shirt were open at the neck to reveal a curly tuft of grey hair. His sleeves were shoved up his muscular arms and tattoos were visible between the black hairs.

Percy considered the man before answering. 'Captain Rowe?'

'That's right. You want passage to England at this time?'

'I want passage to London for myself, my boy and three horses – at this time.'

'Are you a fool or a fugitive?'

Percy shrugged. 'I can always ship at Calais.'

'It'll cost you four pounds six.'

Percy shook his head. 'I can ship at Calais for four shillings.'

'Calais!' the captain scoffed. 'Two and six and we sail tomorrow with the tide!' The Captain started to turn away.

'When's the tide?' Percy asked.

'Mid-morning.' The captain had turned back. 'And let the lads have their fun. Even a monk has a dick which itches now and again. Who are you to say how he scratches it?'

'I don't honestly give a damn, captain, but the Holy Church condemns sodomy and makes some men pay a terrible price for engaging in it.'

Percy was aware of anger pulsing, only barely under control, through his veins. He was thinking of what the monks had done to Father André. He was thinking of the Dominican who had been at his early interrogations, the one who had raped the boy from Saint Pierre. He had forgotten the boy's name but not what they had done to him. He stared at the captain and the captain stared back.

'What are you? A damned scholar?'

Percy had never been accused of that before and smiled wryly. 'Hardly.' He was remembering how angry his tutor had been at his utter inability to decline Latin verbs.

'Well then, what's the point of trying to puzzle out the ways of the Whore Church? Popes can have mistresses and bishops can fuck little boys but watch out if any of us do it, isn't that it? We sail with the tide!' He turned his broad back on Percy and stalked away.

Percy watched him go and then shoved away the remainder of his plate.

'Can I have it?' Alfons asked at once with his mouth full.

'Yes.' Percy hardly bothered answering. His gaze had gone back to the other end of the table, to the sweaty face of the fairest novice as the sailor whispered in his ear and then to the horse-faced friar his eyes closed and mouth agape as one of the sailors worked his backside to hooted cheers and sniggers.

'I can give you a good time, milord.' A high-pitched voice piped in his ear.

Percy started and looked over his shoulder so rapidly that the boy jumped back a little as if in fright. He was no more than twelve or thirteen – or in any case scrawny and stunted. He licked his lips nervously while Percy inspected him, noting the greasy stains on the front of his tunic, the baggy, dirty knees of his woollen hose and the holes in the elbows of his tunic and shirt.

'You can give me a good time,' Percy repeated, wondering if this was how the boy from Saint Pierre had ended after the Dominican was finished with him.

'You know.' The boy smiled encouraging, slipping his middle finger back and forth between the closed fist of his other hand.

Percy's stomach churned not with revulsion but anger. 'How old are you?'

'What difference does that make?' the boy wanted to know, frowning. 'I can do it.' He flung back his bony shoulders and thrust his hips forwards.

'Why?'

'Why what?'

'Why do you prostitute yourself?'

'I ain't no whore! If you don't want it, then leave me alone!' The boy lashed out and then fled to retain his self-respect.

Alfons was gaping at Percy in astonishment. Percy drained his tankard and started to rise.

'I'll bring you more in a minute.' The hostess shoved him back down. Then, bending lower, she added, 'If you want a girl I can give you a room.'

'Forget the girl! We want a room for the night.'

The woman glanced at Alfons and then shrugged. 'As you wish.' Percy told Alfons to finish quickly.

*

They went up a creaking stair that twisted sharply on itself and ended in a dark corridor. The room overlooked the courtyard. There was one lumpy bed, a ragged rug, a chest standing on three legs and a block of wood. The room smelled of garlic, fat and smoke. Percy crossed it rapidly and flung open the shutters, but the air from the courtyard was laden with the smell of manure from the stables and rain hissed on the roof and gurgled along the gutter, sending a damp chill into the room which made him shudder. He closed the shutters again.

Alfons stripped naked and laid himself on a makeshift pallet at the end of the bed. Percy undressed to his braies and shirt and then lay down on the bed. Though he no longer slept by candlelight as a Templar was supposed to do, he still slept clothed, as the Rule demanded. He wasn't sure himself if the Rule, habit or extreme shame of his brand was the reason.

When he woke again it was still dark and the rain had ceased although water still gurgled along the gutter. He could hear the sounds of men laughing in the tavern below, though he could tell by the stiffness of his limbs that he had slept for several hours. He lay still, listening to the night, and then some instinct made him sit up abruptly. 'Alfons?'

There was no response. He flung the covers back and slid out of the bed. 'Alfons!'

Still no response. He looked around the end of the bed: the pallet was empty. His next glance went to his clothes, his sword propped in the corner. He went over and felt inside his surcoat. The purse made fast to the cord belt was still there and seemed heavy enough. He pulled open the purse and poured the coins into his hand. Moving to the window where the light was marginally better, he counted. It was all there – short of fifty sou. He stopped and looked around the room again. Then with a grimace, he started pulling on his hose, gambeson and hauberk. He did not bother with his surcoat and sword, but he took the purse and a dagger and slipped out of the room.

As he passed the entrance to the tavern, he noted that the crowd had thinned substantially. The novices and their male whores were gone. No doubt there were rooms for them too.

Outside it was damp and drizzling, and puddles glistened in the square. Percy made straight for the street he and Alfons had traversed earlier. An eerie reddish light emerged from the end of it.

As he left the openness of the square and entered the alley, he saw that the 'shop' windows on the ground floor of the houses were hung with red curtains, the light from inside casting a red glow over the alley itself. It was like entering hell, a wayward thought told him, and he smiled at his own joke. He started up the alley, with a following wind that blew his cloak against him from behind. A part of his mind was already making fun of the rest of him. What did he plan to do now? Knock on every door and enquire if Alfons were within? He was making a fool of himself. Alfons was old enough to do as he pleased. The fifty sou would simply be deducted from his wages. He stopped.

To his right he could see the silhouetted figures of a naked woman crouching on all fours, her breasts swaying between her arms as a man on his knees rammed at her behind. He looked away and realised that he could see – in silhouette – what was going on inside all the brothels lining the street. Here the girls lounged naked in the window, there they were drinking, and elsewhere they were engaged in copulation in all its forms. Hell indeed. He turned around.

'What are you looking for, milord?' the voice purred from the doorway.

He took a determined step away from her.

'What are you running from?' the voice purred.

He took another couple of steps, faster this time.

'What are you afraid of, milord? Afraid I'll be disappointed?' The laughter cascaded through the night and echoed against the hanging upper storeys.

Percy's mind told him to ignore her. She was unimportant, her insults routine and worn. She was only interested in the coin he would give her. She was no different from the boy earlier this evening. Maybe she was hungry and had nothing else to sell. Maybe someone had raped her too until she had no self-respect left. Maybe she was an insatiable succubus. His footsteps faltered.

'I knew you were more of a man than you pretended.' The voice was closer now and he felt her slip her hands through his arm, her hot breath on his neck. 'Come in and share my wine with me, milord. It will taste better than what you've had till now.' She was pulling him towards one of the houses. The window was red like the others but empty.

He swallowed, but his throat was dry. He cracked his head against the doorframe and cursed soundly.

'You can curse like a Templar, I'll say that for you,' the woman purred and he balked abruptly. 'Come on, come on. You won't notice it in the morning – not with the headache you're going to have anyway.'

'I don't intend to drink.' he told her, surprised at the sound of his own voice.

'Why not?' she asked. 'Afraid you won't be able to get it up if you do?'

'Do you care? You want my purse not… anything else.'

'Do you mean to give it to me?' She held out her hand.

Percy looked at her palm. It was marked with wrinkles. If he could have read palms, he surely could have told her fortune. Then he lifted his gaze to her face and looked at her for the first time. She was no longer young – or at least her face was marked by lines running sharply from her nose to the corners of her mouth, cutting her cheeks in two. Her lips were smeared with some lipstick to make them larger than they were. She had used something to blacken her lashes and it had smudged her cheeks below her eyes. Her hair was a rat's nest of indeterminable colour in the dingy reddish light.

She could read the clinical appraisal in his eyes. She shrugged and her mouth turned down in a sneer. 'Don't you find me pretty enough? Used to nubile little maids of noble birth, perhaps? I don't pretend to be anything more than I am,' she told him proudly. 'I'm Anne and you can fuck me for thirty sou or you can leave.'

Percy was remembering. Before he joined the Order there had been a girl he had visited. She had been sixteen and pretty in her honey-haired, freckled way. She had been flattered at finding favour with a de Lacy, even if he were a younger son. She had made no particular fuss about losing her maidenhead to him. If it hadn't been him, it would have been one of the other lads, someone less noble, less handsome, less kind. Before that there had been a whore in Chester his brothers had taken him to...

He glanced at the room lit by a heavy candle, the red curtains hanging in the window. Then he glanced towards the stairway leading to the upper storey. He nodded towards the stairs.

She shook her head and gestured to the front room.

He shook his head.

'The landlord lives upstairs,' she whispered. 'I'm not allowed to bring customers up.'

Percy entered the room and blew out the candle. She followed him, frowning. 'Do you want to put me out of business?'

'A bird in the hand...'

'All right.' She sat down on the bed. 'How do you want it?'

Percy lay on his back and stared at the ceiling. He had refused to remove his shirt but otherwise he was naked. The air around him was damp and the sheets smelt of sweat and sex.

The whore stood up. 'If you want to stay all night it will cost you more,' she nagged, dissatisfied.

Percy did not look over at her. He was noticing the cobwebs in the rafters of the ceiling and trying to fight down the self-loathing that lay heavy in his stomach. 'You've been lying to yourself, Percy, my lad,' his conscience rebuked him in the voice his maternal grandfather had been wont to use.

He sat up and reached for the heap of clothes by the foot of the bed.

'You're in love with her,' his conscience continued as he drew tight the cord of his braies. 'You love her more than God.'

He shivered and hastened to pull on his gambeson and attach his hose to the points.

The whore stood with her hand outstretched, palm up. Percy counted out the thirty sou and then wrapped himself in his cloak and ducked back outside.

The wind was whistling up the street and had torn the overcast to shreds. As he crossed the square against the wind, he could see stars peeping out between the fragments of clouds, and he drew up. The same stars were shining down on Portugal where she was. Maybe she was even looking up at them now. Percy pulled his cloak tighter and returned to the *Neptune*.

Part Two

Chapter Sixteen

Óbidos, Portugal, April 1309

Félice confronted herself in the small mirror while Rosa, her maid, and Dona Inez, her sister-in-law, fussed about her, preparing her for the royal reception. It was to be her first introduction at the Portuguese court since her marriage, and her sister-in-law was most concerned that she did not disgrace her husband's family. Dona Inez ordered Rosa about in her imperative, impatient voice, while Félice waited nervously. Because she was only beginning to speak Portuguese, she could by no means follow all that her sister-in-law said.

Then, switching to French, Dona Inez snapped at Félice, 'You cannot wear the emerald earrings. They belonged to my mother.'

Félice started and replied defensively, 'but Dom Pedro gave them to me at Christmas.'

'Of course. You are his wife. But he would not be pleased to see you wearing them.'

Félice wondered if Dom Pedro would not be pleased or if it were only Dona Inez that resented it. Dona Inez had never married. No one had explained the reason to Félice, but it could hardly have been lack of dowry. And once, years ago, she must have been a pretty young woman. Now she was over forty, a brittle spinster with a sharp nose and straight black hair she wore parted in the centre of her head and pulled severely away from her face. She favoured sombre colours without decoration. Even tonight, when she was to attend the reception, she was dressed in a garnet red so dark that it was nearly brown, and the only jewellery she wore was a large crucifix of solid gold.

Reluctantly, Félice returned the earrings to the ivory jewellery box. She had made a gown in pale green satin especially to honour the earrings – and to match her grandmother's emerald ring as well.

She had hoped to please Dom Pedro by wearing the earrings, but she was so uncertain about what would please her husband these days that she did not dare ignore his sister's advice.

Dona Inez picked up a gold chain with a simple gold cross and hung it around Félice's neck for her. Then she turned to Rosa and ordered the gown brought over.

Félice stood and, together, Dona Inez and Rosa pulled the pale green satin over her head. In accord with the latest fashion, the gown was close-fitting and low-waisted, with long rows of pearl buttons up the back and from elbow to wrist.

No sooner had Dona Inez started to button her up than she started clicking her tongue. 'I warned you not to make a gown on this pattern!'

Félice's hands went to her back and then to her swollen belly. She was now in her sixth month of pregnancy and felt as big and unwieldy as a old cow. Feeling the gap of over an inch, tears sprang up in her eyes. She had nothing else to wear, nothing else she *wanted* to wear! How could she grow so much fatter in just a week since her last fitting?

'Just button the upper buttons,' she resolved, irritated with her own tears. 'No one will see under the surcoat.'

'Are you mad?' Dona Inez was shocked. 'You can't go to a royal reception with your gown undone like some whore! What are you thinking of?'

'The gown is not undone! There are just two buttons you can't close!'

'Naked flesh!'

'Covered by a surcoat! What else am I supposed to wear? There is not time to make alterations!'

'Why didn't you try on the gown yesterday? You should have known this could happen!'

'How should I have known? I've never been pregnant before!'

'Any good woman knows what pregnancy entails!' Dona Inez turned about abruptly and stormed out of the room, her hand on her crucifix.

Félice felt the tears in her eyes and the tightening of her throat. She bit her lower lip and held her breath, fighting against the desire to cry. It was the pregnancy, she told herself. Why else should she be close to tears over such trivial things? For months now, she had cried at the drop of a hat. She felt so melancholy and tired. For the first time in her life, she wished she could talk to her mother.

Not that Marie would have been inclined to comfort her, but in her brusque, practical way she could have reassured Félice that all was well. What, after all, did Dona Inez know of pregnancy, much less Dom Pedro? Félice could not speak with the servants because her Portuguese was too inadequate.

Rosa said something, dragging her back to the present. With a gesture, she enquired whether she should continue dressing Félice, and at once Félice nodded vigorously. She was being silly. She had looked forward to this reception and to wearing this gown. She wanted to please Pedro with something exceptionally pretty. She couldn't stop now. Besides, it must be getting late and Pedro hated to be kept waiting. Rosa buttoned her from the middle of the back upwards and then helped her slip the salmon silk surcoat, embroidered with gold and dark green, over her head.

Félice immediately started to feel pretty again once her bloated belly was completely hidden under the ample, loose folds of the sleeveless surcoat. She sat down on the stool while Rosa hastened to twist her hair up into a golden crispinette and fit the high-crowned cap, covered with the same silk and embroidery as the surcoat, on her head. Inspecting herself in the mirror, Félice felt pretty. The gold netting of the crispinette set off her red-brown hair and the cap gave her face more length, detracting from the puffiness that had developed since the onset of her pregnancy.

At a sharp knock on the door, she hastened to put the mirror face down on the dresser and turned around guiltily on the stool. As she had expected, Dom Pedro followed his knock into the room. He too was dressed for the royal reception in a red silk shirt and hose over which he wore a silk tunic of cloth of gold. He wore a heavy gold chain studded with rubies and his ceremonial belt and dagger. Everything about him seemed to glitter in the candlelight. Even his shoes were covered with gold embroidery. His glittering finery cast her pastel gown into shadow instantly.

Félice caught herself biting her lower lip and immediately pulled her teeth back inside her mouth. Dom Pedro hated it when she bit her lip: he said it was a childish habit little better than chewing her fingernails – something Félice was also known to do.

Dom Pedro crossed the room with his lithe, quick stride, a frown playing around his brows and lips. Félice wondered if Dona Inez had run to him to protest against her wearing the gown. But he made no reference to it.

'Are you ready? We do not want to be late and the streets are crowded with rabble. They have flooded the town because they expect Queen Isabella to distribute alms generously.' He made this sound like an outrageous affront to the crown.

Queen Isabella was already being called Santa Isabella by many of her subjects because she was liberal with her alms. Rumour had it that the king had ordered his chamberlain to restrict the queen's allowance because all the money which found its way into her hands disappeared into the bottomless pit of charity.

'Yes, my love.' Félice rose to her feet and reddened as she felt Dom Pedro inspecting her.

His lips tightened somewhat and he asked in an exasperated voice, 'Don't you think those colours too pale for a matron? It would have been more appropriate to wear purple or blue – but it is too late now.'

'I thought…' Félice started lamely, but what was the point of trying to defend her evidently worthless taste? She looked down at the gown she had found beautiful only moments before with sudden aversion. How could she have been so foolish not to take Dona Inez's advice? What did she know about fashion and taste? She had spent all her girlhood in a convent with barely two weeks transition from novice to bride. When Pedro had first looked at her with smouldering passion in his eyes, she had felt beautiful and erotically attractive for the first time in her life. Now, when she could feel he was not pleased, she felt ugly. The tears welled up again and she stood indecisively before her table, wishing that she could change into anything else. But already he had taken her elbow and was hastening her from the chamber.

In the narrow courtyard of their townhouse, a litter carried by two white donkeys in bright harness waited for Félice. Since she had become pregnant, Dom Pedro forbade her to ride. He helped her into the litter, where she found Dona Inez already ensconced, a book of hours in her lap although it was impossible to read in this light. Dom Pedro mounted his stallion, and the gates to the street were opened. A groom riding beside the lead donkey guided the litter into the narrow, cobbled street beyond.

The royal residence was located in the white stone castle crowning the highest part of the hill upon which the walled city of Óbidos had been built. It was here that King Dinis had spent his nuptials with his queen in 1284, and he had presented the city to her on the following morning as a wedding gift. The queen had proclaimed the city her favourite ever since, and, considering the amount of time she was wont to spend there, King Dinis had resolved on extensive renovations, turning the powerful fortress which had fought off the Moors dozens of times into a comfortable and luxurious palace.

The reception was being held on the terrace, with a view of the orchard and over the outer walls to the valley beyond. From here it was possible to see the tiled roofs of a half-dozen villages scattered among the vineyards and wheat fields. A light breeze swept this crest, blowing away the heat of the day. The sun was already low over the sea to the west and the temperature was a perfect mix of warmth and freshness. Seeing all this as Dom Pedro helped her from the litter at the foot of the stone steps leading up to the terrace, Félice forgot all her distress over Donna Inez, the earrings and her gown. Her natural optimism bubbled up stronger than all her melancholy. 'What a beautiful view!' she exclaimed happily.

Dom Pedro glanced over his shoulder and then smiled at her. It pleased him when she praised his homeland. He reminded himself that she was just seventeen and a foreigner and forgave her for not knowing better than to dress like an unmarried maiden. Then he glanced at her belly; the swelling was just visible as the breeze blew her surcoat closer to her body. She had proven remarkably fertile and was already carrying the son and heir he needed. For that he must be willing to forgive her anything, he told himself.

Dom Pedro's smile increased Félice's confidence and sent her mood soaring even higher. If only he would look at her again as he had in the first two or three months of their marriage! Then he had seemed unable to take his admiring eyes off her, and he had bedded her more than once a day, sometimes calling a halt to their journey in the middle of the day out of sheer impatience to make love with her. The memories made her flush with a tingling excitement. She was shy of the memories and yet her body, swollen and ugly as it was, quickened at the inchoate memories that wanted to be called to mind more explicitly. But this was not the time or place. Already, Dom Pedro had turned to help his sister out of the litter, and then, giving them each an arm, he led them up the steps to the terrace.

The royal herald announced them as they reached the top of the steps, and they advanced to the improvised dais on which the king and queen waited under an embroidered canopy with the royal arms of Portugal. Félice felt a nervousness quite disproportionate to the event. She had been introduced to the pope and Philip of France, after all. But then it had not been important that she make a good impression. Now she was acutely aware that any *faux pas* would not only damage her husband's status but strain her relations with him as well.

King Dinis was a man approaching fifty and entering the thirtieth year of his reign. Once, as an eighteen year old, he had risen up in rebellion against his father, but no sooner had he ascended the throne than he had shown a reasonable and moderate nature which had brought him a variety of diplomatic successes and enabled him to concentrate on furthering the prosperity of the realm. He had earned the nickname 'the Farmer', which was not meant as a compliment, but it was said that the king was not in the least offended. Unconsciously, Félice had expected someone like her father: a man grown flabby with the routine of daily life and complacent with success. She was surprised to find that the king, though hefty of build, exuded a healthy fitness and that his eyes sparkled alertly in his squarish, bearded face.

As she sank into a deep courtesy before him, he seemed to half-growl and half-bark, 'Humpf! No wonder you've been so long in showing us your bride, Dom Pedro! You will not have wanted to share her with anyone – much less an entire court!' It was a routine phrase, almost standard courtesy for a newly-wed, but it still increased Félice's confidence and made her beam as she righted herself. 'We heard you are from France, Madame.'

'No, Your Grace, from the Languedoc.'

'The Languedoc! You speak the language of the troubadours, child?' He leaned forwards with sudden, sincere eagerness.

'Poor child!' Queen Isabella smiled impishly. 'Now you will be subjected to my lord husband's attempts at poetry. I fear it is not his strong point, but he will not be dissuaded!'

Félice had been too preoccupied with the king to notice the queen before now, but she was even more surprised by Isabella than Dinis. Because of her reputation for charity, Félice had expected someone of saintly austerity and calm. Isabella was plump with lively, teasing eyes. She was dressed in a gown of bright blue with a sky-blue surcoat and a gold gauze wimple encased her head and neck beneath the jewelled crown.

'Hush, woman!' the king answered, with genuine annoyance dulled by evident affection. 'Just because you have no ear for poetry and no understanding of the great tradition of courtly love, is no reason to dismiss the quality of works of art! Let Madame de Meneses be her own judge! And you must be honest with me!' the king admonished Félice with a raised finger. 'We will claim a dance from you and we will discuss the fine points of an art our poor queen is too pious to appreciate! Be prepared!' he warned in mock sternness.

Queen Isabella laughed. 'Welcome to our humble court, my dear. If he gets too tedious, just have a little fainting spell and I will come to your rescue!' The queen then offered her cheek for a kiss, and Félice and Dom Pedro moved on.

There were dozens of noblemen to whom Félice now had to be introduced. Dom Pedro steered her by the elbow from one guest to the next, providing a short, pithy commentary in her ear as they approached. He did not fail to inform her who was important and who was surrounded by scandal or fame. But there were far too many for Félice to take note of all at once. The names and faces blurred and mixed together so quickly that after half an hour Félice was certain she could remember no one.

There were large numbers of clerics among the guests and Félice felt her heart jump at the sight of Templars – free and unabashedly wearing the habit of their Order. Dom Pedro introduced her to a distinguished-looking man with aquiline features and a long grey beard, Dom Alfonso, the commander of the Templar castle at Tomar. Dom Pedro informed Félice that as a young man he had been one of King Dinis's tutors in the arts of war and still had the king's ear. Félice could not help asking him if there was any news about the Templars in France.

The monk considered her seriously for a long moment before saying that, regretfully, there was no change, but King Dinis had sent two of the Portuguese bishops who had investigated the Templars in Portugal – and found them innocent – to the papal court. It was his hope that they would be able to persuade the pontiff – or at least key cardinals – it was imperative for the Holy Father to take control of the trial from the King of France. Indignantly, Dom Alfonso explained, 'The pope is afraid of King Philip and is virtually his captive! When he tried to leave Poitiers for Provence, he was turned back at the gates of Poitiers by the king's soldiers!'

'Félice, why does this concern you?' Dom Pedro admonished, discomforted by the evident depth of her interest in these masculine affairs.

The commander of Tomar took the hint and bowed deeply to excuse himself. 'Thank you for your concern, madame.'

Dom Pedro murmured reprovingly in Félice's ear, 'The persecution of the Templars is much too complicated an affair for you to understand. Surely you have enough to concern you with the birth of our son only months away.'

Félice drew a breath. Did he expect her to think of nothing else? Didn't he realise that the more she thought about the coming birth the more frightened she became? She was saved from replying by the appearance of the king in their path.

'We have come to claim the dance you promised us, madame,' the king announced, holding out his arm peremptorily.

Félice took it gratefully, even eagerly, anxious to avoid any form of conflict with Dom Pedro.

Félice could hear the whispers around them as the king led her in the dance. Many guests did not know whom she was and had to be informed by their neighbours. She noted too some raised eyebrows and wondered briefly if King Dinis was the kind of monarch who did not hesitate to seduce his nobles' wives. But she had heard no such rumours about him and he seemed fond of his queen. She looked up at him with open curiosity.

'What terrible things have you heard about us, madame?' the king asked her, his eyes openly laughing at her.

Félice thought it might be more of an insult to admit how little she had heard so she replied quickly, 'That you are called "the Farmer".'

'You find that terrible?'

'I find it insulting, for surely those who coined the name meant to insult you. They wish to imply that you are simple and cowardly, only because you have taken an interest in agriculture and have encouraged the productivity of your country. Yet, if more kings took an active interest in increasing the yield of the land before they increased their taxes, fewer queens would be driven to give extravagant alms.'

The king laughed so heartily that heads turned all around them to see what was the cause. 'But what does one do with a woman who insists on giving away alms and therefore discourages the poor from working harder? She is our despair! Going against all our policies!'

'Then I must have been misinformed about your policies.'

'Meaning?' He cocked his head in anticipation.

'I had been led to believe that Your Grace's policies were to subsidise irrigation, encourage measures to reduce soil erosion and increase crop diversity in regions which up to now have been characterised by backward, soil-leeching, farming methods. The essence of your policy, I was told, was increasing the productivity of the land not the worker.'

'Dom Pedro told you all that?' The king looked at her sideways.

'No, it was the seneschal at Belmonte, Dom Enrique.'

'Ah. Dom Enrique.' The king considered this a moment and then added. 'You know Dom Enrique is Dom Pedro's uncle, his grandfather's bastard by a Moorish woman.'

Félice had not known. Why didn't they tell her things like this? But it explained the absolute trust her husband had in Dom Enrique's loyalty.

The king was continuing, 'In his youth he was determined to show that his Moorish blood had not impinged upon his Christianity. He was a brave knight and a fierce fighter, but then one day he fell so ill that he was near to death and he had a vision. In the vision our Lady appeared to him and warned him that if he ever touched his sword again he would kill his own brother. When he rose from his bed, he went to his half-brother, Dom Pedro's father, and begged to be given a position on the estates. He grew into a wise and effective administrator. Dom Pedro owes much of his wealth to the good administration of his uncle.'

It was, Félice noted, as if the king thought more highly of Dom Enrique than of her husband.

'Not that Dom Pedro is a spendthrift!' the king hastened to add. 'Dom Pedro is a man of many talents, many interests. It seems sometimes that he cannot make up his mind what he wants. He has a... an impatient nature, a restless spirit. But what are we talking about? You, as his wife, must know him far better than we. Tell us rather what else you heard of us.'

Félice was far more interested in his judgement of Dom Pedro, but at seventeen – and meeting the king for the first time – she did not have the necessary poise and maturity to insist. Instead, she searched her memory rapidly. 'I heard that your negotiations with the English have been very successful. Trade is booming, I'm told, and Porto is growing rapidly.'

'The English are a sensible people. They understand trade almost as well as the Italians do – and they are more reliable. I like doing business with the English,' the king told her candidly.

The music came to an end and Félice dipped into a curtsey of thanks, preparing to return to Dom Pedro.

The king, however, forestalled her irritably. 'You can't go yet! We have not even begun to discuss poetry! Another dance?'

Félice could not say no, and he immediately started quoting from a poem in the langue d'oc, hesitating now and then over a word, but evidently proud of his fluency. Félice applauded, as was expected of a subject for the performance of a king. Then the king started to recite another poem, and Félice suspected it was his own work. Here the use of the langue d'oc was perhaps more awkward, occasionally ungrammatical, but the poem itself was far from trite. Despite the king's talk, it dealt not with courtly love but the death of a child.

'Your Grace has lost a child?' Félice asked as he finished.

The king started and looked at her sideways. 'Our daughter Marilia when she was only three. It is a long time ago now.'

'But your poem has captured the pain for ever.'

The king stopped and bent over her hand, kissing it fervently.

Embarrassed, Félice realised that everyone seemed to be watching them, and, somewhat frightened, she looked for Dom Pedro and the queen. His gesture could so easily be misinterpreted. She found the queen first, but she seemed unconcerned and cast Félice a fleeting smile before continuing her discussion with a bishop. Dom Pedro was scowling at her furiously.

'Your Grace, forgive me, but I fear I weary of the dancing. The babe I carry makes me tire easily.'

The king looked up, alarmed. 'You did not tell us, madame. We did not know.' At once he took her arm and led her back to Dom Pedro. 'My congratulations, Dom Pedro. We had not heard your lady was expecting.'

Dom Pedro bowed his head in acknowledgement, but his expression remained harsh. Félice imagined that she saw a look of disdain cross the king's face. As the king withdrew, Dom Pedro drew her aside and now she saw that Dona Inez was also with him – looking even more hostile.

'Do you think it amusing to disgrace me in front of all the nobility of Portugal?' he demanded with barely suppressed anger.

'What do you mean?' Félice asked, alarmed and hurt. She could not understand what she had done wrong. The king had kissed her *hand*. He had not even been flirting with her! '*How* disgrace you?'

'You should not have danced in your condition!' Dona Inez hissed at her.

'I could not say no to the king!'

'Of course, you could!' Dom Pedro informed her sharply. He was guiding her off the terrace, back down the steps, away. 'You are the Madame de Meneses, not some village girl!'

'But what was the harm in dancing with him? In France it is deemed an honour to be so favoured by the king.'

'You are not in France!' Dom Pedro answered with narrowed eyes. He was beginning to think that Inez was right and he had made a terrible mistake in taking this foreigner for his wife. If it weren't for the child she was carrying, he would have been tempted to have the marriage annulled.

Their grooms had not expected them to come so soon so they had to wait for the litter and horses to be brought up. Dom Pedro and Dona Inez stood, sourly silent, on either side of Félice, and Félice wanted to cry and protest and crawl into a hole and hide. The king had kissed her hand in gratitude, respect – not with any low intentions. Or was she too naïve to comprehend the undercurrents? If only she could have talked to her grandfather! If only she weren't so alone!

Dom Pedro had known her as had no other man. He and he alone had seen her in her nakedness and taken her virginity. Yet he was an utter stranger at this moment. She did not know what he was thinking or feeling or why. She could speculate but she knew that she was trying to see her way blindfolded in the dark. Dom Pedro never *talked* to her about his thoughts and feelings. He told her what she should do and think – or he told her how beautiful, how intoxicating she was. He was voluble only when making love with her. Something he had not done since Christmas...

A sharp pain in her abdomen surprised her and she gasped. Dona Inez looked at her sideways, but Félice held her face rigid. The pain was fading. She did not know what it had been. But it was too soon for delivery. It must... It came again, sharper, deeper. Her gasp now was half-cry and she leaned forwards, trying to ease the pain. Instinctively, she cupped her belly in her hands.

'What is it?' Dom Pedro demanded harshly.

'I don't know. A pain. A...' she drew in her breath sharply.

'You should not have been dancing,' Dona Inez told her self-righteously. 'Any woman with any sense knows that!'

Félice couldn't answer. The pains in her abdomen were so intense that she had no room for any other thoughts. Her face had twisted and she was almost doubled over. Dom Pedro bent, lifted her in his powerful arms and carried her towards the approaching litter. He was not gentle as he set her down inside, but she was grateful to be sitting, thankful to be out of sight behind the curtains.

The pain seemed to ease and Félice tried to sit up straighter. She saw Dona Inez sneering at her from the opposite seat, and she closed her eyes and dropped her head against the headrest. She held both her hands on her belly. This couldn't be normal, could it? Was she making a fuss about something which happened to every pregnant woman? But surely it wasn't the dancing? The dancing had not been strenuous. But what did she know about what was safe? Hadn't Natalie danced when she was pregnant? She couldn't remember any more. The pain was coming back. She tried to remain calm, to relax. Her breathing became laboured, her hands clutched at the side of the litter and sweat broke out on her brow and palms. She moaned, 'Oh God! What is this?'

'Don't you know, you silly goose? You are probably having a miscarriage!'

'No!' Félice protested, but the words sank into her unconsciousness, sending waves of panic to join the waves of pain.

Christ, she was losing the baby – the heir Dom Pedro so desperately wanted. He would never forgive her if she lost the baby. Never. Now she clutched at her belly with a possessive, protective grip.

They drew up in front of the de Meneses palace and Dom Pedro shouted orders again. He flung open the door of the litter and extracted Félice. Flaring torches lit up the hall. A servant ran ahead of them with the torch, Dona Inez following. Voices were echoing in the corridors. Rosa appeared with a worried face. Dom Pedro dumped Félice on the great bed. His voice was angry as he spoke to his sister and the maid. Then he was gone.

Rosa and Dona Inez removed her headdress and crispinette, then her shoes, stockings, surcoat and gown. Rosa spoke soothing words to her which she could not understand. Dona Inez said nothing.

But the pain was rising again. Félice felt as if her insides were cramping up, twisting in upon themselves. She cried out, grasping at the bedposts, clutching the covers. How could it go on? The pain didn't stop. She had always heard that the pain of childbirth came in pulses. But this wasn't childbirth. She screamed as much in terror and protest as from pain.

She felt fluid between her legs and struggled to leave the bed, to get to the garderobe. Rosa pulled Félice's arm over her shoulders and tried to support her, but Rosa was of slight build. They staggered forwards a few steps and then, with a scream, Félice crumpled to the floor. Her insides were knotted and tearing apart, shredding themselves. As she tried to press her hands against the source of the pain, they turned bloody. Blood seemed to be everywhere. And the pain was getting worse.

Rosa was trembling but trying to get her to lie back. The tone of her voice was comforting, gentle. With her bony hand she tried to wipe Félice's hair from her face. She stroked her arms and forehead, murmuring to her. Félice tried to relax, but she was gasping for breath and writhing in agony. She needed to escape the pain, to find some way of stopping it or at least easing it. But nothing she did brought any relief. The pain mounted and mounted. The child was tearing at her insides, pulling her intestines and her stomach with it as it struggled to escape her womb. It was dead but it was killing.

Félice knew intuitively that it was dead. She could sense that the soul had escaped and now the soulless foetus was doing all the damage it could before it was discarded, like the unbaptised half-human that it was. It was scratching, cutting, biting – like a demon trapped inside her womb and determined to get out.

Her thoughts flitted back and forth between the terror of losing the child that Dom Pedro valued above all else and the sheer physical desperation to be freed of pain. The pain would only end when the dead baby was aborted. But if she aborted Dom Pedro's son and heir, he would hate her.

She knew that he did not love her as he had before. She could sense that he was intensely disappointed with her. She kept trying to be the wife he expected her to be, but she kept making mistakes. She wore the wrong clothes, said the wrong things, did the wrong things. No matter what she did, she could not seem to please him any more. If she lost his child – because she had danced – he would despise her.

She could see his harsh, unforgiving face. His black eyes were filled with contempt and hatred. His eyes called her murderess. She had murdered his son and heir by foolishly dancing with the king. His voice came to her, calm and controlled and icy: 'I married you out of remorse for killing your brother. Now you have killed my son. I think all debts are cleared. I don't ever want to see you again.'

She could feel the rejection like an icy wind that made her tremble with cold. Her teeth started chattering. 'Pedro, please! Don't!' What was to become of her? Where could she go? She had no dower portion. She could not return to a drunken father and a ruthless brother. She would be a discarded wife. A social outcast. She had nothing to call her own and she was a thousand miles from home. She was utterly alone. And her dead baby was tearing her insides apart. Why was she worrying about how she would get home?

Her baby was killing her. He was going to take her soul with his to hell.

Maybe that was better than living as an unwanted wife. She had broken her vow to Umberto. Maybe God was punishing her for that. She had given herself to another man and enjoyed it. Umberto's face was indistinct, but he looked upon her as if she were no better than a whore. She was a whore writhing on the floor, soiled with her own blood and the dead foetus of her aborted child. The look of aversion on his face was eloquent. He looked as if he were about to vomit in disgust.

Then, with a shock that made her body jerk, she felt Percy's eyes upon her. They penetrated the bloody, agonised body and shook her soul. 'You have no right to wish for death,' they told her sharply. 'You would not let *me* die!'

'But that was different!' Félice protested.

'How?' Percy wanted to know, his eyes fixed upon her, pinning her down.

'Your life was worth something! Look what you have done! Rescued ten of your brothers, that I know of, and how many more since then?'

'I could have done none of it if you had not saved my life. All that I have done is to your credit. And you are only seventeen! Your whole life is ahead of you. You must go through the pain. Go through it and beyond it – as I did.'

'But I don't know what is beyond.'

'Neither did I. I expected eternal imprisonment and was given your grandfather – and you – instead.'

'But you might have fallen into the hands of the Inquisition.'

'I still may.'

'Then you will curse me for having saved your life.'

'I will never curse you, Felicitas. Don't give up. Not now. Not so soon. Not before we have seen one another again. Please.'

Félice clenched her teeth together. She was trembling and sweating, and the pain was still there – but it was easing.

She heard voices – low male voices – and then the hissing of Dona Inez. Through her tears she made out a stranger in the black robes of a doctor. Then her eyes met Dom Pedro and she knew that she had not been dreaming.

*

'It is quite common for a young woman to miscarry her first child,' the doctor reminded Dom Pedro.

Dom Pedro made a grimace. 'I am no longer young. I need an heir.'

'But your wife is very young. She has decades of child-bearing years ahead of her.'

'If she is not damaged.'

'My examination indicated no reason she should not be able conceive again. On the contrary. She seems a healthy young woman.'

Dom Pedro's expression did not soften, but he took a deep breath and moved back to the bedside to stare down at his wife. She had fallen into an exhausted sleep. Lying in the great bed with her hair a tangled mess around her pale, tear-streaked face, she looked more child than woman. Dom Pedro's lips softened slightly. He remembered abruptly the first time he had seen her: an angelic novice holding an infant in her arms. He had been filled with the same reverence he felt for the Virgin Mary. The memory of the timid, awkward virgin he had transformed into a woman nagged at his consciousness. She had been so innocent, so uncertain, so hesitant at first – and then so surprised, almost baffled – by the response of her own body. Her very inexperience had intoxicated him. He could not get enough of her innocence and he had drunk of it until it was gone.

Now, pale from half a night of haemorrhaging and looking skinny after the loss of their son, she was almost the maiden he had married. He took a deep breath and resolved to give her a second chance.

Chapter Seventeen

Porto, December 1309

The Bishop of Porto watched Dom Pedro from his comfortable armchair by the fire. The rains had settled in again and the episcopal palace seemed to hold the damp cold. The river below was shrouded in clinging mist, and the shouts of the ferrymen and longshoremen came muffled through the shuttered windows. Dom Pedro clearly did not feel the cold, pacing back and forth like a caged leopard, gesturing expansively with his arms while he spoke with vibrant intensity.

'It is the second time in a year that she has miscarried my heir, Your Grace! The doctors assure me that she is perfectly healthy. There is no *physical* reason she should not carry a child to term. But twice in one year! If it is not her body that is at fault, then it can only be God's will!'

The bishop raised his eyebrows eloquently. Even without being a doctor, it seemed to him that Dom Pedro was expecting too much of a seventeen year old girl – and he clearly felt no concern for the girl's health. Only the heir mattered. But Dom Pedro was tearing back and forth across the tiled floor without an eye for his audience.

With his elbows propped on the carved arms of the chair and his fingertips touching, as if forming the peaked roof of a cathedral with his hands, the bishop considered his visitor. He had known Dom Pedro most of his life and he knew his reputation as an impulsive, passionate, restless man. He was doing his reputation full honour now and the bishop was inclined to curb him. But the bishop was also a man of the world. It did not escape his notice that Dom Pedro's amber velvet tunic was lined with sable and trimmed with fox. His collar and belt glimmered with topazes and on his manicured hands he wore massive rings of almost incalculable value. Dom Pedro was wealthy as few men were in Portugal and he did not seem to know what to do with his money. The Church could not afford to offend such a patron.

'Why should it be God's will that your young wife miscarry your children, Dom Pedro?' the bishop asked slowly and probingly. It had not escaped his notice that Dom Pedro spoke of the children as his heirs. Clearly, he harboured no doubts whatsoever about his wife's fidelity.

'Merciful Saviour!' Dom Pedro flung up his arms and turned to face the crucifix hanging prominently between the shuttered windows. 'I have asked myself that question until I cannot sleep! I'm forty years of age, Your Grace! For twenty-three years I was married to a woman too ill to bear me children. I honoured her as was her right, though it was costing me year by year the chance of siring an heir, and I never brought another woman under her roof!'

The bishop noted the careful wording: he had had his pleasures with others, but discretely out of sight and hearing of his stricken wife. What more could one ask of a young man married to a feeble woman whose bed he was, for health reasons, forbidden to share? He had undoubtedly confessed his infidelities to his confessor and received the necessary absolution, so the bishop dismissed this understandingly. 'You have nothing with which to reproach yourself, my son. Everyone knows you were a dutiful husband to Dona Christina.'

'Nor did I defile her memory by marrying immediately. I went instead to France...'

He broke off, his dark brows pulled together fiercely. 'It was a grave error. How often have I begged forgiveness from Him? I have given hundreds of gold marks for the repose of de Preuthune's soul.'

He spun back towards the bishop, his face flushed. 'Your Grace, you need not tell me it was a vain and foolish enterprise. I have vowed never to enter the lists of a tournament again. Never!' He crossed himself. 'But all that was not enough atonement. I sensed it! In my soul, I sensed I must do more.' He held his clenched fists to his breast. 'Blinded by my grief and remorse as I was, I could not think clearly. I saw the boundless grief of his parents and I thought that by marrying his sister I could help the family. I took her without dowry to compensate her grieving parents for their loss.'

The bishop again raised his eyebrows. 'You cannot still grief with gold, my son.'

Dom Pedro let out a moan and sank his face in his hands. 'Now I see that! Now! But you do not know the worst of it!' He tore at his hair and the bishop felt a tremor of aversion. Now he is overdoing it, the bishop thought coolly.

As if Dom Pedro sensed that his dramatic gestures had not been well received, he lifted his head and ran his left hand over his hair and then his clipped beard, smoothing it down unnecessarily. 'You have to understand the situation, Your Grace.' he said in a soft, tense voice, 'otherwise you cannot judge what I have done and advise me how I can best be restored to His favour.'

'Then tell me the worst, my son.'

'When I… I offered to marry the Preuthune girl, she was already promised to the Church.'

The bishop raised his eyebrows yet again, this time higher than ever. 'You mean her parents intended her for the Church?'

Dom Pedro swallowed and ran his hand through his hair. 'No, she... She was already a novice.'

'A novice?'

'A Benedictine novice.'

'Did you know this?' the bishop asked with hard, condemning eyes. It did not escape his notice that Dom Pedro kept his own eyes averted. His hand stroked his beard with increasing nervousness.

'I... I did not know it when I first proposed marrying the girl to Madame de Preuthune. Madame de Preuthune mentioned something about the Church, but she also said it would be no problem. It was only later that I learned that the girl had taken initial vows...'

The bishop did not believe one word of this. Dom Pedro had been perfectly aware of the facts from the start but he had wanted the girl. He must have wanted her very badly not to insist on any kind of dowry – no matter how great his remorse for killing her brother. No doubt his 'generous' offer to renounce any kind of dowry was the trick he used to overcome her parents scruples about breaking their contract with the Benedictines. The bishop sighed.

'Don't you see?' Dom Pedro asked, licking his lips. 'It is because I took her away from the Church that God is angry with me. He is punishing me for stealing His own bride. She will never bear me healthy children, will never give me the heir I need – because she is *His* bride!'

The bishop cleared his throat and squirmed in his chair. A bride of Christ was chaste and pure, whereas Dom Pedro's wife had had two miscarriages already. 'She was *intended* to be Christ's bride,' he corrected Dom Pedro reprovingly, as he started tapping his fingertips together. It was a silent and yet tense gesture, and the muscles around Dom Pedro's eyes and lips had tightened. 'You have sinned gravely, my son.'

Dom Pedro crossed himself and bowed his head in humble acknowledgement.

'And I must say I do not find the punishment you suffer disproportionate. What you did was little better than what the Moors do to captured nuns! You raped Christ's pure and virgin *intended* bride – stole her from Him for ever by defiling her, destroying her purity, corrupting her flesh!'

Dom Pedro swallowed and the palms of his icy hands sweated. He knew that the bishop was right. Félicia was indeed corrupted now. Only recently she had come to him, tried to seduce him, tried to arouse his body only for the sake of satisfying her own. Her shamelessness had appalled and repulsed him. It was the man's part to feel and awake desire. Félicia was corrupt – as corrupt now as a common whore. He despised her and could not stomach the thought of ever sleeping with her again. He dreamt only of sweet Lilita, whom he had met at court this autumn where she acted as maid-in-waiting to the queen. Lilita came of a good Portuguese noble family and she would settle down to being a plump and happy mother concerned only for her children. He could picture her with a dozen plump and happy children around her. She would remain innocent to the end of her days!

'What do you expect me to do, my son?' The bishop brought Dom Pedro out of his thoughts.

'Help me! Advise me, Father!' Dom Pedro went down on his knees before the bishop and held up his folded hands. 'There must be some way of... of freeing both myself and His abducted bride from the hell that binds us together against His will.'

'Some way of dissolving your marriage, you mean.' The bishop wanted to make the request explicit. It was hardly unusual for a nobleman to seek him out in order to dispose of an unwanted wife.

'Yes. Is the marriage even valid, since she had taken initial vows?' Dom Pedro said hopefully.

'Canon law is not entirely clear on that point,' the bishop decided conveniently. Now he pushed himself out of his chair and walked past the kneeling Dom Pedro to the window. He unlatched and flung open the shutter to gaze down on the fog crouching in the river valley.

The Bishop of Porto knew that he would encourage Dom Pedro to petition the pope for an annulment of his marriage. He knew that he would support the petition. But he was not entirely comfortable with the idea. It disturbed him that even a devout and decent nobleman like Dom Pedro could be so overcome with passion for a girl that he would ignore her vows of chastity. It was surely the devil that made women so alluring. Always and again it was women who led men into perdition.

But with a sigh the bishop acknowledged that he could not undo what had been done. The girl had been violated now. The best he could do was to make sure the Church was richly compensated for the loss it had suffered. Dom Pedro would pay a bride-price that even he would feel.

The bishop turned back and faced the nervous Dom Pedro. 'What you did was a grave sin,' he repeated. 'Nor can it be made good merely by discarding your wife.'

'But *is* she my wife, if she was already promised to the Church? A betrothal makes a subsequent marriage to someone other than the betrothed invalid. Surely the same goes for a novitiate? A novice is Christ's betrothed.'

'Yes. That is indeed an argument. You… We will have to put it like that in our petition to His Holiness. But do not think that the matter is as easy as that. You knowingly entered this unholy union with Christ's betrothed, as you put it. *You*, Dom Pedro de Meneses, must do penance for the affront and insult to the injured bridegroom – Our Lord!'

'Anything,' Dom Pedro assured him fervently, crossing himself.

'What if I said you yourself must take monastic vows?' the bishop said sharply, testing him.

Dom Pedro started. 'But I am sole heir to the de Meneses estate!'

'All the more reason. You can bequeath all your estates to the Church.'

Dom Pedro's face hardened and he rose from his knees. He would rather sleep with that whore Félicia until she bore him a living child or died trying. If she died, he would be free to marry again; one way or another, he would get an heir.

The bishop smiled cynically. He could as good as read Dom Pedro's thoughts. 'If you are not willing to consider such a solution, then you must be prepared to make other sacrifices.' The bishop continued before Dom Pedro could storm out in anger, 'First – and assuming you have persuaded His Holiness of your case – you must return your wife to her rightful bridegroom. You must see that she enters the convent of Santa Clara at Vila do Condé and that she is endowed at double the normal rate as compensation for the damage you have done her.'

Dom Pedro nodded fervently. 'I swear!' He crossed himself.

'That is not all, my son!' The bishop warned. 'You must promise that your first-born daughter will be given to the Church and that she will be endowed with fertile and extensive lands which will enrich Mother Church for ever – for the virgin you stole from Christ is eternally lost to Him.'

Dom Pedro hesitated slightly. 'I swear – in as much as I have other heirs.'

The bishop accepted his reservation with an annoyed flick of his hand. 'Last, but not least, you must contribute one thousand gold marks to the papal treasury in gratitude for his mercy in freeing you of the sinful union you entered knowingly and of your own free will.' Dom Pedro tightened his lips in anger but nodded. 'Yes. I will enclose a draft for the sum on an Italian banking house with the petition. When do you think I will have an answer from His Holiness?'

The bishop measured the degree of Dom Pedro's impatience and admitted, 'one of my personal couriers will be leaving by sea on the Feast of Saint Nicholas with Christmas greetings for His Holiness. If your petition is complete by then, it could be delivered the same time as the Christmas message—'

'You will have my petition today, this afternoon – at the latest by tomorrow morning—'

'My son, do you think that you have the necessary familiarity with canon law to argue your case before His Holiness? You cannot plead with him in the same unschooled and vulgar language you have used here with me!'

Dom Pedro stood as if dumbstruck. He was so close to his goal that he was baffled by the slightest obstacle.

'I have in my household a young deacon of exceptional eloquence who possesses a profound knowledge of canon law. I am willing to put his services at your disposal in return for suitable compensation for taking him away from his official duties.'

Dom Pedro gritted his teeth. He knew perfectly well that the bishop was milking him for all he was worth. He would have to pay and pay again to get out of his over-hasty and barren marriage, but he had no choice. He would pay what the Church wanted of him, the sooner the better. Lilita would not wait for ever. He could not wait a day longer than necessary.

'But of course. When can I meet your deacon?'

'I will send for him at once.' The bishop smiled graciously and reached for a silver bell.

Chapter Eighteen

Vila do Condé, Portugal, February 1310

The storm was past but angry waves still swept in from the Atlantic to fling themselves upon the sandy beach with a thump and a snarl. All through the night and the following day, the pounding of the swell and the hiss of the breakers could be heard like the beat of an ominous drum beneath the cawing of the seagulls.

Carlos shook his grey head as he drew the net on to his knees and set about repairing it. His fingers were completely distorted by arthritis, bending in curious ways like old tree roots, but they responded deftly and knowingly.

'Those are dead fishermen's souls,' Carlos declared with a nod towards the open door of his cottage and the cawing gulls he could see hovering on the wind. 'A ship has foundered for sure.'

'Certainly,' his wife retorted tartly, 'somewhere on all the seas a ship will have foundered.'

She was a large-boned, tall woman, with the kind of lean, tough strength common to poor women who have survived into their fifties. She was brown and weathered, with skin that sagged on her fleshless bones. Her nose was prominent, her eyes sunken and her hair was a coarse, unkempt mixture of black and grey. Pounding at the churn between her knees as if she had a personal grudge against the butter, she dismissed her husband's morbid musings as nonsense.

'No, somewhere close by. I can smell it,' her husband insisted, undeterred by her scorn.

With an angry clatter, Theresa left her churn and went to gaze out of the door into the gathering dusk. She stood with her hands pressed to the small of her aching back and surveyed the long beach and the heaving seas, rapidly darkening now that the sun had set. The wind was cold. She hated it when her husband started making morbid predictions. Too often he had been right.

She made out the figure of a woman dressed in black moving along the beach from the north. The wind tore at her gown and cloak and buffeted her violently. Theresa watched with narrow, fascinated eyes. This was the fifth night in a row that she had seen the woman. She came at dusk and walked the whole length of the beach and then went back to the convent of Santa Clara, which was just visible by the light glowing from a dozen narrow, arched windows.

As on the nights before, the woman walked along the border between sea and land, treading on sand wet from the tide, sometimes scurrying back from the edge to keep from getting wet feet. Sometimes she was not fast enough and the last exhausted sheets of water swept right past her, leaving her with drenched feet and hems. Theresa watched her tonight with the same bored fascination as before.

The stupid woman from the convent was moving deeper into the water, her skirts swirling about her on the breakers. She must be a rich woman not to care what damage the salt water would do to her gowns and cloak. And a fool not to care that she would catch her death of cold in this weather!

Or was she looking for crabs swept in by the waves? She was bending over as if looking for something. Maybe she had dropped something. What did that stupid woman think she was doing now? She looked as if she were up to her hips in water walking straight out from the beach. Didn't she realise there was a sharp shelf below the water? The beach fell off abruptly just—

With a cry Theresa started running. She saw the wave gather itself for the kill, then crash down over the woman as she was swept out to sea on the undertow of the wave before. She was lost from sight in the sandy froth of the breaker as it charged up the beach, and then Theresa saw the dark bundle struggling in the white foam. Before the bundle of sand-and-water-laden wool could right itself, the still powerful breaker was rushing back out to sea. The struggling figure in the foam, dragged down by the weight of cloak and gown, was swept along by the ebbing wave. And already the next breaker was preparing its assault.

Carlos had caught up with Theresa and together they plunged into the ocean, Theresa with her skirts hitched up into her girdle so that her legs were bare from the knee down. The pair could not swim but they knew the beach and the nature of waves. They braced themselves against the undertow and plunged confidently into the incoming waves, grasping for any piece of wool or limb of the sodden victim they could reach. Theresa's hands closed first around a corner of cloak and she held fast to it while Carlos went deeper into the water. The next wave broke roughly over them and Theresa almost lost her footing, but she clung to the woman's cloak until Carlos grabbed hold of an arm and began pulling her upwards, trying to get her head out of the water. Theresa got hold of the second arm. With the half-drowned woman coughing and choking between them, the old couple struggled back up the beach.

They collapsed together on the dry sand, drenched and gasping for air. The woman was sputtering and coughing violently, her face purple. Carlos turned her on to her stomach and pressed her shoulders down into the sand to force the water out of her lungs. Her coughing turned into sobs.

*

They had taken her to the abbess's parlour, one of the few rooms in the entire convent with a fire. There they had stripped off her soaked clothes and wrapped her in warm blankets. A lay-sister brought her a pewter mug filled with steaming, spiced wine, which she clutched in both hands. Her teeth chattered and her whole body was convulsed with periodic shudders.

The abbess, Mother Beatriz, considered her charge from the doorway with a mixture of pity and exasperation. Her hair was a mess of matted, sandy tangles, sand still stuck to her face though they had brushed away the worst of it, and the one foot which emerged from the blankets was coated with it.

Mother Beatriz had been abbess at Santa Clara for almost fifteen years and this was the first time she had had to deal with a case like this. She sighed and took a seat opposite her shivering charge. The girl did not look up but continued to stare into the mug she clutched but did not sip.

'Come now!' the abbess urged somewhat impatiently. 'Drink up and you'll get warm sooner.'

Félice obediently lifted the mug to her lips and took a careful sip of hot wine. It was soothing to her raw mouth and throat. She took another sip without lowering the mug from her face. She wished they would leave her alone.

'That's better, isn't it?'

Félice nodded dutifully.

'A very close call, my dear. You owe your life to Carlos and Theresa. You must go down and thank them in the morning.'

Félice nodded again.

'You can take something from the kitchens as a gift as well.' Félice nodded.

The abbess sighed. 'We have to talk, my dear. Theresa says you walked straight into the sea.' She paused as if expecting a denial but none came. 'My dear,' she started in a sharper tone, 'it is a mortal sin to take your own life! You risked your eternal soul if you set out to kill yourself.' Still there was no response. 'I am responsible for you and I insist on an answer: did you intend to kill yourself?'

Félice looked up at her and stared. She did not know the answer to that question herself. She supposed she had meant to kill herself but then again she had been terrified when the wave knocked her down. She had panicked when, every time she opened her mouth for air, water had poured in instead. Water had flooded into her mouth, her eyes, her ears, her nose. She had felt herself being churned about in the waves and she had screamed for help from the very depths of her soul – even if she had been incapable of uttering a sound.

'I did not know the currents were so strong,' She said at last. It was not a lie.

'You can't have intended to go swimming at this time of year!' The abbess did not like the evasion to her direct question.

'I... My feet got wet by accident. And once they were wet, the shock of the cold wore off. I went in deeper...'

Had she wanted to die at that point or had she wanted to tempt fate or she had simply been hypnotised by the waves?

'I am aware that you have had a difficult time. The loss of two unborn infants...'

Félice narrowed her eyes, wondering if the abbess really thought that was the worst of it. Didn't she realise that it was the rejection which hurt more? Félice did not mourn her babies. She associated with them nothing but pain.

They had only been important to her as a means of retaining or regaining Dom Pedro's affection. A merciful God would have let her die with her unborn children rather than subjecting her to this: being discarded by her husband at the age of eighteen.

The abbess got to her feet and went over to the fire. She had been delighted by the news that Dom Pedro de Meneses was sending his cast-off wife to her poor convent. The dowry he had provided was more than the rents the convent lands yielded in a year. She would be able to repair the tithe barn roof and there would still be money for new bedding in the novices' dormitory, and for the silver salter she had wanted for so long… She sighed. She could spend the dowry ten times over in this impoverished, neglected abbey, but what was she supposed to do with such an unwilling sister?

The scandal had been disruptive enough. She had noticed the way the nuns gossiped together, casting excited, curious glances at the newcomer. Amidst her predominately virgin charges, the aura of a discarded wife had been intoxicating, even perversely alluring. She had heard the excited speculation about *why* Félice had been rejected. And now the girl had tried to kill herself! It would be all over the convent by now and the clacking tongues would drown out the chants of vespers!

If Félice had been a nun, she would have disciplined her. She could have confined her to her cell on bread and water for a week at least. But so long as she had not taken vows, Mother Beatriz hesitated to be too harsh for fear she would frighten away the goose that had laid the golden egg.

She took a deep breath and collected all her patience, then turned back to face the half-drowned troublemaker. 'My dear child, it is time you stopped mourning the past and faced the future.'

Félice looked at her with wide, golden eyes. The future was more horrible than the past: it was a great, gaping tunnel running inexorably towards death – cold, empty of joy or pleasure and echoing with loneliness. Félice too had seen the eager, scandalised glances and heard the whispering behind her back whenever she passed. She too had felt the scorn and distaste of the devout sisters and the voyeurism of the less sincere nuns.

'Dom Pedro sent you to our care out of love for you, so that you could be reconciled with God by fulfilling the vows you once made to Him. You promised to become his bride. It is time you kept that promise.'

Félice shrugged. She did not have any choice. She heard Sir Percy's voice begging her not to take vows she didn't mean to a Church that could slaughter its own children and tears blurred her eyes. It was like a memory of another lifetime.

'I do not approve of your attitude, my dear!' Mother Beatriz reproved her. 'It is nearly blasphemy to be so indifferent to Our Lord!'

Félice supposed she was right, but she could not help herself. She cared about nothing any more.

The door crashed open, making Félice jump and Mother Beatriz look over with an angry scowl. A nun fell breathlessly into the parlour.

'Knights and men-at-arms – at least a dozen of them – have just ridden into the courtyard, Reverend Mother!'

'What do they want? If they are seeking accommodation, send them on to—'

'A knight – a foreigner – he demanded an interview with you, Reverend Mother.'

The flustered nun had left the door open behind her, and at this point an armoured knight ducked under the low doorframe and swept past the stunned nun towards Mother Beatriz. The abbess had never experienced such effrontery and it left her no less stunned than Sister Bona gaping by the doorway.

'Forgive me for intruding, madame.' The knight spoke in a fluent, cultivated French, and his voice – in Félice's confused mind – was like Percy's. Knowing this could not be, she glanced up. The knight was advancing into the room and his jerky stride made Félice gasp. No one else in the world walked like that. She wanted to rise up but remembered her nakedness and then Dom Pedro's revulsion at the sight of her. What if Percy looked at her in the same way? She sank back into the chair, pulling her legs up under her and the blankets tighter. She dropped her head to hide her face behind the curtain of her matted, sand-filled hair.

Félice's gasp brought Mother Beatriz out of her shock. 'How dare you enter here uninvited, sir! If you have so little respect for a house of God, you might at least show chivalry towards a noblewoman! This young lady nearly drowned this evening...'

Percy wasn't listening. He too had heard the gasp and he had seen Félice. He crossed over to her before Mother Beatriz could intervene, though she let out a cry of outrage and a flood of shouted abuse. Percy went down on the balls of his feet before the chair in which Félice cowered.

'In the name of God, what have they done to you, Felicitas?' The question was asked so quietly that Mother Beatriz could not even hear it over her own raging.

Félice kept her head down and her eyes shut. She was terrified of Sir Percy's eyes, eyes that could pierce to her very soul. She could hide nothing from him. He would see it all the moment she looked at him. The last time their eyes had met she had been a virgin bride who had just taken her vows to Dom Pedro. Now she was soiled and discarded. The sob that had been pent up inside ever since she had recognised him now escaped her chest, shaking her despised body as if she had been struck.

Percy reached out and gently brushed away her wet, sandy hair, to touch the back of his fingers to her cheek. He could not believe what he saw – the black circles under her eyes, the chapped lips, the dried, splotchy red skin under a fine layer of sand.

'How dare you!' Mother Beatriz had managed to cross the distance between them at last and she snatched his hand away from Félice as if he had been doing her violence. 'Get out of here! Leave the poor child alone!'

The looming, fuming presence of Mother Beatriz and her words, combined with the abrupt removal of his hand made Félice look up sharply, afraid that Percy would leave. She had assumed that he had already backed away and she let out a cry when she found that he was still directly before her, his eyes boring into her, past her outer shell, seeking her soul. But now she could not look away. She stared back, her heart quailing at first, tears trembling in her eyes on the brink of spilling over. And then she began to realise that Percy was not looking at her with anger, contempt or revulsion. He was not even looking at her with pity. His eyes were as soothing and calming as her grandmother's caresses. He didn't hate her. Not even now. She started to breathe more easily and the tears remained unshed.

Mother Beatriz's ranting started to penetrate to her senses. 'I will have you removed by force! You will answer for this!'

Percy abruptly stood. 'That won't be necessary. No force on earth could keep me here. We will leave the moment Lady Félice is dressed and her things packed.'

'Dona Felicia is promised to this convent and is due to take her final vows tomorrow,' Mother Beatriz informed him shrilly. No strange knight was going to steal her prize now – if she had to make the stupid girl take her final vows by beating her black and blue.

'Who promised her? That scorpion who ravaged her innocence and then abandoned her like human refuse?'

The fury in his voice made Félice start. She gazed up at him in wonder. She had not thought her fate could arouse so much passion in him. Percy had always been so silent, so restrained, so... self-contained. And besides, his accusation wasn't fair. Dom Pedro had never ravaged her – she had enjoyed his caresses, craved them with time. Hadn't Percy realised that when he looked into her soul?

'Yes, Dom Pedro made the arrangements out of—'

'Dom Pedro has no right to decide anything for Lady Félice. His marriage to her was annulled at his own request. She is therefore still a Preuthune and it is that family which decides what is to become of her. Sir Geoffrey de Preuthune wants her to come home – unless it is her express wish to stay here.' Percy looked back down at her, questioning and pleading.

Félice shook her head wordlessly. If her grandfather would have her, then she wanted to go home to him. Merciful God, how she wanted to go home to him! Some echo of hope and some reflection of joy flickered across her face and Percy understood instantly.

'I still don't know who you are, sir, nor if you have any right to speak for Dona Félice's family. In Portugal—'

'Madame! I come straight from King Dinis. King Dinis gave his express blessings for my mission to take Lady Félice home to her grandfather as quickly as possible. If you doubt my word, you can ask the royal sergeant in the courtyard.'

Mother Beatriz was beginning to realise she had been completely outmanoeuvred. Among the rumours circulating about this strange girl was that King Dinis had taken a fancy to her. Some gossips even claimed that her second baby had been sired by the king. This, they claimed, was the real reason Dom Pedro had rid himself of her. If the king wanted her back in France, there was little the abbess of an impoverished convent could do. But the dowry came from Dom Pedro so need not be sent with the girl to her parents. She could spend the dowry money as quickly as possible, before Dom Pedro learned what had happened and came to claim it back. He could not have what had already been converted into roofing and bedding. This thought reconciled the abbess to the thought of letting Félice leave; she had proven a troublesome charge in any case.

'If that is His Grace's will…' Mother Beatriz tried to make the best of it. 'Dona Felicia will be ready in an hour – if you would have the decency to remove yourself so she may be washed and dressed.'

Percy hesitated a fraction of a second, half-afraid that if he left Félice alone the abbess would spirit her away or hide her somewhere. He did not trust the church and he was afraid for Félice. They had reduced her to a frightened, spiritless wreck and clearly she could not defend herself against them.

'Madame, I will wait in the courtyard with my men. If the Lady Félice is not delivered to me by compline, I will be back – and I will bring my men with me.'

*

In the courtyard of Santa Clara, Percy waited fractiously. His men had all dismounted and several of them looked longingly towards the refectory windows, spilling light, the sound of cutlery in use and the good smell of braised fish into the courtyard. The sergeants, three Englishmen, four Frenchmen and a Portuguese, waited together, talking in low tones about odd topics. They did not know why Sir

Percy was here at a convent or what they were waiting for, but it did not really matter. Sir Percy was their commander, Templar Marshal of Aquitaine, and whatever he did was right in their eyes.

The three knights, Sir Martin, Sir Hugh and Sir Gilbert, waited with Percy, sometimes exchanging looks as they watched his nervous pacing, but not trying to break into his thoughts or make him speak. They had been with him long enough now to know that Percy always kept his own counsel.

Only Gaston, Percy's 'squire', tagged along behind his lord like a loyal hound, anxiously trying to please him. 'Shall I get you something to eat from the kitchen, sir?'

Percy shook his head and continued to the gate to look out. 'I could get you wine, at least. On a night like this—'

Percy shook his head. 'I'm fine.'

'Should I water, Renaissance?'

'Yes – go see to Renaissance.'

Gaston ran off and Percy sighed with relief. What if they didn't send her out? It was nothing but bravado to claim that he would barge into a convent with his troops. King Dinis had sanctioned his decision to take Félice home but that hardly implied he would also approve of his turning a convent upside down searching for her.

Christ, but the wind was cold. He would have to get her to an inn or another priory for the night. He could not expect her – not in the condition she was in – to sleep in the open as he and his men often did. It was pitch-dark and the wind was still stiff, even if the worst of the storm had blown over. He could hear the surf breaking on the shore. What was it the abbess had said? Félice had nearly drowned? What had she been doing in the water on a cold day like this?

Percy's heart missed a beat as he realised that she must have tried to kill herself. Felicitas! His bright-eyed, quick-witted, vivacious Felicitas had tried to kill herself at the age of eighteen! Christ! he thought, his hand closing around the iron ring of the open gate to maintain his balance: she must have loved her former husband. For eighteen months he had ignored that possibility. He had managed to lock away his memories of her as if she were a sacred relic – perfect and immutable. The memories were something he took out to fondle secretly, but he had never dared think about what she might be feeling and doing in her new life. He had never imagined that she might have fallen in love with her husband.

Percy had come to Iberia to consult the Portuguese preceptors and to raise more funds and volunteers for their activities in France.

Geoffrey had asked him to check on Félice because it had been so long since he had heard from her. He was worried about her. Percy had concluded his business at Tomar first and then gone on to Lisbon to see the king. In parting, he had mentioned that his next goal was a visit to the de Meneses to deliver greetings to Félice from her grandfather. King Dinis had at once informed him of developments, though he himself knew only the barest details: that Félice had miscarried twice in a year; that Dom Pedro had had the marriage annulled to marry a girl barely out of puberty; that he had sent Félice to the Convent of Santa Clara.

Percy had set off for Vila do Condé at once. He too remembered that conversation with Félice in the orchard at Lys-Saint-Georges. He did not want Félice to take vows she didn't mean just because she thought she had no alternative. He knew without asking that Geoffrey would want her to come home. Now that he had seen her, he knew she mustn't stay a moment longer in this place, but he was on his way to Paris not Chanac. And they were under time pressure.

The trial of the Templars was scheduled to begin on 28th March. At that time all the Templars who, despite the threat of being burned at the stake had volunteered to defend the Temple, were to be assembled in Paris. Since it was impossible to conduct a trial with nearly seven hundred defenders, the papal Commission would insist on the defenders electing spokesmen. But, as Geoffrey had managed to learn from certain circles that sympathised with the Templars, the King of France had made certain that not a single senior officer of the Temple would be at the Trial.

King Philip's strategy was to have the Bishops of Narbonne and Albi propose certain candidates as spokesmen to the disorganised assembly of bewildered Templars and induce them to elect as their legal representatives precisely those individuals who were prepared to betray the Temple.

Percy did not judge the traitors. He told himself that they were no worse than he, only unluckier. But Geoffrey and he were determined to thwart the king's neat plans. They planned to spread the word among the imprisoned Templars of the king's intentions and, furthermore, propose alternative candidates. To this purpose, Geoffrey had sent Percy to Portugal to consult the senior officers of the Temple there since the Order had already been found innocent of the charges trumped up by the French king and the Portuguese commanders could act freely.

The result of his discussions had been the selection of two candidates of not only unimpeachable integrity but extensive legal training and recognised rhetorical ability. The Portuguese Templars, who had studied in Paris with one of the priests in question and knew the other by his brilliant tracts, were convinced that if the papal commission were prepared to give the Templars a fair trial, then these were the men best suited to present the legal defence.

The Free Templars now had to get word to the Templars who had volunteered to defend their Order that these two priests – not the candidates who would be put forward by the Bishops of Albi and Narbonne – were the men they could trust to represent them. It meant not only crossing the distance from Porto to Paris in four weeks, but getting access to the Defenders of the Temple in their various dungeons and passing the vital information to them without drawing attention to themselves, arousing suspicion or being detained. Only now did Percy perceive that seeing Félice home to her grandfather was a task that interfered with his larger mission.

Not that he could leave her here, of course. He turned and cast his eye across the austere façade of the stern convent. Where was she? He would have to accompany her at least as far as Bordeaux. She was a capable horsewoman and he would buy her a good mare. The days when he and Geoffrey were short of funds had long since passed. Not only had Master de la More provided him with ample funds and volunteers, but the Portuguese Templars and King Dinis himself had been generous in their contributions.

Nor had Percy the slightest scruple about diverting some of the funds entrusted to him for his activities in defence of the Temple towards Félice. Hadn't she given him the cloak off her back as he lay in the ditch? It had been her dowry and inheritance which Geoffrey had pawned to pay Percy's passage to England. The debt he owed her would never be fully paid.

But could he expect her to travel at the pace they must keep in her present condition? And without so much as a serving maid in attendance? A woman alone in the company of men – so many men at that – would be taken for a doxy and would be exposed to rude advances and contemptuous treatment wherever they went. How could he subject her to such abuse? Yet what choice did he have?

He looked over his shoulder anxiously yet again, and ran a hand through his wind-blown, wiry hair. What in the name of God was keeping her? Were they perhaps trying to persuade her not to come or using force to restrain her?

Gaston had finished with Renaissance and started back towards Percy. Sir Martin caught Gaston by the arm as he ran by. 'Leave him alone, boy, before he loses his temper.'

Gaston looked from Sir Martin to Sir Percy, who was now gazing out to sea with his hands hooked in his sword belt. Sir Percy very rarely lost his temper but when he did it was terrible. 'But—' Gaston started.

Sir Martin shook his head. 'Leave it.'

Gaston stood indecisively for a minute and then returned to the horses. Renaissance stretched out his head, hoping for more delicacies from the hand that often brought him carrots, apples or even sugar lumps. Gaston's hands were empty now so he stroked Renaissance's soft muzzle instead.

Gaston's freedom from the Dominicans had been purchased by the Free Templars only six months earlier. After he had confessed to all the charges against the Temple one after another, the inquisitor had sent him to a Dominican priory where, dressed in the robes of a confessed heretic, he had been 'allowed' to perform the most menial and despicable of tasks, those which the other lay brothers did only with loathing – cleaning the latrines, washing the feet of the beggars who came to the kitchens, emptying the rat- and mousetraps.

Unlike the Templars, the Dominicans had no rule against corporal punishment of menials. Gaston had been frequently subjected to kicks and blows, usually accompanied by sermons on the vileness of his soul. He was a former heretic, worshipper of an idol he had invented in his own agony, a catamite... But the monks who had fucked him in the ass were judges of the Holy Inquisition!

Gaston spat in revulsion and hatred and forced his mind on to other things, looking over his shoulder to the comforting figure of Sir Percy, standing in the arch of the gatehouse. He had recognised Sir Percy instantly. Percy had been the first – and last – Knight Templar he had ever seen before his arrest and that left a lasting impression. He had recognised him even though Percy no longer wore the Templar's white surcoat, tonsure or beard. Sir Percy had arrived at the Dominican priory like any travelling nobleman, demanding accommodation. Percy had caught sight of Gaston gaping and he had asked his host casually, 'What sort of heretic is that, and what is he doing in a Dominican priory?'

They had not been loath to tell him, and Sir Percy had strolled over as if to look at a curiosity in a circus. As he looked directly at a bewildered Gaston, he had mouthed the words, '*Baucent à la recourse.*' Gaston had felt his heart start to pound in irrational hope. Then Percy had turned his back and walked away, but that same night Brother Marius had hauled him from his pallet with the words, 'Your pretty ass caught the fancy of a nobleman! Come on!'

'Pimp!' Gaston had hissed back furiously, knowing that Brother Marius charged a good fee for the services Gaston rendered. He had followed his elder this night, however, with more than the usual inner cramping and frustrated hate. On that night he had been seized with wild confusion, afraid that Percy meant only to use him as the others had, yet unable to suppress the hope his mouthed words had inspired.

Percy had not used him as he had feared. Instead he had provided him with civilian clothes and spirited him out of the priory guest house. Other Templars had been waiting for him in the woods and they had taken him back to the manor of Chanac, along with three other former Templar lay brothers who had also been held by the Dominicans.

Gaston later learned indirectly that there had been considerable controversy about his rescue. Some of the Templars had objected to his rescue because he had confessed without being tortured. Percy had pointed out that for that very reason he was a invaluable witness for the Inquisition and it would be better if he could not be produced. This argument had told, but it had not made those Templars who had been victims of torture feel kindly towards him. Gaston had been subjected to hostile isolation neither so brutal nor so degrading as the treatment the Dominicans had inflicted upon him, but it was all the more wounding because it was delivered by his own brothers.

That had not changed until Percy himself returned to Chanac. Almost at once Percy had grasped the situation and taken Gaston under his own wing, allowing him the duties of squire. And no one, Gaston noticed, questioned Sir Percy except – very occasionally – Lord Geoffrey himself.

Now, the door to the abbess's house opened and a cloaked figure emerged. The door that had briefly spilled light into the courtyard shut again, leaving them all more blinded than before. Percy moved from the gateway with long, jerky strides.

Félice stood in the doorway, sightless in the darkness. The nuns had dressed her in the gown she had worn on the day of her arrival, just over a week ago and stuffed her remaining clothes into a leather sack with a drawstring. Her own cloak had been ruined by the sea and they had given her a lay sister's hooded cloak which still stank of the kitchen, its hem encrusted with manure. The night was cold and dark and she was frightened by the vague shapes of armed men and massive stallions moving restlessly in the dark. The clink of horseshoes on cobblestone, the faint, rapid chinking of chain mail, the deep, gruff murmur of men – it was all frightening. She had not expected this. Who were these men? Where was Percy?

Then abruptly he was towering over her. 'Thank God!' was all he murmured under his breath, and, taking her hand, he led her to the waiting horses.

Chapter Nineteen

Gascony, March 1310

They were still two hours short of Bordeaux when the thunderstorm overtook them. Though they were all used to riding in the rain, the gusting wind and the crashing thunder made the horses nervous, and the pack horses tried to break free. When the rain turned to hail, Percy gestured to a barn and they plunged off the road into the soggy ditch. The horses sank up to their hocks in mud and fought free in panicked lurches. They broke into the barn on the inertia of their chaotic charge, the wind at their backs sweeping in hail and straw and amputated branches with them. It took four men to get the doors closed and they had to barricade them shut with bales of hay. Then, with the sound of the storm howling around them and the hail clattering on the slate roof, they wiped the rain from their faces and took stock of their situation.

The barn was a towering stone structure with a hammerbeam roof and flagstone flooring. It was half-empty at this time of year, but hay, straw, firewood and sacks of oats, barley and wheat were stacked, seemingly randomly, in various bays. On the walls farm implements leaned or were hung on huge nails, and in one of the bays ploughs were parked along with a dismantled grindstone and a winepress in ill-repair.

Soaked through as they were, the lofty, draughty barn felt bitterly cold. The horses shook themselves, despite their burdens of saddle or baggage, and then moved towards the hay with outstretched necks. The men worked quickly to remove their burdens and then used the insides of their own cloaks to wipe them down before hobbling them and leaving them to feed on the hay.

'We can build a fire in that bay there.' Sir Percy indicated a nearly empty bay and, with a nod, four sergeants set about bringing firewood from the far end of the barn, while another brought straw as kindling. Others of his men removed the sacks of grain which lined one wall. Sir Gilbert returned from tending to the horses and reported that one of the pack horses appeared to have pulled a tendon. Percy nodded and then turned his attention to Félice. She stood somewhat forlornly in the centre of the great barn, clutching her cloak about her, her teeth chattering.

For two weeks they had followed the pilgrim routes leading to and from Santiago, staying at the hostels that lined these well-travelled roads. Félice had made no complaint about either the rate of travel or the quality of the accommodation. Without demur she had stayed in the saddle ten hours a day, riding in drizzling rain no less than in sunshine. She had shared their hasty roadside meals and drunk their watered wine with never a hint of dissatisfaction. Without protest she had wrapped herself in her cloak and lain on the straw in the common rooms of the pilgrim hostels. She had either failed to understand or had ignored the rude remarks and insinuations which had been made to her because she was alone in the company of so many men. The Templars had kept watch over her, discouraging – and twice preventing – strangers from trying to approach her while she slept.

Percy had been surprised and relieved to find that she was not only willing but able to travel so roughly. He was acutely aware that she had never in her life travelled in similar circumstances. Now, considering her while she stood shivering in the tithe barn as the thunder cracked overhead and the hail beat at the roof, he felt a stirring of uneasiness. Her indifference to her condition and the world around her was not healthy. Too late it dawned on him that maybe she thought she deserved no better.

'You must get out of that wet cloak, my lady. I'll find you something dry.'

He went to the baggage which had been spread out to drip-dry and untied the lashings holding the canvas cover over his personal belongings. He found and removed a thick, woollen blanket and brought it back to Félice. She had not moved from where he left her.

The other Templars had removed their wet cloaks and the smell of steaming wool rose with the pungent scent of smoke and the subdued murmur of male voices around the fire. Someone made a remark that made the others laugh. Several of the men followed Percy's example and got dry blankets or towels from their baggage. Someone else had thought to bring a wineskin and was passing it around. Félice was staring at them as if they were strangers or as if she were seeing them for the first time.

'I'm sorry, my lady.' Percy handed her his blanket.

She looked up at him and there was a look in her eye he could not interpret. She seemed to be studying him critically, as if he were not the same man whose head she had once held in her lap, helped to walk, and confided in at Lys-Saint-Georges. Of course, she wasn't the same girl any more. Dom Pedro had seen to that. She was no more the girl he had known than he was the proud Templar who set out for Cyprus in early October of 1307.

'My lady, whatever he did to you, you have to get over it.' She lifted her chin sharply and something flickered in her eyes, but whether it was anger, defiance or simply surprise, Percy wasn't sure.

'Maybe you remember, a long time ago, we discussed Sister Madeleine,' he started.

A frown played around her brows, but she did not take her eyes from his.

'Sister Madeleine was not always the woman she has become. You yourself heard her brother's stories about her girlhood and youth. We both know what happened to her. No matter how grateful she was to your uncle for rescuing her, do you think she found it easy to return to Christian Palestine?'

Félice shuddered and wiped away a drop of water trickling down the side of her face from her soaked veils.

'She had been a nun but when she was returned to a convent at Acre she did not feel comfortable there. How could she return to a life of piety and prayer among women who had never known any man, after being raped repeatedly by countless men for over a year? She chose a new path. One which you yourself said was much more meaningful.'

Gaston arrived with the wineskin. 'Here, sir. Shall I get you…' In his eagerness to please, he had rushed over without thinking. The look in Percy's eye made him quail and retreat with a hasty apology but it was too late.

Félice abruptly unlatched the clasp of her cloak and yanked it off as she started towards the fire. Her gown and surcoat were dark across the shoulders and half way down her bodice, where the rain had soaked right through the cloak, but she pulled Percy's blanket around her and sank down on the floor beside the fire, where the others made room for her.

Behind her, Percy sighed. The grumble of thunder came through the drumming of rain overhead and Percy looked up at the roof. The hail had given way to rain again by the sound of things. He moved towards the fire but, though they made room for him, he shook his head. 'I'll go up to the manor and inform whoever's in charge that we have taken refuge here. With luck, we'll be invited into the hall and can put up here for the night.'

'We're just two hours from Bordeaux,' Sir Martin pointed out. 'If it lets up in the next hour, we can still make it before dark. The governor's palace will offer us real beds and a bath.'

Percy glanced at Félice. He was uncertain how she would be received by the constable of Bordeaux and his haughty wife. Percy was a cousin of the Earl of Lincoln and Amerigo dei Frescobaldi was not foolish enough to think that he could afford to offend that powerful English baron, but his wife was the proud daughter of an Italian noble house and she thought herself above everyone in Bordeaux. To a woman like Lucia dei Frescobaldi, Félice's past and present were enough evidence that she was little better than a common whore. She would never believe that she had travelled for two weeks in the company of fourteen men and never once exchanged so much as a chaste kiss with any of them. He could hardly point out to Madame Frescobaldi that they were all monks because they were incognito, and it might have done no good if he could. The behaviour and reputation of too many monks only served to increase suspicions of the type Madame Frescobaldi would harbour about Félice.

'I'll go up and see what the manor is like,' Percy replied at length and started for the barricaded doors. Two of the sergeants at once jumped up to help him get out.

As the door banged shut again behind him, Félice turned to Sir Martin, who with his salt-and-pepper hair and weathered face was clearly a man in his late forties or early fifties. 'You are older than Sir Percy, sir. Why do you defer to him?'

'He is my commander, madame,' Sir Martin answered simply, startled to be addressed by Félice.

The young woman had been a singularly silent companion these past weeks. Except for those words necessary in the course of the journey, she had spoken to none of them. She had answered in the negative or positive to the questions they had been compelled to put to her and she had scrupulously thanked them when they shared their meal, helped her mount or tended to her horse in the evening. But before this moment, she had neither raised a question nor sought a conversation.

Félice seemed to consider this information.

'You know we are all Templars,' Sir Martin added, wondering suddenly if he had made a mistake. Sir Percy had said Félice was Lord Geoffrey's granddaughter and that she had actively assisted in his rescue. Sir Percy said she knew who he was but her question seemed to belie that.

'All of you?' she asked with a sudden jerk of her head, her gaze sweeping around the fire.

'Yes, madame. Your grandfather too.'

'Yes, he wrote to me that he had been privileged to receive admittance after so many years—'

'Admittance? Lord Geoffrey was appointed Preceptor of Aquitaine by the Seneschal of the Order.' Félice looked so amazed that Sir Martin felt compelled to explain. 'The seneschal is on Cyprus and, though he is not free to leave the island, your grandfather sent a messenger to him requesting instructions. He appointed your grandfather Preceptor of Aquitaine and ordered him to organise all the Templars in France not in the hands of the French king. Sir Percy is his marshal.'

Félice took some time assimilating this information. After a few minutes, she asked: 'And how many are you altogether?'

'We are now over one hundred knights, roughly three hundred and sixty sergeants and nearly one thousand lay brothers, including of course the many volunteers from the Empire, England and Iberia.'

'At Chanac?'

Sir Martin laughed. 'Of course not. We have a network of safe manors now. Some belong to relatives of Templar Knights, some are Hospitaller manors and there are sympathisers throughout the Languedoc. It sounds more impressive than it is, my lady. We are all fugitives – outlaws and excommunicates. If we are discovered, the best we can hope for is death. The lay brothers are dispersed throughout many humble manors and in towns as well; they all work for their protectors, many of whom are mere tradesmen. We knights and sergeants are divided into small units and try to maintain contact on the one hand with the Templars outside France and on the other with our imprisoned brothers. We do our best to bring those in custody medical assistance, extra food – especially fresh things – and convey messages from families and friends.

'Lord Geoffrey has also built up contacts in the papal and royal courts which keep him informed of developments regarding the Order as a whole. He has long worked towards seeing that the Order is brought to trial and he is now determined to see that the defence of the Temple proceeds before the papal commission. We are under no illusions concerning the chances of success – least of all Sir Percy.'

Sir Martin dropped his voice as he added, 'But Lord Geoffrey is determined to defend the Temple, as he puts it, "before God and Posterity" – even if our defence is futile in this world.'

Yes, Félice thought, that sounded like her grandfather, and unconsciously she smiled to herself. The smile did not escape Sir Martin's notice either. She would be pretty, he thought with surprise, if she were cleaned up, her skin treated and she smiled.

Félice's thoughts were racing now. 'But if there are one hundred knights now free, then surely many are more senior to both my grandfather and Sir Percy – as you must be yourself. Don't they resent being subordinate to a new knight on one hand and a young man on the other?'

'I cannot know the inner thoughts of all my brothers, madame. It may be that some knights resent them but I doubt it is very many. Without having known him, it seems to me that your grandfather has been a Templar at heart all his life. In any case, his efforts over the last two years are not open to question. Without him, there might be isolated free Templars but no Free Templars. We are all relieved to have at last a wise but dynamic man who is willing to take command and give us direction and hope.'

'And Sir Percy?'

Sir Martin shrugged. 'I could describe him as your grandfather's right hand. Your grandfather will turn eighty this month. His eyes are weakening and more than a couple hours in the saddle exhausts him. He could not have done what he has done without Sir Percy.'

'He must have many men willing and eager to serve him now,' Félice pointed out.

'Yes, of course, but only Sir Percy has his moral authority. Look around you.' He indicated the men collected around the fire. Most were sprawled in various poses of ease and were casually exchanging comments in a good-natured tone, content to be warming themselves while the storm raged.

'We can be divided into two categories,' Sir Martin explained whilst Félice looked carefully at each man. 'Sir Gilbert and Sergeants Rokely, Heydon, Tyler and Silva are all Templars from abroad. They have voluntarily joined our struggle against King Philip. They have never themselves been imprisoned or subjected to torture. The rest – myself, Sir Hugh, Sergeants Pétard, Belot, Tavernier and Roussel and Brother Gaston – all owe our freedom and possibly our lives to Sir Percy. Half of us, you see, are intimidated by the knowledge that they cannot be sure whether they would have withstood the treatment of the Inquisition and the other half are awed by Sir Percy's courage and competence *despite* his torments.

'You have to understand one thing: it is easier for men like Sir Gilbert to risk life and freedom in this struggle because men who have never faced the Inquisition are too naïve to imagine what it means to be chained in a dungeon for months on end. They' – Sir Martin had lowered his voice so that Félice had to lean towards him slightly and strain her ears – 'cannot imagine the pain that we others have endured. And we, who have been through the dungeons, we know that without Sir Percy's example we would never have risked facing it all again.'

'Because of him, it is much easier for us. We are members of an organised unit with officers and safe houses and a network of communication. There is safety in numbers; the herd instinct and our training as Templars take over. We have been drilled to obey orders and help one another.

'But when Sir Percy made the decision to help the prisoners at Chauvigny he had none of that – no orders, no comrades, no networks of well-wishers. When he freed me from the cell at Rodez he and Sir Geoffrey were still virtually alone, and when we freed Father André from the Carthusians we very nearly all came to grief in a single clash with a score of royal troops. Pathetic – or foolhardy – depending on how you look at it.' Sir Martin shook his head at the memory.

'And now?' Félice prompted. Her eyes had taken on an inner sparkle which Sir Martin did not believe had been there before. They seemed lighter now and her face was not so slack. She looked younger than she had before. He had presumed that she was in her mid-twenties but now she seemed as young as nineteen or twenty.

'Now, as I said, we are over one hundred—'

'Forgive me, I meant why must you be in Paris for the Feast of the Annunciation?'

'Ah, that has to do with the opening of the trial. The imprisoned Templars who have declared their desire to defend the Order will be brought before the papal commission and – because there are so many of them – they will be compelled to elect spokesmen. The risk is that without any guidance they will be swayed into letting the papal commission appoint spokesmen for them, and the Bishop of Narbonne and the Bishop of Albi have already identified a number of Templars who are prepared to betray the Order. We have to prevent their election. The bulk of the defenders, after all, are illiterate lay brothers and sergeants. Even the knights are for the most part men like myself, younger sons of provincial knights and lacking any kind of legal training.'

'Did you say the Bishop of Albi?' Félice asked, her lips parted as though slightly breathless.

'Yes – he is one of the king's most unscrupulous minions. He and Narbonne.'

Félice gazed into the fire. Next to her Sir Hugh ventured to offer her the wineskin.

She looked up to thank him and an automatic smile flitted over her features as she accepted. Hugh almost recoiled. She had never smiled at him before. He glanced past her to Sir Martin with an enquiry in his eyes. Sir Martin shook his head to indicate he could say nothing now.

Félice handed back the wineskin to Sir Hugh, seeing him for the first time. Judging by the lines carved in his face, he was a man in his mid to late thirties – but then torture aged a man. He was short and slight of build, with sharp, aristocratic features, thinning fine hair, and a long, drooping moustache. 'Sir Martin says you were freed by Sir Percy.'

'Yes, madame. It is almost a year ago now.' Then, because she continued to gaze at him with openly curious eyes, he explained not unwillingly, 'I had been separated from my brothers because I was so ill they feared... well, not *for* my life but for their own if I died. King Philip wanted us alive, you see. A Hospitaller tended my wounds, and he got word to Sir Percy of where I was being held. It was a former hermit's cell at the back of a chapel – though some say that before that it had been a hiding place for Cathar priests and the chapel was built later. In any case, it was carved out of rock with ostensibly only one entrance from the church. But there was a second entrance – which the local people knew about – through the caves. Sir Percy and two sergeants managed to crawl in, wrap me in a canvas sack and drag me back out through the caves.'

'Sir Percy saved me too,' Gaston announced in a tone that defied the others to contradict him.

The others did not seem inclined to contradict him; rather, they nodded agreement.

'Lord Geoffrey prefers the use of gold to force,' Sir Martin agreed solemnly.

But Sir Gilbert laughed. 'What Lord Geoffrey doesn't know won't hurt him!'

Sir Martin frowned in disapproval, and Félice glanced from one to the other and then at the others around the fire. Now she could identify the two camps perfectly and wondered that she had not noticed it before. For the Englishmen – and the Portuguese – this was an adventure, an important, meaningful adventure, but an adventure nevertheless. For the former prisoners of the Inquisition this was a dance with death. The Frenchmen were in many ways more courageous because they knew the risks they took, not just in their heads but in their bones and bowels. But the Englishmen clearly had the better nerves. Even now, at the sound of someone pounding on the door, the French started sharply while one of the English sergeants responded with natural calm, 'Sir Percy's back,' and went to let him in.

Percy stepped through the door and over the bales of hay. 'There was no one up at the manor but an old steward. He was reluctant to let us into the house. So I paid him for the damage we've done here and promised to move on.' Percy's eyes swept across his company and then settled on Félice. His brows drew together slightly and then his expression cleared. 'The storm has passed and there is clear sky on the western horizon. We could probably still make Bordeaux by dusk.'

The others were already getting to their feet with expressions of distaste or resignation.

'Is that agreeable, my lady?' Percy insisted on putting the question and was totally taken aback when she smiled up at him.

'Of course.'

*

Félice had last seen Bordeaux following her wedding. As they passed through the heavy grey gates to the city and entered the narrow cobbled streets, the memories returned. Indeed, the entire town seemed haunted by the pampered bride she had been. The contrast with her present self sent a shudder of shock and self-revulsion to the marrow of her bones. For the first time since she had left Vila do Condé two weeks earlier, Félice became conscious of the state she was in: drenched, bedraggled, mud-spattered and stinking. How could she sink this low?

At the governor's palace they were received cordially. The steward was sent down to greet de Lacy and see that he and his entourage were comfortably provided for. The presence of a lone woman was reported with disapproval, and Félice was shown to a dingy, none-too-clean room overlooking a dark back alley. The old man who escorted her there made some snickering crack about how many of her 'friends' she planned to receive tonight and then left her. The stink of a nearby garderobe dominated the chamber and a sudden scratching and darting in the darkened corners suggested that mice or rats were scurrying for cover.

Félice sank down on the sagging bed, with its dusty, threadbare covers, lacking sheets or comforters. She stared out through the narrow arched window at the last patch of semi-light sky. The room in the bishop's palace just beyond the square, where Dom Pedro had draped her with jewels and stripped her of clothes for his love making was vivid before her eyes, and suddenly it struck her as no less repulsive than this chamber.

What was the difference between the woman she had been then and an Arab harem slave? Dom Pedro had taught her sexual pleasure and smothered her in luxury, but her only function had been the breeding of sons – just like an Arab concubine.

The comparison made her think of Sister Madeleine. Nothing she had experienced in the last year and a half could compare with what Sister Madeleine had suffered. Félice had been a wife not a slave. She had been seduced not raped. She had been rejected not sold. When Madeleine had been restored to her Christian sisters, they must have whispered even more maliciously and cruelly than ever the nuns at Vila do Condé had. Félice squirmed uncomfortably, ashamed of her self-pity, but it also occurred to her for the first time that Sister Madeleine might have preferred the company of lepers – indeed, felt like one herself.

Félice considered the leper hospital at Lys-Saint-Georges in a new light. She conjured it up before her eyes and forced herself to remember the sight of the lepers themselves. Could she go there now without the inner revulsion she had felt before? Surely, she too had become a leper? Her fingers curled around the edge of the mattress as she concentrated. Maybe that was what Percy had been trying to say: she should be like Sister Madeleine and devote herself to the lepers to give her life meaning.

But it had been Percy who had once told her to be herself. He had urged her *not* to try and imitate Sister Madeleine.

But Percy had said that to a virgin novice, not the violated and discarded woman she was now.

And yet Percy *didn't* scorn her. She could sense that now as much as she had two weeks ago – and that despite the wreck she had become. She looked down at her mud-splattered skirts and smelt the sweat which had saturated the cloth under her arms and then the manure from the hemline. Her memory jarred and she remembered abruptly the state Percy had been in when she found him. Of course he did not despise her. He knew what it was like.

No, she corrected herself, swallowing with an ever greater sense of shame: he had known much worse. They had stripped him of all human identity and then forced him to betray himself. Nothing Dom Pedro had done to her could be compared to that. She took a deep breath. If Sister Madeleine and Sir Percy could rise up again from the gutter into which other people had thrust them, then so could she. The first thing to do was to get out of these travel-stained clothes, bathe and wash her hair, and then get into something presentable.

★

The following morning, Percy deposited most of the funds he had raised in Portugal with the banking house of Peruzzi, and then returned to the governor's palace. He had decided to have Sir Hugh and Gaston escort Félice to her grandfather while the rest of them continued on to Paris. He would give Félice ten louis for her own use during the journey and Sir Hugh another one hundred, to be turned over to Geoffrey.

In the courtyard of the palace, he found his men already loading the pack horses, while the tethered riding horses stamped impatiently and alertly considered the world. Félice was dressed in a blue velveteen gown with a russet surcoat and had apparently persuaded Madame Frescobaldi to give her a cast-off cloak which she was now wearing. As soon as she caught sight of him, she came over.

Percy drew up beside his knights and jumped down. He handed the reins over to an attentive Gaston. Félice's appearance at dinner the night before in a crumpled but beautiful silk gown had done more than startle the assembled company. It indicated to Percy that she had started to recover from the near fatal wound her husband had delivered when he rejected her. Percy smiled at her. It was the same, tight-lipped smile he had adopted since the extraction of three teeth by the Inquisition, but it was not laden with sadness any longer.

Félice licked her lips somewhat nervously as she announced, 'Percy, I hope you won't be angry. I've engaged a girl to wait on me.'

Percy tensed slightly and looked about to locate the girl she had hired, at once on the alert for possible betrayal.

'I know there is a risk to it,' Félice continued quickly, watching the way his eyes narrowed and his lips tightened, 'but she is young, frightened and very desperate. I think that mere kindness will win her loyalty very soon.'

Percy had located the girl in question. She was standing beside Félice's mare and looked hardly more than a waif – dirty, underfed, clutching a bundle of belongings in her trembling hands. Her big, frightened eyes met his and she dropped into a curtsey. Félice must have warned her that her employment depended on his assent. Percy turned back to Félice. 'Sir Hugh and Gaston will be escorting you to Chanac. Think what is at stake if she is not trustworthy and dismiss her before you reach Chanac if you have any doubts.'

'I want to come to Paris with you,' Félice answered steadily.

'No. We have business in Paris—'

'I know – the papal commission. Sir Martin told me.'

Percy looked sharply over at Sir Martin, who had moved up beside them.

'You said she knew about us. That she could be trusted,' Sir Martin explained himself.

'Of course,' Percy answered, 'but that is no reason to burden her with information which could endanger her.' He was angry, in his quiet, impenetrable way.

'Listen to me!' Félice drew his attention back to herself. 'When I insisted on rescuing you, *I* made the decision that I would rather die excommunicate than live damned. I am neither a child nor a chattel. I have a right to decide what to make of my life. That is what *you* urged me to do only yesterday. To make something meaningful of my life, as Sister Madeleine has done.' She spoke softly so they would not be overheard by the others but she spoke fervently. Once before her grandfather had tried to protect her by not telling her where he was taking Sir Percy. She had never fully forgiven him for it.

Percy swallowed and he was aware of a dangerous tightening in his chest. 'Yes,' he said with a calm he did not feel. 'Yes. You must make your own decisions. If you prefer to go to Sister Madeleine, then I can have Sir Hugh—'

'No. You were the one who told me not to imitate someone else. You told me to be myself. Do you think differently now?'

'No, of course not.'

'Than let me come with you to Paris.'

'What does that have to do with your future?'

'Everything. I can help you and Grandpapa.'

Percy caught himself just before he dismissed this with an angry rebuttal. How dare he deny that she could help them? She had done it when she found him, when she warned them of what Marie intended, and she had alerted them again when she brought word that the Inquisition was searching for his corpse. 'How?' The question came out somewhat gruffly because his throat had gone tight.

'Sir Martin told me that the Bishop of Albi is on the papal commission.'

Percy blinked. Albi was a name that still sent shock waves through his nervous system. 'Yes.'

'The Bishop of Albi was my confessor – when he was still Dean of Poitiers. I am certain I can request an audience with him and I am positive that he will receive me.'

Percy could feel Sir Martin watching him with burning, probing eyes. She must have told Sir Martin what she wanted to do. 'And then?' he asked, swallowing to wet his dry throat.

'The Templar defenders from Albi are in his custody,' Sir Martin answered for her. 'They will be held in the dungeons of his Paris residence.'

Percy looked at the older man and then at Sir Gilbert, who had come up behind him. The Englishman wore the alert look of a hunting dog that thought it had caught a whiff of game.

'You can escort me to the episcopal palace for my audience and then withdraw while I seek the advice of my former confessor alone,' Félice told him.

Percy did not dare to look at either Sir Martin or Sir Gilbert. Sir Martin knew what he was going through – it would have been as if they had asked Sir Martin to return to Rodez. Sir Gilbert did not understand why Percy hesitated. He was already straining at the leash. Not for the first time, Percy recognised that without the English he too would surrender to his own ghosts. The bishop had never seen him. There was no reason to think he would be in any more danger in his palace than anywhere else. And as Félice's cousin he would have an excellent disguise. He lifted his head slightly and his facial muscles tightened.

'All right.'

Sir Gilbert broke into a smile, and Sir Martin gazed at Percy with a mixture of admiration and pity. Percy turned away from them and lowered his eyelids so they could not see the fear already eating at his stomach.

Félice touched the back of his hand very lightly. It startled him so much that he spun about and met her eyes. 'Thank you, Percy.'

Chapter Twenty

Paris, March 1310

Umberto di Sante massaged his temples with his fingers, trying to alleviate the headache that plagued him. The pain which seemed to cleave his skull and numb half of his brain made it almost impossible to concentrate on the documents before him. The neat script of the scribe seemed to blur before his eyes and the letters ran together so that the figures transmitted no sense at all. Irritably, he shoved the documents aside with the tense gesture of a man in pain and pushed back the stool.

The headaches were getting worse and part of him knew that they were not entirely attributable to excessive quantities of the bishop's wine the night before. The headaches came even when he had not joined the bishop in his 'private circle', and it was this which frightened him. A mere hangover was easy to banish with fresh air and a raw egg but these headaches defied all easy remedies and robbed him of his strength, causing even his stomach to rebel.

He left the carved writing desk and went to the window to look out on to the Seine. The episcopal palace faced Notre Dame from the left bank of the river and the windows of the scriptorium offered di Sante a splendid view of the cathedral. To the left, the spire of Saint Chapel pointed to heaven, and beyond the Isle de la Cité he could see all the way to the massive tower of the Temple. That was where the bulk of the Templar prisoners were now being held, in their own former headquarters – if in slightly different style than that to which they had once been accustomed.

Everyone had been unprepared for the number of Templars who had volunteered to defend their Order last autumn. No one had expected that after two full years in the dungeons of the king so many of the wretches – men who had sworn to every conceivable heresy and sin their interrogators had suggested to them – would suddenly retract their own confessions and declare the Order innocent of all charges. It had been a serious setback for the king and he had made sure that the Bishops of Albi and Narbonne felt his displeasure. The Bishop of Albi had been subjected to the most vicious verbal abuse at the hands of his kinsman Nogaret and to this day he had not fully recovered either his standing at court or his own equilibrium.

Not for the first time di Sante wondered whether he should leave the bishop's service and find a new patron. He had come into contact again with Father Elion and sometimes he toyed with the idea of approaching him. However, the disgrace of vomiting at his first interrogation and then the whole humiliating incident with the escaped English Templar inhibited him. Otherwise, he had not come into contact with anyone more influential than the bishop himself. He was not going to give up his extremely good position here unless he had something better to go to.

With the trial of the Temple about to commence, his chances of attracting royal favour had never been better. He would be allowed to attend the hearings. The opportunity might even arise for him to raise a question; or, better still, refute some argument of the defenders. Up to now the bishop had not allowed him to meet Nogaret in person but at the trial it would be unavoidable. Di Sante would not need the bishop's patronage if he could attract the notice of the king's most powerful minister.

The arrival of a barge at the water gate to the palace distracted di Sante from his thoughts. The barge was one of the many barges one could hire and had that semi-dilapidated look of rented property. The helmsmen and the six oarsmen wore jerkins of the same reddish-brown over red hose rather than a proper livery. As di Sante watched, a tall knight in a blue and purple surcoat over a long-sleeved hauberk and over-the-knee blue suede boots sprang on to the landing and turned to help a lady disembark. The lady wore a purple velvet cloak trimmed with black fur that seemed somewhat too large for her. Hampered by her skirts and the cloak, she scrambled awkwardly over the gunnel and then stopped and looked up at the towering façade of the episcopal palace.

Di Sante felt his heart lurch in his chest and he pressed his face directly to the glass of the window. It was Félice de Preuthune!

Di Sante had heard about her wedding to the man who killed her brother in a jousting accident – and he had heard about the annulment as well. At the time he had thought it was what she deserved for breaking her vow to him, and he had felt bitter and vindictive. But now the mere sight of the wide, golden eyes in her heart-shaped face as she gazed up at him – as if she knew he were there – banished all his resentment.

Umberto jumped down from the window niche and ran to the spiral stairs. He took the steps two at a time and then dashed along the cloister arcade. She had come back to him! And now, as a deflowered and cast-off bride, she would not dare reject – indeed she must welcome – what he could offer her.

He would rent lodgings for her in the student quarter so he could visit her regularly, whenever his duties allowed.

He burst into the entrance hall, where the porter and a sergeant of the guard were already receiving the visitors. A boy was sent scampering up the stairs opposite; Umberto nearly called out to him that he was here. But then he let the boy be, preferring not to attract attention to himself. Instead, he slowed his steps and advanced with sweet, nervous anticipation towards the waiting visitors. He took the time to enjoy each second, to observe each tiny detail.

A year of marriage had not seemed to touch Félice at all. She still had a frail, girlish figure, made all the more delicate by the oversized cloak. Why was she wearing something far too large for her? She must have been aware that the cloak was not flattering because she was already pushing back the hood and undoing the clasp at her neck. As she drew off the cloak, she revealed a white chiffon surcoat embroidered with pink and silver roses worn over a deep purple velvet gown. Amethyst earrings dangled from her earlobes, very evident for she wore her hair confined, like a married woman, in a crispinette under a snug hat held by chiffon scarves wound under her chin.

The sight of her with confined hair made Umberto catch his breath and his stride faltered slightly. The images of countless couplings came to him and in that instant the full impact of her marriage hit him like a blow. There was an instant of anger that someone else had laid hands on her purity, followed almost instantly by an anticipatory excitement. She was a woman now and she would need no coaxing and coddling. She had come to him.

He stepped boldly on to the glazed tiles of the hall, his head held high, his cowl flung back from his head.

'Mademoiselle de Preuthune!'

She turned towards him, startled, and her eyes widened. Her surprise was total. He smiled and extended his stride.

Félice recognised him instantly. Umberto had not changed much in two years. With his dark eyes sparkling from the joy of seeing her, he seemed more the student she had loved than the haughty Dominican she had last seen. The robes of his novitiate had been replaced by the robes of a friar but the perfectly oval face under the rich, dark hair of his tonsure was still youthful. It was so hard to believe that this was a man who had tortured innocent villagers. And then she heard Percy choke and his spur scrape sharply on the tiles. Félice glanced up at him over her shoulder. His nostrils had flared and his head was pulled back like a stallion smelling death.

Umberto was before her. He took her hands in his and lifted them to his lips. 'I had not dared hope.' He met her eyes and something made him suddenly uncertain. He did not see his joy reflected in them. She was staring at him very, very strangely. 'Lady Félice?' he asked.

'Umberto.' She uttered his name almost inaudibly. Then, as if collecting herself, she added, 'I have come to see His Grace, Monsignor de Saint Laurent. I did not know you were still in his service.'

I *should* have known, she reproached herself. I should have been prepared for this. And behind her she could feel Percy's rigidity, as if he interpreted the warm greetings of a Dominican to mean that she had betrayed him. 'This is my cousin, Sir Percival de Thune, from England. My grandfather sent him to bring me home from Portugal.'

She indicated Percy, and Umberto spared the tall knight an uninterested glance. Then another thought struck him. She hadn't fallen in love with this man, had she? A woman who had been rejected by her husband might grasp at the first alternative. Umberto subjected Percy to more intense scrutiny and was forced to conclude that women might find him attractive. Furthermore, his eyes were hostile, which suggested that he was jealous, and that at once mollified Umberto slightly. If the knight had the sense to be jealous, then he could not be overly certain of Félice's affections.

Maybe she only needed to know that he forgave her for her marriage and then she would discard this brainless brute.

'Let me take you up to His Grace's audience room.' Umberto started in his most gracious tone, a hospitable smile tossed with self-assurance to the stiff knight.

He led them, gliding along the long corridors of the palace, his habit gracefully rippling around his legs as he strode on purposefully. He did not fail to point out sculptures, frescos and tapestries of particular value and interest as they proceeded. He casually enquired when they had arrived in Paris and where they were lodged. Did they plan to stay long?

In the ante-room of the audience chamber, a half-dozen other petitioners sat upon the stone bench lining the wall beneath the windows in various poses of boredom or impatience. Umberto indicated that Félice and Sir Percy should wait just a moment and then he advanced towards the double doors giving access to audience chamber, but his entrance was forestalled by the doors crashing open and the bishop himself striding out of the room.

Di Sante and the bishop both drew up in shock at the unexpected near collision, but the bishop recovered first.

'I should have suspected you would be sniffing about already!' the bishop snarled, adding with a jerk of his head: 'Get out!'

Then he turned to Félice and smiled with every appearance of sincerity. 'My dear girl! It is a delight to receive you. Come along. The rest of you can come back tomorrow!' The bishop dismissed the other petitioners with a wave of his hand, and then stopped abruptly as his eyes met Sir Percy's. 'And who are you?'

Félice answered before Percy could open his mouth. For some reason she was afraid to let him speak. 'My cousin escorted me here, Your Grace, but… but I would like to speak with you alone.'

'By all means. You can wait here,' he told Percy, pointing to the now empty benches.

'I will wait on the landing,' Percy answered. 'The air is better.' Then with a bow that did not take the sting out of the insult, he turned and strode out of the chamber.

'A singularly rude young man, my dear, but I suppose we don't choose our relatives.'

The bishop had taken Félice's hand through his elbow and was leading her through the audience chamber on to the dais and out through the side door leading to his private apartments. These were located around a small gallery that looked down on the cloisters below. On a warm day it would have been delightful to sit in the shade of the arches but there was still a bite to the March air despite the bright sun. The bishop therefore led Félice into a carpeted room with wainscotting that kept at bay the chill of the Seine and stained glass spattering jewels of light across the floor. At the ringing of a bell, a servant appeared, who was ordered to stoke the fire and then bring refreshments. The bishop indicated the chairs before the fire.

'You may not know that I have always had a special interest in your well-being, my dear,' the bishop opened as Félice, with just a touch of trepidation, settled herself in the offered chair. 'I have been kept informed of your whereabouts. The wedding was… shall I say, ill-advised and very unfortunate.' He shook his head. 'Not that you are to blame for it! I know that you had nothing to do with the choice. You need not fear that I thought otherwise. I know what a dutiful daughter you are. What I don't understand is how your father could make such a disastrous decision. He must have been mad with grief over your elder brother. Nothing else can explain such a misguided choice! I must say that it shocked me very much at the time.'

'I'm not sure that I understand, Monseigneur.' Félice managed to put in at last. 'My father was indeed grieving too deeply to think straight. It was my mother who made the decision. Dom Pedro offered to take me without a dowry.' She paused just long enough to make sure that the bishop registered this and then added, 'But what is so shocking about it?'

'Well, I mean, you had already taken your novice's vows, had you not? The abbess of Saint Radegonde was quite understandably outraged!'

'Yes, but novices frequently don't take final vows. While I was at the convent school at least three of the novices returned to their families and subsequently married.'

'Subsequently, yes. But you had not really left the convent, had you? You had been given leave to attend your brother's funeral. But I suppose these are fine points of no particular importance in the long run. Are you in Paris with your parents now? What has brought them here?'

'I have come straight from Portugal, Monseigneur. I asked Sir Percy to bring me here before taking me home. I wanted to seek your advice.'

The bishop was an ambitious man. No one would have accused him of softness, but he was nevertheless flattered by Félice's trust, perhaps because it was so rare. The look on his face softened visibly and he answered sincerely: 'I am honoured.'

'Monseigneur.' Félice pulled all her courage together and looked him in the eye. 'You know that I gave my husband only two dead – indeed not even that – children.'

The bishop looked somewhat discomforted at this. 'Yes… well… I heard something about a miscarriage—'

'Two miscarriages, Monseigneur, although the doctors swear there is nothing wrong with me.'

'Many women miscarry more than once, my dear. I don't think there is any reason to think there is something wrong with you.'

'But it must be God's will!' Félice persisted.

'Yes, of course, it is always His will.'

'And He will have had his reasons, will He not?'

'Indeed – but we are often too unworthy to be granted the capacity to understand His design. We must trust in Him and retain our faith, not demand answers to our questions. He will reveal His will to us in His own time.'

'But...' This was not the answer Félice had wanted, and she chewed unconsciously on her lower lip for a moment before plunging ahead. 'But couldn't it be that he was punishing me?'

'It might be – but it must not be. What have you done in your short, sheltered life that should so offend Him?'

The bishop made the question sound rhetorical but it gave Félice the opportunity she needed. In a low, anguished voice she revealed to him, 'I broke a vow, Monseigneur.'

The bishop went stock-still and studied her with narrowed eyes. 'You don't mean your novice's vow, do you?'

She shook her head, eyes lowered, her hands clutching one another in her lap, a picture of nervous courage.

'What vow did you break?'

'I... Monseigneur, try to understand! I was a young girl and I... It is quite normal, is it not, for young girls to fall in love or think they have?' She lifted her eyes and looked at him hopefully.

The bishop cleared his throat and adjusted himself in his chair. Then he reached for his wine and took a sip while he considered his answer. As soon as she had mentioned a broken vow, he suspected it must have something to do with a young man. The abbess had even made some reference to an incident with a young man. 'It is, as you say, "normal" but very dangerous, my dear. Why else do you think parents go to so much trouble to try and protect their daughters from these childish follies? The basis of such supposed "love" is nothing more than the base, carnal instincts which develop in consequence of the biological maturing of your body.

'When young people – male or female – reach the age of physical maturity, their primitive biological urge to reproduction asserts itself. This response is identical to what one sees in cats, dogs, cattle and other beasts when they reach reproductive age. Through the grace of God, however, humans are given the will to resist these urges, to rise above the animal and seek the divine. This is a lifelong struggle and one in which we all suffer many setbacks. Which is why, I repeat, parents must take great care to protect their immature children from their own carnal instincts until they are strong enough to fight them on their own.'

'You must not think that I went to my bridal bed other than a virgin.'

'I never doubted it, my dear. And yet you spoke of a "love" that I presume did not focus on your husband. You did not know your husband before your marriage, if I was informed correctly.'

'I met Dom Pedro two weeks before we were wed. I learned to love him afterwards. But while I was in Poitiers, I had… I had…'

'Become infatuated?' the bishop supplied.

'Yes, perhaps that is the right word,' Félice agreed but her expression suggested that she did not fully subscribe to the description. 'In any case,' she continued, 'I met and became very fond of a certain student. He seemed to return my affections and I foolishly imagined that my parents might be persuaded to give me to him. He came of a good family and he had prospects as steward of a great estate.' The bishop's eyes had narrowed slightly, but he only nodded encouragement for her to continue. 'At least that is what I thought. But then one day, quite without warning, he joined the Dominicans.'

The bishop drew in his breath and held it, his eyes boring into Félice with such hostility that she faltered.

'Go on,' he urged, slowly releasing his breath. 'What happened then? You never saw him again and plunged into your marriage still heart-sick?'

'I wish that that were the case, Monseigneur. Then I should truly have nothing with which to reproach myself – except a childish fancy, which, as you so aptly put it, was the effect of biological maturity and so, surely, not in itself a sin.'

The bishop could not entirely stifle a snort of approval. The girl had lost none of her brains.

'But my lover sought me out *after* he had become a novice.' The bishop's face became dark with disapproval and his lips tightened grimly, but he did not interrupt her. 'He had my cousin fetch me and he met me in Notre Dame la Grande. In a confessional, Monseigneur! There he enquired whether I loved him still and begged me not to abandon him.'

'A Dominican novice?' the bishop enquired, his eyes slits in his pudgy face, his lips pressed together in fury.

'Yes, monseigneur. But I hoped then that he would not take his final vows. I hoped he would change his mind. I still loved him or thought I did. When he begged me to vow that I would never take another man, I... I agreed. There – in such a holy place – I promised that I would never give myself to someone else.'

'But surely you knew that your parents might decide otherwise.' The bishop seemed to have overcome his anger. His tone was normal now, almost casual.

'He – my lover – said that they could not force me. That the Church only recognises a marriage to which both parties consent. He said I need only refuse to marry.'

'Easy advice from a young man, I dare say.' The bishop was evidently disgusted. 'And did your parents compel you to marry?'

'No.' Félice looked down at her hands and spoke very softly.

'I see.' The bishop raised his eyebrows. 'Or rather I don't see. You took a vow not to marry anyone else and then broke it without hesitation at the first opportunity? I would not have expected that of you. I thought you had more character.'

'Monseigneur. When I took the vow, I still hoped that—
'

The bishop cocked his head.

'That my lover would change his mind about joining the Dominicans. I hoped he would not take his final vows, that we would be free to marry. But it soon became clear that he intended to go through with his vows. So I asked myself what right did he have to bind me with a vow that did not bind him?'

'As a Dominican, he could not give himself to any other either.'

'But that was *his* choice, monseigneur. Why should I be forced to do something against my will and against the will of my parents because a young man to whom I was neither related nor otherwise indebted had decided to enter the Dominicans?'

'Force had nothing to do with it. You vowed your fidelity to him of your own free will.'

'But on false assumption,' Félice insisted steadily. She had lifted her head and the look in her eyes was anything but frightened or uncertain now.

'You *presumed* that he might not take final vows, my dear. That was your error – unless he explicitly gave you reason to think otherwise.'

'He promised me that he would find a way for us to be together. Was I to think – even imagine – that a young nobleman who had vowed his love to me meant anything dishonourable?'

The look on the bishop's face could only be called sceptical. Félice hurried to agree with his unspoken thoughts.

'In retrospect, monseigneur, I can see now that I was extremely naïve. As he pursued his career, I realised that he only intended me to play the same role as the Countess of Périgord – at a lower level, of course. Should I have been forced into such a disgraceful and sinful position because I made a naïve vow as a fifteen year old girl?'

'You argue your case very well, my dear. But if you were so sure of yourself, I do not think you would be here seeking my advice.'

Félice winced. In her eagerness to defend herself, she had forgotten the alleged purpose of her visit.

'I... I am confused, monseigneur. I do not feel any guilt for what I did. I regret the vow, not my marriage. But when I experienced two painful miscarriages, and my husband used these as an excuse to set me aside, I started to wonder, if maybe... Monseigneur, tell me if I acted wrongly and how I can make amends?'

The bishop nodded, satisfied. 'It is not a simple case. Your conscience is well developed. Your sin was not marriage to the man your parents chose for you – no matter how unwisely – but the vow to a man who was not free to bind you. You should have refused to even meet a Dominican novice – much less under such compromising and blasphemous circumstances! You insulted Our Dear Lord by converting a confessional into the site of an illicit tryst.' The bishop's words were sharp and disapproving but his tone of voice was matter-of-fact. The bishop was a practical man and not prone to exaggerated moralising.

'Come, help yourself to refreshments.' He indicated the table, which had been discreetly set with a variety of pâtés, jellies and breads while they talked. 'And let me think this over.'

*

On the landing, Percy was told that his two men-at-arms had gone off to the kitchens. He scowled, cursed under his breath and set off to look for them – as if this had not been their task from the start. He found them comfortably drinking ale with the crumbs of leftover pasty still clinging to their beards, and, at a wink from Heydon, he turned his attention to the episcopal sergeant who was acting as host. 'Have my men been imposing too rudely on your hospitality?'

'Not in the least, sir.' As he spoke the sergeant shoved back his stool and started to rise in the presence of a knight. Percy waved him to sit down and climbed over the bench nearest him to sit down himself.

The sergeant at once called over his shoulder to one of the scullery boys to bring another tankard of ale. 'Or would you prefer wine, sir?'

'Ale will do.'

'You'd best have a bite to eat too, sir. The bishop just sent for refreshments and that means it could be hours till Lady Félice is ready to leave,' Pétard suggested solicitously.

Percy frowned but nodded. Their host called out for more meat pasties.

'Sergeant Jourdan was just telling us that there are three Templars being held here – men who have just arrived from Albi after retracting their confessions because they want to defend their Order.'

Percy raised his eyebrows and turned stiffly to their host. He could feel his blood pulsing at an unnatural rate and wondered if he were red. His fingers were ice cold. 'Do you know their names, by chance?'

'Names? Nay. No idea. Why?'

'I had... have a cousin – Lady Félice's uncle to be exact – who is a Templar. He has not been seen or heard from since that Friday the 13th.'

'Poor bastard.' The sergeant shook his head. 'I never cared much for the Templars one way or another. They were arrogant asses sometimes, but, you know, not really worse than the Dominicans. And by God they could fight!'

'Then you don't believe the confessions?'

'Ach!' He made a dismissive gesture. 'You know, if they'd done to me half the things they did to them, I'd have sworn my own mother was a witch or the Virgin Mary or both! Anything they wanted to hear!'

The three disguised Templars stared at him, nonplussed by his candidly sympathetic reaction. Then both Templar sergeants looked at Percy, waiting for him to respond.

Percy found that he could hardly breathe. 'My cousin was in the Languedoc, I don't know exactly where. You don't think it's possible he is one of your prisoners, do you?'

'Do you want to go down and see?' The offer was so alacritous that Percy was instantly suspicious.

'Not if it would get you into trouble in some way. The chances are, after all, very slight.'

Jourdan shrugged. 'I don't have anything to worry about. The bishop hasn't said they can't have visitors. I'll take you down after you've finished.' He indicated the cold meat pie and ale that the kitchen boy had just clunked down in front of Percy.

Percy stared at both with a sense of inner revulsion. His stomach was in no state to face either at the moment, but, with a smile, he lifted the tankard to his host and then forced himself to drink in long, thirsty gulps.

'The worst of them is that pretty boy you saw in the hall,' Jourdan was continuing in a chatty tone. 'They say he vomited at his first interrogation...'

Percy choked and thumped the tankard down, coughing violently. Pétard hastened to whack him on the back. Percy shook his head, tears in his eyes from the coughing, and gasped, 'Swallowed the wrong way.' He wiped his mouth on the back of his hand and looked at the sergeant expectantly, his face still red.

'Yeah, they say di Sante vomited at his first interrogation but he soon got over his squeamishness. He became the bishop's favourite interrogator and was sent all around the countryside looking for renegades and heretics. They say he once had a woman, some poor peasant accused of hiding a fugitive, hung up by her breasts over a fire. You wouldn't think it to look at his angel face, would you?'

The look the strange knight gave him made Jourdan falter slightly. Then he continued, 'An arrogant bastard too! He never looks at you when he gives his orders – like he's trying to hold his nose closed as if you were a piece of shit!'

Percy finished the ale and forced himself to confront the meat pasty. His heart was pounding in his chest as if it wanted to escape.

Heydon came to his assistance. 'A lot of Dominicans are like that, if you ask me.'

'True, but this one's so damned young! And he's utterly subservient to the bishop. If he catches you saying or doing anything the bishop wouldn't like, you can be sure that the bishop will hear of it. A regular rat!'

Percy wiped his greasy hands on his hose and stood up still chewing. 'Can we go? Even if you're right about it taking a long time, I'd hate the Lady Félice to send for us while we are still in the dungeon.'

The moment they passed through the door leading down into the dungeon, the stink of mould and mildew was noticeable in the air and Percy felt his hair stand on end. Rather than the refreshing nature of a stiff breeze or the clear cold of snow and ice, the chill that greeted them was a stagnant, penetrating, damp iciness which rose from the pits of hell.

They descended a narrow flight of uneven stone stairs covered with rat and bat shit. At the foot of the stairs they started along a corridor. The rough-hewn walls were slimy with mildew, and now the stench of soiled straw mixed with the smell of dank walls.

Jourdan was leading with a torch but Percy turned sharply and looked at Pétard. He had gone pale as death and sweat glistened on his face. Percy could see his pulse fluttering at the base of his throat and one eye had started rapidly blinking in an unnatural manner. Christ help us all, if I look like that, Percy thought. He jerked his head and ordered Pétard out.

Jourdan had stopped when he noticed the others were not directly behind him.

Percy caught up. 'The man's got night-blindness: he can't see in this dark,' he explained brusquely, facing the corridor ahead of them rather than Jourdan himself.

'Were you close to your cousin?' Jourdan asked unexpectedly.

'Not particularly; why?'

Jourdan shrugged and started forwards again. They passed an open door and Percy glanced in automatically. He immediately regretted it. He caught sight of a table with leather straps hanging off it – and secured on opposite walls were two iron bars one about a foot off the ground and the other directly under the ceiling. The shackles waited at one end of the bar and iron balls of various weights were neatly lined up against the side of the room. Sweat was now running down his back and his hands were so cold that he had to clench them to keep them from going numb. Ahead of him, Jourdan had inserted his long key into a lock.

As he shoved back the heavy door, it creaked and the smell of shit and urine and something worse came out of the room into the dank corridor. Jourdan stood back and glanced up at the strange knight. For the first time he noticed how exceptionally tall he was. The knight did not meet his gaze but ducked into the dungeon.

It was utterly dark. The floor was strewn with dirty straw and vermin scuttled for cover as a giant intruder invaded their space. It was a small chamber, much smaller than the public jail at Albi, and it housed only three men. One was lying on his back on the far side of the chamber. One sat with his arms hugging his knees and his back against the narrow wall. The third was curled up in the corner with a wasted arm over his face.

All three pairs of eyes instantly went to Percy as he stepped into the room. The man clutching his knees lifted his head sharply while the two men on the floor merely stirred enough to be able to look at the unexpected visitor. Behind him, Heydon was making small talk to Jourdan, deftly distracting him from what was going on in the cell.

The man clutching his knees frowned at Percy. Of the three prisoners, he was the only one in armour, and the look in his eyes was hostile and wary at once. He waited tensely for what Percy would do or say. It was the man curled up in the corner who responded most dramatically to the presence of the young knight. With the rustle of straw and the clank of chains the man managed to pull himself upright. 'Sir Percy?'

Percy turned to him at once and looked more closely. The man had long white hair framing a sunken, grey face with a matted, grey beard. An open sore swelled his right eyelid so that only a tiny corner of the iris showed and pus oozed out of the corner on to his cheek. The man was struggling to get to his feet, hampered not so much by his chains – one bound his right wrist to the wall and another bound his feet together – as by his own shattered bones. His right hip seemed to have collapsed in upon itself and the thigh bone protruded from it at an awkward angle, only to wrench around at the knee. The shin was a shortened stick, gnarled where it had been broken in three places and from this hung a useless, deformed foot.

Percy's stomach turned itself inside out, but he had recognised the voice: 'Brother Gautier?'

'Yes! God bless you! They let you go? Your king interceded?' Brother Gautier, sergeant-commander of Saint Pierre, sounded genuinely pleased. There was no trace of jealousy that he was maimed for life and still in chains while his guest of long ago stood tall and tanned and free in front of him.

And that was the worst of it.

Percy crossed the distance between them to catch the man in his arms as he tried to rise. He pressed him to his strong chest, unable to express the conflicting emotions of guilt, gratitude and overwhelming pity. The night of his arrest was abruptly vivid in his mind. Brother Gautier had refused to tell where the keys to the treasury were until the royal soldiers started beating him. After that he and Gautier had spent months together in the jail at Albi. Brother Gautier had helped lessen the loneliness by telling him about himself and all the other brothers so that one by one they had become men rather than strangers. Gautier's calm narratives had done much to distract Percy from his own terror. Gautier had held his head and poured water down his lips when he had been too weak to drink after the torture. Gautier had said psalms over him when he was trembling with fever after they burned the base of his feet. Gautier had... Percy heard the voices outside the door and remembered the present.

Loosening his embrace but not letting go, he forced himself to look Gautier in the eye and spoke in a low voice. 'You must not address me by name. The Inquisition and the pope think I died in the spring of '08. I go by the name of Sir Percival of Thune here.'

Somewhat louder, he asked, 'You have retracted your confession? Intend to defend the Order before the papal commission?'

'Yes!' It was the knight behind him who answered most decisively and Percy turned around without letting go of Gautier, who clung to him as if afraid he would disappear.

'I am François de Fontaine,' the knight on the floor told him with pride still in his deep voice. He was more powerfully built than Percy, with broad shoulders and big bones that even near starvation could not shrink. His hair was streaked with grey but still predominantly brown. 'I remember the last night they took you out for an interrogation,' he announced, and Percy glanced sharply towards the door, but Heydon had apparently succeeded in luring Jourdan back down the corridor. Their voices came to him only very faintly. The captive Templar continued coldly, 'You could not walk and your chest was bloody from an unhealed brand wound. Your gums were bleeding too. We heard your screams and were encouraged because, as always, you said "no" to everything. But then, after the loudest "no" of all, everything went silent. The sheriff returned to his bed but you were not brought back. You confessed, didn't you?'

Percy stared at the man sitting on the straw, chained, like the others, to the wall by his right wrist. His face was disfigured by scurvy that had turned his lips to open sores. The stench of his breath reached Percy even in the foul-smelling room. But his tone was admonitory, and Percy was reminded of the shame of his confession.

'Yes,' he admitted. He was still too ashamed to even challenge his accuser, to ask whether he had never weakened under torture. At the time of his own confession two years ago, François had been the only other knight who had not yet succumbed, but was it possible that he had held out for another two years and was not crippled?

Percy remembered that François, now in his mid-forties, had been a youth at Tortosa when Acre fell. More than any of them, he had been determined to die rather than confess to lies. And he had been the one who had led them in Templar battle songs which conjured up the days when the Temple had been great. François had kept them all from despairing by telling them about the Templars who had been held in Saracen prisons or sold into Egyptian slavery. He had made them feel like heroes even in their worst degradation. Percy had admired him with all his heart and envied him his strength. To look at him now it was clear that he was strong still, and Percy was duly humbled.

'And after you confessed, still you weren't returned to us,' François continued in an accusatory tone. 'Why was that? What deal did you strike with the Inquisition?'

Percy was neither startled nor insulted by the implication. He considered François' reaction more natural and more intelligent than Gautier's uncritical acceptance of him. But he had no answer that would banish the doubts François harboured. Whatever he did or said could be interpreted as mere disguise or lies.

From the far end of the corridor came the distinctive creaking of an empty rack and François' body seemed to shrink of its own accord. Heydon must have asked to see the torture chamber, Percy noted with a mixture of approval and alienation. It was a good ploy to distract Jourdan but the morbid curiosity repelled him. And François had broken out into a foul-smelling sweat.

Percy tried not to let him know that he had noticed his reaction. 'Is there anything I could say which would convince you I never made any special deal with them? Should I bring you some of the brothers I have – with the help of God – freed? Would their testimony about what we have done to build up a secret network of Free Templars convince you? Would a letter from the Seneschal of the Order accredit me in your eyes? Or de Sonnac's sword from Mansourah—'

'De Sonnac's sword? De Beaujeu gave that to Commander Jean de Preuthune, but he lost it at Acre while trying to save de Beaujeu.'

Percy handed the sword to him.

François had difficulty lifting the heavy weapon but he stared first at the sword then at Percy. 'I don't understand.'

'Jean de Preuthune lied to Master de Molay. He did not lose it at Acre – he returned it to his father, who had received it from de Sonnac himself. His father, Geoffrey de Preuthune, rejoined the Order and has been appointed Seneschal of Aquitaine and preceptor of all Free Templars in France.'

'Then it's true?' François asked hesitantly.

'What?'

'That there are Free Templars? That there is an organisation? That some of our brothers have been rescued?'

'It's true.'

'We'd heard rumours. The guards talked about it, grumbling because their duties had been increased and the inspections were more frequent,' François explained, staring at Percy with a mixture of awe and mistrust still.

'Have you come to help us get out?' Gautier asked, his grip on Percy suddenly more fierce, as if a surge of hope had seized him and given him new strength.

Percy felt his heart constrict within his chest, ashamed and full of self-loathing. How could he come here not even planning to offer them this option? How dare he raise their hopes, only to deliver instructions from an Order that had not protected them from this? What right did he have to ask anything of them? They had withstood two more years of the treatment that had broken him in six months. And they were risking death by fire.

But Percy could not lie to Gautier. 'No, that is not why I came. I was told that you wanted to defend the Order—'

'We do!' Came the chorus of voices.

'All of you?' Percy now looked over his shoulder towards the third brother lying on the floor.

Brother Gautier nodded solemnly. 'Yes, all three of us.'

In answer to Percy's gaze, he added, 'You remember Brother Thomas – the porter at Saint Pierre.'

Percy started sharply. He remembered not only the jovial, bald porter who had greeted him talkatively the night of the arrest, but also that Brother Thomas's feet had been burned till the bone showed. Could he, of all men, now be willing to risk the auto-da-fé? He looked more closely at the man on the floor.

A bald, toothless skeleton grinned back at him. 'Yes, it's me, sir! Not so fat as I once was, as you see. And I'll never be footsore again either.'

Percy could not find the strength to even smile much less respond. Brother Thomas had no feet left at all. The burn wounds must have festered and his feet had been amputated well above the ankles.

Brother Gautier clutched Percy tighter again, this time in a gesture of comfort, but the stoicism of the two men ignited a fury in Percy's breast that he could not suppress. 'God damn them!' It burst out of him as he broke free of Brother Gautier. 'God damn them!'

'Amen to that, sir. But if you don't want us all to end up in there with 'em, can I ask you to keep your voice down?' Sergeant Jourdan spoke from behind him in the doorway, and Percy glanced over, remembering himself. He saw Heydon's worried face as he crossed himself.

Percy heard his own laboured breathing and then glanced up at the mouldy barrel-vaulted ceiling over his head. Up there the sun shone and the air was clean. There was wine and fresh fruit and white bread. Overhead, the Bishop of Albi was entertaining Félice in his well-appointed apartment and the Dominican dog was gliding about on his soft shoes, his fine robes fluttering about him as gracefully as a woman's skirts.

Percy had been in dungeons more than once since his own escape but the men he had visited had been strangers. Too late he realised that there was a world of difference between seeing strangers in these familiar conditions and seeing men he knew as individuals – as worthy and good men. The anger that had been latent or merely simmering for so long was boiling over.

But he could not afford anger now. He forced it back down, deep into his chest, down into his belly, down where it could not endanger him at the moment.

He lowered his gaze and looked over at Jourdan. 'My apologies. I should not have shouted.'

'Are you nearly finished, sir? We shouldn't stay much longer. We might be missed and people may wonder where we are.' Heydon was clearly getting nervous – and that was saying a lot for the battle-hardened English veteran.

Percy nodded. 'Give me just two more minutes alone with my kinsman.'

Jourdan looked indecisive for a moment but then he said, 'We'll be at the foot of the stairs,' and they moved away.

Percy turned back to the three prisoners. 'I can't stay but I will try to return with something for your eye, Brother Gautier – and fresh fruit. It will clear up the sores in your mouth, François.'

'Why did you come, if not to free us?' Thomas asked the question that oppressed all three prisoners.

Percy took a deep breath. 'I came to pass on the following information: because there are so many of you who have volunteered to defend the Order, you must elect representatives. The Bishops of Albi and Narbonne will attempt to pressure you into electing spokesmen of their own choosing. The men they favour are in their pay. The preceptor in Portugal recommends electing Peter de Bologna and Renaud de Provins instead. They are both highly trained in ecclesiastical law and can be trusted to conduct the defence most effectively.'

François nodded, looking Percy directly in the eye. The hostility was now completely gone. 'Even I have heard of Renaud de Provins. He was a brilliant scholar – too brilliant, they said, for the Templars. The Dominicans tried to convince him to join them.'

'I must go.' Percy glanced towards the door, and then, returning to Brother Thomas, he knelt and gave him a kiss on each cheek. 'God is with you, brother. Is there anything I can bring you?'

'Will we be allowed to see a priest?' Brother Thomas asked hopefully. 'If there are priests among the defenders, will we be allowed to confess to them?'

'I don't know – but I will see what I can do.'

Percy rose and went to Brother Gautier. They embraced again.

'I'm so glad you got out!' Gautier insisted. 'It was an accident that you were ever arrested. If you had only been one day farther along, in Provence, you would have made it safely to Cyprus.' Percy smiled his tight-lipped smile. 'I'm glad I did not make Cyprus. There our brothers are free but helpless to do anything.'

When he turned to take his leave of François, he found that the old knight had gone down on his knees.

'May I kiss the Hand of the Baptist?' he begged.

Percy dropped on to his own knees and held out the hilt of de Sonnac's sword.

Chapter Twenty-One

Paris, March 1310

Sergeant Jourdan had the watch until midnight and he was expecting Percy. As soon as Percy had delivered Félice's gift to the bishop, he found his way to the guardroom door. Jourdan left his two companions playing dice and escorted Percy down the now familiar stairway into the dungeons.

'We have to hurry,' Percy urged Jourdan. 'I have only delivered a gift and await an answer.'

Jourdan shrugged. Percy consciously avoided looking into the torture chamber as they passed, and he handed an astonished Jourdan an orange as he swept into the chamber where his brothers were held. 'Wait for me here. I won't take more than five minutes.'

Inside, the three men hardly seemed to have moved since he left them, but both François and Gautier started to rise at the sound of Percy's voice.

'Brother! You shouldn't take too many risks for our sakes!' Gautier admonished, and Percy embraced him.

'I won't.' He opened his cloak and started digging about in a deep leather pouch which he wore slung over his left shoulder, resting on his right hip. He removed a glass vial and handed it to Gautier. 'This should clear up the sore on your eyelid. If not, try this.' He took out a second, smaller bottle. He next removed five oranges, to the gasps of the three prisoners.

'Have you robbed the royal treasury?' François asked half in jest, as Percy pressed one into his hand. Oranges were too expensive for all except the very rich. Neither Gautier nor Thomas had ever eaten one in their lives, and Percy had to show them how to peel and divide their first orange. Thomas chewed with his toothless gums somewhat sceptically, while Gautier insisted that he should have saved the money to help other prisoners.

Percy had no time to argue. 'Eat them – they will stop the bleeding in your gums faster than anything else.'

He was still unloading his pouch. He had three large loaves of bread and fresh cheese. Last but not least, he removed holy wafers and wine. These he brought to a wide-eyed Brother Thomas.

'It is blessed, brother.'

The old man seemed to gasp and then started to tremble. He turned his head towards the wall without accepting Percy's offering.

Percy squatted down. 'What is it, brother?' He laid a hand on the man's shaking shoulder.

'I… I… can't! You know that!' He was sobbing soundlessly. 'I am unclean, unconfessed.'

Percy went stock-still, aware of the others staring at his broad, muscular back. They were no less shocked than Thomas. 'I consulted a priest,' he lied. 'He assured me that if you had been denied confession but were not excommunicated, you could receive the Body and Blood. He said that God knows your sins, your repentance and your anguish. He would want you to share in the comfort of the Communion.'

Thomas turned his face back from the wall. Tears glistened on his sunken, colourless cheeks. His eyes glittered with an almost feverish hope. He wanted to believe the young knight but he was still afraid. 'Commander? May I?' He deferred the difficult decision to his superior.

Gautier stirred uneasily and glanced at François. 'Sir?'

Percy held out the wafers again. 'Please, for His sake – who died for our sins.'

'Commander?' Thomas almost screamed for guidance.

'Yes,' Gautier croaked as he sank on his knees to the rustle of straw, the clink of chain and an uncontrollable groan of pain.

Thomas tried to sit up, and Percy slipped his free hand under his lice-infested head to help him. Thomas stuck out his tongue. His breath made Percy swallow his instinctive recoil but he placed the wafer on his tongue and recited, 'The Body of Our Lord Jesus Christ, which was given for thee, preserve thy body and soul unto everlasting life. Take and eat this in remembrance that Christ died for thee, and feed on him in thy heart by faith, with thanksgiving.'

He then handed Thomas the wineskin. Thomas looked up at him, confused and frightened. Not since his acceptance into the Order had he been granted the privilege of partaking of Holy Wine. Percy nodded and pressed it on him. 'The Blood of Our Lord Jesus Christ, which was shed for thee. Drink this in remembrance that Christ's blood was shed for thee and be thankful.'

Thomas crossed himself fervently and started to recite the Pater Noster. Percy stood and then repeated the ritual for Gautier and François. As he rose, he saw Jourdan staring at him from the doorway.

'It's been ten minutes already,' the sergeant warned in a strange voice.

Percy nodded, replaced the wineskin in his bag – there were no wafers left – and then embraced each of the prisoners again, before facing Jourdan. The sergeant had not moved from the doorway. Percy collected his courage and advanced steadily towards him. He expected him to slam the door shut in his face and turn the lock. He felt the hilt of his longsword under his cloak. He would kill himself if he had to. He would not spend another day in a dungeon.

But Jourdan stepped back at the last moment and let him out. The door clanged shut, the sound seeming to reverberate louder than ever in the corridor. Percy stood facing Jourdan.

'You are brothers, aren't you?'

'What do you mean?'

'You're a Templar, aren't you?'

'Why do you say that?'

Jourdan merely shook his head. 'If I told the bishop you would be arrested, tortured—'

'I know what arrest means – better than you do. Do you have a price or do I have to silence you with this?'

The blade rasped in its sheath as it was drawn, and Jourdan jumped back to get out of range.

He held up both his hands. 'I am unarmed!'

This was not strictly true. He wore a short sword and a knife, but he was veteran enough to know that neither was much use against the knight's longsword. Jourdan was a middle-aged man who had spent the last twenty years riding escort to a bishop and keeping watch over episcopal prisoners. He had never used his sword in anger – unless you counted bar-room scuffles when he had been younger. Percy was not only fifteen years younger, eight inches taller and in peak condition, he was a trained knight, a Templar. Jourdan was not a fool.

Percy held the sword at the ready, his eyes wary. Jourdan had retreated farther down the corridor. The minute Percy turned to leave he would expose his back. He would hear an attack coming but in the confined space and the dark he could not be sure that he could spin around and meet the challenge effectively. He was also running out of time.

Jourdan could not know what was going through Percy's head but he could see he was thinking and that frightened him. A knight who could administer the sacraments was an awesome man in his eyes. 'Listen! I won't betray you – on one condition!'

Percy lifted the corner of his lips. He had bought so many jailers, guards, stewards and even captains over the last year that he was almost disappointed. 'Name your price,' he replied wearily.

'I said condition, not price. I'm sick of the bishop's service. Find me another position – at the same pay. I have a wife and four children to support.'

Percy was surprised – pleasantly so. 'Very well,' he agreed, acutely aware that Jourdan might see him out and then run straight to the bishop. But nothing could prevent him from doing that anyway. He either had to kill Jourdan or take a risk. He was not prepared to kill Jourdan, for he had been cooperative, even sympathetic. So he had no—

'Water!' An agonised croak reached his ears from behind him not from the cell where his brothers were confined but farther away. His hair stood on end.

'Guard! Please!' The croak was louder, more rasping.

Percy recognised the state of desperation and panic which was several stages before the end of one's real strength and yet at the end of one's self-control. 'There's someone in the torture chamber.' He managed to put his horror into words.

'Nothing to make you worry,' Jourdan replied with a shrug. 'It's di Sante! The bishop learned that he had been carrying on with some lady against his express instructions.'

Percy could only stare.

Jourdan continued, 'The bishop ordered him strung up for three days and three nights – in honour of the Holy Trinity.'

Percy spun around blindly and found his way to the entrance of the torture chamber by the inarticulate groaning that emanated from it. He still held his sword in his right hand only because he had forgotten it entirely.

Di Sante was naked except for his braies and these were obviously soiled. He was suspended by his wrists, which were shackled to the upper bar, and his feet were chained to the lower bar and stretched apart so that he was spreadeagled. His head hung forwards on his chest.

At the sound of someone entering, he lifted his head and tried to make out who it was, but the light from Jourdan's torch was behind Percy turning him into an ominous but evidently armed silhouette.

'Sergeant?' he croaked in a hopeful and frightened voice. His face and the top of his head were covered with three days growth of hair. His lips were cracked and swollen.

'Water but nothing to eat were the bishop's orders,' Jourdan said behind Percy. 'Shall I give him water, sir?'

'Yes,' Percy agreed without moving.

The sergeant started to move past him and Percy snapped the torch out of his hand and gestured for him to put it in a bracket in the corridor. Jourdan understood at once, nodded and obeyed.

Jourdan re-entered the chamber, removed a tin dipper from a hook on the wall and removed the lid of a barrel. Percy heard the dipper plunk into the water and he swallowed. He had not been suspended comfortably like the Dominican but with his hands tied behind his back – and they had never brought him water. He had been expected to speak, to answer questions, hour after hour, but there had been no water, not even when his mouth was so dry that his answers were dusty, painful whispers which not even flame could turn into audible screams. His arms had been wrenched from their sockets, his elbows disjointed, his hips pulled apart from the weights on his feet. There were no weights on the Dominican's feet. They were still lined up neatly against the wall.

Jourdan lifted the dipper to di Sante.

Di Sante had ordered an innocent peasant woman to be hung by her breasts over a fire. Di Sante had witnessed his own confession knowing that it was a lie. At least the first half. Di Sante was part of the Inquisition.

'Sergeant.'

'Sir?'

'Do me a favour.'

'Sir?'

'Shorten the hand chains six inches – and attach the one hundred pound weights to his feet.'

Percy did not wait for an answer. He turned on his heel and started back out of the dungeon. He had got halfway up the stairs when a wailing howl came chasing after him. It overtook him, surrounded him in the confines of the stairs and he tripped. His chin banged on the step and his hand slipped on the mouldy walls as he tried to catch himself. The howl came again, drawn out and accusing. Percy righted himself and paused. His conscience was begging him to return and retract his orders. But he couldn't. His hatred was stronger than his pity. He continued up the stairs and out into the refreshing night air. A last whimper followed him and then the door swung shut.

Chapter Twenty-Two

Paris, 27th March, 1310

It was eight months since the seneschal of the Temple had named him Preceptor of Aquitaine and invested him with supreme and absolute authority over all Free Templars in France, but Geoffrey was still unused to the marks of honour his subordinates paid him.

As he and his small escort turned into the street, the wooden gates giving access to the cobbled courtyard of a Flemish merchant's grand house swung back. No sooner had he passed under the stone arch than men swarmed around him, taking the reins of his greying stallion, holding his off stirrup, reaching up to help him down from the high saddle. An engraved silver goblet with wine was offered to him as his weary feet touched the ground, and all around him the welcoming murmur of blessings and greetings could be heard.

'Let me take you up to your chamber, my lord,' Sir Gilbert offered. 'Master de Winter has put his best guest chamber at your disposal. Will you be wanting a rest before dinner?'

'Yes, I need to rest, but then I would like to' – Geoffrey's eyes swept the courtyard, which seemed overflowing with disguised Templars trying in some way to please him, but Percy was nowhere to be seen – 'to see you all and hear what you have accomplished. Will the trial open tomorrow as planned or has the king managed to interfere?'

It had taken Geoffrey three weeks to make the journey from Chanac. He was worried that the king might have intervened to prevent or postpone the trial.

Sir Gilbert smiled and shook his head. 'Everything is proceeding as planned. We have established contact with nearly all the Defenders and the mood is good, my lord.'

Sir Gilbert had been impressed and inspired by the courage and confidence of the imprisoned defenders. They believed that the pope had finally intervened on their behalf and that at last they would have a fair chance to clear their Order of the spurious charges. The proof of the existence of Free Templars had in several instances contributed to an almost euphoric sense of impending triumph, which had in turn infected the men now clustered eagerly around Geoffrey.

Even the usually cautious Sir Martin was smiling broadly. 'Welcome to Paris, my lord. I think you will find you have not come in vain.'

'Ah, Martin, no matter what happens tomorrow, I had to be here.'

Geoffrey had slept poorly these past nights because his body was troubled by the aches and pains of riding and his thoughts by all the imponderables of the impending trial. Geoffrey knew that the pope was as weak and indecisive in his defence of the Temple as the king was fanatically determined to destroy it. Geoffrey vacillated between righteous indignation which demanded a hearing, even if it sent them all to their deaths, and guilt at the knowledge that other men than he were risking the flames.

Master de Winter himself, an old friend of Geoffrey's, was standing in the doorway to give Geoffrey the kiss of peace and welcome him under his roof. Geoffrey enquired with genuine concern if they were not too many and too much of a burden, but de Winter dismissed the problem regally. The majority of the sergeants were housed in the tavern which abutted his warehouses from the street behind. Sirs Percy, Martin and Gilbert were welcome guests, and it was a great pleasure to finally meet Geoffrey's favourite grandchild, the Lady Félice.

In a large, loud group they made their way up the groaning wooden stairs to the second storey and along the narrow corridor to a spacious chamber with wooden floors, wainscotting and panelled ceiling. Everything here seemed to gleam from recent polishing, even the cupboard bed built into the far wall.

Geoffrey thanked his host and promised to come down to the hall when he was washed and rested. He asked if he could have a bath and his host promised to have one sent up at once. Niki took the luggage from the sergeant who had carried it upstairs and closed the door firmly, conscious of how much Geoffrey needed peace and quiet after the long journey.

Félice had been waiting anxiously for this moment, and now she knocked timidly. Annoyed, Niki reopened the door, but at once broke into a smile at the sight of her. Niki backed up with the words, 'My lord, it is Lady Félice.'

Félice saw her grandfather's eyes light up at once. He held out his arms to her and she ran to them. Then, frowning, he held her at arm's length and scolded, 'You deserve a good whipping, do you know that? You promised to write if there was…' Too late he saw the tears that flooded her eyes. 'Ah, no!' He pulled her back into his arms more tightly than ever and swivelled gently back and forth from the waist, cursing himself while she sobbed.

'I wanted to… but I didn't have the money… for a courier. And—'

'Hush!' He kissed the top of her head. 'Child, forgive a stupid old man. I didn't mean it.'

But Félice couldn't stop crying. She had not cried in anyone's arms since she had left home. All the nights spent crying in her empty bed at Belmonte had merely left her exhausted and conscious of her utter isolation. She needed the comfort of her grandfather's embrace. She needed to cry all the coldness left by her failed marriage out of herself.

Geoffrey started to understand. He backed up to a leather armchair and sank down into it, pulling Félice on to his lap. She was somewhat heavy for his thin thighs, but for the moment that didn't matter. She buried her face in his neck and her tears were warm and wet on his sagging skin. Niki discreetly withdrew to see to his lord's bath, sensing this was a reunion that even a loyal squire had no right to witness.

'I... I knew that he didn't love me any more,' Félice stammered; all her woes came pouring out between gasps for air. 'It wasn't just the miscarriages. Even before that he had stopped loving me. But he wouldn't have... If either of the babies had lived. But if I couldn't have children he had to get rid of me so he could... could marry...'

She broke down again and Geoffrey rocked her back and forth. Her tears were trickling down inside his shirt, growing colder as they descended.

'If I were a young knight – like your brother – I would kill Dom Pedro for what he's done to you.'

'No, Grandpapa! I don't want him dead. I still love him. If only I could have regained his affection – but I didn't know how! I don't even know *why* he stopped loving me!'

The anguish in her voice made Geoffrey still more angry. How could any man be indifferent to the pain he caused? For pity's sake alone, Dom Pedro should have taken her back. There was no excuse in Geoffrey's eyes for such callousness to a woman.

'It was before the first miscarriage.' Félice had to tell someone in a desperate effort to understand herself. 'I... felt it. He looked at me differently. I was his wife and I was carrying his heir so he treated me respectfully, but something was different – gone. It happened so suddenly! How can love die so fast?'

She lifted her head and looked directly at her grandfather. She expected him to explain this to her as once he had explained geometry and Greek.

'It can't,' Geoffrey told her simply.

'But it did!' she insisted, tears spilling down her splotched and salt-streaked face. 'One day he was passionately in love with me and interrupted dinner to take me to bed and then the next morning... he was different! He looked at me and said he didn't like my dressing gown – though it was the one I'd always worn.'

Geoffrey pulled her back into his arms and Félice continued pouring out her misery in a flood. She told him of Dona Inez's constant criticism, how she could do nothing right. She told how Dom Pedro refused to let her ride or show an interest in his estates. She explained that he expected her to think of nothing but the baby. Geoffrey concluded that, after all, it was better the marriage had ended. The thought of Félice being treated like a heifer for the rest of her life offended him almost as much as the callousness of her rejection. Félice began telling him about the night of her first miscarriage, when she danced with King Dinis and her husband had claimed this had caused the miscarriage.

'Ridiculous!' Geoffrey retorted, irritated by such nonsense.

He gently set Félice back on her feet and went across the room to get the carafe of wine and a chalice. Returning with both, he sank down on the rug before the fire and gestured for Félice to join him on the floor. Here he could put his arm around her shoulders without having to bear her weight on his tired legs. Then he poured the wine and passed it to her. She hiccuped, took a deep breath and sipped the dark Burgundy.

When she seemed calmer, Geoffrey said carefully, 'Hugh says you tried to kill yourself. Is that true?'

Félice didn't answer and Geoffrey held her closer and then gave her a little shake. 'How could you do that? How dare you?'

Félice was looking down at her hands and a single tear made its way down her face. She swallowed. 'If... if Dom Pedro could turn against me, stop loving me, then there must be something wrong with me. Something that will make other men turn away from me as he did. I was afraid that maybe even you – now that you've become a Templar at last—'

'Félice!' It was a cry of pain. 'You couldn't think that!'

She bit her lower lip and tears swamped her eyes.

Geoffrey pulled her into his arms again and started rocking her. 'I used to think you were the brightest of all my grandchildren, but sometimes you are very, very stupid. Do you know that? Well, you are. I am an old man and there are some people who will tell you that I am senile – your mother for one. But your mother is the last person on earth who understands the meaning of the word "love".'

He could tell that he had her attention. She still had her face buried in his shoulder but she was holding her breath to stifle her sobs.

'Dom Pedro *never* loved you! He must have desired you; he was very probably infatuated with you. That is what infatuation is like: it takes hold of you instantly, is irresistible and then just as suddenly it is gone!' He snapped his fingers to emphasise his point.

Félice stiffened in his arms, but he was making sense and she knew it.

He stroked her head. 'Love isn't like that, Félice. Do you think I could have fallen out of love with your grandmother even if I tried? I *did* try! But I couldn't stop loving her, so I turned my back on the Temple and took service with King

Louis so I could win the right to marry her. And Sister Madeleine has loved your Uncle Jean ever since he bought her out of slavery over twenty years ago though they have never known each other carnally. Love doesn't have anything to do with making love – though that can enhance it. And sex without love, as Sister Madeleine can testify, is an act of violence and contempt. From what you have told me, Dom Pedro desired your body but he never even tried to know – much less love – your soul. Did he?'

Félice thought about this and was forced to shake her head in agreement. Whenever she tried to talk to him about anything substantive, he'd told her – indulgently at first and with irritation later – not to trouble her pretty head or to think of their child.

'Now, I'm going to ask you a difficult question, Félice,' Geoffrey continued gently. 'Did you love Dom Pedro – or did you love your husband?'

Félice frowned. 'But Dom Pedro was my husband!' she protested, and then catching Geoffrey's raised eyebrow, she grasped what he meant.

She bit her lower lip while she tried to sort out her emotions. She had not known Dom Pedro when she married him. His passion had startled and flattered her at first, but she had spent most of her married life simply being afraid of displeasing him. 'I so wanted to be a good wife,' she admitted. 'I didn't want to fail.'

Geoffrey nodded and held her closer. 'Sometimes – in the long run – it is better to fail. Now you are back with the people who love you, Félice. And we cannot stop loving you no matter what Dom Pedro or his sister or anyone else on earth thinks of you. You can hurt us, disappoint us, even anger us, but you can't make us stop loving you.'

Félice looked up and straight into his eyes. 'But you're the only one in the world who loves me, Grandpapa! My mother has always hated me and my father...' She shrugged. There wasn't even any point in mentioning Norbert or Umberto. Félice knew that the one did not even pretend to love her and the other only thought he did.

'And Percy?'

Félice started and caught her breath. 'You think Percy loves me?'

'Oh, child! Can't you see it?'

She was remembering Percy's eyes on the day of her wedding, the dream she had had during her miscarriage and the day he had rescued her. But he had never looked at her with desire – not the way Umberto and Dom Pedro had. 'But he's never—'

'Said anything? Of course not! He is a monk. He would not dishonour you by saying anything. But he carries his love for you around in his heart; it hurts him sometimes but it also gives him strength. Now, I want you to be honest with me, Félice. Why did you try to kill yourself? Because you had lost Dom Pedro or because you hated yourself?'

Félice thought back to that night in Vila do Condé. She hadn't thought of Dom Pedro at all. 'It was because I couldn't face the future,' she admitted in a whisper.

Geoffrey nodded with relief. 'But that is better now, isn't it? I don't have to worry about your trying something like that again, do I?'

'Oh no! Percy has given me a reason to live. I want to help you both.'

Her grandfather understood her better than she did herself. He smiled sadly.

When they brought up the bath and buckets of steaming water, Geoffrey gently dismissed Félice. No sooner had the door closed behind her than there was a knock on the door and a familiar voice asked, 'May I assist you, my lord?'

Geoffrey spun around, delighted. Percy fell on to one knee before him and bowed his head.

'Not that! Not from you!' He bent to lift Percy up and embrace him.

As always, Geoffrey's warmth confused Percy. He had never known it from his own harsh father, much less his embittered mother. His heart responded with a lurch of affection that almost hurt and yet his arms hardly dared return the hug. He doesn't know what I have done, Percy reminded himself, feeling ashamed and contaminated by his mercilessness. Geoffrey would never have done what he had to the Dominican.

Geoffrey missed the open affection which had been so much a part of his relationship with Eleanor. But Geoffrey knew that Percy's reticence was not the product of inner reservations but an inbred shyness he had to struggle to overcome. Usually Percy took a moment to overcome his inhibitions and then relaxed. Today, the relaxation did not come.

Geoffrey stepped back and looked at Percy more closely. 'What's wrong?'

Percy averted his eyes. 'Nothing. Let me help you.'

He started to unbuckle the back of Geoffrey's leather brigandine. Niki, frowning, managed to elbow Percy aside at this point. Percy turned to the boys who were hanging a cauldron of water over the fire and asked them to leave. 'I will see to my lord's bath.'

The boys left the chamber. Percy went to the steaming cauldron and tested the temperature of the water while Niki helped Geoffrey undress. When naked, Geoffrey stepped into the tub and settled down. He watched Percy as the younger man conscientiously performed the menial task of filling the bath.

The bath three-quarters full, Percy stripped down to his shirt, tossing surcoat, hauberk and gambeson carelessly aside. He rolled his sleeves back over his elbows and took the bar of soap in his long-fingered but calloused hands.

Geoffrey at last breached the silence, testing the water of Percy's explicit humility carefully. 'I've seen Félice. She was hurt very badly by that man Marie married her to.'

'She tried to drown herself in the Atlantic just hours before we arrived at the convent… She must have loved her husband very much,' Percy ventured carefully, trying to sound neutral.

'No.' Geoffrey did not want him to suffer unnecessary pain. 'It was not love for him but shame at her failure that robbed her of the courage to go on living.'

Percy glanced up with a flicker of relief in his eyes.

Geoffrey continued simply. 'You were right to bring her to Paris.'

'She insisted on coming. She says she wants to help us. She has already helped us…' Percy fell silent, his eyes averted.

'What is it?' Geoffrey asked again in a lower, coaxing voice.

Percy still would not meet his eyes. 'I wish that I could clean my heart as I can my body.'

'And what would you cleanse from your heart?' Geoffrey asked, half-afraid of the answer. Geoffrey believed in the power of love even if it were unspoken and forbidden. He believed that any man who could learn to love another person was a step nearer to God. He disagreed with the Church which thought that universal love was easier if specific love was denied. He did not want Percy to deny or abhor his love of Félice.

Percy did not stop in his task but he took his time answering. At last, holding Geoffrey's left arm and rubbing it with soap, he said, 'Bitterness. Hatred.'

Geoffrey let out his breath slowly. He was relieved that it was not love Percy wished to expunge but he was conscious of a new danger.

'I was in the Bishop of Albi's Paris dungeon—'

'Albi's?' Geoffrey asked, alarmed, sitting up straighter. He did not think Percy should have taken such a risk. 'Couldn't someone else have gone?'

Percy shook his head. 'I… had to go. There are three men there – defenders – whom I know from the time of my own imprisonment. Two were arrested with me at Saint Pierre. Brother Thomas has lost both his feet – they must have been amputated because they had been burned to the bone.' As he spoke his voice had hardened more and more. 'Father André warned me,' Percy continued. 'He begged me to forgive them – but I can't!' It burst out of him and his hand made a violent motion, splashing water and drenching his face. Percy wiped the drops away with the back of his sleeve.

'Father André is an exceptional man,' Geoffrey pointed out, adding simply, 'I have not forgiven them either.'

'But you would never lower yourself to their level,' Percy told him definitively.

Geoffrey was not sure what he meant and Percy could not bring himself to be more explicit. He started soaping Geoffrey more vigorously, his eyes averted, his tongue probing the hole left by his extracted teeth.

Geoffrey could sense the explosive conflict of emotions simmering near to overflowing beneath the calm exterior and he felt a chill go through him. It was de Sonnac who had once told him that the heart is a battleground between good and evil. Geoffrey had come to understand that as a conflict between love and hate. Percy might not explicitly want to expunge love from his heart but if hatred got the upper hand it would die of its own accord.

Chapter Twenty-Three

Paris, 28th March, 1310

It was a sunny day and the trees which reached skywards behind the high stone wall enclosing the Bishop of Paris' garden had taken on a faint greenish tinge. Before the open gateway, the street was congested with the arriving litters of the papal commissioners, the king's 'witnesses' and the first cartloads of defenders. The bishop of Paris, as host, was standing just inside the open gate in full episcopal regalia, the sun glinting on the gold threads of his embroidered cope and mitre as he nodded his head and clasped hands with his brother bishops.

The Bishop of Albi disdained a litter despite his bulk and his episcopal robes. He arrived upon his heavy-boned Flemish gelding and swung his leg over the cantle to the groaning of leather. One of Paris's grooms in a white and gold livery sporting a bishop's staff and a paschal lamb in gold thread, rushed to hold the bridle, and Albi strode towards Paris with a wide grin on his face. He clasped the other man's frail hand in his own giant one. 'A fine day! Excellent weather. The Lord shines on our efforts to bring these repulsive heretics to justice!'

'Indeed. Indeed.' The bishop of Paris extracted his hand from the burly grip of his fellow bishop; all the bones felt crushed where the heavy rings had been ground into his fingers. 'If you would take your place upon the platform, brother.' The Bishop of Paris graciously indicated the wooden platform completely clothed in white linen and covered with a canopy of white and gold, where seven armchairs had been set up for the commissioners. The Bishops of Narbonne and Trent were already present, standing behind the row of chairs chatting comfortably while menials set wine and water on tables before the commissioners. Stools were lined up behind the chairs for the bishops' various secretaries and below the raised platform other tables had been set up for the official scribes who would take the minutes of the proceedings. To the right of the platform another row of chairs under a blue canopy had been set up for those of the king's ministers who would attend. For the defenders of the Temple there were no seats provided: they would have to stand before the tribunal.

Umberto di Sante could follow his master only slowly. As he gently let himself down from his horse, his arms and shoulders protested with searing pain that made him groan inwardly. He dropped his arms as quickly as possible and swallowed the bile that rose in his throat. Then, turning, he kept himself rigidly upright as he snapped at a groom to take his horse 'this instant!' The groom gave him a sullen look but did as he was told. Let him think it was just arrogance, anything but that he should notice Umberto did not have the strength in his tortured arms to control the powerful beast. He watched as his horse was led away, then turned and moved very stiffly forward, his face a mask. Each step was agony for him. His hips seemed to grind in their sockets and his ankles felt as if they would buckle under him any moment.

Umberto was certain that the bishop did not know what it felt like to be suspended from one's arms with a one hundred pound weight attached to shackles on one's ankles. He would have given his very soul to make sure that the bishop learned.

Advancing very slowly, looking from side to side so others would think his pace was dictated by curiosity not pain, he noticed a number of men astride well-bred and well-groomed horses waiting in the background. The horses stamped irritably and rubbed their faces against their forelegs in evident boredom while the riders watched the proceedings with ill-disguised intensity.

Something about them made a chill run down Umberto's spine and he was reminded of all the rumours about Free Templars who were running wild these days. There could be no question that here and there prisoners had 'disappeared'. The officials responsible for the prisoners usually had some transparent story about sudden mysterious fevers or even suicides, but the whispers simply became louder. And now and then – as at that Carthusian monastery near Poitiers or, more recently, just north of Toulouse – the guards holding Templar prisoners had been overwhelmed by force. Although these incidents were officially kept secret, no fewer than seventeen men were known to have lost their lives to mysterious brigands who released Templar prisoners. The king had furiously decreed that these were common outlaws acting unpolitically and had simultaneously degraded the sheriffs in whose territory the assaults occurred. To an insider like Umberto, there could be no doubt that there were Free Templars at large and that they were becoming increasingly bold.

Bold enough to risk being here? Would they try to free the prisoners being brought up in cartloads? Over five hundred of them? Not this handful of men surely. But Umberto's stomach contracted nervously and he studied the men more closely still. The knight nearest him seemed vaguely familiar but he could not place him at first – until he recognised the old man beside him: Félice's grandfather! The young knight was the man who had escorted Félice from Portugal. But they weren't Templars. Umberto sighed with relief. Félice had a Templar uncle. No doubt that was the reason her grandfather was here. Maybe he hoped to find his son among the many prisoners and, of course, he had an escort, including his kinsman. For all Umberto knew the knight might even be the illegitimate son of Félice's uncle. Now that the men were explained and no longer ominous, Umberto wondered if it wouldn't be polite to pay his respects to Monsieur de Preuthune. He could send greetings to Félice.

But with a nervous glance towards the Bishop of Albi, he decided against it. It was on account of Félice that the bishop had ordered his 'chastisement' in the dungeon. Umberto would never forgive him for that. His entire energies since his release had been directed towards thinking of some way to escape the bishop's service. When he had a new, more powerful patron, he would flaunt his relationship with Félice! The bishop would see that he could not break a di Sante as if he were a peasant or a heretic! He would live to regret the day he had humiliated Umberto di Sante!

Strengthened by this thought, Umberto forced himself to step out more vigorously, his face stiff with the effort of suppressing all indication of pain. The features of his face seemed more prominent under his waxy, white skin and his lips were bloodless.

Beside him, a cart carrying prisoners drew to a halt. The smell of unwashed bodies saturated the air and Umberto gagged. The bishop had not even let him down from his chains to relieve himself! He had been forced to soil himself for three days! He would certainly never forgive him for that!

The soldiers guarding the Templars opened the back of a cart and ordered the prisoners to climb down. Their legs still chained together, they clambered only awkwardly to the clanking of chain and the curses of the guards.

'Why are these men still chained?' The voice was authoritative, angry and it cut through the air like a knife.

Everyone looked over. Di Sante frowned. Who did Félice's cousin think he was to interfere with a papal commission?

'They couldn't pay for the removal of the shackles. It costs a sou a piece.' The guard who had been shooing the prisoners out of the cart explained defensively.

Umberto could see the man was nervously trying to identify the knight, unsure whether he was a high official of some kind. He wore no coat of arms but the breeding of his stallion, the glitter of gold spurs and the quality of his blue-and-purple surcoat was enough to make any commoner pause.

The knight was already reaching for a leather purse that hung from his sword belt but Félice's grandfather forestalled him. The old man the took his own purse from his hip. He gave the guard a coin and kept his stallion looming over him until he had unlocked the fetters of all his prisoners. Then he backed the stallion away with the slow deliberation of a good horseman.

Di Sante remembered how this man had challenged the pope himself in an audience almost two years ago, and he looked curiously to see if he still wore the spurs Saint Louis had given him. From this distance it was not possible to make out the *fleur-de-lis* but the spurs glittered as though studded with diamonds. Félice was right to be proud of her grandfather – but he was taking such terrible risks. It was very dangerous to show so much open sympathy for the Templars. Di Sante looked over his shoulder to see if any of the king's officers had witnessed the incident and was relieved that Nogaret did not appear to be present.

Umberto reached the gateway and passed into the garden with a nod to the Bishop of Paris. No one questioned a

Dominican. He made his way to the steps leading up to the platform and went to take his seat.

'Ah, there you are!' The Bishop of Albi greeted him. 'I was wondering where you'd got to.'

Umberto inclined his head slowly but did not deign to answer.

'Still sulking?' the bishop retorted. 'Well, please yourself.' He turned away, annoyed that di Sante was playing the martyr, but satisfied that he wouldn't be insubordinate again – judging by the way he still minced around after a mere three days in chains! Albi shook his head in disgusted contempt. Maybe he'd made a mistake. Di Sante was soft and self-pitying. Not good material after all.

More and more prisoners were being crowded into the garden before the platform. The stink emanating from them was becoming correspondingly stronger and Albi noticed that several of his fellow bishops discreetly sniffed at perfumed cloths which they kept tucked in their sleeves or embroidered gloves.

Albi disdained such pampering and let his gaze sweep across the filthy, hairy, skeletal figures that shuffled into the garden. They squinted in the unaccustomed bright light and their hands were still in chains even if their feet were free of shackles for the moment. Various rags, no longer identifiable as either habits or surcoats, left their dirty, emaciated bodies more exposed than covered. Several of the men held their hands in front of their genitals in evident shame at the inadequacy of their attire.

Yet for all that, there could be no denying the excitement which possessed these creatures as they entered the garden. Though the strong sunlight made their darkness-accustomed eyes stream with tears, they still looked about with open curiosity and alertness. They talked eagerly amongst themselves, exchanging greetings, enquiring after those who were absent, raising questions such as: 'Will we be given a fair trial?'; 'Where is the master?'; 'Have you seen any of the preceptors?'; 'Did you hear from the Free Templars?'

Albi could not make out individual conversations but he could sense the hope that hung as tangibly in the air as the stink of the dungeon. The Bishop of Narbonne called the assembled company to order and Albi settled back into his chair. It would be interesting to see how long it took before their hope was blown away.

A prayer was said for guidance and blessings for all the commissioners and then the papal edict setting up the commission was read aloud and entered into the minutes. Finally the charges were read aloud – in Latin. The priests and other literate Templars were compelled to translate these charges for their less literate brethren, which meant that the reading of the charges was accompanied by an increasingly loud undertone of babbling from the defenders. Now and then men even raised their voices to shout out their protest: 'Lies! Slander!' And, as men do, they took courage from one another so that more and more of the Templars risked venting their anger in shouts of, 'Not true!', 'Lies!' or even the occasional, 'We were tortured!' It became increasingly difficult for the clerk reading the charges to make himself heard. The Bishop of Narbonne used his crook to pound on the platform and call for order. The reading of the charges resumed:

The Templars renounced God. 'Never!'

The Templars renounced Jesus Christ. 'Christ is Our Lord!'

The Templars denied the virginity of Mary. 'Lies!'; 'The Virgin is our patron!'

The Templars denied the saints. 'Not true!'

The Templars worshipped Satan in the form of a cat. 'Lies!'; 'Not us! 'The Dominicans worship a dog!'

That was at least original, Albi noted and glanced over his shoulder at his own Dominican dog to see how he had reacted. Di Sante sat with his arms crossed as if he were totally detached from the proceedings.

The Templars denied the ability of Christ to grant salvation. 'He is our only Salvation! The Resurrection and the Life!'

The Templars believe Christ died for his own sins. 'For our sins! For our sins and *yours*!'

That was almost an accusation. Albi looked over to see if he could find the man who had shouted so vibrantly. But all the bearded, haggard faces looked alike.

The Templars denied the sacraments. 'Not true!'

The Templars did not bless the host at mass. 'Lies! Base lies!'

The Templars were absolved of their sins by the master, preceptor or commander rather than their priests. 'Why have priests then?'; 'Where is Master de Molay?'; 'We demand to see the master!'

The cries for de Molay became so loud that the Bishop of Narbonne signalled for the guards to intervene. Roughly shouting for silence, the guards used force to silence those they saw yelling. The clamour came to a ragged halt.

'De Molay has refused to testify before this commission despite our repeated efforts to persuade him,' Narbonne told them before ordering the scribe to proceed.

At their initiation, Templar recruits were compelled to kiss the officer in charge of their reception on the navel and the base of the spine and on the penis. 'Slander!'; 'Lies!'; 'Never!'

The initiation of members was kept secret to hide these shameful practices. 'We had nothing to hide!'

Sodomy was practised and encouraged. 'More by the Franciscans and Dominicans!'; 'Look to your own house!'; 'Only he who is without sin…'

Various idols were worshipped. 'Christ and His Mother were worshipped!'

Templars who failed to worship the idols were imprisoned or killed. 'There were no idols!'

The Templars swore never to discuss the secrets of the Order with outsiders.

Confused murmuring followed this. It seemed perfectly harmless to most of the accused. How else could they have kept their military plans from falling into the wrong hands, and why should the Hospitallers know the secrets of training, weapons and navigation the Temple had developed?

Just before the scribe continued, someone called out, 'Our Rule was no secret – every pope has seen and confirmed it since the Order was founded in the presence of Saint Bernard!'

Albi made a sour face and looked for the speaker – he was obviously an educated man.

Templars could only confess to their own priests.

Again there followed a confused muttering among the prisoners. Wasn't that true of any Order?

'The pope himself gave us priests for that very reason!'

Despite the enormity of the sins of the Order, the members had failed to report them to the Church authorities. 'We owe obedience to the pope alone!'; 'The Order committed no sins!'; 'We had nothing to report!'; 'The Order is innocent of all charges! Innocent!'; 'We are innocent!'

It was becoming a chant and Narbonne pounded angrily with his staff.

'Your master and preceptors and visitors have *all* confessed!' Narbonne shouted above the clamour. 'Your officers have all confessed! You have all confessed!' Narbonne was screaming in French and the defenders no longer needed interpreters. The response was correspondingly more immediate and greater. From hundreds of throats came denials: 'Not all of us!' Or, more pervasive: 'Under torture!'

The Bishop of Narbonne called for order again. 'Do you deny the charges?'

'Yes!'

This was shouted so loudly from so many throats that it came clearly over the wall to the anxious cluster of riders waiting outside in the otherwise deserted street. They exchanged worried glances. Unable to hear the questions, the suddenly positive response was confusing.

'Do you wish to defend your Order?'

'Yes!'

'Even though your master has refused to do so before this commission?'

'The master is correct to insist upon the jurisdiction of His Holiness.' The voice that answered was cultivated, precise and had an Italian accent. Albi and Narbonne both sat up straighter and searched for the speaker with a sense of alarm. 'Who said that?' Narbonne demanded sharply.

'I did.' A man started forwards and his brothers made way for him. He was dressed in the remnants of a priest's cassock. He had curly brown hair that flowed to his shoulders mixing with his long beard. He looked about forty years of age and had black eyes and a prominent nose. He would undoubtedly have been handsome if he had been cleaned, and there was no denying his dignity. He stood straight with raised head, his mangled hands held in front of him.

'Who are you?' Narbonne asked, scowling.

'My name is Peter di Bologna.'

A ripple of comment went through the Templars and men strained to get a look at the man.

On the platform, Albi hissed angrily over his shoulder towards di Sante, 'Isn't that one of our men?'

'Pierre de Boulogne sur Mer is in our pay,' di Sante told him with conscious ambiguity.

This Italian was not in their pay but Pierre de Boulogne was. If the bishop were too stupid to note the difference, it was his problem. The bishop settled smugly into his chair again and di Sante smiled behind his back.

'You deny the authority of this commission?' Narbonne was demanding angrily.

'Certainly. Only His Holiness himself or a Church Council can pass judgement on the Poor Knights of the Temple of Solomon at Jerusalem. Master de Molay would be remiss in his duties if he did not insist upon this point. We poor brothers, however, have gathered here to give testimony to your excellencies in the fervent hope that your findings will persuade His Holiness of our innocence and induce him to take up the cause of his humble, loyal and most cruelly misused servants.'

For a moment, Narbonne was unsure how to respond to this mixture of defiance and conciliation. With a glance towards Nogaret, he decided to ask sternly, 'Do you recognise the authority of this commission or not?'

'To hear evidence and testimony, yes.'

Narbonne glanced now at Albi and Trent, the other two bishops who were unquestionably loyal to the king. Both seemed to nod to him.

'Do you represent your brothers?' he asked Bologna.

'No, Your Grace.'

But Bologna's own denial was lost in the affirmative answer shouted by many of the others.

Narbonne gestured irritably for silence. 'Not all of you can defend the Temple. You must elect representatives. Do you agree on Peter di Bologna?'

The clamour of approval was unambiguous.

'I cannot assume this burden alone,' Bologna protested. 'According to—'

Narbonne cut him short. He had no intention of letting Bologna alone represent the Templars. That would be too dangerous no matter how confident Albi was. Men whose treason could be bought were inherently untrustworthy. 'Three other defenders must be elected.'

Someone in the crowd of Templars shouted out a name and Narbonne quickly asked, 'Objections? None? Very good. Two more names.'

'That was somewhat over hasty.' The Bishop of Le Puy noted, leaning forwards across the Bishop of Trent.

Le Puy was a man who owed his appointment not to Philip IV but to Louis IX. He had himself been on crusade; Narbonne thoroughly mistrusted him.

'What do you mean? No one objected!'

Narbonne pressed ahead ruthlessly, trusting the men planted among the prisoners to shout out the names of reliable men prepared to work in the king's interests in exchange for a promise of 'clemency'. They had all been assured that they would face nothing less than life imprisonment.

When he asked for nominations, several voices were raised at once, causing Narbonne to frown angrily and glance at Albi in reproach. He was supposed to have this organised.

'Renaud de Provins!' came distinctly and was repeated by several men. But other names were being called as well.

Albi turned on Umberto. 'I thought you had this organised!'

'I wasn't exactly free to see to your affairs during the last three days, was I?' di Sante pointed out in a venomous voice despite the sweet smile on his angelic face.

'Damn you!'

Narbonne was calling for order, his face flushed, and Nogaret had crossed his arms in an attitude of displeasure. Narbonne ordered all the names recorded and had the secretary bring them to him. He passed them down to Albi.

Albi signalled for Umberto. 'Which of these men are in our pay?'

Umberto considered the list. He briefly considered lying but decided upon the truth. He indicated two of the five names. Albi nodded curtly and passed the list back to Narbonne with a brief commentary.

Narbonne read out the first name. 'All in favour say "aye".'

Scattered voices started to shout 'yes', faltered and fell silent.

Narbonne frowned. He could feel Le Puy leaning forwards again, his eyes narrowed with suspicion.

Narbonne called out the name of the second trustworthy candidate. This time only silence greeted him. Nogaret leaned forwards ominously and Narbonne found that he had started sweating despite the fresh breeze.

'Renaud de Provins!' someone shouted from the crowd and this time many took up the call.

'Who the hell is this Renaud?' Narbonne demanded of Albi.

Albi could only shrug.

'A nice mess!' Narbonne commented.

'It seems the third man has been elected,' Le Puy decided for him. 'You may record the name.' He told the scribes, who looked somewhat bewildered. Before he was made even more of a fool, Narbonne nodded agreement to the scribe and then read out the next name. The candidate received wholehearted support from one corner of the garden, which spread with increasing enthusiasm to the others. Bowing to the inevitable, Narbonne had his name recorded as well and then adjourned the session. 'The next hearing will be on April 7th.' He ordered the four spokesmen taken to his own palace and all the other defenders returned to their various dungeons. He stood and started to depart.

Le Puy caught his arm. 'I would be honoured to have the four spokesmen under my roof, brother. You are so burdened with prisoners, while I have so few.'

'I assure you it is no burden to enforce the will of His Majesty and His Holiness.'

'None whatsoever, I quite agree. You will therefore not begrudge me the desire to share in the blessing of serving our secular and ecclesiastical lords?'

Narbonne narrowed his eyes but could not think of a good reason to decline. 'They must be kept under strict guard. If they escape—'

'They condemn their Order,' Le Puy pointed out. 'Which is hardly what they were elected to do, is it?'

Narbonne realised that he was trapped. 'Sergeant! Turn the four spokesmen over to my dear colleague of Le Puy.' Furiously, he descended from the platform, his robes fluttering about him and his mitre starting to slip backwards.

Nogaret cut off his retreat and raised his eyebrows. 'Do you know the defenders' spokesmen?' he enquired.

'Two are in our pay and can be trusted to do the bidding of the king.'

'Which is to say that two are not. I'm not sure the king will be satisfied with these results, Monseigneur.' Nogaret turned his back on the bishop and departed.

*

No one was more bewildered by his election than Renaud de Provins. Round-faced, short-sighted and pock-marked to the point of complete disfiguration, Renaud never sought any kind of limelight. He was short, with a waddling walk, and a very high voice, the result of castration at the age of twelve. The bishop had sought thereby to preserve his angelic voice for the cathedral choir indefinitely, but the pox which struck two years later had taken the beauty from his voice as well as his face.

To these innate or old disabilities were added the indignity of the fact that he had been seized on Friday, 13th October, 1307, when wearing nothing but his nightshirt. This was now a filthy rag that did very little to cover his misshapen, hairy legs and tended to reveal his mutilated genitals when he moved. His ankles were bruised and bloody from the shackles which had not been removed until the strange knight had intervened shortly before the opening of the hearing. His naturally drab but fine hair hung in greasy strands almost to his shoulders and lice visibly crawled about his head and on his dirty body. Renaud could see the repulsion and disbelief with which the other spokesmen looked at him while they were carted back to Le Puy's palace in a two-wheeled donkey cart which one of Le Puy's secretaries had hired. Renaud could only shrug in answer to their stares and smile embarrassedly – revealing a nearly toothless mouth.

William de Chambonnet was the last of the four to have been elected. He had been deputy commander at the commandery of La Nouée in Brittany. He had not yet confessed to any major charge and it had been his fellow prisoners who, knowing his steadfastness and his burning loyalty, had nominated him. His wrists, like his ankles, were running sores and he held his arms across his chest because his shoulders had been dislocated so often that it hurt to let his arms hang freely. His face was like the jagged peaks of the Alps and his eyes burned with inner fire. He looked at Renaud askance and finally asked, 'To what do we owe the honour of *your* company?'

Renaud shrugged again helplessly and tried to smile stupidly. This expression of simplicity had often averted abuse and insults in the past. 'I didn't elect myself,' he pointed out, adding a breathy giggle that made his high-pitched voice seem all the more effeminate.

'If you are one of Nogaret's paid traitors, I'll find a means of killing you!' de Chambonnet told him bluntly.

Bertrand de Sartignes – who had indeed agreed to serve the interests of the king – started. He was an illiterate knight, now nearing sixty, and he couldn't understand what was happening. He was a knight – or he had been. Now he was a heretic. No, no; they had said he was not after all. They said he was to retract his confession. But if he retracted his confession, he was a relapsed heretic and then the secular authorities could burn him at the stake. His hands started to tremble and he scratched at his lice bites, a confused frown on his face. They had promised not to kill him if he helped the king. And they would kill him if he didn't cooperate. And this other knight would kill him if he did. He started stroking his beard in fitful little pats. Then, feeling the dark, molten eyes of the Italian priest boring into him, he stopped like a guilty child and sat on his hands. 'I didn't do anything wrong,' he told Bologna defensively. Already his nervous hands had come free and were tugging at his beard and then at the neck of his habit.

'It's all right, brother,' Bologna told him with an inner sigh.

He had seen the symptoms too often before. He closed his eyes to pray: 'Father, forgive them.' Then opening his eyes, he fixed them on Renaud. 'Are you Renaud de Provins?'

'Provinz – country-bumpkin.'

Renaud smiled his simpleton's smile but Bologna was not deceived. Like the Portuguese Templars who had recommended Renaud for the defence, he was familiar with Renaud's publications. Publications had no faces, no voices and no sexuality that could be either beautiful or ridiculous. Not one of the men who had recommended

Renaud for the defence of the Temple had ever seen him: they had judged him by the way he wrote.

And Renaud wrote in a witty, provocative style, his best works being hypothetical dialogues in the confessional between a 'stupid' peasant and his parish priest. Misspelled and ungrammatical Latin turned the priest's monologues into texts which could make students roll on the floor with delighted laughter. Some quotes had become so popular that they were bandied about the Sorbonne and could be guaranteed to disrupt lectures whenever students got bored. But the theological questions they raised were both intellectually challenging and highly relevant. Peter di Bologna welcomed the assistance of Renaud – even though he too was initially taken aback by his appearance and mannerisms.

'It is an honour to meet you, Brother,' Peter said honestly, overcoming his initial surprise.

Renaud dropped his silly grin, moved by the sincerity in Bologna's voice. 'I hope I can help you – at least in collecting the legal basis for our defence. You'll have to do the actual talking for us, I'm afraid.' He smiled apologetically. 'Who would take me seriously, after all?'

Bertrand looked from one priest to the other, bewildered.

'Renaud is a very distinguished scholar, Brother Bertrand.' Bologna told the knight. 'He will be an immense asset.'

'Assuming we are given access to the documents we need. How can we be expected to prepare a defence without copies of the indictment, the testimony of our brothers and officers and all relevant papal edicts regarding the Temple? The charges of secrecy, confessing only to our own priests and absolution from the master and other officers are the most dangerous.'

Bologna nodded. 'Assuming it is a *fair* trial, yes.'

Their donkey cart jolted through a rut and then started bumping along a poorly cobbled, back alley. Bertrand moaned in agony and William clutched his arms tighter across his chest.

'Do you doubt it then?' Renaud asked.

'You saw the way Narbonne tried to manipulate things.'

'The Free Templars got word to us that Narbonne and Albi are both the king's creatures,' William reported.

Renaud opened his eyes. '*Are* there Free Templars?'

'They sent a message telling us to mistrust Narbonne and Albi, and to elect the two of you to be our spokesmen,' William told them bluntly.

Renaud and Peter looked at one another in surprise and then both broke into smiles. Bologna even laughed and then shouted so that passers-by turned and stared: '*Baucent à la recourse!*'

Chapter Twenty-Four

Sunday, 21st May, 1310

Across the city the bells were clanging for mass, most loudly and tonelessly from the church of Saint Hippolite on the corner. The sergeants housed in the tavern in the next street were already waiting in a group before the de Winter shop as the porter shoved back the gates to the courtyard to let the mounted knights depart for mass.

From the corner of his eye, the porter caught sight of the leper who had been hanging about in the street the night before. Outraged by such impudence, he let out a string of oaths and threatened to call the watch. 'You have no right to endanger good Christians with your blight!' The porter was thinking of the young master's newborn infant. Infants were vulnerable to any evil and the presence of this most repulsive of all illnesses so near the doorstep horrified the loyal servant in the extreme. To emphasise his point, he bent to pick up a loose stone he could throw at the monster.

Abruptly, a hand gripped his shoulder.

'Let him be.' From his stallion, Percy had bent down to stop the man from throwing his stone.

The porter stared in disbelief at the knight, torn between respect for a social superior and outrage at his interference.

Before he could protest, however, Percy had jumped down and, leading his stallion, he crossed the street to the leper, crouched in his tell-tale, hooded robes with the identifying bells. Sirs Martin, Hugh and Gilbert drew up and waited for him impatiently as he took his purse from inside his surcoat. Gaston, however, stirred uneasily to see his lord approach a leper so closely. He looked to Félice for support and was dismayed to find her opening her purse as well.

Percy took a coin and held it out to the man.

'God bless you, my lord,' the beggar answered, holding out his battered tin bowl. Percy let the coin fall into the bowl and was about to turn away when the muffled voice of the leper said, 'Sister Madeleine sends her greetings.'

Percy swung back sharply. 'You know Sister Madeleine of Lys-Saint-Georges?'

'She sent me to find the Holy Grail, my lord – or he who has found it.'

'You mean Sir Percival?'

'She said he would know where she built her first hospital.'

'In Paphos on the isle of Cyprus.'

The leper reached a rag-covered hand inside his robes and removed a sealed letter. It was addressed to 'Sir Percival de Preuthune'. Percy took the letter and inspected the seal: it was that of Sister Madeleine's brother.

The bandaged hand was still outstretched, and, remembering himself, Percy removed his purse a second time and this time gave the man a louis. The hooded figure bobbed his head and uttered repeated thanks and blessings but Percy had turned away, breaking open the seal. The letter was dated 30th April.

'Monsieur,' Sister Madeleine wrote, the Abbot of Arbroath came to me this day with letters and news. He was in Poitiers on behalf of his king, where certain information came to his ears. He has begged me to forward the enclosed letter to you. It is urgent and vital. In haste, your devoted and faithful Madeleine.'

Inside her letter was another message, folded even smaller than the first and addressed to 'Parzival, Chevalier'. Frowning slightly, Percy studied the seal of this letter but was none the wiser, being unfamiliar with Scottish ecclesiastical seals.

The others had closed curiously around him.

'The man was sent by Sister Madeleine to deliver an urgent message,' he explained as he broke the seal of the second letter.

He stared at the tight, neat script covering the page. It was Latin. He swallowed and glanced up at the others. They looked back expectantly. 'I can't read it,' Percy admitted. 'It's Latin.'

The three knights looked blankly at one another and then back at Percy. Geoffrey had ridden to Rouen to see Charles of Valois and was not expected back before midweek. None of the others were literate in Latin.

'I can read Latin,' Félice reminded them and held out her hand. She translated into French as she read aloud:

> Bernard, Abbot of Arbroath and Chancellor of Scotland, sends his respectful greetings to the noble Sir Percival de Lacy, brother of the Poor Knights of the Temple of Solomon at Jerusalem and marshal of said Order in Aquitaine. He begs indulgence that he has the impertinence to write although personally unknown to you and offers as excuse the vital and urgent nature of his message. The good and noble Jean de Preuthune and his own beloved King Robert would not forgive him if he did not pass on the information which came to his ears quite accidentally whilst attending upon His Holiness Pope Clement V in Poitiers this past week. There he was, by chance, in the presence of His Holiness when the latter was in receipt of a message describing the ambitions of

> the Bishop of Cambrai to become Archbishop of Sens—

'That's the younger Marigny. He's already been consecrated at the age of twenty-two!' Sir Hugh exclaimed angrily. Félice glanced up and the wind lifted the green chiffon veils that fell from the back of her crown-like cap.

'Go on,' Percy urged.

> The Bishop of Cambrai has promised to burn as relapsed heretics all those Templars in his jurisdiction who have had the courage to defend their Order—

'The Archbishop of Sens controls Paris!'

'And Chartres and Orléans!'

'Christ – that's over five hundred men!'

'That is the backbone of the defence!'

'That is the *end* of the defence!'

'But how can he interfere with a papal commission?'

'We must get word to Bologna.'

Percy was staring at Félice. She had gone chalk-white and her hand was trembling so violently that the parchment fluttered. She did not meet his eyes but stared at the letter in her hand.

'Does it say more?' Percy pressed softly but intently.

Félice swallowed but her throat was so tight that she thought she would choke. Despite all their talk about the risks, she had not believed it – not until she read the tight Latin script of an unknown Scottish abbot. They meant to burn the Templars like heretics. As they had burned the Cathars. As they had burned her great-grandmother de Najac.

'Does it say any more?' Percy insisted, his hand gently touching Félice's knee.

Félice tried to read but the text seemed to become jumbled and confused. Her thoughts were on fire. Her grandparents had both carried the scars of fire on their bodies and souls.

'What more does it say?'

'Nothing.' she gasped out at last. 'Only, only that the pope and the king of France will be stained with the blood of martyrs if Cambrai is allowed to pursue his goals, but the abbot prays fervently that the pope will resist the pressure of King Philip—'

Percy laughed bitterly and turned his back abruptly to collect his reins and point his boot in the stirrup.

'The abbot writes that you are welcome in Scotland. That King Robert guarantees the safety of all Templars in his kingdom.'

Percy was in the saddle again. Félice looked up at him. Her white face was framed by the green scarves tying her cap under her chin. Fear was in her wide, golden eyes. 'Percy, what are you going to do?'

'First, I need you to gain me admittance to the spokesmen of the defence in the palace of the Bishop of Le Puy.' Up to now Geoffrey, an old acquaintance of the bishop, had been their contact with the spokesmen of the Templar defenders. 'And then I will assemble all the Free Templars in Paris.'

*

It was the first time the papal commission had ever been convened on a Sunday, but Bologna was so insistent that the seven commissioners soon found themselves taking their places in flustered haste. Since their transfer to Le Puy's custody, the four Templar spokesmen had been provided with decent clothes, food and lodging. They were clean, shaven, deloused and no longer marked by the deathly pallor of the dungeon. Peter di Bologna had been transformed back into the strikingly handsome man he was, while William of Chambonnet had won back the proud bearing of a knight. Even Bertrand de Sartignes appeared less bewildered and nervous. He kept his lips tightly shut and his eyes on Bologna, nodding sharply and emphatically whenever Bologna made a point. Only Renaud, conscious that no amount of washing or dressing would transform his pockmarked face or lower his piping voice, was careful to keep behind the others and say as little as possible.

The commissioners, muttering among themselves and scowling with displeasure, hardly gave the spokesmen time to enter the low-vaulted chamber where the hearings were held before demanding the meaning of this unprecedented request for an 'emergency' session. 'What "emergency",' Narbonne scoffed, 'could possibly require an extraordinary meeting of a papal commission?'

'An assault upon the authority of His Holiness and this commission itself,' Bologna answered readily. 'I think, my lord archbishop, you will agree that the attempt by any outside authority to interfere with the careful and honest deliberations of this exalted commission is an affront to the Holy Father, the commission itself and to its members.'

'Indeed.' Narbonne replied leaning back in his armchair.

'What assault?' Albi demanded.

'The pope set up this commission to investigate certain charges against the order of the Poor Knights of the Temple of Solomon—'

'We know what business we were appointed to conduct!' Narbonne interrupted.

Bologna smiled and bowed his head. 'His Holiness, in his wisdom, recognised that the Temple could not be investigated without the testimony of its members. That is why he invited all Templars to speak up in the defence – or the condemnation – of their Order. The witness of the Templars themselves is crucial to any investigation.'

'Certainly. This is hardly new and hardly urgent. You are wasting our precious time!'

'But the Archbishop of Sens intends to take action against those very Templars who have agreed to cooperate with this commission and provide testimony on behalf of the Temple.'

'How do you know that?' Narbonne demanded with a sharp look in the direction of Le Puy.

Le Puy himself looked thunderstruck.

'Does that matter? Surely the issue is—'

'I didn't come here to discuss rumours. I have more important things to do. I must read mass.' Abruptly, he got to his feet and collected his robes around him.

The Bishop of Trent coughed and got to his feet as well. 'Quite. Mass. I must read mass.' He hastened after Narbonne.

Albi started to rise and then thought better of it. He sank back into his chair and turned to Bologna. 'You called us together because of some rumour? I want to know where this rumour came from.'

'I don't think the source of this information is at all relevant,' Le Puy intervened. 'We all know that the Archbishop of Sens has called a council of bishops for tomorrow.'

'We don't know the agenda, and it's not our business anyway! The Archbishop of Sens has the right to convene a council of his bishops as often and whenever he likes!' Albi growled back.

'But surely,' Bologna pressed urgently, 'if he intends to prevent witnesses from appearing before the Commission it is of vital importance to you! The issue is the very ability of this commission to conduct its business faithfully and in accordance with the wishes of the Holy Father! If action is taken against those Templars who have volunteered to testify, then these invaluable witnesses will be prevented from appearing before the commission. The commission will be entirely lamed.'

'You underestimate us,' Albi retorted bluntly.

'But surely you do not wish to be handicapped in your endeavours. The witnesses – whether Templars or not – must be guaranteed immunity from persecution so long as the commission's investigation is in progress.'

'Freedom from persecution is not freedom from justice – though I can well imagine that you are ill able to discern the difference.'

'Be that as it may, even the testimony of a confessed murderer may be so valuable that a deserved sentence is suspended until testimony can be given and recorded. We ask no more.'

'It is a fair request,' Le Puy declared.

'But not ours to grant.' Albi dismissed it. 'We were appointed by His Holiness to investigate the Templars. We were specifically denied jurisdiction over the fate of individuals. These remain the sole responsibility of their respective ecclesiastical and secular authorities. The bishops of France are responsible for investigating and rooting out heresy in their respective sees. If the admirably vigorous Archbishop of Sens wishes to purge his domain of heretics, I can only congratulate him on his devotion to the true faith.'

'Even if his "devotion" prevents His Holiness from investigating a much more serious and potentially dangerous source of widespread heresy?' Bologna asked.

His words were drowned out by William of Chambonnet, who could stand the polite discussion no longer. 'Damn it! If the Templar defenders are not immune from being condemned as heretics then this whole trial is a farce!'

'Please, Will!' Bologna tried to calm Chambonnet.

'If you insult this commission you will be put in chains for contempt!' Albi flung back at the outraged knight.

'Are you bishops or puppets of King Philip?' William roared as Bologna pulled urgently at his arm.

Albi got to his feet and pointed at Chambonnet. 'You confessed to denying Christ! You confessed to spitting upon his image! You confessed to trampling upon the cross! You dare to question my authority? You will burn in hell for your heresy! You will burn!'

Renaud thought he was going to be sick. They were going to burn them all. They were going to burn him alive. He felt the sweat on his face, smelt the stink of his sweat rising from his armpits. He suddenly needed to urinate.

'I think you are getting carried away.' Le Puy's cold voice cut through the room. 'This commission – as you so aptly said yourself – is not authorised to investigate the sins of individuals. Must I remind you that none of these men fall under your jurisdiction as Bishop of Albi?'

Albi looked daggers at Le Puy and then dropped back into his chair.

'Now, I think we should consult among ourselves about the appropriate response.'

The remaining three bishops nodded with relief and all withdrew from the room.

As the door closed, Bologna turned on Sir William. 'Although I sympathise with your feelings, Will, I must beg you to refrain from such outbursts.'

'You don't have to lecture me!' Chambonnet retorted, red in the face. He turned his back on them and stalked across the room.

Bologna turned to Renaud and their eyes met. They both knew that the law was against them.

The bishops filed back into the room. The Templar spokesmen looked over expectantly.

The Bishop of Limoges announced, 'In light of the fact that your information is of dubious veracity and from unknown or unnamed sources, it is our opinion that no action should be taken by this commission at this time. We sincerely regret the dilemma posed by the prospect of action against Templars who have volunteered to defend their Order but we must stress that a bishop is by office compelled to protect the souls of his flock as a good shepherd protects his sheep from wolves. It is not the mandate of this commission to interfere with the efforts of our brother bishops in pursuit of their sacred office.'

Even Bologna's energy failed him and he found no reply. The bishops left the chamber with obvious relief.

Only Le Puy paused long enough to shake his head and say, 'I'm sorry.'

Chapter Twenty-Five

Paris, Tuesday, 23rd May, 1310

People were still streaming towards the Porte Antoine, some obviously hurrying now, afraid to be too late for the spectacle. Félice watched them with cold detachment. For over an hour she had sat here in the window seat, watching the crowds that surged slowly towards the fields outside the Porte Antoine where fifty-four stakes had been hastily erected overnight. Yesterday the Archbishop of Sens had condemned fifty-four Templars to death by fire for retracting their earlier confessions of heresy.

Her heart was numb but her mind noted with meticulous clarity that the crowd was composed of more than the usual low life of Paris. Not only apprentices and servants dodging work swarmed in loud blustering groups but guild masters and journeymen had turned out, proudly wearing the distinctive colours and caps of their guilds. In addition to the usual street pedlars offering relics, hot sausages or candied fruits, there were gaggles of clerics in solemn vestments. Students, as always, were in abundance, and there were knights on horses among the burghers. They were all going in the same direction with the same intention: to watch men die.

Félice got abruptly to her feet, aware that she had let the thoughts of what was happening only half a mile away come too close to her consciousness. She daren't think about it. If only her grandfather had not insisted on going!

He would have understood what she was going through. He would have been able to help her.

If she climbed to the attic, would she have a view of the sky to the east? Would she be able to see the tell-tale trails of black smoke from fifty-four funeral pyres for living men.

She had to find some distraction! But wasn't distraction an insult to the men who were dying? Didn't she owe it to them to at least think about them in this, the hour of their worst torture? If she did not have the courage to go and do homage to them as her grandfather was doing, the least she could do was think about them.

Where in the name of God were Percy and his knights? He had wanted to raise the Free Templars – but it was just two days ago that they had learned what the Archbishop of Sens intended! Two days! Percy could hardly have reached the Loire – and only that if he'd ridden Renaissance to foundering. He wouldn't have had time to even get word to the others, much less assemble them.

Why had Sister Madeleine sent a leper with an urgent message? Why hadn't she sent one of her servants, one of the former Templars on one of the draught horses? Why hadn't she come herself? If only they had known sooner...

Then Percy and his handful of knights and sergeants would be out there trying to defy the King of France before the very gates of Paris. Had she gone mad? What did she think he could achieve? He would kill himself and all the others he had so painfully rescued and rallied over the last two years. She should thank God that they had not had the news a day earlier. There was nothing any of them could do now...

★

The common crowd did not surprise Umberto as he surveyed it from his position on the tribunal platform, but he was amazed that the archbishop had managed to assemble so many of the relatives of the condemned. These had been escorted by royal soldiers to a space beside the tribunal and just outside the crude fence erected around the fifty-four stakes. The stakes were set up in five rows of eleven, the last short by one. Faggots were heaped around the inside of the fence; and wagons loaded with the bundles of kindling were still arriving and being unloaded by peasants at the back of the enclosure.

The tribunal was crowded with dignitaries. In the centre, the young Archbishop of Sens had taken a large, high-backed chair. In full archiepiscopal regalia – but flanked by his two hounds – he chatted with Nogaret, who stood beside his chair. The Bishops of Chartres and Orléans were in attendance, along with the Provost of Paris, the captain of the king's archers, the Dean of Notre Dame and the king's own confessor from Sainte Chapelle. Brother Elion was looking more pale and strained than ever as he hovered at the foot of the tribunal platform. He fussed with his hood, apparently undecided if he should wear it up over his head or back on his shoulders. He carried an evidently very expensive book in his left hand and repeatedly flipped it open as if trying to memorise his lines. Umberto smiled cynically at that, remembering how very carefully and painstakingly he prepared all his speeches. No doubt he had not slept since the bishop's sentence had been passed. Father Elion would have the honour of trying one last time to persuade the Templars to repent.

Wagons with Templar prisoners from every jail where defenders were held were now arriving. These were not the condemned but men who were to witness and bear witness to what was about to happen. These men were evidently bewildered – and cowed. The mere sight of the stakes and faggots were enough to turn their blood to ice. Gone was the hope, optimism and tinges of defiance that had been so tangible at the opening of the inquiry. The men who now stumbled – still chained – from the wagons were more animal than human. They cowered, they flinched, they trembled in their rags; they were relieved to be herded to a place in front of the eager spectators but outside the crude fence.

The wagon carrying the condemned was now creaking up before the tribunal. These men too were still chained. It began to dawn on Umberto that someone must have paid for the prisoners to be released from their chains at the opening of the enquiry. He remembered the angry question from Félice's cousin, and then the way her grandfather had paid for those few who came still chained. But today no one interceded on the Templars' behalf.

Like criminals they came stooped and humiliated, smelling of the dungeon. The chains inhibited their movements. Their ankles were rubbed raw and bleeding from the unaccustomed necessity of moving in their shackles.

Umberto understood about shackles now. He knew that they bruised and cut; he knew how quickly one could rub one's skin raw against their cold metal edges. Unconsciously, he rubbed at the back of his left ankle with his right foot. The open sores were long since healed and the bruises had faded, but the scars were in his heart for ever.

Umberto looked at the prisoners in their filthy, stinking rags and was reminded of how he too had been forced to wet himself for three days. His face flushed at the mere memory of his shame, and he forced himself to acknowledge that these were men who had not chosen the filth in which the Inquisition had clothed them.

The archbishop rose and read the sentence of the Church turning these 'relapsed heretics' over to the secular arm.

'"And the chief priests and scribes stood by earnestly accusing."' The voice pierced the chill of the early morning stillness and there was no one on the tribunal who did not recognise the quotation from the Gospel of Saint Luke. They understood that they were being compared to the Jewish priests who had turned Christ over to Pontius Pilate and they turned towards the crowd, searching for the source.

But how could they find the speaker in a crowd ten thousand strong?

Irritated, the Archbishop of Sens cleared his throat and repeated his last sentence.

'Their blood is upon your head, Philip de Marigny! The blood of innocents is upon you and upon your king!'

This time the archbishop hissed angrily at Nogaret, 'Can't your soldiers silence that man? He interferes and he could sway the opinion of the stupid masses!'

Nogaret turned and said something to the captain of the royal archers who was responsible for order in the crowd.

Meanwhile, the Provost of Paris had taken over from the archbishop and was reading the sentence for 'relapsed heretics'. He emphasised that every one of the condemned men had 'freely' confessed.

This was greeted by more than one derisive cry from the crowd: 'As you would on the rack!'; 'Let me put *your* feet to the fire!'; 'Lies!'

The men on the tribunal exchanged irritated glances tinged with worry. A ripple of uneasiness swept through the crowd. The students, apprentices and other rowdies were clearly ready to take up any chant which would discomfort the representatives of law and order.

Umberto searched more intensely than before for the speaker. Now he did not turn his attention to the provost's loud barking, but searched the crowd, waiting with anticipation for the next cry of defiance. The provost announced that the condemned would be burned at the stake.

'Where is your silver bowl, Pontius Pilate? Where can you wash your hands of innocent blood?' the voice called out, almost cracking under the weight of the emotion it carried.

Now Umberto thought he had located the general area from where the voice originated. He focused his attention on the area without blinking. He was fascinated by the man – so obviously educated – who would risk showing sympathy for the condemned before Nogaret and the Provost of Paris.

Father Elion was speaking in his most vibrant, eloquent voice. He urged the condemned to reconsider their terrible decision. They had spat upon Christ in the past but still He forgave them. He loved them. He longed for nothing more desperately than that they turn to Him again in love and submission.

'The Resurrection and the Life lies not in the mouths of the Pharisees who condemn you for your love of Christ! Your kingdom is not of this world. It is with Him – beyond the reach of Nogaret and his Godless henchmen!'

Umberto was almost certain that he had spotted the man shouting – a frail, old man with a clipped white beard. He stretched his neck and squinted his eyes, straining for a better view, while beside him the occupants of the tribunal cursed and whispered angrily among themselves. The mocking hoots and shouts of students and rebellious journeymen came like an echo of the lone challenger. Umberto did not dare take his eyes from the man he had identified, but he could hear the others muttering that the prisoners too had clearly been affected by his words: 'Look at that! Now they want to be defiant!'

Father Elion also seemed to sense that his own eloquence was being outclassed. The prisoners were now being led to the stakes and tied to them. It was a long, tedious process, but the crowd was fascinated. With parted lips and unblinking eyes they gaped at the spectacle of filthy, mishandled men being bound to rough-hewn stakes.

Father Elion still harangued the prisoners to think of their souls. 'The agony of your bodies is short and insignificant in comparison to the agony your soul will suffer! Spare yourself both of these cruelties! Return to the bosom of the Church!' He held up a crucifix and genuine tears wet his sculpted cheeks.

'He who has never left the path of righteousness need not return!' came the voice from the crowd, and this time Umberto – who gazed unblinkingly upon the old man he had identified – saw him lift his chin and open his mouth.

Jesus God! Umberto recognised Félice's grandfather! Almost at the same moment, soldiers of the king plunged into the crowd and laid their hands upon him. He was roughly seized and pulled out of the crowd. Without thinking, Umberto left his place on the platform and clattered down the stairs, holding his robes out of his way. The old man was a courageous old fool! Didn't he recognise the danger?

The soldiers had wrenched his hands behind his back and bound them together. They shoved him forwards, cursing and insulting him. Umberto blocked their way as they emerged from the crowd.

'This is a nobleman!' he intervened sharply.

The guards glanced at the Dominican blocking their path with evident surprise.

'So?' came the defiant answer. 'He was interfering with the king's justice.'

'He is a senile old man and cannot be held responsible for his actions!' Umberto insisted.

'That's for the captain to decide,' the archers retorted, shoving Geoffrey forwards.

Geoffrey was frowning at Umberto with a mixture of anger at the insult and puzzlement at the intervention. He could not remember ever having seen Umberto before.

Umberto fell in beside the archers as they escorted Geoffrey to the tribunal platform. The relatives of the condemned had been let loose to try and plead with their obstinate sons and brothers. The hysterical sobbing of one woman could be heard over the lower murmur of men.

Geoffrey lifted his head and filled his lungs with air to shout, '"The hour cometh when the dead shall hear the voice of the Son of God and they that hear shall live—"'

Outraged, the archers turned on him. One delivered a blow to his mouth and the other to his gut.

Geoffrey doubled over and blood burst from his split lips. He had not the wind to shout but he finished the quote nevertheless and the guards no less than Umberto heard him gasp, '"They that have done good things shall come forth unto the resurrection of life; but they that have done evil—"'

'Shut up, you bag of bones!'

'He is quoting the Gospel of Saint John,' Umberto informed the guards, but they only shrugged.

The captain of the king's archers, seeing that the disrupter had been found and arrested, hastened down from the tribunal and confronted Geoffrey. Around them a murmur of excited anticipation went up. Not one of the Templars had succumbed to the pleas of Father Elion or their relatives. The torches were being put to the brittle kindling.

'Your name?' the captain of the king's archers demanded of Geoffrey.

Geoffrey was silent.

'Did Christ answer when he was brought before Pontius Pilate?' Umberto intervened angrily. 'This is Sir Geoffrey de Preuthune, Lord of Najac. He was knighted by Saint Louis during the Seventh Crusade.'

'You know him?' the captain asked Umberto with raised eyebrows. The captain knew that Umberto was an intimate adviser and associate of the Bishop of Albi and he was clearly representing his bishop here.

'Yes. He's a senile old man, but he is harmless.'

'Harmless? Didn't you hear what he shouted?'

'We can hardly condemn a man for quoting scripture.'

'I don't know about that. My job is to keep order and this man was disruptive.'

'Yes, I know that, but surely it would suffice to remove him—'

A startled cry went up from the enclosure just then and the crowd stirred restlessly, straining for a better look, exclaiming excitedly, 'The flames have reached them! Look! Look!'

A cracked voice tried to take up a hymn. Another scream might have been a cry to Christ. The sound of crackling wood and the smell of smoke reached the men at the foot of the tribunal.

Umberto saw Geoffrey draw a deep breath, and he seized him before he could shout whatever it was he intended. 'For Félice's sake shut up!' Umberto hissed at him in Latin.

Geoffrey was stunned into silence. He stared at Umberto. How did he know Félice? Who *was* this Dominican?

A voice took up the Lord's Prayer and it was joined by other strained, rasping voices. The prayer was obliterated time and again by screams of unbearable agony which dissolved into whimpering and moans. One of the Templars managed to curse the Archbishop of Sens by name.

Geoffrey had gone very stiff.

Umberto turned to the captain again. 'Come. Let the old man go. The execution is going according to plan and he can't do anything to stop it now.'

'He should be questioned. Maybe he is one of the Free Templars,' the captain insisted.

'There are no Free Templars. And the purity of his faith is a matter for Holy Church not the secular authorities.'

'I think we'd better keep him in custody till this is over,' the captain decided. 'Put him over there where he has a good view,' he ordered his soldiers, adding: 'And if he makes another peep, I'll have you on extra duty for the next fortnight.'

The soldiers prodded and shoved Geoffrey to the space provided for the relatives of the condemned.

Umberto went with them. He spoke in a low voice, in Latin, 'My lord, I beg you, hold your tongue. There is nothing you can do, and think of your granddaughter. What would become of her if you were arrested?'

The hysterical mother of one of the condemned had apparently been removed by her other sons and another woman had fainted. The remaining relatives of the dying watched with stony, rigid faces. Geoffrey was glad to be among people who took no pleasure in what was being done. Someone, seeing his bleeding lip, offered him a cloth to wipe away the blood. 'Your son?' another asked in a low voice.

'They are all my sons,' Geoffrey answered.

The stench of burnt flesh was starting to overpower the acrid smell of smoke and several people covered their mouths and noses with their sleeves or some other cloth. The wind shifted and a shower of ashes fell upon the crowd, who at once let out a scattered protest as sparks burned clothing and skin. The short pinpricks of pain created outrage among the 'innocent' bystanders. Behind them the tribunal was emptying. The bulk of the dignitaries was satisfied that justice had been carried out and they had other duties to attend to.

The crowd too was growing thinner. The honest and wealthy had seen enough and were returning to their business. Only the skulkers and pedlars, still trying to milk the crowd, remained.

The Templar witnesses were kept in place by their guards but they seemed rooted to the ground in any case. The captain of archers was giving orders to save the remaining kindling and start clearing the back of the enclosure. As the wind had been blowing towards the back most of the time, these men had burned first and they were now charred and shrivelled corpses hanging like crude black sculptures upon their stakes.

'Grandpapa!'

Geoffrey and Umberto looked over in shared horror. Félice, escorted by Niki, was making her way against the flow of the departing crowds. The hearts of both men stood still at the sight of her. Her white veils and silken sleeves fluttered wildly in the mounting breeze and her hair was free, curling and whipping about under her veils. The sun highlighted the burgundy tones of her dark hair, and glinted on her gold earrings and emerald ring as she lifted her skirts to hurry forward.

'Félice! What in the name of God—'

'Monsieur,' Niki interrupted, 'I didn't know what else to do! When they arrested you…' He nodded towards the guards flanking Geoffrey.

'Where is the captain?' Félice enquired. 'I will… Umberto?'

Umberto took her hand to his lips.

'My lady Félice.'

The look in his eyes made her want to withdraw her hand. She did not want his love. She did not want anything to do with him. 'What are you doing here?'

'I was sent to represent the Bishop of Albi – fortunately. I think I convinced the captain to release your father as soon as this sad spectacle is over.'

Félice swallowed and kept her eyes rigidly averted from the enclosure. She could not close her nose or ears but fortunately the last whimpers and moans had ceased. Only the crackling of the fire and the shouts of the peasants responsible for seeing that the flames did not spread could be heard.

'Go home, Félice!' Geoffrey urged in a tight voice.

'Yes, return to the safety of your lodgings,' Umberto agreed. 'I will see to your grandfather's safety.'

'Let me speak with the captain.' Félice looked up at the tribunal and directly into the eyes of the Archbishop of Sens.

'What can I do for you, mademoiselle?' Since Félice had left in such a rush that she had not bound her hair, the archbishop naturally assumed that she was still a maid. His leering eyes reminded her of her immodesty, but she knew that only courage would help her now.

'I have come to take my grandfather home, my lord archbishop. His squire sent for me.' She indicated Niki.

The archbishop looked from Félice to Niki to Geoffrey and then Umberto. He raised his eyebrows. 'And what have you to do with all this, brother? Aren't you Albi's secretary?'

'My lord. But I recognised Monsieur de Preuthune when he was arrested. I am an old friend of the family.'

'He was the one disrupting the proceedings, was he not?'

'Yes!' the guards and Umberto answered simultaneously.

'My uncle is a Templar, my lord,' Félice explained. 'My grandfather cannot believe what is said about them. Please let me take him home.'

'But of course, my child.' The youthful archbishop smiled and waved his gloved and ringed hand in a gesture of regal indulgence. 'Guards! Release the prisoner.'

Although the archbishop had no authority over them, the archers deferred to his manner and, besides, he stood high in the favour of the king at the moment. With a shrug they unbound Geoffrey's hands. Félice slipped her arm through his and turned him away from the charred remains of fifty-four men still chained to the stakes on which they'd died.

'I will escort you,' Umberto announced.

'That won't be necessary.' Félice insisted, but Umberto ignored her and fell in on her far side while Niki flanked Geoffrey.

Geoffrey said nothing so Félice was compelled to listen to Umberto's version of events. Despite his admiration for Geoffrey's education and courage, he made it very clear that Geoffrey was mad to show his sympathy for the Templars.

'Even if the charges were totally fictional – which I assure you they are not – there is no point in defying the king. He is determined to destroy the Templars and anyone who gets in his way will be eliminated.'

'But the papal commission is not subject to the king,' Félice pointed out hesitantly.

'And you see how he got around it! If today's example does not induce other Templar defenders into withdrawing from the defence, the Archbishop of Sens will not hesitate to send more to the stake. And, meanwhile, the other bishops of France feel compelled to prove they are no less diligent in their condemnation of heresy. Albi has already sent the Templar prisoners he brought up to Paris for the trial back to Albi. You can be sure that they will be condemned as relapsed heretics if they persist in wanting to defend the Temple.'

Geoffrey caught his breath and broke stride.

Umberto paused solicitously. 'Is something wrong?'

Geoffrey shook his head. The prisoners from Albi were men Percy knew. Percy would not let them burn. And how could he argue against the use of force? His helplessness oppressed him, crushed the very breath from his lungs. He felt as if he could not breathe. His grip tightened on Félice's arm. He stumbled.

'Grandpapa!' Félice looked into his face and sensed more than saw that he was fighting for breath. His face had gone red. His right hand clutched at his heart. His lips parted and worked silently.

As he slowly crumpled up, Niki caught him in his arms. 'We must get him home, Madame!'

'I'll send a physician,' Umberto offered. 'Where are you staying?'

Félice had no time to think of an alternative solution. She told Umberto the address but spared him neither a glance nor thanks. Geoffrey had closed his eyes and was pressing both hands to his heart. Christ help him! Félice prayed. She was terrified of losing him. She couldn't imagine life without him. But he was eighty years old! He couldn't live for ever. Oh, God, not now! Not here in Paris! Not with Percy away! No, no, no!

*

Hours later, after the physician had come and gone, after Umberto had officiously promised to light candles for Sir Geoffrey's recovery and return the next day, Félice was still kneeling beside the bed. Her maid, Nannette, had urged her to rest in her chamber, but she preferred to rest her head on her arms here, near her grandfather.

She dozed, thoughts and dreams mingling together incoherently. She remembered her grandmother's peaceful death and tried to convince herself that Geoffrey too had the right to die. Hadn't he done all he'd come for? He was a Templar at last. There was nothing more he could do. The Order couldn't be saved. The king was determined to destroy it. Their whole struggle was hopeless. It was time to recognise that and give up.

Besides, Eleanor would be waiting impatiently. Félice was no longer a child. She had no right to cling to her grandfather. And wouldn't he look after her even after he was dead? She had believed that as a child; where was her faith now?

'Félice.' She lifted her head with a gasp and met her grandfather's glittering dark eyes. 'You need not keep vigil. I'm not ready to die – not yet.'

'Thank God!' She was struggling to her feet, her feet tangling in her skirt and hanging sleeves, her hair hanging uncovered in thick strands.

'Is there water somewhere? I have a terrible thirst.'

Félice's relief found its expression in a flood of tears. She bent over the bed and put her arms around Geoffrey. Then she drew back to gaze at him, smoothing his wrinkled face with her hands. Her hair hung down, enclosing them both.

'Do you know you look very much like your grandmother?'

'You only wish I did!' Félice retorted, smiling through her tears. 'Let me pour you water.'

She withdrew, wiping her tears away with her sleeves. She found the water and a goblet by the bedside. She held out the water to her grandfather and he righted himself enough to drink.

'I'm worried about Percy. We must keep him here in Paris. We must convince him that the trial is more important than the defendants from Albi. I know he has disobeyed me more than once and used force to rescue some of our brothers. But the men we have rescued were never important prisoners, never well guarded. The defenders will be guarded as closely as de Molay and the other officers. The execution of relapsed heretics will always be a public affair like today. We cannot hope to rescue men under such circumstances. It would be suicide. But I fear he will try. Only the trial, the prospect of doing more good here than he can do in Albi, will keep him here.'

'Don't worry about that, Grandpapa.' Félice stroked his forehead. 'We saved him once before – we can do it again.'

Geoffrey smiled faintly. 'Last time he was helpless. He is anything but that now. He has a will of his own – and a mighty soul. Sometimes it frightens me.'

Félice bent and kissed his forehead. 'You've no need to fear, Grandpapa, Percy loves you.'

'I know, but not enough to obey me.' Geoffrey fixed his eyes on her and spoke very deliberately: 'He might listen to you.'

She did not meet his eyes, but she coloured. He could see it even in the darkness.

'When the time comes, will you try?'

Félice nodded.

Chapter Twenty-Six

Paris, 24th May, 1310

Renaud Provinz could not sleep. He had not been able to sleep since he had witnessed the burning of his brothers. His eyes stung and his body felt heavy from exhaustion, but his nerves were stretched like bowstrings – like a man on the rack.

Renaud turned over on his pallet for the hundredth time, feeling guilty for the rustling the straw made. He did not want to keep the others awake. Fortunately, Bertrand was snoring on the other side of the room and William too had fallen asleep, judging by his deep, slow breathing. But Peter was not sleeping, he could tell. He took a deep breath and tried to calm himself.

Maybe the flames wouldn't really be so much worse than the rack had been. After all, the smoke from the fumes seemed to have killed several of the knights before the flames consumed them. And even at its worst, it had not lasted more than twenty or twenty-five minutes. He had been on the rack longer than that. And once they had kept him suspended by his wrists with weights on his feet for over four hours. That was when he had confessed to everything.

Renaud pulled his thin blanket over his head and buried his face in his elbow. He had confessed and confessed and sworn that he had adored idols and that he had fucked all his brothers. He, the castrato! That had made even the guards laugh; and the inquisitor had been furious because it revealed the whole confession for what it was – a desperate plea for mercy at any price. Since the confession had been discredited by his own hyperbole, the whole thing had to be wrenched out of him again. They had put him to the rack.

Renaud threw back the blanket, gasping for breath. He wouldn't be able to stand the flames. He would retract his retraction and accept a life of imprisonment. He would disgrace the Order as none of the Templars had done yesterday.

Who had been the voice in the crowd reminding them of Christ freed of the corrupt Church? It had been a great comfort to know that they weren't entirely alone. Had he been one of the Free Templars or just a righteous man?

The sound of heavy footsteps and then the clank of keys in the door brought Renaud bolt upright. They had never been disturbed in the middle of the night before – not since they had been transferred to the sympathetic Bishop of Le Puy's custody.

The light of torches suddenly lit up the room and set a thousand shadows dancing. Renaud saw that Bologna too was sitting upright on his pallet, waiting alertly. A knight ducked into the room and for a brief moment Renaud hoped it was the young Free Templar who had brought word of Marigny's planned action. But it was a stranger.

'Which of you is Peter di Bologna?' he asked, looking around the room at the two sitting and two sleeping men.

His voice drew William de Chambonnet from his sleep with a start and he sat up abruptly with a grunt.

'I'm Peter di Bologna,' Peter said.

'And which of you is Renaud Provins?'

Renaud squeaked in answer.

'Come on, get up,' the knight ordered with a wave of his hand.

'Why? Where are you taking us?' Peter protested.

Renaud felt his knees start to tremble.

The knight ignored the question and signalled for his men to seize the two priests. Although unresisting, the guards handled them roughly. Their arms were yanked behind their backs and their wrists bound more tightly than necessary.

'What is this? Why only Bologna and Provins?' William wanted to know.

'Those are my orders. I don't question His Grace.'

'His Grace? The bishop?' Bologna asked in astonishment. They had only had the best treatment from the Bishop of Le Puy.

'The *Arch*bishop – of Sens,' came the answer with a half-laugh of satisfaction at the effect these words had on the prisoners.

And then they were shoved out of the door of their chamber and taken, blindfolded, out of the palace to be loaded on to a wagon.

Renaud kept trying to order his thoughts but his brain had ceased to function. All he heard was the pulsing of his blood and with each beat of his heart it hissed: 'Burn, burn, burn'.

They had come for him in the middle of the night when he was twelve, Renaud remembered suddenly. His memories overpowered the chanting of his panicked pulse. He had been sleeping soundly and contentedly in the novices dormitory with no premonition of what was to come. Why should he have a premonition? He had slept in that same bed since his parents had turned him over to the abbey at the age of seven, and it had never betrayed him before.

The abbey had been his home. He had been safe, well fed, clothed no worse than the others. He had played, prayed and learned with the other novices without cause for complaint. There were stern, unfriendly monks whom the novices hated, and cold, frightening monks whom they avoided. There were foolish monks whom they teased mercilessly and there were kindly monks who told them stories and comforted them in their childhood troubles. It had been a big, boisterous family under the stern but benevolent care of the abbot.

Renaud had been like the half-score other novices, except that he had an exceptional voice which brought tears of joy to the abbot's eyes when he sang. Renaud had been proud of that – and grateful for the extra sweets and pats on the head the abbot occasionally gave him. Otherwise it had been a childhood like any other, full of tears and laughter, lessons and pranks. He had never dreamt that it could end in a single night when the men who had nurtured him held him down on the kitchen table and amputated his genitals with a butcher's knife.

Renaud had not reached maturity and he had been raised to the monastery. It was not the loss of his sexual organs as such but the cold-blooded manner in which they had done it to him which had destroyed his world. He could not forgive them for not explaining what they wanted, for not seeking his consent. After letting him live among them like a younger brother for five years, they had treated him like a piece of livestock.

He had tried to punish the abbot by refusing to sing or singing off-key and out of time. The abbot had retaliated by threatening to expel him from the abbey. He did not know the name with which he had been born or where his parents lived. He had no skills at an age when most boys had been apprenticed for five or six years. He would have starved to death outside. So he had revenged himself upon the world by accepting all the marks of favour the abbot showered on him. He no longer had to fast with the others; he no longer had to attend matins; he no longer slept in the dormitory. He was provided with fine woollen robes; he had stockings and shoes in winter; he shared the abbot's wine and table. He revelled in his luxuries and his status, lording it over the other novices, who came to hate him.

When the Lord had struck him down with pox, he had been almost prepared to accept the justice of it. He had been prepared to sacrifice the loss of his angelic looks to the righteous indignation of God at a youth who had grown overweening. But when it became clear that he had also lost his voice, the comfortable world he had believed secure collapsed around him for a second time.

The abbot could not bear the sight of him, so he had been given two louis and a letter of introduction to one of the abbot's friends teaching at the Sorbonne. Renaud supposed that no fifteen year old would have found it easy to go out into the world after growing up in the cloisters of an abbey, but for a castrated, pock-marked youth the world was a nightmare of mocking laughter, slammed doors and disgusted sneers. He had learned hunger and loneliness and fathomless humiliation until he had lain on his belly in his own vomit after drinking himself senseless. He had realised then that he was on the brink of slipping irretrievably into an abyss which would only make those around him laugh – as they had the night before. So he had fled into his learning.

His first 'confessions' had been nothing more than dialogues he held with himself about the meaning of God, mercy and divine justice. Slowly, as he started to enjoy the writing for itself, the puns and the irony crept in. By the time he ventured publication, his style had been honed by countless hours crouched over his desk in a draughty attic. When he learned that one of the senior scholars of the Temple had enquired after him, he had been flattered. When he was – despite his voice and his disfigurement – offered admittance to the Temple, he had rejoiced beyond all measure.

At the time, he admitted to himself as the bonds on his wrists rubbed his wrists raw, he had been flattered to be courted by such a mighty and mysterious Order. His pride had become puffed up again. Yet what he had craved most was the companionship of brothers. As a Templar priest he had been permitted to leave the isolation of his garret and rejoin a religious community. The knights and sergeants had looked at him askance, but the other priests and the lay brothers had accepted him. He had been allowed to continue his studies and his writing – until the night of his arrest.

That too had been in the middle of the night, he remembered. And for a third time his world had been destroyed – not only his personal world but the very foundations upon which his personal world had been built. Like an earthquake, the destruction of the Temple had brought so much misery to so many that his personal fate seemed insignificant. If he were to burn tonight or tomorrow, he reminded himself, at least he would not burn alone.

The end of the journey came when the prisoners had long since lost the feeling in their fingers. Their tortured joints ached and Renaud's blindfold was soaked with the tears of self-pity he had shed.

They were pulled off the wagon with more indifference than cruelty and shoved, still blindfolded, down a staircase. No one had to tell them that they were being returned to a dungeon. The dank dampness told them where they were even before the foul stench of unwashed humanity and uncleaned latrines met them at the foot of the stairs.

Abruptly, Bologna resisted. He balked and then tried to fight free, cursing and spitting venom. Renaud had never known the self-possessed Italian priest to lose his self-control before.

Renaud stumbled over the step down into the cell itself. They cut free his swollen, lifeless hands and clamped the cold, rusting shackles on his raw wrists. Then they removed the blindfold. Renaud looked about blinking in the torchlight. It was a small cell, no more than ten feet square. Peter and he were the sole occupants, chained to opposite walls.

Peter was still screaming at the guards that he was the elected spokesman of the Templar defenders. He demanded to be taken to the Bishop of Narbonne. He insisted that an emergency session of the commission be convened. He ordered and commanded and they ignored him as if he were no more than a yapping hound. They withdrew taking their torches and the metal door clanged shut behind them. Peter roared and lunged towards the door. His chains yanked him violently back. He flung out his arms and, howling, beat his chains against the walls of the cell. 'You can't do this! Open up! Let me out!'

'Peter,' Renaud spoke softly. 'Peter, it's no good. They aren't going to let us out of here.'

'They have to. The trial—'

'They'll come for us when it's time.'

'But we can't work here! Not chained! Not in the dark!'

'Peter, try to save your strength. We will need it.'

Bologna's raging deafened him to Renaud's high, squeaky voice. 'How can God be so unjust!' Bologna demanded furiously, pounding the walls with his chains again. 'Why? Why? Why?'

Renaud didn't have an answer but over the years he had grown tired of asking the question. He sighed and closed his eyes, trying not to feel the rust of the shackles grinding into the open wounds on his wrists.

'Guard!' Bologna shouted. 'I confirm my confession! The Knights Templar were idol worshippers! We kissed ass!'

Renaud couldn't believe his ears, and neither could the guard.

The sliding shutter over the barred window in the door of the cell cracked back and a gruff voice asked, 'What did you say?'

'Bring me before the papal commission!' Peter demanded. 'I will confirm my confession. I will—'

'Peter, don't!' Renaud squeaked in desperation.

'The papal commission is in recess until November,' the guard told Bologna, 'but I could call a Dominican—'

Bologna collapsed on his chains, his head flung back against the mouldy walls, his eyes closed. 'No,' he answered in a whisper they could hardly hear. 'No.'

*

Paris, 27th May, 1310

Gaston had never been so bone-tired in all his short life. His seat was bruised and his knees blistered from the long days and nights in the saddle. He had blisters on the palms of his hands from trying to control strange horses. The dirt of a thousand miles on dusty roads was thick on his hair and tunic, and his neck and wrists were grimy with the mixture of dust and sweat. His eyes were bloodshot and his lips cracked. Never in all his life had he ridden so far, so fast and so hard as in the last week.

As they pulled the bell cord at the de Winters' townhouse, Gaston felt immensely proud to be still in the saddle. His very weariness and the marks of the ride were badges of honour which made him feel like a real squire. He, who as a boy had only admired horses and riders like creatures from a fairy tale, had kept up – no matter how ungracefully – with his lord.

Glancing at Percy now, Gaston felt a confused surge of admiration and anxiety. Percy had slept even less than he had himself. More than once he had awakened in the saddle to find that Percy had his horse on a lead. As the days went by and Gaston's strength gave out more frequently, Percy had done the duties of squire himself – feeding and watering their horses, untacking and tacking when they changed mounts, buying wine, cheese and bread for their journey.

In Tours the news of the execution of the Templars in Paris caught up with them. Percy had drawn up, listened to the town criers passing on the news sent by royal courier, and then, without a word, he had turned back, on the road to Paris.

Percy had never been a talkative master, and certainly they had been in too much of a hurry for talk on this journey, but he had never been so silent as on the return. Gaston had naïvely believed that if the Archbishop of Sens had already carried out his threat, there was no need for hurry. But Percy had pressed them even harder on the way back. And there was a look on his face which frightened Gaston – a harsh, intense, fanatical look that reminded Gaston of the inquisitors. Once he had ventured, very timidly, to ask what Percy planed to do now.

Percy had stared at him with burning, bloodshot eyes and shaken his head. Gaston had been afraid to ask what that meant.

The porter opened the gates for them, and Percy nodded his thanks as he ducked under the heavy beam of the gate. He rode into the stables rather than dismounting in the yard, and the smell of straw and sound of munching horses greeted them. Renaissance, who had carried Percy only as far as Étampes and had then been left in a tavern stable until they returned, whinnied a friendly greeting to the assembled horses.

Gaston jumped down with a surge of relief to be back in this familiar barn. Lord Geoffrey and Lady Félice would welcome them. They would have a good meal and a real bed tonight – and a bath too. Gaston led his gelding into a vacant stall and undid the girth. His weary arms could hardly hold the heavy saddle as he slid it off his gelding's back, so that it fell with a loud clunk to the stable floor. He removed the bridle and then, with an unconscious grunt, hoisted the saddle on to his forearm and left the box. Only then did he notice that Percy still sat astride Renaissance, though the long-legged stallion had made his own way into an empty stall and snatched at the hay hanging invitingly in a hay net.

'Can I help you, sir?' Gaston asked hesitantly.

In answer, Percy leaned forwards over the pommel and withdrew his feet from the stirrups. In slow motion he swung his right leg over the rump of the stallion and dropped down – to collapse in the straw at his stallion's feet.

Gaston dropped his saddle and bridle and rushed into the stall. 'Sir!'

Percy lay coiled up clenching his teeth together. Geoffrey had warned him that his ankles would be weak for the rest of his life. More than once, several days of hard riding had left them swollen and tender. Since Wednesday, they had caused him ceaseless pain and he had hardly been able to walk when he dismounted last night. Now he could not stand at all.

Gaston was bending over him. 'Sir? What is it? What can I do?'

'It's just my legs,' Percy managed, forcing himself to uncoil slightly.

The sharp, burning pain from the jolt of dropping out of the saddle was receding, leaving only the continuous ache with which he had lived for days. He opened his eyes and saw Gaston's frightened face behind the layer of dirt. 'Go and find Niki, Lord Geoffrey's squire. He'll be able to help me upstairs.'

'Are you...' Gaston swallowed his protest, recognising that he was not big or strong enough to support the tall knight. 'I'll be right back!' He scrambled to his feet and was gone.

Percy took a deep breath and closed his eyes again. He drew in the scent of hay gratefully. Renaissance needed to be untacked and rubbed down. Where were the grooms? Then his thoughts drifted to Lord Geoffrey. He must be back from Valois by now. Percy had dispersed all the other Templars of his own escort with orders to muster the Free Templars at Melun. It would be dangerous to keep them there together for long. He had to learn if Sens intended to send more men to their deaths and when. He had to talk to Bologna about the response of the papal commission. He had to...

The sound of voices distracted him. Two men had entered the stables. He could not see them from where he lay but he recognised the voice of Master de Winter. 'I assure you I will use all my influence to persuade him to return home. You are quite right; he needs peace and calm and good, clean country air – all things he cannot find in Paris.'

'He came because of the papal commission investigating the crimes of the Templars. You must tell him that the commission has announced a recess until November.'

Percy started at this news and then strained harder to hear what was being said. This second speaker's voice was unfamiliar. It was young, educated, with a faint foreign lilt. It reminded Percy of Bologna but would the Templar defender be casually standing about in de Winter's stables? Had Le Puy allowed him to visit Lord Geoffrey here?

'Has it?' de Winter asked, astonished.

'Yes, ostensibly in protest against the actions of the Archbishop of Sens and to consult with His Holiness. In reality, because the Bishops of Narbonne and Albi are anxious to prove to King Philip they are no less ardent opponents of heresy than Sens.'

'Does that mean they will be burning Templars in their dioceses as well?' the good merchant asked in horror.

'Yes,' the stranger admitted with no more than a hint of mild regret. 'It would be better if Lord Geoffrey didn't hear of that. After what he did on Tuesday, I fear he might try to disrupt the autos-da-fé somewhere else.'

Percy smiled with relief and gratitude: Lord Geoffrey had *tried* to do something. They hadn't died thinking no one cared. In his exhausted, weakened state, his love for Geoffrey almost unmanned him. He felt the weight of all he owed this one old man with his immense heart.

The stranger was still speaking. 'I don't think he realises the danger he is in – and the danger in which he thereby puts Lady Félice. It took all my powers of persuasion to convince the captain of the king's archers and the Archbishop of Sens to release him. If he were to fall into the hands of the authorities a second time, no arguments on earth will convince them that he is merely senile.'

'We all know how much we owe you, Brother Umberto,' de Winter assured the stranger.

Percy opened his eyes with a start and the tension that possessed his body made his legs twitch. Renaissance snorted as if to calm him, but he held his breath listening.

The voices were coming nearer, walking slowly. He could make out the distinctive scrape and slap of a man in sandals. His heart was pounding in his ears.

'I could hardly stand by and watch such a gallant chevalier being mishandled, especially knowing that he was Lady Félice's grandfather. I was, of course, concerned about her safety as well. You can't imagine my horror when she arrived in person! That squire should be whipped for dragging a young lady into such a situation. Why didn't he turn to you?'

'I was not at home at the time, and Niki knows how clever and devoted Lady Félice is to her grandfather.'

'Which is all the more reason not to expose her to such acute danger – not to mention of the horror of an auto-da-fé! Lady Félice is much too gentle and pitying to enjoy the sight of men dying such a death!'

Percy's stomach was cramping and his lungs wanted to break apart for want of exhaling. He could not bear the possessive way this stranger spoke of Félice, and already his heart suspected what his brain refused to admit.

'She is a courageous young woman. She did not leave her grandfather's side until he had regained consciousness late in the afternoon. I cannot imagine why any man in his right mind would divorce her!' de Winter exclaimed in sincere outraged perplexity.

'A boor indeed! And he has hurt her badly… What? My God! There's a man…'

They had spotted Percy where he lay and it took only a moment for Master de Winter to recognise him through his unkempt beard and the dust of the road. 'Sir Percy! What are you doing here? Are you hurt?' De Winter's face at once crumpled with concern. Raising the lantern to better light the stall where Percy lay, he grasped his voluminous, rich robes so he could come to Percy's assistance.

Umberto hung back, recovering from the shock of the unexpected discovery and puzzled by a memory he could not place. The dirty, bearded man lying in the straw reminded him of someone, but he could not think who. Not Félice's tall, arrogant cousin in his expensive chain mail and silken surcoat, but someone he had seen likewise filthy and unkempt and lying…

Percy's eyes were fixed on Umberto. He saw the pale oval face under the silky dark tonsure, wide black eyes under thin, arching black brows and a straight, strong nose that was neither too long nor too short. His chin was shaved to satin and his long neck sank into a hooded black cowl of the finest angora wool. The white linen robes beneath the cowl were spotless and stiff from pressing. His sandalled feet were clean and pedicured. He was beyond all doubt beautiful, and he stared at Percy with eyes that widened in horror.

Umberto was remembering that Templar who had disappeared not far from Najac. The very Templar Lord Geoffrey had told the pope he had found – and buried. Oh God! Umberto felt a panic rising in him that made his knees weak. Lord Geoffrey had lied! He had managed to hide the Templar until he was restored to health. And he harboured him still under his roof – passing him off as a distant relative, entrusting his own innocent and unknowing granddaughter to his care!

Umberto's shock was passing, turning into a blinding fury against Lord Geoffrey. Poor Félice had been in Poitiers the whole time, terrified at the thought that Free Templars might lurk in the woods around her home! If Félice ever found out the true identity of her 'cousin' she would be horrified! She, who loved her grandfather so deeply, would feel betrayed. She, who had turned to him rather than her own father when her husband repudiated her, would be left without an anchorage in the midst of a dreadful emotional storm.

Umberto's active imagination already pictured her crying her heart out on his chest. He would comfort her. He would remind her that her grandfather was attached to the Temple. He could hear Félice's angry protest: 'But to endanger us all! My parents, my brothers and myself! If he is discovered, we will all pay the price.' Umberto would assure her of his protection. He would intercede on her behalf. She would cling to him, desperately grateful, and then – feeling like an orphan with nowhere else to go – she would beg him to take her in…

'It's just a broken ankle,' Percy was reassuring Master de Winter. 'I've sent for Niki to help me upstairs. Do I understand correctly that Lord Geoffrey has been ill?'

The voice was strong but slightly raw, like someone whose throat was parched. Umberto remembered with unwonted clarity that the sheriff had ordered the guards to bring 'good' water after the Templar's first confession. And then, with a shudder, he remembered how he himself had begged for water when Albi had chained him in the dungeon for three days. He swallowed.

'Lord Geoffrey's heart failed him briefly on Tuesday,' de Winter answered in a low solicitous tone. 'He attended the executions and – it was too much for him.'

Percy managed to sit upright while de Winter explained. 'But he is recovering well, thanks to the excellent care of Lady Félice.'

'Give me a hand.' Percy held out his own and the merchant took it, braced himself and pulled the young man to his feet. Percy's face went rigid and white with the effort of overcoming the pain in his ankles, but he forced himself to stand. He flung one arm over the back of his stallion to keep upright and gazed at last *down* on Umberto. The two men stared at one another and this time they both knew who the other was.

Umberto could sense the malevolence smouldering in the Templar's heart, turning his clear blue eyes murky with malice. Some instinct made the hair stand up on the back of his neck but Umberto suppressed his fear. What had he to fear from an outlawed and excommunicated heretic? A broken man who had begged for mercy and wept like a child? He need only go to his superiors – or to Nogaret himself – and say that at Master de Winter's...

But it would not be fair to drag the innocent and kindly merchant into this affair. And Félice, she thought this man was her cousin. And the pope and Albi thought he was dead and buried. If Umberto now claimed he was alive, he would have to have some proof.

Another thought suddenly struck him: if he had indeed been hidden and nursed back to health by Lord Geoffrey, then Albi would blame Umberto for failing to find him two years ago. Umberto felt his throat constricting. All those people he had tortured in his attempts to find this man must have lied to him! He had failed to find out what dozens of people must have known! Albi would blame him for that, just as he blamed him for the escape in the first place. It had been Lord Geoffrey's story of having buried him a week after his escape which had rescued Umberto from disgrace two years ago. To shatter it now would be to destroy his own reputation and future as well as Lord Geoffrey's. Umberto recognised that he was trapped.

Master de Winter, remembering his manners now that Percy was on his feet again, turned to Umberto. 'Brother Umberto, I don't believe you've met Sir Percival—'

'—de Lacy, isn't it?' Umberto forestalled him. Even if he knew he could not turn the bastard over to the authorities, he could still put fear in the man's heart by showing what he knew.

De Winter merely looked puzzled. 'No, de Thune. An English cousin of Lord Geoffrey,' he explained.

Percy lifted the corners of his lips and continued to stare at Umberto without a trace of uneasiness.

'Brother Umberto di Sante managed to secure Lord Geoffrey's release from arrest on Tuesday,' Master de Winter was explaining to Percy. 'It was very fortunate that he was present.'

'I'm sure it was not the first time Brother Umberto witnessed the torture and murder of innocent men.'

Master de Winter caught his breath at such effrontery and flashed Percy a look of reproach and warning. Too late he registered that Percy was not merely dirty and bearded from a week in the saddle, but that his face which had always struck the merchant as noble and intelligent had taken on a brutal quality. The prominent nose was beak-like and the deep eyes ruthless.

Before Umberto could find an answer, there was a commotion behind them as Gaston returned with Niki. 'Here!' Gaston led the way breathlessly. Then, catching sight of the Dominican in the light of the lantern, he stopped so abruptly that Niki bumped into him.

Percy broke eye contact with Umberto and shook his head slightly but imperatively to Gaston. Gaston started to withdraw backwards, his heartfelt loathing for anyone in the black and white robes of the Dominicans openly written on his young face.

To distract attention, Percy addressed Niki. 'Thank you for coming, Niki. I could use your shoulder on the way upstairs.'

De Winter was relieved by the distraction. 'Shall I send for a groom, Brother Umberto?'

'Please.'

And while their host went towards the tack room shouting for the grooms, Umberto bowed his head and smiled to Percy, asking the cynical question, 'Have your legs been badly hurt?'

'No!' Percy retorted, and then, slipping his arm over Niki's broad shoulder, he limped past the Dominican and into the merchant's house.

Chapter Twenty-Seven

Minerve, June 1310

They had spent the night at Labastide-Rouairoux and the day winding past the last bastions of the Haut Languedoc. The horses were exhausted and the sky behind them dark with threatening rain as they started down from Sainte Colombe. The countryside was notably drier and the scrub brush among the chalk-white outcroppings was parched with thirst. They were soon coated in the white dust thrown up by sergeants Rokely and Pétard, who were leading them.

As the dusk closed in upon them, they followed a corniche, a dry gorge running ever more steeply beside their treacherous trail.

'Where are we going, madame?' Nannette asked fearfully, pressing her docile but weary mare closer to Félice's own.

'We're almost there,' came Percy's voice from ahead as he emerged out of the darkness, pointing straight on.

Against the lingering light, a tower loomed up ahead of them, and Félice inexplicably felt her heart in her throat and her hair standing up on the back of her neck. Her mare, sensing her rider's aversion, balked instantly. Percy looked back sharply. Félice's face was ghostly pale in the darkness and her hands were trembling. She made no effort to overcome the stubborn refusal of her mare to continue.

'What is it?' Percy asked with a touch of irritation. After such an arduous journey, he was anxious to reach their destination.

'I smell smoke.'

Percy lifted his head and drew a deep breath, but there was not a trace of smoke in the air.

'Come.' He reached over and took Félice's reins over her mare's head to lead her. Félice let him lead her to a tall, narrow gateway of crumbling, ill-fitting stone that blocked their way.

Now she could feel that a gorge fell nearly as sharply away to their right as their left. They were on the spine of a ridge far narrower than that of Najac village, and she mistrusted whatever was beyond this crude gate, evidently built from rubble.

Sergeant Rokely rapped upon the wooden gateway and a challenge answered his knock. He gave the agreed answer and the gate swung open. They rode through in single file, Rokely and Pétard, Geoffrey, Percy leading Félice, Nannette and then the others.

Beyond the gate the street was crudely paved. There were frequent missing cobbles and weeds grew between the remaining uneven stones, but it was easy to follow the street for it led straight along the spine of the corniche, lined on the left with abandoned houses. The doors and shutters hung upon their hinges; here and there they stood completely open, offering a glance into the yawning darkness. To their right were the walls of what had once been a castle but the battlements had been damaged and the windows were like the eye sockets of a skull, offering an insight into nothingness.

They passed a second gate and here the corniche suddenly broadened, enabling a second street to peel off to the right. But the road ahead of them was lined with men holding torches. The chorus of male voices that gave voice to a ragged cheer sent a chill down Félice's spine. Geoffrey drew rein abruptly and his stallion threw up his head. He looked at Percy as the younger man drew up beside him, his eyes glittering with anger. Percy did not meet his gaze. Instead, he rode on through the cheering ranks, towards the church, which stood to the right some one hundred yards farther on, a small square nestling beside it.

Here the sergeants and knights stood shoulder to shoulder brazenly wearing Templar surcoats. They too cheered as Percy and Geoffrey emerged at the head of the arriving party. The cheer turned to a chant: *Baucent! Baucent!*

At the entrance to the church were collected all the knights of superior rank and the priests of the Free Templars: Friedrich von Feldburg, who had brought four other knights and seven sergeants from Tempelhof in the Mark Brandenburg; Don Juan de Segovia who commanded eighteen Castilian Templars; Dom Sergio with his thirteen Portuguese; Sir Reginald, senior of the sixteen English knights; and Sirs Norbert and Pierre, who had once been commanders at Cahors and Mas Deu respectively and had been liberated by the Free Templars.

Geoffrey dismounted stiffly and ignored the hand Percy offered him. With a rigid face, he advanced to exchange the kiss of peace with the men collected in his honour. Then he turned abruptly and held out his hand. 'Félice.'

The men who had already closed in around him parted, somewhat startled, and Niki sprang to take Félice's horse from her. Félice nodded to Nannette, and together they passed between the astonished Templars. Geoffrey tucked her hand in his elbow and then stepped into the church. The officers of the Free Templars and their priests followed with lighted candles and behind them came all the knights and sergeants – in the little church there was no room for the lay brothers who remained outside. Altogether they were roughly seven hundred men Geoffrey estimated quickly.

The church had been stripped when the king's men came on Friday, 13th October. The priest and his deacons had been arrested along with the serving brothers, and the tenants evicted from their homes throughout the bastide. The king's men had then plundered the houses and carted away the stores held in the warehouses and barns. Wine had run in the gutters and a bonfire had been built for all they could not consume or carry including the pews and the choir stalls. Now the church was naked except for the stone table that formed the altar and the mocking beasts which curled around the capitals of the squat pillars. Overhead, disturbed swallows fluttered amidst the cobwebbed beams of the peaked wooden roof. The priests behind Geoffrey had taken up a hymn and the light of their candles gradually drove back the shadows.

Geoffrey leaned hard on Félice's arm. He was furious with Percy for organising this demonstration of force, furious with him for bringing so many men together, allowing them to wear their robes flagrantly. He was taking unnecessary chances. He was trying to push Geoffrey into a direct confrontation with the Crown.

But Geoffrey wouldn't have been half so furious if he hadn't felt so frustrated. Geoffrey had placed all his hopes in the papal commission and the trial of the Temple. He had allowed himself to hope that they could clear themselves of these ridiculous charges. He had convinced himself that the very presentation of evidence – the proof of the torture, the bribes, the falsification of testimony – would sway public and ecclesiastical opinion in their favour. He had been aware that this would not influence the king, who had ordered it all, but he had promised himself that a stalemate could be attained. He had never believed that the Temple would be restored to its former properties and power, but he thought that if it were cleared of the charges it might be allowed a new start, impoverished but intact.

Percy had always been sceptical. Percy had obeyed orders but he had privately expressed his belief that the trial would not bring any meaningful results. He had been right, and he would now demand that Geoffrey acknowledge this by endorsing more direct confrontation with the king.

Did it have to come to this? Geoffrey remembered how humbly they had started. He had first contemplated the rescue of prisoners sketching his plans in the dirt of Sister Madeleine's garden. He had never dreamt that one day he would see nearly seven hundred men gathered in an abandoned bastide that had once belonged to the Temple – and all under his command. Back then, he reminded himself, Percy had not wanted to fight at all. Percy had only joined him out of gratitude and love.

Geoffrey closed his eyes in defeat. This was his fault and his alone. He had gone too far: step by step he had led them here. He could not send them 'home' – disperse them and order them to watch in silence and inactivity whilst their brothers burned. But to order any other course of action was suicide. It would destroy everything he had saved. It would send the men he had rescued from the dungeons to their deaths.

Strong, raw, male voices filled the barren church. Geoffrey had reached the altar. He turned and looked back down the nave. Behind the priests and knights with their candles stood sergeants with torches. Here assembled, the light of candles and torches glinting on chain mail and scabbards, they looked impressively mighty. Geoffrey knew how intoxicating such an illusion of strength could be. His memory touched half-forgotten scenes of a greater army still: Saint Louis' assembled Christian forces on the eve of embarking on the disastrous Seventh Crusade. They too had gathered in the tiny chapel in Limassol and it too had been so overfilled with knights that their power seemed magnified. But it was an illusion – now as then. They were as insignificant as insects in comparison with the powers that stood against them.

The hymn came to an end with a long 'amen' and then there was an expectant shuffling and rustling throughout the church. Geoffrey knew he had to speak. He could not use Félice as a shield any longer.

He searched among the faces nearest him for someone who had been in Paris and knew Félice. Seeing Gaston, he signalled to the youth. 'See that my granddaughter is given the best accommodation available.'

Gaston did not know whether to feel honoured or angered, but he could not disobey. He led Félice and Nanette back out of the church. Geoffrey faced the assembly alone.

He raised his voice and thanked them all for coming and for the welcome they had given him. Him? He wondered even as he spoke; or Percy? And at last he spared a glance for the tall Englishman who stood symbolically and literally immediately to his right. Percy was his right arm. Percy had organised this night.

There was a slight, crooked smile on Percy's face and the light of torches glinted in his eyes. Geoffrey's eyes fell to the hilt of his sword and he shuddered. While Saint Louis advanced up the Nile at a snail's pace and the Mamelukes attacked them with impunity, de Sonnac had lost his patience and, disregarding the king's explicit orders, had led his Templars in a charge that left hundreds of startled Saracens dead but not a single Templar. But at Mansourah that same de Sonnac pride and contempt for orders had led to utter disaster. He had known that the assault of the city was doomed to failure. He had known it was against the orders of the king. He had foreseen the consequences of the Count of Artois' folly. And he had knowingly sacrificed all the Templars of the van in a gesture of haughty contempt. The look in his eyes then was the look in Percy's now.

Geoffrey forced himself to stop remembering, to face the present with as much calm and dignity as his office demanded. 'I have convened this chapter to discuss what course of action we should take in the face of the latest developments. I wish to hear your opinions.'

Don Juan appeared to have been awaiting this invitation because he immediately stepped forward. 'My lord, can there be any question? We must avenge our brothers!'

His words were greeted with a burst of cheers.

Geoffrey glanced towards the enthusiastic assembly and sighed. 'Avenge?' he asked when the audience had calmed down. 'What exactly do you mean, brother Juan? Should we perhaps burn the Archbishop of Sens?'

'That's exactly what I mean!' Don Juan retorted.

'And may I ask how you propose to gain control over the worthy archbishop?' Geoffrey asked with raised eyebrows.

'We should surround his palace and set it afire. I have been to Paris and I am certain it can be done. We could set fire to the stables and kitchens and—'

Geoffrey raised his hand. 'There is no need to discuss details until we are agreed on the principle. We now know your opinion. Are there other suggestions?' Geoffrey searched the faces of the men nearest him looking for contradiction.

Dom Sergio at once stepped forward. The Portuguese felt patriotically compelled to disagree with the Castilians. 'The Archbishop of Sens is a puppet of King Philip and Nogaret. We must strike at them! We should send word to the Assassins and arrange for them to eliminate both men. Then public opinion will be reminded that the real enemy is the Muslims who still contaminate the Holy Land and half of Iberia. They will rise again in support of a new crusade. They will turn to the Templars to lead them!'

'And meanwhile other men will burn!' Sir Hugh pointed out heatedly, cutting off the beginnings of a cheer.

The church was suddenly deathly still instead.

'Continue, Sir Hugh,' Geoffrey said after a moment.

Hugh flushed, reminded that he had spoken out of turn and without being properly recognised. 'Revenge must wait until we have done all we can to prevent further deaths.'

'How do you propose to do that?' Sir Norbert enquired with evident nervousness. 'The Defenders are well guarded and the executions are public. We must persuade the pope to intervene.'

'Set the assassins on the pope!' someone called from the ranks of the sergeants, causing a brief storm of violent disagreement among the men at the back.

Geoffrey had to call for order repeatedly before things calmed down and he could acknowledge Sir Friedrich from the Commandery at Tempelhof.

'I believe the king expects us to try and prevent the executions. They are bait to lure us into the open. We should not do what is expected but use these executions as a distraction to strike elsewhere. While all eyes are focused on the fires, we should free Master de Molay and our senior officers.'

'Do you think the Grand Master would want to pay for his freedom with the lives of those who have offered to defend the Order?' Sir Pierre asked angrily.

'De Molay refused to defend the Order!' Sir Reginald boomed in a deep baritone, and he did not bother to disguise his anger. Geoffrey registered that the Englishman apparently shared his son Jean's dislike for de Molay.

'Master de Molay was right to insist—' Brother Norbert of Mas Deu started hotly, but Geoffrey held up his hand to prevent the debate from becoming undisciplined and misdirected.

'We are not here to discuss the master's actions. Sir Pierre's question is the right one: what would he want us to do?'

'That is *not* the question.' Father André limped forwards, leaning heavily upon a cane. 'The question is what *He'* – he pointed to the altar – 'would want us to do. Do you think *He* wants us to shed Christian blood?'

'The Archbishop of Sens sheds Christian blood!' Sir Gilbert retorted hotly.

'And that blood is upon his head. Our martyred brothers are with God now, while the Archbishop of Sens faces an eternity in hell. Where do you want to spend eternity, brothers? With all those thousands of our brothers who have died for their *Faith,* whether on the Horns of Hattin, at Mansourah and Acre or in Paris on the 23rd May? Or do you wish to spend eternity with the Archbishop of Sens and Philip of France in hell?'

'You expect us to let our brothers burn?' Sir Martin demanded, and many of the French knights clearly sided with his outrage.

'They will be with God before you, Sir Martin,' Father André answered calmly.

'Their martyrdom does not excuse our inaction!' Sir Reginald answered impatiently, and there was a grumble of support from his English knights and sergeants.

'My lord?' Sir Cyprian, who stood farther back in the crowd, lifted his voice and caught Geoffrey's eye. Geoffrey nodded for him to speak. 'We – the Free Templars of France – should not forget that any or all of us might now be facing the auto-da-fé – if it weren't for yourself and Sir Percy. Do we have the right to distance ourselves from the fate of the others who were less fortunate?'

'Many are called but only a few are chosen,' Father André answered.

'Chosen for martyrdom or life?' Sir Cyprian asked, frowning.

'That is your choice,' Father André returned.

An excited, youthful voice asked in outrage from the door, 'You want us to stand by and watch while Commander Gautier and Brother Thomas burn?'

These remarks were almost drowned in an eruption of abuse.

'Bugger! If you hadn't kissed ass—'

'Percy!' Gaston shouted desperately. 'You won't let them burn, will you? Tell them that you won't let them burn!'

'I won't let them burn,' Percy said simply. A deep silence fell briefly before a loud rapturous cheer erupted. The sergeants started stamping their feet and soon the serving brothers and knights were stamping too. *Baucent! Baucent!*

Geoffrey looked at Percy, feeling all of his eighty years. 'Have you got what you came here for?' he asked wearily in a low voice which could barely be heard above the clamour of approval.

'Not entirely. I want your blessing too.'

'Have you thought what will happen if you fail?'

'I think of nothing else,' Percy responded harshly.

Geoffrey closed his eyes. He was weak and helpless in the face of so much bitter determination. He opened his eyes again and met Percy's: bloodshot, sharp and fanatical. What was it Percy had said? He wished that he could cleanse his heart of bitterness and hatred as easily as he could cleanse his body.

But he couldn't. Geoffrey shook his head in helplessness and boundless regret but then he made the sign of the cross over Percy, stepped down from the altar platform and walked through the cheering ranks of Templars with his gaze fixed on the door.

Outside the night was mild after the hot day. The stars glinted in the now blue-black sky and the Milky Way was a murky smudge arching overhead. Geoffrey took a deep breath of the clean air and then started as a shadow separated itself from the other shadows to his left and came towards him. Félice's face was like a detached moon surrounded by the transparent veils that swathed her neck and hair.

'Grandpapa, what's happened?'

'Percy's won.'

'What do you mean?'

'Listen to them!' He gestured irritably towards the church, where a new burst of cheering rumbled out of the door and down the steps. 'They are all blinded by their own good luck. They think they can defy the King of France openly. They want to rescue their brothers from the flames. And they will all die trying.' There were tears in his eyes and his voice.

Félice wove her fingers into his, and her wide-set golden eyes in her heart-shaped face looked earnestly up at him. While she had been waiting, she had discovered a Cathar dove scratched into the pavement of the square, and she knew now that this had been a Cathar village before it had been given to the Templars. She knew with inner certainty that it had been Simon de Montfort who had destroyed the castle and that here in this square the Inquisition had burned Cathar heretics. That was the smoke she had smelt: the smoke of the Inquisition. Was it any wonder that Percy wanted to fight back?

'Is it really so hopeless?' she asked. 'Surely there are ways to rescue at least some of the victims without risking everything? Percy has been successful in the past, hasn't he? Think how many men you have rescued without losses.'

Geoffrey sighed. 'Yes, no doubt I am just a weak old man. Fretful as an old woman. Of course, we must do something to try to help the others but I am afraid of losing what we have, afraid of losing the lives we have saved. Afraid more for the one who is like a son to me than for the hundreds of others I do not know. I am not fit for the office they have given me!'

'That's not true!' Félice flung her arms around him, wrapping him in her voluminous silk sleeves. 'You aren't weak! You aren't in any way unfit! You are wise and we are foolhardy.' What had the resistance of the entire nobility of Languedoc ever brought but disinheritance, imprisonment and death? An entire nation had been conquered and humiliated – subjugated by the Inquisition. What hope did this band of Free Templars have?

Geoffrey clung to her, his eyes fixed on the star-strewn sky. 'Dear God, now I understand Master de Molay! He was afraid to risk what he had in a confrontation and that is why he lost everything.' Geoffrey stared blindly at the stars, taking strength and comfort from Félice's warmth. His thoughts drifted from himself and his own timidness to Percy's strength. The Percy he had seen tonight was not the same thoughtful young man he had watched recover from the injuries inflicted by the Inquisition. 'Do you know the worst of it?' he asked Félice abruptly. She lifted her head to look at him questioningly. 'His soul is being warped and deformed by hatred. It is consuming him from the inside.'

Chapter Twenty-Eight

Albi, June 1310

The organisation of an auto-da-fé is considerably more complicated than it appears, and the Bishop of Albi was determined to make his burnings more notable than the hasty affair the Archbishop of Sens had arranged in Paris. Furthermore, Albi intended to use the burning of the unrepentant Templars as a reminder of the fate of the Cathars and a symbol of the power of the Church – in particular that of its bishops.

This meant that not only the usual crowds of curious, morbid and hungry had to be among the spectators but the important merchants and, above all, the nobility of the region. The bishop was sensitive to the fact that the nobility of the Languedoc still considered itself more civilised than their French langue d'oïl occupiers. This sense of superiority had been a principal factor inducing Catholic noblemen to support the Cathars, or at least tolerate them, for a long time. It had persuaded them to actively oppose the crusade called against the Cathars. And when the crusade was at last successful and the nobility had to pay for their intransigence with their lands, the dispossessed had often sought honour and security among the Knights Templar.

The Templars had drawn their strength from the region right from the start. It was here in the Aquitaine that they had had the largest number of manors and commanderies. The bulk of these had been bequests by wealthy citizens –

gentry, nobility and bourgeoisie – which might otherwise have gone to other religious orders. The bishop had calculated that if all the bequests to the Temple had gone to the diocese, his income would have increased by fully thirty-eight per cent! Unfortunately, the king seemed determined to keep the Templar properties for his own enrichment and the pope inclined towards turning them over to the Knights of Saint John, but that was another issue altogether.

What was important was that the nobility of the region be compelled to see the once mighty Templars were now as helpless as the Cathars had been. Whatever the nebulous links between the Cathars and the Templars might have been, their fate was the same. Holy Mother Church, in her unerring righteousness, was again triumphant.

Since the bishop could hardly compel the nobility to come, he had to lure them. So with a shrug he disregarded the papal ban on tournaments and sponsored one of his own. Nothing was more certain to lure knights, lords and ladies in great numbers than this most demanding of all bloodsports.

With forethought and precision, the bishop selected the site for the jousts. For the ladies, the bishop organised a troubadour contest to be held in his own palace. For the commoners there was to be a variety of entertainments including three-legged races, wrestling matches, bear-baiting and acrobats. The entire series of events was organised so that the troubadour contest was on Saturday and the mêlée on Monday so that virtually everyone was certain to be in attendance on Sunday – the day the Templars were to be burned.

Umberto found himself flattered against his own will by the trust the bishop placed in him. Umberto was entrusted with drafting the public statement the bishop planned to read before turning the Templars over to the sheriff. Most flattering of all, Umberto had been designated to make the last appeal to the condemned – the role Father Elion had played in Paris.

Umberto worked long, hard and late into many nights preparing the bishop's statement and his own plea. The bishop's speech was supposed to be a succinct legal indictment of the crimes confessed to and their heretical nature. The law was clear, the evidence was overwhelming so the Church had no choice but to turn over the dangerous relapsed heretics to the secular arm. The bishop's role was that of the just but unforgiving Father. To Umberto was left the role of the pitying and forgiving Son.

Umberto found it much easier to put himself in this role than he had expected. He imagined that he could understand the defiance and pride that induced many Templars to deny the confessions which had been torn from them under humiliating circumstances. Umberto was even willing to admit to himself that many of the individual Templars were very likely innocent of true heresy. They had, no doubt, believed their Master could absolve them of confessed sins, and sodomy would have been no less widespread among the Templars than in other religious orders. But he personally suspected that only very few of the Templars had really worshipped idols. As for denying Christ at their initiation, he wondered if it weren't really some ritual based on Saint Peter's denial of Christ.

Umberto was prepared to secretly admit that many men who had incriminated themselves under torture were in fact innocent, and he could understand that innocent men might indeed retract their earlier confessions. He did not think it right to send them to their deaths. And if he could persuade just one man to back down, to throw himself on the mercy of the Church, Umberto would attain such fame that he could leave the Bishop of Albi's service.

The priest who could outdo Father Elion's eloquence and achieve better results, would attract the attention of the king and the pope and the curia. Umberto would be able to pick and choose between posts – he might even be offered a bishop's staff.

Sometimes, when Umberto could no longer find the erudite Latin phrases for the bishop's statement or his own eloquence seemed flat and unconvincing, his thoughts drifted. He saw himself walking in doeskin slippers on the marble pavement of a cloister. The purple silk of his vestments billowed in a light breeze and sun glinted on the gilding of his cope. Félice was beside him in a sheer, rose-coloured silk gown, her silver surcoat shimmering. She wore her hair free and uncovered because she was 'at home'. In his daydream, he was explaining some point of theology to her and she was asking her pert and provocative questions with the admiring expression he remembered so well from Poitiers. Then a young deacon interrupted them: 'Your Grace, a royal courier has just ridden in…'

⋆

Umberto was disappointed when Félice was not among the many noblewomen who came to the tournament. Her brother Norbert came with a half-dozen household knights. Umberto politely enquired after his family and Norbert informed him candidly that his father was drunk most of the time and his mother suffered from swelling of her joints. He clearly regarded himself and behaved as the Lord of Najac in all but name.

Umberto wiped the sweat from his face with the inside of his sleeve. On second thought, it was probably better that Félice had not come. He had no desire to deal with her grandfather during the auto-da-fé this afternoon. This great, carefully planned show must not go wrong in any detail.

Of course, if Lord Geoffrey were arrested, Félice would certainly come to plead for him. She would turn to Umberto for help. He could then reveal to her gravely and with due regard for the shock he would give her that her so-called 'cousin' was in fact a dangerous escaped Templar for whom her grandfather had risked life and soul in defiance of King and Church. She would turn against him in her horror at his betrayal. They would let him pay the price of his lies, treason and defiance...

And if Percy de Lacy himself dared come, if he risked any action in support of the Templars, then there would be every reason to arrest him too. They could put him to the question – as indeed they would Lord Geoffrey as well. Sir Percy had broken last time and he would again. Then they would have him, and Umberto – because of his eloquence and success with the other Templars – would be able to shrug at the bishop and say, 'You believed Lord Geoffrey's story and called me off his trail. Otherwise we would have had him in our hands years ago!' Then he would turn his back on the raging bishop and go out to join Nogaret in the courtyard, and ride away to his consecration.

The seven stakes for the condemned had been erected during the previous night and the faggots had been piled professionally and coated with pitch to ensure a good, enduring fire. A crude platform ran along behind the stakes, which enabled the guards to lead the condemned men to their respective stake, make them fast and then withdraw. Any of the condemned who succumbed to Umberto's eloquence could be removed via the same platform. For those who remained obdurate, the platform would soon become nothing but further fuel for the flames sending them to hell.

A flimsy fence enclosed the area where the stakes had been erected and it was heavily guarded for crowds of the curious milled about from the moment the work of erecting the stakes began. By midday the square was filled with excited spectators, and pedlars were doing a brisk trade in trinkets, wine and sausages.

While the bishop and the nobility attended mass, the sheriff had brought the prisoners from the dungeon. The prisoners were divided into two groups: the larger group consisted of those who had confessed and never retracted their confessions and seven men who had repudiated their confessions. The latter seven, including the three men who had offered to defend the Temple, were together in an open wagon, which was driven into the enclosure and drawn up in front of the stakes immediately opposite the austere east end of the cathedral.

The procession of clergy, dignitaries and high-born left the cathedral by the south door and made its way along the base of the imposing brick structure to collect at the base of the choir. The bishop and his intimates mounted the wooden platform erected for them and Albi rested his hands on the railing, gazing down at the seven Templars chained hand and foot – except for Brother Thomas, who had no feet and so was kneeling – before him.

A hush fell over the assembled crowd. The bishop raised his staff and made the sign of the cross. Then he opened his mouth and delivered in lilting Latin the concise statement Umberto had written for him in a deep-timbred voice that reached the edges of the square and fled down the streets converging upon it. It ended with the question, in French, of whether any of the men denied the truth of what he'd said.

The condemned could not understand Latin. They gazed up at him, pale as death itself beneath the grime of the dungeon and their unkempt beards. Their eyes burned in bloodshot eyes. Their lips were cracked and bleeding. They stared. They swallowed. They did not answer. With a shrug of resignation which even the most distant spectator could see, the bishop turned to the sheriff and delivered the relapsed heretics into his hands.

The sheriff was an efficient man. He gave curt orders to his men and the prisoners were hustled to the back of the stakes and up the ladders. It was with forethought that the platforms and ladders had been provided. The prisoners seemed unable to move their own limbs and the guards were forced to drag and carry them, a task which would have been twice as difficult if they had not had the sure footing provided by the platform.

Once the first bonds had been passed around the prisoners' waists, the chains on their hands and feet were removed; they could be reused for other prisoners. Then the Templars were secured with rope to the stakes, their hands behind their backs. Brother Thomas caused considerable trouble since he lacked feet. He could not stand and he sagged so heavily that the ropes hardly held him. The guards had to bind him at his shoulders, hips and knees as well as at the waist and hands.

Umberto's moment had come. He rose nervously, swallowing and clearing his throat. The text of his appeal was rolled in his sleeve but he knew it would make a bad impression if he read it. His appeal must appear spontaneous.

While Umberto made his way to the gate of the enclosure, a group of younger knights clattered into the square. They had scorned the piety of attending mass, preferring to spend the afternoon in the lists training for the main event of the tournament tomorrow. Now they were anxious not to miss the entertainment of the auto-da-fé and rudely forced their sweating and snorting horses through the dense crowd.

Umberto cast them a look of disgust and noticed the raised eyebrows of disapproval on the bishop's face. Umberto half-smiled at the thought that the bishop would punish these arrogant fighting men; very likely he would ban them from the tournament on the morrow. Of course, the bishop would first have to find out who they were. They still wore their helmets and dirty training surcoats, devoid of heraldic arms.

The citizens grumbled loudly enough to be almost provocative as the knights insisted on the privilege of their better birth and forced their way to the front of the crowd, almost against the enclosure fence. The stallions fretted, tossing their heads and spattering saliva all the way to where Umberto had taken up his position opposite the central stake.

He closed his ears and thoughts to the rude knights and concentrated on his task. He let his eyes linger on the faces of the condemned, one after another. They were all old, haggard men seemingly similar in their scraggly beards, long dirty hair and rags. The footless man was completely bald. Another of the prisoners had hideous open sores all over his face. They were all piteous.

Umberto raised his head and flung open his arms. 'Brothers! Hear me! The Apocalypse is come!'

The sheriff's men brought lighted torches and took up their positions, two at each of the stakes.

'Hear the voice of Our Dear Lord when I *beg* you to repent! Repent of all your sins! God knows your heart!' Umberto reminded them. He wanted them to repent of their *real* sins, not the fictional ones that had been tortured from them. By asking them to repent in so ambiguous a manner, he hoped to give them a way out, an escape that was not entirely dishonest. 'He knows the sins you have committed. He asks only that you sincerely repent of them and return to his bosom! He longs to enfold you in his arms like the prodigal son! He longs to—'

The crash made Umberto jump and, despite himself, he looked over his shoulder. He saw four massive destriers smashing against the railing of the fence enclosing the pyres. The beams, hastily hammered to the temporary fence posts, gave way and the posts tipped backwards – the whole fence was being torn out of the ground! The stallions plunged forwards tossing their heads angrily at the reins that held them back despite the driving spurs. In his astonishment, Umberto almost waited a moment too long before fleeing towards the cathedral.

The sheriff was shouting orders. His men were stuffing their torches into the faggots and drawing their swords. Those men who had been guarding the streets into the square tried to fight their way through the half-excited, half-panicked crowd to reach the shattered enclosure. The bishop was screaming something Umberto could not understand over the general noise, and some of the other spectators were loudly asking who these men were. None of the knights who had been to mass made any effort to come to the sheriff's assistance. They had attended mass unarmed.

The leading mounted knights were clashing with the sheriff's men – at a clear advantage despite the better odds of the royal forces because they were mounted. Those knights who were not engaging the guards were already cutting free the first and second Templars, pulling them down from their stakes and dragging them roughly over their saddles. The flames had caught on the faggots all along the line, however, and the horses started to shy.

Umberto could see the fury with which two of the knights tried to drive their stallions forwards towards the next burning pyre, but the fear of fire is a deep instinct, greater than all the training in the world, and the stallions refused. Only one of the knights managed to ride close enough to the third stake to reach the condemned with his sword. Leaning far out of the saddle, he slashed and blood was drawn but the prisoner was struggling now. The prospect of rescue was so real, no near, and the horror of death by fire so compelling, that he found strength. The rescuing knight forced his stallion in once more and lashed out again. The man's feet were free.

The crowd was cheering – for the Templars. The bishop was screaming. The flames at the far end of the line were leaping up now and one of the condemned let out a howl that wafted over the square above all the rest of the clamour.

The rescuers tried to press forwards, running down two of the sheriff's men, but as they pressed in towards the now billowing flames of the last four stakes one of the stallions reared up and overbalanced. He went crashing backwards on to his rider.

The rescuers were losing cohesion. The three who had managed to haul condemned men over their saddles were now forcing their way through the crowds, who parted willingly, and were soon galloping downhill towards the bridge. Another rescuer had drawn up and jumped down to help his fallen colleague, who had apparently been knocked unconscious or broken something vital when the stallion went over backwards. Two were fighting wildly with the sheriff's men, their stallions bleeding from the wounds inflicted. The remaining four men were still trying to reach the men being slowly consumed by the flames.

One of the rescuers had vaulted to the ground. He clambered up a ladder engulfed in flame. The other three turned to keep the sheriff's men from reaching the man attempting the rescue. Then one of these jumped down from his terrified stallion and ran to the base of the stake to receive the prisoner his colleague cut down. The victim was unceremoniously pushed, coughing, half-conscious, off the front of the platform.

Percy sprang down himself and ran to the next stake. Again he mounted the steps through the flames, but the platform itself was already starting to burn. His foot broke through the charred planking and he nearly fell through. He struggled back to his feet. The crowd was cheering him. His dagger worked feverishly at the bonds around Thomas's chest. The planking under his feet gave way for a second time with a crash. He was plunged into the inferno itself. Above him Thomas wailed in one last piercing protest against God.

Percy tried to clamber back up the burning faggots towards Thomas but Martin and Gilbert were dragging him off the pyre. 'It's too late! You can't do any more! We can't do any more!'

They were stronger than he. They had him out of the flames. His surcoat was gone, the edge of his gambeson singed, but he was aware of neither fact. Hugh, still mounted, managed to drag a terrified, resisting Renaissance towards him. Heydon was shouting that he couldn't hold the sheriff's men much longer. Rokely confirmed, 'We've got to break for it now!'

Percy dragged himself into the saddle from the right side. The others grabbed their own stallions and vaulted up, swinging their stallions to face north before even their seats touched the saddle. Percy flung his worthless dagger from him and drew de Sonnac's sword.

Too late the others realised he wasn't with them. He had not turned towards the river. He rode straight at the platform before the cathedral and he guided the Baptist's hand, or vice versa. The sword gleamed in the afternoon sun and glowed in the flames devouring three of his brothers.

The bishop stood with his hands upon the railing, shouting at the crowd, the sheriff, his guests, his God. He saw the danger too late or perhaps he was too stunned by the effrontery to respond. He stopped shouting and stared for a short moment in sheer astonishment. The most elegant battle sword he had ever seen – and the only one he had ever seen used in earnest – cut the air in two and sent his soul to hell.

Chapter Twenty-Nine

Minerve, June 1310

It was three days since sergeant Roussel had returned with two of the four rescued men, and still they had neither word from or of Sir Percy. Father André held an almost perpetual vigil in the barren church, attended intermittently by the others. The men of Lord Geoffrey's staff could be seen huddled together in worried discussion when they were not pacing the walls of the dilapidated bastide on a watch of uncertain purpose. Sir Geoffrey himself had spent hours questioning Roussel and the rescued men, and when he was not praying he too haunted the slowly crumbling walls. Waiting.

Félice walked the ramparts like the others, her gaze fixed upon the panorama that lay spread before her in all its rugged, barren beauty. It was high summer. The weather had been hot and dry for almost four weeks now. On the floor of the gorges which enclosed them, fingers of shallow water trickled across their gravel bed. She felt a wave of homesickness for the rich green valleys of Najac. This was a desert in comparison. And it had been lack of water which had driven the inhabitants to surrender to Simon de Montfort after a five week siege. She knew the story from the shepherd who supplied them with cheese and wine. It was exactly one hundred years since the bastide had fallen. They had surrendered from thirst and then one hundred and forty men and women had been condemned to the auto-da-fé for their faith. Just as her great-grandmother had been.

Now all of the Languedoc belonged to the conquerors. Their Gothic churches were spread like outposts across the countryside. The Inquisition demanded tribute in every town. Even Najac was in the hands of the enemy. They had driven her grandfather away and her father to drink, and it was Marie and Norbert who controlled all which once had been her grandmother's. She was alone in the world, but for a man of eighty and an outlaw monk...

And Percy might be dead. With each passing day and hour, the probability that he had been killed or taken captive increased. If he were captured, he would be tortured and put to death. Félice was forced to pray that he be allowed to die quickly, if he had to die. But why did he have to die? Why couldn't he return safely? She felt a desperate need to see him again, speak to him, touch him...

Despite the heat and the blazing sun, she saw again the snowy road in the gathering gloom of a February night. She knelt in the wet snow and took his louse-ridden, unkempt head in her lap. She would give her soul to be granted the same privilege again...

Nannette, bored and confused by a situation no one had bothered to explain to her, busied herself with cutting climbing roses from the crumbling walls of the castle ruins. Pleased with her harvest, she made her way to the large rectangular cistern which the Templars had dug after they took over the bastide. Laying the roses on the rim, she released the rope securing the bucket and started to lower it down the well. Out of the depths of the well a distorted and disembodied voice shouted, 'Hallo!'

Nannette dropped everything and screamed, 'Spirits!'

Geoffrey was emerging from the church with Gaston, and at Nannette's shout he hastened towards her, limping from kneeling on the hard church floor.

'What—'

'In the well! I heard a voice! It must be someone who drowned! They did that to heretics! Sank them in the wells of their own towns! This was a Cathar bastide, wasn't it? That's why it was abandoned!' Nannette's fears had all come together and she was trembling despite the heat.

Geoffrey leant over the well. 'Hallo!' he shouted. Then, 'Percy? Dear God! Percy?'

Geoffrey could hear the voices now, though distorted by the echo. The source was invisible but the words distinct: 'Send down a ladder and a sling.'

'At once!' Geoffrey promised.

Already Gaston was breaking away. 'I'll fetch them!' he promised.

'Get the others!' Geoffrey ordered.

Soon they were all assembled around the well and a rope ladder was carefully lowered. From below, they were directed to move it more to the left until, abruptly, they could feel the tension of someone grabbing it from below. Two of the sergeants held it fast and the first of Sir Percy's men climbed up out of the cave which opened into the well shaft some twenty feet above water level.

The men emerged chalky and caked with mud. A cheer greeted not just the first of the men to emerge, but each one of them: Sergeants Gaujac, Tavernier and Pétard, followed by Sir Hugh. Then came the English sergeants, Rokely, Heydon and Tyler. When they were safely on the surface, they called for a sling and helped lower this carefully. After what seemed like a long time a shout was given to draw it up again, and those above ground soon had sergeant Belot at the surface. His shoulder was wrapped in a bloody bandage and his face ashen. He was followed by Sir Jean of Vaour and Jacques of Réalmont, men who had been rescued from the auto-da-fé and now had raw and bloody feet.

While the tedious process of bringing the men up out of the wellshaft was still under way, Geoffrey gave orders for a meal, wine, clean clothes and beds to be prepared. Sir Cyprian, the most skilled of them in tending wounds, had gone to get his instruments as soon as he saw sergeant Belot. Even Father André had hobbled out of the church, a wooden crucifix in his crippled hands.

The men brought out of the well were talking all at once, the men around them interrupting to ask questions that could not be fully answered before the next one came. One of the lay brothers arrived with a jug of cooled wine and it was passed from man to man. Fragments of their tale were scattered upon the pavement: the sheriff's pursuit of them to the abandoned château at Hautpoul; the assaults; the ruse with the torches; the dummy they had nailed to a charred cross; the escape route out of the well which Percy had known about from the start – as he knew of this entry. Geoffrey found himself wondering how Percy knew, but then de Sonnac had been born and raised in this area, at Lastours.

The men explained that the two caves were, unfortunately, not connected. They had been nearly lost underground. They had been inadvertently rescued by a stray sheep whose bleating had shown them the way out. They had travelled on the surface, afraid of discovery in their suspicious condition. At length, Sir Percy and the two men they had rescued from the auto-da-fé could walk no longer and had to be carried.

Geoffrey leaned over the well again. 'Percy?'

'We'll send him up next – in the sling,' came the echoing answer from the well. It was Sir Martin's voice.

They lowered the sling again and, though the others continued to chatter excitedly, Geoffrey, Félice and Gaston waited nervously while the precious bundle was slowly hauled, hand over hand out of the depths of the well.

It was Niki who leaned past his lord to grab Percy under the arms and haul him on to the rim of the well. With an arm around Niki's neck to keep himself from falling back down into the well, Percy swung his swollen and limp feet over the rim, to sit facing outwards. Behind him, Sirs Martin and Gilbert were already starting up the ladder. Not one man had been lost.

Geoffrey had eyes only for Percy. He saw the smoke stains along his hairline, the creases around his eyes and the rings of his hauberk. He saw the dirty stubble of his week-old beard and smelt the sour-sweet mixture of mud and sweat. A sword had slashed open his right sleeve just above the elbow and the chain mail hung open from the tear, the broken links gaping and exposing the bloody rag that had been wrapped around the wound. Then their eyes met and the joy and triumph Geoffrey had been feeling choked in his breast.

There was no sense of victory in Percy's eyes. Nothing but a blank bitterness.

'They burned Thomas, François and another brother,' he told Geoffrey.

'You saved four men when no one in his right mind thought you could save any! Let us thank God and all his saints! You are back safe! Not one man lost! This is the greatest miracle I have ever been allowed to witness!'

'Amen!' Father André added fervently and the others, falling raggedly silent, crossed themselves as they echoed him.

Percy stared at Geoffrey and then at Father André. The corner of his lips lifted just a fraction. 'I am astonished by your blessings, father. Or didn't Roussel make it back?' He lifted his head slightly, his back stiffening.

'He has been here for three days with Brothers Michel and Gautier.'

'Didn't he tell you?' Percy asked, lifting his eyebrows in evident astonishment.

Geoffrey let out a warning croak. Roussel had told Geoffrey, but Geoffrey had kept the information to himself.

'Of course,' Father André was answering in his gentle, forgiving voice. 'He said you'd saved four men! And Brother Gautier told us about... Brother Thomas.' Father André continued in a tone full of sympathy and faith, 'He is in heaven, my son. There is nothing with which to reproach yourself—'

'No – except that I was too late! That I was too slow! That I'd failed to foresee the panic of the horses! That I—'

'Percy!'

At the sound of his name Percy snapped upright and clamped his mouth shut. He turned his head towards the voice and the others stood back startled – even Gaston.

Félice stepped beside him and sank down on her heels at his feet in a rustle of silk. The fragrance of crushed roses came from the folds of her gown, which had been packed in rose petals for the journey from Paris. She took hold of one of his feet and Percy gasped at her touch. She gently unbuckled first one spur and then the other. Then she stood and announced simply, 'I must see to your injuries, sir. You can talk later.' Over her shoulder she ordered Gaston and Nannette to draw a bath.

'My lady!' Father André protested. 'Sir Cyprian—'

'No!' Geoffrey gripped the priest's forearm so sharply that he gasped in pain. 'No,' Geoffrey continued more calmly, but loud enough for all to hear, 'Sir Cyprian must see to the others. Come.' He began herding the others towards the long warehouse along the north side of the square which they used as a refectory.

The others went willingly, the excited, relieved babble of their adventures tumbling from them as they gave way to the hunger and thirst they had suppressed for days. The men who had returned were so grateful to be safe and back among their comrades that their exhaustion was momentarily forgotten. Nor had they any reason to worry about Sir Percy now that he was safe and in good hands. As marshal and nobleman, it was only natural that he separate himself from lesser men as soon as the crisis was past. Besides, only Sirs Gilbert and Martin had heard the content, much less the tenor, of the exchange between Percy, Geoffrey and Father André. These two knights exchanged a look. Sir Gilbert then gave Geoffrey a more penetrating appraisal, while Sir Martin glanced in Percy's direction and saw that Félice had taken his arm across her shoulder and that he was staggering more than walking towards the house she occupied.

Father André stood indecisively by the well, his eyes riveted on the troubling image of Sir Percy with his arm around a young woman. Just as he decided that he must follow and bring him to his senses, Geoffrey called out his name from behind. 'Father André! You will join us *now*!' Then, as if he could see the hesitation which was the beginning of defiance, without raising his voice he added, in an unmistakable tone. 'You vowed obedience, father, and I am ordering you to come!'

Father André spun about and glared at Geoffrey furiously. This old man, who had been a Templar barely two years, had no right to use that tone, much less so tactlessly impute that he was disobedient. Geoffrey left Sirs Martin and Gilbert standing and strode back to the reddened, furious priest.

'You cannot order me to ignore the peril to a man's soul!' Father André greeted him before Geoffrey could speak.

'Whose soul?' Geoffrey asked sharply, his dark eyes glinting challengingly beneath his white eyebrows.

'Sir Percy is one of the most noble knights I have ever had the privilege to know, but he is weak – terribly weakened from this ordeal. Can't you see the danger? Do you think your granddaughter is not a child of Eve? Or – if you are so indifferent to Sir Percy's immortal soul – you might take more care of your granddaughter's honour!' This was flung at Geoffrey as a man of war might have flung a gauntlet.

Geoffrey scorned the transparent attempt to distract him from the issue. His voice was calm in comparison to Father André's. 'My granddaughter's honour is not at risk – Percy's soul is.'

'Then you *do* see the danger!' For a split second Father André was relieved, then he realised that this only made matters worse. 'You see the danger and you would turn your back, leave him – in his weakened condition – at the mercy of his latent lust? Percy is a young man. Too often he has proved he does not have his emotions in hand—'

'Tell me, father, as a *priest,*' Geoffrey stressed the last word, 'what did Our Lord come to earth to preach? Did he beg us to hate – or to love – our fellow man?'

'What sophism is that? The love he preached has nothing to do with the carnal lusts of animals—'

'Never!' Geoffrey cut him off for now he was becoming angry. 'But whether you are capable of understanding the love between man and woman or not, you must concede that hatred is the greater sin.'

'Greater than the breaking of a holy vow? That is what we are talking about! Not the fornication of an ordinary man, not the adultery of a scorned and divorced woman, but the violation of a monk's sacred vow!'

Geoffrey had trouble not exploding in fury, but after eighty years he had learned to keep his temper in check better than when he was twenty. 'Are you blind? Percy's heart is being consumed by hatred. If my Felicitas can not break the grip it has upon his heart then he is lost – more surely than if he were to seduce a hundred maidens!'

Father André drew back, baffled by reasoning he could not follow.

'Percy killed the Bishop of Albi!' Geoffrey exploited Father André's confusion to deliver a blow that left the priest dazed. Father André mouth opened but he could only stare. 'When he failed to get Brother Thomas down from the stake in time, he remounted and hacked the bishop in two from shoulder to waist.'

'God have mercy! Christ have mercy! Mother Mary have Mercy!' Father André crossed himself and his lips moved in prayer while his eyes stared in horror at Geoffrey.

'Do you think he would stop at doing violence to the king or even the pope in his present state of mind?'

'We must stop him!'

'Don't you remember what happened here two weeks ago?' Geoffrey pointed to the now empty church. 'They all want revenge! They want to strike at the king, the pope, at Nogaret, at the spineless cardinals and papal commissioners! They will cheer him on! They will follow him! They will drive him to the end of his own strength! Don't you see that? Ask any of *them*' – he indicated the men in the improvised refectory – 'what they think of the murder of the Bishop of Albi! They approve! They revel in it! And as long as they can ride on the coat-tails of Percy's anger, they will let him blaze a path of violence to make the Assassins blush!'

Father André stared at Geoffrey; his righteous indignation was extinguished, replaced by a look of torment.

Geoffrey's anger died out as quickly as it had flared, leaving only the simmering rancour left by Father André's insults. 'If my granddaughter can turn him from that path, then I think even you should have the grace to thank Him for His great gift of love.'

Then he turned on his heel and walked towards the improvised refectory, certain that this time Father André would follow him.

Chapter Thirty

Minerve, July 1310

Twice Gaston turned away the sergeant who came enquiring after Percy, but then Lord Geoffrey himself crossed the sunny square. Gaston stood nervously blocking the doorway into what once had been a shop on the market square of the little bastide. He nervously licked his lips and shook his hair out of his eyes as Lord Geoffrey drew up before him. Lord Geoffrey was dressed in the full splendour appropriate to his rank as Seneschal of Aquitaine, in white surcoat and mantle, his sword at his hip.

'I have come for Sir Percy,' Geoffrey informed the boy.

'He's still asleep,' Gaston told the venerable figure of authority, his tight, high voice betraying his discomfort.

'Then it's time we woke him,' Geoffrey answered simply and he pushed past the boy into the cool, dim chamber beyond.

The bath still stood in the corner, the bare wooden boards around it dark with spilled or leaking water. The linen screens had been left standing to one side. Percy's dirty hose, shirt and gambeson lay in a heap next to his boots, which had been sliced open to free his swollen legs and feet the night before. His sword was propped up against the wall in its scabbard, the belt hanging limply. His hauberk lay across a bench, and it was evident from the wire brush, grease and rags on the bench beside it that Gaston was in the midst of cleaning it. Across the room a straw pallet with a woven cover and sheets was empty. Geoffrey nodded to himself and crossed the room, to start up the narrow wooden stairs leading from the back of the chamber to the room overhead.

On the darkened stairs, Nannette rose up with a gasp of alarm. She looked up at him, tufts of hair escaping from her braid and her eyes wide as saucers.

'What are you doing here, child?' Geoffrey asked gently. 'You didn't sleep here, I hope?'

'Yes,' Nannette squeaked in a frightened voice.

'Why didn't you go below? There was a perfectly good pallet made up. Go on down and wash and rest,' he urged her, pressing himself against the wall to make room for her to get past him.

Nannette cast a frightened glance over her shoulder and then, flushed and confused, slipped past him down the stairs. As she reached the foot she glanced up once more and saw Geoffrey try the door. It was bolted from the inside. She hesitated, feeling that there was something she ought to do or say to warn her mistress but it was too late.

Geoffrey knocked twice and then spoke through the door in a normal voice. 'Let me in.'

It was Félice who opened it for him. She wore a white cotton shift but was barefoot and her hair was loose to the waist. She backed into the room and closed the door behind him. Geoffrey's eyes went immediately to the bed, where Percy lay on his stomach, his head on his arms and his legs entangled in the sheets except for one foot – swollen and bruised – hanging off the edge. He was apparently sleeping soundly.

Geoffrey turned his attention to his granddaughter who was standing with her back to the door, her eyes full of unfamiliar hostility.

'Félice! What's the matter?'

'It's morning.' Félice stated the obvious. 'And you've come to take him away.' Her eyes ran hostilely across his Templar habit and Geoffrey sighed. He remembered with painful sharpness Eleanor's hatred of the Temple. Why couldn't his women understand? Why did they have to see the Order as a hated rival? Because it was – or had been. He sighed and shook his head ambiguously.

Then he turned back towards the bed and advanced carefully. At the bedside he stood looking down for a long time at the young man slumbering there. Percy had never fully regained his weight after his imprisonment. Lying here stripped of padded gambesons, chain mail hauberks and billowing surcoats, he was a bony young man with prominent shoulder blades and the knobs of his spine standing out under pale skin. His nose was peeling from too much southern sun and his wiry hair was bleached and dry.

With a start, awareness of Geoffrey's presence reached Percy's subconscious and his eyes snapped open. He shifted his head and saw Geoffrey standing over him. He turned over and sat up in a single sharp, alarmed gesture. The scar of his branding seemed to burn upon his naked chest and Geoffrey's gaze was automatically drawn to it. Percy pulled the sheets up over it as if it were a disgrace without taking his eyes from Geoffrey.

'You have to face the Chapter,' Geoffrey said at last.

'I know,' Percy answered.

'We will be waiting in the church.' Percy nodded.

'Don't take too long in coming,' Geoffrey advised as he reached the door and stopped to look again at Percy sitting on the bed, draped haphazardly in sheets.

Then he turned to Félice, still standing by the door, and he smiled. 'God bless you.' He leaned over and delivered a kiss on her forehead before letting himself out and heavily descending the stairs.

Percy and Félice were left gazing at one another. Félice tried to swallow her tears and get hold of herself. Percy noted the sun flooding through the open window and falling across the Persian rugs. He saw the roses stuffed in a chipped pottery vase on the table beside her, and it struck him that roses were representative of both romantic love and the Virgin. He lifted his eyes to meet Félice's and he did not know what he should say to her.

Abruptly, she left the door behind her.

'I'll bandage your feet so you can walk.' Already she had opened the chest and removed two rolls of clean white bandages. She knelt beside the bed and Percy sat on the edge so that she could bind his feet and ankles. She worked deftly and efficiently, as Sister Madeleine had taught her.

When she had finished she went to stand, but Percy caught the hand she put on the edge of the bed. He took it to his lips and she sank back to the floor and hid her face in the bedcovers hanging off the edge of the bed. Percy stroked the back of her head; his fingers reached through her hair to the base of her neck and massaged her tense muscles. After a few minutes Félice felt strong enough to rise and help Percy dress.

Gaston brought clean braies, hose and shirt and the not-yet-clean hauberk. Then he was sent to fetch a surcoat and mantle. Since his boots were ruined, Gaston and Félice helped Percy into chain-mail leggings and bound these with garters at the knee to keep them from sagging.

At the foot of the stairs, Nannette stood open-mouthed for a moment, before remembering the bread and ale she had fetched. She offered these to Percy but he shook his head. With a deep breath, he squared his shoulders and advanced slowly and deliberately towards the door, hesitating between each step to collect the strength for the next.

They watched him until he had crossed the square to the church and disappeared inside.

'What will they do to him?' Félice asked, turning to Gaston.

Gaston shook his head and swallowed. Nannette looked, baffled, from one to the other. It was Félice, as the woman, who had committed the greater sin in her eyes and she did not understand why no one seemed to be shocked or angry with her. Félice's own grandfather had found her in bed with a man to whom she was not married and yet he had neither beaten nor berated her. It baffled her no less that Félice herself did not appear frightened or penitent.

Abruptly, Félice remembered that Gaston too belonged to the Order. 'Shouldn't you be there?' she asked him. Gaston hesitated, apparently looking for an excuse not to attend this fatal chapter meeting. 'You can speak for him, Gaston! Someone should speak up for him!'

Gaston drew a breath to explain that his voice would only harm Percy's cause, but then he thought that someone on Percy's side ought to at least *be* there, and, without a word, he darted out into the sunlight and ran across the square to the church.

The echoing sound of his shoes scraping on the flagstone and his panting came back to him like the rasping of a giant from the ceiling. In a circle before the altar his brothers stood, all in their white and red habits. Percy lay face down in the centre, his head towards the altar and his arms outstretched like a cross.

Father André was speaking in his raw yet educated and melodic voice. He was intoning Latin, which Gaston could not understand.

Gaston tiptoed up the nave and attached himself to the circle of Templars behind the other serving brothers. He let his eyes sweep along the faces opposite: Lord Geoffrey and the six knights, Gilbert, Martin, Hugh, Cyprian, Sebastian and Donald. Then came the sixteen sergeants and the ten serving brothers. Beyond the standing Templars, Gaston noticed that the four men they had rescued at Albi were also present, sitting on the steps up to the choir behind Lord Geoffrey and Father André. The faces of all the men were grave but not really hostile, Gaston thought.

Father André suddenly abandoned Latin and spoke in French. 'Do you wish to confess your sins and transgressions here before your brothers?'

'I do.'

'What sins do you wish to confess?'

'I have killed Christians.'

There was a stirring among the men, raised eyebrows and exchanged glances.

'Christians!' Father André repeated, apparently quite disconcerted.

'I don't know how many. A dozen, I guess.'

'Alone?' Father André asked in surprise.

'I alone am responsible for what we did. On my head and on my hands are the blood and consequences.'

There was a trace of de Lacy pride in those words that made Gaston's heart thrill and Father André frown.

Sir Hugh was the one who spoke next. 'With certainty one of the men killed was mine.'

'We archers inflicted the highest casualties,' sergeant Rokely pointed out jealously.

'And still I would claim two men as mine own,' Sir Gilbert spoke up hotly, unwilling to be outdone.

'I killed a bishop,' Percy said from the floor and the others fell silent.

Gaston caught his breath at this news and glanced about hastily, but he saw that all the men who had been with Percy wore stiff, belligerent expressions – they seemed to dare Father André to criticise Percy for this. He glanced at Lord Geoffrey and saw that the seneschal was neither shocked nor apparently disapproving. He looked almost amused.

Father André looked immeasurably worried as he put the next question. 'Do you repent?'

'Yes,' Percy answered simply – to Father André's apparent relief.

'Sincerely repent? Do you regret what you have done? With all your heart?' the priest pressed him further.

'I regret what I did. I beg for the forgiveness of my brothers—'

'You'd do better not to ask!' Sir Gilbert declared. 'It was the best day's work I've ever seen!'

There was a rumble of assent from the others. Father André and Geoffrey exchanged a glance.

Geoffrey took over from the priest. 'Do I understand that the will of the chapter is to forgive Brother Percy for his violence against an unarmed priest?'

'That murdering bastard was armed with twisted laws, twisted logic and a twisted tongue! He put more Christians to death and inflicted more unspeakable misery on helpless servants of God than most Muslims have ever done!' came the decisive retort of Sir Gilbert.

'Three innocent men burned to death on his orders and he stood watching it without a trace of compassion!' This was called from the altar steps by one of the rescued men.

'The Baptist would not have lent his hand to such a task if the bishop were not long since an instrument of the devil,' sergeant Gaujac suggested.

Geoffrey started slightly at this remark and glanced down at Percy. He had come to face the chapter unarmed, as was proscribed. De Sonnac's great battle sword was still propped against the wall in the abandoned shop. Then, nodding, he assumed his responsibility as Percy's superior.

'Brother Percy, to the extent that I am able, I hereby absolve you of any guilt for the violation of our Rule regarding the taking of Christian life. For the Absolution of your sins, you must seek the office of a priest.'

They all said 'amen'.

'Have you other transgressions you wish to confess?' Father André asked in a sharp voice, as if he were afraid they would all now say a last prayer and disperse.

'Yes,' Percy admitted.

The stillness was so absolute that it was like a trumpet blast. Gaston felt his stomach cramp. How dare they judge Percy! There was not one of them, not even Lord Geoffrey, who was so brave and good as he.

'What transgressions, my son?' Father André prompted him gently. He was leaning forwards and his face was strained with pity. He tried to convey by his tone of voice that he would not be unduly harsh or demand unbearable penance, if only Percy would confess and repent.

'I have violated my vow of chastity and various – probably all – articles of the Rule dealing with contact with women.'

Father André closed his eyes and gave a short prayer of thanks. 'And you repent,' He put the words in Percy's mouth.

They were not repeated.

Several of the men shifted uneasily. On the altar steps there was a small commotion as Guichard struggled to his feet so he could see better what was going on.

'Do you repent?' Father André asked more sharply.

Percy pulled his arms in under himself and pushed himself up off the floor. He stared at Father André and then looked at Geoffrey. Geoffrey could have – should have – ordered him to resume his pose of penitence. But Geoffrey seemed to be waiting curiously for what he would do next. With some difficulty and obvious pain, Percy got to his feet. He looked from one man to the next. They met his eyes questioningly.

Two hundred years had passed since the Order was founded. None of these men – with the possible exception of Father André – shared the rabid piety of the founders. The crusading knights who had filled the fanatical Father Bernard of Clairvaux with admiration for abhorring cleanliness and refusing even to be buried beside men who 'consort with women', had little in common with their institutional descendants.

Not that the men now gathered in the abandoned bastide took Percy's transgression lightly. They had been shocked, each in his own way, as the news had spread this morning. But they had had several hours to think about it and discuss it among themselves.

These men recognised, if only intuitively, that the world itself had changed since the founders of the Order had banded together for the protection of pilgrims. The Order had grown rich, powerful and haughty – and the Holy Land had been lost. The Church itself had lost ever more sanctity. Parish livings were accumulated by powerful and wealthy clerics who banked the income and never set foot in the parishes nor once preached to the souls entrusted to them. More lucrative church offices were openly bought and sold. Bishops and archbishops were appointed in defiance of the canon laws by secular lords. And the pope himself lived openly with his concubine!

Sirs Martin and Gilbert now exchanged a glance. They had agreed not an hour earlier that there was no one else who could possibly hold the Free Templars together. With no disrespect for Lord Geoffrey, the Free Templars needed a man who could fight and lead them, not just advise them.

Percy looked again at Father André and shook his head.

'You are weak, my son. You have been bruised and battered by fate. You accepted comfort and care, and had no strength to ward off the seduction that—'

'I crawled up the stairs on my hands and knees to get to her!' Percy cut him off harshly.

Even Geoffrey was shocked.

'Do you understand?' Percy looked at each of them, one at a time. 'I was not seduced. Lady Félice tended the wounds of my body and then withdrew with her maid to her chamber. Nothing happened against my will or against my wishes. I sought her out because I needed her. And she, in her pity, tended to the wounds of my heart and soul. She has stopped the bleeding of both. I do not regret going to her.'

Geoffrey glanced at the others and, seeing his own sympathy reflected in their faces, announced, 'Then go and sin no more.'

Percy shook his head and fixed his gaze on Geoffrey. 'I do not intend to repay Félice's generosity with contempt and rejection.'

Again Sirs Martin and Gilbert exchanged glances, and there was an uneasy stirring among the others. Gaston strained to get a clearer look at Percy, but he could only see his back.

'What do you mean?' Geoffrey asked in a tone that was harsher than before.

'I mean that I will treat Félice as my lady... love.' Percy found it hard to voice the word, but having said it he lifted his chin slightly defiantly. He would not do to her what Dom Pedro had done: use and discard her.

'You would live with her in open concubinage?' Father André asked in horror, and Geoffrey too looked shocked and worried.

'Damm it! If the pope can do it, why not Sir Percy? He's done a damned sight more for his fellow man than Clement ever has!' The outburst came from Sir Gilbert and was heartily seconded by a half-dozen men.

'Silence!' Geoffrey snapped at the impertinent Englishman. Then he addressed Percy again. 'How do you reconcile your actions with your oaths?'

Percy unclasped his mantle and held it out to Geoffrey.

Geoffrey stared at it, and the others held their breath.

Sir Martin was worried now. This was the worst turn events could take. 'Lady Félice is not like other women,' he declared. 'For all the help she's given us, she is as good as one of us.'

The others looked at him curiously. His logic was badly flawed. Templars were not allowed intercourse with each other any more than with strangers or women. And yet he had struck a chord, particularly among the men who knew Félice. She was indeed 'different'. It was not as if Percy had been found with some strange woman, someone they could associate with evil influence and carnal excess.

Geoffrey felt his heart palpitating as he tried to decide what he should do. He had not foreseen this development, and he was not sure how he felt about it. He had assumed that Percy would drink of the comfort of love and then, equilibrium restored, return to his duties. Instead, Percy was placing Félice above his oath and his Order. Jean had not done that for Madeleine; he himself would not have done as much for Eleanor. If he had been under oath when they met, he was certain that he would never have known her. And he would not have been here now. But what did that have to do with anything?

Geoffrey was acutely aware of the others watching him, of the moments slipping by. He was demonstrating indecisiveness, Showing his age…

Martin and Gilbert exchanged another glance and then Sir Gilbert raised an eyebrow at Sir Donald while Sir Martin caught Sir Cyprian's attention. The sergeants stirred uneasily.

Geoffrey met Percy's eyes and saw what looked like sympathy in them.

'Forgive me, my lord.' Percy broke the uneasy silence, and his voice was a sharp contrast to his haughty defiance of a moment before. 'I have disappointed you grievously. You saw in me a greatness which I do not have.'

Geoffrey stiffened and flung back his shoulders. No. He had not made an error. Percy had descended into hell itself – for what else were the torture chambers of the Inquisition? – and he had climbed up into the flames of the auto-da-fé. Who else among them had done that? Who were they to judge him? 'No!' Geoffrey announced so forcefully that the others ceased their whispering and looked over guilty. 'I made no mistake, Sir Percival. Keep your mantle.'

Percy hesitated slightly, unbalanced by the conviction in Geoffrey's voice.

Geoffrey smiled at him. 'Go on, put it on again – or did you hope I would accept it?'

Percy felt the embarrassment of not knowing himself what he had wanted. He hastened to fling the mantle over his shoulders again so he could break eye contact and avoid Geoffrey's penetrating gaze.

Someone cheered and the others joined in, and, while the others cheered Percy's victory, Geoffrey smiled contentedly to himself, aware that it was he, not Percy, who had won.

Chapter Thirty-One

Avignon, France, July 1310

Pope Clement V knelt before the high altar of the Dominican convent where he had resided since his arrival in Avignon in March. It was dark. Only the sanctuary lamp flickered dimly, swaying slightly in a dank breeze that came out of the darkness behind the altar.

The pope noted that his nose was running and he sniffled irritably, his hands clasped in prayer. But the chill was getting worse and he shivered under the weight of his gold-embroidered robes. They weighed down his shoulders, bending him like an old woman. The weight of his mitre pulled his head forwards. His neck bent, aching under the weight.

Abruptly, something crashed behind him – like a heavy wooden door falling closed. He twisted around, still on his knees, and saw a knight approaching. The knight was in full armour and wore a great helm so that he seemed like a faceless, inhuman monster, oversized head and arms glittering with steel scales. A loose, long surcoat, split up the front fluttered about the mailed muscular legs as he strode forwards. The surcoat was plain white except for a dark cross emblazoned on the breast. The cross glistened as if it were wet.

The knight advanced up the choir towards the kneeling, shivering pope. Slowly and deliberately, the mailed fist went to the hilt of the massive longsword hanging at his hip. With a rasp that ended in the singing of metal, the great sword was drawn. The blade dazzled in sudden sunlight. The choir was so bright that it seemed to dissolve. The knight was looming over the kneeling Clement. The cross on his chest was formed by blood.

The knight leaned over the pope, enfolding the pontiff in shadow despite the brightness behind him. He raised his sword. It was dripping blood. Clement V screamed with all his strength, but only a weak croak came out.

'Holy Father?'

He woke from the nightmare to find his body-servant, the Franciscan friar Brother Bernardo, leaning over his bed holding a silver chalice dripping condensation.

Clement shook his head sharply and wiped sweat from his face with the sheets. Then seeing that the casement window had been opened, letting in a draught, he irritably ordered Brother Bernardo to close it at once.

'In this heat, Holy Father, I thought—'

'I don't care what you thought. I will catch my death of cold in such a draught – or have you been paid by Cardinal di Rienzo to send me to an early grave?'

It was no more than a petulant rebuke, but the friar crossing himself, fervently swore his innocence.

Satisfied, Clement pushed himself more upright and took the chalice before gesturing again for Bernardo to close the window. He sipped the cooled wine laced with mint and juniper.

His heart was still palpitating from his nightmare, and he concentrated his thoughts upon it. The interpretation of dreams was a delicate business. There were only a few gifted men who – like a good astrologer – were capable of extracting the divine message from the confusing and ambiguous signs contained in every dream.

Was the assassination attempt he had just experienced in his sleep a warning or a threat? Was he destined for martyrdom like Saint Thomas à Becket of England? Saint Clement of Avignon. The pope did not dislike the sound of it – yet the assassin had worn a cross. A bloody cross.

Perhaps it had been the Church Militant? Perhaps the attack had been intended to represent Christ's wrath? Had he incurred His wrath in some way? He couldn't think of anything he had done which could be so displeasing to the Lord. He always confessed his breaches of chastity with the Countess of Périgord and was routinely given absolution by his confessor. He had no other sin on his conscience. He dismissed the idea of Christ's wrath.

Still, the assassin had worn the white of the archangels – and of the Templars.

Damn them! Damn them all! Clement pulled his sheets around him as if they could offer protection from the military order. Ever since he had learned of the Bishop of Albi's murder, he had lived in fear of the Templars. This dream had been so vivid, so real, so personal. What if the Templars had supernatural powers?

The Bishop of Albi's murderers had disappeared into thin air. Throughout France the rumours were spreading that it was no mortal who had cut down the bishop. Some insisted that Grand Master de Beaujeu others Hugh de Payens himself had come back from beyond the grave. Others said it was the Archangel Gabriel, others Saint George. Officially, Clement dismissed such notions as ignorant superstition. Why should a saint – much less an archangel – intervene on behalf of condemned heretics?

But what if they weren't heretics? What if they were innocent men? Could they then come back from the dead to torment those who had condemned them? Would He send His archangels and saints to do battle on their behalf?

But *he* had not ordered the burnings, Clement comforted himself, flinging his sheets aside and swinging his bony legs over the edge of the bed, only to be gripped again by the images from the dream. It had to have some meaning. He must talk to someone adept at interpretation!

Bernardo hastened to relieve him of the empty chalice and bent to put silk slippers on the pope's feet, which dangled a good eight inches above the platform on which the bed stood.

'Father Elion,' Clement remembered, 'is said to have experienced divine visions.'

'Indeed, Your Holiness,' Bernardo confirmed solemnly. 'Thrice he has been visited by Our Saviour himself. The first time was in Nazareth. The Lord warned him to flee just before the Saracens closed the city to all Christians and forced the monks in the city to renounce Christ or die. The second time was on the isle of Cyprus, when he was told to return to France and pursue the enemies of the Church – that was when he left the Holy Order of Saint Francis to join the Dominicans and on his return applied to your predecessor to be appointed to the Holy Inquisition. The third time was just this last year when he… he dreamt of some impending catastrophe which has not yet occurred.'

'Where is Father Elion now? In Avignon?'

'Not that I know of, Your Holiness. Should I make enquiries?'

'No, send for my secretary. We will command Father Elion's attendance from wherever he is.'

The pope and the friar walked together in the shade of the arcade surrounding the cloister garth. Clement was dressed in fine silk robes of white and purple. With each step, he revealed doeskin shoes embroidered with silk and silver. His white gloves were also elaborately decorated. His close-fitting cap, which tied under his chin, was by contrast devoid of decoration because it was usually worn under the conical hat of the papacy or a mitre.

Father Elion wore homespun with a cord at his waist. The dust of the road clung to the skirts of his habit and sweat had saturated the sleeves and sides, leaving lines of salt and permeating the cloth with body odour. The feet in the well-worn sandals were blackened with ingrained dirt.

While Clement would have been offended by the smell and appearance of the man had he been anyone else, in recent months Father Elion had turned mystical, so the pope overcame his inner revulsion.

Father Elion listened to the pope's account of his dream intently, asking pointed questions, but in the end he announced, to Clement's suppressed disappointment, 'There was nothing visionary about your dream, Holy Father. You had a nightmare. The murder of the Bishop of Albi has scandalised all Christendom. It is only natural that you should fear for your own life. But a vision – a divine vision – is different.'

'How different?' asked the offended pope.

'First, it never occurs when sleeping but whilst you are awake. Second, you never lose touch with your reality. You know where you are – continue to see your environment – but are paralysed and see imposed upon reality a vision which others cannot see. Nor is a true vision ambiguous in meaning. God knows what we can be expected to understand, and, since he wishes to communicate with us, he is careful to speak in a language – whether directly or allegorically – which we instantly comprehend. He *graces* us with understanding. Otherwise a vision is worthless. I assure you, Your Holiness, you had nothing but a bad dream.'

Clement could hardly dispute this verdict delivered with such conviction from a man of known holiness, but he did not like being dismissed like a child.

'It is said, you know, that no mortal could have killed the bishop – much less have mounted burning pyres and carried off men unharmed. Many believe that the murderer of the Bishop of Albi was none other that Saint George. Others claim it was the Archangel Gabriel himself.'

'I assure you, Your Holiness,' Father Elion declared a touch disdainfully, 'that Christ abhors the Templars who took up arms in defiance of his ultimate commandment. Christ chose the path of peace not war. The Templars who claimed to fight in His name were and are anathema to Him. You need not fear He would send His angels or saints to their defence.'

'But the men who disrupted the auto-da-fé at Albi disappeared into thin air as soon as the sheriff ran them to earth.'

'They escaped the sheriff and we have not yet been able to pick up the trail again, but it would be folly to equate the sheriff's failure with supernatural powers. The murderer of Albi was neither saint nor angel – he was a creature with a black heart who will pay for his outrage in the worst tortures of hell for all eternity!' Father Elion was now employing his preaching voice, which was rather too loud for the circumstances, and Clement pulled a face.

'No one saw his face,' the pope pointed out stubbornly. 'And he climbed upon a burning auto-da-fé and removed a man already as good as dead without injury to himself. I do not count that an ordinary feat! And it was witnessed by hundreds! If this were not the work of Our Saviour then it could only have been the work of the Devil.'

'Nonsense!' Father Elion frowned angrily. 'I have interrogated many witnesses of the incident. The rescuers of the condemned heretics were ordinary men – they were wounded, they bled and burned.'

'In which case they must be Templars who escaped arrest,' the pope concluded. 'For who else would risk his life for the sake of condemned heretics?'

Father Elion drew back his lips in a grimace. 'I fear you are right, Your Holiness. But it can only be a handful of desperadoes.'

'A handful strong enough to risk attacking a bishop in a public square full of spectators – and capable of holding off the sheriff's men for a day and a night.'

'A dozen, at most a score of knights, Your Holiness.'

'A dangerous dozen!'

Now it was Father Elion who had to concede to the pope. He bowed his head in a gesture of defeat, only to lift it again with new fervour lighting his eyes. 'It is time you stopped hesitating and procrastinating, Your Holiness. You must destroy the Devil's Order once and for all!'

'The commission will resume its investigation in November,' Clement retorted with a petulant edge to his voice. He had had enough of 'people' – namely King Philip – pressing him to speed things up.

'You will be at risk until the day you find the Temple guilty and disband it entirely!'

'I cannot just disband it!' Clement snapped back. 'I would discredit myself. All would claim that I had only yielded to the king's pressure. It would undermine my authority throughout Christendom and make me look like a mere puppet of the French king!' The vehemence with which he spoke revealed how sensitive he was on the point.

Father Elion could only bow deeply. To have opened his mouth again would have been to risk speaking the truth: that Clement was already viewed as the king's puppet.

After swallowing his thoughts he continued, 'If you must go through with the enquiry and trial, Your Holiness, then you should make sure that Peter di Bologna is not in a position to defend the Temple. He has the Devil's own gift for rhetoric and someone must have supplied him with all relevant documents and legal references. His defence of the Temple was swaying even loyal supporters of the Crown and the Church – and the masses were dazzled by him.'

'You mean I should let the Archbishop of Sens burn him? He has been begging me to give him permission for months now.'

'No.' Father Elion shook his head solemnly. 'An auto-da-fé is a public affair. It would give Bologna a perfect platform to make a last impassioned defence of his corrupt Order. Such a man – already condemned to eternal damnation – would not hesitate to go to his death with lies about the innocence of the Temple on his charring lips. But the impressionable masses always assume that a man's last words are absolute truth. We cannot risk burning him in public. Rather, bring him here and let him rot in obscurity. But he must never be given the chance to speak before the public – much less the Commission – again.'

*

Father Elion had been provided with a cell in the Dominican convent housing the pope and was consulted by Clement V at least once a day. When he was sent for by the influential Dominican, Umberto di Sante came promptly – though with mixed feelings of excited hope and nervousness.

He hoped that he had been singled out for a purpose, that his talents had been recognised and were about to be rewarded. Yet Umberto could not face Father Elion without remembering the disgrace of that night two and a half years ago when he had vomited during the interrogation of the English Templar.

If the inquisitor remembered the incident, he made no reference to it now. Instead he opened with the words, 'You were one of the witnesses closest to the Bishop of Albi's murderer.'

'I was nearly trampled to death when they broke through the barriers,' Umberto reminded him with a touch of offended pride. He might have disgraced himself during his first interrogation, but he had come a long way since then.

'You are not one of these superstitious fools who thinks they were spirits or saints, are you?'

'Of course not! I am almost certain I know who those men were – or at least who led them. Yet no one listens to me; and I have no evidence.'

'What do you mean?' Father Elion lifted his head sharply and his eyes bored into Umberto.

Now he was going to have to refer to the night of his humiliation. Umberto took a deep breath. 'You remember that English Templar who, ah, disappeared?'

'Yes, of course. A dreadful embarrassment and a severe setback.'

'You remember too the nobleman who claimed to have found and buried him?'

'Yes.'

'Well, he was the man who tried to disrupt the burning of the Templars on 23rd May. I trailed him to his lodgings and discovered that the English Templar was in his company, disguised and passed off as his nephew from England.'

Father Elion's eyes widened. 'Are you certain?'

'Very.' Umberto could see the inquisitor's mind at work and he hastened to provide the rest of the information he had. 'He had recovered from his, um, interrogation, and was full of hatred and defiance. I am certain that he led the knights who disrupted the auto-da-fé in Albi, and I went in search of him after the bishop's murder – but he had disappeared. He was neither on his protector's estates nor in Paris and no one, not even his daughter-in-law, who hates the old man and would give much to see him brought to justice, could give me any information concerning his whereabouts.'

Father Elion stared for a long time at the young man and Umberto began to fidget uncomfortably under his glare. It was as if the inquisitor could look past his words and knew that his chief concern had not been bringing Lord Geoffrey or even the Englishman to justice but rescuing Félice from their evil influence and dangerous company.

But if the inquisitor had read Umberto's soul correctly, he chose not to discuss it now. 'You cannot search all of France, Brother. Nor do we need to. They will come to us.'

'Lord Geoffrey and the Englishman?'

'Yes – and the others who are their accomplices.'

'How?' Umberto asked bluntly, his disbelief imperfectly disguised.

'Very simple. The Templar Defenders, Peter di Bologna and Renaud de Provins, are to be transferred from the custody of the Archbishop of Sens to the custody of His Holiness here at Avignon. If the word is allowed to slip out – cautiously, you understand, as if it were a secret – that they are destined to be put to death, then they will serve as bait. You will see. The Free Templars will come to us and fall like ripe fruit into our hands.'

*

Umberto considered the two men heaped in the straw of the wagon, and felt pity. Their skins were almost transparent and they peered up at him from eyes so screwed against the light of day that they seemed no more than a welter of wrinkles in sunken eye-sockets. Their heads were louse-ridden and their scalps were red and flaking. Sores swelled their lips. Their wasted bodies reeked of sweat and urine. He was glad that his mission was to bring them safely to Avignon and not dispose of them in some way. It gave him licence to be merciful. Feeling both brave, with a hauberk of mail over his habit, and saintly, he ordered his guards to give the prisoners fresh water and bread.

As they made their way south at a snail's pace, Umberto found himself fantasising about the rescue attempt that was sure to come. He imagined running into the deceitful Lord Geoffrey during one of their nightly halts; Félice would be with him. Umberto could tell by the looks the matrons and maidens cast him as he passed through village and town that he cut a fine figure in his mixture of habit and coat of mail. Félice would cast him an admiring glance and then, ashamed of her own desire, quickly shade her eyes with her lashes – only to steal glimpses of him at every opportunity. The old nobleman would greet him with apparent kindness, enquire disingenuously after the purpose of his journey. Umberto would at first dissemble, pleading confidentiality, and then – when Félice had retired to her chamber – confide his 'secret'.

He would then know that the attack would occur the next day. To be forewarned is to be forearmed, as the saying goes. It had long since been arranged that only half his escort travelled with the wagon while the other half stayed out of sight, ready to close in at a prepared signal.

Of course, neither Lord Geoffrey nor Félice would take part in the actual assault. The Englishman would attack. They would take him captive – if he were not killed in the initial clash of arms. Then they would return with their wounded prisoners – for Umberto knew it would be a bitter fight and much blood would be spilled – to the inn of the night before where Lord Geoffrey and Félice would be waiting. Umberto would then order Lord Geoffrey's arrest.

Félice would be horrified and shocked. She would be angry with him. She would plead fervently for her grandfather's release. But Umberto would demonstrate the strength and conviction necessary in an inquisitor. He would be gentle but firm. The protection of the Holy Church was more important than mere family ties.

Félice would become hysterical. He would have to shake her to make her come to her senses. He would take her firmly by the shoulders and shake her sharply, calling to her to get hold of herself. Abruptly, she would go still – suddenly aware of her own hysteria. Then she would collapse into tears of helpless despair – in his arms. He would comfort her tenderly but with restraint. His mail had transformed him into a man of authority and strength. He would not succumb to the temptation she offered him, not at that point. He would comfort her, but when she started to cling to him, he would gently but firmly distance himself from her. He would send her to her chamber while he conducted 'important business'. Later he would seek her out...

Renaud too dreamed of rescue. Peter was convinced that they were being taken to the pope so they could clear the Order of all charges. Renaud did not exactly contradict him, but privately he found himself wishing that he would just be spirited away to some safe place where he could live in peace and freedom.

While Peter talked and fantasised about the arguments to be used with His Holiness, Renaud pictured a pretty village with a humble church. He would have a timbered vicarage with a cosy hall and fireplace and a bedchamber on the floor above, beneath the thatched rafters. From his bedchamber he would look out across the village common, and in the mornings he would wake to the lowing of cattle and the cackle of hens.

Renaud pictured himself being greeted by the matrons as he hung out his washing and the children who would cluster around him as he collected water at the well in the yard. They would ask him questions and he would make them all laugh. Everyone would greet him with 'Father', and they would come to him in their sorrow and their distress, seeking his advice and comfort. Was there any profession more satisfying than that of parish priest?

But the rescue never came. Just over four weeks after leaving Paris they crossed the Pont Saint Bénezet, with its twenty-two arches spanning the Rhône, and entered the walled city of Avignon.

The city was already benefiting from the presence of the pope. The papal court, not to mention the countless petitioners of papal favour and messengers of secular and spiritual lords, kept the inns overflowing. Shops, tradesmen and brothels enjoyed a boom such as the town had never before known. Many tradesmen and merchants from the surrounding countryside came up to Avignon to take advantage of the flourishing trade, and their makeshift stalls and pedlars' wagons clogged the already crowded streets. Despite his blustering and insistence on the right of way, Umberto's party made only slow progress through the streets.

Before the gates of the Dominican convent Umberto dismounted stiffly, and, with a sense of anticlimax and uneasiness, went to report to Father Elion.

The guards dismounted contentedly. One man was sent to fetch ale for all of them, while the others stretched and chatted about what they would do now that their long escort duty was over. They took no notice when a pedlar drew up his wagon and gazed at the prisoners with curiosity.

'And who might you be?' he asked the prisoners directly.

'My name is Peter, called Peter di Bologna.'

The pedlar frowned and leaned closer to the wagon. 'There was a Templar priest who went by that name.'

'I am he.'

The pedlar looked sharply at Renaud. 'Are you the other one, Raymond or—'

'Renaud de Provinz.'

'Hey, you!' One of the guards had noticed the inquisitive pedlar. 'Get on with your business! Or do you want to answer to the Inquisition for trafficking with heretics?'

The pedlar crossed himself hastily and then spat at the prisoners. 'May you burn in hell for denying Christ!' Then he cracked the reins of his wagon on the rump of his spavined horse and set off without a backward glance.

Umberto emerged from the convent and ordered the prisoners removed from the wagon. They were taken through the gatehouse and into the cramped ward. A cluster of Dominican sisters gossiping on the steps up to the church turned and craned their necks at the spectacle of two filthy priests in leg-irons with their hands bound behind their backs. Renaud was ashamed. He could not have said why it was worse to be paraded before these nuns in his present state than through all the towns of France between Paris and Avignon, but he felt as if he had been stripped naked before them.

The Templars shuffled forwards on skeletal legs unused to walking, weighed down by the chains on their ankles. The nuns stared after them. They were taken through a doorway and into the cloisters. The bubbling fountain reminded Renaud of his thirst and he looked wistfully towards the water lapping in the basin of the fountain. They were shoved along the cloisters and through a door that led to a narrow, twisting staircase, the guards urging them on from behind. They started climbing.

Renaud counted the steps. After twenty-three, he could go no farther. Not on his weak legs, not with the chains. They cursed and kicked him. He started to crawl. Forty, forty-five, fifty. He stopped. The guard went to kick him again. The Dominican of their escort forestalled him. 'Let him catch his breath.'

After a few minutes Renaud started crawling again. His knees were bruised, but it was still easier than trying to walk. Sixty, sixty-eight. He stopped again. No one said anything. Even the Dominican was panting. They resumed their climb. Renaud had no energy to wonder where they were being taken or why. He only wished that the stairway would end. Eighty-eight. The guards too stopped for breath. One hundred, one hundred and sixteen. They reached a locked doorway.

The Dominican unlocked the door and pushed it open. A disturbed bat flapped angrily. Dust hung in the air, visible against the light that filtered through the shutters in the double-arched windows of the square tower. They had evidently climbed to the top of one of the two towers flanking the nave of the church.

Brushing aside cobwebs with a grimace of distaste, the Dominican led them to the opposite side of the tower, removed their chains and then opened the shutters. Then he stood back and gestured for the prisoners to come forwards. Puzzled and bewildered, they obeyed.

'Go on,' he ordered irritably, his eyes averted. 'Climb through the window.'

Renaud and Peter looked at each other and slowly advanced to the window. Neither of them was prepared to simply jump to his death – but they were also aware that they could hardly stop the guards from throwing them. To their surprise, they found that a wooden platform was built outside the tower just at the level of the window. It was roofed with wood and had open sides except for the beams holding roof and floor together. A cage.

Peter looked back at the Dominican. 'What is this?'

'Your new place of residence. The pope thought you would enjoy the fresh air and light.'

If it was an attempt at a joke, the Dominican did not bring it off well. He looked almost as sick as Renaud felt.

'Get on with it!' one of the guards now urged irritably. 'I have better things to do with my evening!'

Peter and Renaud looked at one another in disbelief. The guard was urging them forwards again, taking hold of Renaud by the scruff of his bony neck and thrusting him through the window. With his knee, he shoved Renaud's buttocks after his head, and, without any hands to catch himself, Renaud fell on to the wooden platform with a thump. The platform swayed out from the wall and Renaud screamed instinctively at the sensation of instability. The cage was evidently suspended from some point overhead rather than made fast to the side of the tower. Peter followed Renaud in the same unceremonious manner, and then the shutters were slammed behind them. They could hear their escort clattering back down the stairs.

Peter pulled himself to his knees. The roof over their heads was roughly four feet over the floor so they could not have stood even if they had managed to pull themselves to their feet. He looked around in disbelief. He had heard of such cages. Edward of England had imprisoned the sister and daughter of his enemy Robert the Bruce in such cages.

Renaud crawled to the edge of the cage, letting out a sharp cry as the cage adjusted to his weight by tilting slightly. The cage stabilised. He lay on his chest with his arms bound behind him and gazed down on to the tiled roofs of the expansive convent below. So this was the essence of papal Grace: to be allowed to starve to death in the sunlight and fresh air rather than burn at the stake.

Chapter Thirty-Two

Avignon, August 1310

It was raining. It never rained in Provence in August yet it was pouring. Peter lay with his head hanging out of the cage, catching the moisture directly on his lips. Renaud preferred to lick it from the staves.

'God has not abandoned us,' Peter croaked when his tongue was moist enough to allow speech.

They had been in the cage for three days now and if the rain had not come they would surely have died before the week was out.

Renaud did not answer. Though he lapped up the water running down the staves of the cage with an animal desperation, his mind was capable of noting with detachment that the rain only prolonged their ordeal. The rain did not constitute redemption nor even a reprieve from agony. Rather, it robbed him of the delirium that had numbed his senses, and, as he quenched his thirst, he was aware that his hunger was becoming increasingly acute.

⋆

The rain eased off during the night; though the next day broke overcast, by noon the powerful Provençal sun was beating down again from clear heavens and the last puddles were evaporating rapidly. Renaud gazed out between the bars of the cage into the distance. His mind was blank.

A click and scrape directly beside him startled both prisoners. The shutters over the windows were opened and a nun looked out of the tower and directly into the cage. Renaud shrank back in shame but Peter had not given up hope.

'Mercy, sister. Bring us water and food. Please.'

The nun put her finger to her lips, glanced over her shoulder and then climbed up on to the window ledge to pass a loaf of bread and a bunch of grapes through the window.

With their hands still bound behind their backs, neither Peter nor Renaud could reach for her offerings, but Renaud fell forwards on to his face in an effort to tear grapes from the stem with his teeth. The nun, meanwhile, removed a small eating knife from her girdle and signalled for Peter to come nearer to the window. He advanced on his knees to the side of the tower, the cage shifting under his weight. The nun leaned out and started sawing at the ropes around his wrists. The nun's knife was sharp and the bonds gave way rapidly and easily. Peter's arms fell uselessly to his sides. He gasped in horror and sought to grasp the window pillar. His arms twitched but his hands remained limp. While he struggled to overcome the paralysis of his limbs, the nun turned her attention to Renaud.

'Come, father,' she called. 'Let me cut you free as well.'

Renaud, who had been concentrating on the grapes, had not realised what she was doing. Now he abandoned the grapes and came forwards on his knees. She cut the cords holding his wrists.

Beside her, a novice had passed a wineskin full of spring water through the bars of the cage and was helping Peter drink. She smiled at Renaud and offered him the water as soon as Peter had drunk as much as he could. She tipped the wineskin ever higher for him until it was empty. Then, passing a second full wineskin through the bars, she withdrew with the nun, closing the shutters behind her. They could hear the two women's retreating footsteps.

Peter and Renaud stared at one another in disbelief. It was like a mirage yet the bread and grapes still lay on the floor of their cage, and now, painfully, feeling was returning to their freed arms. Peter reached for the loaf of bread but his hands could not grip. He caught the loaf between his wrists and, pressing his wrists together, carried the loaf to his mouth. He tried to bite through the crust, but he could not hold the loaf steady enough. Renaud scooped up the grapes with his numb hands – the fingers as useless as dead flesh – and devoured the grapes while Peter struggled with the loaf of bread. They did not exchange a word. And then the cage lurched.

Peter dropped the loaf and Renaud cried out in terror. It lurched again and with a scraping sound it started down the side of the tower. The prisoners stared at one another. They could hear a pulley squeaking in protest overhead as the cage caught here and there on the masonry, started to tilt and then abruptly jerked free, tossing the prisoners down. They lay on their bellies, terrified by the unnatural motion of the cage while their minds hoped for rescue. They were too far gone to understand how it would work. What would happen at the bottom of their descent? Who would greet them?

The cage clunked on solid earth. In the same instant a crash from overhead sent splinters showering down on them. Renaud looked up just in time to see a second axe blade smash through the roof of the cage and then a third. The planking was raining down on them. A mailed fist reached inside and grasped him under the arm. He screamed in pain as the fist closed around his fleshless bones and started to haul him out of the cage. His head was dashed against the end of a broken board. Another hand had him under the other arm, hauling him upwards. A horse whinnied. Someone was shouting. He was dumped over the withers of a dark horse. He could smell horse sweat and oiled chain mail.

'The gates! Close the gates!'

Hooves clattered on cobbles. He was being bounced violently up and down as the horse sprang into motion. He turned his head to the side. Beyond the rider's mailed leg, he could just make out a carved portal giving access into the convent. Sergeants of the papal guard armed with cross-bows spilled down the steps. One lifted his crossbow. Renaud at once closed his eyes and tried to make himself as small as possible.

'Percy! Help me!'

'You can't! Ignore him!' a male voice barked.

'Get them out of here!' came the answer.

Renaud's rescuer put spurs to his horse and suddenly they were galloping. It took all of Renaud's meagre strength and concentration to cling in desperation to the saddle. The clatter of hooves, the snorting of the horse and the rushing of his own blood in his ears all but drowned out the high-pitched wail of a woman screaming. 'Percy! Noooo!'

*

The convent had no dungeon and no torture chamber so they took the prisoners to the smoke-room – empty at this time of year. In the windowless, conical chamber, blackened with smoke, they left the prisoners with their hands tied behind their backs and fastened to their bound feet.

'Jacques, report to Father Elion and I'll go to His Holiness at once,' the sergeant was saying as they departed, slamming the door.

Percy lay paralysed by terror on the floor coated with a layer of charcoal. A part of him still could not believe that he was here, could not grasp the extent of his miscalculation. How could he have been so stupid? So overconfident? So filled with a sense of invincibility? How could he let himself be cut off and then overpowered. He had sworn that he would kill himself rather than fall into their hands again.

But in that fatal instant between realising that the gates were closed and the moment when they brought Renaissance down and overpowered him, he had hesitated. Six, twelve or twenty-four months ago he would have taken his life instantly, but that was before Felicitas had given him her love. Father André was right after all. She had softened and weakened him and robbed him of his most potent weapon: his indifference to death.

But death would have been better than this. He could not withstand what he knew was to come. It would have been one hundred times better to have killed himself. How could a man's brain and heart be so confused?

Felicitas! They had hold of Felicitas.

When he had been arrested the first time, he had been alone among utter strangers. The emotional isolation had been his worst enemy and he had felt sorry for himself. Now his agony exceeded all that fathomless loneliness precisely because he was not alone. They had hold of Felicitas.

Damn, damn, damn! He beat his head against the stone floor. They had removed his helmet and his coif had been knocked back on to his shoulders, so his unprotected skull was subjected to the pounding – until he managed to stop himself. He drew a breath, aware that he was on the brink of complete collapse. His thoughts trod on the edge of a precipice; he knew that if he let them slide down the abyss – picturing what they could and would do to Felicitas – he would go mad. He clung to the edge, forced himself to concentrate on his surroundings. He became aware of a curious chafing sound. He squirmed until he could see

Gaston, bound as he was, on the floor beside him. Gaston was trembling so violently, that his clothes made the chaffing sound as they rubbed on the floor.

'Gaston?'

'Sir?' Gaston sobbed.

'It was my fault. I shouldn't have let you come with us. It was no business for untrained youths.'

'I… begged… I'm so… sorry… A peasant – worthless…' he was crying and Percy had no means of comforting him.

Percy sighed. 'You aren't worthless.'

'What are they going to do to us?' Gaston was already asking.

Percy preferred not to answer the question. He could not lie. He advised instead, 'Say you are an orphan. That I hired you for wages. You were never a Templar.'

Percy meant it as advice but Gaston took it as rejection.

'But I was! I am!' Gaston cried out with wounded pride. It was bad enough that he had failed to play the role of squire to which he aspired, but the fact that Percy wanted to expel him from the fellowship of the Order seemed an added humiliation and an unjust punishment. 'You can't deny me! Only the chapter can!' It was a futile protest in Gaston's own ears. He knew the chapter would reject him instantly if Percy no longer held out his protective hand.

'That's not what I meant,' Percy tried to explain. 'But if you claim you were only my servant, they will go easier on you. There is no way they can prove you were a Templar.'

'But I am!' Gaston insisted stubbornly, too obsessed with not being rejected to see the sense of what Percy was advising.

There was no opportunity for further discussion. The door crashed open again and Father Elion swept into the room, his dirty white, homespun robes fluttering around his gaunt body, his eyes ablaze with excitement.

He swept in to stand towering over Percy, gazing at him with intensity.

'Strip him naked to the waist!' he ordered sharply to the papal soldiers.

Two of the guards bent over, unbuckled Percy's empty sword belt and then roughly hauled his shirt, hauberk and surcoat up and over his head to bunch on his arms behind his back. His naked chest was exposed to the Inquisitor. Father Elion's eyes widened in elation as they saw the brand in the shape of the Templar cross that he had himself ordered made and applied.

'It *is* he! Sir Percival de Lacy! Returned from the grave!' He added the last in a mocking tone.

Turning to the guards, he ordered them to cut Percy's hands free of his feet and suspend him from one of the meat hooks instead. 'The other one too,' he ordered as an afterthought.

As they hauled Percy up off the floor, wrenching his muscles and joints unnaturally, Father Elion watched his face intently. He could see that Percy was straining not to moan or cry out as his joints creaked in protest. Sweat started to gleam on his well-tanned skin.

Gaston's sharp cry of pain as they pulled him up by his bound wrists distracted Father Elion. He looked at the youth for the first time, noting that he was young and blond with that kind of prettiness which only youth has in the borderland between childhood and manhood.

'Is the youth your lover, sodomite?' he asked Percy mockingly. He had been told that Percy had turned back at the youth's cry for help.

'No!' Gaston shouted, his face contorted with pain and anger. 'Only… damned Dominicans! *You* did it! Never my brothers!'

Father Elion was genuinely astonished by this outburst, and glanced from Gaston to Percy. Then, out of curiosity, he asked the youth, 'Who are you?'

'Brother Gaston.'

'A Templar?'

'Yes!' Gaston insisted vehemently, as much for Percy as for Father Elion.

'And you admit to being a sodomite?'

'*You* forced me to become one!' Gaston told the inquisitor more vehemently. 'You raped me!'

'I have violated neither male nor female,' Father Elion retorted primly. 'My chastity is intact.'

'The Inquisition raped me!' Gaston insisted.

'Then you have been in the hands of the Inquisition before?'

'Yes. I was imprisoned with all my brothers from Saint Pierre. Along with Sir Percy.'

'And how did you get free?'

Gaston bit his lip and closed his eyes.

'Do you too admit to denying Christ?'

'No!' Gaston retorted sharply, his face bright red and dripping sweat.

Father Elion held out his arm to one of the guards holding a torch without removing his eyes from Gaston. He snapped his fingers, and the guard gave him the torch.

'Leave the boy alone!' Percy intervened before he could even apply the torch to Gaston.

Astonished but instantly alert, Father Elion turned his attention back to Percy. He held the torch close to Percy's face, forcing him to draw back from the heat and the acrid smoke. Every movement caused Percy's muscles and joints to be wrenched and strained anew. The smoke cut off his access to good air and he started to cough. Each cough sent sharp stabbing pains through his shoulders, chest, elbows and wrists. He writhed against the heat and the smoke and his writhing brought new pain to his limbs.

'You *are* the youth's lover, aren't you?'

'Is that the only kind of brotherly love you understand?' Percy spat out and thereby inhaled so much smoke that he had a new coughing fit.

'How did you escape the bishop's guards in the spring of '08?' Father Elion snapped back.

Percy clamped his teeth together and did not answer.

Father Elion smiled to himself, his eyes lit with satisfaction. 'I can make you talk, Sir Percival. You know I can. Why don't you spare us both the trouble and time and talk now?'

Percy made no response.

'Let's start with the easy questions, things we both know. Did you deny Christ at your initiation to the order of the Poor Knights of the Temple of Solomon?'

'Yes.'

'Did you spit upon the crucifix?'

'Yes.'

'Did you worship an idol?'

'With cat's ears and feet!' Percy spat out, and something about the way he did it made the guards laugh.

Father Elion looked around sharply and the guards suppressed their merriment, but Father Elion could not escape feeling that Percy had just made a fool out of him. He had made the very charges sound so ridiculous that his confession sounded like mere sarcasm.

Angry, Father Elion held the torch so close that Percy could not escape it. He was seized with a fit of coughing.

'Did you murder the Bishop of Albi?'

Percy tried to pull his head away from the flame. Father Elion held the torch closer. 'You murdered the reverend Bishop of Albi, didn't you?'

Percy's left eyebrow sizzled and fizzed into nothing.

'You command the Free Templars who murdered Albi, don't you?'

The skin around Percy's left eye started to blister.

'You have the Bishop of Albi's blood upon your hands, don't you?'

Percy was contorting himself ever more on his protesting limbs to evade the flames. He had another coughing fit and could not get any air. He grew desperate and panic took over.

'Yes!' he choked, willing to say anything to get air again.

Father Elion moved the flame just a little. It was proving *too* easy. He found that he was vaguely disappointed. He had promised himself a more satisfying challenge. His attention drifted back to the youth. Father Elion held the torch under Gaston's nose and asked, 'Did you deny Christ?'

'No!'

Father Elion pressed the torch closer under Gaston's nose. Like Percy before him, Gaston started coughing and squirming. He groaned audibly as his muscles and joints protested.

'Did you deny Christ?'

The torch was scorching his chest and neck.

'Yes!' Gaston sobbed, unable to stand it any longer.

'How did you escape the Inquisition?'

Gaston just screamed, unable to take the pain and unwilling to betray his rescuer.

'I released him!' Percy answered for him.

'You? How? With two broken legs? Who helped you? Hid you? Nursed you?'

Father Elion started to transfer the torch from Gaston to Percy and then thought better of it. Instead, he pressed the torch directly against Gaston's chest, eliciting a howling shriek that echoed and reverberated in the chimney of the room almost drowning out Percy's infuriated shouting.

'*Leave him alone*!'

'Then answer my questions!' Father Elion retorted, removing the torch and rumpling his nose at the stink of burned flesh. 'Who gave you assistance when you escaped the Bishop of Albi's guards?'

'God.'

The answer was so impudent, so blasphemous, that Father Elion lost his temper. He struck out with his free hand, boxing Percy's face from the left and then the right. 'How dare you?'

'Do you want me to do that?' a burly soldier offered. As a professional, he knew that Father Elion was too frail from his fasting to do a proper job of beating anyone – much less a strong young man like this prisoner.

Father Elion got hold of himself. 'No.' He took a step back. 'No.' Father Elion's professionalism took over again. He considered Percy with narrow eyes, noting the tan and the well-developed muscles along his contorted chest and shoulders. He had recovered from his last imprisonment. He had grown strong and arrogant again. It would be wrong to give him the satisfaction of an open clash of wills. It was always better to weaken and humiliate a man before applying torture. 'No,' he repeated a third time. 'The prisoners need time to contemplate their situation. Let them hang for a day or two without food or water. Then we will see if they dare take His name in vain!'

He turned and strode from the room in a flutter of black and white habit and the guards followed him with a shrug.

Chapter Thirty-Three

Avignon, August 1310

They had confined Félice in the convent punishment cell, a room four foot by eight with a single grilled window near the ceiling which opened at ground level on to the street. A chamber pot and a wooden bench were the only furnishings. A mouldy blanket was rotting in one corner, but, it being August, Félice was not tempted to make use of it. She sat instead on the bench and stared at the blank wall.

Sister Madeleine had had the sense to keep her mouth shut and had managed to disappear in the confusion. She and the others would get to her grandfather, and Félice felt certain that he would react immediately. He would demand her release. And even if he didn't or couldn't get her out, the worst which could happen to her would be that she was forced to take the veil. But Percy...

No matter how she looked at it, she could not see how they could get Percy out. Not with the brand on his chest marking him irrefutably and eternally for what he was.

And every minute of his imprisonment was a moment in which he was at *their* 'mercy'. Whether it was merely active imagination or genuine telepathy, she knew that he was being tortured. Of course he was being tortured! They had done it before and they would do it again. They might already have destroyed his legs – again. Or mangled his hands as they had Father André's. They might be tearing the remaining teeth from the mouth she loved. Or they might choose to rape him as they had Gaston... She jumped to her feet and then stood, bewildered, in her stone cage.

What could she do? She paced to the wall beneath the window and lifted her face. Should she scream; attract attention to herself?

No, she could picture too well the mocking curiosity of the street urchins peering through the grille, kicking refuge and dung down on her. She had no illusions about the pity of the common man. She had seen the merriment of crowds as they watched the hands hacked from thieves – or the Templars burnt alive.

She turned away from the window, from the images of her memory. They would burn Percy if he failed to confirm his confession. Percy, don't be brave! she pleaded with him mentally. Not for an Order already condemned and convicted. Percy, please give them the answers they want to hear. Please! Don't give them the chance to mutilate you again! Please.

The crack of the bolt being shot back brought her to an abrupt, breathless halt. She stared at the door like a captive panther. It creaked open slowly.

A voice enquired cautiously, 'Félice?'

The voice was vaguely familiar, but she couldn't place it. She waited unmoving, holding her breath. A figure in the robes of the Dominicans slipped into the cell. Now she recognised Umberto. She felt her muscles tensing again.

'Félice?' Umberto asked as he gazed at her in disbelief. She was more enchanting in person than in his dreams. The white veils of a novice framed her heart-shaped face and made her straight dark brows stand out sharply. In the darkness of the cell, her eyes were wide, almost consumed by the black pupils. And her habit could not disguise the hourglass fullness of her figure. She was no longer a nubile girl. She was a delectable woman.

'It *is* you!' Umberto was declaring, letting the door fall closed behind him and coming to take her hands in his. 'My poor, sweet Félice,' he murmured, kissing her hands and letting his pitying eyes devour her. She was evidently terrified. She seemed hardly to recognise him in her frantic state. 'You need not fear. I will protect you from harm,' he assured her, feeling his own strength and power and virility.

'Umberto,' she murmured, trying to think how best to exploit his presence and apparent affection for her.

'Yes, sweetheart, it's me.' He laid his arm around her shoulders and drew her against his chest. His heart was pounding with the intoxicating excitement of holding her to him at last. He felt a mixture of pride, amusement and embarrassment at the instant response of his loins. The abrupt flinching of her hips away from his indicated that she too had felt the hardness of his genitals. He eased his clasp slightly, charmed by her shyness despite the fact that she had been married and must know the pleasures of the flesh – or had her husband been a boor who had only hurt her and offended her sensibilities?

Ah, that would be luck! She would surrender stoically, expecting nothing in return, and would be so astonished. She would be enraptured by the pleasure he would give her! His lips twitched at the memory of other women who had fallen under the spell of his sexual skills. But he did not want to think about the others now. He turned his thoughts to Félice again. She had drawn back from him and eyed him with evident suspicion. 'Félice, you mustn't fear.'

'Who sent you?'

'No one. I came of my own. I couldn't be sure it was you. I didn't know you had decided to take the veil again.'

'Ah.' Félice shook out the skirts of her habit absent-mindedly. She was still desperately searching for the right strategy to employ with this unexpected visitor. There had to be some way she could use him to gain access to Percy – or the pope.

'I came to see His Holiness,' she blurted out. 'To petition His Holiness regarding my... my dowry. Dom Pedro did not return my dowry when he annulled our marriage and now I have no dowry for the Church.'

'Ah, that explains things. I wondered what you were doing here.'

Umberto was relieved that she had not been directly involved in the rescue of the Templar priests. If she had been, it might have proved more difficult to secure her release. Father Elion was too much of a fanatic to release anyone – even a beautiful noblewoman – who was tainted with heresy.

'And then there was such a commotion and I saw them clubbing my cousin and dragging him from his dying stallion! Why, Umberto?' she demanded challengingly, her chin lifted and her eyes flashing with indignation.

Umberto wanted to grab her flushed, angry face in his hands and cover it with kisses of delight. How he loved her when she was angry! But he restrained himself, forced himself to sound stern and disapproving. 'Don't you know?'

'Know what?'

'Know what he did?'

'What could he possibly have done to deserve such treatment? He is a brave and noble knight!'

'Félice,' Umberto said in the solemn tone he had practised again and again for this very situation. 'I think you should sit down. There is something I have to tell you.'

'What?' she asked impatiently, frowning slightly.

She was always so impatient, he thought indulgently. 'Please sit down. This is not going to be easy for you.'

'Then stop tormenting me. Tell me what it is!' She sounded as if she were going to stamp her foot like a spoilt child any minute, and Umberto had to suppress his desire to laugh in delight.

'Your… your cousin, Sir Percy, is not really your cousin.'

She looked at him askance, a frown on her brow. 'What do you mean? My grandfather says Percy is his uncle's grandson.'

'I know what your grandfather says – but it is not the truth.' He said this slowly but deliberately. How often had he made this speech in his imagination.

Félice looked at him blankly. 'Why should my grandfather lie?' she demanded after a moment.

'Because… because he was trying to protect you.' Yes, this was better than condemning her grandfather, Umberto realised, instantly changing his tactics. She would never believe that her grandfather had meant her harm. 'He was trying to keep you from learning the awful truth.'

'What awful truth?'

'That Sir Percy is an escaped Templar – a man for whom we have been searching for years – and is very likely the murderer of the Bishop of Albi.'

Félice drew back from him in feigned terror. 'I don't believe you! It can't be! You're lying!'

She was reacting exactly as he had expected. Umberto was prepared for her indignation. He nodded reassuringly. 'I can understand your disbelief, but I have proof—'

'Proof? How can you have proof?'

Christ, if they knew Percy had murdered the Bishop of Albi then nothing – not even abject confirmation of all the charges they laid against the Temple – would save him. Félice's desperation was reflected in her voice as she insisted almost hysterically, 'the murderers disappeared. They never even found a trail. They were devils or angels! It has nothing to do with Percy!'

She sounded so much the indignant, schoolgirl with whom he had fallen in love in Poitiers that Umberto could not resist pulling her into his arms and kissing the top of her head – even if it meant abandoning the role of solemn and wise protector he had intended to play. She fought free of him but he was not offended. He knew that she was still in the resisting phase, and the more vehement her resistance now, the more complete would be her surrender when it came.

He reverted to the role he had chosen for himself and spoke with profound patience. 'I understand that you must think that – he is tall and handsome in his way. And, I remember, he came for you in Portugal after your unfortunate marriage was dissolved.'

Against her will Félice found herself stiffening in fury at Umberto's patronising tone. He spoke of the worst humiliation of her life as if it were a petty misfortune.

'Of course, you think of this Percy as your knight in shining armour, but if you could see him now, your illusions would be shattered.'

Christ! What had they done to him? She had to do something immediately. Félice's brain seemed to dash about frantically in an empty head – a rabbit caught in an enclosed garden with a pack of hounds at its heels. She plunged towards the only hole that looked like a possible escape. 'I demand to see His Holiness! Only he can convince me that what you say is true.'

Umberto was taken aback by her vehemence. In his fantasies she had always accepted his word. But when he thought about it, it might be better if she heard the truth from the mouth of His Holiness. Besides, this gave him the opportunity to show her how well connected he was. 'All right,' he agreed in his controlled, solemn tone. 'I will arrange an audience with His Holiness in which you can approach him about both your dowry and your alleged cousin's identity.'

'When?' she asked, clutching at his hand fiercely.

'As soon as possible, of course, but His Holiness is a very busy man. It could be a day or two—'

'And I am to stay here until then?' she protested, almost hysterical. Every hour that went by was an hour in which they might be shattering Percy's bones or tearing apart his limbs!

Umberto looked back at her desperate, frightened face and then gave the cell a cursory glance. 'You can share my chamber, if you prefer,' he told her in a soft tone with just a touch of a smile.

Félice started so violently that Umberto was offended. She was supposed to fall into his arms in gratitude, not react as if held slapped her across the face.

'I… I am intended for the Church!' Félice managed to gasp out. She had only just recognised the danger that lurked in Umberto's affection for her. He could make all his assistance dependant upon her giving herself to him.

Umberto leaned closer, his dark eyes burning with open desire.

'We both know that you are no longer the innocent virgin of Poitiers.'

Félice answered defiantly, 'What does that have to do with a vow of chastity? Many a widow of more than one husband has joined the Church – and her vow of chastity is no less sacred than that of the purest virgin. A vow is a vow. You too are vowed to chastity.'

Umberto smiled. 'The pope no less than any of us. Do not play the naïve fool, Félice. It doesn't suit you.'

'I am not playing the fool. I am asking you to respect my wishes.'

'Your wishes? I thought you wanted to escape this cell?'

Her pent-up anger, her taut nerves, her natural temperament all betrayed her in that instant. 'I do, but not at the price of selling myself like a whore!'

Umberto responded as if she had spat in his face. He drew back sharply and gazed at her in offended outrage. How could she compare his offer of protection to the wages of prostitution? But in the next instant he noticed that she was trembling and his pity overpowered his anger. Maybe her husband had so misused her that she was genuinely appalled at the thought of physical intercourse. He wanted to take her in his arms and comfort her, but, understanding her problem, he resisted the temptation. He withdrew with dignity. 'I will never force you, Félice. I want you to come to me of your own free will. But if you will not accept my offer, then I must leave you here for the present.'

'Let me speak to His Holiness!'

'I will do my best,' he promised vaguely, and Félice was suddenly struck with the thought that he might intentionally leave her here for days and weeks to make her more 'pliable'. But it was too late, Umberto had withdrawn, bolting the door behind him.

*

Pope Clement V looked from Father Elion to the captain of his guard. He wished them both to hell in this moment, and his fingers drummed nervously on the arm of his great carved chair. He was dressed only in a loose cotton nightshirt over which he had flung a red-velvet cloak. In the room behind him, the Countess of Périgord was waiting impatiently and he detested keeping her waiting. But he was even more furious because he had been interrupted in his intimate rendezvous with the countess by a bloodcurdling scream that had made the hair stand up on the back of his neck – and more important organs go limp.

'It is not possible to put a man to the question without risking such a response,' Father Elion was explaining indignantly to the pontiff. Even if all of Christendom knew about the pope's affair with the countess, he still found it offensive to be confronted by a pope in this state of disarray. 'If a man is not cooperative, then sharper methods must be employed – and unfortunately most men howl and scream like beasts before their reason induces them to escape pain by telling the truth.'

'That is all very well when the questioning takes place in a proper dungeon but must I remind you that this is a convent for gentlewoman? Think what terror you will have struck into the hearts of innocent maidens! They will think some monster is lurking in the shadows, ready to rape or murder them in their sleep! I'm sure the mother superior will be clamouring at my door before long! Which reminds me; you said you arrested a Benedictine novice as well. What does she have to do with anything?'

'She evidently knew the Englishman – calling to him by name. I have not yet had the opportunity to question her myself,' Father Elion answered, trying to keep his temper under control. 'I will do so at once, if you—'

'Good God, no! Do you think I want a nun to be stripped and mishandled before the eyes of common soldiers! You are overzealous, Father! Captain, fetch the girl to me here.' The countess had specifically asked about the girl.

Father Elion opened his mouth to protest but the pope gestured imperiously for him to hold his tongue. He was in one of his petulant moods – and he was always more decisive and imperative when he knew the countess was within hearing.

Father Elion was cursing himself for not questioning the girl earlier. He had thought that a couple of days of neglect in the punishment cell would soften her for questioning and had ordered Brother Umberto to keep an eye on her. He knew nothing but what Umberto had told him – that she was the granddaughter of the nobleman who had apparently sheltered Sir Percy and that she thought the Englishman was her cousin.

At the sound of voices and footsteps beyond the door, Clement pulled his cloak more primly around his indecently clad body and tucked his bare feet out of sight in the abundant folds. Then he squinted to sharpen his failing eyesight in the inadequate candlelight as the door opened and the girl was escorted into the chamber. She was as white as her habit and her lips were bloodless. Huge dark eyes dominated her face, and as she came near enough to fall on her knees before him and kiss the hem of his cloak, he could see that she was trembling.

'A chair for Mademoiselle!' the pope ordered irritably, as he bent and touched her veiled head with his long fragile fingers. 'Peace, my daughter. You have nothing to fear.'

Father Elion rolled his eyes towards heaven in despairing supplication. Why did He allow men – a pope – to be so easily manipulated by the charms of corrupt female flesh? Just one look at this female and the pope was clearly lost in her spell. He would be incapable of rational thought. What almighty power the Evil One had in his army of females.

Félice lifted her face towards the pope but remained on her knees before him. 'Your Holiness, I beg you...' Her voice faltered. She was faint from lack of sleep and nourishment – and from fear. It was three days since they had been taken captive. In three days they could have broken every bone in his body, emptied his mouth of teeth, torn off all his finger- and toenails... She was so afraid this audience had come too late – and afraid that she would fail.

'Come, my daughter.' Clement leaned forwards in his chair and slipped his hand under her elbow, indicating that she should stand.

She shook her head sharply. 'I beg you, Your Holiness. Do with me what you please but release Sir Percy and Gaston.'

Félice knew she was taking a risk but it was a calculated one. The fact that they had not even shown her a torture chamber and the pope's tone and expression gave her every reason to think that they would not apply 'sharper methods' even if they chose to punish her. She hoped, however, that a gesture of abject submission would do much to sway opinion in her favour.

She was right.

'But my dearest child!' The pope was leaning low over her. He could see the dark circles under her eyes and her chapped lips. Her breath was slightly sour and her habit soiled and crumpled from lying and sitting in the mouldy cell. 'Why should we wish you any harm? I'm sure this is all some kind of mistake. Bring Mademoiselle a glass of wine. She needs something to fortify her.'

Félice shook her head. 'Your Holiness, I have had no food since my arrest, and wine—'

'What? Sir, how dare you treat a daughter of the Church, a noblewoman, in such a manner! You will answer for this!'

'They were Father Elion's explicit orders, Your Holiness,' the knight in charge of the papal guard answered a fraction sullenly. He had questioned his orders at the time and been sharply rebuked by the Dominican.

'Father!' Clement swung on Father Elion in a mixture of genuine and exaggerated outrage. 'Whatever gave you the right to issue such orders? In the name of the Sweet Virgin, how could you order such a vile thing?'

The inquisitor sighed. 'Mademoiselle de Preuthune was arrested for her apparent complicity in the rescue of the Templar Priests, Holy Father,' Father Elion reminded the pope. 'I did not put her to the question – as I am entitled to do under the circumstances. I simply left her to fast and contemplate her sins.'

Pope Clement frowned. He had forgotten the Templar priests and prisoners and did not like being reminded of them. 'I can't imagine that this poor girl had anything to do with the Templars,' he declared. 'Fetch water, wine and some light refreshment for Mademoiselle,' he ordered a servant, and again indicated that Félice should sit in the chair provided for her.

Félice rolled back on her heels and stood somewhat unsteadily. She stepped backwards towards the chair and slowly sank down on it, her eyes fixed on the pope. Her heart was racing from the strain of knowing how much depended on her skills of persuasion. She clearly had the papal sympathy, but just as clearly he detested the Templars; somehow she had to convert his sympathy for her into compassion for Percy.

'Now, my daughter, tell me what brought you to Avignon.'

'Word was brought to my grandfather that you were holding two Templar priests, the priests who had been elected to represent the Templar defenders before your Commission, Holy Father.'

Father Elion quickly put his hand to his face and feigned a cough to disguise his chortle of delight at the horrified look on Clement's face. The pope had been so certain that the girl was innocent and then she walked straight into the noose. It was priceless!

'Your grandfather? Who is your grandfather and what does he care about the Templars?'

'Lord Geoffrey de Preuthune of Najac, Holy Father. He was knighted by Saint Louis at Mansourah.'

'Ahhh.' The pope remembered abruptly and glanced at Father Elion who bowed his head smugly. He turned his attention back to Félice, who had stopped speaking. 'But what does your grandfather have to do with the Templars?'

'He believes with all his heart that they are innocent of any wrongdoing and is determined to help them in any way he can. That is why he gave shelter to Sir Percy, nursed him back to health and supports him still.'

'Sir Percy?'

'Sir Percival de Lacy, Your Holiness. He is an English Templar who was arrested on his journey to Cyprus by the Bishop of Albi. He escaped from Albi's soldiers when being transported from Albi to Poitiers some six months after his arrest.'

Father Elion could hardly believe his ears. She was naïvely confessing everything – and they hadn't even had to threaten her with torture. Women were so weak! So stupid!

'You know it is a crime against the Crown and Holy Church to give aid to a Templar.' Pope Clement told her sternly. 'Your grandfather committed a grave crime and a deadly sin when he defied his Sovereign and myself. Did he think that being knighted by a saint entitled him to question the wisdom of Christ's vicar on earth?'

Clement wanted the girl to be duly intimidated, but, on the contrary, she seemed considerably less frightened than when she had first been brought into the chamber. She gazed at him with wide, calm eyes. All trace of trembling was gone and the pallor of her face was strangely luminous.

'Your Holiness, it was I who found Sir Percy on the roadside – his legs broken from the ministrations of the Inquisition, his body wasted with neglect and more naked than covered despite the snows of winter.'

'But you could not know he was a Templar!' the pope hastened to excuse her.

'Did it matter?' Switching easily to Latin, Félice quoted from Saint Matthew. '"For I was hungry, and you gave me to eat; I was thirsty, and you gave me to drink; I was a stranger, and you took me in. Naked, and you covered me; sick and you visited me: I was in prison, and you came to me."'

Clement started violently.

Father Elion gasped and then hissed furiously at this serpent clothed in the robes of Holy Church, 'How dare you blaspheme!'

'Blaspheme, father?' Félice turned her steady gaze upon Father Elion and her eyes made him quail inwardly. Eyes full of fathomless wisdom. 'Is it blasphemy to quote His Holy Word?'

'It is blasphemy because you twist the meaning!' Father Elion retorted hotly.

Clement gestured for him to be silent with an angry wave of his hand, asking Félice instead, 'What are you trying to say?' He sensed some hidden meaning to her words but he had been in positions of power too long, his head filled with the more pressing business of politics and administration, to remember the text she was quoting.

'Holy Father.' She turned back to the pontiff. 'I am trying to explain why I did not hesitate to help Sir Percy when I saw him sick and all but naked, a stranger and a prisoner. I am trying to explain why neither King Philip nor – with your forgiveness – even you can convince me that I did wrong.'

'But I have just told you that you committed a deadly sin! You can be excommunicated for aiding a heretic – and the Templars are condemned heretics!'

'Condemned, Your Holiness? But the commission has not even completed its investigation.'

'They are condemned out of their own mouths!' Father Elion answered passionately for Clement – who was clearly taken aback to have a young woman respond so self-confidently and unabashedly to his pontifical reproach.

Félice turned again to Father Elion. 'Why, Father, it would please me to hear what *you* would confess to if your legs were being relentlessly twisted until the ankles and then the shinbone broke, or would the touch of red-hot iron—'

'How dare you!' Father Elion took a step nearer and very nearly raised his hand against her in his outrage. She was the most repulsive creature he had ever encountered: an angelic face and a sadistic temperament crowned with a serpent's tongue.

'If you can withstand your own torture, Father, without denying Christ, then we can discuss whether human weakness is heresy. I do not see that it matters.'

She turned back to the astonished pope and, leaning forwards, drew him into her eyes. Her voice was low, melodic, almost intimate as she spoke to him, but it betrayed no trace of desire or allure. Rather, it was sexless and disembodied and it blotted out all other sounds and thoughts. 'Holy Father, I found Sir Percy – a stranger – hungry, thirsty, sick and a prisoner. And I took him in, gave him to eat and drink. I tended his wounds and I set him free so that on the Day of Judgement *He* could not say to me: "Depart from me cursed, into everlasting fire… for I was hungry and you gave me not to eat; I was thirsty, and you gave me not to drink. I was a stranger and you took me not in; naked and you covered me not."'

Clement was trembling. He knew now how the text continued: 'Amen, I say to you, as long as you did it not to one of these my least brethren, neither did you do it to me.' He was staring at the girl, oblivious to the outraged protests of Father Elion.

'Set them free.'

'Your Holiness?' The question was posed by the astonished commander of the papal guard.

Angrily, Clement broke eye contact with the girl and spun on the knight. 'I said set them free! This Sir Percy and the other one. Set them free!' He was fighting for the salvation of his soul.

Félice closed her eyes and let out her breath very slowly. The relief was so great that she did not entirely believe it.

'Holy Father! Have you gone mad?' It was the protesting voice of Father Elion. 'This is the man who murdered the Bishop of Albi! He is a dangerous threat – not least to your own safety.'

Félice opened her eyes again, every nerve of her body ringing with strain. She saw the pope's eyes widen with fear, saw him lose confidence in his decision at once, saw him open his mouth to rescind his order...

'Your Holiness, that is a lie. I swear it – and I can prove it.'

'How? You can hardly claim to have committed the act yourself!' Father Elion scoffed at her. 'And besides, he has already confessed to the crime.' He too had seen that the pope was on the brink of rescinding his order to release the prisoners.

'Bring me his sword,' Félice insisted, closing her mind to the implications of such a confession. What had they done to him to make him confess?

'What?'

'Please, Holy Father.' She fell on her knees again and caught at the hem of his cloak. 'Send for Sir Percy's sword.'

'Bring the sword.' Clement gestured to one of the guards. 'Now, sit, child.'

Her proximity made him nervous. He was too acutely aware of his own near nakedness and the sins of the flesh which he had been so willing and anxious to commit just prior to this frightful audience. She had completely confused him, making him more frightened for his soul than Father Elion made him fearful for his body.

Félice was trembling again. The food which had been sent for arrived, but she could not eat. She sipped the water and then the wine.

The sergeant returned with the sword and on his face was a look of consternation. He held it with evident respect and presented it to Clement, hilt first.

Clement gasped.

Father Elion stepped closer. 'What new blasphemy is this?'

'It is the finger of Saint John the Baptist,' Félice told them steadily.

'Of course. The relic belonged to the Temple since the Fourth Crusade. I wondered why it was not found among the items taken into custody,' Clement commented. Most of the relics which had been seized when the Templar Commanderies were sacked by Philip IV's soldiers had already been turned over to the pope.

'It was Master de Sonnac's sword, and he used it against the Saracens on the seventh Crusade until he gave it to my grandfather at his knighting. My uncle carried it in the Holy Land and it was bloodied in the defence of Acre. My grandfather gave it to Sir Percy – as you can see. Holy Father, do you believe that Saint John would ever lend his hand to the murder of a man of God?'

There was a deathly stillness in the chamber. Father Elion had the word 'nonsense,' on his lips, but somehow he couldn't get it out. Clement was gazing at the relic as if it were the first time he had ever seen anything so holy. Then he looked again at Félice.

She answered his gaze with the words: '"Watch thee therefore, because you know not the day nor the hour of His coming".'

Clement nodded and pushed himself to his feet. 'Set them free and restore his sword to him. I do not fear it, nor he who wields it. Go in peace, my daughter.'

For a third time Félice fell to her knees and kissed the hem of Clement's cloak. Father Elion was protesting vigorously again, but his words only annoyed Clement. The man was obsessed with the persecution of men already defeated and disarmed. He understood nothing. Clement suddenly decided that he was hardly better than the common soldiers who applied the instruments of torture. What had the girl said? Until he had withstood his own torture without denying God, he had no right to assert that these confessions were genuine. His own faith had never been put to the test! He looked over at Father Elion and saw how filthy his robes were, how blackened his sandalled feet. He noticed the stench of his body and wrinkled his nose in distaste. The man was offensive.

'Father, you forget yourself!' He interrupted the protests of the fanatic as soon as Félice had departed with the captain of the guard. 'We have made a decision. Leave us.'

'Holy Father! My conscience demands that I speak! You cannot let a dangerous criminal escape! A man who will strike again!'

'You exaggerate, father. We have, after all, achieved the objective you yourself set: Peter di Bologna has disappeared and cannot testify before the commission. The commission will have to adjourn and I will convince the church council, that is convened for Vienne next spring, to condemn the Templars. That is a better solution all around. The whole Church will condemn and revile them, and no one can blame me.'

Clement was highly pleased with this inspired idea – which must surely be divine – and resolved to banish the Dominican from his court. He did not like him any more.

*

The papal summons for Father Elion had interrupted the torturers so unexpectedly that they hardly knew how to respond. The soldiers who were holding Percy against the wall so he could see what they were doing to Gaston relaxed their efforts the minute Father Elion and their Captain were gone. Then after a few minutes, they looked about for some means of keeping him in place without any effort on their part. They finally decided to hog-tie him again. He cried out once as they pulled his arms behind his back, the pain so sharp that it dizzied him, but then they dumped him on the floor and left him.

At the fire, the man tending the irons asked if he should keep them glowing or let them cool. The sergeant who had been left unexpectedly in charge shrugged and wiped the sweat from his forehead with the back of his arm. 'Let them cool. I need something to drink.'

There was a murmur of agreement from the other four men, and the sergeant, wiping his face again, ordered, 'Bert, guard the door, and we'll bring you something from the kitchens.'

They all left the room, banging and bolting the door behind them. The only sound echoing in the conical chamber was Gaston's sobbing.

Gaston could not have said why he was crying: the pain was enough to make him cry but that was not the whole of it. He had confessed again. And he had told them about Lord Geoffrey and Chanac and Minerve – but they didn't believe him. They wouldn't stop until Percy confirmed all he said. And so he had begged Percy to tell them. He couldn't help himself! He couldn't take it. Even now the pain was driving him mad. He wanted to scream, but his throat was so parched that he couldn't. He would have done anything – even let them fuck him – for a glass – for a sip – of water. But nothing he offered them was enough to make them stop. Only Percy could release him from his agony. And even as he begged Percy to say what they wanted to hear, he hated himself for it. He hated himself so much he wanted to die. Why didn't they just kill him?

'Gaston.'

'Pardon, monsieur.'

'I'll say anything except what endangers the others. Do you understand?'

Vaguely, Gaston did understand. Percy had confessed to all the charges against the Temple, even idol worship and sodomy. It was the questions about Lord Geoffrey, their safe houses and the source of their funds which he had not answered – though he had bellowed and screamed at them to leave Gaston alone until his voice failed him. Gaston understood, but he couldn't take any more! Sobbing, he prayed for God to take him to Him so Percy would not betray the others.

Percy lay listening to Gaston's sobs and asked the Nothingness what he should do. What could he do? Why didn't they torture him? Why Gaston? To be forced to choose between oneself and the safety of the others was fair, but they were forcing him to sacrifice someone else, someone weaker and more innocent. But if he heeded Gaston's pleas for help, he would betray Lord Geoffrey and all the others. No matter what he did, he was betraying someone who loved him. No matter what he did or said he was committing a crime against Love. If only they would let Gaston alone!

The bolt was shot back, and Percy lifted his head and tried to twist his head enough to see the door. He saw the hem of a once white habit, grimy now with mould and dirt, and a shoe of doeskin that could only clothe a woman's foot. Suddenly he knew what was coming: they were going to hang Félice before his eyes and apply the branding iron to her breasts. He went mad. He beat his head against the stone floor, seeking with all his strength to knock himself unconscious.

He imagined her hands cupping his face. She kissed his forehead, his eyes and his lips. 'Percy, it's all right.'

Someone was sawing at the bonds holding his wrists and ankles together. They worked roughly and furiously, and he could hear their rasping breathing in his ear as if they were sobbing from the effort. His numb limbs sprawled uselessly on to the floor and she kissed him again; he felt her tears on his face.

'What are you standing about gaping at?' Félice demanded of the four astonished soldiers and the wide-eyed sergeant who stared at her open-mouthed from the doorway.

She could not guess that when they saw her take the half-naked, limp body of Sir Percy on to her lap they saw a thousand *pietà* come to life and were struck dumb with wonder.

'Cut the boy down at once and bring water!'

Now they fell over themselves in their haste to obey.

Gaston screamed as they let him down, the pain of his arms being moved overpowering all his other agonies. Félice left Percy long enough to press a kiss on Gaston's forehead and stroke the side of his face.

'My lady?' He tried to speak. She put her finger to his lips and shook her head. Then she demanded water again in a voice so shrill it would not have disgraced a fishwife.

The sergeant almost tripped in his haste to bring it to her, and she spilled it as she tried to hold Gaston's head in her lap and control the long-handled dipper with one hand. It didn't matter. A good part of the water found its way into his gasping mouth and the rest cooled his sweaty face. Then easing him down and placing a last kiss on his forehead, she shoved the ladle back at the sergeant. 'More! And see that a stretcher is made ready and my mare.'

'Félice?' an astonished voice asked from behind the sergeant, who turned to carry out her orders as if she had been the Mother of God herself. 'Whatever...' Umberto gazed at her kneeling beside Sir Percy, holding his head in her lap, and he too was reminded of a *pietà* – except that Percy was struggling to overcome his helplessness, insisting in a rasping whisper that he could ride.

'His Holiness has ordered their release,' Félice told Umberto bluntly.

'But...' Umberto was bewildered. 'How? Why?' Just an hour ago she had been safely in her cell and Father Elion had been on the brink of getting the information he needed.

'Ask His Holiness,' Félice answered, indifferent to Umberto, whom she no longer needed.

The sergeant was back with a second ladle of water.

Percy could not bear lying at her feet like an invalid or a child – not with Umberto in his flawless white robes, clean and handsome, gazing down at them. He managed to get his feet under him. His legs would hold. And he took the water from the sergeant.

'But don't you see!' Umberto protested frantically. 'See the brand! He is a Templar – the murderer of the Bishop of Albi.'

'My shirt and hauberk.' Percy returned the empty ladle and gestured with his head towards the heap of silk and chain mail that lay where they had been dumped three days earlier. One of the soldiers sprang to bring it to him and, seeing that Percy could not lift his arms for pain, helped him dress.

'The Cross of Our Lord,' Félice answered Umberto.

'He is a heretic! A murderer!' Umberto had to make her see the truth. He could not understand how she clung to her fantasies in the face of so much evidence.

'The Bishop of Albi suffered less than poor Gaston here, not to mention Father André and Brother Gautier, and the serfs you tortured, Umberto, and all the others.'

'What are you talking about?'

'Let him who is without sin throw the first stone, Umberto.'

Umberto could not follow her silly, feminine reasoning, and he was torn between annoyance and enchantment as he realised that she, with her limited education and female brain, had mixed up and misinterpreted the teachings of the Church. 'This has nothing to do with sin! Leave theology to priests and stop straining your pretty head with issues you can never properly understand. Come!' He held out his hand to take her away from this charred and stinking chamber.

Félice starred at his white manicured hand and then lifted her eyes to his well-proportioned face, his perfectly shaved tonsure, the silky black hair crowning his smooth, oval face. She knew that he had never meant to hurt or humiliate her; he was simply incapable of putting himself in her shoes. He was too convinced of the validity of his own vision of the world to be able to see it from anyone else's perspective. Poor Umberto. She shook her head. 'No, Umberto. I am going home with Sir Percy and Gaston.'

Umberto could not understand what she was saying. She was here at last, alone and vulnerable, and he had demonstrated to her that her so-called cousin was a fraud. She *must* fall into his arms in gratitude for his protection. She did not belong with the others.

Percy was towering behind her and his breathing was heavy with the strain of overcoming his pain and renewed humiliation. His hair and face were filthy with the charcoal dust of the curing-room and his face was disfigured: the entire left side was swollen, red and blistered under a missing eyebrow. The stubble of a three-day beard gave his face a brutal, unkempt look and he stank abominably. Félice could hardly see him as some kind of chivalrous hero. As for the boy, he lay at her feet, crying helplessly. His bony chest was a morass of burns created by a hot poker applied judiciously on Father Elion's orders. He was piteous, to be sure, and might have appealed to her maternal instinct – if he hadn't reeked so disgustingly. Umberto looked at Félice more bewildered than ever.

The soldiers who had gone to fetch a stretcher arrived and nudged Umberto aside with muttered apologies. They set the litter down beside Gaston and lifted him on to it as gently as they could. No one watching them would have guessed that they were the same men who had applied the glowing iron to his chest and denied him the water for which he pleaded. Someone thought to tuck his shirt and gambeson beside him on the litter and someone else laid a clean linen towel over his chest, covering the open wounds.

Félice glanced at Percy and he nodded. The soldiers lifted the litter and Félice led them out of the room, Umberto backing out before her. They crossed the kitchen garth in a little train that aroused curious glances from the papal servants lounging before the brewery. But they passed quickly out of the kitchen gate into the back courtyard.

The cobbled courtyard at the back of the convent complex was littered with rubbish from countless deliveries of supplies for the voracious papal kitchens. Stray cats and dogs slunk about, and two draught horses stamped irritably at flies while they waited for the wagon behind them to be offloaded. Félice's mare and Gaston's gelding were just being led from the stables as they arrived.

'Should we tie the stretcher to the gelding's girth?' the soldiers asked, and Percy nodded.

They brought Félice's mare and held the off stirrup. Félice was helped up on to her saddle and then swung about to watch the soldiers attach long lines from the handles of the stretcher to the girth of Gaston's shaggy gelding on either side of its ample rump. With obvious difficulty, Percy was trying to get himself into the saddle without having to strain his arms. One of the soldiers finally gave him a boost from behind. Then, turning the gelding towards the open gate with the pressure of his legs, Percy glanced over his shoulder to see that the stretcher was following without tipping Gaston on to the cobbles. Félice fell in behind him where she could keep an eye on Gaston.

Umberto was so stunned by what he had seen that she was almost through the gate before he could overcome his paralysis and ran after her shouting, 'Félice! Stop! Don't leave!'

Félice drew up and looked back at the young man chasing after her. She waited for him.

He grasped at her leg and held it to his chest. 'Félice! You can't leave! What will happen to you out there – with them?' He pointed contemptuously to her disreputable-looking companions. 'I can protect you! I can keep you in comfort! I've been nominated for dean of—' She was shaking her head, and he grew even more desperate. 'But I love you!' he protested, almost angry that he had to humble himself before her. Things were standing on their head. She was supposed to declare her love for him, cling to him, not the other way around.

'Ah, Umberto, don't you see?' she asked him, smiling sadly. 'You don't love *me!* You don't even *know* me. You are in love with a figment of your own imagination – with a girl who wears my face but thinks and does only what *you* want her to think and do.'

'No, that's not true!' he protested hotly. 'I love you! I've forgiven you for marrying Dom Pedro and for what you said after your arrest. I know you think you are doing right, but you must trust me to know what is right for you. You are making a terrible mistake.'

'Then it is my mistake. Percy is my lover, Umberto. I belong to him now.'

She squeezed her calves on her mare's flanks and the little Arab sprang forwards, forcing Umberto to let go.

As her words sank into his dazed brain, he shouted after her with the stinging bitterness of unexpected betrayal, 'Whore!'

Chapter Thirty-Four

Near Lyon, October 1311

Percy knelt before Geoffrey and fastened the leather garters under Geoffrey's knobbly knees to hold the chain-mail leggings in place. Then, taking the blue enamel spurs with the diamond *fleur-de-lis*, he slipped one over each heel and drew the buckles tight. Finished, he drew himself upright and considered the old man standing stiffly before him.

Geoffrey was in his full amour. It was old-fashioned armour: chain-mail leggings and hauberk with an attached chain-mail coif. The chain-mail had been scrubbed free of the last specks of rust, oiled and polished so that it gleamed even here in the dimness of the tent, but no plate reinforced the skin of linked steel, not even at knees and elbows. The coif was made fast to Geoffrey's head with a band of red leather that bound it tightly like a crown, the leather ties hanging down the back of his head. The chin flap was hooked shut so that only the oval of his face was uncovered, his white beard hidden under the chain mail encasing his throat and chin. Only the white of his moustache and eyebrows – and the rugged, deeply gouged crevices of his face – revealed his age.

The eyes that gazed out of the bronzed face were young and blazing with the light of hope and dedication. Percy averted his own to concentrate on tying the chain-mail mittens to the end of the long sleeves of the hauberk.

'You disapprove,' Geoffrey concluded, as he saw Percy look away.

'No, my lord, I do not disapprove—'

'But you think it is pointless,' Geoffrey supplied the words that Percy could not bring himself to utter.

Percy kept his gaze averted. He did not want to confirm Geoffrey's words. How could he know if his pessimism were not sheer cowardice, an overpowering, unmanning terror at the mere memory of the Inquisition. He could not bear the thought of going willingly – openly and unarmed – into a city held by the King of France and housing the pope. He trusted neither the king nor His Holiness, but he had not dared to raise his voice against the venture in chapter for fear of being called a coward. If he were so much a coward that he feared the scorn of the men he supposedly led, then he had no right to raise his voice here in private.

'You don't have to tell me what you think. I understand.' Geoffrey grasped Percy's shoulders and made the younger man look at him. The deep brown eyes in his tanned face were like molten chocolate – warm and sweet with affection. 'But try to understand me as well. His Holiness tried to condemn the Order and the only support came from Philip's creatures! The majority of even the French bishops and abbots voted with the English, German, Hungarian and Iberian delegates against any condemnation of the Order without further evidence. The vote went against the pope and Philip by over five to one! The council furthermore explicitly denounced the burnings, scoffing at the papal commission which had allowed its principal witnesses to be taken out of their custody to their deaths. Ah, Percy! They *insisted* on hearing the case themselves! They *demanded* the reopening of the investigation. They have *challenged* us to come to our defence, and they *guaranteed* our safety! If we don't come forward now, we have condemned ourselves! Surely you see that?'

'Yes.' Percy did see all that. 'But King Philip has sent his troops across international boundaries to strike at clerics he found displeasing in the past and he will do it again. He has been behind at least one pope's death and possibly two. Why should he hold back from striking at men he finds inconvenient merely because a church council has offered its questionable protection? Which noble bishop or rich abbot do you expect to see standing between you and the points of royal pikes?'

'None.' Geoffrey answered Percy's bitterness with profound calm. 'If the king strikes, then our miserable lives are lost but the Honour of the Order is intact – stronger than ever. What could make it clearer to the assembled church council that the king fears our testimony?'

Percy drew a breath, but Geoffrey stopped him from speaking by gently touching his chest and shaking his head. 'I have outlived my usefulness. This is my last gesture, and I am proud and honoured to have such a meaningful opportunity of departing this life. Don't deny it to me, Percy.'

Percy shook his head and abruptly flung his arms around the old man, holding him closely for a moment. Geoffrey felt tears prick his eyes. In the three and half years they had known each other, it was the first time Percy had ever initiated an embrace. Then, as if ashamed, Percy released Geoffrey and took a step back.

Geoffrey turned and reached for his sword.

'Let me get de Sonnac's—'

'No, his sword must not fall into the hands of our enemies.'

Geoffrey buckled on his own, standard-issue Templar sword over his white, woollen surcoat with its red cross on chest and back. Then he tucked his leather gloves into his belt and drew the wide, white mantle over his shoulders.

The red cross of the Temple had been sewn upon his chest. With a nod he led them out of the tent.

A cheer went up as Geoffrey emerged through the tent flap. The Free Templars were assembled here in the forest outside Lyon at nearly full strength. Waiting directly before the tent were the six other knights Geoffrey had selected to accompany him to Vienne. He had not named Percy, which had surprised many of the other knights until they learned that Percy was being left in command of all the Free Templars in Geoffrey's absence.

Furthermore, each of the selected knights were, like Geoffrey himself, men who had never been in the hands of the Inquisition. They had not confessed to a single charge, much less admitted to heresy, and as a consequence, in the event of their arrest, none of them could be deemed relapsed heretics and condemned to death by burning. Last but not least, Geoffrey had been careful to choose one knight from all the principal provinces of the Order in the West: England, Portugal, Castile, Aragon, Germany and France. Hungary and Italy were not represented because they had no Hungarian or Italian knights among them. His choice had been duly confirmed in chapter as representing all the Free Templars.

The six men honoured with the defence of the Order before the Council of Vienne were dressed, like Geoffrey, in the full splendour of cleaned armour and new, white surcoats and mantles. The wool had been purchased especially, and Félice had spent most of the night sewing on the red crosses.

As the selected Templar Defenders saw Geoffrey, they gathered up their reins and pointed their mailed feet in their stirrups to mount. Niki led forwards Geoffrey's greying destrier. The old warhorse lifted his head and snorted in excitement at the sight of his master dressed for war. Geoffrey smiled and stroked the heavy neck, before letting Percy help him up into the saddle.

From the high saddle, Geoffrey looked benignly down into Percy's tortured face and smiled. '*Shalom.*'

The word was drowned out in the cheer of *'Baucent à la recourse!'* from the others.

Geoffrey lifted his head and his hand to wave to them all as he put his jewelled spurs to his impatient stallion and rode out of the camp, the others falling in behind him in pairs.

*

Two hours away, in the little walled town of Vienne, the church council was again in session. The bright autumn sun blazed down harmlessly upon the white walls of the town and the watch at the West gate had just settled down to a game of dice when, out of nowhere, the shadow of armed men fell across them. They looked up startled and their eyes widened in terror.

Looming over them on sweaty but by no means weary stallions was a party of knights in glittering armour, and they brazenly wore the surcoats and mantles of Knights Templar. It was years since Templars had haughtily ridden the streets of Europe. The sight of seven such men was like an apparition out of an already mystical past.

What was more, they seemed so pure and invincible in their clean white habits that the humble men who scrambled hastily to their feet in uneasy respect were uncertain if they were dealing with men or spirits. Each of them was remembering the eerie rumours following the murder of the Bishop of Albi about superhuman rescue, revenge and escape. But the men who had disrupted the auto-da-fé in Albi had been in civilian garb – in gambesons dirty from the tiltyard – not pristine white.

The knight at the head of the little column let his stallion prance just inches from the dice left scattered at the base of the gate. Though apparently an old man, he spoke forcefully, asking to be directed to the church council.

One of the garrison at once offered to lead the party of knights to the guildhall which housed the deliberating bishops and abbots of the council. As they made their way through the narrow, cluttered streets, the sight of Templars riding two abreast behind their white-haired leader brought conversation and bargaining, gossip and quarrels, laughter and anger to a sudden halt. The townspeople gaped in open wonder at the apparition as it passed and dared only whisper their astonishment and speculation after the spectre was past.

Yet the whispers spread out from the streets the Templars rode, along the alleys and the courts, from gable to gable, and soon people were running to catch a glimpse of them. Boys and young men who had heard only lurid tales of Templar greed and perversion rushed to catch a glimpse of these self-proclaimed worshippers of Satan. And old men who could remember the glories of Saint Louis' crusades and the tragedy of the Fall of Acre dragged their aching bones away from their hearths in disbelief.

The imposing guildhall, built by rich merchants proud of their independence, faced a square already thronged with crowds of petitioners, servants and pedlars who waited on the worthy council members closeted inside. These crowds were thickened by the curious, and all turned to watch as Geoffrey led his party of knights across the square to the steps of the guildhall.

Unaccustomed to the weight of armour, Geoffrey was stiff as he drew up and dismounted slowly.

A curious boy was alacritously nearby, holding out his hand. 'I'll hold him, sir.'

'Thank you.' Geoffrey turned over the reins and glanced back at his companions. They were acutely conscious of the thousands of eyes upon them. After a short whispered exchange, they dismounted simultaneously. It was neat gesture, and a ripple of approval went through the crowd. How pitifully easy it was to impress the rabble, Geoffrey thought with a sad smile. Other boys hastened forwards to hold the remaining six stallions as Geoffrey started up the steps to the doorway guarded by two sergeants in papal livery.

The pikes crossed in front of him sharply. Geoffrey looked from one sergeant to the other.

The elder man seemed to flush, the younger man thrust out his lips insolently. 'No one is allowed admittance without an invitation from His Holiness,' the elder man announced officiously, keeping his eyes averted.

'We were invited,' Geoffrey answered. 'His Holiness and the entire council invited us to come.'

The sergeant swallowed, nervously. 'Whom should I announce?'

'My name is unimportant. Tell the council that the elected representatives of the Poor Knights of Christ and the Temple of Solomon at Jerusalem have come to defend their Order.'

The sergeant jerked his head to the younger man, ordering him to carry this message to the hall on the floor above, where the council was meeting. Two minutes later, the guard returned and confirmed the invitation. The sergeant stepped back and Geoffrey passed by without a further glance. From his calm and deliberate pace, no one could have guessed that his chest was so tight he could hardly get any air.

The wooden stairs creaked under the weight of the seven men in armour, and at the top of the stairs the gabble of excited voices reached them even before they emerged from the stairwell into the splendidly painted hall with its soaring hammerbeam roof. Along both walls, benches had been placed for the princes of the church while the pope sat flanked by his cardinals upon the dais. The light streaming in from the windows on the east side of the hall caught and glinted upon the gold of the richly embroidered robes of the assembled abbots and bishops. White, red, purple and green silk spilled in graceful folds over the assembled company. Mitres wagged and dipped as the agitated clerics argued and consulted among themselves until the presence of the visitors drew their attention. Startled faces turned towards the entrance and all conversation died upon their lips. A deathly silence gradually but certainly took hold of the room.

Geoffrey waited until it was complete. Only then did he advance up the length of the hall with his knights behind him. The sound of their heavy footsteps upon the beams of the floor were like muffled drumbeats. Clement was pale as a ghost.

Geoffrey knelt before His Holiness and went to kiss the papal foot, but Clement yanked his foot back in horror.

Geoffrey kissed the hem of his robe instead. Then rising without waiting to be bid, he announced in a voice that was not raised but in the silence carried to the rafters, 'We are here at your bidding, Your Holiness, to answer all the charges so unjustly levelled against ourselves, our brothers and our Order.'

'Who are you?' Clement managed to ask in a thin, high voice.

'We are Knights Templar, Your Holiness.'

'Yes,' Clement croaked, clutching the arms of his chair. 'But *who* are you? Where do you come from?'

Geoffrey was glad to oblige. His companions had swung out to flank him on either side, so that he formed the point of an arrowhead aimed at Clement. Turning to the right, he introduced each of the three men to his right, stating their Christian name and the commandery from which they came: Paulo of Zaragoza, Juan of Segovia, Gilbert of Willoughton. He repeated the procedure with those on his left: Friedrich of Tempelhof, Sergio of Pombal and Pierre of Richerenches.

The silence was broken now. Behind them, the whispering of the excited clerics was like the hissing of water on a long beach.

'But how is it you can come in here?' Clement demanded, his voice wobbling in his anxiety and confusion.

'We were invited by this council,' Geoffrey answered, turning deliberately to look the clerics on the side benches in the eye.

More than one voice was raised in the affirmative, and a tall man with a hawklike face in the robes of an archbishop pointedly reminded Clement that this was true and went on to explicitly welcome Geoffrey and his companions. Geoffrey bowed graciously in thanks. Not to be outdone by Canterbury, several other archbishops joined the Englishman in expressions of welcome and even thanks.

Clement was scowling. 'What significance does the testimony of seven knights have against the thousands of confessions that have already been so meticulously recorded?' Clement demanded of his insubordinate fellow bishops.

'The testimony of seven unfettered and unbroken men is worth more than a hundred thousand confessions emanating from the torture chamber!' the Archbishop of Canterbury thundered back.

He was a close friend of William de la More. He had seen de la More fight in Scotland. He had used all his powers of persuasion to convince de la More that if he would confess to just one minor charge, the bishops of England would find the Templars innocent of all the rest.

In the end, this plea bargaining had worked with the majority of Templars – who had admitted to only one count of the indictment: to believing their master could absolve them of sin – but de la More had remained stubborn to the last. Nothing less than the absolute and complete exoneration of his Order would satisfy him even as he wasted away from the consumption he had contracted in King Edward's service.

There was a clamour of approval for Canterbury's assertion, and Clement hated King Philip for putting him in this distasteful and senseless predicament. Philip had harvested the gains from destroying the Temple and Clement all the unpleasantness!

'The testimony of these seven knights would be no different from that of the others if they were put to the question!' Clement told his insubordinate council, reaping a wave of laughter.

The redoubtable Archbishop of Canterbury overcame the laughter by shouting, 'And the testimony of the tortured would be no different from that of these seven men if they had been granted the immunity to which their sacred office entitled them!'

'The arrest and torture of consecrated monks by the secular authorities constitutes the most ruthless and dangerous assault on the independence of the clergy since Henry Plantagenet claimed the right to try clerks in secular courts!' the Archbishop of York asserted militantly.

The German bishops took up the cry, reminding the pope of the long history of struggle with the Holy Roman Emperor over the authority of secular powers to control sacred offices. They asked him whether he had lost his senses or if he had intentionally sought to diminish the dignity and power of the Church!

'The Inquisition acted without even consulting the bishops of the dioceses in which they operated!' an outraged Italian bishop pointed out heatedly before Clement could recover from his indignation at the German charges.

The Bishop of Porto was meanwhile reminding the assembled company that the Templars had been found innocent in Portugal, Cyprus, and throughout the Holy Roman Empire.

A bishop from Aragon was trying to remind the company that there were still Saracens in Iberia. Without the Templars and Hospitallers, he tried to shout over the increasing confusion of competing conversations, the Moors would have driven Christianity back across the Pyrenees. Islam had knocked once before at the gates of Poitiers!

Clement blew his nose in frustration and sent an angry silent prayer to heaven. Why did these bishops care about an Order that was already obliterated, exterminated, dead? He cast a furious glance at the Templars still standing before him and started violently.

The young men flanking the leader stood with their feet apart and their hands hooked casually in their belts. Their right hands were thus just inches from their hilts. It was a stance of relaxed but pointed vigilance. Clement's blood ran cold, remembering his dream of over a year before. They had come to kill him! In terror he lifted his gaze from their mailed fists to their faces, scanning them one at a time.

The young men had dark, serious faces with blank, obedient eyes, but the old man was looking at him with eyes that burned like hot coals. Why did the face seem familiar? He knew he had never seen this Templar before, or had he? When de Molay had come about the crusade perhaps? Clement frowned, searching his memory hopelessly.

'Who are you?' he demanded in a whisper that only Geoffrey could hear.

'Geoffrey de Preuthune, Your Holiness. We met once before – before I had the privilege to be received into the Order of the Poor Knights.'

'Preuthune! You gave refuge to that Englishman!'

'It was my privilege.' Geoffrey bowed his head slightly.

Clement was now remembering the girl. She had eyes like his, lighter in colour but just as intense and penetrating. She had argued for the Englishman's life as if he had been Christ himself when in fact she – a nun – was nothing but his whore. He lashed out now at the old man. 'Your granddaughter is a whore, Monsieur!'

Geoffrey, surprised by the attack, flushed and snapped back without thinking, 'No more than the Countess of Périgord!'

Clement almost leapt from his seat in outrage. Sputtering with rage, he pointed his finger at Geoffrey. 'You will burn in hell!'

'Then I will keep you company.'

Clement sprang to his feet. 'How dare you!'

Geoffrey shrugged, but the pope's outraged cry had drawn the attention of the council back to centre stage. The disorganised discussion died away and the assembled dignitaries gazed at the curious figure of the fragile but furious pope gazing red-faced at the calm Templars.

Clement, aware that everyone was staring at him, tried to regain his dignity. He swallowed his fury, sniffed lightly to clear his running nose and raised his voice. 'Geoffrey de Preuthune, who are you to question the testimony of your own Grand Master and all the senior officers of the Temple?'

'I am a free man, Your Holiness.'

The answer was greeted with hoots of open delight from some of the foreign bishops, though the Archbishop of Sens now tried to come to the pope's assistance by asking in a pointed voice, 'Where are the Templars elected defenders?'

'Here!' Geoffrey answered swinging about to find the speaker, recognising at once the voice of the spoilt young man who had ordered the burning of fifty-four of his brothers. Geoffrey hated Sens even more than Clement V. 'We represent roughly two thousand *Free* Templars including Fathers Peter di Bologna and Renaud de Provins.'

Even Sens was startled, and the exclamations of amazement, disbelief and excitement which now erupted cast the earlier commotion into shadow.

'What do you mean *Free* Templars?' Sens spluttered, sounding silly even to himself.

'I mean there are nearly two thousand Templars gathered near Lyon – men who have escaped or been helped to escape from the clutches of the King of France or who have freely left the countries where they were safe to stand by their brothers of France in this struggle for the survival and honour of our beloved Order. Two thousand Templars, Your Grace,' Geoffrey spat out the title as if it were an insult, 'who are not starved, scourged and chained. Men you cannot destroy with a wave of your beringed hand. Men no less ready to die for their faith than the men you sent to Paradise, but not bound like martyrs to the stake. Men with their swords in their hands.'

'Arrest these men!' Clement screamed hysterically. 'Arrest them! Arrest them!'

The pandemonium that followed would have been comic if it hadn't been so tragic. Clement and the Archbishops of Sens and Narbonne were genuinely terrified for their lives. The pope flung over his chair to trip presumed pursuers as he fled the chamber, although only Sens and Narbonne were on his heels. The papal guards were stunned by the abrupt order and wary of seven fully armed men. The majority of the delegates were outraged by this flagrant violation of a safe conduct they had themselves issued. They protested loudly, but – as Percy had predicted – not one of them was willing to put his own mortal body between the Templars and the pikes of the papal soldiers.

The knights with Geoffrey closed protectively around him. Their hands were upon their hilts.

'Do we fight free?' Friedrich of Tempelhof asked roughly, starting to draw his sword.

'No.' Geoffrey laid his hand sharply on his forearm, preventing him from drawing his sword.

'My lord!' Paulo of Zaragoza tried to protest.

'No!' Geoffrey repeated. 'It was agreed!'

He had told them when he selected them that they must be prepared to sacrifice themselves and they had all vowed they would do so. The papal guards were quick to take advantage of the situation, wrenching their arms behind their backs, binding their wrists and disarming them. Geoffrey was startled by the sudden, sharp pain in his chest as they yanked back his arms.

The protests of the other delegates were, however, growing louder and shriller. Some of the clerics tried to order the papal guard to release the prisoners while others threatened the papal guards with excommunication and damnation. The soldiers closed their ears to all the clamour and hustled their prisoners towards the foot of the hall and the stairway to the floor below. Geoffrey staggered. The pain in his chest was so great he was unable to breathe.

'This arrest is proof enough that they are innocent!' Someone shouted.

'See French justice! The trial of the Templars has been a farce!'

'The Templars are innocent!'

It was the last thing Geoffrey heard as he blacked out.

As the old man suddenly sagged, unconscious between them, the two guards who were holding him cursed and tried to bring him to with cuffs to his head. The sight of the guards mishandling their seneschal elicited roars of rage from the other Templars, and the knights who had meekly followed Geoffrey's orders now started to struggle in earnest. The result was even greater chaos as one or two of the younger abbots now found the courage to try and intervene in defence of the disarmed, old man.

It was one thing to ignore the protests and threats of the assembled clerics and another to use force against them. The papal guards were thus thrown into confusion. The shouts to free the Templars were mounting in volume. The guards looked helplessly at one another. One of them lost his nerve and with a single jerk of his knife cut Friedrich of Tempelhof free. The German at once attacked the men who were still trying to 'revive' Geoffrey, grabbing one around the throat and choking him in the angle of his elbow. The other Papal soldier holding Geoffrey at once dropped his prisoner to try and come to his companion's assistance.

The bellowed order of 'Let them go!' might have come from one of the delegates or from their own sergeant. The guards didn't care any more. They were concerned only with getting out of this absurd situation. They released the prisoners and shoved them roughly in the direction of the stairwell.

Two of the Templars took hold of Geoffrey and at the stairs lifted him on to the back of José of Pombal, the largest of them. José staggered down the stairs with the unconscious Geoffrey on his shoulders, followed by the others, with the exception of Friedrich, who continued to hold the guard in his elbow until he was certain the others were safely below. Then he thrust the guard away from him so violently that he tripped and sprawled face first on to the floor as Friedrich bolted down the stairs two at a time.

To his amazement he found the courtyard before the guildhall free of crowds and in the next instant he realised with horror that it was completely ringed with armed and mounted men. They were trapped! Friedrich looked quickly over his shoulder, wondering if it would be wiser to seek the protection of the council members again. They could return and throw themselves at their mercy. They must force the king to send his soldiers against the council as a whole and not just seven Templars.

He lifted his head to give the order to retreat, but to his amazement saw that his stallion was being led forwards. The man leading his stallion was one of his own knights. Beyond him they were lifting the unconscious Geoffrey on to his stallion. Friedrich looked again and realised with amazement that the men cordoning off the square were disguised Templars. He wanted to laugh, but there wasn't time. Percy was already sending the men holding Geoffrey in his saddle out of the square and the others were at their heels. The cordon was closing in. Friedrich vaulted into the saddle and spurred his stallion after the others.

*

Geoffrey was still unconscious when Percy carried him to his tent. His face was ashen and his skin sagged on the bone structure, lifeless and alien. His jaw was slack. The temples were unnaturally prominent. His limbs hung limply from Percy's arms as lifeless as the chain mail that encased them.

Percy went down on one knee and gently laid Geoffrey upon the pallet. He arranged the limbs neatly and then looked up to meet Félice's wide golden eyes. He saw his own grief and dread reflected in them.

Brother Cyprian was already ducking into the tent with his satchel full of herbs, and Niki was fussing about the coal brazier, trying to get a fire going against the chill of the autumn afternoon. Félice took the blanket folded at the end of the pallet and laid it over her grandfather's lifeless body. Brother Cyprian went down on his heels beside Percy and took Geoffrey's wrist to feel his pulse. Then he lifted an eyelid and inspected Geoffrey's eyes. 'Were you pursued?' He asked as he continued his methodical inspection.

'No.'

'Good. He should not be moved. If he comes to again, you can give him some wine and broth, nothing heavy. Which of the priests would he want?' The question was directed to Félice.

'Father André.' Félice's voice caught as she spoke, but she managed to bite back her tears for a bit longer.

Brother Cyprian drew himself to his feet and gazed down at his commander. Then he crossed himself, and, turning to Percy, stated the obvious. 'There is nothing I can do.' He left the tent.

Percy looked again at Félice. Her eyes were shimmering with unshed tears. 'Stay with him. I must see to the watch.'

He left the tent, and Félice settled herself on the canvas flooring of the tent, clutching her knees in one arm and holding Geoffrey's hand in the other. She vaguely heard muffled orders from beyond the canvas, the low anxious voices of men, the snort of contented horses, the chant of a prayer.

Father André limped into the tent on his cane. For all that he disapproved of Félice's liaison with Sir Percy, he could not deny her devotion to her grandfather. As she sat with the long, full sleeves of her woollen houppelande sweeping over her knees and her face framed in the prim white veils that shrouded her neck and hair under a snug cap, she certainly did not look like a seductress. He sighed at his own confusion and painfully let himself down on his knees. He crossed himself and began to pray. After a while,

Percy returned to the tent and stood respectfully just inside the flap.

As it grew dark, Niki brought candles and moved the brazier closer to the pallet. Percy brought a fur-lined cloak and laid it over Félice's shoulders. He poured wine for Father André. Outside, Father Pierre of Bologna was saying mass. They could hear the chorus of the responses. Then the other Templars collected around the cooking fires, their voices a low comforting murmur like a running stream. The smell of roasting hare and onions came on the light wind. Niki brought them all bread and stew, but without exception they turned it away untouched.

The men outside dispersed to their own tents. The cooking fires were allowed to go out. Félice dropped her head on to her knees and dozed. She was woken by the voice of Father André. He was reciting the last rites clearly and forcefully. Geoffrey's responses were hardly audible. Lifting her head, she saw that the priest was bending his ear over Geoffrey's lips, straining to understand his words. She looked towards the tent entrance. Percy too was awake, watching the ritual with a stiff, expressionless face. At last Father André was satisfied. He blessed Geoffrey and kissed his forehead.

Father André tried to pull himself to his feet and Percy at once came forwards to give him a hand. The priest looked down at Félice and with a sigh he advised her to get some rest. 'He is confessed and can go to God in peace. There is nothing you can do.'

Félice just stared at him. Father André sighed again and made his way slowly towards the tent door. There he turned to look back at the two young people standing on either side of the dying man and shook his head in confusion. Then he left them.

Percy replaced Father André at Geoffrey's side. He stared at the old man, aware of a storm of emotions that made his heart ache in his chest. Overcome with remorse for all the things he had failed to say and do, he bent forwards and kissed Geoffrey's forehead. 'Forgive me, my lord! I failed you!'

'Nonsense,' Geoffrey answered clearly, if softly.

Percy and Félice both started.

Geoffrey smiled. 'We've won, Percy. Did you hear? The whole council proclaimed our innocence.'

Percy swallowed hastily. The others had reported what had occurred. He glanced at Félice, and then answered with a forced smile, 'I heard. We have been completely exonerated. *You've* won.'

Geoffrey lay smiling with his eyes closed, but with his right hand he felt the blanket as if looking for something. 'Félice?'

She had let his hand fall from hers while she dozed. Now she seized it again guiltily. 'I'm here Grandpapa.'

He smiled. 'I knew you were – but Eleanor is getting impatient. She has waited a long time, don't you think? Much longer than she deserves. You wouldn't want me to keep her waiting any longer, would you?'

'Of course not.' Although Félice formed the words bravely, the only sound that came out was a garbled sob. Tears were flooding down her face hopelessly, her nose was running and her whole chest heaved for breath.

'That's not fair!' Geoffrey protested, teasing. 'You were braver when Eleanor died.'

'But you weren't,' Félice reminded him between sobs.

'How true…' He murmured the words so softly that neither of the others could hear him over the sound of Félice's sobbing. Still he managed to convey a slight pressure to her hand, a last gesture of comfort, as he slipped away from them, smiling in anticipation.

*

In the morning they laid him out in the glen before the tent, a watch of six Templars standing vigil while the others filed past to pay their last respects. It was another brittle, bright autumn day and the light fell sharply through the leaves of green and gold from a sapphire sky of cloudless brilliance. The air was aromatic with the scent of fallen leaves and a touch of smoke from the cooking fires of the night before.

Félice sat on a leather folding stool beside the corpse. She wore one of the gowns that had been dyed for mourning after Petitlouis' death. Her face was swathed in veils of black. Though she no longer wept, none of the men who cast her timidly curious glances as they passed her grandfather's body doubted that she had cried through the night.

Throughout the morning the sound of hammers and saws provided an accompaniment to the solemn procession of mourners as three Templar serving brothers prepared a coffin for their late commander. In the afternoon, the sound of carpentry was replaced by the chink and thud of the grave diggers.

They held the funeral service at the hour of sundown, the forest already in the grips of shadow with only a faintly pinkish light filtering through the trees. A chill rose from the earth like the breath of the grave. Félice shuddered so violently that her bones seemed to rattle.

In the next instant a slight commotion drew attention briefly away from the open grave. Six or seven horsemen emerged from the shadows, their horses snorting and stamping as they smelt death. Besides the secretary to Cardinal di Rienzo, who was their principal informant from the papal court and their spy at the Council of Vienne, Félice was amazed to see Dom Alfonso, the Templar Commander of Tomar. The others recognised Brother Robert, and the stirrings of alarm were quickly silenced.

The new arrivals dismounted and knelt, further reassuring the assembled company that the newcomers were not harbingers of danger. Father André finished the service. He nodded to the brothers waiting at the ropes slung under the coffin and they untied these from the stakes holding them and started to ease the coffin into the grave.

'Halt!' It was Percy's voice and instantly obeyed. The sergeants stood holding the strain of the coffin, while Percy advanced to the edge of the grave. His face was pale in the surrounding darkness. In the dusk it was hard to see exactly what he was doing but then Félice realised that he had ungirded his sword and was placing it on top of the coffin. The gesture terrified her.

'Percy?' she ventured, but her voice was inaudible – or he blocked it out.

She was not the only one who was shocked by the gesture. Several of the commanders raised their voices to stop Percy.

'That is a sacred relic!' Father André protested scandalised.

'It is sorrow enough to lose our master' – no one took offence at the title Geoffrey had never officially carried – 'but it is wrong to cast away our talisman as well!'

'We need the Baptist's hand more than ever!'

'He gave you the sword, sir! He meant you to carry it—'

'In defence of the Order!' Percy spun round on the protesters, his face a mask of fury such as Félice had not seen since the Paris burnings. 'Don't you realise the Order is dead? Ask Brother Robert!' He pointed to the cluster of newcomers. 'The Council of Vienne has been adjourned and Pope Clement has dissolved the Order on his own authority!'

Then, because the disbelief around him was so tangible, he added more forcefully, 'The Knights Templar no longer exist! We are nothing but outlaws. I will not raise the

Baptist's hand in mercenary service! Do you understand?' he roared.

Then, seeing the shock and bewilderment on their stunned faces, Percy tried to soften the blow he had just delivered. 'The Order has been dissolved, not condemned. We can be received back into the Church. We can go our own ways.'

Then he raised his voice again, challengingly and threateningly. 'But if that means I must earn my keep by selling the services of my sword, then God forbid that I slaughter for pay with a Templar sword – with de Sonnac's sword! With the Baptist's hand!'

The pain in his voice made Félice want to scream. He might as well have turned the sword upon her and driven it through her heart. He might as well have turned it upon himself. She could hear his self-hatred, and she recognised too late that Percy had no identity and no self-respect outside the Templars. The cold seemed to reach to the marrow of her bones.

'Well said, my son.' Dom Alfonso had pulled himself upright and made his way through the ranks of the others to embrace Percy. 'But I am here at the explicit request of his grace King Dinis of Portugal with the following message: the Knights Templar may be suppressed but their spirit cannot die. Remember that He was crucified, dead and buried but on the third day He rose again from the dead. So too can the Knights of Christ rise from the ashes of their brothers, rise from the hell of the French king's dungeons, rise up to splendour and honour in the service of the King of Kings. Come back with me, all of you!'

He turned to face the anxious and confused company of Free Templars but Félice noted that he had not let go of Percy's arm.

She was paralysed with cold, but her eyes were sharper than ever. She could see them all so clearly. Dom Alfonso had Percy in his tough old hand. Percy, a man who for over three years had managed to confound the forces of the French king by rescuing men from his dungeons – even from the flames of the auto-da-fé – was a man of proven military ability. Dom Alfonso might not approve of his having killed a bishop, but he would find a way to justify it. Dom Alfonso needed competent commanders, men of proven courage and cleverness, men who could command the loyalty of other men. And Percy needed a reason for living, a cause, a justification for his existence – and a sense of identity.

She saw Dom Alfonso take de Sonnac's sword off the coffin and hand it back to Percy. She saw Percy take it in his hand, but the cheering from a thousand throats no longer reached her. She heard only the breakers on the beach at Vila do Condé.

Chapter Thirty-Five

Saint André du Gard, October 1311

Father Renaud mounted the narrow wooden stairs of the rundown parish church to ring vespers. The tin clang of the little bell hardly carried across the morass between the slate-roofed cottages which beyond the village became a road again. It was a sharp contrast to the melodic clang of the great bells of the convent at Avignon and the contrast never failed to make Father Renaud break into a sour sweat. Each time he made this climb and rang the bells for mass, he was reminded of the cage in which they had confined him, and the terror returned. But he made himself climb the stairs and ring the bell in penance for his lost faith.

God had granted him all his prayers: he had been freed from the cage, taken out of the hands of the Inquisition and been given his own parish. Lord Geoffrey had arranged that. He had his humble but dry parsonage. He had his living and his own church. He ought to be boundlessly grateful. He ought to be filled and overfilled with praise for God, who had worked these miracles. But the only emotions he felt intensely were self-pity and a growing listless depression.

Father Renaud forced himself to remember the cage in all its lurid details as he hauled on the hemp rope. He made himself conjure up the images of the dungeons in which he had been chained. How dare he bemoan his present fate? What did it matter that the church roof leaked in a dozen places? That mould was slowly blotting out the frescos on the walls? Or that none of his parishioners bothered to come to mass? That he was scorned if not simply ignored by his flock?

The living here had been vacant for almost twenty years, and the villagers had become accustomed to going to the next village or not attending mass at all. To be fair, there were usually a dozen people in church on important feast days, and occasionally one of the women attended mass on Sunday. But on this rainy Wednesday there would be no response to the clanging of the bell. It was days since he had exchanged a word with anyone.

Renaud let go of the bell rope and the bell fell silent almost at once. Grabbing his cassock in his right hand and using his left to steady himself, he started back down the stairs into the damp chill of the church.

At the foot of the stairs he caught sight of Jacques, one of the village boys, peeping around the door, and Renaud's spirits lifted. Jacques was eight or nine, a scruffy, neglected son of a usually drunken father, whose second wife clearly intended her own children to usurp Jacques' place. He had been curious from the day of Renaud's arrival but much too shy at first to venture inside the church. Renaud had slowly won him over with honey cakes and raisins – delicacies he had never known before.

Renaud smiled encouragingly at Jacques. 'Hello, Jacques. Do you want—'

'Gelding! Gelding! Gelding!' the boy called out and then he fled.

The giggles of the other boys could be heard from the street. Renaud understood. The other boys of the village had ridiculed Jacques for his tentative friendship with the priest, and Jacques – in a desperate bid for the acceptance he had never enjoyed – had sacrificed the dubious friendship of the ugly castrate for the prospect of acceptance by his peers. But understanding the boy's motives did not make it easier to bear. Father Renaud stood paralysed where he had been struck by the boy's words, doubled over with inner pain.

After a while he managed to right himself slightly and start up the nave of the church. A single widow knelt in the first pew. Renaud avoided looking at her, afraid that she would be able to read the self-pity on his face. A priest was supposed to exude faith, calm and wisdom. He was supposed to offer comfort and advice – not himself feel helpless against the petty blows of fate.

Renaud forced himself to go through the routine of mass. He did not need to concentrate upon his actions or his words, but the mere necessity of performing the service forced him to stop thinking about himself – at least for the length of time it took to read mass. Finished, he went to extinguish the candles.

'Father, will you hear my confession?'

The voice made him nearly jump out of his pock-marked skin. It was a clear, young voice, deeply melodic, and so unquestionably educated, that he spun about sharply.

The widow stood at the foot of the choir, her ivory face framed in black silk veils and wearing a well-tailored gown of fine cashmere wool, but she must have ridden far in the drizzling rain for it was soaked through. Her folded hands were chapped and red. Her eyes were bloodshot and her face was splotched with patches of dried, flaking skin.

'Of course, my daughter,' Renaud answered automatically, and in that instant, he forgot Jacques' treacherous taunt and the leaking roof and the empty church. What did it matter that he was pock-marked and castrated? His consecration gave him the awesome power to take away the sins of others, and what gift could be greater? He indicated the decrepit confessional with its moth-eaten curtain. If he could give this young widow the comfort of forgiveness for whatever sins she had – or imagined she had – committed then his life had meaning after all.

The widow preceded him and disappeared inside the cubicle. Renaud took his place opposite her behind a screen made of a flimsy panel of wood with holes irregularly drilled into it. He waited, but from the other side of the screen there came only a harsh, rasping cough.

Finally the voice said, 'I have loved a monk. I have known him, and it is his loss to the Church that makes me want to tear my heart out of my breast and trample it underfoot. I would that I could stab my heart with a hundred daggers so that the love it feels would drain away from the hundred wounds. I wish to God I could understand what is wrong with loving a man so deserving of love!'

The intensity of her pain tore open his own heart. Renaud could hear the loneliness, the sense of rejection, the self-hatred in her voice, and at once he lost confidence in his abilities to comfort – no matter how much absolution he was prepared to grant just to ease this poor woman's pain. He knew that he had to try to explain a world which he did not himself understand and he stuttered helplessly.

'It… it isn't the loving… that… that is a sin.' Renaud tried to help her. 'It is the desire to express that love physically.'

'Why is that a sin?'

'Because… because…' Renaud heard his own high voice squeaking and thought how ridiculous it was for a castrate to judge physical love. 'Because it is selfish,' he managed at last.

Silence answered his statement, and then another fit of coughing that became increasingly muffled. A sixth sense filled Renaud with alarm and without thinking he flung back the curtain and plunged out of the confessional to tear open the curtain on the other side. The woman had sunk down on the floor and was burying her face in her skirts.

Renaud reached out to her, but drew back his fingers in alarm. She was feverish. He had to get her inside, somewhere warm. She must get out of her wet clothes, drink something hot, go to bed. But there was no manor house, not even an inn, within ten miles. He could hardly turn her over to one of his parishioners. She was too obviously of gentle birth. He would have to take her to the parsonage. It stood directly beside the church, and it was comparatively clean – at least it had a second storey with a wooden floor.

'My daughter,' he started hesitantly. 'You must get dry and warm. Come with me.'

She did not respond at first. He reached out timidly to her again, afraid and nervous to touch a female who was both young and of gentle station. He managed only to pat her skirted knee twice. 'Come with me,' he repeated.

She had ceased coughing, and without meeting his eyes she started to struggle to her feet. 'Niki is outside,' she announced strangely. 'He was my grandfather's squire, you know. We are alone now.'

'You can both stay with me until you are well,' he assured her, and she followed without further protest.

*

She woke in the darkness. She would have to go on living, she admitted with a certain fatalism. Then she tried to move and found that her limbs were stiff, as if she had not moved in hours, and that her shift stuck to her. She threw back the heavy comforters, aware that she was sweating, and heard a angry cry from what turned out to be a tabby cat, which jumped down indignantly from the bed.

She looked around the room, her eyes adjusting to the darkness. On a crude table stood a pottery washbasin and pitcher. A chamber pot stood on the floor beneath the table. The plaster of the walls was cracked and chipped, especially on the wall against the chimney. Father Renaud had lined his sandals, clogs and old leather shoes neatly against the wall beneath his nightshirt and a spare cassock. Poor, dear Father Renaud, she thought. Was this his reward for enduring so much injustice?

The tabby cat was furiously licking herself beside the bed. From the stairway came a mellow, golden light, the smell of boiled chicken and the sound of men's voices. Félice became aware of her hunger, and, knowing that it could only be Niki and Father Renaud below, she slipped off the bed, took her still damp cloak and slipped her feet into Father Renaud's large sandals. It was not easy to walk in them but still better than using her wet shoes or going barefoot on the earth floor below.

Father Renaud and Niki looked up in alarm as they saw her descending the stairs, and Niki rushed to give her a hand. 'Are you feeling better, my lady?'

'Yes, thank you. Is there any broth left?'

'Of course!' Father Renaud jumped up to take a pewter bowl off the mantleplace and fill it from the iron pot suspended over the low fire. As he set the bowl before her, he gave her a new, wondering look, and she looked back at the priest, for the first time seeing him in all his unsightliness: his pock-marked skin; his eyes permanently squinting in his round face; dandruff clinging to greasy hair encircling his shaven tonsure. He had yellow teeth and a neck that was too short over hunched, rounded shoulders. And despite all that he was not bitter?

'Niki has told me who you are,' Father Renaud admitted as he handed her a large pewter spoon.

Félice stopped in mid-motion and her eyes narrowed slightly, her lips drawing tight. She had had many identities in her twenty years: her father's daughter, her brother's sister, Dom Pedro's lady and then his discarded wife. She had been a maiden, a novice, a wife and the mother of dead children. She had been her grandfather's favourite, Umberto's love and Percy's whore. 'Who am I?'

'You brought me water in Avignon.' Renaud answered simply.

Félice felt tears sting her eyes, then she managed to smile at Father Renaud. 'Thank you.'

Chapter Thirty-Six

Lys-Saint-Georges, November 1311

The Lord of Lys-Saint-Georges put two rooms of the south-west tower of his chateau at Félice's disposal. In the upper chamber, with a view down the hill to the hospice from one window and over the orchards from the other, she kept her personal belongings and slept. In the lower room she worked.

Sister Madeleine was an angel of mercy, as her brother was wont to say, but she hated numbers. Her hospital lived entirely on charitable grants and alms, and somehow there was always enough money at the right time to buy the necessities. 'Somehow' very often meant that Sister Madeleine's brother had to produce the necessary funds, and over the years he had become increasingly insistent that his sister try to keep better control of her finances.

Félice, who still could not bear the sight of the lepers, had decided that this was her task from now on. So she had had all the accounts and ledgers of the little leper hospital carried up to the tower chamber. She was determined to put Sister Madeleine's books to right.

Looking at the heaps of disorganised parchment with near illegible scrawls crowded upon them, however, Félice began to lose heart. The day was drawing to a dim end and the ticking on the heavy panes of glass suggested that the rain had turned to snow. She would need more wood for the fire and more candles if she were to work here this evening. She stared at the table which seemed to sag under the weight of the work she had cut out for herself; she wanted to go upstairs and crawl into bed. Sleep. Escape.

A hound set up a fervent yapping and at once several others joined in. The sound of voices came up from the base of the tower, and Félice, grateful for the distraction, stepped into the window niche and pressed down on the iron handle holding the glass shut. She pulled the glass inwards and leaned out into the fine snow to see what had caused the commotion. A cowled priest leading a shaggy, brown nag was walking along beside the moat, heading for the drawbridge. Priests were common guests.

She drew her head back inside and latched the window shut. As she left the window niche, she pulled the curtain closed to reduce the draught. Then, with a sigh, she faced the mound of accounts and forced herself to start sorting through them.

Sister Madeleine had made sporadic attempts at creating order, which included occasional inventories of her supplies. Then there was a roll on which she entered all her purchases. There were also clearly incomplete notations of donations.

Félice sat frowning over the notes in the fading light, chewing on the end of her quill-pen, trying to sort out the disparities between accounts. Was this item a discount, a 'donation' or merely a miscalculation? The knock on the door startled her, but she did not look up as she intently added the column of figures once again. 'Come in. Forty-three and sixteen minus seventy-six'

'You'll ruin your eyes in this light.'

The hair stood up on the back of her neck and she jerked her head around to look towards the speaker.

He stood in the doorway, his wind-ruffled, snow-flecked hair almost brushing the arched frame. Snow dusted the shoulders of his cloak, though it was starting to melt and turn to glistening drops of water. His over-the-knee boots were muddy.

She gazed at him in wary disbelief, afraid of her emotions.

Her dark eyes seemed huge in her pale face, and he saw the look of wariness come over them. 'I'm sorry. Perhaps I should not have come.'

'Why have you come?' She carefully set down her pen. She was sitting very upright on her stool – straight and stiff and brittle.

'You left without farewell.'

'I couldn't bear it.'

His brows came together slightly and his eyes seemed to search her face without finding what they were looking for. Once he had been able to read her soul itself, but now he was illiterate.

She noted that his face was red with cold and he was breathing heavily. 'I'm sorry. I'm being inhospitable. Shall I send for wine?'

He shrugged. 'It's not necessary.'

'Have you come to see Sister Madeleine?' she queried, trying to explain his presence without awakening false hopes.

'I brought Father Renaud. He was no longer wanted in Saint André. I thought he might serve the patients here.'

Félice nodded. It was a good idea. But it was odd that they were talking about Father Renaud. Why couldn't they talk about themselves? 'When do you leave for Portugal?'

Percy shrugged. 'Does it matter?'

'Have the others left already?'

'We have dispersed. Each man will go his own way. The Germans prefer the Teutonic Knights on the whole and most of the French and English will join the Hospital. Dom Alfonso took only a score of knights and a half-hundred sergeants with him. He was, I think, disappointed.'

Félice lifted the corner of her lips. 'He wants you – not the others.'

'He has the Baptist's hand.'

'But no one to hold it.'

'To murder bishops? What makes you think he would let me keep it?'

'He gave it back to you.'

'It was a gesture for my grieving brothers.'

She had no answer.

'May I sit down?'

'Of course.' Félice stood up, looking about for a chair to offer him. But her 'office' was sparsely and functionally furnished. Aside from her table, stool and the window seat there was nowhere to sit. Percy sank down where he stood and sat in the door frame without taking his eyes off her. She reseated herself on her stool.

'So you have decided to stay here and help Sister Madeleine after all,' he stated.

'Do I have a choice? Oh, yes, I could turn myself over to my brother Norbert and let him auction me to the highest bidder. Or I could throw myself on the mercy of my sister Natalie. That is where I found a position for Nannette, since she did not fancy life at a leper hospital…'

'Ah…'

Félice cocked her head curiously.

Percy shook his head in answer. 'Nothing important.'

Félice lifted an eyebrow.

'Gaston is in love with her, and apparently she with him. She left Gaston a message, saying where to find her. That was how I tracked you to Father Renaud, and he told me you were here.'

'You might have thought of it on your own. You wanted to bring me here from Vila do Condé.'

'And you made it clear that you didn't want to come. Then you preferred the dangerous and dubious company of outlaws and excommunicates...'

'It was a noble fight against injustice.'

Percy tried to smile. 'Geoffrey was proud of you.' For a moment they were both silent, overcome with shared grief, but at last Percy managed to ask, 'What made you change your mind?'

'About what?'

He gestured vaguely. 'About Lys-Saint-Georges, and your usefulness here?'

'Father Renaud. He reminded me that charity is the essence of goodness. And the source of true joy.'

'You shame me.' He looked away.

'Why?'

He looked at his palms; he turned his hands over and looked at the back and then the palms again. 'They have blood on them.'

'The blood of tyrants.'

'Tyrants?'

'Albi, the minions of the Inquisition, the mercenaries of King Philip.'

Percy drew a deep breath and pulled his lips up in his crooked smile. 'The blood of mercenaries is not cheap but it is worthless.'

Félice shuddered as if a shadow had just crossed her grave. She rose slowly to her feet. 'What are you talking about?'

He looked up at her. Her hair was decorously braided down her back and she wore a neat cap that sat like a crown tied under her chin by scarves. The outer sleeves of her houppelande cascaded down to the floor and her inner sleeves extended beyond her wrists to cover the base of her hands. She was every inch a lady and it was inconceivable that he had held her naked in his arms.

He smiled faintly. 'I was only reflecting that you are too good to be a mercenary's bride – or widow.'

'But not too good to be a monk's whore?' she retorted with sudden, searing anger.

'Whore? Did I ever pay you?'

They were staring at one another and their emotions were so violent that they singed the very air.

'Does the judgement of that Dominican still mean so much?'

'Umberto means nothing to me! How dare you be jealous after Avignon?'

'You left me.'

'To avoid being discarded again!'

'What have I ever done to deserve a comparison to Dom Pedro?' Percy's anger was sharpened with pain.

Félice looked down at her hands, ashamed. He was right. There could be no comparison and yet she knew he could not be both a monk and her lover.

'You don't honestly think Dom Alfonso will turn the blind eye my grandfather did and allow me to have a chamber and place at table in Tomar, do you?'

'No, I wouldn't want you to.'

Percy looked away, and it was a moment before Félice realised that he was speaking into the darkness of the empty stairway. '...I felt the way I did when they broke my second leg.'

She held her breath to try and hear what he was saying. Never had he spoken of his torture before.

'I was still in shock from what they had done to my left leg, and when they put the iron stirrup on the right leg, I... I... I was utterly alone... Surrounded by strangers who wanted to destroy what was left of me. But there wasn't anything left. I was nothing... Your grandfather's death left me in shock, and then still dazed from that, I discovered you too were gone. I couldn't grasp it. I kept expecting you to return. When I realised that you *had* left, it felt like when they broke my second leg. I was utterly alone... and I was nothing...'

She waited but nothing more came. He looked back up at her.

'You were surrounded by your brothers,' she reminded him.

He shook his head. 'No one there knew me as you do.'

'Percy! You are not what the Inquisition made of you – you are the Marshal of Aquitaine!'

'Marshal of a non-existent province for a disbanded order that I never wanted to join in the first place?'

No one had ever told Félice that Percy had not wanted to be a Templar. 'But Dom Alfonso—'

'—wanted me to bind myself to an institution dedicated to God. But I don't believe in Him any more.'

Félice caught her breath.

'Does that shock you?'

She shook her head slowly. 'You told me that the night we met.'

'So I did,' he remarked, not really remembering. 'But you still believe in him, don't you?'

Félice nodded, embarrassed. She felt as if she had no right to believe in God if Percy rejected him.

'Why? How? After all we've gone through? All the men His Church burned and broke only because they loved Him! How can you believe in God?'

'Because he has always answered my prayers,' Félice whispered.

Percy could only stare at her in incomprehension.

'I didn't pray for the others – only you,' she confessed in a small, shamed voice.

Percy stared at her stunned – horrified – and then he pointed out gently, 'He didn't save me – you did.'

'But only with His help,' Félice countered.

Percy closed his eyes. He wished that he could find faith again, but it was gone. There had been nothing but silence at the other end of his prayers for so long that he had long since ceased to pray. Ever since the night they broke him and he had denied Christ for the first time, it had become increasingly easy to deny Him until it was not even a conscious act of denial. He had simply ceased to have any relevance. Percy realised that his life had come to revolve around Geoffrey and Félice and their joint crusade for justice. And now both were as inaccessible as his dead faith.

She took a deep breath. 'What now?'

He shrugged, opening his eyes but still not looking at her. 'I had thought to go to King Robert the Bruce. We got on well when I went to Scotland to deliver your grandfather's letter to your uncle. He promised me that I would always have a place at his court. He holds most of his country now, but he must still have employment for mercenaries.'

'And you would prefer that?'

'Yes. I – foolishly it seems – assumed you would be with me…'

Félice stopped breathing.

Percy looked up at her, pleading.

Slowly Félice sank down on to her knees and timidly she leaned forwards to lay her head on his chest. 'Where else should I be?'

He put his arms around her and held her fast.

Historical Note

The principal characters in this novel – the Preuthunes, Percy, Umberto and the Bishop of Albi – are fictional. The persecution of the Knights Templar by King Philip IV of France and the subsequent dissolution of the Templar Order is historical fact.

On Friday, 13th October, 1307, the Templars throughout France were arrested without warning. The surprise was complete. The king's troops came in the dead of night. The provincial houses were unfortified and the Templars predominantly lay brothers or ageing sergeants and knights. Men of military value were stationed on Cyprus, preparing for the next crusade. There was no notable resistance, and only a few scattered Templars escaped arrest.

The motives for the French king's move were so patently financial that no further motives are necessary to explain his actions. Philip IV arrested and possibly murdered one pope to gain access to Church revenues; he carried out wholescale expropriations of property held by Italian bankers on two separate occasions; he devalued the currency repeatedly, and in 1306 he ruthlessly confiscated the property of all French Jews and expelled them from his kingdom. The Templars with their reputed riches but lacking – since the loss of the Holy Land to the Muslims in 1291 – a justification for their existence were a logical target.

The charges brought against the Templars were more or less the routine accusations made against Philip IV's enemies – including Pope Boniface VIII, the Jews, and Bishop Guichard of Troyes. All were accused of denying Christ, profaning the sacraments, engaging in perverted sexual activities and conducting sorcery and/or worshipping idols. There is no historical reason to suspect that the Templars were any more guilty of these standard charges than Pope Boniface VIII or Bishop Guichard of Troyes.

There is no question that the Inquisition, which investigated the alleged crimes, was taking its orders from the King of France. The Inquisitor General was, incidentally, Philip IV's confessor. The use of torture is recorded, criticised even by contemporaries and never denied by the prosecution. The methods of torture described in this novel – with the exception of the branding – are recorded. Brother Thomas is based on a real case: one Templar defender had no feet as a result of their having been burned to the bone during interrogation and subsequently amputated.

In those countries where the ruling monarchs did not share Philip IV's interest in seeing the Knights Templar destroyed such as England, various Iberian kingdoms, Cyprus and the Holy Roman Empire – the arrest and trial of the Templars was conducted either half-heartedly, as in England, degenerated into an open attempt to enrich the respective royal treasury or established the complete innocence of the Order. Edward II of England explicitly refused to employ torture on the grounds that it had no precedent in England, and initially sent away the French Inquisitors with the explanation that English law required trial by one's peers. Later, Edward and the English bishops engaged in plea bargaining: in exchange for confessions from lay brothers regarding the right of the Grand Master to grant absolution of sins, the Templars were found innocent of all other charges. In Aragon and Castile, after initial resistance to the French king's advice, the respective kings decided to exploit the situation to seize Templar wealth – only to meet organised resistance. They were forced to lay siege to Templar castles and take them by force. The Templars died in the defence of their castles – and honour – or were hanged for treason, but they did not confess to the alleged crimes and could not be condemned as heretics. In Metz the archbishop conducting the judicial enquiry was confronted by twenty Knights Templar in full battle array offering to defend the Order in trial by combat. It wasn't necessary – they were found innocent without the combat. Indeed, in all countries where no torture was applied – such as Cyprus, Portugal, and the Holy Roman Empire – Templars were found completely innocent.

Meanwhile, Pope Clement V, who owed his election to Philip IV, played the vacillating and cowardly role described in the novel. Philip IV openly threatened him with the same fate as Boniface VIII and for a time used troops to prevent his moving from Poitiers, located in France, to Avignon, a papal fiefdom. Some historians suggest that at this time a deal was struck between the French king and the pope in which the pope agreed to condemn the Templars in exchange for Philip dropping his resistance to a posthumous rehabilitation of Boniface VIII. Certainly, all Clement's actions suggest that his principal concern was not justice but the preservation of his papal – and personal – dignity and prerogatives. By 1310 he was ordering the use of torture in England and overturning the verdict of innocence delivered on Cyprus on the grounds that no torture had been employed.

The papal commission investigating the alleged crimes was not opened until nearly two years after the initial arrest of the Templars in France. It was apparently assumed that men who had broken under torture and spent the remaining two years in dungeons would not offer further resistance. The authorities were clearly overwhelmed by the number of Templars – more than six hundred – who even at this late date and despite the treatment they had endured retracted their confessions and declared their willingness to defend their Order. They elected four spokesman, the priests Peter di Bologna and Renaud de Provins and the knights William and Bertrand. Bologna particularly is described as educated and eloquent. It is a matter of historical record that either one or both of the two priests 'disappeared' some time between May 1310 and the autumn of 1311. Although there were rumours of an escape by Peter, the most likely explanation – if not the one provided in this novel – is that they were murdered by the minions of Philip IV or died in consequence of torture intended to elicit confessions.

Whatever the fate of the individual spokesmen, the public execution by fire of Templars as relapsed heretics caused the collapse of the Templar defence. Fifty-four Templars were burned in Paris on 23rd May, 1310. Other bishops followed the example of the Archbishop of Sens and carried out public burnings in their own dioceses. Altogether one hundred and twenty Templars were condemned to the stake. Only two 'repented' to escape the flames. There are no recorded incidents of rescue. The murder of the Bishop of Albi is entirely fictional.

By contrast, the appearance of Templars at the Church Council in Vienne in October 1311 is historical fact. The assembled clerics had not been willing to accept Pope Clement's judgement of the Templars or his 'evidence,' and the Council insisted on re-opening the trial. They invited the Templars to defend their Order, and, to the astonishment of all, seven (some accounts say nine) fully armed and armoured Templars rode into the city of Vienne to do exactly that. What is more, these men claimed to represent between fifteen hundred and two thousand 'free'

Templars hiding in the forests near Lyon. There is no way of knowing to what extent this number was an exaggeration or a mere figure of speech, but it so frightened Pope Clement, who evidently gave it credence, that he took flight, doubled his personal guard, ordered the arrest of the Templar defenders and dissolved the Council.

The fate of the seven knights and the 'Free Templars' they claimed to represent is unrecorded. Rumours and legends about 'Free Templars' abound – including whole shiploads of Templars arriving in Western Scotland in time to assist Robert the Bruce at Bannockburn. The establishment of new military orders in the Iberian peninsula clearly provided an outlet for many knights, and the Teutonic Knights were still engaged in a crusade in Prussia while the Knights of Saint John were active in the Mediterranean. But the majority of any Free Templars, like the majority of their imprisoned and mistreated brothers, would have been lay brothers and these could have disappeared into the other religious orders or civilian society without a trace.

Less than six months after the appearance of the Free Templars and before the Church Council was reconvened, Pope Clement dissolved the Order of the Knights Templar on his own authority. The Order was suppressed after four and a half years of persecution without being officially found guilty of the charges. Public opinion, initially anti-Templar, had swung so much against the king that in 1314 he decided to stage a public reaffirmation of the confessed crimes by the Grand Master and three other senior officers of the Temple still held in royal dungeons. On the steps of Notre Dame, before a huge crowd the Grand Master, Jacques de Molay and the Preceptor of Normandy, Geoffrey de Charney, instead retracted their confessions. They were burned at the stake the next day. According to legend, Jacques de Molay cursed the king and pope from the flames, challenging them to meet him before the throne of God within the year. Both Philip IV and Clement V died within months.

978-0-595-43271-4
0-595-43271-9

Lightning Source UK Ltd.
Milton Keynes UK
UKOW02f0501151216
289985UK00002B/247/P

9 780595 432714